S. J. PARRIS

Treachery

HarperCollins*Publishers*

HarperCollins*Publishers*
77–85 Fulham Palace Road,
Hammersmith, London W6 8JB

www.harpercollins.co.uk

Published by HarperCollins*Publishers* 2014
1

Endpapers map © Nicolette Caven

A catalogue record for this book
is available from the British Library

ISBN: 978 0 00 748119 4

Set in Sabon by Palimpsest Book Production Limited
Falkirk, Stirlingshire

Printed and bound in Great Britain by
Clays Ltd, St Ives plc

MIX
Paper from
responsible sources
FSC˙ C007454

Find out more about HarperCollins and the environment at
www.harpercollins.co.uk/green

From aboard Her Majesty's good ship the *Elizabeth Bonaventure*, Plymouth, this Sunday the twenty-second of August 1585

Right Honourable Sir Francis Walsingham

After my heartiest commendations to you, Master Secretary, it is with a heavy heart that I pick up my pen to write these words. You have no doubt expected fair news of the fleet's departure by now. It grieves me to tell you that we remain for the present at anchor here in Plymouth Sound, delayed at first by routine matters of supplies and provisioning, and awaiting still the arrival of the *Galleon Leicester* to complete our number, which we expect any day (and with it your son-in-law). Naturally, in a voyage of this size such minor setbacks are to be expected. But it is a far graver matter that weighs upon me now and which I feel I must convey to Your Honour, though I ask that for the present you do not reveal these sad circumstances to Her Majesty, for I hope to have the business resolved before too long without causing her unnecessary distress.

Your Honour perhaps knows, at least by reputation, Master Robert Dunne, a gentleman of Devon, sometime seen at court, who proved a most worthy officer and companion when I made my voyage around the world seven years since, and was duly rewarded for his part in that venture. I had invited Dunne to join my crew for this our present voyage to Spain and the New World, though there were those among my closest advisers who counselled against it, given the man's personal troubles and what is said of him, which I need not elaborate here. Even so, I will not judge a man on hearsay but on his deeds, and I was determined to give Dunne a chance to recover his honour in the service of his country. Perhaps I would have done well to listen, though that is all one now.

From the outset Dunne's manner was curious; he seemed much withdrawn into himself, and furtive, as if he were afraid of someone at his shoulder, not at all the man I remembered. This I attributed to nervous anticipation of the voyage to come; to leave home and family for the far side of the world is not a venture to be undertaken lightly, and Dunne knew all too well what he might face. Last evening, he had been ashore with some of the other gentlemen. While we remain here in harbour I consider it wise to allow them the natural pursuits of young men and such diversions as Plymouth affords the sailor – there is time enough for them to be confined together below decks and subject to the harsh discipline of a ship's company once we haul anchor, though I make clear to the men under my command – as do my fellow captains – that they are expected to conduct themselves in such a way as will not bring the fleet into disrepute.

Dunne was brought back to the ship last night very much the worse for drink, which was also out of character; God knows the man had his vices, but I had confidence that drink was not among them, or I would not have appointed him to serve with me on Her Majesty's flagship. He was in the company of our parson, Padre Pettifer, who had found Dunne wandering in the streets in a high degree of drunkenness and thought best to bring him direct to the ship – a decision I would not have made in his position, for I am told they had the Devil's own work to help Dunne into the rowboat and up the ladder to the deck of the *Elizabeth*. There they were met by my brother Thomas, who had taken his supper with me aboard and was on his way back to his own command. Knowing I was in my quarters, at work on my charts with young Gilbert, and thinking this matter not fit to trouble me with, my brother and the parson helped Dunne back to his cabin to recover, though Thomas later said Dunne appeared very wild, lashing out as if he could see enemies invisible to the rest, and addressing people who were not there, as if he had taken something more than wine. But, according to Padre Pettifer, almost the moment he lay down upon his bunk, he fell into a stupor from which he could not be woken, and so they left him to sleep off his excesses and repent of it in the morning.

What happened between that time and the following dawn is known only to God and, it grieves me to say, <u>one other</u>. The weather was foul, with rain and high winds; most of the men were below decks, save the two who kept the watch. At first light, my Spanish navigator, Jonas, came knocking at my door, in a fearful haste. He had tried to take Robert Dunne a draught of something that would restore him after the night's excesses, but the cabin was locked and Dunne would not be roused. I understood his concern – we have all seen men in drink choke on their own vomit unattended and so I went with him to see – I have a spare key to the private cabins and together we unlocked Dunne's door. But I was not prepared for what we found.

He was facing away from us at first, though as the ship rolled on the swell, he swung slowly around, and it was then that I noticed – but I run ahead of my story. Dunne was hanging by the neck from the lantern hook, a noose tight around his throat. Jonas cried out, and spilled some of the philtre he was carrying. I quickly hushed him, not wishing to alarm the men. With the door shut behind us, Jonas and I

3

lifted Dunne down and laid him on the bunk. The body was stiff already; he must have been dead some hours. I stayed with him and sent Jonas to fetch my brother from his own ship.

The death of a man by his own hand must be accounted in any circumstances not only a great sorrow but a great sin against God and nature. I confess that a brief anger flared in my breast that Dunne should have chosen this moment, for you know well that sailors are as devout and as superstitious as any men in Christendom, and this would be taken as an omen, a shadow over our voyage. I did not doubt that some would desert when they learned of such a death aboard, saying God had turned His face from us. Then I reprimanded myself for thinking foremost of the voyage when a man had been driven to such extremes of despair in our midst.

But as I waited for my brother to arrive, my anger gave way to a greater fear, for I looked more closely at the corpse and at once I realised what was wrong, and a great dread took hold of me. I had no need of a physician to tell me this death was not as it first appeared. And so you will understand why I confide this to Your Honour, for I must keep my suspicions to myself until I know more. If a ship should be considered cursed to count a suicide on board, how much the worse to harbour one guilty of an even greater sin?

For this reason, I ask you for the present to keep your counsel. Be assured I will inform you of progress, but I wanted Your Honour to have this news from my own hand – rumour will find its way out of every crack, often distorted in some vital particular, and as I know you have eyes and ears here I would not wish you to be misinformed. It has been given out among the crew that it was self-slaughter, but there must be a coroner's inquest. You see that I cannot, with due care for my men and the investment of so many great nobles, including Your Honour and our Sovereign Queen herself, embark upon a voyage such as this believing I carry a killer among my

4

crew. If Her Majesty should hear we are delayed, I pray you allay any fears for the success of the expedition and assure her we will set sail as soon as Providence allows. I send this by fast rider and await your good counsel.

I remain Your Honour's
most ready to be commanded,
Francis Drake

ONE

'There! Is that not a sight to stir the blood, Bruno. Does she not make you glad to be alive?'

Sir Philip Sidney half stands as he gestures with pride to the river ahead, so that the small wherry lurches to the left with a great splash and the boatman curses aloud, raising an oar to keep us steady. I grab at the bench and peer through the thin mist to the object of Sidney's fervour. The galleon looms up like the side of a house, three tall masts rising against the dawn sky, trailing a cat's cradle of ropes and rigging that cross-hatch the pale backdrop of the clouds into geometric shapes.

'It is impressive,' I concede.

'Don't say "it", you show your ignorance.' Sidney sits back down with a thud and the boat rocks alarmingly again. '"She" for a ship. Do you want Francis Drake thinking we have no more seafaring knowledge than a couple of girls? You can drop us here at the steps,' he adds, to the boatman. 'Bring up the baggage and leave it on the wharf, near as you can to the ship. Good fellow.' He clinks his purse to show that the man's efforts will be rewarded.

As we draw closer and Woolwich dock emerges through the mist I see a bustle of activity surrounding the large vessel:

men rolling barrels and hefting great bundles tied in oil cloth, coiling ropes, hauling carts and barking orders that echo across the Thames with the shouts of gulls wheeling around the tops of the masts.

'I am quite happy for Sir Francis Drake to know that I cannot tell one end of a boat from the other,' I say, bracing myself as the wherry bumps against the dockside steps. 'The mark of a wise man is that he will admit how much he does not know. Besides, what does it matter? He is hardly expecting us to crew the boat for him, is he?'

Sidney tears his gaze away from the ship and glares at me.

'Ship, not a boat. And little do you know, Bruno. Drake is famed for making his gentlemen officers share the labour with his mariners. No man too grand that he cannot coil a rope or swab a deck alongside his fellows, whatever his title – that's Drake's style of captaincy. They say when he circumnavigated the globe—'

'But we are not among his officers, Philip. We are only visiting.'

There is a pause, then he bursts out laughing and slaps me on the shoulder.

'Of course not. Ridiculous suggestion.'

'I understand that you want to impress him—'

'Impress *him*? Ha.' Sidney rises and springs from the wherry to the steps, while the boatman clutches an iron ring in the wall to hold us level. The steps are slick with green weed and Sidney almost loses his footing, but rights himself before turning around, eyes flashing. 'Listen. Francis Drake may have squeezed a knighthood out of the Queen, but he is still the son of a farmer. My mother is the daughter of a duke.' He jabs himself in the chest with a thumb. 'My sister is the Countess of Pembroke. My uncle is the Earl of Leicester, favourite of the Queen of England. Tell me, why should I need to impress a man like Drake?'

Because in your heart, my friend, he is the man you would

secretly like to be, I think, though I smile to myself and say nothing. Not long ago, at court, Sidney had failed to show sufficient deference to some senior peer, who in response had called him the Queen's puppy before a roomful of noblemen. Now, whenever Sidney walks through the galleries or the gardens at the royal palaces, he swears he can hear the sound of sarcastic yapping and whistles trailing after him. How he would love to be famed as an adventurer rather than a lapdog to Elizabeth; I could almost pity him for it. Since the beginning of the summer, when the Queen finally decided to commit English troops to support the Protestants fighting the Spanish in the Low Countries, he has barely been able to contain his excitement at the thought of going to war. His uncle, the Earl of Leicester, is to lead the army and Sidney had been given to believe he would have command of the forces garrisoned at Flushing. Then, at the last minute, the Queen havered, fearful of losing two of her favourites at once. Early in August, she withdrew the offer of Flushing and appointed another commander, insisting Sidney stay at court, in her sight. He has begged her to consider his honour, but she laughs off his entreaties as if she finds them amusing, as if he is a child who wants to play at soldiers with the bigger boys. His pride is humiliated. At thirty, he feels his best years are ebbing away while he is confined at the Queen's whim to a woman's world of tapestries and velvet cushions. Now she sends him as an envoy to Plymouth; it is a long way from commanding a garrison, but even this brief escape from the court aboard a galleon has made him giddy with the prospect of freedom.

I am less enthusiastic, though I am making an effort to hide this, for Sidney's sake. Hopping from the wherry to the steps is close enough to the water for my liking, I reflect, as I falter and flail towards the rope to keep my balance. My boots slip on each step and I try not to look down to the slick brown river below. I swim well enough, but I have been in the Thames by accident once before and the smell of it could knock a man out before he strikes for shore; as to what floats beneath the surface, it is best not to stop and consider.

At the top of the steps, I stand for a moment as our boatman ties up his craft and begins to labour up the steps with our bags. Mostly Sidney's bags, to be accurate; I have brought only one, with a few changes of linen and some writing materials. He has assured me we will not be gone longer than a fortnight, three weeks at most, as we accompany the galleon along the southern coast of England to Plymouth harbour where it – or *she* – will join the rest of Sir Francis Drake's fleet. Yet Sidney himself seems to have packed for a voyage to the other side of the world; his servants follow us in another wherry with the remainder of his luggage. I have not remarked on this; instead I watch my friend through narrowed eyes as he hails one of the crew with a cheery hallo and engages the man in conversation. The sailor points up at the ship. Sidney is nodding earnestly, arms folded. Is he up to something, I ask myself? He has been behaving very strangely for the past few weeks, ever since his falling out with the Queen, and I know well that he does not take a blow to his pride with good grace. For the time being, though, I have no choice but to follow him.

'Come, Bruno,' he calls, imperious as ever, waving a lace-edged sleeve in the direction of the ship's gangplank. I bite down a smile. Sidney thinks he has dressed down for the voyage; gone are the usual puffed sleeves and breeches, the peascod doublet that makes all Englishmen of fashion look as if they are expecting a child, but the jacket he has chosen is not much more suitable, made of ivory silk embroidered with delicate gold tracery and tiny seed pearls. His ruff, though not so extravagantly wide as usual, is starched and pristine, and on his head he wears a black velvet cap with a jewelled brooch and a peacock's feather that dances at the back of his neck and frequently catches in his gold earring. I make bets with myself as to how long the feather will last in a sea breeze.

A gentleman descends the gangplank, his clothes marking him apart from the men loading on the dockside. He raises one hand in greeting. He appears about Sidney's own age, with reddish hair swept back from a high forehead and an impressive beard that looks as if it has been newly curled by a barber. As he steps down on to the wharf he bows briefly to Sidney; when he lifts his head and smiles, creases appear at the corners of his eyes, giving him a genial air.

'Welcome to the *Galleon Leicester*.' He holds his arms wide.

'Well met, Cousin.' Sidney embraces him with a great deal of gusto and back-slapping. 'Are we all set?'

'They are bringing the last of the munitions aboard now.' He gestures behind him to a group of sailors loading wooden crates on to the ship with a system of ropes and pulleys and much shouting. He turns to me with a brief, appraising look. 'And you must be the Italian. Your reputation precedes you.'

He does not curl his lip in the way most Englishmen do when they encounter a foreigner, particularly one from Catholic Europe, and I like him the better for it. Perhaps a man who has sailed half the globe has a more accommodating view of other nations. I wonder which of my reputations has reached his ears. I have several.

'Giordano Bruno of Nola, at your service, sir.' I bow low, to show reverence for our difference in status.

Sidney lays a hand on the man's shoulder and turns to me.

'May I present Sir Francis Knollys, brother-in-law to my uncle the Earl of Leicester and captain of this vessel for our voyage.'

'I am honoured, sir. It is good of you to have us aboard.'

Knollys grins. 'I know it. I have told Philip he is not to get in the way. The last thing I need on my ship is a couple of poets, getting under our feet and puking like children at the merest swell.' He squints up at the sky. 'I had hoped to be away by first light. Still, the wind is fair – we can make up time once we are into the English Sea. Have you sea legs,

11

Master Bruno, or will you have your head in a bucket all the way to Plymouth?'

'I have a stomach of iron.' I smile as I say it, so that he knows it may not be strictly true. I did not miss the disdain in the word 'poets', and nor did Sidney; I mind less, but I would rather not disgrace myself too far in front of this aristocratic sailor. Puking in a bucket is clearly, in his eyes, the surest way to cast doubt on one's manhood.

'Glad to hear it.' He nods his approval. 'I'll have your bags brought up. Come and see your quarters. No great luxury, I'm afraid – nothing befitting the Master of the Ordnance, but it will have to suffice.' He makes a mock bow to Sidney.

'You may sneer, Cousin, but when we're out in the Spanish Main facing the might of King Philip's garrisons, you will be glad someone competent troubled themselves with organising munitions,' Sidney says, affecting a lofty air.

'Someone competent? Who was he?' Knollys laughs at his own joke. 'In any case, what is this "we"?'

'What?'

'You said, "when we're out in the Spanish Main". But you and your friend are only coming as far as Plymouth, I thought?'

Sidney sucks in his cheeks. 'We the English, I meant. An expression of solidarity, Cousin.'

I notice he does not quite meet the other man's eye. I watch my friend's face and a suspicion begins to harden in the back of my mind.

Knollys leads us up the gangplank and aboard the *Leicester*. The crew turn to stare as we pass, though their hands do not falter in their tasks. I wonder what they make of us. Sidney – tall, rangy, expensively dressed, his face as bright as a boy's, despite the recently cultivated beard, as he drinks in his new surroundings – looks no more or less than what he is, an aristocrat with a taste for adventure. In my suit of black, perhaps they take me for a chaplain.

We follow Knollys through a door beneath the aftercastle, where we are ushered into a narrow cabin, barely wide enough for the three of us to stand comfortably, with two bunks built against the dividing wall. It smells, unsurprisingly, of damp, salt, fish, seaweed. If Sidney is deterred by the rough living arrangements, he does not allow it to show as he exclaims with delight over the cramped beds, so I determine to be equally stoical. Behind my back, though, my fists clench and unclench and I force myself to breathe slowly; since I was a child I have had a terror of enclosed spaces and to be confined here seems a punishment. I promise myself I will spend as much time as possible on the deck during the voyage, eyes fixed on the sky and the wide water.

'Make yourselves at home,' Knollys says, cheerfully waving a hand, enjoying the advantage his experience gives him over his more refined relative. 'I hope you have both brought thick cloaks – the wind will be fierce out at sea, for all it is supposed to be summer. I shall leave you here to get settled – I have much to do before we cast off. Come up on deck when you are ready and say your farewells to London.'

'I'll take the bottom bunk, I think,' Sidney announces, when Knollys has gone, tossing his hat on to the pillow. 'Not so far to fall if the sea is rough.'

I lean against the doorpost. 'Thank you. And you had better tell him we will need another cabin just for your clothes.'

Sidney eases himself into his bunk and attempts to stretch out his long legs. They will not fit and he is forced to lie with his knees pointing up like a woman in childbirth. 'You know, one of these days, Bruno, you will learn to show me the respect due from a man of your birth to one of mine. Of course, I have only myself to blame,' he continues, shifting position and knocking his hat on the floor. 'I have bred this insolence by treating you as an equal. It will have to stop. How in God's name am I supposed to sleep in this? I can't even lie flat. Was it built for a dwarf? I suppose you will have no problem. God's wounds, they have better accommodation at the Fleet Prison!'

I pick up his hat and put it on at a jaunty angle.

'What were you expecting, feather beds and silk sheets? It was you who wanted to play at being an adventurer.'

He sits up, suddenly serious. 'We are not playing, Bruno. I am the Queen's Master of the Ordnance – this is a royal appointment. No, I am not in jest now. And you will thank me for it, wait and see. What else would you have done with the summer but brood on your situation? At least this way you will be occupied.'

'My *situation*, as you put it, will be no different when I return. Unless I can find some way to stay in England independent of the French embassy, I will be forced to return to Paris with the Ambassador in September. It is difficult not to brood.'

I try to keep the pique from my voice, but his casual tone is galling, when he is talking of my whole future, and perhaps my life.

He waves a hand. 'You worry too much. The new Ambassador – what's his name, Châteauneuf? – can't really throw you out on the streets, can he? Not while the French King supports you living at the embassy. He's just trying to intimidate you.'

'Well, he has succeeded.' I wrap my arms around my chest. 'King Henri has not paid my stipend for months – he has more to worry about at his own court than one exiled philosopher. The previous Ambassador was paying it himself from the embassy coffers – I have been surviving on that and what I earn from—' I break off; we exchange a significant look. 'And that is another problem,' I say, lowering my voice. 'Châteauneuf as good as accused me of spying for the Privy Council.'

'On what grounds?'

'He had no evidence. But they suspect the embassy's secret

correspondence is being intercepted. And since I am the only known enemy of the Catholic Church in residence, he has drawn his own conclusions.'

'Huh.' He draws his knees up. 'They are not as stupid as they appear, then. But you will have to be careful in future.'

'I fear it will be almost impossible for me to go on working for Walsingham as I have been. The previous Ambassador trusted me. Châteauneuf is determined not to – he will be watching my every move. He is the most dogmatic kind of Catholic – the sort that thinks tolerance is a burning offence. He will not keep someone like me under his roof. Those were his words.'

Sidney smiles. 'A defrocked monk, excommunicated for heresy. Yes, I can see that he might see you as dangerous. But I thought you were keen to return to Paris?'

I do not miss the insinuation.

'I wrote to King Henri last autumn to ask if I might return briefly. He said he could not have me back at court at present, it would only antagonise the Catholic League. Besides,' I lean against the wall and cross my arms, 'she will be long gone by now. If she was ever there.'

He nods slowly. Sidney understands what it is to love a woman you cannot have. There is no more to be said.

'Well, you can stop brooding. I have an answer to your problems.' The glint in his eye does not inspire confidence. Sidney is well intentioned but impulsive and his schemes are rarely practical; for all that, I cannot suppress a flicker of hope. Perhaps he means to speak to his father-in-law Walsingham for me, or even the Queen. Only a position at court would allow me to support myself in exile. Though she cannot publicly acknowledge it, I know that Walsingham has told the Queen how I have risked my life in her service over the past two years. Surely she will understand that I can never again live or write safely in a Catholic country while I am wanted by the Inquisition on charges of heresy.

'You will speak to the Queen?'

'Wait and see,' is all he says, with a cryptic wink that he knows infuriates me.

Sidney was appointed Master of the Ordnance early in the spring – a political appointment, a bauble from the Queen, no reflection of his military or naval abilities, which so far exist largely in his head. Over the summer he has been occupied with overseeing the provision of munitions for this latest venture of Francis Drake's. So when the Queen received word that Dom Antonio, the pretender to the Portuguese throne, was sailing for England to visit her and intended to land at Plymouth, Sidney volunteered immediately for the task of meeting and escorting him to London, so that he might see Drake's fleet at first hand.

The plan is that we sail with the *Galleon Leicester* as far as Plymouth, where the ships are assembling, spend a few days among the sailors and merchant adventurers while we wait for the Portuguese and his entourage, so that Sidney can strut about talking cannon-shot and navigation and generally making himself important, then return by road to London with our royal visitor by the end of the month, when the royal court will have made its way back to the city after a summer in the country. I am grateful for the diversion, but I cannot help dwelling on the reckoning that will come on our return. If Sidney can find a way for me to stay in London, I will be in his debt for a lifetime.

The sun is almost fully above the horizon when Knollys calls us back to the deck, its light shrouded by a thin gauze of white cloud. I think of a Sicilian lemon in a muslin bag, with a brief pang of nostalgia.

'We shall have clear weather today, God willing,' he says, nodding to the sky. 'Though it would not hurt to pray for a little more wind.'

'You're asking the wrong man,' Sidney says, nudging me. 'Bruno does not pray.'

16

Knollys regards me, amused. 'Wait until we're out at sea. He will.'

The ship casts off smoothly from her moorings; orders are shouted, ropes hauled in, and from above comes a great creak of timber and the billowing slap of canvas as the sails breathe in and out like bellows. For the first time since we boarded, I am truly aware of the deck shifting beneath my feet; a gentle motion, back and forth on the swell as the *Leicester* moves away from the dock and the children who earn pennies loading cargo and running errands cheer us on our way, scampering as far as they can run along the wharf to wave us out of sight. Knollys laughs and waves back, so Sidney and I follow suit as the sun breaks through in a sudden shaft that gilds the brass fittings and the warm grain of the wood and makes the water ahead sparkle with a hundred thousand points of light, and I think perhaps I will enjoy this after all. But each time I move I am reminded that the ground under my feet is no longer solid.

'Occupy yourselves for the present,' Knollys says, 'as long as you don't get in anyone's way.'

'I am fully ready to pull my weight, Cousin, just let me know what tasks I should take in hand. I have heard how Drake likes to run his crews and we are not here to sit about watching honest men toil while we drink French wine in the sun.' Sidney beams, spreading his hands wide as if to say, Here I am.

I look at him, alarmed; there had been no mention of this in the invitation. I glance up to the top of the mainmast, where a pennant with a gold crest flutters above the lookout platform. I hope he has not just volunteered us for shinning up rigging and swabbing decks.

Knollys looks him up and down, taking in the silk doublet, the lace cuffs, the ornaments. He smiles, but there is an edge to it.

'Good – the wine is strictly rationed. I must say, Philip, I

17

am surprised Her Majesty has allowed you to leave court for so long. In the circumstances.'

Sidney looks away. 'Someone has to bring Dom Antonio to London. He wouldn't make it in one piece on his own. You know Philip of Spain has a price on his head.'

'Even so. Given that you and she are at odds at present, I'm amazed she trusts you to come back again.' Knollys laughs, expecting Sidney to join in.

There is a pause that grows more uncomfortable the longer it continues. Sidney studies the horizon with intense concentration.

'Tell me,' I say, to relieve the silence, 'what kind of man is Francis Drake?'

'Stubborn,' says Sidney, without hesitation.

'A man of mettle,' Knollys offers, after some consideration.

'I have sat on parliamentary committees with him over the past few years,' says Sidney, 'and he is as single-minded as a ratting dog when he has his mind set to something. Pragmatic too, though, and damned hard-working – as you'd expect from a man raised to manual labour,' he adds, examining his fingernails.

'There is a combative aspect to him,' Knollys says thoughtfully, 'and a fierce ambition – though not for personal vanity, I don't think. It's more as if he enjoys pitting himself against the impossible. He can be the very soul of courtesy – I have seen him treat prisoners from captured ships with as much respect as he would pay his own men. But there is steel in him. If you cross him, by God, he will make you pay for it.' He sucks in a sharp breath and seems poised to expand on this, but apparently thinks better of it.

'Is he an educated man?' I ask.

'Not formally, though he is learned in matters that concern the sea, naturally,' Knollys says. 'But in his cabin he keeps an English Bible and a copy of Foxe's Book of Martyrs, as well as the writings of Magellan and French and Spanish volumes on the art of navigation. He is excessively fond of music and makes sure he has men aboard who can play with some skill. Why do you ask?'

'Only that he is Europe's most famous mariner,' I say. 'I am intrigued to meet him – he has changed our understanding of the world. I imagine he must be a man of extraordinary qualities.'

Knollys nods, smiling. 'You will not be disappointed. Now, the two of you can watch the sights while I go about my business. God willing we shall have calm seas and a good wind and we will be in Plymouth inside two days.'

He waves us vaguely towards the front of the ship. I follow Sidney up a few almost vertical stairs to the high deck. As soon as Knollys has turned his back, Sidney disregards his command; he greets the nearest sailor heartily and presses him with questions about his business – why does he tie that rope so, what does it signify that the topsails are still furled, what is the hierarchy of men in the crew, where is the farthest he himself has been from England – barely pausing to draw breath, until the poor fellow looks about wildly for someone to save him from this interrogation.

Smiling, I leave them to it and find myself a quiet spot at the very prow. I do, as it happens, know one end of a ship from the other – I spent part of my youth around the Bay of Naples – but I reason that the more useless I make myself appear, the more I will be left to my own devices. What does pique my interest here is the art of navigation; I should like to have the opportunity to talk to Knollys about his charts and instruments, if he would allow. Since sailors for centuries have calculated their position by the stars with ever more precise calibrations, and since for those same centuries all our charts of the heavens have been based on erroneous beliefs about the movement of the stars and planets in their spheres, I am curious to know how navigators and cartographers will adapt to the new configuration of the universe, now that we know the Sun and not the Earth lies at its centre, and that the fixed stars are no such thing, their sphere no longer the outer limit of the cosmos. I wonder if these are ideas I could discuss with an experienced sailor like Knollys. He circumnavigated the globe with Drake in 1577, according to Sidney, on the voyage that made them famous and wealthy men; surely in the course of such a journey the calculations they made must have added up to confirmation that the Earth turns about the Sun and not the reverse? Drake and the men who sailed with him are forbidden by the Queen from publishing accounts or maps of their route, for fear they would fall into the hands of the Spanish, but perhaps Knollys might be persuaded at least to discuss the scientific discoveries of his travels with me in confidence, as one man of learning to another.

Ahead the Thames gleams like beaten metal as clouds scud across the face of the sun and their shadows follow over the water; in this light, you could almost forget it is a soup of human filth. I rest my forearms on the wooden guardrail and look down. I must check myself; with my state so precarious, it behoves me to be wary of what I say in public, until I know how it may be received. Knollys is, by all accounts, a good Protestant, like his brother-in-law Leicester and Sidney, but I would be a fool to imagine that these ideas of the Pole Copernicus have been accepted by more than a very few. Only two years ago I was openly ridiculed at the University of Oxford for expressing such a view in a public debate. Just because the Inquisition cannot reach me in Elizabeth's territories, it does not follow that all Englishmen are enlightened.

We make steady progress along the river as it widens towards the estuary, here and there passing clusters of dwellings little more than shacks, where fishing boats bob alongside makeshift jetties. To either side the land is flat and marshy, pocked with pools reflecting the pale expanse of the sky.

London gives you a sense of being hemmed in, pressed on all sides; there the sky is a dirty ribbon glimpsed if you crane your neck between the eaves of tall houses that lean in towards one another across narrow alleys, blocking the light. As we move further from the city, I feel my shoulders relax; the air freshens and begins to carry a tang of salt, and I inhale deeply, relishing this new sense of space. The sounds grow familiar: the snap of sailcloth, the creaks and groans of moving timber, the rhythmic breaking of waves against the hull as we rise and fall, the endless skwah-skwah of the gulls.

After supper, while Sidney settles to cards with Knollys and his gentlemen officers, I excuse myself and return to the deck. The wind is keener now and I have to wrap my cloak close around me against the cold, but I had rather be here in the salt air than confined in the captain's cabin, with its fug of tobacco smoke and sweet wine. Directly ahead, the sun has almost sunk into the water, leaving the sky streaked orange and pink in its wake. To our right, or what Sidney insists I call starboard, the English coast is a dark smudge. To the left, on the other side of the endlessly shifting water, lies France, and I narrow my eyes towards the distant clouds as if I could see it.

The boards creak behind me and Sidney appears at my side, a clay pipe clamped between his teeth. He takes out a tinder-box from the pouch at his belt and battles for some moments to light it in the wind.

'Thinking again, Bruno?'

'It is a living, of sorts.'

He grunts, takes the pipe from his mouth, puffs out a cloud of smoke and stretches his arms wide, lifting his chest to the rising moon.

'Nothing like fresh sea air.'

'It was before you arrived.'

He leans with his back to the rail and grins. 'Leave off, you sound like my wife. She always complains about the smell of a pipe. Especially now.' He sighs and turns to face the sea again. 'By God, it is a relief to be out of that house. Women are even more contrary than usual when they are with child. Why is one not warned of that in advance, I wonder?'

'This time last year you were fretting you might not manage an heir at all. I'd have thought you'd be glad.'

'It is all to please other people, Bruno. A man born to my station in life – certain things are expected of you. They are not necessarily your own choices.'

'You don't want to be a father?'

'I would have liked to become a father once I was in a position to support sons and daughters myself, rather than still living in my father-in-law's house. But . . . well.' He laces his fingers together and cracks his knuckles. 'They will not let me go to war until I have got an heir, in case I don't come back. So I suppose I should be pleased.'

The sails billow and snap above us; the ship moves implacably forward, stately, unhurried. After a long silence, Sidney taps his pipe out on the rail in front of him.

'I put a group of armed men and servants on the road to Plymouth two days ago. They will meet us there and escort Dom Antonio back to London.'

My earlier suspicions prickle again.

'Along with us,' I prompt.

Sidney turns to me with a triumphant smile, his eyes gleaming in the fading light. He grips my sleeve. 'We are not going back to London, my friend. By the time Dom Antonio is warming his boots at Whitehall, you and I shall be halfway across the Atlantic.'

I stare at him for a long while, waiting – hoping – for some sign that this is another of his jokes. The wild light in his eyes suggests otherwise.

'What, are we going to stow away? Hide among the baggage?'

'I told you I had a plan for you, did I not?' He leans back again, delighted with himself.

'I thought it might be something realistic.'

'Christ's bones – don't be such a naysayer, Bruno. Listen to me. What is the great problem that you and I share?'

'The urge to write poetry, and a liking for difficult women.'

'Other than those.' He looks at me; I wait. 'We lack independence, because we lack money.'

'Ah. That.'

'Exactly! And how do we solve it? We must be given money, or we must make it ourselves. And since I see no one inclined to give us any at present, what better way than to take it from the Spanish? To come home covered in glory, with a treasure of thousands in the hold – the look on her face then would be something to see, would it not?'

For a moment I think he means his wife, until I realise.

'This is all to defy the Queen, then? For not sending you to the Low Countries? You plan to sail to the other side of the world without her permission?'

He does not answer immediately. Instead he looks out over the water, inhaling deeply.

'Do you know how much Francis Drake brought home from his voyage around the world? No? Well, I shall tell you. Over half a million pounds of Spanish treasure. Ten thousand of that the Queen gave him for himself, more to be shared among his men. And that is only what he declared.' He breaks off, shaking his head. 'He has bought himself a manor house in Devon, a former abbey with all its land, and a coat of arms. The son of a yeoman farmer! And I cannot buy so much as a cottage for my family. My son will grow up knowing every mouthful he eats was provided by his grandfather, while his father sat by, dependent as a woman. How do you think that makes me feel?'

'I understand you are frustrated, and angry with the Queen—'

23

'The fellow she means to give the command of Flushing is my inferior in every degree. It is a public humiliation. I cannot walk through the galleries of Whitehall knowing the whole court is laughing at my expense. I am unmanned at every turn.' The hand resting on the rail bunches into a fist.

'So you must come home a conquering hero.'

'What else is there for an Englishman to do but fight the Spanish?' When he turns to me, I see he is white with anger. 'It is no more than my duty, and she would prevent me for fear of letting her favourites out of her sight – she must keep us all clinging to her skirts, because she dreads to be alone. But I would be more than a pet to an ageing spinster, Bruno.' He glances around quickly, to make sure this has not been overheard. 'Picture it, will you – the thrill of bearding the King of Spain in his own territories, sailing back to England rich men. The Queen will not have gifts enough to express her thanks.'

I want to laugh, he is so earnest. Instead I rub the stubble on my chin, hand over my mouth, until I can speak with a straight face.

'You really mean to do this? Sail with Drake to the Spanish Main? Does he even know?'

He shrugs, as if this were a minor detail. 'I hinted at it numerous times as I was assisting him with the preparations this summer. I am not sure he took me seriously. But I can't think he would object.'

'He will, if he knows you travel without the Queen's consent and against her wishes. He will not want to lose her favour.' But I am not thinking of Drake's advantage, only my own. The Queen will be livid with Sidney for flouting her command and if I am party to his enterprise, I will share her displeasure. Sidney will bounce back, because he is who he is, but my standing with her, such as it is, may never recover. And that is the best outcome; that is assuming we return at all.

'Francis Drake would not be in a position to undertake this venture if it were not for me,' Sidney says, his voice low and urgent. 'Half the ships in his fleet and a good deal of the funds raised come from private investors *I* brought to him, gentlemen *I* persuaded to help finance the voyage.' He jabs himself in the chest with his thumb to make the point. 'He can hardly turn me away at the quayside.'

I shake my head and look away, over the waves. He is overstating his part in the venture, I am sure, but there is no reasoning with him when he is set on a course. If he will not brook objection from the Queen of England, he will certainly hear none from me.

'I have no military experience, Philip, I am not a fighter. This is not for me.'

He snorts. 'How can you even say so? I have seen you fight, Bruno, and take on men twice your size. For a philosopher, you can be very daunting.' He flashes a sudden grin and I am relieved; I fear we are on the verge of a rift.

'I can acquit myself in a tavern brawl, if I have to. That is not quite the same as boarding a ship or capturing a port. What use would I be at sea?'

'What use are you in London now that the new Ambassador means to watch your every step, or kick you out altogether? You are no use to anyone at present, Bruno, not without patronage.'

I turn sharply away, keeping silent until I can trust myself to speak without betraying my anger. I can feel him simmering beside me, tapping the stem of the clay pipe hard against the wooden guardrail until it snaps and he throws it with a curse into the sea.

'Thank you for reminding me of my place, Sir Philip,' I say at length, in a voice that comes out tight and strangled.

'Oh, for the love of Christ, Bruno! I meant only that you are of more use on this voyage than anywhere else, for now. Besides, he asked for you.'

'Who did?'

'Francis Drake. That's why I invited you.'

I frown, suspicious.

'Drake doesn't know me. Why would he ask for me?'

'Well, not by name. But this summer, in London, he asked me if I could find him a scholar to help him with something. He was very particular about it, though he would not explain why.'

'But *you* are a scholar. Surely he knows that?'

'I won't do, apparently. He is looking for someone with a knowledge of ancient languages, ancient texts. A man of learning and discretion, he said, for a sensitive task. I told him I knew just the fellow.' He beams, slinging an arm around my shoulder, all geniality again. 'He told me to bring you to Plymouth when I came. Think, Bruno – I don't know what he wants, but if you could do him some sort of service, it might smooth our way to a berth aboard his ship.'

I say nothing. When he invited me on this journey to Plymouth, he showered me with flattery: he could not dream of going without me, he said; he would miss my conversation; there was no one among his circle at court he would rather travel with, no one whose company he prized more highly. Now it transpires that he wants me as a sort of currency; something he can use to barter with Drake. Like a foolish girl, I have allowed myself to be sweet-talked into believing he wanted me for my own qualities. I also know that I am absurd to feel slighted, and this makes me all the more angry, with him and with myself. I shrug his arm off me.

'Oh, come on, Bruno. I cannot think of going without you – what, left to the company of grizzled old sea dogs for months on end, with no conversation that isn't of weevils and cordage and drinking their own piss? You would not abandon me to such a fate.' He drops to one knee, his hands pressed together in supplication.

Reluctantly, I crack a smile. 'Weevils and drinking our own piss? Well then, you have sold it to me.'

'See? I knew you would not be able to resist.' He bounces back to his feet and brushes himself down.

26

Our friendship has always been marked by good-natured teasing, but his earlier words have stung; perhaps this is truly how he views me. Nothing without patronage.

'Seriously, Philip,' I turn to look him in the eye. 'To risk the Queen's displeasure so brazenly – are you really willing? I am not sure that I am.'

'I swear to you, Bruno, by the time we come home, the sight of the riches we bring to her treasury will make her forget on the instant.' When I do not reply, he leans in, dropping his voice to a whisper. 'You do realise the money Walsingham pays you is not charity? He pays you for information. And if the Baron de Châteauneuf has as good as banished you, how can you continue to provide it?'

'I will find a way. I always have before. Walsingham knows I will not let him down.'

'Come, Bruno!' He gives me a little shake, to jolly me along. 'Do you not yearn to see the New World? What good is it to dream of worlds beyond the fixed stars if you dare not travel our own globe?' He pushes a hand through his hair so that the front sticks up in tufts, a gesture he makes without knowing whenever he is agitated. 'You're thirty-seven years old. If you want nothing more from life than to sit in a room with a book, I can't think why you ever left the cloister.'

'Because I would have been sentenced to death by the Inquisition,' I say, quietly. As he well knows. But how do you explain to a man like Sidney the reality of a life in exile? 'And what of your wife and child?' I add, as he stretches again and turns as if to leave.

He looks at me as if he does not understand the question. 'What of them?'

'Your first child is due in, what, three months? And you mean to be halfway across an ocean.' With no good odds on returning, I do not say aloud. Even I know that Francis Drake's famous circumnavigation returned to England with only one ship of six and a third of the men. But Sidney is as

27

irrepressible as a boy when he sets his heart on something; he clearly believes there is no question but that we will return triumphant with armfuls of Spanish gold.

He frowns. 'But I have done my part. She will have the child whether I am there or not, and there will be nursemaids to take care of it. God's blood, Bruno, I have done what they asked of me, I have got an heir, that is why they have had me cooped up at Barn Elms for the past two years. Am I not permitted a little freedom now?'

I am tempted to observe that he has possibly misunderstood the nature of marriage, but I refrain; I am hardly qualified to advise him about women. Besides, there is no profit in making him more irritable. His anger, I see now, is not at me, but at everyone who would voice the same objections: his wife, his father-in-law, Francis Drake, the Queen. He is rehearsing his self-justification. I have great affection for Sidney, and he has many qualities I admire, but he can be spoilt and does not respond well to being thwarted.

'It might be a girl,' I reply.

He makes a noise of exasperation. 'I am going back down for a drink. Are you coming?'

'I think I will stay here for a while.'

'As you wish.' At the head of the stairs to the main deck he turns back, one hand on the guardrail. 'You know, I am trying to find a way to help you, Bruno. I thought I might have a little more thanks than this.' He sounds wounded. In my amazement at his mad scheme, it had not occurred to me that I might have hurt his feelings.

'Forgive me. I am grateful for your efforts – do not think otherwise.'

'You are coming, then? To the New World?' His face brightens.

'Let me get used to the idea.'

He disappears to the lower deck and I return my attention

28

to the restless black water that surrounds us. Two weeks of this had seemed a diversion; months on end is another proposition entirely. In sunlight, the sea looked benign, obliging; now its vastness strikes me as overwhelming. To challenge it, to attempt to best it with such a small vessel, appears grotesquely presumptuous. But perhaps all acts of courage look like folly at first. The breeze lifts my hair from my face, and I realise that the sun has fully set and the horizon is no longer visible on either side. There is no divide between sea and sky, nothing but endless darkness and the indifferent stars.

TWO

We round the headland into Plymouth Sound two days later, early evening on 23rd August, as a cheer goes up from the men on deck. The wind has not been on our side since we passed the coast of Kent and moved into the English sea, making our progress slower than Knollys had predicted, but now the sky is clearer overhead, the sun glistening on a broad bay, surrounded on three sides by gently sloping cliffs, dark green with thick tree cover. Sidney and I have been standing at the prow for the past hour, craning for the first sight of the harbour, but nothing could have prepared me for the spectacle of the fleet anchored in the Sound.

Some thirty ships of varying sizes, the largest painted black and white and greater even than the *Galleon Leicester*, stand at anchor; between the great painted fighting ships and merchantmen, ten or so smaller pinnaces rock gently on the swell, sails furled, pennants snapping, their heraldic colours bright against the pale sky. The water sparkles and the whole has the appearance of a marvellous pageant. I find myself staring open-mouthed with delight like a child, Sidney likewise, as the crewmen on deck send up another cheer at the sight of their comrades. Until this moment, I would not have claimed any great interest in seafaring, but the assembled fleet is truly a sight to stir a sense of adventure. I picture all these ships sailing out in formation at Drake's command, pointed towards the New World, Sidney and me at the prow, squinting into the sun towards an unknown horizon. And returning, to the salute of cannon from the Plymouth shore, our pockets bursting with Spanish gold. Sidney really believes this is possible; now that we are here, it is hard not to be infected by his conviction. All about us, a volley of shouted commands is unleashed, followed by the heavy slap of canvas as sails are furled, ropes heaved, chains let out with a great clanking of metal on metal, and the vast creaking bulk of the *Galleon Leicester* slows almost to a standstill as her anchors are dropped and rowboats lowered down her sides to the water. Knollys turns to us, eyes bright with pride, as if this show is all his doing.

'There, gentlemen, you see the flagship, the *Elizabeth Bonaventure*, Sir Francis Drake's own command. And there, the *Tiger*, captained by Master Carleill.'

He points across the Sound; Sidney shoots me a sideways look and a grimace. Half the investors in this expedition he knows from court, many of the officers men with connections to his own family. He will have to keep his plans quiet until the voyage is underway, for fear of Walsingham finding out.

Knollys continues, oblivious, his outstretched arm casting a long shadow over the deck as he gestures: 'Across the way you have the *Sea Dragon*, the *White Lion* and the *Galliot Duck*, and there the little *Speedwell*, and beside her the *Thomas Drake*, named for the Captain-General's brother and under his command.'

We are near enough to see the crews of the other ships, men scuttling up and down rigging and swarming over the decks like insects. Now that we are at ease in the shelter of the harbour, the breeze has dropped and I feel the warmth of the sun on my back for the first time since we left London.

'And what is that island?' I ask, pointing to a mound of rock in the middle of the Sound. Sheer cliffs rise to a wooded crest, and at the summit, a stone tower peeps above the treeline.

'St Nicholas Island,' Knollys says, shading his eyes, 'though the locals call it Drake's Island. Sir Francis has been trying to raise money to improve the fortifications in case of invasion. There was a garrison there in years past, though I believe it has fallen out of use for lack of funds. But come – the Captain-General, as we must call him on this voyage, will be expecting us.'

He leads us down a flight of stairs below deck, where he calls for rope ladders to be dropped over the side through a hatch. These are thin, precarious-looking contraptions, but Knollys swings himself easily into the gap and shins down to the two stout sailors holding the end of the ladder steady in the rowboat below. Sidney nudges me to follow, and a silent sailor hands me through the hatch, where I climb without looking down, gripping the ropes until my palms burn, placing one foot below the other, conscious all the while of Sidney's impatient feet inches above my head.

The oarsmen negotiate a path between the anchored ships and from this vantage point, at the waterline, you understand the immensity of these galleons; their hulls the height of a church, their masts disappearing to a point so high you have to crane your neck until you are almost lying horizontal to see the top. Navigating through them you feel as if you are in a narrow lane between high buildings, if buildings were uprooted from their foundations and could lurch and heave at you. A hearty melody of flutes and viols carries across the water, accompanied by raucous singing that collapses into laughter after one verse. A few more strokes of the oars and our boat cracks against a sheer wooden cliff scaled with barnacles, where another ladder sways, awaiting us. I glance at my palms. Sidney notices and laughs.

'Don't expect to go home with the soft hands of a gentleman, Bruno.'

'I'm not sure I have ever had the soft hands of a gentleman,' I say. I hold them out and regard them on both sides, as if for evidence. My fingertips are stained with ink, as always.

'That's not what the ladies of the French court say,' he replies, with a broad wink. It is one of Sidney's favourite jokes: that I worked my way through the duchesses and courtesans of Paris before turning my keen eye to England. It amuses him that I was once a monk; he cannot imagine how I managed to keep to it all those years, the most vigorous years of my youth. He can only picture how he himself would have been, and so he likes to joke that, since leaving holy orders, I go about rutting everything in sight like a puppy on a chair leg. It amuses him all the more for being untrue.

Knollys precedes us up the ladder; Sidney follows and I am left to bring up the rear. This ship is higher even than the *Leicester*; my arms begin to ache and the ladder shows no sign of ending. I dare not look anywhere except directly in front of me, at the snaking ropes and the wooden wall that grazes my knuckles each time the swell knocks me against it. As my head draws level with the rail, I reach out to grasp it and my hand slips; for a dizzying moment I fear I may lose my footing, but a strong hand grips my wrist and hauls me inelegantly over the side.

'Steady there.'

I regain my balance, take a breath, and look up to face my rescuer.

'And who is this, that we nearly lost to the fishes?' he asks, not unkindly. As he smiles down a gold tooth flashes in the corner of his mouth.

'Doctor Giordano Bruno of Nola, at your service.' My heart is pounding with relief, or shock, or both, at the thought that I might have fallen the full height of the ship. 'Sir,' I add, realising whom I am addressing.

33

No introduction is needed on his part; the quiet authority of the man, his natural self-assurance, the way the others stand in a deferential half-circle around him, leave me in no doubt that I am speaking to the one the Spanish call *El Draco*, the dragon. England's most famous pirate smiles, and claps me on the shoulder.

'You are welcome, then, to the *Elizabeth Bonaventure*. Are you a doctor of physick?' His expression is hopeful.

'Theology, I'm afraid. Less useful.' I offer an apologetic smile.

'Oh, I don't know.' He looks at me, appraising. 'We may yet find a use for you. Come, gentlemen – are you hungry? We will take supper in my quarters.'

Knollys bows his head. 'Thank you. There is much to discuss.'

'Ah, Captain Knollys.' Francis Drake rubs his beard and his smile disappears. 'More than you know.'

There is a heaviness in his voice, just for an instant, that catches my attention, but he turns away and calls orders to one of the men standing nearby. It is an opportunity to study the Captain-General unobserved. He is broad-shouldered and robust, taller than me though not as tall as Sidney, with an open face, his skin tanned and weathered by his years at sea. There are white creases at the corners of his eyes, as if he laughs so often that the sun has not been able to reach them. His brown hair is receding and flecked with grey at his temples and most visibly in his neat beard; I guess him to be in his mid-forties. I see now why Sidney, despite his bluster about rank, is so keen to impress this man; Drake radiates an air of quiet strength earned through experience, and in this he reminds me a little of my own father, a professional soldier, though Drake cannot be more than ten years my senior. I find I want him to like me.

Drake turns back to us and claps his hands together. 'Come, then. You should at least quench your thirst while we wait for the food.'

34

As we follow him to the other end of the deck, the crew pause in their duties and watch us pass. I notice there is an odd atmosphere aboard this ship; a sullen suspicion in the way they watch us from the tail of their eye, and something more, a muted disquiet. There is no music or singing here. The men are almost silent; I hear none of the foul-mouthed, good-natured banter I have grown used to among the crew of the *Leicester* on our way down. Do they resent our presence? Or perhaps they are silent out of respect. I catch the eye of one man who stares back from beneath brows so thick they meet in the middle; his expression is guarded, but hostile. Something is wrong here.

Drake leads us to a door below the quarterdeck, where two thick-set men stand guard with halberds at their sides, staring straight ahead, grim-faced. Light catches the naked edges of their blades. I find their presence unsettling. I guess that Drake and the other officers keep items of value in their quarters and must have them defended, though such a display of force seems to show a marked lack of faith in his crew. He leans in to exchange a few words with one of the guards in a low murmur, then opens the door and leads us through into a handsomely appointed cabin, proportioned like Knollys's room aboard the *Leicester*, but more austerely furnished. Trimmings are limited to one woven carpet on the floor and the dark-red drapes gathered at the edges of the wide window that reaches around three sides of the cabin. Under it stands a large oak table, spread with a vast map, surrounded by nautical charts and papers with scribbled calculations and sketches of coastline. Behind the table, bent over these charts with a quill in hand, is a skinny young man with a thatch of straw-coloured hair and small round eye-glasses perched on his nose. He jolts his head up as we enter, stares at us briefly, his Adam's apple bobbing in his throat, then begins sweeping up the papers with as much haste as if we had caught him looking at erotic prints.

'Thank you, Gilbert – get those cleared away and leave us, would you?' Drake says.

The young man nods, and takes off his eye-glasses. Without them, he is obliged to squint at us. He rolls up the charts with a practised movement and gathers the papers together, stealing curious glances at me and Sidney as he does so.

'That is the Mercator projection, is it not?' I say, leaning forward and pointing to the large map as he begins to furl it. He peers at me and darts a quick glance at Drake, as if to check whether he is permitted to answer.

'You know something of cartography, Doctor Bruno?' Drake says, looking at me with new interest.

'Only a little,' I say hastily, as the world disappears into a blank cylinder under the young man's ink-stained fingers. 'But anyone with an interest in cosmography is familiar with Mercator's map. The first true attempt to spread on a plane the surface of a sphere, measuring latitude with some mathematical accuracy.'

'Exactly,' the young man says, his face suddenly animated. 'It is the first projection of the globe designed specifically for navigation at sea. Mercator's great achievement is to alter the lines of latitude to account for the curvature of the Earth. It means we can now plot a ship's course on a constant bearing—' He catches sight of Drake's face and swallows the rest of his explanation. 'Forgive me, I am running on.'

'My clerk, Gilbert Crosse.' Drake gestures to the young man with an indulgent smile as he eases out from behind the table. 'Gilbert, these are our visitors newly arrived on the *Leicester* – Captain Knollys, Sir Philip Sidney and Doctor Giordano Bruno.' The clerk smiles nervously and nods to each of us in turn, though his red-rimmed eyes linger on me as he locks the papers away in a cupboard and backs out of the room.

'Very gifted young man there,' Drake says, nodding towards the door after Gilbert has closed it behind him. 'Came to me via Walsingham, you know. Take a seat, gentlemen.'

Behind the table, wooden benches are set into the wall panelling. We squeeze in as Drake pours wine into delicate Venetian glasses from a crystal decanter. The young clerk has left a brass cross-staff on the table, an instrument used to determine latitude; my friend John Dee, the Queen's former astrologer, kept one in his library. I pick it up and, as no one seems to object, I hold one end against my cheek and level the other at the opposite wall, imagining I am aligning it with the horizon.

'Careful, Bruno, you'll have someone's eye out,' Sidney says, sprawling on the bench, his arm stretched out along the back behind me.

I lower the cross-staff to see Drake observing me with interest. 'Can you use it?'

'I have been shown how to calculate the angle between the horizon and the north star, but only on land.' I set it back on the table. 'I don't suppose that counts.'

'It's more than many. An unusual skill for a theologian. Can you use a cross-staff, Sir Philip?' he says, turning to Sidney, mischief in his eye.

Sidney waves a hand. 'I'm afraid not, Drake, but I am willing to learn.'

Drake passes him a glass of wine with a polite smile. He cannot fail to notice that Sidney does not give him his proper title; both are knighted and therefore equal in status, though you will not persuade Sidney of that. I watch Drake as he sets my glass down. The tension I sensed among the men on deck has seeped in here, even into the refined and polished space of the captain's cabin. I think of the armed men outside the door.

The latch clicks softly and Drake half-rises, quick as blinking, his right hand twitching to the hilt of his sword, but he relaxes when he sees the newcomers, a half-dozen men with wind-tanned faces, dressed in the expensive fabrics of gentlemen. Leading them is a man of around my own age, thinner but so like Drake in all other respects that he can only be a relative. He crosses to the table and embraces him.

'Thomas! Come, join us, all of you.' Drake points to the bench beside Sidney. There is relief in his laughter and I observe him with curiosity; what has happened to put this great captain so on edge? 'You know Sir Philip Sidney, of course, and this is his friend, Doctor Bruno, come to greet Dom Antonio, whom we expect any day. Gentlemen, I present my brother and right-hand man, Thomas Drake. And this is Master Christopher Carleill, lieutenant-general of all my forces for this voyage,' he says, gesturing to a handsome, athletic man in his early thirties with a head of golden curls and shrewd eyes. I see Sidney forcing a smile: this Carleill is Walsingham's stepson, who – though barely older than Sidney – is already well established in the military career that Sidney so urgently craves.

After Carleill, we are introduced to Captain Fenner, who takes charge of the day-to-day command of the *Elizabeth Bonaventure*; though Drake sails on the flagship, he is occupied with the operation of the entire fleet. Behind Fenner are three grizzled, unsmiling men, more of Drake's trusted commanders who accompanied him on his famous journey around the globe and have returned to put their lives and ships at his service again.

Knollys is delighted to be reunited with his old comrades; there is a great deal of back-slapping and exclaiming, though the newly arrived commanders seem oddly muted in their greetings. To me and Sidney they are gruffly courteous, but again I have the sense that our welcome is strained, the atmosphere tainted by some unspoken fear.

'Now that the *Leicester* is here, I presume the fleet will sail as soon as the tide allows?' Sidney asks Drake.

Drake and his brother exchange a look. There is a silence. 'I think,' says the Captain-General slowly, turning his glass in his hand, 'we are obliged to wait a little longer. There are certain matters to settle.'

38

Sidney nods, as if he understands. 'Still provisioning, I suppose? It is a lengthy business.'

'Something like that.' Drake smiles. A nerve pulses under his eye. He lays his hands flat on the table. The room sways gently and the sun casts watery shadows on the panelled walls, reflections of the sea outside the window.

A knock comes at the door; again, almost imperceptibly, I notice Drake tense, but it is only the serving boys with dishes of food. These sudden, nervy movements are the response of someone who feels hunted – I recognise them, because I have lived like that myself so often, my hand never far from the knife at my belt. But what does the commander of the fleet fear aboard his own flagship?

I had been led to believe that all ship's food was like chewing the sole of a leather boot, but this meal is as good as any I have had at the French embassy. Drake explains that they are still well stocked with fresh provisions from Plymouth, for now, and that in his experience it is as important to have a competent ship's cook as it is to have a good military commander, if not more so, and they all look at Carleill with good-natured laughter. 'Although, if—' Drake begins, and breaks off, and the others lower their eyes, as if they knew what he was about to say.

The tension among the captains grows more apparent as the meal draws on. Silences become strained, and more frequent, though Sidney obligingly fills them with questions about the voyage; the captains seem grateful for the chance to keep the conversation to business. It is only now, as I listen to their discussion, that I begin fully to realise the scale and ambition of this enterprise. I had understood that the official purpose of Drake's voyage was to sail along the coast of Spain, releasing the English ships illegally impounded in Spanish ports. What he actually plans, it seems, is a full-scale onslaught on Spain's New World territories. He means to cross the Atlantic and take back the richest ports of the Spanish Main, ending his campaign with the seizure of Havana. Soberly, between mouthfuls and often through them, Drake throws out figures that make my eyes water: a million ducats from the capture of Cartagena, a million more from Panama. If it sounds like licensed piracy, he says, with a self-deprecating laugh, let us never lose sight of the expedition's real purpose: to cut off Spain's supply of treasure from the Indies. Without his income from the New World, Philip of Spain would have to rein in his ambitions to make war on England. And if that treasure were diverted into England's coffers, Elizabeth could send a proper force to defend the Protestants in the Netherlands. I understand now why some of the most prominent dignitaries at court have rushed to invest in this fleet; its success is a matter not only of personal profit but of national security. It is also clear to me that Sidney has effectively found an alternative means of going to war, and that he expects me to follow.

When the last mouthful is eaten, the captains excuse themselves and leave for their own ships. Only Thomas Drake and Knollys remain behind.

Sir Francis pushes his plate away and looks at Sidney. 'I must be straight with you, Sir Philip. It would be best if you were to leave Plymouth as soon as possible with Dom Antonio when he arrives. He will no doubt wish to linger – he and I are old comrades, and he will be interested in discussing this voyage – but in the circumstances it is better you hasten to London. For his own safety.'

Sidney hesitates; I fear he is weighing up whether this is the time to announce his grand plan of joining the expedition.

'What circumstances?' I ask, before he can speak.

By way of answer, Drake raises his eyes to the door and then to his brother.

'Thomas, call them to clear the board. Then tell those two fellows to stand a little further off.'

Thomas Drake opens the door and calls for the serving boys. While the plates are hurried away, he exchanges a few words with the guards, waits to ensure that his orders have been obeyed, then closes it firmly behind him and takes his seat at the table. Drake lowers his voice.

'Gentlemen, I have sad news to share. Yesterday, at first light, one of my officers on this ship was found dead.'

'God preserve us. Who?' Knollys asks, sitting up.

'How?' says Sidney, at the same time.

'Robert Dunne. Perhaps you know him, Sir Philip? A worthy gentleman – he sailed with me around the world in '77.'

'I know him only by reputation,' Sidney says. His tone does not make this sound like a compliment.

'Robert Dunne. Dear God. I am most sorry to hear of it,' Knollys says, slumping back against the wall, shock etched on his face. 'He was a good sailor, even if—' He breaks off, as if thinking better of whatever he had been about to say. So this accounts for the subdued atmosphere among the men.

'The how is more difficult,' Drake says, and his brother reaches a hand out.

'Francis—'

'They may as well know the truth of it, Thomas, since we can go neither forward nor back until the business is resolved.' He pours himself another drink and passes the decanter up the table.

'Dunne was found hanged in his quarters,' Drake continues. 'You may imagine how this has affected the crew. They talk of omens, a curse on the voyage, God's punishment. Sailors read the world as a book of prophecies, Doctor Bruno,' he adds, turning to me, 'and on every page they find evidence that the Fates are set against them. So a death such as this on board, before we have even cast off . . .'

'Self-slaughter, then?' Knollys interrupts, nodding sadly.

'So it appeared. A crudely fashioned noose fastened to a ceiling hook.'

41

'But you do not believe it.' I finish the thought for him.

Drake gives me a sharp look. 'What makes you say that?'

'I read it in your face, sir.'

He considers me for a moment without speaking, as if trying to read me in return. 'Interesting,' he says, eventually. 'Robert Dunne was a solid man. An experienced sailor.'

'He was a deeply troubled man, Francis, we all know that,' Knollys says.

'He had heavy debts, certainly,' Drake agrees, 'but this voyage was supposed to remedy that. It would make no sense to die by his own hand before we set sail.'

'A man may lose faith in himself,' Sidney says.

'In himself, perhaps, but not in his God. Dunne was devout, in the way of seafaring men. He would have regarded it as a grievous sin.' Drake pauses, holding up a warning finger, and lowers his voice. 'But here is my problem. I have allowed the men to believe his death was self-slaughter, as far as I can. They may talk of inviting curses and Dunne's unburied soul plaguing the ship, but I had rather that for the present than any speculation on the alternative.'

'You think someone killed him?' Sidney's eyes are so wide his brows threaten to disappear. Drake motions for him to keep his voice down.

'I am certain of it. He did not have the face of a hanged man.'

'So he was strung up after death, to look like suicide?' I murmur. 'How many people know of your suspicions?'

'The only ones who saw the body were the man who found him, Jonas Solon, and my brother Thomas, who I sent for immediately. I also called the ship's chaplain to ask his advice. He offered to say a prayer over the body, though he said there was little he could do for a suicide in terms of ritual.'

'But no one else thought the body looked unusual? For a suicide by hanging, I mean?'

'If they did, they said nothing. I only voiced my disquiet

42

to Thomas in private later and he said he had thought the same.' Drake takes a mouthful of wine. The strain of anxiety is plain in his face, though he is doing his best to conceal it.

'Dunne did not show the signs of strangulation, though it was evident he had been hanging by the neck for some time,' Thomas says, keeping his voice low. 'The eyes were bloodshot and there was bruising around his nose and mouth. But he did not have the swollen features you would expect from choking.'

'My first thought was to have him buried at sea that same day, to spare him the indignity of a suicide's burial,' Drake continues. 'But Padre Pettifer, the chaplain, and my brother here talked me out of it – though the death happened aboard my ship, we are still in English waters and it would be folly to disregard the legal procedures. Besides, we could hardly keep it a secret. So I had him rowed ashore and handed over to the coroner. A messenger was dispatched to his wife the same day – Dunne was a Devon man, his family seat no more than a day's ride away. The inquest will be held in three days, to give her time to travel.' He twists the gold ring in his ear. 'You see my difficulty, gentlemen? If Dunne was killed unlawfully, I must find out what happened before we set sail, but without jeopardising the voyage.'

'You mean to say it could have been someone in the crew? He might still be here?' Sidney asks in an awed whisper.

'This is what we must ascertain, as subtly as possible,' Drake says. 'For my part, I do not believe any stranger could have done it. We have a watch throughout the night and they swear no unknown person came aboard after dark.'

'If it was someone among your men, surely it is all to the good that he believes the death is taken for a suicide?' Knollys says. 'He will think himself safe, and perhaps make some slip that will give him away.'

'That is my hope. Either way, we cannot sail until this is resolved.' Drake pinches the point of his beard and frowns.

'He may strike again.' He glances at his brother. I wonder if he has some particular grounds for believing this. 'But neither do I want the inquest to conclude that Dunne was murdered and set the coroner to investigate it. The fleet could be delayed indefinitely then. Men would desert. The entire expedition could be finished.' He looks to Sidney as he says this. Given how many of Sidney's friends and relatives at court have invested in this voyage, he knows as well as Drake what is at stake. He nods, his face sombre.

'But the family will not want a verdict of *felo de se*,' Knollys murmurs. 'It would mean he died a criminal and his property would be forfeit to the crown. If there is the slightest doubt, his widow would surely rather it were treated as unlawful killing. At least then there is the prospect of justice.'

'The coroner *must* reach a verdict of *felo de se*,' Drake says sharply, 'or we are looking at sixty thousand pounds' worth of investment lost.' He waves a hand towards the window, where the other ships of this expensive enterprise can be seen rising and falling on the swell. 'To say nothing of the faith of some of the highest people in the land, including the Queen herself. This is the largest private fleet England has ever sent out. If we should fail before we even leave harbour, I would never again raise the finance for another such venture. I *must* determine whether there is a killer aboard my ship before the inquest.'

'And what will you do when you find him?' Sidney asks.

'I will decide that when the time comes.'

Knollys looks as if he is about to offer another argument, but at the sight of his commander's face he falls silent. I watch Drake, fascinated by his flinty expression. To lead a company of ships and men to the other side of the world must require a character that inspires loyalty. But what other qualities must it demand? Ruthlessness, in no small measure, I imagine; the willingness, if necessity forces your hand, to declare that the law is whatever you say it is. On board a ship, thousands of miles from shore, you must believe yourself the king of your own small kingdom, and keep your subjects obedient by any means necessary. You would have to act without compunction, and make your decisions without wavering.

'Why before the inquest?' Sidney asks.

'I was mayor of Plymouth four years ago,' Drake says. He rests his elbows on the table. 'I know how the functionaries of the Town Corporation work. The Devonshire coroner could not find a felon if one were hiding behind his bed-curtains. The kind of ham-fisted investigation he would carry out aboard my fleet would achieve nothing but to sow discord and mistrust among the crews and allow the killer every chance to escape. No.' His right hand closes into a fist and the muscles tighten in his jaw. 'I mean to find this man myself.'

He looks around the company as if daring anyone else to question his judgement. The others lower their eyes; there is a prickly silence.

'How many men do you have on board the *Elizabeth*?' I ask.

'At present, while we wait in harbour, around eighty men,' Drake says.

'And no one saw or heard anything? It would seem strange, on such a busy ship, that a man in good health could be subdued and hanged in his own cabin without anyone hearing a disturbance.'

Drake looks at me. 'You are right. But Dunne was very drunk the night he died. He had gone ashore with a few of the others. They said he was acting strangely even before they had come within sight of a tavern.'

'Strangely, how?'

'Some of the men said he had a blazing argument in an inn yard, ending with punches thrown on both sides. Then Dunne stormed away and the others didn't see him again until later. Padre Pettifer, our chaplain, found him wandering in the street and brought him back to the ship. Thomas met them as they were trying to climb aboard.'

'I was returning from dinner with Francis,' Thomas says. 'I thought only that Dunne was extremely drunk. He was swaying violently and his talk was very wild.'

'In what way?'

'Like a man in the grip of fever. He kept saying they were at his heels, and pointing out into the night.'

'Who was at his heels?' Sidney says, leaning forward. Thomas glances at him with disdain.

'Well, if he'd said, we might have a better idea of who to look for.' He jabs a forefinger into the air. 'He just kept pointing like a madman, like so, and saying "Do you not see him, Thomas Drake?" When I asked who, he opened his eyes very wide and said, "The Devil himself."'

'Did you notice anything about his eyes?' I ask.

'His eyes? It was dark, man,' Thomas says. Then he seems to relent. 'Though in that light they appeared very bloodshot, and the pupils dilated. The eyes of a drunken man, as you'd expect.' He sucks in his cheeks. 'It is strange. Dunne had his faults, but the bottle was not one of them. It had clearly gone to his head – he even started addressing me as his wife—'

'God help her, if you are easily mistaken in looks,' Sidney says. Thomas glares him into silence.

'I helped him to his cabin. Told him to sleep it off. Just before we reached the door, he pointed ahead and said, "Martha, why have you brought that horse aboard this ship?" Then he vomited copiously all over the deck and his legs went from under him.'

'We've all had nights like that,' Sidney says.

'Yes, it would be an amusing story, if he had not been found dead the next morning,' Drake remarks, his face stern. Sidney looks chastened.

'Between us, we laid him on the bed,' Thomas says. 'He seemed to fall asleep right away.'

'And no one saw or spoke to him after he returned to his cabin? No one heard anything unusual? Though I suppose it would be difficult to ask too many questions.' I rub the nail of my thumb along my jaw and think again that I must visit a barber soon.

'*You* ask a great many questions, Doctor Bruno,' Thomas Drake mutters. 'Anyone would think you were the coroner.'

Sir Francis regards me with shrewd eyes.

'You perceive my problem exactly. Having given out that he died by his own hand, it becomes difficult then to press the men too closely as to what they saw or heard without arousing suspicion.' He sighs, and pushes his glass away from him. 'Already some are saying they want to leave while they still can, that this is now a doomed voyage. I have persuaded them to stay for now, but if it is presumed to be murder, it would be impossible to hold a crew together, each man looking at his fellows, wondering who among them is a killer. I must tread very carefully.'

'But one of them *is* a killer, so you believe,' Sidney says, a touch of impatience in his tone. 'So you must find him, or risk him killing again.'

'Thank you, Sir Philip,' Drake says, with impeccable politeness, 'but the situation is perhaps more complicated than you understand. In any case, be thankful it is not a problem that need disturb your sleep. You will have your hands full with Dom Antonio. The poor man spends his life running from assassins already – I do not want him staying in Plymouth if there is another close at hand.'

I see in Sidney's face the effort it takes not to respond to this courteous dismissal. I half expect him to stand up and announce his intention to travel with the fleet, but perhaps I should give him more credit; even he can see that this is not the time. I frown at the table, already assembling the evidence in my mind, querying the how and the why. In part I am curiously relieved by the news of this death; surely with this shadow cast over the voyage Sidney will not be able to elbow his way aboard and I will be given an easy excuse without having to defy him. And yet there is another part of my brain that snaps to attention at the prospect of an unexplained death to be riddled out – already I am picturing the scene on deck, the last movements of the dead man as he enters his cabin, the ship dark and still. I shake my head to silence the buzzing questions in my mind. This man's death is not my business, as Drake has made clear enough.

As if he shared my thoughts, Sidney sits forward and points down the table to me.

'Well, perhaps we are in a position to help you, Sir Francis. You are fortunate that my friend Bruno here is better than a hunting dog for following the scent of a killer. When it comes to unexplained murders, he is your man.'

He leans back, beaming at me. At this moment, I would willingly push him overboard.

Drake arches an eyebrow. 'Is that so? A curious talent for a theologian.'

'I fear Sir Philip exaggerates. On one or two occasions I have happened, by chance, to be—'

'He will not boast of it because he is too modest,' Sidney cuts in. 'But I could tell you some tales – Bruno has a prodigious memory and the subtlest mind of any man alive for finding a murderer and bringing him to justice. Why, only last summer—'

'Yes, but these are nautical matters, Sir Philip, and I have no experience of such things,' I say quickly, before Sidney can volunteer me for the task. 'Sir Francis is right – this sad business is not our concern.'

I expect Drake to concur, but instead he studies me carefully, still pulling at the point of his beard. 'You are a scholar, though, Sir Philip assures me? You are familiar with ancient languages?'

I bow my head in acknowledgement, recalling what Sidney

had told me about Drake's interest in me. 'Some. It would depend which you have in mind.'

'That is the issue. I'm not sure.'

Thomas Drake raises his hand again. 'Francis, I don't think—'

'Peace, Brother.' Drake pinches the bridge of his nose between his thumb and forefinger. He looks up and smiles at the company, with some effort. 'Well, gentlemen. I wish you could have found us in better cheer. I am sorry to have dampened your spirits, but I thought it best you be informed. I have faith that we will resolve this matter as soon as possible. And now, you will want to get ashore, I suppose, and settle for the night.'

Sidney looks from Drake to Knollys, confused. 'But we have a berth aboard the *Leicester*.'

Knollys clears his throat.

'Philip, I must make some adjustments to my crew now we are here and will need that cabin for another officer. I had thought, once we arrived in Plymouth, you would prefer the comfort of an inn.'

'I will have some of the men row you ashore. They are expecting you at the sign of the Star – don't worry, it's the best inn in Plymouth. I should know – I own the lease.' Drake laughs. 'I stay there myself when I am in town. Mention my name and they will do whatever they can to oblige you.' He rises, sweeping his smile over both of us, but his gaze rests on me, as if he is debating whether to say something more.

Sidney's face is taut with the effort not to protest. 'That is gracious of you,' he says, in a clipped tone. 'I wondered, Sir Francis, if we might speak privately before we leave?'

Thomas Drake looks set to step in; it seems that he has appointed himself his brother's counsellor, monitoring what he says and to whom. Drake, who does not appear to require such careful protection, waves him back.

'Of course. Perhaps we may take the air? I feel the need

of it.' He nods us towards the door. 'Wait for me on the quarterdeck – I will join you shortly.'

Sidney hesitates, then bows in acceptance. Thomas Drake opens the door for us. True to their orders, the guards are standing a little way off, close enough to keep an eye on the captain's quarters but not, you would suppose, near enough to follow the conversation within. I wonder if they have been in these positions throughout the meal. If it were me, I would have had my ear stuck to the door as soon as it was closed. I say as much to Sidney once Thomas is back inside.

'Of course you would,' he says, laughing. 'The surest way to get Bruno to do anything is to tell him he must not, in case he learns something forbidden.'

'Whereas you are the very model of obedience, as Her Majesty will soon discover.'

He hisses at me to keep quiet. We emerge on to the upper deck at the stern of the ship, the part reserved for officers. Below us, the men sit in groups, some playing at dice, some whittling away at pieces of wood with pocket knives, others leaning over the rail and staring out across the Sound at the other ships.

'It must be hard to keep discipline among the men while the ships stand idle here,' I remark.

Sidney pounces on me, his eyes lit up again with a new scheme – one I can guess at before he even speaks.

'Exactly! And Drake will be bleeding money keeping the crews fed so they don't desert. This is why we must resolve this situation for him so that the fleet can leave as soon as possible. Then he will be in our debt.'

'No.' I take a step back. 'You will not appoint me to find this killer, Philip. You have already persuaded me to join the voyage against my better judgement – though I see no sign of an invitation from Drake yet. Quite the opposite, in fact.'

He flaps a sleeve in my direction. 'That is what I mean to discuss with him. Besides – what better way to demonstrate how indispensable we are?' He squints into the low evening sun. 'Listen – the fleet cannot sail until Drake determines who was responsible for the death of Robert Dunne. A good many persons of high standing have put up their own money for this venture, at my behest, including my uncle Leicester and Lord Burghley, not to mention the Queen herself. If the ships are stuck here in Plymouth, they lose the best part of their investment. But if we were to find this killer, Bruno, we would save the voyage.' He gives my arm a little shake to press the point.

'You overpraise my abilities,' I say, pulling away. 'Once or twice, I grant you, I have been fortunate in finding out a murderer, but it is not work I seek out for the love of it. Mostly I find myself in these situations with no choice.'

'What about Canterbury? You went there willingly to seek out a killer, for the sake of a woman. But you will not do it for a friend, is that it?'

I look away. There is nothing to be said on the subject of Canterbury. He tries another tack.

'You may not wish it, Bruno, but this is something you have a talent for, just as some men have a gift for making money or singing. If God has given this to you, He intends you to use it. I see that sceptical look. But remember the parable of the talents.'

'I am only wondering when you became my spiritual adviser.' I shake my head. 'This is not our business. You heard what Drake said – the man had debts. No doubt one of his creditors grew tired of waiting. Or it is some quarrel between sailors – you think if anyone among the crew knows something, he would confide in a foreigner who has never sailed further than Calais to Tilbury? Let Drake take care of it according to his own judgement, as he said.'

Sidney nudges me to be silent; the Captain-General's head appears at the top of the stair ladder.

'Gentlemen! Thank you for waiting. It is more pleasant out here, is it not?'

He sweeps an arm round to encompass the view. The evening is still light, with charcoal streaks of cloud smudged across the deepening blue of the sky. White gulls circle around the topmast, loudly complaining; to either side the green slopes rise from the water and smoke curls from the chimneys of scattered cottages. Before us, out to sea, the other ships of the fleet rock gently at anchor, sails furled; behind us, the small town of Plymouth huddles into the bay. A thin breeze lifts my hair from my face and flutters the lace at Sidney's collar.

Drake joins us by the rail. He turns and considers me again, as if weighing me up, then returns his gaze to the horizon. 'What is it you wish to discuss, Sir Philip?' Something in his tone suggests to me he already knows full well.

Sidney knots his fingers together, giving them his close attention. When he eventually speaks, he lifts his head and looks across the harbour, not at Drake.

'Sir Francis, you recall in London, when you came to me to discuss the ordnance? We spoke of another matter then too, concerning my involvement with this voyage.'

He is careful with Drake's title now that he wants his favour. Drake frowns, then turns to Sidney with an expression of confusion or amusement, or perhaps both.

'But, Sir Philip, I thought that was just talk. I recall you proposed that you should come with us, but we both agreed Her Majesty would never give her consent.'

'And I said to you, that being the case, we would have to take care she did not find out until we were well under way.' Sidney keeps his voice low and steady, but I recognise the tone: determination edged with petulance. It is a matter of honour for him now not to back down.

Drake rubs the back of his neck. 'I assumed that was a joke. I laughed when you said it, as I remember.'

'I thought you were laughing in agreement.'

There is a long silence, during which we all watch the gulls.

One lands on the rail a little way along from us and regards us with hauteur.

'Well, look,' Drake says eventually, placatory, 'we misunderstood one another, but no harm done. In any case, you are needed to escort Dom Antonio to London and my fleet is sailing nowhere while this matter remains uncertain.' He passes a hand through his hair and raises his eyes to the clouds, as if some explanation might be found there.

'Sir Francis.' Sidney is firm now, all business. 'You will not deny my part in raising capital for this expedition. Therefore I have earned my passage with you, I think, and my friend's.'

Drake's gaze flits to me in alarm. You as well? his raised eyebrow asks.

'But if that is not sufficient for you, let us prove ourselves further. I was not in jest when I said that Bruno has a nose for unearthing murderers keener than a pig after truffles.'

'A gracious comparison,' I murmur. Drake smiles.

'The Queen herself would vouch for him, if she were here.' Sidney is relentless. 'If we can find this killer for you, no one will be out of pocket, the fleet can sail, and we will have earned our place in it.'

'And the Queen? She expects you back at court with Dom Antonio, does she not? She will not look kindly on you or me when he arrives alone and informs her that you are halfway to the New World.'

Sidney shrugs. 'But she will have forgotten her anger by the time we return, when she learns we have captured the Spanish ports.'

Drake closes his eyes briefly, as if willing himself to be patient.

'Nothing is guaranteed on a voyage like this. Her Majesty likes the idea of Spanish gold, to be sure. But she is cautious of any act of aggression that may provoke King Philip to war.'

'As if he is not committing acts of aggression every day of the week!' Sidney cries, outraged. 'He has been impounding

English merchant ships in Spanish ports and confiscating their cargos, ships going about their legal trade. We have no choice but to respond.'

Drake lays a hand on his arm. 'I have in my quarters a royal commission of reprisal, signed by the Queen's own hand, permitting me to enter Spanish ports, free the impounded English vessels, and recompense our merchants for their losses.' He pauses. 'She is not to blame if I choose to interpret recompense in my own robust way. That is precisely why she leaves the wording ambiguous. But if we are to take the ports of the Spanish Main, we must proceed with caution.'

'I always prefer cautious piracy, given a choice,' I say. 'The aggressive kind puts everyone in a foul temper.'

Drake turns to me, unsure whether I am mocking him; after a moment he laughs and claps me on the back.

'What about you, my friend?' he asks. 'Our scholar. Do you also dream of looting Spanish ships, weighting down your purse with emeralds fat as grapes? Would you risk scurvy, cabin fever, heatstroke, drowning, shipwreck, for the chance to stick a cutlass in a Spaniard?'

I look up and meet his eye. Sidney skewers me with a warning glare; here is where I am supposed to second his enthusiasm.

'I have never dreamed of sticking a cutlass in anyone, Sir Francis. But I confess I have a yearning for new horizons, and here is as good a place for me as any.' I tap the planks of the decking with my boot to make the point. 'I wouldn't say no to the fat emeralds either.'

He gives us a tired smile. 'Well, they are there for the plucking. Big as this.' He makes a circle with his thumb and forefinger. Then his hand falls to his side and his face grows serious. 'Is it true, then, that you have a gift for finding out a killer? Discreetly?'

'I would not call it a gift, sir. More a series of coincidences.'

'I have disputed with my brother just now,' Drake says, eventually. 'He thinks I should not confide my suspicions of the Dunne business with those outside the command of this voyage. I hardly need say that I must swear you both to secrecy on this matter. But I would ask your advice, since you have offered your services. Because you are educated men, and God knows I am not. The only pages I read are nautical charts.' There is something pointed in the smile he gives Sidney as he says this, as if he is well aware how Sidney views his status. To my friend's credit, he lowers his eyes, embarrassed.

'Connected with the death of Robert Dunne?' I ask.

Drake glances over his shoulder and leans forward on the ship's rail so that we are obliged to huddle in to hear him.

'I do not know exactly whose hand moved against Dunne that night, but I suspect I know who was behind it. And if I am right, there will be more deaths. Ending with my own, if he is not stopped.'

A cold gust of wind cuts across the deck; I shiver, and feel it is the effect of his words, though he speaks matter-of-factly.

'Hence the guards,' I say.

'Those I keep anyway. But now I keep more of them. I cannot help but suspect Dunne's death was a warning to me.'

'How do you conclude that?' Sidney says. 'If he had bad debts, could it not be—'

Drake's look silences him.

'I know it, Sir Philip, because I have made many enemies in my life, and they have vowed vengeance. All our past deeds, gentlemen, one way or another, will be washed up on the shore of the present.' He stares out across the water, where the fading sun has brushed a trail of light in its wake.

I exchange a glance with Sidney.

'Can you be any more specific?' I say.

Drake half turns his head. 'Oh yes. There is a particular story here, but I will not keep you longer tonight, gentlemen. Tomorrow we will speak further. I would like you to look at a book for me, Doctor Bruno,' he says, then glances again over his shoulder. Though no one else is on the quarterdeck, still his face grows guarded. 'Not here. We will dine tomorrow at your inn. Oh – one more thing. Tomorrow my wife arrives from Buckland with her widowed cousin. They think they are coming to see us off – I did not have the chance to warn her. This death has given me much business to attend to in Plymouth – I may prevail upon your gallantry, gentlemen, to keep the ladies company while I am occupied.'

I make a little bow of acquiescence; there seems nothing else to do. Sidney remains silent, but his affront is almost palpable. I put a hand on his arm as if to restrain whatever outburst I sense brewing, and he shakes it off as if it were a wasp.

'Give you good night, gentlemen,' Drake says, his smile and handshake businesslike once more. 'Until tomorrow, then.'

We follow him to the head of the stairs and I see the armed men waiting at the bottom, staring straight ahead like a pair of statues at the door of a church.

THREE

Sidney is obliged to tamp down his anger while we take our leave of Knollys and the others, which he does with faultless manners, though I sense him bristling beneath the courtesy. As two of the crewmen row us to shore in a small craft, he presses his lips together and says almost nothing; it is left to me to respond to the sailors' cheerful advice about where to find the best whores in Plymouth and which taverns water their beer. From the broad bay of Plymouth Sound they take us between the great ships and through a harbour wall into a smaller inlet they tell us is called Sutton Pool. Here fishing boats jostle one another at their moorings, their hulls gently cracking together; the sailors ease us deftly between them to a floating jetty, where we stumble out and make our way to the quayside. Standing on solid ground for the first time in days, my legs feel oddly unreliable; when I look at the line of houses facing the harbour wall, they shift and sway as if I had been drinking.

Once the sailors are away from the quay and out of earshot, Sidney plants his legs astride, hands on his hips, and allows himself to vent.

'Do you believe the face of that man?' His expression is almost comical; I have to bite the inside of my cheek not to laugh. He takes off his hat, grabs a fistful of his own hair and pulls it into spikes. 'I come here as Master of the Ordnance and he thinks I am fit only to amuse his womenfolk? If he had a child I dare say he would appoint me its nursemaid, all the while telling me he is not sure there is a place for me on the voyage I helped to finance!'

'I have never known you to scorn the company of women.'

'It is not fitting for a gentleman, do you not see that, Bruno? No, perhaps you don't.' Because I am not a gentleman, he means. He lets out a dramatic sigh. 'Some old widowed cousin. And his wife – they say she is young, but she cannot be much to look at or he would not entrust another man with the care of her.'

'Perhaps he trusts her to resist you.'

He looks at me with a face of mild surprise, as if this idea is a novelty. 'Huh. Still, it is an insult. Even this' – he waves a hand vaguely towards the narrow streets behind us – 'he supposes I am so soft I cannot live without a feather bed, does he? We should be out *there*, Bruno, with the men. Well, we shall be soon enough – I will see to it.'

He crushes his hat between his hands as he makes an effort to master himself, but I see how much our exclusion from the ship has wounded him; he takes it as another humiliation. First the Queen, now the farmer's son; does everyone think he is fit only for the company of women? And this wounded pride is dangerous; it makes him more reckless in his desire to prove himself.

'It does seem that he is not keen to take on extra mouths to feed,' I say. 'And maybe he has reason – it is not as if we would be the greatest assets to any crew.'

'Speak for yourself.'

'I do. I have told you already, I would be no use at sea. They would rather conserve the rations, I'm sure.'

'And yet.' Sidney regards me with his head on one side, as if an idea has just struck him. 'He is interested in you. He asked me to bring you. What is this book he wants to show you in particular, I wonder?'

'Something to do with ancient languages.'

'Odd – he doesn't strike one as the type to pore over antique texts. He seemed to imply it was connected to the murder.' His eyes grow briefly animated, until he remembers his grievance. 'Well, either way, we must give him what he wants, Bruno. Let us find his killer, read his book, whatever we must to show him we have skills he can use.'

I say nothing, only pick up my bag and begin walking, with a strange lurching motion, in the direction of the houses. Sidney falls into step beside me with his long loping stride, pensive and silent. I see clear as day what he does not, or will not acknowledge: Drake does not want him on this voyage. Even if we found Robert Dunne's killer tomorrow and presented him to the Captain-General bound and gagged by dinner, I do not think it one whit more likely that Drake would take us on board. There is no point in saying this to Sidney.

'You know, tomorrow,' he mutters, as we turn into a narrow cobbled street that curves steeply upward from the harbour wall, 'I think I will make it my business to visit all the larger ships of the fleet and discuss the armaments with their captains. That way they will know I am here as Master of the Ordnance, not merely an escort to exiled princes and Drake's womenfolk. I will not have these sailors laughing at me behind their hands.'

'But you don't know anything about ordnance. Not when it comes to using it. They may laugh directly in your face if you pretend to knowledge you don't have.'

He glares at me, then breaks into a grin. 'If you affect to know what you are doing, most people will take you at your own evaluation. I believe it was you taught me that, Bruno.'

I smile, to concede the point. 'I am not sure that will work with men who have sailed around the world once already.'

We find the sign of the Star readily enough on Nutt Street, a broad thoroughfare lined with tall, well-appointed houses.

Sidney explains his connection to Drake and pays for a room, demanding – as if in parody of himself – linen sheets and a feather mattress; while he is haggling with the landlady over the best chamber I glance around the entrance. It is a fine building, perhaps a century old or more, and grand in the plain style of the times: broad flagstones on the floor, strewn with rushes; limewashed walls; a high ceiling with wooden beams. The candles in the wall sconces are beeswax, not cheap tallow, and there is a warming smell of roasting meat and spices drifting from the tap-room. And yet I find I do not like the place. Some nameless instinct makes my skin prickle; my fingers stray to the small knife I carry at my belt and stroke its smooth bone handle for reassurance. I sense something here that makes me uncomfortable, though I cannot explain why. When I remark on this to Sidney as we climb the stairs to our room, he only laughs.

'Relax, Bruno – Robert Dunne's murderer is back on the *Elizabeth Bonaventure*. He's not going to come creeping in here in the night looking for you. Besides, this is the only decent inn in Plymouth – I'm not moving because you have a feeling in your waters, like the village wise woman.'

I laugh with him; he is probably right. But I can't shake the notion that someone's eyes are on us, and they are not friendly. When we come down to the tap-room for a last drink before bed, I pause in the doorway while Sidney finds a seat, scanning the tables, the other men ranged on benches. The inn is busy; anyone within twenty miles who has produce to sell will have heard that Drake's fleet is at anchor here, and know that where there are ships, there is an insatiable demand for provisions. Two thousand five hundred hungry men altogether in the fleet, according to Knollys, and for every day the voyage is delayed, those men have appetites of all kinds that must be fed.

I push through the crowd while Sidney goes to the serving hatch, my eyes still sweeping the room for a seat, when a knot of people suddenly parts and I see a figure at the end of a wooden bench, in the shadows of a corner, close to the outer door, staring at me. I don't have a clear sight of his face; he wears a shapeless hat pulled low, and a black travelling cloak, though the room is stuffy. All I see is that he is looking directly at me, but there is something about the shape of him, the way he hunches into his chest, trying not to be noticed, the way his eyes burn from under the brim of his hat, that echoes in my memory; I feel certain I have seen him before. I turn to Sidney to point the man out, but someone blocks my view and when I look back he is gone and the door is banging hard. Without waiting, I shove past a group of merchants, ignoring their aggrieved cries, and fling myself out into the inn yard, wheeling around for a sight of the stranger in his cloth hat.

The yard too is busy; horses, carts, stable lads, travellers dismounting. Boys cross back and forth hefting bales of straw or gentlemen's panniers, sidestepping to avoid one another, their timing as precise as a dance. There is no sign of the man in black. Dodging the bustling people and the piles of dung, I chase out of the high gates and into the street, looking left and right. He is gone, and the light is fading. Clouds have crept in and banked up over the town while we were indoors. Sidney arrives beside me, a tankard in each hand, following my gaze with a perplexed frown.

'What are you doing out here?' he says.

'That man in black, skulking in the corner. You saw him?'

'I saw a good forty men in that room, at least half of them wearing black. What about him?'

I shake my head. 'He was watching us. I am certain of it. When he realised that I had seen him, he ran.' I hold my arms out to indicate the empty street. 'But where to?'

'Who would be watching us?' Sidney follows my gaze up the street, sceptical. 'No one knows we are here.'

'I don't know. Though I have seen him before, I am sure of it.' But as I look around, watching the last few passers-by making their way home as night falls, I begin to doubt my conviction. I have made enemies during my time in England, but none of them could have known I would be here. The years I spent on the run in Italy, when I first fled my monastery, taught me what it meant to live always looking over your shoulder, watching every crowd for a hostile face, for the man with his hand tucked inside his cloak. I had thought in England I would be free of that, but the work I have done for Walsingham has meant that, even here, there are those who hate me enough to want to kill me. I take a deep breath; last year, when I thought I was being followed around London, I vowed I would not become one of those men who jumps at shadows and draws his knife each time a dog barks. But the man in black was real enough. I only wish I could place him.

'Well, you're supposed to be the memory expert,' Sidney says, cheerfully. 'If you can't remember a face, what hope for the rest of us?'

'I didn't see his face. It was more – his demeanour.'

He gestures towards the inn with his ale. 'For God's sake, come in and have a drink. You can sleep with your dagger drawn if it makes you rest easier.'

He thinks, though he would not say so, that I have imagined the man in black, or at least imagined his interest in us. Perhaps he is right. We make our way back in silence. There is no sign of the man when we pass through the tap-room, though the same sense of unease lingers. Any doubts I had about the voyage have only been redoubled by the day's events and the prospect of entangling ourselves in another murder, and one that is no business of ours. Sidney stays below in the tap-room, drinking with strangers; I lie on my bed, staring at the map of cracks in the ceiling plaster. Everywhere I turn, it seems, my life is in jeopardy, whether out to sea, back to France or even here in Plymouth. I do not sleep with my knife drawn, but I keep it beside my bed, and when Sidney rolls in later, he finds me sitting bolt upright the instant the latch creaks, one hand already reaching for it, and the sight makes him laugh.

FOUR

I break my fast alone the next day; Sidney is ill-tempered after his late night, and lies moaning and tangling himself in sheets while I wash. He says he is not hungry. I take some bread and cheese and small beer at a long table with other travellers in the tap-room. My fellow guests regard me briefly with bleary eyes, before returning their attention to their food; I am by no means the only person with a foreign aspect here and I reflect that this is one advantage of a port town. The sky outside is dull, the grey-yellow of oyster flesh, and in the flat light my fears of last night shrink and lose their substance, until I can almost laugh at myself. I glance occasionally to the seat by the door where the man in black had been sitting, and wonder if I did imagine his malevolent stare after all.

The morning passes slowly. Sidney frets and chafes like a child kept from playing outside, waiting for some word from Drake. He suggests walking down to the harbour and finding someone who will row us out to the ships for a fee, but I talk him out of it, reminding him that Drake said he would dine with us at the Star at midday. Until then, there is nothing to do but wait. I try to read but his pacing up and down the room muttering makes that impossible; eventually I suggest a walk and he agrees. Overhead the clouds threaten rain; I glance up, pull my cloak closer around me and think with longing of the skies over the Bay of Naples.

The quayside is a bustle of activity. Small fishing boats negotiate their way around one another in an elaborate dance as they move toward the harbour entrance; men call out from the jetties as ropes are thrown to and from vessels and barrels of fish hauled ashore. Broad, red-faced fishwives are gathered with their trestles and knives at the dockside where the goods are unloaded, their hands silvered and bloody. Ever optimistic, the gulls circle boldly a few feet above their heads, screeching like a Greek chorus. The smell of fish guts carries on the wind.

We walk along the harbour wall as far as the old castle with its four squat towers, built on the headland to defend the harbour. Ivy and creepers hang like cobwebs from its stonework, giving it a neglected air. The sight of the ships out at sea only serves to darken Sidney's mood.

'I had far rather be out there, Bruno, whatever work they put me to.' He waves a hand towards the Sound, where the *Elizabeth Bonaventure* bobs like a child's painted toy.

'I know. You have said so.'

Then his face brightens. 'I had some interesting conversation in the tap-room last night after you retired. Concerning our friend Robert Dunne. Do you want to hear?'

'Ah, Philip. Is that wise? Drake wants the man's death regarded as a suicide – he will not thank you for fuelling speculation among the townspeople with too many questions.'

'Before you start chiding like a governess, I asked no questions – as soon as the traders in the bar learned I was connected to the fleet, there was no holding them back. And if Drake thinks he has silenced all speculation with the report of suicide, he is sorely mistaken.' He rubs his head and winces. 'By God, that ale is strong. We should turn back, you know. Drake may be there already, waiting for us.'

The sun lurks dimly behind veils of cloud, almost directly

overhead. We turn and follow the path back towards the town.

'The townspeople talk of murder, then?'

'Murder, witchcraft, curses – you name it. The sailors are not popular in Plymouth, for all the people here depend on them for a living.' He glances around for dramatic effect, though there is no one else out walking. A sharp wind cuts across the headland; up here it feels more like November than August.

'So it seems,' he continues, 'that our friend Dunne—'

'Stop calling him that.'

'Why?' He frowns. 'Why are you so irritable today? I'm the one who's been poisoned by that ale.'

'He wasn't our friend, and we have no reason to be poking about in the business of his death. It sounds as if you are making light of it.'

Sidney takes me by the shoulder. 'His death, as I have already explained to you at least three times, is our ticket on board that ship there.' He points. 'A ship that in a year's time will come back to this harbour so weighed down with gold you'll barely see the bowsprit above the waves.'

I do not bother to argue. 'Go on, then. Dunne.'

He clicks his tongue impatiently and pulls his hat down tighter against the wind. 'Robert Dunne was well known in Plymouth, they said. He had been living here for the past few months, though his home was in Dartington, a day's ride away.'

'Not on good terms with his wife, then?'

'That's part of it.'

The path begins to slope down towards the street that runs alongside the inner harbour, where the little fishing boats are moored. Below us, men sit on upturned barrels on the quay, mending nets or examining sailcloth. A group of small boys are scuffling on the harbour wall, fistfighting or trying to hit gulls with their slingshots. Occasionally a pebble goes astray, and one of the fishermen raises a fist and shouts a bloodthirsty curse as the boys dart away in a gale of raucous laughter. I wait for Sidney to elaborate.

When he is certain I am paying attention, he leans in closer and lowers his voice.

'Apparently Dunne was a regular at the town's most notorious brothel. A place they call the House of Vesta.'

'Really? After the Vestal Virgins of Rome, I suppose. Very subtle. So his wife found out, climbed aboard the ship in disguise, and strung him up?'

'Try to take this seriously, Bruno. Dunne had been seen more than once in the company of the same two men.'

'In the brothel?'

'No – in the taverns. No one knows who they were. And these Plymouth merchants and traders, believe me, they make it their business to know everyone. They knew who I was before I'd opened my mouth. But Dunne's companions remained a mystery.'

'Was one of them a man in a black cloak?'

Sidney rolls his eyes. 'Actually,' he says, tapping a finger against his teeth, 'they did say one of the men always wore a hat. Even indoors. Did your phantom last night have a hat?'

'Yes – a black one, pulled low over his ears. And both he and his hat were quite real, I assure you.'

Sidney considers this. 'Every one of those foul-breathed fishmongers last night claimed to have seen Dunne with his companions around and about, yet not one of them got a close look at their faces.'

'Well, at least we know one of them had a hat. That narrows it down.'

He grins. 'Not much of a start, is it?'

'Drake said Dunne got into a tavern fight the night he died. Do your reliable sources know anything about that?'

He leans in. 'The favourite theory is that these strangers were using Dunne to get at Drake's treasure.'

66

'What treasure?'

'Drake is famous in Plymouth, as you'd expect, and well liked with it, he has done a great deal for the town, but of course elaborate theories multiply around him – that when he came back from his trip around the world he gave up only a fraction of his booty to the Queen and has hidden the rest somewhere nearby.'

'And these honest souls would like to recover it and hand it over to Her Majesty?'

Sidney laughs. 'I'm sure that's exactly what they plan to do with it. But you should hear the stories they tell about what else Drake brought back with him.'

'Such as?'

'Books written by the hand of the Devil, birds with feathers of real gold, young women with two heads who give birth to children that are half-dragon, half-man. The sort of things everyone knows they have on the other side of the world.'

'Oh, those. Where is Drake supposedly keeping this diabolical menagerie?'

'I don't know. I suppose they think that's what Dunne was being paid to find out.'

We follow the street along the quayside by the row of limewashed houses and taverns facing the water. Suddenly Sidney elbows me in the ribs and nods to the path ahead, where two well-dressed young women are walking towards us arm-in-arm, followed at a discreet distance by a manservant. One is tall, with red-gold curls pinned back under a French hood, the other darker, with pale skin and strong brows. From their glances and shared whispers it is clear that they have also noticed us. Sidney is about to embark on an elaborate bow, when one of the ladies cries out, her hand flying to her mouth; she is not looking at us but beyond, to the harbour wall. Wheeling around, I see one of the boys who was fighting; he is calling urgently and pointing down. The smallest of his companions has fallen from the quay into the water, where he flails and splutters, attempting to cry out.

'It's my brother, he can't swim. I never meant to push him in,' squeals the boy on the quay, hopping up and down and flapping his hands.

The blond head in the water sinks below the surface, bobs up again in a brief frenzy of foam, then disappears. Without thinking, I tear off my doublet and plunge in, fighting to open my eyes in the murky water, my ribs jarring at the shock of the cold. At first I can see no sign of the child, then I look down and see his little body sinking in a silver chain of bubbles, his smock shirt billowing around him. I surge forward and grab at his waist, dragged back by the weight of my wool breeches in the water; he is surprisingly heavy, but once I break through the surface, gasping at the air, it is not far to the wall. Hands reach out to lift the boy; he is laid on the cobbles, while one of the fishermen bends his ear over the boy's face. I haul myself on to the quay and kneel on the stone to recover my breath, water coursing from my clothes and hair. The boy lies there, unmoving; the man beside him tries shaking him to provoke a response.

'Is he dead?' wails the child who pushed him, clawing at his shirt in anguish. 'Mother will kill me.'

'Here.' I kneel beside the boy and press hard several times on his chest. 'I have seen this done in Venice, when a boy fell in a canal.' The child promptly raises his head and vomits over the shoes of the man beside him, who lets out a surprised curse and cuffs the older boy round the head.

'Do that again, you little bugger, and I'll throw you in after him,' he says, as the boy howls even louder. 'Give us all a fright like that. If this gentleman hadn't been so quick you'd have lost your brother, and I wouldn't have liked to be the one to tell your mother her darling was gone.'

It strikes me that this distinction may have prompted the boy's desire to push his brother in the first place, but I keep silent. The fisherman turns to me. 'Thank you, sir. My nephews – always scrapping where they shouldn't be. Their mother's a widow. If you hadn't been here – I can't swim myself, see.' He glances back at the murky water with a grimace. 'Amos Prisk, sir. That's my boat there.' He points, then wipes a hand on his smock and holds it out to me. He has a firm grip, though somewhat slippery. I try not to think about fish guts. 'I would stand you a drink, only my sister's not back from the market with the day's takings.' He lets go of my hand and turns his palms out, empty.

'No need,' I say, embarrassed. Quite a crowd has gathered to watch the drama; at its edge, I see the two attractive women looking at me and whispering to one another. I wipe my hand surreptitiously on my wet breeches, push my dripping hair out of my face and give them an awkward smile. The taller one leans over to whisper something to her friend and they both laugh. I glance away and, over their heads, some distance off, I glimpse a figure in black, standing between two houses at the mouth of one of the alleys that curves down from the town towards the harbour. He remains completely still, observing the scene, his face cast into shadow by the brim of his hat. I take a step forward, but Sidney cuts across my line of sight.

'Heroic of you, Bruno. You've got seaweed on your face. Here.' He picks off the offending plant, folds his arms and nods, as if impressed, though he can't quite disguise the irritation in his voice. I motion him out of the way, impatient, but the man in black has disappeared. Sidney has my doublet draped over one arm.

'I'm sure you'd have done the same if your clothes were less valuable,' I say, reaching down to wring out my breeches. He gives me a pointed smile.

'We had better get you away from the ladies – the way that shirt is clinging to you verges on indecent.' He takes my arm and steers me towards the houses. As we pass, he bows

69

to the two women, but I notice the darker one is watching me with an intent expression.

'That was very brave,' she calls, as if on impulse, as we are almost past them.

Sidney turns his most gracious smile on her, placing his hand carefully on my shoulder. 'My friend is celebrated from here to the Indies for his bravery. Please do not think of falling in the water, ladies, unless he is at hand.'

I catch the woman's amused glance, and shake my head in apology.

'But, sir,' she says, with mock concern, 'how shall we know where to find you, if we should happen to think of falling in?'

Sidney raises an eyebrow at me. 'You may find us at the sign of the Star, madam.'

'Well, that is a coincidence,' says the auburn-haired woman. 'We too will be staying there tonight. Good day, gentlemen.' She takes her companion's arm and turns elegantly, flashing a smile back at Sidney over her shoulder.

He watches her walk away, then turns to me with a low whistle.

'They were a couple of bold ones, weren't they? Pretty, though. And expensively turned out. Courtesans, do you think?'

'Here?'

'Where there are sailors . . . But maybe you're right. Women of that quality would cost more than a sailor makes in a year, unless his name's Francis Drake. Staying in our inn, too. That dark one was eyeing you, Bruno, though you have the look of a drowned dog. Damn you!' He raises a fist, grinning. 'I should have moved faster. Nothing like saving children or animals to make women fall at your feet.'

'Next time we see them, I will drop a kitten down a well so you can prove yourself,' I say, rubbing my arms and shivering as my wet clothes chill against my skin. He drapes my doublet over my shoulders and cuffs me gently on the back of the head, the way the fisherman did with his young nephew. I decide not to tell him about the man in black, for now.

At noon we descend to the tap-room of the Star to look for Drake, and the serving girl points us towards a private dining room across the entrance hall. I am dressed in a russet doublet and breeches of Sidney's while I wait for my clothes to dry, and feel like one of those pet monkeys the ladies at court keep on a leash, trussed up in little silk jackets and jewelled collars. The breeches are too big, and the rustle of silk as I walk is unfamiliar and disconcerting; at every step I find myself turning, thinking I am being followed, until I realise again the strange susurration is coming from my own legs.

Sidney pushes open the door and is not quite quick enough to disguise the drop of his jaw when he sees the guests gathered around the table. Francis Drake sits at the head of the table. Thomas Drake is present too, with a fair, round-cheeked man in clerical dress, and an expensively dressed man of around forty. But Sidney's eye is caught by the two young women from the quayside, who sit demurely at the table, mischievous smiles hovering at their lips. For a moment I am confused; Sidney's earlier speculation has lodged in my mind and my first thought is that Drake has hired the women. Then I see him lay his hand over the delicate white fingers of the auburn-haired woman and the truth slowly dawns. She wears a wedding band on her left hand.

'I hear you are quite the knight errant, Doctor Bruno.' Drake raises his glass to me as we edge around the table.

'The mothers of Plymouth need not fear for their children while you are in town,' says Thomas Drake. He is seated to the right of the dark-haired woman, who is still watching me with that secretive half-smile. I sense that Thomas Drake would prefer it if we were not there.

'I fully expect Bruno to be offered the freedom of the city

71

by the time we leave,' Sidney says, flashing the beam of his smile around the company.

I shrug, embarrassed by the attention. 'Anyone would have done the same.'

'I would, of course, if I'd noticed in time,' Sidney agrees, sweeping off his hat. 'You were just that bit quicker, I'm afraid.'

'Oh, but it would have been a pity to ruin such a fine feather for the sake of a fisherman's child, Sir Philip,' the dark-haired woman says, with a perfectly sincere expression. Her friend bites down a smile, then raises her eyes to meet Sidney's. Drake looks from one to the other with amusement.

'I believe you are already acquainted,' he says, gesturing to the two women.

'We were not formally introduced, dear,' the auburn-haired one says, patting his hand.

'My wife Elizabeth, Lady Drake,' he says, with pride, and the woman inclines her head modestly, before glancing up at Sidney from under her lashes. He looks like a man who has bet the wrong way in a dog fight.

'And her cousin Nell, Lady Arden.'

The dark-haired woman nods to Sidney, then looks directly at me. 'Widow of the late Sir Richard Arden,' she adds. I cannot help feeling this is for my benefit. So much for the notion of Drake's plain wife and her ageing widowed cousin. I suspect that Sidney's enthusiasm for the task of chaperoning the women around Plymouth has increased significantly. In fact, it is likely that I will have to chaperone them from Sidney.

Drake waves Sidney to an empty chair at his left hand, opposite his wife. I take the remaining seat, between the clergyman and the one who looks like a courtier, placed diagonally opposite Lady Arden, who smiles again, as if she is enjoying some private joke. I guess her to be in her mid-twenties, of an age with Drake's wife; her pale skin is smooth and flawless and beneath those dark brows her green eyes

72

glint with a suggestion of mischief, and miss nothing. In an instant, Plymouth has grown considerably more interesting.

'So you are the renowned Doctor Bruno?' The man in clerical robes sets down his cup and regards me with a placid expression. Reluctantly, I turn my attention from Lady Arden to look at him. He has that high colour in his cheeks, peculiar to some Englishmen, that makes it seem he is permanently blushing or flustered. His fair hair is thinning severely on top, but the smoothness of his face suggests he is no more than his early thirties. There is no obvious edge to his words, but I cannot help interpreting them as provocative, though that probably says more about my character than his.

'I was not aware that my renown, such as it is, had reached as far as Plymouth,' I say, offering a polite smile.

'We had heard whispers that Sir Philip Sidney was bringing with him a famed Italian philosopher,' he says, returning the smile, though it does not touch his eyes. 'Ambrose Pettifer, chaplain on the *Elizabeth Bonaventure*.' He extends a hand, as if he has just remembered the correct etiquette. I grasp it; his handshake feels unpleasantly moist.

'Giordano Bruno of Nola. Though you know that.'

'I understand you are a fellow priest. A Dominican, if I am not mistaken?'

'I'm afraid you are,' I say. 'I left my order almost a decade ago. I no longer consider myself in holy orders.'

He raises a pale eyebrow. 'I did not think that was permitted?'

'It's not. That's why I was excommunicated.'

'Ah.' His eyes widen briefly. He takes a sip of wine. 'I hear you are condemned as a heretic by the Church of Rome for the ideas in your books.'

My smile is growing strained. 'Generally by those who have not read them. In any case, I am in good company – the Pope also regards your queen as a heretic. And everyone who shares her religion.'

'Yes,' he persists, 'but is it true that in your books you draw on ancient magic, and you write that man can ascend to become like God?'

I glance around in case anyone should overhear this. 'I write about cosmology and philosophy, and the ancient art of memory. I have never argued that man can become like God.' Not in so many words, anyway.

'Good,' he says primly. 'Because that sounds like a Gnostic heresy to me. Even so,' he continues, toying with his empty cup, 'I would rather the crew did not learn that you were a Catholic priest. Englishmen are superstitious, you know, and sailors more than any. Under duress, it is the old faith they turn to. Many of them carry relics and holy medals, though they know these are forbidden, and I often hear them crying out to the Holy Virgin along with every saint in heaven.' He folds his hands together. 'I close my eyes and ears to it, of course, but it would not help if they knew there was a priest of the old religion aboard. You understand?'

'Don't worry, Padre,' Sidney says, leaning in to catch the end of this, 'Bruno is a long way from the priesthood now. He will not try and sneak the sacraments to them when your back is turned, I give you my word.'

I laugh, grateful to Sidney for trying to lighten the conversation, but Pettifer is not to be deterred.

'You may joke, Sir Philip,' he says, raising a finger, 'but a man died by his own hand aboard the *Elizabeth* only two days ago. Imagine how this has affected the men. They talk of curses and omens and God's punishment, and it makes it all the harder to keep them to the true path of faith. I have their souls in my care, you see.'

'Well, I will do my best not to add to your burden,' I say, reaching for the jug of wine. God, the man is insufferably pompous.

He gives me a tight little smile in response. 'In any case,' he says, 'I presume you will be back on the road to London as soon as Dom Antonio arrives? Sir Francis will hardly be in a position to offer him much hospitality, in the circumstances. I dare say you would all be better off back at court.'

'I dare say,' Sidney agrees breezily. Fortunately, we are spared any further exchanges on this subject by the arrival of a trio of servants carrying dishes of salad leaves and manchet bread, followed by platters of fish poached in wine.

'Caught off these shores, brought in this very morning,' Drake says, indicating the fish, as proudly as if he had caught it himself. I see Sidney and the other well-dressed gentleman looking at it with suspicion; they regard fish as a penance, to be eaten on Fridays and in Lent when good Christians forego their meat, but Drake tucks in as if it were the best venison. After a year at sea, Sidney will have gained a new appreciation for fresh fish, I think, smiling to myself as I am served.

'Do you mean to stay long in Plymouth, Lady Drake?' Sidney asks, leaning across the table.

'My cousin and I grow tired of our own company at Buckland Abbey when my husband is away,' she says. 'When we received word that the fleet was to be delayed in Plymouth, we thought we would pay a visit. Not that Plymouth has a great deal to recommend it, saving your gracious company, masters. But we are grateful for a change of scene. We may even take the opportunity to call by the drapers' and buy some cloth.'

'We ladies have to take our entertainments where we can find them,' Lady Arden adds, with a dry smile.

Drake looks at his wife and beams approval. I watch her, curious.

'And you, Sir Philip? How long will you stay?' calls my neighbour, the newcomer. He has the imperious voice of a man accustomed to talking over others. His beard is carefully trimmed to a point and flecked with grey and he wears his hair cut very short in an effort to mask his encroaching baldness, but he is still handsome, in a weathered sort of way. I notice his upper lip is swollen, with a fresh cut.

'At least until Dom Antonio arrives, Sir William,' Sidney says, leaning down the table to offer a courtly smile.

'Oh good God, is that Portuguese bastard still hanging about?' Sir William says, rolling his eyes and holding out his glass for more wine. 'You'd think he'd have given up by now. I can't understand why Her Majesty goes on tolerating him, still less giving him money.'

'Because he has a better claim to the throne of Portugal than Philip of Spain does.' Sidney's face grows serious and he sets down his knife. 'If Dom Antonio became king, he would be our much-needed ally. You must know that since Spain annexed Portugal on the death of the old king, it now commands the biggest navy in Europe. It is clearly in England's interest to oppose that.'

Sir William grunts. 'It was a rhetorical question, Sir Philip. Besides, not even Dom Antonio believes he has a hope of regaining the Portuguese throne. Spain has bought off the whole of the nobility in return for their support. Pass the wine.'

'Do you stay long yourself, Sir William?' Sidney asks.

'Me? I stay until the fleet sails.'

'And then back to court?'

Sir William barks out a sharp laugh. 'And then I sail with them, Philip. I have a berth aboard the *Elizabeth*.'

'What?' Sidney's manners can't quite keep pace with his emotions; his gaze swivels from Drake to Sir William, mouth open, until he composes himself and fixes Drake with a simmering glare.

'Sir William Savile has invested very generously in this voyage,' Drake says, although he has the grace to look a little sheepish. 'And he has valuable military experience.'

'Thought it was time for a bit of adventure,' says Sir William, with a broad grin that makes him wince, as his split lip stretches. He dabs at it with a forefinger. 'A chap can grow soft and idle, hanging about at court all summer with only women for conversation. Saving your presence, my ladies.' He nods to Lady Arden, who says nothing, though her eyes dance with indignation. 'At least, that was my intention, until this unfortunate business with poor Dunne—' He looks over at Drake and breaks off; Drake is shaking his head, as if to warn him off the subject, presumably for the sake of the women.

'How horrible,' Lady Arden says, with a dramatic shudder. 'What would make a man do that? Take his own life, I mean.' She looks up at me, green eyes wide.

'Despair,' I say, since no one else seems inclined to answer.

'Or fear,' remarks Sir William Savile, tearing at a piece of bread.

'Why do you say that?' I ask, turning to him. He regards me, apparently surprised to be addressed so directly. He appears to weigh up my status before he condescends to answer.

'Well,' he says, eventually, 'I suppose a man may be driven to a point where he considers death an escape from something worse.' He looks into his glass as he speaks.

'Worse than death?' says Lady Arden, scorn in her voice.

'There are many kinds of death, my lady,' he replies. 'Who knows what demons Robert Dunne was fleeing from.'

'Did you know him well?' I ask.

He shoots me a sharp glance. 'Not well, no. He had lands in Devon, as do I. We had conversed on nautical matters a number of times, so I was pleased to discover I had been given the cabin next to his aboard the *Elizabeth*. I had thought we would have more time to talk during the long months at sea, but alas . . .' He spreads his hands in a gesture of helplessness.

'Did you speak to him the night he died?' I lean forward, perhaps too eagerly. Savile frowns.

'I think, gentlemen,' Drake cuts in, 'that the memory of our late comrade is not honoured by discussion of his death in this way. Especially over dinner.' He smiles pleasantly but I catch the same warning tone in his voice that I noticed the day before. Savile meets his eye briefly and gives a curt nod of agreement.

The rest of the meal passes in ship talk, but the shadow of Dunne's mysterious death hovers at the edges of the conversation, the subject we are all consciously avoiding. Whenever Drake talks about being able to set sail, I am conscious that he means when he has identified Dunne's killer. It would seem that Savile and the women are still under the impression that Dunne hanged himself. If Savile had the cabin next door, Drake must have asked him about any unusual disturbance the night of Dunne's death – and if he has not, perhaps it is because he has doubts about confiding in Savile. I could not blame him; there is something unconvincing about the man's bluff bonhomie. I tell myself I should discuss this with Drake before I blunder in asking questions; then remember that I have sworn not to get involved in this business.

Further down the table, Sidney is regaling Drake and his wife with anecdotes of court life. Drake looks politely bored; his wife, by contrast, is hanging on Sidney's every word, laughing with delight as if on cue, her eyes fixed on his. If that were my wife, I think, I would keep her well away from Sidney; at this rate, he will be writing her sonnets by supper. I watch Drake: his broad, tanned face, his big red hands that dwarf the wine glass he clasps between them. I don't suppose she has a lot of sonnets from that quarter. When I look up, Lady Arden flashes me a knowing smile, as if she is following my thoughts.

As the servants are clearing the board, Drake leans in to whisper something to his wife and together they stand, excusing themselves as Drake announces he must now attend to his wife's comfort and will see us later back on board. Savile's moustache twitches with a smirk at Drake's choice of words.

'And who will attend to your comfort, Lady Arden?' Savile says, from the side of his mouth, with a slight leer. 'I am sure I could oblige.'

'How gallant, Sir William,' she says, with icy courtesy. 'I'm afraid as a widow I must fend for myself. Now, if you will forgive me, gentlemen, I think I will retire to my room for a while. The emotion of discussing nautical charts at such length has quite worn me out.' She smiles sweetly around the table and pushes her chair back.

The rest of us rise to our feet as the ladies and Drake take their leave and I turn to find Thomas Drake at my shoulder.

'Sir Francis attends you and Sir Philip upstairs, in his wife's chamber,' he murmurs. 'He wishes to speak with you in private.'

Padre Pettifer is just leaving, but he turns and catches my eye as Thomas is speaking. I am certain he has overheard. Again, I sense a hostility in the way he looks at me.

'Rich as Croesus, that one, since the old man died,' Savile mutters to me, jerking a thumb in the direction of the door.

'I beg your pardon?'

He leans in with a wolfish grin. 'Ah, no need to pretend. I saw how you looked at her. We're all trying, believe me. Who wouldn't want a ripe young widow with money in her coffers? But I tell you – Bruno, was it? – once a widow, there's little incentive to become a wife again. They get a taste for independence, y'see.' He nods a full stop, as if to confirm his disapproval. 'She'll make you work for it. They enjoy wielding their power. Still, may the best man win, eh?'

I smile. 'The field is all yours, Sir William. I am in holy orders.'

'Good God. Are you really?' He draws back and squints at me as if I have just told him I have a tail. 'Man of the cloth, eh? Whatever prompted you to do that? Still, don't worry' – he slaps me on the shoulder in that hearty way Sidney has – 'Her Majesty positively encourages priests to marry these days. You stay in England, you might yet find yourself a nice little wife. Not a woman of rank, mind, but someone. I'll keep my eye out for you.'

'That's very good of you, Sir William. Although you will be at sea for the next twelve months, at least. I fear the options will be limited.'

'True, true,' he says, rolling the tip of his moustache between his fingers. 'Well – when I come back. A governess or some such might do you nicely.'

'I humbly thank you.'

At the door, Sidney catches my eye and nods towards the stairs.

'Where are you two going with such eager expressions, eh?' Savile asks. 'Don't fancy some cards, I suppose? I'm bored witless on that ship.'

'Have you been starting brawls for entertainment?' Sidney asks, indicating his lip.

'What, this?' Savile reaches up and gingerly touches the cut. 'It was nothing. A misunderstanding. Idleness frays tempers.' He lowers his voice. 'The men just want to set sail, you know. I understand Sir Francis wants to pay his respects to Dunne's family, but really, there's the rest of the fleet to think of, not to mention the investors. The longer we delay, the greater the chance one of Philip of Spain's spies will catch wind of what we're up to and slip him a warning. We won't get as far as the Azores before some Spanish fleet jumps out on us.'

'What spies?' I ask.

'They're everywhere,' he says, with a theatrical gesture that takes in the inn's wide entrance hall. I look around. The place is empty, save for us. 'Well, they're bound to be – port full of foreigners, easy for them to slip into the crowd. Drake even keeps a damned Spaniard on his own ship – have you ever heard anything so absurd? I'll wager he's tipping off his countrymen somehow – terrible shifty look about him, y'know? Well, they all do, the Catholics – it's those black eyes they have. Can't tell if they're looking at you straight.'

I regard him impassively with my black eyes until he gives a little cough. 'Saving your presence.'

'I'm afraid we must pass up the card table for now, Sir William,' Sidney says, to cover the awkward pause. 'We are going up to read some poetry.'

'Oh, good Lord,' Savile says. '*Poetry*. I'd rather put my balls in a wine press. God save you, gentlemen.' With a brisk bow, he strides away to the tap-room.

'Perhaps your man in black is one of these Spanish spies that have infested the place,' Sidney muses, as we climb the stairs. I send him a withering glance. 'Stop looking at me with your shifty Catholic eyes,' he says, and skips out of the way before I can land a punch in his ribs.

FIVE

The room is larger and better furnished than the one I am sharing with Sidney; I see his gaze wandering around it with a touch of envy. There is no sign of the women. Drake sits on the end of an ornately carved bed. On his lap he holds a leather bag, his hands spread protectively over it, as if someone might try to snatch it from him. He looks up with a distracted smile and waves us to a chair with tapestried cushions by the fireplace. There is only one; Sidney sits, I lean against the mantelpiece. Thomas Drake stands with his back to the door and nods to his brother.

'Gentlemen,' Drake says. 'There is something I wish to show you, but it must be done in confidence.'

'Does it touch on the death of Robert Dunne?' Sidney asks, sitting forward to the edge of his chair. Drake hesitates.

'I believe so. I am hoping you might clarify that.'

From his place by the door, Thomas Drake makes a barely audible sound of disapproval. Drake looks up. 'My brother feels strongly that what I am about to share with you should remain a secret. But I have explained to him that you gentlemen are scholars, as we are not. And I believe we may trust you. After all, you want something from me, do you not?' He fixes Sidney with a knowing eye. 'A passage to the New World?'

Sidney nods, silent.

'Well, then.' Drake smiles. He pulls at his beard, considering. 'The question is where to begin.'

'The letter,' Thomas prompts. He does not sound enthusiastic.

'Yes.' Drake purses his lips, then takes a deep breath, as if he is about to embark on a difficult venture. 'The same day we discovered poor Dunne's body – that very evening, in fact – I received a message. It was brought to me on board the *Elizabeth* by my clerk, Gilbert, who collects letters that arrive for me every day from this inn. Here.' He reaches inside his doublet and draws out a sheet of paper, which he holds out. I step forward and take it from his hand, as I am nearer. The paper is rough along one edge as if it has been torn from a notebook, folded in three and had been sealed with crimson wax, though there is no mark impressed in the seal. I unfold the paper and lower it so that Sidney can see it too. The message says simply,

Matthew 27 v 5

'Cryptic,' Sidney mutters, taking the paper from my hand and turning it over. 'What is the verse? Bruno?'

'I'll wager he knows,' Drake says, catching my expression and pointing at me.

'"And he cast down the pieces of silver in the temple, and departed, and went and hanged himself,"' I murmur. 'The death of Judas Iscariot.'

Drake looks impressed. 'Do you carry the whole of the scriptures in your head?'

'Oh, Bruno is a master of the art of memory,' Sidney says, with what might be a hint of pride. 'He has devised his own system. It is what passes for entertainment where he is from. He can do you the whole of Homer if you find yourself bored one evening.'

'That will make the voyage fly,' Thomas Drake says, arching an eyebrow.

I return his sarcastic smile, and tap the paper in Sidney's hand. 'This verse. You think it is some reference to Dunne, I suppose?'

'The day he dies, apparently by hanging himself? I see no other way to read it,' Drake says.

'According to the Gospel of Matthew, Judas Iscariot hanged himself from remorse after he betrayed his master,' I say, running through the text in my mind. 'Is this mystery correspondent trying to imply that Dunne did the same? That he hanged himself out of guilt? Had Dunne betrayed anyone, that you know of?'

'But we don't believe Dunne did hang himself,' Sidney points out.

We look at Drake. He sighs heavily and opens the bag on his lap.

'Betrayal. Perhaps. Or it may refer to something else.' He reaches in and withdraws a bound manuscript. I straighten immediately, feeling goosebumps rise on my skin. In my thirteen years at the monastery of San Domenico Maggiore I spent much of my time in the scriptorium and among the archives of their library, and later among the booksellers of Venice; I can recognise manuscripts almost by touch and smell, and tell you their provenance by the feel of their bindings, their vellum, their ornamentation. I do not need to touch the one Drake now holds carefully between his fingertips to know that it is both old and unusual. Instinctively, I step forward and reach out for it.

He raises a hand. 'Bear with me, gentlemen, while I tell you a story that will help to explain what I am about to show you.'

Sidney clasps his hands around his knees like an eager child at his grandfather's chair. I shift my position against the mantel and give Drake my full attention.

'It begins eight years ago, at the beginning of my voyage to circumnavigate the globe,' Drake says. 'Does the name Thomas Doughty mean anything to you?'

He directs this question to Sidney, who sits up, surprised.

'Doughty? But of course – he used to work for my uncle Leicester. Before he was—' he checks himself, looking at Drake, uncertain. 'Before he died.'

'He was executed,' Drake says, brusquely. 'In a godforsaken place called Port San Julian, in Patagonia, at the end of the world. He was beheaded on my order in plain sight of all my crew, and with good justification, whatever gossip you may have heard at court.' He juts his chin out, as if challenging us to argue. Sidney shrinks back slightly into his chair.

'But that is not the beginning of the story,' Drake continues, his voice softer. 'Early in our voyage, not far from the Cape Verde islands, we captured a small ship, the *Santa Maria*. She was on her way to the Americas, so there was nothing of great value in the hold, but she was worth the trouble for the provisions she carried and for the use of an extra vessel. I packed her crew into the longboats and set them adrift to shore – despite the reputation Spain wants to give me, I prefer to get where I'm going without bloodshed, if I can. But there was an unfortunate incident during the capture.' He pauses and rubs the back of his neck, as if it discomforts him to recall. 'On board the *Santa Maria* was a young priest travelling out to the colonies, a Jesuit. He barricaded himself into one of the private cabins when we boarded, even though the captain had surrendered almost immediately. Thomas Doughty and his brother John broke the door down. The young priest was backed into a corner, they said, holding a dagger in one hand, and with the other clasping to his chest a wooden casket. Naturally they assumed its contents must be of value – they asked him repeatedly to give it up to them, but the priest refused. When Doughty took a step towards him, the priest ran at the brothers with his weapon, calling down all manner of curses upon them. It was an act of reckless desperation – both the Doughtys were armed with swords and when the priest lunged with his little dagger, Thomas Doughty ran him through. When the Jesuit realised he was fatally wounded, he tried to throw the casket out of the window, but John Doughty managed to stop him. You may imagine their disappointment when they discovered that the casket contained only this old manuscript, in a language neither of them could read.'

He pauses, and motions to his brother to bring him a glass of wine. Thomas Drake pours from a jug on a small table by the door and offers it to us; Sidney accepts, though I shake my head, wanting Drake to continue his story. Already my mind is racing ahead, my eyes still fixed on the manuscript under Drake's hands; if a priest was willing to sacrifice himself to save those pages, or even throw them into the sea to keep them from being found, they must possess their own kind of value. One perhaps only another scholar can assess.

'Since none of us could read it, the manuscript was consigned to the hold of the *Santa Maria*,' Drake says, after a long drink, 'and placed in a locked chest to be inventoried with the rest of the spoils. The incident with the priest was regrettable, and did not sit well with the crew, for all their dislike of the Spanish. Thomas Doughty was not popular among the men – he was high-handed and did not believe a gentleman should shoulder his share of the manual work. We had barely left Plymouth before word had reached me that Doughty was criticising my command in front of the men, and I was obliged to reprimand him, which created open resentment between us. The crew began to mutter that the murder of a priest would bring curses on our voyage – some said the priest had invoked the Devil with his dying breath.

'The *Santa Maria* was rechristened the *Mary*, in honour of my first wife, and I gave Thomas Doughty command of her, thinking this responsibility might persuade the men of my confidence in him, and quiet his rebellious mutterings against me.

86

This was a grave error on my part, as I soon came to realise. I had instructed my brother to bring me the manuscript, together with some other items of value from the hold, for I did not altogether trust Doughty.'

'He caught me taking them and accused me of stealing,' Thomas Drake cuts in. 'He and Sir Francis had a great row about it, with Doughty accusing me and my brother of helping ourselves to plunder which rightly belonged to all the men who had helped take the *Santa Maria*. While they were shouting, one of the crew whispered to me that they had seen Doughty coming up from the hold more than once, but no one had dared challenge him. Sure enough, we found a few rings and coins from the *Santa Maria* in his cabin. He claimed the prisoners had given them to him as gifts, but no one believed him, save his brother and a few malcontents they had won over to their side.' He clenches his teeth; clearly the memory of the Doughty brothers still stirs his blood.

'I deprived Doughty of the *Mary*'s command and moved him to another ship,' Drake says, taking up the story again. 'There he and his brother began to stir up a mutiny against me in earnest. Thomas Doughty spread the story that I had commanded him to kill the priest so that I could steal the Devil's book. John Doughty told the men that he and his brother were versed in witchcraft, and when it pleased them, could conjure up the Devil to make a storm that would destroy my flagship and every man who defied them. According to others, Thomas Doughty promised them substantial rewards when we arrived back in England if they would side with him to mutiny and make him commander of the expedition. He boasted to some that before he was done he would make half the company cut one another's throats.' He folds his fingers together and presses them against his lips. 'Tell me, was I supposed to tolerate such an open threat to my authority?'

He looks from Sidney to me with questioning brows; I

suppose it is a rhetorical question, but we shake our heads vigorously nonetheless.

'No indeed. I had him bound to the mainmast, to show him I was serious. When he was freed, I sent him to one of the store ships where I thought he could do no harm. We sailed sixty days south-west across the Atlantic without seeing land, and all the while I knew Doughty's brother and his supporters were still murmuring against me for my treatment of him. The discipline of the voyage was in jeopardy. So when we reached Port San Julian, I empanelled a jury to try him for treason. You know the rest.' He takes a sip of wine and looks away, as if he does not want to recount the end of the story.

Silence settles on the room, as Drake and his brother privately revisit their own memories of those events. I watch the Captain-General; he speaks as if he regrets the business with Thomas Doughty, but that unflinching ruthlessness is visible just below the surface. Drake is not a man you want to fall out with, I think, not for the first time.

'And what of the manuscript?' I prompt, nodding to it. Drake turns to me and blinks, as if working out where to pick up the thread of his story.

'The manuscript,' he says, considering. 'Well. I kept with us the navigator from the *Santa Maria*, a Spaniard named Jonas. He had sailed to the coast of Brazil before and I thought his knowledge might be useful. He spoke English well and he agreed to act as translator. It was from him that I learned a little about the young priest Doughty had killed. His name was Father Bartolomeo and he was a Spaniard, but had joined the Jesuit College in Rome and from there found a position in the Vatican library. He had boarded the *Santa Maria* at the very last minute, arriving the day before they set sail and begging passage to the Indies, claiming he needed urgent conduit to the head of the Jesuits in Brazil. The only baggage he carried was that wooden chest that he never let out of his sight. Father Bartolomeo was some distant relative of the captain, so he was found a berth as a favour. Jonas said he had kept to himself, refusing to leave his cabin, but that from the little he saw of him, he thought the Jesuit acted like a man in fear for his life. He was edgy, always looking over his shoulder, even once they had cast off. The crew had started to wonder if he had stolen whatever was in that chest and was running away to escape justice. When the cry came that the *Santa Maria* was under attack from my ship, Jonas said the priest locked himself in his cabin, but everyone on board could hear him crying out to Jesus, Mary and all the saints to forgive him for bringing the wrath of God on the voyage.'

'What did he mean by that?' Sidney asks.

Drake shrugs. 'If he'd lived, he might have been able to explain. Or at least tell us something about this book. But the Doughty brothers made sure he took his explanations with him to his Maker.'

'May I see the book?' I ask softly, unable to contain my curiosity any longer. Drake hesitates.

'I am no scholar, gentlemen, as I have told you. But even I know that a man does not throw away his life lightly over a book. I kept it under lock and key in my cabin for the rest of the journey, but with Doughty's trial and everything that came after, the book was almost forgotten.'

I am still holding my hand out for it, nodding encouragement, as you might coax a child to part with a favourite toy. Drake smiles.

'You are keen, sir. And you are not alone in your eagerness to get hold of this book. But first, I want a promise of your complete secrecy. You too, Sir Philip. Whatever this book contains, two men have already died for it. The fewer people who know I have it here, the better.'

'I give you my solemn oath,' I say. 'On everything I hold sacred.'

Sidney sends me an amused glance from the corner of his

eye; I guess he is wondering what it is that a man like me could hold sacred. For all he likes to believe himself an adventurous thinker, Sidney is obediently orthodox in his Protestant faith.

'And I,' he says. 'On my life, I swear.'

This seems good enough for Drake, who crosses the room and lays the manuscript in my lap as tenderly as if it were his own newborn. The leather of the covers feels stiff under my fingers; I realise as I open it that for what feels like an age, I have forgotten to breathe.

'If you can shed some light on this book, Bruno, it may explain certain things,' Drake says. 'At the very least, I would like to know what it is. I don't even know what language it is written in.'

'It is a Coptic text, of some antiquity,' I murmur, skimming the first couple of lines. And then my heart appears to stop beating.

'What?' Sidney says, leaning over my shoulder. 'What is it, Bruno? You've gone pale as a corpse.'

I look up, staring at Drake, temporarily robbed of speech or movement. When I finally find my voice, all I can manage is a croak.

'Have you shown this to anyone?'

He frowns. 'Very few people.'

'I mean – to anyone who might have an idea what it is?'

'I had a bookseller value it,' he says. 'Dunne suggested him.'

'Robert Dunne?'

'Yes.' He looks faintly impatient. 'After we returned from the circumnavigation, I forgot about the book. It was in a chest with many other things I brought back. With Her Majesty's blessing, you understand, not all of what we took from the Spaniards went to the Tower to be inventoried.'

I nod, brushing this aside.

'It was only when I bought the old abbey at Buckland that it came out of storage. For the first time I had a library, as befits a gentleman' – here he grins, for Sidney's benefit – 'and the manuscript was put on a shelf. I always meant to have it valued, but life threw more urgent matters in my path. My first wife died, I was elected mayor of Plymouth then Member of Parliament, I was forever on the road up and down to London, all the while trying to finance a new expedition to the Americas. The book slipped my mind. Until Dunne came out to dine with me at Buckland – his family seat was not far away. He asked me if I still had the manuscript and if he might look at it. I dug it out of the library – it was thick with dust – and he studied it for some while. Then he offered to take it to London and have it examined by an associate of his, a book dealer, who knew about such things and might be able to give me a good price for it.'

'Could Dunne read it?' I ask. A cold knot is growing in my stomach. 'Was he a scholar? Did he know what it was?'

'What *is* it?' Sidney asks, tugging at my sleeve like a child. I ignore him, waiting for Drake's reply.

'I don't think so,' he says slowly, his eyes fixed on the manuscript as if he were now wary of it. 'But he could not disguise his interest sufficiently. So, naturally, I became suspicious – it was clear he had been talking to someone about the book and believed it to be worth something.' He sighs. 'Dunne was a good sailor, God knows it serves no one to speak ill of him now, but his one great weakness was gambling. He had run up heavy debts in Plymouth and in London and was always looking for ways to keep his creditors at bay. I knew if I let him take the manuscript I would not see the half of its value, if I ever saw a penny. So I told him I would take it to this bookseller myself next time I was in London and give Dunne a commission if it turned out to fetch a good price.'

'But you didn't sell,' I say, almost in a whisper, stroking my fingertips over the parchment as delicately as if it were a woman's skin.

'I didn't trust this dealer an inch, once I met him.' Drake sits back on the edge of the bed, watching me. 'I took it to him all right. He feigned great disappointment – told me it was not what he'd been led to believe, it was not worth much after all. He offered to buy it nonetheless, and for a price that was supposed to make me feel he was doing me a favour. But there was a look in his eye – hungry, you know? He couldn't hide it.'

'Did he tell you anything about it?'

Drake shakes his head. 'He said that it was an old legend about Judas Iscariot. Of interest only to theologians. I told him I would have it valued elsewhere and he doubled his offer immediately. So I told him it wasn't for sale.' He pauses for a draught of wine. 'Less than a month later, we had a robbery at Buckland.'

'Were they looking for the book?'

'I believe so. My library was turned over. But nothing taken, as far as I could see – and I have more obviously valuable objects in the house that were left untouched. This manuscript was in a strongbox in my treasury while I decided what to do about it. I hired more armed watchmen to guard the house after that, but I was sure it must be connected to that man Dunne had sent me to.'

'This bookseller . . .' Doubt prickles at the back of my neck. 'Do you remember his name?'

Drake frowns. 'I'm not sure I ever knew it. Dunne took me to meet him in Paul's Churchyard – if we were formally introduced, I have forgotten the name he gave. I will tell you one striking thing about him, though.'

'Yes?' I raise my eyebrows, though I am almost certain I know what he is going to say.

'He had no ears.'

Sidney and I look at one another.

'It was another reason not to trust him,' Drake continues, though he has not missed the glance. 'You don't lose both ears by accident. He'd clearly been punished as a common criminal at some point, though for what I don't know.'

'Sedition,' I say, almost without thinking. Drake stares at me. 'You know this man?'

'Possibly.' My fingertips stray to my throat as my memory flashes back to my time in Oxford.

'How many book dealers have had both ears cut off?' Sidney says, turning to me. 'It must be him.'

'It's a good thing you didn't sell it to him,' I say. 'Though that won't stop him trying to obtain it by any means, if we are talking of the same man.'

'Then it *is* valuable?' Drake leans forward, a gleam in his eyes.

'For the love of Christ, Bruno – tell us what it is,' Sidney says, exasperated.

I take a deep breath, trying to keep my voice even.

'If it is genuine, this is a book the Holy Office swore did not exist. Bishop Irenaeus of Lyon mentioned it in the second century, in his treatise against the Gnostic heresies, but to the best of my knowledge, that is the only surviving reference. The Vatican library has always denied its existence, though that has not stopped scholars pursuing the scent of it—'

'Spare us the lecture, man, cut to the point,' Thomas Drake says, from his post by the door. 'Tell us what it is.'

I look at him until he looks away, then I begin to read, keeping my voice as low as I can:

'"*The secret account of the revelation that Jesus spoke in conversation with Judas Iscariot three days before he celebrated Passover.*"'

Thomas Drake just blinks, and shrugs. Sir Francis peers at the manuscript, his brow creased, as if he is trying to puzzle out the meaning. Only Sidney regards me with a glimmer of understanding.

'The testimony of Judas Iscariot.' He hesitates. 'But it must be a fiction, surely?'

I rub the parchment gently between my finger and thumb. 'Not necessarily.'

'I am still none the wiser, gentlemen,' Drake says. 'Would you care to enlighten us poor sailors?'

I look at him, considering where to begin.

'The holy scriptures contain four accounts of the life and death of Jesus Christ, those we call the gospels of the four evangelists, that were accepted by the Church Fathers as true and divinely inspired and which more or less corroborate each other. This we all know.' I tap the book on my lap. 'But there were many other accounts circulating in the early years of the Church, alternative gospels that fell outside orthodox doctrine and so were suppressed, destroyed, forbidden. Among them was rumoured to be a Gospel of Judas.'

Drake looks from me to the book and back. 'Written by his own hand?'

'Some think so. Legends have grown around its substance. The Gnostics believed it vindicated Judas Iscariot, unravelled the whole story of salvation and would overturn the foundations of the Christian faith.' My hands are trembling on the page as I speak. If this manuscript should be genuine, if it should prove that the story of mankind's salvation has been based on false accounts, *if there were another version of the story* . . . what then?

'What should be done with it?' Drake says. His expression suggests he is struggling to take this in.

'Best to keep it under lock and key, for now. And on no account sell it to that book dealer with no ears.'

'Why, what does he want with it?' Thomas Drake demands.

'I don't know yet.' I look down at the manuscript; there is no way of assessing its significance without reading it in its entirety. 'He may want to sell it to the highest bidder. Or he may have other plans.'

'Oh, no, no, no. If there is a high price to be had for this book, I shall be the one doing the selling.' Sir Francis sets his jaw and fixes me with a defiant eye.

'The Jesuit already paid a high price for it. He worked for the library of the Vatican, you say?'

'According to Jonas,' Drake says. 'Why?'

'Then it would seem reasonable to assume that he found the book there. So why was he taking it away, to the other side of the world? With the knowledge of his superiors, or without? Either way, someone must have noticed it missing and followed its trail. It would not surprise me to learn that the Holy Office has agents out looking for this book, even now.' Voicing this aloud causes a chill to run through me. If there is one quality the Roman Inquisition can never be accused of lacking, it is tenacity. And are they still looking for me, I wonder? I lower my eyes and take a deep breath. I am a free man, in a Protestant country; it is nine years since I ran from my monastery in Naples, rather than face the Inquisition. Surely they have forgotten me by now? But I already know the answer: the Inquisition never forgets. 'This book could tear the Church apart,' I add, looking up and meeting Drake's frank gaze. 'It could plunge Europe into war, if its contents are made known. You may be sure the Vatican wants it back, at any price.'

'Europe is already tearing itself apart over the interpretation of the scriptures,' Sidney says, as if the whole business bores him. 'Bread, wine, flesh, blood. Purgatory, Pope, predestination. How much difference can one more gospel make?'

I look at him with reproach. 'You can say that because your country has never had the Inquisition.'

'We had Bloody Mary,' he retorts. 'Plenty still alive remember what she did in the name of pure faith.'

Drake watches us, his chin resting on his fist. 'Perhaps the best thing would be to hand it over to Her Majesty. She can have her scholars examine it and dispose of it as she thinks fit. I would not for all the world give it back into the hands of the Pope.'

'Perhaps. But someone should read it first,' I say quickly. 'And make a copy, in case anything should happen to this one.'

'By someone, I suppose you mean you?' Thomas Drake says, with that sardonic tone he saves for me and Sidney.

'Unless you can read Coptic script, Thomas Drake, I see no one else for the job,' Sidney fires back, in my defence.

Thomas narrows his eyes at him. 'So your friend is proposing we hand the book to him. What guarantee do we have that we will ever see it again? He seems to know this book dealer well, and have a shrewd idea of its value. And – saving your presence, master – he *is* Italian.'

'You have my word of honour, which should suffice among *gentlemen*,' Sidney says as he stands, his right hand straying instinctively to his sword. Thomas Drake takes a step forward, chest out. He has not missed Sidney's emphasis, and its implication.

'Peace, both of you,' Drake says, with a warning glance. Chastened, Sidney sits and Thomas retreats to his position by the door post. 'Of course Bruno must be the one to read it. But you will have to do it in my cabin on board the *Elizabeth*. A wise man told me not to let it out of my sight.' He smiles, to draw the sting from any offence.

'But what has any of this to do with Robert Dunne's death?' Thomas says, though with less bluster than before.

Drake shakes his head.

'Has anyone looked through Dunne's personal effects?' I ask.

'No,' Drake says. 'I had thought to gather them up for the family when they arrive, but I have not had time. The cabin has been kept locked since the body was taken out.'

'Good. He had been seen about the town in the days before he died, meeting two strangers. It would be worth seeing whether he kept any correspondence, or anything that might identify them. Though I suppose we have an idea now.' I grimace at Sidney. 'We must see if we can find out who brought that Judas letter to the Star to be delivered to you. And I would like to talk to your Spanish translator about the young Jesuit.' My mind is already moving ahead, outpacing my own objections.

'I told you – Bruno will find this killer in no time,' Sidney says, rubbing his hands together with satisfaction.

Drake nods, though he does not look entirely convinced.

'You can do this discreetly? I do not want the men further alarmed with suspicions of murder. Nor Dunne's widow, who will be here any day – better she accepts that he died by his own hand, or we shall be caught in all manner of judicial snares and this fleet will never depart.'

Once again, I am struck by his lack of sentiment.

'Never fear, Bruno is as cunning as the Devil himself when he chooses,' Sidney says breezily.

I am about to protest the comparison when there is a sharp knock at the door. We all start; Thomas Drake jumps back just as the door is flung open and Lady Drake glides in, peeling off her gloves, followed by her cousin.

'You might at least wait until someone calls "Come",
Elizabeth,' Drake grumbles, though he looks relieved. 'There is a fellow supposed to be guarding the door – does he not do his job?'

'I pointed out to him that this was my chamber and he could not very well keep me from it,' Lady Drake says, offering her smile around the room. 'Have you finished your secret council? We grow bored, and the sun is out.' She glances at the book on my lap and then at me, with enquiring eyes. 'So – is the mystery solved?'

'We are giving it due consideration,' Drake says, before I can respond. He takes the book from my hand and places it carefully back into the leather satchel. I feel a pang as it leaves my hands; at this moment, I would give up almost anything for the prospect of an afternoon alone with that manuscript.

'Sir Francis, you promised us the company of these fine gentlemen for our visit,' Lady Arden says, in mock reproach, 'and yet you keep them to yourself all afternoon. You must learn to share.' She sends me a dazzling smile and curls the ribbon of her hood around her finger. I notice that this does not pass Thomas Drake by.

'Very well. I had better be getting back to the ship, in any case. Don't want to find they have all deserted by the time I return.' Drake pats Lady Arden on the shoulder, indulgent. 'Let us go down, gentlemen.'

Together, we bow to the ladies.

'We will join you in the entrance hall shortly,' Lady Drake says. 'I think we should make the most of the fine weather and walk along the Hoe while we can, do you not agree, Sir Philip?' She looks at him from under her lashes, her hands folded demurely together.

'As you wish, my lady,' Sidney says, bowing again. Drake seems satisfied; these are the kind of proper, courtly manners his new wife expects, and he is pleased to have found an escort of sufficient quality to flatter her with the appropriate deference. Only I see the look in Sidney's eyes. I hope Drake will not have cause to regret it.

The armed guard follows Drake and his precious bag down the stairs. I cannot help peering along the corridors and over my shoulder, alert to the slightest movement. If that book should fall into the wrong hands before I have a chance to look at it, I could never forgive myself, and it seems that someone here in Plymouth – more than one person, perhaps – wants it as much as I do. Even enough to kill for it, I have no doubt.

SIX

The sky is clearer over the harbour when we emerge on to the quayside, all of us walking together to see Drake and his brother into the boat that will row them back out to the *Elizabeth Bonaventure*. Patches of blue appear between banks of cloud, reflected in the water like fragments of coloured glass. The fishing boats rock gently at their moorings, accompanied by the constant slap of sailcloth and halyards in the breeze and the clanking of iron fixings. While Thomas Drake seeks out their oarsmen and Sir Francis bids farewell to his wife, I draw Sidney aside.

'Can it be him?'

He looks at me. 'Rowland Jenkes? I don't see that it can be anyone else.'

I rub at the stubble along my jaw, remembering the book dealer I had encountered in Oxford, the man who had been nailed to a post for sedition and cut off his own ears to escape, who now made a living importing forbidden Catholic literature and would not hesitate to kill anyone who stood in his way. 'We know he disappeared from Oxford before he could be caught. He had contacts with all the Catholic exiles in Paris and the French seminaries. If there were rumours of this book going missing from the Vatican library, they would reach Jenkes's ears in no time. So to speak.'

Sidney grins, though his face quickly turns serious. 'Does that mean he is in Plymouth, then?'

I shrug. 'It sounds as if someone here is after that manuscript, and Robert Dunne was involved in some way. The two men Dunne was seen meeting – Jenkes could be one of them. Were they using him to steal the manuscript, do you think?'

'Your man in black last night. Is it Jenkes?'

'It could be. I was sure I had seen him before. We will have to watch our backs – if it is, he will want to revenge himself for Oxford.'

Sidney frowns. 'In any case, that still makes no sense of Dunne's death. Drake says no stranger would have been able to board the ship without the watchmen alerting the officers. He could only have been killed by someone on the *Elizabeth* – someone working with Jenkes, perhaps?'

'But if Dunne was working for Jenkes—'

We are interrupted by a call from Drake; he and Thomas are already seated in the rowing boat, their armed escort poised at the prow, his eyes scanning the water.

'I will send a boat for you later this afternoon,' Drake calls. 'Meanwhile, the ladies will be glad of your company.'

I raise my hand in a half-wave, half-salute, though I cannot keep my eyes from the leather satchel he clutches to his chest. For all their charms, I would gladly abandon the ladies to the mercies of the port for a few hours alone with that manuscript. Only one woman ever had the power to distract me from a book as important as the one I watch recede into the glittering distance, as the rowing boat pulls slowly out towards the harbour wall, and she is long gone.

'You would rather be out to sea with the men, I think?' Lady Arden's voice startles me back to the present. I turn and she is beside me, disconcertingly close, a sly smile hovering over her lips.

'Not at all,' I say, attempting to mirror it. She laughs; a

bright, unforced sound, and begins walking away from the quayside. I fall into step beside her.

'You don't have to lie to spare my feelings, you know. It is a wretched business, being a woman – you men always regard our company as inferior to that of your own sex, because you think we have no opinions worth hearing on politics or navigation or war or any of the topics you value. Until the night draws on and you have taken a few glasses of wine – only then do you find you can tolerate our presence.'

'And have you?'

'Have I what?' She cocks her head to look at me.

'Opinions worth hearing on politics and war?'

'Oh, hundreds. And I shall tell you them all as we walk, before you have a chance to dismiss me as another flighty girl.' She slips her hand through my arm.

'I look forward to hearing them, my lady,' I say, aware of the light pressure of her fingers on my sleeve. 'I think any man who tried to dismiss you would do so at his peril.'

'You learn quickly.' She laughs again, and squeezes my arm tighter. 'So – did you read the book?'

'Which book?' I am not sure how much Drake has told his wife about the manuscript. I do not want to be the one to alarm her.

Lady Arden gives me the sort of look a nurse would give a child. 'Oh, come. The book Sir Francis thinks someone wants to steal from him. Lizzie guesses he must plan to sell it because he needs more money for the voyage. We are speculating that Sir Philip wants to buy it and that you are to make sure he gets a fair price.'

'Do I look like a book dealer to you?'

'Not a dealer. A scholar.' She pauses, looks me up and down. 'Or you did this morning. Before you fell in the water. Now you look more like . . .' She considers Sidney's clothes.

'A dressed-up monkey?'

101

'Like Sir Philip, I was going to say.' She giggles. 'Although perhaps there is not a great deal of difference.'

'Well, I will consider that a compliment. And I did not fall in, by the way. I jumped, on purpose. Just to be clear.'

She smiles again. 'Of course.'

As if to confirm the story, a chorus of shrill voices calls out from behind us. I turn to see the little boy I dragged out of the harbour that morning running up to me, barefoot, holding out what looks like a handful of leaves between his cupped hands. The larger boy, his brother, hangs back, sheepish, with a group of children of a similar age. When the small boy draws closer, I see that he is presenting me with a collection of strawberries.

'For you, master.' He proffers them, his face hopeful. A thin trail of snot runs from one nostril to his lip, but he can't wipe it with his hands full, so he twists his tongue up to try and lick it away. I look at him and am struck by the thought that this child almost didn't live to see the afternoon. His hair is still stiff with salt.

'Thank you,' I say, crouching to his height and making a basket of my hands for the fruit. 'What is your name?'

'Sam.' He puffs his chest out and looks expectantly from me to the strawberries.

I sense that I am expected to sample his gift, so I rub the dirt off one and put it in my mouth. They are bullet-hard and not yet sweet, but I make a show of relishing it.

'Sam, I think these are the best strawberries I have tasted in England.'

The child looks delighted. He wipes his nose on his sleeve and coughs, then scampers away over the cobbles to his friends, who crowd around him, chattering and pointing.

'You have made a friend for life there,' Lady Arden says.

'Strawberry?' I hold out my hands. She regards them with a delicate curl of the lip.

'Not if he picked them with the same hand he uses to wipe his nose.'

102

I smile. 'You can barely taste it. You don't like children?'
She glances back at the huddle of boys.

'I have no strong feelings about them either way. My sister
has four and I am quite happy to indulge them, for a short
time. But it was regarded as a great failing on my part not
to have produced any myself before my husband was so care-
less as to die. Whenever I see children – especially healthy
males like those – I feel implicitly reproached.'

I am not sure how to answer this, so I remain silent. When
I am sure the children are out of sight, I drop the strawberries
at the side of the road and Lady Arden takes my arm again.
We walk on for a while, Sidney and Lady Drake walking
ahead of us along the path that leads towards the castle. She
does not take his arm; instead they walk at a respectful distance
from one another, leaning their heads in to hear the other's
conversation. They are, of course, both married. I am conscious
that between Lady Arden and me there are no such restrictions. Is it proper for her to walk with me in this way? She
appears not to care; it is I who feel awkward, as if we are
breaching some rule of decorum.

'My late husband has a cousin, who is at present the only
heir to his estate and title. He has been gallant enough to offer
me marriage.' She sucks in her cheeks and gazes out to sea as
she says this.

'You are not elated by the prospect, I think.'
She makes a face.

'My husband only died last year. He was a decent man, in
his way, but it was not a match of love. He was nearly thirty
years older than me. Such arrangements are rarely successful.'
She glances at Lady Drake and looks a little guilty. 'I was a
wife for seven years, and gave him no cause for complaint.
But as a widow, his estate belongs to me while I live and I
am my own mistress. I should like a while longer to enjoy
that position, before I sign my freedom over to another man.
Besides' – she screws up her mouth – 'my husband's cousin

looks like a boar. You think I mean this figuratively, but you are wrong. He actually looks like a boar. Bristles and all. Every time he opens his mouth to speak, I want to stuff an apple in it.'

I laugh abruptly, and she joins in, leaning her weight into me. Lady Drake and Sidney stop and turn, amused, though I notice Lady Drake seems piqued.

'What is the joke, Nell?' she calls. 'Share it with us, won't you?'

'I was just telling Doctor Bruno about Cousin Edgar the boar,' Lady Arden shouts back, and follows this with a magnificent impersonation of a grunting pig. Sidney stares at her. Quite possibly he has never seen a well-born lady pretending to be a boar.

Elizabeth Drake laughs and shakes her head. 'Oh God, *him*,' she says. 'No, we all think you could do better.' Her gaze flits to me for an instant, and to the way Lady Arden leans on my arm. Do I qualify as 'better' than a titled cousin who looks like a boar, or not? Her expression gives no clue.

'Lady Drake has been telling me a little about Robert Dunne,' Sidney says, with a meaningful look at me as we fall into step alongside them.

'Did you know him well?' I ask her.

'Not so very well,' she says. 'But all the Devonshire families know one another to a degree. Robert Dunne was the younger son. Feckless with money, went to sea to make his fortune. He was a hero for a while after he came back from the voyage with Sir Francis, even married himself an heiress. But then he gambled away everything he brought home. Terribly sad that he should take his own life, though.' She says this in the same tone that she might say it was terribly sad the village fair had been rained off. 'It would be awful if the whole voyage fell through because of it. Sir Francis would be devastated.'

And you? I wonder, watching her. Are you anticipating a year or so of relative freedom in your husband's absence? I look from her to Lady Arden. Perhaps this is all women really want: the freedom to be their own masters, the way they imagine men are. But none of us is truly his own master in this world of dependency and patronage. Just look at Sidney.

I catch his eye; clearly Drake has not wanted to alarm his wife with the truth about Dunne's death.

'I suppose my husband claims his death is the curse of John Doughty at work again?' Lady Drake says, as if she has read my thoughts.

'John Doughty? I understood his name was Thomas?' I say, confused.

'Thomas was the one Sir Francis killed for mutiny,' says Lady Arden.

'*Executed*,' Lady Drake corrects, automatically. 'John is his brother. He came back alive from the voyage, and as soon as he reached London he tried to bring a legal case against my husband for unlawful killing. It was a great scandal at the time.'

'I remember that,' Sidney says, nodding. 'John Doughty and his supporters claimed Sir Francis had never been able to prove that he had the Queen's commission to pass the death sentence while at sea. It was a dangerous precedent, some said, because the Doughtys were gentlemen and Sir Francis – saving your presence, my lady – at the time was not. Though of course we all regard him as such now,' he adds hastily. I give him a sideways look.

'John Doughty brought the matter to court,' says Lady Drake, ignoring this, 'but the case was thrown out on a technicality. Doughty believed the Queen herself had intervened to quash his suit so that the glory of my husband's achievement would not be sullied by his accusations.'

'And did she?' I ask.

'Few doubt it,' Sidney says. 'She was publicly defending Drake against accusations of piracy and murder from the Spanish – she could hardly countenance the same from one of his countrymen.' He shakes his head. 'One could almost pity John Doughty – not only did his case fail, but shortly after that he was accused of taking money from Philip of Spain's agents to kidnap or kill Sir Francis. He was thrown in the Marshalsea Prison. He may still be there, for all I know.'

'He is not,' Lady Drake says. 'He was released early this spring. Someone must have bought his freedom for him.'

'Was it true that he took Spanish money?' I ask.

'Who knows?' she says. 'Spain has a high price on my husband's head, that much is certain. There are plenty would put a knife in him for that sort of money, and with less cause than John Doughty. All we know is that, when Doughty came out of prison, he vowed revenge on Sir Francis and all those men of the jury that condemned his brother to death. He sent a message to my husband, signed in blood, saying that he had called down a curse on him and every ship he sailed in, and would not rest until he had my husband's blood in payment for his brother's. Sir Francis feared his time in prison had turned his wits.'

'He has a flair for drama, this John Doughty,' I say. 'You could play this story on a stage, the crowd would roar for more.'

'So I tell my husband,' Lady Drake says, seeming pleased. 'But John Doughty claimed to practise witchcraft. Some that testified against him said he had uttered spells to call down the Devil during the voyage. Sir Francis affects to scorn such things, but underneath he is as superstitious as any sailor. Especially since the others died.'

'Which others?'

'Two of the men who served on that jury have died prematurely in the past few months. One, apparently in perfect health, was taken by a sudden stomach pain and was dead by morning. The other, an experienced horseman, was thrown while out hunting and broke his neck.' She shrugs and holds out her hands, palm up, as if to return an open verdict.

'But these sound like accidents. They could happen to anyone.'

'So I say to Sir Francis. But both have happened since John Doughty was freed. And now there is Robert Dunne.'

'He was also on the jury?' Sidney asks.

Lady Drake nods. 'My husband says Dunne was driven to despair by his gambling debts. But I can see in his eyes that he does not believe it. Why should a man kill himself on the eve of a voyage which promises to mend his fortunes? I am sure he suspects that Dunne was murdered, and it has fuelled his fears.'

'Perhaps you underestimate his courage, my lady,' I say, trying to sound soothing. She turns to me with a sharp look.

'Then why does he delay the fleet's departure?'

I shake my head. 'I could not presume to know his reasons.' What I think, but cannot say, is that John Doughty's curse has nothing supernatural about it. The deaths of these other jurymen were possibly accidents, possibly not. A man bent on revenge could surely find opportunity to slip someone poison or startle a horse. And now Robert Dunne, hanged in his own cabin. If this John Doughty is passing his own death sentence on those he holds responsible for his brother's murder, one by one, then with Dunne he has drawn terrifyingly close to the greatest revenge of all – Drake himself. No wonder the Captain-General is afraid. But what has this story, if anything, to do with the Judas book?

A cold wind knifes in from the sea; Lady Arden shivers and pulls her shawl tighter around her shoulders. The castle looms up on our left, its four squat towers brooding over the town to the north and the Sound to the south. Out in the harbour, the *Elizabeth Bonaventure* sways on the waves; on board is a manuscript that might crack the foundations of the Christian faith, I think, and a strange apprehension grips me, somewhere between thrill and fear.

Sidney drops back to walk with me and the women go

on ahead, arm in arm, heads bent close together as they share their confidences. Sidney watches them with narrowed eyes.

'I wager you'll have her before we leave Plymouth,' he says eventually.

I smile. 'I wish you would speak plainly, Philip.'

'Well, why should I not be blunt about it? She is hardly troubling to disguise her liking for you. I don't think it would require an elaborate courtship on your part.' He wraps his arms around his chest, his eyes still fixed on the women. 'Widows,' he says, the word weighted with all the tangled desire, contempt and fear men feel towards women who intimidate them. 'The most dangerous kind of woman, Bruno.'

'Why?'

He hesitates. 'Because they don't need us.'

I laugh aloud, but he is deadly serious, and I am reminded again of the difference between us. With neither name nor land to pass on, I have never been the sort of man that women need for an advantageous marriage. In the years since I abandoned holy orders, there have been those who have liked me for my face, but to women of good birth, like Lady Arden, I can offer nothing beyond a fleeting dalliance, a diversion while they wait for a more suitable match. Sidney envies me this, and wonders why I don't make better use of it.

'She is expected to marry again,' I say. 'Some cousin of her husband's.'

'You should take advantage, then, before she becomes someone else's property,' he says.

I only smile and shake my head. It is a strange way to regard women, but perhaps I think this because I spent thirteen years as a monk, and lack experience in the transactions of marriage. Or perhaps because the only woman I ever thought of marrying would sooner die than be considered anyone's property.

'I would say the most dangerous kind of woman is another

man's wife,' I remark, looking ahead. Sidney slides a glance at me from the tail of his eye.

'They expect you to flirt with them,' he says. 'Compliment them. Flatter their vanity. It's all part of the game, nothing more. She understands that.'

'Does her husband?'

'Does Drake understand the dance of courtly manners? What do you think?'

We pass the castle and follow the path along the curve of the promontory as the clouds begin to drift inland. After a few more yards the women want to turn back. Sidney leaves me to take up his position by Lady Drake's side, still keeping a discreet distance; the cadences of their conversation drift back to us on the wind, but not the words.

'You are preoccupied,' Lady Arden says, beside me. She has to do a little half-run every few steps to keep pace with me; without realising, I have picked up speed as we make our way downhill to the town, eager to deliver our charges to the inn so that Sidney and I can return to the ship.

'Forgive me,' I say, turning to her and forcing my attention back from the grey-green water beyond the castle, from Judas and his testament. If it *is* his testament. Her bosom rises and falls, constrained by its tight bodice, with the effort of walking so fast. 'I am too used to the company of my own thoughts. I lack my friend's courtly manners, I fear.'

She waves the comment away and slips her hand through my arm again. 'What you call courtly manners is just formalised insincerity. Gallantry from a courtier is meaningless – it is no more than a script he has been taught from boyhood. I had much rather talk to someone who thinks before he speaks, and means what he says. What are you thinking of now, for instance?'

'The past,' I say, looking out to sea.

She nods, and we walk on for a few paces, before she turns to me again.

'You were a monk, Sir Francis says?'

'Many years ago now.'

'Why did you leave?'

'I found it – restricting.'

She lets out a knowing laugh and blushes pleasingly. People always find that answer amusing; as if there is only one sense in which holy orders might constrain a man.

'I asked too many questions,' I add.

'And do you still?' she says, with a playful smile.

'Not as many as you, my lady.' I mean it as a joke, but the smile falters and she withdraws her hand, briefly stung. She regains her composure quickly enough, but she does not ask me anything else. I walk beside her in silence towards the quayside, angry at myself; there is something perverse in me that feels compelled to push away any woman who shows an interest, though whether this is the legacy of my vows or of my failed experiments in love, I cannot say.

She turns to me as we reach the cobbled street that runs along the harbour front.

'Forgive my impertinence, Doctor Bruno,' she says. 'It is so rare for me to find a man I enjoy talking to, I forget that some of you do not relish chatter as much as women do. But I have one last question for you, if you will permit me.'

'Please.' I spread my hands wide, though I find I am preparing myself to lie.

'Will you and Sir Philip take a glass of wine with us this evening at the Star? Sir Francis has arranged that Elizabeth and I should have supper with the Mayor and his wife – her social duty, it can't be avoided – but I have hopes that we will be able to leave early, before we pass out from boredom.' Here she glances around, as if the Mayor or his wife might be eavesdropping from an alley. 'Do say yes. It would at least give us some spur to get through the evening when we feel our spirits flagging.'

I smile; my limited experience with English provincial

dignitaries allows me some sympathy. 'It would be a pleasure. But I don't know what time we expect to be back from the ship.'

'Naturally, you have more important demands on your time,' she says, her tone clipped, and I curse myself again; would it cost so much to be a little more gallant?

'My lady – are you not concerned that people would think it improper?'

She makes a noise through her nose that suggests derision. 'Which people? The people of Plymouth, you mean? Merchants and fishwives and fat aldermen puffed up with their own importance – should I care for their idle gossip?' She turns her face up to the uncertain sky and laughs. 'Besides, you are perfectly respectable, are you not?' The sly grin has returned; she looks at me as if we are complicit.

'I was not thinking so much of you,' I say, in a low voice, as Sidney and Lady Drake arrive beside us.

'Let us hurry, I fear it will rain,' Lady Drake says, squinting up at the clouds massing overhead. 'Doctor Bruno, you have already had one soaking today, I'm sure you don't want to ruin another suit of clothes.'

'Especially one of mine,' Sidney adds.

'Until tonight, then,' Lady Arden says to me, as we reach the inn. I don't think Sidney has ever looked so impressed with me. The women exchange glances. I leave Sidney to make his farewells while I slip away to the tap-room.

The landlady, a solid, broad-hipped woman in her fifties with the weathered face of those who live by the sea, is engaged in chiding one of the serving girls for her slovenliness. She stops, her mouth open in mid-scold, when she catches sight of me, and her expression softens.

'Yes, sir, what can I get you?' She wipes her hands on her apron.

'I wondered if I might have a word with you in private?' I offer up my best smile; it has served me well with older women.

111

She smooths down her skirts and simpers. 'Well, of course – get along with you, slattern,' she adds, to the girl. 'And don't let me catch you shirking your duties again – there's plenty would take your position here if you were to lose it.'

The girl mumbles something, bobs a curtsey and scurries away. The landlady turns to me, hands on hips. 'These girls – act like they're the ones doing you a favour, turning up at all. Now – what is it, sir?'

'Mistress, I was with Sir Francis Drake earlier and he expressed some concern about a small matter.'

Immediately her face stiffens; she folds her hands together as if in prayer.

'Was it the dinner? If it was in any way lacking, please assure him—'

'No, no – there was no fault with the dinner. It was fit for Her Majesty herself, Sir Philip Sidney said so.' She relaxes and her expression unfolds into a smile. 'No, it was only that a couple of days ago he received a letter. It was left here for him. Sir Francis was anxious to know where it came from.'

She frowns.

'People do deliver letters here for him sometimes. His clerk drops by to collect them, but I don't remember each one.'

'It was two days ago. Sunday. There can't be that many people delivering letters on a Sunday, surely?'

'You'd be surprised. When a fleet like this is preparing to sail, there's no such thing as a day of rest. I've no recollection. You could ask the girl, she sometimes delivers messages.' She gestures to the door.

In the corridor outside I find the sullen maidservant sweeping the flagstones, her features set in a pout. She glances up as I pass and I make a face, nodding behind me to indicate her mistress. The girl breaks into a smile.

'Do you recall someone bringing a letter here on Sunday for Sir Francis Drake?' I ask.

She leans on her broom. 'Who wants to know?'

'I do, obviously.'

She looks me up and down, her eyes coming to rest on the money bag at my belt. Her manner is pert, but her expression, when she looks me in the eye, is shrewd.

'Are you the Italian?' She says it as if she has heard mention of me, a thought that makes me uneasy.

'Who wants to know?'

She gives a brief laugh. 'Fair enough. No, I don't recall any letters being left on Sunday.' She eyes my purse again. 'Now you have to answer my question,' she says, when it becomes clear that the purse is staying shut.

'As you wish. Yes, I am Italian.'

'And you travel with Sir Philip Sidney?'

'You are very well informed. Where did you learn this?'

She shrugs, nodding to the door. 'Mistress Judith said. Her in there.' Her gaze slides away from mine as she says it. I dislike the thought that people are gossiping about us already, but I suppose it is to be expected, with all the interest around Drake's expedition. This girl is sly, there is no doubt, but servants' knowledge can be valuable; they slip in and out of private rooms unobserved, and usually have sharp eyes and ears.

'You must see everyone who comes and goes in this place,' I say, casually, as she resumes her sweeping. Her head snaps up and her eyes narrow.

'Most of them,' she says. 'Why?'

'I wondered if you had noticed a man in black, wears his hat pulled low, even inside. I saw him the other night in the tap-room.'

She shrugs, purses her lips as if considering. 'Can't say as I recall. Lot of men come and go round here.' There is a challenge in her gaze as she waits for me to make the next move.

Reluctantly, I draw out a groat and hold it up. 'Perhaps you could try to recall.'

She eyes the coin. 'I know the man you mean. Smallpox scars. Bright blue eyes. That the one?'

I nod, slowly, a chill creeping up my neck. She is describing Rowland Jenkes. 'Did you notice his ears?'

'What about them?'

'He doesn't have any. That's why he wears the hat.'

'Well, then, I wouldn't have noticed, would I?' She holds a hand out for her payment. I withdraw it slightly.

'Is he a regular here?'

She shrugs again. 'He's been in a few times. Not seen him before the last fortnight, though.'

'Listen – what's your name?'

'Hetty. Sir,' she adds, making it sound sarcastic.

'If you see this man again, Hetty, or you can discover anything about him or where he lodges, let me know and there could be more of these.' I hand over the groat; it vanishes into a fold of her dirty skirts. 'You'll find me around the place. I'm staying here.'

'I know,' she says, regarding me with the same level stare. I bid her good day, but I can feel her eyes on me as I walk away.

SEVEN

Climbing the rope ladder up to the *Elizabeth Bonaventure* seems easier this time; the sudden swaying and the knocks against the barnacled wood of the ship take me by surprise less often and my hands are growing hardened to the coarse fibres of the rope. I find I can shin up it quicker than before, and though I still feel giddy at the drop when I glance down from the ship's rail, I am in no danger of slipping. Thomas Drake is there to welcome us aboard with his usual lack of warmth.

'My brother is occupied with Captain Carleill at present. I will take you to him when they are finished.'

'In the meantime,' Sidney says, with a pleasant smile, 'perhaps we could look at the cabin where Robert Dunne died? Sir Francis thought it might be useful to see if there is any indication among his belongings as to who could have wished him harm.'

'Keep your voice down.' Thomas glances quickly around. He does not seem inclined to oblige. 'His belongings need to be boxed up for his relatives to take. But I am certain that, if there was anything to be found, we would have seen it. He had very few possessions with him.'

'Perhaps not,' Sidney says, still beaming. He seems to have

115

decided that aggressive charm is an effective way to irritate Thomas Drake. It is proving successful so far. 'The most telling items are often so small as to be overlooked. And of course your brother would have been concerned with the dead man and not in examining his possessions. Fortunately, Doctor Bruno here has just the kind of sharp eye that is suited to this task. I do distinctly remember Sir Francis saying it would be a good idea for Bruno to take a look at Dunne's cabin.'

Thomas Drake hesitates, weighing up whether to dig in his heels, then appears to relent. 'I will fetch the key. Wait here.' He turns abruptly and disappears up the ladder that leads to the captain's quarters.

'You enjoy baiting him,' I observe, leaning on the rail and looking out to sea.

'He invites it. He makes his dislike of me so clear, I can't help rising to it. He enjoys the fact that he has some small authority here – it is the only place where he could speak as he does to a man of my estate. Jumped-up little farm boy, riding on his brother's glory.'

'He is a captain in his own right, Philip.' I sigh.

'Yes, and why is he never on his own ship? He seems to believe he must be all over his brother's business, as if it will unravel without him. I wonder Sir Francis tolerates it.'

'I don't like his manner either, but if you keep antagonising him, he will do his best to make sure you are kept off this voyage. And whose part do you think Sir Francis will take?'

'Have you noticed how reluctant he is to allow us to look into Dunne's death?' Sidney says, ignoring my question. 'Every time the subject is raised, he makes an objection, though Sir Francis seems keen.'

'I wouldn't say keen, exactly—'

'But Thomas is actively trying to keep us away from it,' Sidney persists. 'Do you think he has something to hide?'

'For the love of God,' I say, turning back to him. 'You can't possibly think Drake's own brother would—'

Sidney digs me sharply in the ribs and I see the man in question approaching us.

'Follow me, then,' he says, looking from one to the other of us with narrowed eyes before leading the way towards the officers' quarters. He climbs a ladder to the deck below the captain's cabin and stops in front of a low door, which he unlocks with a key taken from inside his doublet. He turns to us, one hand resting on the latch.

'See that you treat everything with respect,' he says, raising a finger in warning. 'Sir Francis will have to account to the family for all Dunne's effects.'

Beside me, I can feel Sidney bristling at the implication.

'Rest assured we will leave everything just as we find it,' I say, in a soothing voice, laying a restraining hand on Sidney's arm.

Thomas regards us for a moment, then nods and opens the door to reveal a small cabin much like the one Sidney and I shared aboard the *Leicester*. Sidney elbows past him to enter; I mutter an apology as I squeeze in behind. The smell hits us like a fist.

'Sweet Jesus!' Sidney says, pressing his sleeve over his mouth and nose. The room is thick with the stench of urine and vomit, intensified by the damp.

'I wish you joy of your labour,' Thomas says, through his sleeve. He stands in the doorway, blocking the light. The ceiling beams are low enough that Sidney is forced to stoop; I can stand upright, but only just. If I breathe through my mouth, the air is almost bearable.

'There is no room for a man to hang in here,' I remark, stating the obvious. Even if Robert Dunne was my height, he could barely have swung from one of the rafters without his feet scraping the floor. 'Where was the rope fastened?'

'There.' Thomas Drake indicates an iron hook fixed into the ceiling for hanging a lantern. I reach up, take hold of it with both hands and lift my feet off the floor.

'It would hold a man, but there is no room for the body to drop,' I say, indicating the height from floor to ceiling. 'At best he would have strangled slowly as his own weight pulled the noose tight.'

'Exactly. And the face did not have the appearance of strangulation, as my brother told you.'

'Was he a heavy man?' I ask.

Thomas Drake tilts his head and appraises me. 'Of a height with you, I would say, though much stockier. He had broad shoulders, and something of a paunch.'

'He would have been solid, then. Not easy to lift.' I look up at the hook again.

'If the killer meant it to look as if he took his own life, hanging seems a curiously elaborate charade,' Sidney says. 'Why not choose something more subtle, like poison?'

I turn slowly and look at him, eyes wide.

He presses his sleeve back to his face with a quizzical look, but I am suddenly aware of the presence of Thomas Drake and reply with a minute shake of my head.

Thomas is no fool; he senses that there is an unspoken conversation being kept from him here, and it only serves to increase his distrust. He takes a step further into the small room and folds his arms.

'Go about your business, then.'

'I can't see a thing in this gloom. Do you mean to stand in the doorway the whole time, blocking what little light there is?' Sidney draws himself up to face Thomas, forgetting the restrictions of the cabin and hitting his head on the ceiling. '*Shit!* Do they build these for dwarves?'

'They build them for sailors, who know how to accommodate themselves to the confines of a ship,' Thomas says drily. He unfolds his arms, then appears at a loss what to do with them, so crosses them again. 'Do you suppose I would leave the two of you here to rifle through the man's possessions unsupervised?'

Even in the poor light of the cabin, I see the anger constricting Sidney's face. The battle of wills at play here is almost audible in the silence that follows. Thomas seems to realise he has mis-spoken; his eyes grow uncertain and he opens his mouth as if to speak, but Sidney takes one stride across the cabin and stands with his face barely an inch away from Thomas's. When he speaks, his voice is quiet and controlled.

'Let me remind you, Thomas Drake, that I am a knight of the realm and Master of the Queen's Ordnance. You will forgive me' – he gives a charming little laugh – 'but I thought you were implying that I was likely to steal a dead man's belongings? Is this your assessment of me, or my friend?'

Thomas does not back away, but his self-assurance wavers.

'Of course, that was not my meaning, Sir Philip,' he says, lowering his eyes. 'I must beg your pardon, but I have been at sea enough to know that the best of men can be tempted by a trinket that can be slipped inside a sleeve or a jacket. It is our responsibility to protect Dunne's possessions for his family,' he adds.

'Pity you didn't take more care to protect his person while he was still alive,' Sidney says, stepping back. 'Well, Thomas, I am not one of those men corrupted by trinkets and nor is my friend Bruno. Your brother said he was content for us to examine Dunne's cabin in case we can shed some light on his death. Which is all but impossible with you filling the doorway.'

Thomas appears to weigh up his choices, and eventually takes a step back, out of the cabin.

'It's still damned near dark in here,' Sidney protests. 'Could you see about a lantern?'

'I am not your chambermaid, Sir Philip.' Thomas's voice is tight, but after a moment, he adds, 'I will see if one can be found.' He hesitates, watching us, then turns and moves away from the door. Sidney immediately closes it behind him.

'I can't see a thing now,' I say, barking my shin on what I take to be a wooden chest on the floor.

'We're supposed to be doing this discreetly,' Sidney says. 'Drake doesn't want the whole ship to see us going through the dead man's cabin. What would they make of that? Though Thomas has already drawn more attention than necessary, all that fuss just now. And now what do you say about him?' He jerks his thumb towards the door. 'I tell you, Bruno – he does not want us looking into this business. Why is that, do you suppose? Come now, you are the philosopher.'

'I think he takes exception to the way you speak to him,' I say. 'And he regards us as outsiders. I do not think it any proof he is involved.'

'How should I speak to him, then?' Sidney's voice rises, indignant. 'When he will not show me the proper deference, and speaks to me as if I am some pampered child under his feet?'

I keep my face neutral. 'But the question of deference is a thorny one at sea, is it not? The distinctions of class mean less than the degrees of authority aboard ship, it seems. That was the problem with the Doughty brothers, as I understand it. Thomas Drake evidently believes he outranks you here, and if you want his brother to take you to the New World, you will have to swallow it for now. But you cannot possibly imagine he would jeopardise his brother's voyage by killing a fellow officer? What possible reason could he have?'

'Perhaps he had a grudge against Dunne. Or perhaps he knew something about him—' His speculation is interrupted by a timid knock at the cabin door. Sidney throws it open to reveal Drake's young clerk, Gilbert, holding a lantern and a tinder-box.

'Captain Drake asked me to bring this,' he ventures, proffering the items. 'Captain *Thomas* Drake, I should say.' Sidney nods and takes them with curt thanks, and is about to close the door again when Gilbert steps forward, clearing his throat. 'Pardon me,' he begins, then threads his fingers together and hesitates. 'May I ask what you are looking for?'

'No,' Sidney says, putting his hand to the latch. I motion to him to be quiet and move out of the shadows to see Gilbert more clearly. Without his eye-glasses he is obliged to squint, which gives him a permanent frown. He has the pallor of a man who spends his life bent over books, not wind-lashed on the deck of a ship. Again, I find myself curious about his presence here.

'I knew Robert Dunne well from court,' says Sidney, relenting. 'Sir Francis asked me to pack up his belongings for his widow, who is due to arrive any day. So, if you wouldn't mind . . .'

'Yes, of course,' Gilbert says, though he doesn't move. His narrowed eyes flit around the walls of the cabin. 'Poor woman. An awful tragedy to bear. That a man should die in the sin of self-slaughter. Although . . .' He hesitates, dangling the bait.

Beside me, I hear Sidney tut with impatience. I lay a hand on his arm. Gilbert Crosse evidently wants to share his thoughts.

'Although what?' I ask, with an encouraging smile.

He glances back at the deck before taking a step closer.

'I cannot help wondering if Sir Francis entertains some doubts on that score,' he says, in a confidential tone.

'Really?' I keep my expression unmoving. 'Has he said as much?'

'Not to me.' Gilbert shakes his head. 'But he seems uneasy. He has been asking subtle questions about who was on the watch that night, who was the last to speak to Dunne, that sort of thing.'

'I expect he wanted to ascertain his state of mind,' I say.

'Perhaps. Or it may be that he does not take Dunne's death for what it appeared to be.' He plucks at the cloth of his sleeve. 'And I wish I knew for certain because, you see . . .' He bites his lip, and his gaze flickers over his shoulder.

'What is it, Gilbert?' I prompt gently. It seems that he wants

121

to unburden himself but is afraid of saying too much. 'Because what?'

'I know someone is not telling the truth. In answer to Captain Drake's questions.'

'Really?' Sidney bounces forward, suddenly interested. 'Who?'

There is a pause, heavy with anticipation, while Gilbert twists his hands together and debates whether to say more.

'I was out on deck that night before Robert Dunne died,' he says. 'I saw them come back.'

'What were you doing?' Sidney asks, so brusquely that Gilbert jumps as if stung.

'I was – taking measurements,' he mumbles. Sidney glances at me. I can tell he has taken a dislike to Gilbert, but I am inclined to hear him out; someone who is so eager to voice his suspicions to strangers may have something useful to impart. Or else his eagerness might be worth noting in itself.

'I thought it was raining that night?' Sidney says.

Gilbert blushes and looks flustered. 'Later. Before midnight it was quite clear still. I just like to practise taking readings with my astrolabe. It's much harder to use when the ship is in motion and the wind is strong, and I am not experienced at sea, so I want to be prepared.'

'You have a mariner's astrolabe?' I look at him with new admiration. These instruments, designed for calculating latitude out at sea from the stars, are rare and expensive. I find myself wondering what kind of clerk this young man is. 'So do you navigate as well as copy Captain Drake's letters?'

He squirms and looks at his shoes. 'Oh, I just help with the calculations, that's all.'

'Go on with your story, if it is worth hearing,' Sidney says, impatient.

Gilbert stammers an apology and continues. 'Padre Pettifer, the chaplain, had brought Dunne back to the ship. Even in the dark, I could see he was hopelessly drunk. He could barely stand – the priest was holding him up. Thomas Drake helped Pettifer take Dunne to his cabin. Padre Pettifer stayed with him for a while, and after he left I saw the Spaniard Jonas knock on the door and go in. He was carrying one of his potions.'

'What potions?' Sidney says.

'Jonas has some skill with herbs, they say.' Gilbert glances between us, his eyes anxious. 'He can make up a draught to cure seasickness or the effects of ale. I have not tried them myself. It all smacks a bit too much of the village wise woman for my liking, and I am a man of science.'

He draws himself up. Sidney snorts.

'So Jonas took a draught of something to Dunne that night?' I ask, with a sharp look at Sidney.

'I suppose he must have,' Gilbert says. 'The thing is – I heard Jonas tell Captain Drake that he only looked in on Dunne, saw he was passed out and left again, taking his remedy with him.' He drops his voice to an urgent whisper. 'But that is not the truth.'

'You mean, Jonas stayed there longer?'

Gilbert bites his lip and nods. 'I was on deck for at least a half-hour more, until the rain came on, and I did not see the Spaniard come out before I returned to my quarters. It was only the next day, when they said Dunne had hanged himself, that I thought of it . . .' His voice tails off and he stares at his feet.

'So, you are saying . . .?' I prompt.

He shakes his head quickly. 'Nothing. I meant only that Jonas might know something of Dunne's state of mind that night. Perhaps they had some conversation.'

'Have you told Sir Francis that you believe Jonas is lying?'

He looks at me in alarm. 'Oh no – I may have been mistaken. And I would not want to sow doubts in Captain Drake's mind if he has none.' He chews at the quick of his thumbnail. 'I just wondered if perhaps he had voiced any doubts to you?'

Now we come to it. Beneath all the awkward fidgeting, this young man is sharper than he looks; he is fishing for gossip. The question is, why?

'To us? No – we have only just arrived,' I say.

'He is hardly likely to confide any such doubts to us if he has said nothing to his own crew,' Sidney agrees.

Gilbert looks chastened. 'Of course. I meant no offence.'

'Why do you speak of doubts at all?' I ask, in a lighter tone. 'Did Robert Dunne not strike you as a man likely to take his own life?'

He purses his lips. 'I did not know him well, you under-stand. We did not really mix in the same circles. But on reflection, I would say he did not.'

'He had heavy gambling debts,' Sidney remarks. 'That could push a man to despair.'

'Yes, that was common knowledge,' Gilbert says, with a disapproving expression. 'But he seemed so optimistic about the voyage, on the few occasions I spoke with him. This would be his last expedition, he said. He'd be away long enough to avoid his creditors and when he returned, he said his fortunes would be mended and he would finally be able to put his life right.'

'Fortunes? He meant whatever treasure he brought back, I suppose?' Sidney says.

Gilbert shrugs. 'I don't know. I assume so.'

'Did he have friends on board the *Elizabeth*?' I ask. 'People he was close to?'

He blinks at me. 'I often saw him talking with the Spaniard Jonas. They knew one another from the circumnavigation in '77. Beyond that, I don't know what he did when he went ashore. You would have to ask the men. I don't really associate with them much.' He casts his eyes down as he says this and I realise that he is lonely aboard the *Elizabeth*; he belongs neither with the hardened sailors nor with the gentlemen officers. It would be a long voyage for him to the New World, I thought, with only his astrolabe for company.

'Though if anyone would know whether Dunne seemed of a mind to take his life, I suppose it would be the chaplain, Padre Pettifer,' Gilbert adds. 'Some of the men do seem to confide in him.' The curl of his lip as he says this suggests he cannot fathom why.

'But not you?'

'No,' he says, firmly. 'I would rather confess my sins directly to God, when the need arises.'

I nod, turning away to hide a smile. The silence is broken by a crackle and a flare from behind me; I turn to see Sidney lighting the lantern. Already, I sense his impatience; he has decided this over-earnest young man is no more than a gossip, lurking to see what details he can scavenge. But I have a feeling that Gilbert has not told us everything. I rest my hand on the latch, as if to close the door, but he seems reluctant to leave.

'I understand you have written books on cosmology, Doctor Bruno, and that you argue the universe is infinite?' He shuffles as he says this, and blushes, as if he were asking a girl to dance. I acknowledge the truth of it with a tilt of my head. 'They say your theories have caused a good deal of controversy.'

'So did Mercator's projection of the globe when he first published it,' I say. 'It is hard to persuade people that the world may look different from the way they have always perceived it.'

He nods vigorously, his face alight. 'Yes, indeed. I would like so much to discuss these ideas with you in detail, Doctor Bruno. You can imagine, I'm sure, how starved one grows of intellectual discussion among men like this. I pray we will have the chance while you are in Plymouth.'

I respond with a non-committal murmur and hold the door open for him.

'Well, I shall leave you to your sad task,' he says, after a pause. He turns, casting a look back at the cabin. 'Perhaps you may find something of interest in there.' He smiles, still trying to peer over my shoulder. I return the smile, and politely close the door in his face.

'What sins could a milksop like that have to confess – coveting his neighbour's astrolabe?' Sidney rolls his eyes. 'God's tears. Do you know what we used to do with fellows like him at Oxford?'

'I wouldn't like to guess.'

He grins. 'Well, that's you taken care of for the voyage, Bruno. You two can have a wild old time with your measurements and your instruments. Starved of intellectual discussion! He has a fine opinion of himself for a bloody clerk.'

'Ah, leave him alone,' I say. 'Help me lift this chest on to the bunk.'

'Oh, I see – just because he's heard of your books.' Sidney folds his arms and nods. 'Suddenly he's your best friend. Well, *I* think he's odd.'

'I don't disagree. But let's concentrate on this for now.'

Between us, we grip the ends of the wooden chest and heft it on to the rumpled bed. It weighs less than I had expected, and we almost lose our balance.

'He was very eager to share his misgivings,' I remark, watching as Sidney lifts layers of clothes out of Dunne's chest.

'Probably just glad to have someone listen to him,' Sidney says, without looking up. 'I can't imagine the rest of the crew have much time for a whey-faced scribbler like that.'

'He seemed sincere, though, do you not think?' I lean against the wall, running through Gilbert's uninvited confidences in my mind. 'If he truly suspects that Dunne didn't kill himself, it must be a relief to unburden his fears. I imagine Drake put an end to any such speculation the minute it was voiced.'

'He wanted to be sure we knew about the Spaniard, though. Do you think there's anything in that?'

'You mentioned poison earlier as the simplest way to kill

a man without suspicion. I wondered why we had not thought of that before. And now we have a resident herbalist who took him a philtre the night he died.'

'But apparently they were friends,' he points out.

'Gilbert said he saw them talking. That is not necessarily the same thing.' I suck in my cheeks. 'I don't know how we go about asking this Jonas questions without putting him on his guard. Especially if he does have something to hide.'

'You have a knack for that sort of thing,' Sidney says. 'That's why Walsingham values you so highly.'

'I'm not the only one Walsingham values on this ship, apparently.'

'Yes.' He nods towards the door. 'We'll have to keep an eye on that clerk. He's bound to be reporting back. He must not know of our plan to sail with the fleet until we are underway – I don't want him tattling to Walsingham. Now then – what's in here?'

He lifts the last of the clothes out of the chest and throws them down on the bunk with a disgruntled noise. 'Nothing except shirts, and not very good ones at that.'

'There must be something else.' I turn slowly, taking in the bare cabin. The yellow light throws sickly shadows up the walls as it sways on its hook with the ship's motion. Already I feel my own balance knocked off-centre now that we are back on board; that same sense that everything certain and solid has been pulled away from under me. I reach out a hand and lay my palm against the rough wooden wall of the cabin to steady myself. There are so few possessions here, so little to give us any sense of the man whose life had ended swinging from a ceiling beam like a side of beef. I shudder. 'He was certainly travelling light for someone who expected to be away for a year.'

Sidney stuffs the clothes into the chest without bothering to fold them and lifts it off the bunk. The ship gives a sudden shift back and forth as if on an unexpected wave, and he

127

staggers with the weight of the chest, dropping it to the floor, narrowly missing his foot. The movement causes the cone of light from the lantern to lurch wildly from side to side, briefly illuminating the shadowy recesses of the cabin.

'*Dio mio*, what is that?' I grab the lantern from its hook and fling myself across to the bunk, pulling back the rumpled sheets where a dark red stain blooms on the white linen.

'What have you found?' Sidney crowds in beside me, curious, his shadow falling across the bed.

'Move back, I can't see. Here, hold this.' I hand him the lantern and lift the sheet closer to my face. The stain is dry, the fabric stiff. I lean in and sniff it.

'Wine,' I say, letting the sheet fall back to the bed. 'For a moment I thought it was blood.' I pull the top sheet away to reveal a bottle of dark-green glass, empty, and two stoneware mugs. Both have the dried dregs of wine inside. I stick my nose inside one and sniff.

Sidney grins. 'You are better value than a hunting dog, Bruno, just as I told Drake.'

'This smells odd,' I say, passing it to him. 'Sweet. It's familiar, but—'

He inhales, his face in the mug. 'Christmas, that's what it smells of. The wine must have been spiced. It fits, I suppose. Everyone said Dunne was drunk that night. He must have put this away in his cabin before he even left for shore.'

'But there are two mugs here. It looks as if he was drinking with someone.' I sniff the mug again. He is right; the lingering sweet smell calls to mind winter spices. 'Might someone have slipped something into his drink? Something that would account for the wildness of his behaviour?'

'So they could kill him while he was out of his right mind, you mean?' Sidney scratches the back of his neck. 'I suppose that's possible. What do you think – the Spaniard and his herbs again?'

128

I frown. 'Who knows? I would like to talk to this Jonas, before we make up our minds against him. But it seems he would have had the means. Wait – what's under here?'

The space beneath the bunk, where it is built into the wall, has been converted into a cupboard for storage. I open one of the doors, but the cavity appears to be empty. 'Give me the light, would you?'

Sidney crouches beside me, shining the lantern into the corners. I lay on my front and wriggle my head and shoulders into the hole, pressing my hands around the boards on the floor and sides.

'What are you looking for?' Sidney asks, passing the light in to me.

'I don't know. But where would you hide anything valuable, if not in the chest? There must be something in here.' My voice is muffled by the enclosed space. 'He was going to sea for a year or more, you'd think he would have brought some personal possessions with him. Some memento of home. This room is so spartan, it seems wrong.'

'Maybe he didn't want to be reminded of home,' Sidney says. 'Maybe he saw it as a chance to escape all that.'

I say nothing. I have a feeling he is not thinking about Dunne. Just as I am on the verge of conceding defeat, I notice some scratch marks on one of the wooden planks at the back of the storage cavity. I place the light beside me, stretch awkwardly to my belt for my knife, and slip the blade in under the board to prise it up. It lifts easily to reveal a small recess. I reach in and retrieve a fat leather-bound book with an ornate jewelled clasp.

'What have you got?' Sidney asks, impatient.

'An English testament, by the look of it. Here, hold this.'

I wriggle out backwards, hand him the lantern and brush myself down. We sit together on the bunk, heads bent close over the book. He undoes the clasp and opens the stiff cover to the first page.

'Well, I'll be whipped,' Sidney whispers.

A hole has been cut in the pages of the book, very precisely, identical on every page, all the way through to the back cover. Inside it is a velvet purse with a drawstring. I lift it out and test the weight.

'Let's have a look,' Sidney says, holding out his hand. I tip the purse up and five bright coins jangle into his open palm. Sidney whistles.

'Five gold angels. Christ's bones! I thought Robert Dunne was supposed to have gambled away his last groat. Where would he get a sum like this?'

'Perhaps he won it.'

'Unlikely, from everything we've heard. We should take this to Drake. It's an old trick, this, you know.' He pokes the cavity cut out of the book. 'This is how Catholics often smuggle vials of chrism and holy water through the ports. Revenue officers don't think to look inside books. Let's see if there's anything else under there.' Sidney rests one knee on the planks and leans in with the lantern to grope around in the space beneath the boards. 'Ha! What have we here?'

He passes me a folded paper and reaches back inside, bringing out a tarnished metal coin.

'Look at this.' He holds it out on the flat of his palm. Peering closer, I see that it is about the size of a sovereign, but of cheap metal, imprinted not with the Queen's image but with an insignia depicting a flame above a dish. 'What do you make of that? It looks like no coin I've ever seen. Foreign, do you think?'

I shake my head. 'I don't think it's a coin at all. More likely some sort of token – a private currency, perhaps? Though it is not a symbol I recognise.'

He examines it, shrugs. 'Let's take a look at the paper, then.'

The letter has been sealed with crimson wax, and the seal is neatly broken in two. I unfold it and hold it out so Sidney can read it with me.

Will Bryte
Edward Morgan
Abe Fletcher
Robert Dunne
Francis Knollys
Thomas Drake
Francis Drake

A line has been drawn through the first three names on the list. Sidney looks up at me, a glint of excitement in his eye.

'What do you make of this?'

I scan the list. 'I'd like to know if Bryte, Morgan or Fletcher were either of the two men Lady Drake mentioned – the jurymen from Thomas Doughty's trial who died this year.'

'I don't recognise those names, but that was my first thought. I'll wager you are right. Is this list in Dunne's own writing, I wonder?'

I open the book again. On the top right-hand corner of the inside cover, the name *R. Dunne* is written in ink, and below it, *Plymouth 1577*. The curling loops on the R and D are quite different from the script on the list of names.

'If Dunne wrote his own name in his book, then I would say no. Turn the paper over.'

Sidney holds out the back of the sheet, where the paper was folded and sealed. In the same hand is written 'Master Robert Dunne'.

Sidney bends closer to examine the wax. 'No imprint. Whoever sent it knew it would mean something to Dunne. But why send him a list of names that includes his own?'

'A threat, perhaps. Letting him know that his time is coming. Though it seems odd to give a man warning that you plan to kill him.'

'And implying that you intend to strike at Drake and his brother as well,' Sidney says, rubbing his chin. 'Why did Dunne say nothing to Drake?'

131

I look sideways at him. 'Perhaps he had good reason not to.'
'How so?'

I sit on the edge of the bunk, tracing the raised pattern the jewels make on the book's cover with my fingertips. 'What do we know of Robert Dunne? A gentleman, though deeply in debt. One of the jurymen who condemned Thomas Doughty to execution seven years ago. Which makes him one of John Doughty's targets for revenge.'

'If the John Doughty story is true,' Sidney says, leaning against the door. 'It might be nothing more than rumour and coincidence.'

'True. But I am just trying to set out all the possibilities. We know that Robert Dunne was an obsessive gambler, and that he was using this voyage to escape his creditors.'

'We also know that he expected to come into money in the not too distant future, if your twitchy friend the cartographer is to be believed.'

'He's not my friend. But yes. Dunne may have meant his spoils from the voyage, but what if he meant something else? And we're told that he had been seen more than once in the company of a couple of strangers – meetings he clearly didn't want his fellow sailors to know about.'

'Then there's the Judas book, and the dealer we presume to be Rowland Jenkes. Dunne was mixed up in that, don't forget. And now this mysterious purse. Maybe he stole it from someone, who killed him in revenge?'

'Or maybe it was some kind of payment.'

Sidney looks at me expectantly. When I make no reply, he shrugs. 'It's a tangle.'

I tuck the letter inside my doublet. 'We should ask Drake about this list. If this is the jury that condemned Thomas Doughty, it may shed some light. Didn't you say John Doughty went to prison because it was alleged that the Spanish had recruited him to assassinate Drake?'

Sidney narrows his eyes. 'So it was said at court, but—'

132

'And suppose that were true? If you were John Doughty, bent on revenge, how would you go about it? Drake travels with armed men wherever he goes, and he would recognise you a mile off, so how would you ever get near him? If you were clever, might you not recruit someone to do the job for you? Someone who could get close to Drake without him suspecting anything?'

He stares at me. 'Someone like Robert Dunne, you mean?'

'It is no small task to persuade a man to take another's life. Especially when the man concerned is considered a hero. You would need to find someone who is vulnerable to coercion in some way. This might be an advance payment.' I tap the purse with my forefinger.

'Philip of Spain has offered twenty thousand ducats to the man who rids him of El Draco. That would be incentive enough for many. You think John Doughty aimed to use Dunne to assassinate Drake, for a share of the reward?' He shakes his head. 'It's quite a convoluted theory, Bruno.'

'I know.' I place the purse back inside the book and tuck it under my arm with a sigh. 'I would be glad to hear a simpler one, if you have it.'

He presses his lips together. 'Not yet. We should show all this to Drake, see what he makes of it.'

'He may not thank us for suggesting he is next on the murderer's list.'

'I doubt he will lose much sleep over the idea. If Drake feared the assassin's knife he would never set foot outside his own door.' Sidney affects indifference, but it is plain he is impressed by Drake's bravery.

Holding up the lantern, I close the cupboard door and take a last look around the dead man's cabin. A sudden melancholy sweeps over me at the bareness of it, the thought that a life can leave so few traces. Hard not to think of what I would leave behind me, if someone came for me in the dark watches of the night. No widow, no child, no land. Nothing but the books I have written. At least, I suppose, that is some sort of mark in the sand. I am about to leave when something flashes on the floor; a brief wink as I move the light.

'Wait – what was that?'

I crouch and retrieve from between the floorboards a small pearl button in the shape of a flower. I hold it out on my palm for Sidney to examine.

'Did this come from any of the shirts or doublets you took out of the chest?'

'Don't think so. This is not a cheap thing, and Dunne's clothes were shabby, for the most part. But let us look again.'

He prises open the chest and dumps an armful of the dead man's clothes on the bed. Between us we lift up the meagre collection of shirts and doublets. They give off a stale, damp odour.

'The shirts all lace at the neck,' I point out.

'And these doublets have buttons wrapped in thread,' he says, dropping them back in the chest and wiping his hands. 'Unless it belonged to the clothes he died in, it's not his.'

'So we might conclude that someone else lost this button in here. Perhaps in the course of a scuffle.'

'Torn off while hoisting him to the ceiling?' Sidney suggests. 'That can't have been an easy task.'

'Hold on to it,' I say. 'And look closely at the buttons of everyone on board from now on. Its owner may not realise it is missing.'

Sidney drops the button into his purse for safekeeping, along with the coin. I slip the list of names inside my doublet and tuck the prayer book back under my arm.

We emerge on to the deck just as the door of the next cabin opens and Sir William Savile appears, fastening a short green cape to his shoulder. He looks surprised to see us in Dunne's quarters but greets us with his usual heartiness. Again I detect a faint hint of irony in it, as if we are all agreed that we are acting a part. Or perhaps I am too ready to be suspicious.

134

'Gentlemen. What are you up to in there – looting?' He grins, nodding to the book, and I curse myself for not having thought to conceal it.

'Sorting through Dunne's belongings for his widow,' Sidney says, with a touch of hauteur. Savile raises an eyebrow.

'Ah. I see the Captain-General is not afraid of setting you to menial tasks,' he says, but his eyes are still fixed on the book. 'For my part I have told him I will keep the watch once in a while, but I draw the line at scrubbing out the heads. Is that a book of Dunne's? I never saw him read anything except a hand of cards.'

'It is a testament,' I say. 'Perhaps he preferred to keep his devotions private.'

He inclines his head. 'Looks like a handsome book. Costly. For a fellow who claimed he didn't have a shilling. And died owing me, I might add, among others. May I see?'

He meets my eye with an expectant smile as he holds out a hand. I make no move to release the book.

'You played cards with him, then?'

Savile gives a short laugh. 'For my sins. His enthusiasm for the card table was in direct proportion to his lack of talent for it, poor devil. The first night we docked in Plymouth, Sir Francis took a private room at the Star and we gentlemen dined together. There was a game after supper. Dunne went out early, and lost with a very bad grace, I must say. I was among those he promised to repay. He stormed away in a great fury. Not what you expect from an officer, but then some of these country gentlemen are rather unpolished, don't you find?' He addresses this question to Sidney, who refuses to return the slick smile, despite the fact that he almost certainly shares Savile's views. There is something unpalatable about seeing one's own snobbery reflected so nakedly in another.

'Were the stakes high?' I ask.

He turns and allows his glance to slide up and down me

before resting on my face. 'As high as befits the status of the players. But etiquette demands that you don't enter into a game unless you can meet the stakes. Very bad form otherwise.'

'Did Dunne leave the game owing a lot to the rest of the company?'

'Not enough to make it worth killing himself,' Savile says. 'Or to make it worth anyone's while to kill him.' One side of his mouth curves into a smile.

'Why – has someone suggested that is what happened?'

'I thought that's what *you* were implying. But one always speculates in these matters, don't you think? Anyhow. Mustn't speak ill of the dead,' he adds, without sincerity. 'Where are you fellows bound? Off to see the Captain-General?' He looks as if he means to join us. I glance at Sidney; we would not be able to discuss anything with Drake if Savile tags along.

'I intend to visit the rest of the fleet this afternoon in my capacity as Master of the Ordnance,' Sidney says, with a little swagger of the shoulders. 'Doctor Bruno will be helping Sir Francis with his charts.'

Savile looks at me with a flicker of interest. 'Navigator, are you?'

'I know something of astronomy.'

'Huh. I thought he had a fellow for that. The whey-faced boy with the spectacles. Well, I think I shall come with you, Sir Philip. If I have to spend another afternoon in my cabin I fear I shall do away with myself out of boredom.' He stops when he sees our expressions. 'Sorry. Thoughtless. But really, it's enough to drive you out of your wits, cooped up here all day. And the attractions of Plymouth are soon exhausted.'

'I'm not sure there will be many more entertainments laid on during the months at sea,' I say.

'Ah, but that is different. At least we will be in the thick of it then. The journey itself is the adventure! Come, Sir Philip. Where shall we begin?'

Sidney throws me a helpless look as Savile takes him by the arm.

'I can deliver the key to Sir Francis,' I say, biting down a grin as I take it from Sidney's hand. 'I would not want to keep you from your official business, Sir Philip.' He purses his lips and glares at me. If he was hoping to ask discreet questions about Dunne as he toured the other ships in the fleet, Savile's company will be an unfortunate handicap, but that is Sidney's problem. He can find his own way out of it; my thoughts now are bent on the book in Drake's cabin.

EIGHT

'Ah, Bruno. Come in. I hope the women didn't wear you out with their chatter this afternoon.' Drake is sitting behind his vast table, a raft of papers spread out before him. Gilbert Crosse is at his side, canted over with a pencil in his hand and his spectacles balanced on his nose. Thomas Drake stands by the window, hands clasped behind his back. He nods acknowledgement without a smile. Sidney is right; the man truly is his brother's keeper. Gilbert glances from me to Drake in alarm, and moves to gather up the papers. Drake lays a hand on his arm.

'Don't worry, Gilbert,' he says. 'Doctor Bruno is not here to spy on your charts.'

Moving closer, I see that the papers are covered with detailed drawings of a section of coastline, all marked neatly with latitudes and meridians and carefully labelled with place names. I twist my neck to read and realise I am looking at the coast of north-west Spain, from Cabo de Finisterra to the mouth of the Vigo river. Gilbert watches me reading the map and touches his fingers to his temple, as if the anxiety were giving him a headache.

'Did you draw these?' I ask. He must catch the admiration in my voice, because he blushes all the way to his hairline

138

and lays a hand on the edge of one of the pages, a proprietorial gesture.

'But whose map is it from?' I peer at it, intrigued. 'It does not look like any of the extant maps I recognise.'

Gilbert looks at Drake for permission to answer.

'I should hope it does not,' Drake says with a smile, resting a hand on the boy's shoulder. 'These drawings are original. Not copied from existing *mappa mundae*, but sketched from the true calculations and bearings of real navigators and pilots.'

'You are remaking the map?' I stare at them. It was common knowledge that the elaborate and often fanciful maps drawn up by cartographers, even the most skilled such as Gerard Mercator, bore little relation to the true shape of the world's countries and especially their coastlines, as navigated by experienced mariners. Master cartographers more often than not copied their drawings from existing maps, so that the errors were replicated. It had always seemed to me absurd that there was not more collaboration between the adventurers and merchants of different nations when creating new maps – such collaboration would mean enormous leaps in our understanding of the world and how to travel it. But a navigator's local knowledge is a prized resource, closely guarded; to share it with a rival nation would be to give away military and commercial advantage.

'War with Spain is inevitable, sooner or later,' Drake says, giving me a sober look. 'If not this year, then the year after, or the one after that. I suggested to Master Secretary Walsingham that Her Majesty's fleet would be a good deal more confident when the time comes if we had accurate maps of the key Spanish ports and coastline. To say nothing of better charts of the Spanish Main and every other vital stronghold. He sent me Gilbert.'

The young man attempts to look modest, but I can see he is glowing.

'You have some skill in cartography, then?' I ask, regarding him with new interest.

'Gilbert is a master draughtsman,' Drake says, with as much pride as if he had trained the boy himself. 'And has studied mathematics and cosmography. All he lacks is the experience of seeing a coastline up close, from the deck of a ship. This we hope to remedy.' He claps the boy on the back.

'I studied with a master cartographer in Antwerp, who had himself trained with Abraham Ortelius,' Gilbert explains, puffing out his chest a little. 'Though for the purposes of this journey, I am merely Captain Drake's clerk,' he adds quickly.

'Yes. These maps do not exist,' Drake says, tapping the papers on the table and fixing me with a warning look.

I bow to show that I have understood, recalling that the Queen had forbidden Drake to publish any map or account of his voyage around the world, lest it fall into Spanish hands. If these maps of Gilbert's are to give England an advantage, Spain must not know of their creation. They are, in effect, military intelligence.

'What have you there, Doctor Bruno?' Gilbert says, blinking over his eye-glasses, pointing to the book under my arm. 'Did you find that in Robert Dunne's cabin?' He lays down his pencil and looks at it with interest.

Drake glances sharply from me to Gilbert, assesses the situation, and with one practised movement he stands and rolls up the charts on the table, sending Gilbert's pencil spinning to the floor. While the cartographer scrabbles beneath the seat in search of it, Drake gives me the minutest shake of his head.

'Thank you, Gilbert. We will continue after supper, if we may, with the approach to the Vigo river.'

Gilbert accepts the dismissal, though he squirms on the spot, his face anxious.

'I had planned to go ashore this evening, sir,' he says, a slight waver in his voice. 'To Evensong, as I always do. Though, of course, if you . . .'

Drake waves a hand. 'No, forgive me, I had forgotten. Far be it from me to stand between a man and his prayers. I dare say we will have time enough to discuss the matter before we ever near the coast of Spain.' He grimaces, as if he sees the prospect receding before his eyes.

Gilbert eases out from behind the table. He gives me a shy smile as his gaze flits again to the book in my hands. If our aim was to avoid speculation over the nature of Dunne's death, we are making a poor job of it, I reflect; soon the whole ship will be murmuring about Sidney and me rummaging through the dead man's belongings, and wondering why. Although, after our conversation with Gilbert and Savile, it seems clear that speculation is rife already.

When the door is firmly closed behind Gilbert, Drake pushes both hands through his hair in a distracted gesture, and motions for me to take a seat opposite him.

'Where is Sir Philip?' he asks.

'Gone to speak to the other captains about ordnance. Sir William volunteered to accompany him.'

Drake chuckles. 'Let them get under each other's feet. What have you turned up in Dunne's cabin, then?'

I hand over the book, explaining where I had found it. He nods when he opens it to see the cut-away hiding place and the purse. 'Yes, I have seen such things before. A good way to hide valuables, though better done with a less showy book, I would think. I wonder where Dunne got this kind of money.'

'Not at the card table,' Thomas says, with conviction. It occurs to me that the dead man may have owed him too.

'However it came into his hands, it suggests that the killer was not interested in valuables,' I say. 'It was not much of a hiding place – it would have been short work to find that money. We also discovered this beneath the boards of his bunk.' I hand him the list. As he scans it, his composure falters and his face grows pale.

'Thomas, take a look at this.' Drake hands him the list. Thomas reads it and looks up at his brother, his expression fighting between anger and shock. They exchange a long look, before Sir Francis turns to me.

'Do you know what this is?'

'A list of jurymen from Port San Julian?' I venture. 'Those who condemned Thomas Doughty to death?'

'How could you know that?' Thomas Drake snaps his head up from the paper. He crumples it in his fist and glares at me.

'Lady Drake mentioned something about it today when we were out walking.'

'Did she?' Drake raises an eyebrow and nods, as if this does not surprise him. 'You know, then, that John Doughty, who was fortunate not to share his brother's sentence on the voyage, has been seeking his revenge since we returned to England. His attempt to prosecute me failed, and he vowed then to take the law into his own hands.' He pauses, and his shoulders heave with the force of his sigh.

'I understood he had spent time in prison?'

'That was none of my brother's doing,' Thomas Drake cuts in, so fast and defiant that it as good as confirms the opposite. Sir Francis gives him a warning glance.

'John Doughty was accused of taking money from the Spanish for my death or capture. To this day I don't know if there was truth in it – some said the charges were fabricated to silence him. The reward is real enough, mind – twenty thousand ducats, Philip of Spain has offered for my head.' There is a flash of gold tooth as he grins briefly, proud of the fact, before his expression grows serious again. 'John Doughty was imprisoned in the Marshalsea. Worst place for him – it's my belief he ended up among Catholic recusants with sympathy for the Spanish, which only served to double his hatred of me. He was released in February of this year. That's when the letters started.'

'He sends you threats?'

Drake presses his lips together. 'Always the same theme – I am guilty of murder, blood demands blood. I would pay them no mind, except that he never fails to include some detail to prove he knows what I have been doing recently.' He grimaces. 'That is hard to ignore – especially when he makes reference to my wife.'

'He threatens her?'

'Not overtly. He will mention that she looked well in the yellow dress she wore to church on Sunday, that sort of thing. To make clear that he watches her closely. For that I am obliged to take him seriously. Especially since I heard the news about Will Bryte.'

'What happened to him?'

'Thrown from his horse, supposedly. Even then, I would not have paid it any heed, if I had not had word that Edward Morgan had died barely a month later. In his case it was a stomach sickness. So they said.' He falls silent and smooths out the list on the table, staring at it.

'He is picking us off one by one,' Thomas Drake says, his voice flat.

Drake looks up at his brother, and then at me.

'Elizabeth said I was being foolish, making too much of accidents and coincidence. But when I heard of Morgan's death, I felt the breath of fear at my collar. And now there is Robert Dunne . . .' He spreads his hands out, indicating help-lessness. 'I said to my brother, John Doughty is behind this somehow, mark my words.'

'And you think he is in Plymouth now?'

'I said it could not be,' Thomas cuts in, stepping closer. 'There is no question of Doughty boarding this ship – there are too many among our crews who know his face. I refused to believe it. But this—' He leans in and stabs at the list with a forefinger.

'Fletcher too, Thomas,' Drake says, shaking his head. 'I

always wondered.' He sees my expression. 'Abe Fletcher had testified against Thomas Doughty during his trial. He was washed overboard during a tempest in the Strait of Magellan, though no other men were lost. He was sailing on the same ship as John Doughty.'

'He was the first, then,' Thomas says. He keeps his composure, but he darts a quick glance at the cabin door and his fingers are interlaced so tightly that the knuckles are white.

The atmosphere in the room has changed; fear has insinuated itself among us, and we can all sense it hovering. We look at one another. No one seems to know what to say next.

'Is this handwriting the same as your letters?' I ask, to break the silence.

Drake squints at the paper. 'The letters I received were in a wild hand, full of scrawls and strange symbols. The writing of a madman, you'd say – though that might have been for show. I burned them, of course – I didn't want them upsetting Elizabeth.'

'But why was this list in Dunne's possession? Meant as a threat, I suppose,' Thomas says, answering his own question as he looks to his brother for affirmation. 'And why did Dunne not say anything? If he had been given reason to fear that his life was in danger, and those of others, why would he not mention it to the Captain-General? We could have done more to protect him.'

'Pride, perhaps,' Drake says. His mood is sombre.

I hesitate. 'Perhaps there is another reason.' Both brothers look at me. 'What if that list was not a warning but an instruction?'

Drake understands me first, amazement dawning in his eyes. 'You mean to say that Dunne . . .?' He frowns, glances at Thomas. 'No, not Robert. It is not possible. He was a loyal shipmate.'

I hold out my hands, palms up. 'It is only a theory. But

John Doughty must have realised he had little chance of getting close to you or your brother. What if he coerced Dunne, with the promise of sparing his life? Dunne would have been your close companion for months at sea. He would have had ample opportunity and you would not have suspected a thing.'

Drake looks at his brother and shudders.

'But Robert Dunne's own name is on that list.' Thomas Drake shakes his head. 'And even supposing he did plan on killing Sir Francis – he is dead himself now, and your extravagant theory brings us no closer to knowing why, or who killed him.'

'But we cannot avoid the conclusion that it was someone on board this ship,' Drake murmurs. We all glance at the door.

'Gilbert mentioned that the Spaniard, Jonas, went to Dunne's cabin that night after Dunne came back early. I wondered whether he might know anything.' I couch the question carefully, not wishing to sound as if I share Gilbert's suspicions.

'Yes, I sent Jonas to see him,' Thomas says, sounding defiant. 'The Spaniard has some skill with herbs – he can make infusions which take the edge off an excess of drink. I asked him to prepare a remedy for Dunne.'

'Did he say how Dunne seemed when he left him? This Jonas may well have been the last person to see Dunne alive. Apart from his killer.' I do not need to add that they may be one and the same.

Thomas shakes his head. 'He said only that Dunne had been sleeping when he left.'

'You can speak to him yourself if you like,' Drake offers.

'This is a bad business, Francis.' Thomas gives his brother a hard look. 'If the men have begun murmuring against the story you gave out—'

'It is a bad business altogether!' Drake pushes the table away and stands, flushed by his outburst. He takes a deep breath and lowers his voice. 'It has been since the minute we found him.

But we can go neither forward nor back until we learn the truth about his death.' He exhales slowly. 'And now, Bruno,' he says, turning to me with an effortful smile, 'the Judas book. Perhaps you will find something there to shed light on this matter.'

He crosses to a corner of the cabin and unlocks a cupboard set into the wooden panelling. From it he retrieves the package we had seen earlier at the Star. I feel a tremor of anticipation in my fingertips at the prospect of opening those fragile pages. He places the book on the table in front of me.

'Thomas, let us leave Doctor Bruno to his scholarly work. I will make a tour of the ship, speak to the men. You might do the same aboard your own vessel. Reassure them that all is in order.'

I like to think I detect a gentle note of admonition in this last sentence, and smile to myself.

'You intend leaving him alone with it?' Thomas points at me, apparently outraged.

Drake turns to his brother. 'What do you imagine he is going to do – jump out of the window? There is an armed guard outside the door, he would not get very far. And if anyone tries to steal it from him, well – Sir Philip assures me no sane man would attempt to best Bruno in a fight. Isn't that right, Bruno?'

'I can defend myself if need be, Sir Francis,' I say, hoping I will not be called upon to prove it.

Reluctantly, Thomas Drake moves towards the door, with a last glance over his shoulder that seems designed to let me know he has the measure of me. Drake nods once, and closes the door behind them.

Afternoon drifts into early evening. At intervals the sun pushes through the clouds and fractured light scatters in liquid patterns across the wooden panels of the captain's cabin and the wide desk. I have almost stopped noticing the gentle rocking of the ship, the creaking of timber, the hundred other noises that belong to the sea. Losing track of time, I forge on, sentence by sentence, absorbed in the words before me as my hand copies them to a fresh paper, transforming the curlicues and spirals of the Coptic letters into robust Latin. Frequently I have to pause, take a deep breath, collect myself. These words could be more volatile than all the powder and shot stored in the holds of all these ships put together.

My thoughts are disturbed by a sharp knock on the door. I look up with a start; it must be a visitor for Drake. I have been so absorbed in the book that I have no idea whether the guards are still outside. Shoulders tensed, I turn the paper face down, grasp the handle of my knife and call 'Come!'

The door opens a crack to reveal a man who could be one of my countrymen. His hair is black and curls to his shoulders, his face is tanned a deep olive brown and his eyes are so dark it is hard to tell where the pupil begins and ends. He wears a gold ring in each ear and his beard is unevenly trimmed. Between his cupped hands he carries a covered pewter tankard. Wisps of steam drift from beneath the lid. His expression when he looks at me is wary, more so when his eyes flit to my hand on my dagger. I remain still, watching him.

'Captain Drake tell me I bring you this,' he says indifferently, indicating the tankard. He speaks English with a thick accent. This can only be Jonas, the former prisoner now elevated to the status of translator.

'*¿Qué es?*' I ask, pointing at the tankard.

'*¿Usted habla español?*' His face relaxes a little and he steps forward, though his eyes are still fixed on the knife. I let go of it and gesture to him to come in. He closes the door and holds the tankard up, explaining in Spanish that he has made an infusion of herbs beneficial for settling the stomach. '*Para el mareo,*' he adds, with an encouraging nod. I am about to explain that I am not seasick, when it occurs to me that this must be a ruse of Drake's, to give me a chance to talk to the Spaniard in private.

'You know about medicine?' I ask, in Spanish.

He shrugs. 'My mother was a gypsy. She taught me how to use herbs for healing. I know a little of poultices and infusions. Enough to be of use to men at sea.' He gives a diffident smile and lifts the hinged lid of the tankard; steam gusts out, with a strong scent of fennel and something else, a sickly-sweet tang I can't place. I think of the two mugs in Robert Dunne's cabin, the smell of spices, the reports of his strange, wild drunkenness, and my hand freezes in the act of reaching for the tankard. This man was in Dunne's cabin the night he died, was quite possibly the last person to see him alive, and he may already know that Sidney and I have looked through the dead man's belongings. I glance down at his woollen jerkin. The buttons are all made of wood, and intact. Even so, perhaps I would be wise not to touch whatever is in this mug.

I smile nonetheless and take it from his outstretched hand, inhaling the steam.

'It's good,' he says, seeing my hesitation. 'Everyone asks me for this when we are at sea, trust me. I am Jonas,' he adds, with a little bow.

'Giordano Bruno of Nola.'

'I know.' His eyes stray over my shoulder to the wide table behind me, where the manuscript and my notes lie spread out in full sight. 'You are making a translation of the book?'

I follow the direction of his gaze. 'Yes. Where are you from?'

'Cadiz, once. But I have been at sea since I was a boy.' He pauses; that same half-smile again. 'I have never felt at home anywhere on dry land.'

'But you feel at home on an English ship?'

He does not miss the sceptical tone and immediately his face closes up; I have impugned his loyalty, to his country, or to Drake, or both, and he is offended. 'Do *you*?'

'I would not claim to feel at home on any ship. But for now I have no choice.'

'No more do I,' he says meaningfully. He sighs and folds his arms across his chest. 'Ah, I know what you think. They all think the same. El Draco – he captured my ship, insulted my motherland, stole everything. Why would I stay with him, if I am a true Spaniard, if not to betray him? I see how they watch me. They think I spy for my country, for King Philip. You are thinking the same. But I tell you this, Italian.' He looks away to the window, as if he doesn't care either way. 'If there is a spy on this ship, it is not me.'

The strangeness of this remark does not escape me.

'There are enough men in this fleet who know of Captain Drake's plans for the Spanish Main,' he continues. He points through the window to the town. 'Plymouth crawls with merchants and traders from Europe, the harbour is full of their ships. Yet if letters find their way into Spanish hands, all eyes will fall on me.' He keeps his gaze firmly fixed on the window, his voice low. 'To be a foreigner among Englishmen is always to be guilty of something. The crime itself doesn't matter. You understand this, perhaps?'

I nod with feeling, recalling my brush with English justice last summer. 'In London, barely a day passes when I am not called a filthy Spanish dog.'

He laughs. 'Take it as a compliment, my friend, to be thought a Spaniard.'

'Why do you stay with him, then?' I ask, sensing that his guard has relaxed a little.

'That first voyage, when he captured the *Santa Maria*, he kept me with him because I knew the waters of the Spanish Main, and I can translate. He needs me to negotiate with the Spanish.'

'I heard he negotiates with a sword.'

He waves this aside. 'These are stories told by the Spanish. We are fond of exaggeration. Like you Italians, in my experience.'

I acknowledge the truth of this with a smile.

149

'El Draco is courteous, though it suits my countrymen to say otherwise. When he took my ship, he put her crew in the longboats and sent them home unharmed.'

'Except for the priest,' I say, thinking of the Doughty brothers running the frightened young Jesuit through with a sword.

'That was not Captain Drake's doing,' Jonas says, with some ferocity. 'The Spanish claim he cuts off the hands of prisoners. I never saw any such thing. I had better treatment from him in one voyage than I ever had from a Spanish captain in all my years at sea. Consider – I was a prisoner, but at the end of the voyage he paid me as one of his crew. So.' He shrugs. 'I stayed in England. There was nothing left for me in Spain.'

And Drake had paid you for switching your loyalties with money stolen from Spanish ships, I think, watching him. No wonder you couldn't go back. But I can't help questioning how deep this new loyalty runs. There is something in Jonas that strikes a chord with me; I recognise myself in him, and not just because we look alike. In his eyes I see the same restlessness, the hunted look of the exile, the man who knows he has nowhere truly to call home. For the present, it seems he has thrown his lot in with Drake, but I know well how easy it is to deceive with appearances. I am trying to think of a way to broach the subject of Robert Dunne without making him suspicious, when he unfolds his arms and points to the tankard.

'You need to drink while it's hot. Otherwise it's not so beneficial.'

'I prefer to wait for it to cool a little.'

He watches me in silence, then lets out a sudden laugh. 'You don't trust me, huh? Even you – you think, what is he making me drink, this Spaniard? Perhaps he means to poison us all one by one, in the name of King Philip?' He shakes his head, still laughing, but there is a bitter twist to it. 'If I were going to poison anyone for Spain, would I not start with El Draco? He is the one with the twenty thousand ducat reward on his head, not you.'

Jonas takes the tankard from my hand and drinks a long swig of the steaming concoction before calmly handing it back to me and wiping his mouth on his sleeve. When I see that he has swallowed it, I feel I have no choice but to follow suit. It tastes woody, with a strange sweet aftertaste that makes me wince.

'See? No one has died.' He grins. 'Yet.'

'I apologise. I meant no offence. Another death aboard this ship would certainly seem like a bad omen.'

He gives me a sharp look. 'A bad omen? Yes, that is how they speak of it. Poor Robert. God rest his soul.'

'You were friends?'

Again, that sideways glance, as if he knows I have an ulterior motive. 'We were shipmates for nearly three years when we sailed around the world. He was a good man. You don't expect—' He throws his hands up in a sudden, savage movement. I sense that there is some emotion at play here that he is doing his best to hide, though he lacks the practice of the English in that regard.

'Did you speak to him before he died?'

'Why do you want to know this?' His eyes narrow to dark slits. Where Gilbert Crosse couldn't wait to spill his suspicions, this man is unusually sensitive to intrusive questions.

'Only that it is all people are talking about since we arrived.' I try to sound casual.

'And what are they saying?'

'That everyone finds his suicide unexpected.'

'Yes. It was surprising.' The bitter edge infects his voice again, or perhaps it is sarcasm.

'Because he didn't seem like a man who would take his own life?'

'I would not have said so. But who knows what passes in another man's thoughts. You should finish your drink,' he says, pointing. 'They say the wind will freshen tonight, there

151

will be more of a swell. You will thank me then. Although the wind will do us no good if we cannot sail.'

Reluctantly, I take another sip under his watchful eye, and try again.

'I heard Robert Dunne was very drunk the night he died. In drink, sometimes one is overtaken by melancholy. Perhaps he just . . .' I mime a snapping motion.

He takes a step forward, eyes flashing, but he speaks quietly. 'You know nothing of it. Don't judge a man you never met because some people on this ship amuse themselves by gossiping like laundrywomen.'

'I am sorry. I only meant—'

He exhales, and his temper subsides. It is hard to tell if he is angered by my questions because they are impertinent, or because he does not want to discuss the subject. 'Yes, I saw him that night. Thomas Drake found me and asked me to make something for Robert. He said he had been drinking hard and seemed out of control. I took an infusion, a purgative, to his cabin but there was no reply.'

'Was he . . .?'

'No. Not at that point. The door was not locked so I went in. He was face down on his bed, passed out. I didn't like to wake him so I took the cup away again. But I should not have left him.' He presses his lips together and lowers his eyes to the floor.

The Spaniard is giving a plausible impression of someone distressed by the sudden death of a shipmate, but I can't shake the feeling that he is keeping something to himself. Understandably; we have only just met, after all, and the fact that I can speak to him in his own language is not grounds enough to trust me yet. Even so, Jonas's story does not tally with Gilbert's; it would take only a moment to see that Dunne was unconscious on the bed and leave the cabin. But Gilbert said that the Spaniard stayed in there for some time. One of them is lying.

'You could not have known,' I say, trying to sound sympathetic. 'He must have woken in the night and decided on an impulse.'

'Well, it does no good to wonder now,' he says, his voice brisk. 'He is gone and we must bend our minds to the times ahead.' A shadow passes across his face. 'War is coming. Only a fool could ignore it. Whatever we do on this voyage will be regarded as an act of war by King Philip. So we had better make sure we succeed.' His fists are clenched, his jaw tight. *We*, I think.

'Will you fight with the English, when the war comes?'

He tilts his chin and gives me a long look. 'You find it hard to believe? Let me ask you something – why are *you* not at home in your own country, Giordano Bruno?'

'I am not welcome there at present.'

'Well, then. You should understand that the business of loyalty is sometimes complicated. Do you consider yourself an Englishman now? Who would you choose, if you had to, between this English queen and your countrymen?'

'England is not at war with Italy.'

'She is at war with the Pope.'

'I suppose I would say that my enemy's enemy becomes my friend.'

He nods. 'Exactly. A man may learn to love a country that is not his own, if his own rejects him.'

I want to ask why he feels Spain has rejected him, but fear if I intrude too far he will clam up. 'Despite the weather,' I say instead, looking at the banks of grey cloud through the window.

He smiles, an unexpected flash of white in his tanned face. Unlike most sailors, he still has most of his own teeth. 'True. I will never learn to love the English rain. But soon, God willing, we will feel Spanish sun on our backs.' He gestures towards the table. 'So, what does it say?'

'What?'

'The manuscript, of course. That is the book that was taken from the *Santa Maria* when I sailed with her, no? The book that Padre Bartolomeo died to protect.' His tone when he speaks of the dead priest is respectful, but curiosity burns in his eyes.

'Did he tell you anything about it?'

Jonas shakes his head. 'We did not even know he had brought it aboard until he was killed. But he was a strange one. A priest who acted as if the hounds of hell were at his heels.'

'Captain Drake said that, when the ship was boarded, he was heard crying out to God for forgiveness,' I say, careful to tread gently.

'Does not everyone who fears he is about to die?'

'In particular, Drake said, he begged forgiveness for bringing the wrath of God on the ship,' I persist. 'Did he mean the book?'

Jonas does not reply, only looks at me as if trying to read my face, until his mouth curves into a sly smile. 'You tell me. No one has been able to read it until now.' When I do not respond, the smile fades. 'It is valuable, no?'

'I don't know.' I keep my voice flat. 'Captain Drake told me Robert Dunne tried to persuade him to sell it. A friend of his, a book dealer, was keen to buy it.'

Something chases across the Spaniard's face, but he quickly masters it and shrugs. 'I don't know what they spoke about in private. I did not even know Captain Drake had it with him on board.' His eyes stray to the manuscript again with renewed interest. I feel an urge to cover it with my arms, to protect it, even though I know he can't read it.

'I should get back to work,' I say. 'Thank you for this.' I hand back the tankard. He looks disappointed when he sees how little I have drunk.

'You should thank Captain Drake,' he says. 'It was his idea. I just do as he asks.'

'Where do you keep your herbs?' I ask, as a thought occurs.

He frowns. 'In my quarters. Why do you ask?'

'Are they locked away?'

'Why, are you planning to steal some?' He laughs, but it peters out as he catches my face. 'Yes, I keep them in a box with a lock, under my bunk. I think they are quite safe there. Bunches of dried herbs are no good unless you know what they are and how to use them. I ask you again – why do you want to know?'

And does somebody on this ship know how to identify herbs and use them? Robert Dunne had a drink with a companion in his cabin the night he died. He was later reported to be wildly drunk, to the point of hallucinating; did that person slip something into his drink before he left the ship – some substance that might have ensured he would be in no fit state to fight off his killer? I do not say any of this aloud, because the most obvious suspect is Jonas himself.

'I only wondered – are there any that could be dangerous? If taken in the wrong quantities, I mean?'

'Any medicine can be dangerous in the wrong quantity. That is why not everyone has the skill to use them. But if you are asking, could a man do himself harm by taking my herbs, I suppose the answer is yes. It is a strange question, Giordano Bruno. It makes me think you still believe I mean to poison somebody.' He says this with a half-smile, but he watches me keenly with eyes of stone.

'It was more a question of whether a person might use your herbs to cause harm to others,' I say evenly.

'As I have said, only someone who knew what he was doing,' he replies, with equal politeness. 'But what could have put that in your mind?'

'I was only curious.' I shrug, and offer an innocent smile. We are circling one another, each waiting for the other to make an advance. But I have no solid accusation against him, and I lack the authority to ask more probing questions – to do so would only make him more defensive, and Drake has

155

warned us against arousing too much suspicion among the men. Jonas is already spiky, alert to any insinuation – so touchy, you might almost think he has something to hide.

The door creaks and Jonas gives a start, as if he has been caught out. Drake stands in the doorway, broad and bluff, rubbing his large hands together as if in anticipation of a spectacle.

'Ah, Jonas, good lad,' he says. 'You have taken care of Doctor Bruno's seasickness, then?' He catches my eye over Jonas's head and I feel a weight of relief; whatever I have just drunk was at least made for me on Drake's orders.

'He will weather any storm now,' the Spaniard says, with a smooth bow.

'Good, good. Let us hope it won't come to that tonight, at least. Now leave us. I may have need of you after supper.'

Jonas bows again and backs away, casting a last glance at the book on the table as he goes.

'Useful?' Drake mouths, nodding in the direction of the door as it closes behind the Spaniard.

'The potion, or the conversation?'

'Either. I've heard men swear by his concoctions in rough seas. Did he have anything to say about Dunne?'

'He says Dunne was passed out from drink when he went to his cabin the night he died, so he never gave him any remedy. Does it not trouble you that he keeps all these herbs and medicines aboard the ship?' I ask. 'He tells me some are potentially deadly, if you know how to use them. And given how much you . . .' The sentence tails off as I search for a diplomatic way to phrase it.

'Given how much I am worth dead?' He seems amused. 'You are not alone in your concern, Bruno. When we took Jonas from the *Santa Maria*, my brother wanted to keep him bound and on prisoner's rations for the entire voyage, and others voted with him. I argued that is not the way to win a man to your cause. This time Jonas comes with us of his own

156

free will, as a paid crewman, but there's more than one good sailor refuses to sail with a Spaniard on the ship. Fearing he will rise up and attack us single-handed, I suppose.' He rubs the back of his neck.

'He wouldn't need to,' I say quietly. 'If he found a way of dispatching you, Sir Francis, the whole voyage would be undermined. It would be no great difficulty to slip some deadly mixture into your food or drink, with his knowledge.'

Drake frowns at me, then bursts out laughing and claps me on the shoulder. 'God's blood, Bruno, I already have one wife to fret over me. Not to mention Thomas. I thought you had determined Dunne was out to assassinate me, now you worry about Jonas. Which is it?'

'For twenty thousand ducats, it might be any of them.'

He laughs again, but there is a tension underlying it. 'I have my food tasted before every meal. I eat only from the common dish. I sleep with armed guards outside my door. I take every precaution a man whose death is worth twenty thousand ducats can reasonably take, Bruno. Jonas Solon has proved himself a reliable shipmate, and I will treat him as such. Certainly he is no more or less to be trusted than any other man here just because he is a Spaniard. You of all people must understand that.'

I nod, but do not reply. Drake seems to make the same assumption as Jonas himself: that I should not think ill of the Spaniard because he and I are fellow outsiders, brothers in exile. For me to suspect him is apparently a breach of solidarity.

'Now – I want to hear what you make of this manuscript. Come, sit.' He unlocks a cupboard and takes out two crystal goblets and a decanter, from which he pours a generous measure of red wine. I cannot help but regard it with suspicion before I sip; the more I learn about the potential threats to Drake's life, the more everything on this ship comes to seem a murder weapon in waiting. 'You're quite safe to drink this, my friend, I keep it locked away. It's good Rhenish,' he says,

157

with a twinkle, seeing the way I sniff at it and hesitate. He pulls out a chair and gestures to me to sit opposite him at the large table, where my notes and my translation are spread out.

Though he is not a theologian nor a scholar, the Captain-General listens attentively through my explanation of the manuscript, his chin resting on his bunched fist, frowning as I explain the context of the story told by the author, the writer who claims to be Judas Iscariot. He asks intelligent questions, which I attempt to answer in the same spirit, and he nods thoughtfully, pulling at his beard and rubbing his finger beneath his lower lip as he tries to comprehend all the ramifications of the pages that lie between us, tattered and salt-damaged but still largely legible.

Drake swirls the dregs of his wine around the glass and peers into it. 'What does he say about the resurrection?'

'Didn't happen. Not according to Judas.' I tap the parchment. 'He's covered himself too – he says Christ showed him a vision of himself, Judas, being persecuted to death by the other apostles after Christ's crucifixion, because they wanted to silence his message. He knew he was destined to be history's scapegoat, but he was content to accept this destiny because only he knew the truth.'

'I thought he was supposed to have hanged himself after the crucifixion? When did he find the time to write this?'

'That verse from the Gospel of Matthew, the one in your anonymous letter, is the only source for the story of Judas hanging himself,' I say, 'though it has become accepted as truth. The other three gospels don't mention his death. This account says he went into hiding after the crucifixion, for fear of reprisals from the other disciples, and wrote his version of events in secret.'

Drake pushes his chair back and crosses to the small cabinet in search of the decanter. 'Sounds like codswallop to me.'

'Perhaps. Though you might say that about any of the gospels.'

158

He turns and stares, the glass bottle in his hand, shock freezing his face for a moment before a short bark of laughter erupts.

'True, true. They ask us to believe a lot. Virgins giving birth, blind men seeing, dead men walking. Impossible, to our understanding. But then they said it was impossible for a man to sail the circumference of the Earth and survive.' He flashes me a triumphant smile and lifts his glass as if in a toast to himself. 'Now – feeding a crowd of five thousand with five loaves and two fish – that one is hard to swallow if you know a thing or two about making rations go round.' He laughs at his own joke, pours himself another drink, then lifts the decanter in my direction, eyebrows raised in a question. I nod, and hold out my glass. 'Few would be bold enough to say so, though,' he says. His face turns serious and he points an accusing finger at the manuscript. 'What should be done with this, do you think?'

'It should be studied further. But . . .' I hesitate, unsure how my suggestion will be received. 'It might be best if it were delivered into the Queen's keeping as soon as possible. It could be useful for bargaining with the Vatican. They will want it back, you may be sure of that. But if it should be lost at sea . . .' I leave the sentence hanging.

He considers this. 'Yes, I have thought of that. It has been around the world once and survived, perhaps we should not tempt fate. But who should I trust to take it to London, then? It might just as easily be lost on the roads, especially if this book dealer is as unscrupulous as you say.'

'I could take it for you, Sir Francis. Sidney has four armed men on the way to Plymouth to escort Dom Antonio to the Queen. I could travel back with them.' The idea takes shape as I speak; with letters of introduction from Drake, might I not even persuade the Queen that I am the man to study the manuscript? She would want such a volatile document examined and understood, and there would be few men in England with the knowledge and experience to probe its mysteries.

Certainly none of the half-wits I had met in Oxford were up to the task. It might, at least, give me a reason to stay in London, and a means of showing the Queen she had need of my skills. And it would be a legitimate reason to leave Plymouth.

Drake narrows his eyes, but I see he is suppressing a smile. 'My brother will not countenance that, I fear, now that he knows how valuable it is. He already thinks me a fool to leave you alone with it. Besides, Sir Philip wants a berth aboard my ship to the New World. One for you too. He will be sorely disappointed if you abandon him.'

'He can always bring me back a souvenir.'

Drake laughs, and drains his second glass. 'Not that we will be going anywhere until this business with Dunne is resolved. And his widow arrives in Plymouth tomorrow,' he adds, in the same heavy tone, glancing at the window. 'She is bound to oppose a verdict of suicide, and the coroner may feel obliged to consider her case.'

We are interrupted by a knock at the door. Drake gathers up the manuscript in one swift move and replaces it inside the cupboard, which he locks with a key from his belt just as the door opens and Gilbert enters. I bow in greeting; he responds with a bashful smile and turns to Drake.

'The captains are here for supper. Shall I show them in?'

Drake nods, then motions to my notes still scattered across the table. 'Clear those away, Bruno. Should I keep them here under lock and key?'

I gather the papers into a pile. 'Better I keep them in my lodgings, Sir Francis. That way we have two copies, in case anything should happen to one.'

'Can you keep them secure?' He looks doubtful.

'Secure enough. Besides, no one except us knows I have made this copy.' No one except Jonas, I think, as I tuck the pages into my leather bag.

NINE

Out on deck, the wind has freshened and the ship's motion is more insistent. To the west, the light is fading and heavy clouds are massing on the horizon, obscuring the setting sun. There is quite a party bound for Plymouth this evening from the *Elizabeth*: Sidney and Savile are waiting on deck, along with Gilbert Crosse, Jonas, Thomas Drake and Pettifer the chaplain.

'Planning a night of revelry ashore, Padre?' Savile says, with a wink. The clergyman blinks slowly and stares at him, unsmiling.

'I am going to pray, Sir William,' he replies. 'My soul feels the need of sustenance in our present troubles.'

'Don't blame you, sir. Savage company like this.' Savile jerks his thumb in the direction of the main deck. 'We could all do with a little elevation.'

'And where will you look for yours, Sir William, in Plymouth?' Sidney sounds charming, as always, but there is a bite to his tone. I deduce that he and Savile have not spent the most harmonious afternoon together.

Savile raises an eyebrow. 'There is only one place in Plymouth fitting for a gentleman, Sir Philip. One must seek the sacred flame.'

Pettifer tuts loudly and turns his face away. I catch Sidney's eye as understanding dawns.

'You mean the House of Vesta?' I say to Savile. 'It is a whorehouse, is it not? Is the sacred flame its emblem?'

Savile looks down at me and cocks his head. 'The cognoscenti do not have to ask such questions, my friend.' He offers a condescending smile.

'Surely a great scholar has his mind on higher things,' Jonas says, laughing. I sense he is trying to deflect any tension.

'You do not know many scholars then,' Savile replies, his tone dry. 'Every one I ever met goes to it like a street dog. Every priest, too,' he adds, with a nod to Pettifer, who scowls and exhales through his nose, as if his patience is being tested to its limit. 'Isn't that so, Gilbert?' Savile nudges the young clerk. 'All this talk of Evensong is just a cover, surely?'

Gilbert stares at him, alarmed, a fierce colour spreading up his face. 'I don't know what you mean, Sir William,' he falters.

'Come on – you're off to a bawdy house later, surely, fine young lad like you?'

Gilbert looks distraught at the very idea. Sidney claps him on the shoulder. 'He is teasing you, Master Crosse. Pay him no heed. He would benefit from a couple of hours in church himself,' he adds, glancing at Savile.

'Wouldn't we all, Sir Philip,' Savile says, with a rueful smile. 'Though you will not have time, I fear – are you not appointed to entertain Lady Drake and her cousin while they are here?' He asks the question innocently enough, but I see Sidney's face harden.

'The boat is below, my masters,' Jonas says quietly, indicating the rope ladder. He throws one leg over the side and begins to make his descent. One by one, we move to follow him.

The sea is choppy, even in the Sound; one of the oarsmen holds the small rowing boat as steady as he can against the hull of the *Elizabeth* while I climb in, with Pettifer following, but he has to cling hard to the rope ladder as the waves buffet us in contrary directions. The ladder sways and I have to half turn and jump into the boat, setting it rocking wildly, as a wave thumps it hard against the hull of the ship and spray hits us full in the face. I am glad we have only a short journey to make, though we will surely be soaked by the end of it; the wind is high now and the oarsmen's faces strain with the effort of pulling us through the white-flecked water.

'You have packed up Robert Dunne's belongings for his widow, Sir Philip?' Gilbert Crosse leans towards Sidney and shouts into the spray. Both Pettifer and Jonas look across at us with interest.

'That's right,' he shouts back. 'She arrives tomorrow, I believe. Poor woman.'

'Did you find anything?' Gilbert persists. 'I mean, anything that might explain why he took his life?' The conspiratorial look he gives me is so lacking in subtlety he may as well be acting it in a playhouse.

'No letter or any explanation, if that is what you mean,' I say. 'Any such thing would surely have been found already. We only put away his possessions and made certain nothing was left behind. It was a service Sir Philip wished to perform for an old friend.' I glance at Sidney, who lowers his head in a solemn nod.

'Remind me how you knew him again, Sir Philip,' says Savile lightly, 'for I never heard him speak of you.'

'Family connection,' Sidney says, with a wave of his hand, as if this covered every possibility. Savile does not press the matter, just watches him with an expression of knowing amusement. I begin to suspect that Savile is a good deal shrewder than his public face would have people believe, and that we should keep an eye on him.

'We may never know what drove a man to such a dreadful sin,' Pettifer remarks, assuming a righteous expression. Jonas scowls at him, though the chaplain appears not to notice.

'If anyone were to know the state of his mind, it would be

163

you, Padre, surely?' Savile says.

The chaplain blinks at him, his eyes wary. 'How so, Sir William?'

'Did you not visit him later on, the night he died? I was restless and thought to take some air on deck, and I was certain I saw you coming from his cabin – this would have been past midnight, I suppose.'

'Well – yes, I did – that is, I went to see how he was. I wanted to be sure he was recovering, given the state he was in earlier.'

'And was he?' Sidney asks.

'He seemed a little better. So I stayed to pray with him.'

'Pray?' Sidney looks sceptical. 'He was awake, then?'

'Yes, Sir Philip, obviously.' If Pettifer had at first been caught off guard by these questions, he quickly regains his composure. 'He felt the need of spiritual comfort. A man cannot help but consider the frailty of the flesh as he sets out to sea, and remember how completely he must trust himself to God's mercies. I have found that many sailors wish to unburden their conscience and set it clear before their Maker when the journey begins.'

'Unburden? You mean he made his confession to you?' I ask – too quickly.

'I do not hear confession, Doctor Bruno – that is a sacrament of the Catholic Church.' He purses his lips and gives me a reproving look.

'Of course,' I say, smiling. I make up my mind to speak with him in private as soon as I can. A man who wants to unburden himself to a minister of religion because he fears death is making a confession, however much Pettifer may dance around the word. What did Robert Dunne have to confess? I catch Sidney's eye as the wind lifts his hair from his face; he furrows his brow and I return his look with a minute shake of my head. I have no answer, except to glance around at the men hunched down in the rowing boat against the wind, and wonder which of them is lying. The prow rises to cut through a wave and drops back with a flat thud, before rising again; spray slaps us hard in the faces and Sidney and Savile curse aloud as they check their satin and velvet for salt marks.

'Now you thank me,' Jonas says in Spanish, raising his voice over the noise of the wind and pointing to his stomach with a grin as the boat heaves over another wave. 'Are you feeling sick?'

'Not yet.' I smile, grudgingly acknowledging his point.

'I promise you,' Jonas continues, looking pleased, 'take a little every day and you will be as much at home in the water as a mermaid.'

'A mermaid? Oh God, has he made you drink his seasickness remedy?' Savile asks, overhearing. When I nod, he mimes putting a finger down his throat. 'That's a mistake you only make once – no tempest could have you bringing up your supper faster than a draught of whatever he puts in that. Eh, Jonas?' he says, winking at the Spaniard.

'Wait until we are out in the Atlantic, Sir William,' Jonas replies, in English this time, leaning back and stretching out his legs. 'You will be begging me for a cup of it.'

'A hundred crowns I will not.'

The oarsmen steer us through the harbour entrance to Sutton Pool and all the passengers slump with relief as we move into flat water. Sidney is looking a little green and is unusually quiet. This gives me an impish pleasure; if he discovers he lacks the stomach for seafaring, perhaps he may change his mind about this escapade. But as we approach the wooden jetty, I watch his face as he struggles to master himself, takes a deep breath and assumes his usual good cheer as he stands, one hand on Gilbert's shoulder, surveying the harbour with a satisfied expression, as if he were a homecoming hero. It would take more than a bout of seasickness to sway him once he has determined on a plan, I realise with a sigh. Church bells echo across the pool from somewhere behind the houses, funereal in the fading light.

A wooden ladder leads down from the jetty into the water; I stand behind Gilbert Crosse waiting to disembark and the man before him pushes off too hard as he steps out to the ladder, causing the small boat to lurch suddenly and send us stumbling into one another. Gilbert loses his footing and falls backwards; I catch him around his ribs to keep him upright and he twists away sharply, almost like a reflex, as if I have grabbed him in a sore place.

'Sorry, I didn't mean to hurt you,' I say, helping him to regain his balance. He pulls away from me, brushing himself down.

'No – I'm quite all right, thank you.' He adjusts his jacket and steps quickly to the ladder. I watch him as he pauses on the jetty to adjust his clothing once more. He seems to fear that our impromptu embrace has disarranged his shirt, which he now takes pains to tuck firmly into his breeches. As he straightens up, he meets my eye and gives me a tense, embarrassed smile as he scurries towards the dock.

Pettifer and I are the last out of the boat. I try to keep Sidney in my sights but I turn and see that Pettifer is hanging back as the others walk on ahead, as if he wants to speak with me alone. Taking the hint, I slow my steps. When he judges the rest to have moved out of earshot, he lays a hand on my arm.

'May I ask you a question, Doctor Bruno?' He is making an effort to sound more courteous, and this in itself piques my interest.

I stop and turn to him. 'Of course.'

He hesitates, as if unsure how to frame it.

'There is talk aboard the *Elizabeth* that Captain Drake has brought you here to unfold the secrets of the Jesuit's book. The one he took from the *Santa Maria*.' He looks at me with an anxious frown, awaiting confirmation.

'Sir Philip Sidney brought me here to keep him company.

I never met Sir Francis until yesterday.' I look him in the eye, to lend weight to my words, wondering who could have started this rumour. Aside from Drake and his brother, only Jonas has any firm knowledge of the reason for my visit to the captain's quarters.

'But you do not deny, sir, that the Captain-General has put you to work translating a book he keeps locked in his cabin? An ancient book?'

'It were best, perhaps, that you ask Sir Francis directly about his books,' I say, smiling to take the sting from my reply. 'As his chaplain, you are surely in his confidence.'

'He is much preoccupied with other matters at present,' Pettifer says, steepling his fingers together and pressing the tips to his lower lip. 'And once rumours begin aboard a ship . . .' His expression asks for sympathy. 'You understand, I'm sure, that as chaplain I have the men's souls in my care.'

I say nothing; only raise an eyebrow as I wait for him to explain what he wants me to do about the men's souls.

'Sailors are, for the most part, simple men,' he continues, his fingertips still pressed to his lips. 'Not educated, like you and me. I have no doubt they worship as the law demands when they are at home, but their superstitions remain vivid. And once out at sea, days or weeks from land, many of them look for comfort to the faith they learned from their grandfathers. When waves are crashing over the ship or a Spanish pinnace is firing on you, how do you tell a man he must not cry out to Our Lady of the Sea or Saint Brendon the Navigator for succour, because we are Englishmen and the Queen forbids it?'

'You have been in such situations many times, I suppose?'

'I speak from experience, yes.' He nods, to affirm his own sincerity. 'You ask if I hear confession – the truth is, I hear many. I cannot offer absolution, but that seems to matter little – often I have seen how a man fearing death wants simply to unburden himself of his sins, whether he gives it that name or no. So you see, I must walk a fine line when it comes to balancing spiritual authority with spiritual comfort.'

'I see that. But why are you telling me this?'

He sighs, as if wearied by the effort of spelling it out.

'It is supposed by the men,' he continues, carefully, 'that the book Captain Drake keeps locked in his cabin is a book of heresy. Some say it contains invocations to call down the Devil. Some say it curses the name of Christ.'

I laugh. The sound is snatched away by the wind. 'They have read this book, then, these simple sailors? They know enough Coptic to surmise its contents?'

'Coptic? So it *is* the same book,' he says softly. I swear inwardly at my own stupidity.

'These are vivid superstitions – you said it yourself.'

'A priest was murdered for that book, Doctor Bruno, and that alone is enough to make it a bad talisman for a sailor.' He grasps my sleeve again. 'Tell me this much, then – *is* it a work of heresy? Because, God knows I am no superstitious deckhand – I took my degree at Cambridge, you know – but as a churchman I cannot help but wonder what Captain Drake is about, dabbling in such matters?'

'Perhaps he regards it as a curiosity,' I say, keeping my eyes on the rest of our group as they progress along the harbour wall towards the town. 'And in any case – one man's heresy may be another man's gospel.'

'Gospel.' He whispers the word as if tasting it, and nods to himself. 'And you, Doctor Bruno?' he says. 'Who were once in holy orders – do you not ask yourself if what you do is right, bringing a heretical text into the light? A book that may shake men's faith in their salvation?'

'Why would you suppose it contains any such matter, if no one has yet read it?'

'How do you square such work with your conscience?' he fires back, as if I have not spoken.

'My conscience is principally concerned with the advancement of knowledge.'

'*Knowledge.*' He presses his lips together and nods, as if he expected such a response. 'I have met priests like you before, Doctor Bruno, in the universities, who prize intellectual ambition over humble obedience to God's law. You would no doubt argue there should be no limit to human knowledge – but at what price? Do you consider that?' His fingers tighten on my sleeve and his tone is so portentous that I am compelled to turn and look at him. Gently I extract myself from his grip and begin walking briskly after the others, so that he has no choice but to keep up.

'May I ask you a question in return?' I say, without looking at him, as he scurries alongside me. A fine drizzle has begun to fall, whipped into unruly patterns by intermittent gusts of wind. The boats in the harbour knock together, their chains clanking like forlorn ghosts over the water.

'If I am permitted to answer in the same elusive fashion you favour,' he says, with a flicker of a smile.

'I deserve nothing less, I suppose.' I return the smile, in the hope that this will soften him.

'Well?'

'When Robert Dunne unburdened himself to you, the night before he died – did you sense then that he . . .' I pause, considering how best to phrase it. 'That he saw his own death imminent?'

'Of course not.' He stops dead and blinks rapidly at me. 'Else I would have done something. You think I would have left a man I feared might hold such intentions?'

'I was not suggesting you were to blame.' I hold up a hand to show I mean no offence. He is defensive, certainly, but what does he fear being accused of? 'But you do not consider it surprising that he took his own life a short time later? You said he wanted to confess—'

'Why, has someone suggested otherwise?' When I do not

reply, he nods slowly and the half-smile hovers over his lips again. 'Well, you have me in a cleft stick here, sir. If I say I have no doubt he took his own life, I am admitting that I abandoned him to his despair, since it seems I must have been one of the last to speak with him. And if I were to say that he did not seem like a suicide, I cast doubt on the manner of his death and suspicion on the whole crew.' He leaves this hanging in the air, then shakes his head. 'Better I say nothing. Especially to a stranger,' he adds.

'What did he despair of?' I ask, lowering my voice.

He gives a condescending laugh. 'I may not be able to give the sacrament of absolution, sir, but I still respect the sanctity of a man's last confession. If that is what you want to call it.'

'Do you think he knew it was his last confession?'

Pettifer makes an impatient noise with his tongue, as if he considers this a question too far. 'Dunne was troubled. Many sailors are troubled on the eve of a long voyage such as this. They know they are putting their lives into God's hands, and naturally that leads them to reflect on how they would stand before God, were they to face Him. I did not perceive Robert to be on the brink of committing such a grievous sin, but his conscience was certainly weighed down . . .' He hesitates, pulling nervously at his ear. I have the sense that this is not the whole story.

'Was he troubled by something in particular that night?'

He responds with a thin smile. 'You asked for one question, sir. You have already far exceeded your allowance.'

I acknowledge the truth of this and we begin walking again. He has taken against me over the Judas book, though how he knows as much as he does about its contents, I have no idea. And he is over-sensitive on the matter of Dunne; perhaps he fears he will be accused of failing in his pastoral duty towards the dead man, or perhaps there is more to it than that, since it seems now that the chaplain was the last to see Dunne alive.

170

'One more question,' I press him. 'And in return, when I have read more of Captain Drake's book I will be better placed to tell you whether it poses a danger to anyone's soul.'

A flash of greed lights his eyes at this and he nods. 'A fair exchange. What, then?'

'When you went back to him, was he still under the influence of drink? And did it seem to you the normal behaviour of a drunken man?'

'That is two questions, by my count.' He passes a hand across his receding hairline and sighs. 'When I found him in the street, he was very much the worse for drink. Naturally one sees this all too often with mariners, but it was unusual for Dunne – I had not seen him so lost to the bottle before.' He runs the tip of his tongue around his lips. 'When I knocked, he was still groggy, but he spoke coherently enough. Perhaps he had slept the worst of it off by then.' He tilts his head to one side and gives me a long look. 'But I have discussed all this with Sir Francis. I do not believe you knew Dunne.'

'No. I'm afraid I am afflicted with insatiable curiosity.' I peer ahead through the rain to where the others have disappeared around the corner of a house into one of the crooked streets leading up into the Barbican.

'Well, that is always a curse,' he says. 'An unbridled hunger for knowledge was the downfall of our first father in the garden.'

'So it was,' I say, with a tight smile.

Ahead of us, Sidney reappears from the side street, arms folded. 'For the love of God, Bruno, what are you hanging about for? We have company awaiting us.'

Pettifer glances back to me. 'I suppose he means to visit that brothel,' he says, lowering his voice. It is clear that he has already judged us for it.

I look at him. 'Sir Philip is married, Padre Pettifer.'

'Doesn't stop most of them.' He sniffs. 'No business of mine, of course, but you might tell him to give it a wide berth.

171

Whatever Sir William says, it is no place for a respectable man. Dangerous too, so I hear.'

'In what way?'

'Aside from the usual?' He wrinkles his nose. 'Cutpurses,' he whispers, tapping his belt.

Sidney calls again, and I turn to take my leave.

'Well, this has been most interesting, Doctor Bruno,' Pettifer says. 'I look forward to speaking further with you, as promised.' I glance back; the look he gives me is weighted with unspoken meaning. He sounds as if he believes himself to have won.

'What were you talking so closely to him about?' Sidney asks, when we are safely around the corner.

'Robert Dunne, what else?'

'You did not make him suspicious?'

'It is impossible to talk about the man without someone becoming suspicious. But that chaplain is defensive enough already. You know he heard Dunne's confession the night he died. So he says.'

'I heard you mention confession in the boat, but I couldn't catch his answer. You think he's lying?'

I hold out my hands. 'Someone is lying. Jonas says Dunne was passed out beyond all hope of waking when he went to his cabin. Pettifer says he prayed with him not more than an hour later.'

'It's not impossible. Perhaps Dunne woke with the drinker's guilt and wanted spiritual comfort.' He stretches his arms out. 'Though I must say, I would not turn to that insipid fellow, if it were me.'

'Listen – whoever killed Dunne must have done it while he was unconscious, to avoid any struggle. Pettifer said Dunne seemed troubled that night. He could be saying that to make the suicide idea more plausible.'

'So it could have been Pettifer. Or perhaps Jonas slipped something into that potion that needed a while to take effect. He could have gone back later, after Pettifer left,

172

knowing Dunne would be under the influence.' Sidney sighs. 'We still don't know why any of them would have reason to kill him.'

'Something he knew. Something he had that they wanted. Why did he have so much money hidden in that book, for instance?' I push my hands through my hair. 'Someone could have been looking for that.'

'There are eighty men on board,' he says, throwing his hands up.

'But how many of those could enter Dunne's cabin unremarked? And on a crowded ship there seem always to be people around. Any of the common sailors near an officer's cabin would surely have been noticed.'

'Maybe not in the dead of night. And if he was passed out from drink he could have left the door unlocked. It would only take a moment to slip inside.'

I shake my head.

'The chaplain knows more than he is willing to say, that much is certain. And so does Jonas the Spaniard.'

'Well.' He lays a hand on my shoulder. 'Leave off worrying about it for now. A brace of beautiful ladies are expecting us at the Star. One of whom, I happen to know, is very keen to enjoy your company while we are in Plymouth.'

'I'm afraid you will have to make my apologies to the ladies.' I slow my pace and he stops, eyebrows raised.

'Why? Where are you going now?'

'To church.'

'*What?*'

I set off up the hill, turning only once to glance over my shoulder and enjoy the look on his face.

The rain is easing now, orange streaks appearing between the clouds over the bay. The hour cannot be much past seven but the streets are still busy, as people with carts and baskets make their way uphill from the harbour and new arrivals, mostly men, spill in from the other direction, coming in from the sea or outlying roads and heading in groups for the taverns and whorehouses. Their coarse voices trail after them, singing and cursing, pumped with lust and aggression, snatched away in fits and starts by the wind that whistles down the narrow streets in search of the sea. The wet cobbles are slippery underfoot; ahead of me I see a man, already far gone in drink, lose his footing and clutch at his companion, howling with laughter. The evening sounds of a port town, nothing out of the ordinary. And yet I keep my hand close to the knife at my belt; I sense a tension in these streets that seems more concentrated tonight, as if building towards some kind of climax. Perhaps it is just the combined presence of so many men, so many sailors and soldiers, cooped up, frustrated, eager to be away, to discharge that raw energy into hauling ropes, swabbing decks, knifing Spaniards in the guts – energy that threatens to spill out here into tavern brawls and street fights instead. No wonder the citizens of Plymouth resent the presence of the fleet, anchored impotently day after day, sending boatloads of these men ashore every night with appetites that demand to be slaked. It is a night to stay indoors and keep the door barred, especially if you are trussed up in silk and lace like a child's doll, as I am. I quicken my steps, alert to every movement in the shadows from side streets and doorways.

Above the roofs to the west rises the square crenellated tower of a church, the largest to be seen in the close-knit streets around the harbour. The large west door has been pulled shut and the bells have fallen silent.

I slip into the back of the church, the great door creaking on its hinges as it closes behind me. A few people turn at the sound, but I tuck myself away out of sight, in the shadow of a thick stone pillar. Along the broad nave, an avenue of columns and pointed arches leads to the altar. The air smells musty, that scent of old stone that, in the absence of incense, always makes English churches feel uninhabited. For an instant I am

174

reminded sharply of the crypt of Canterbury Cathedral, and it takes some effort to push the unwelcome memories from my mind. Though there are tall windows to either side, the church is still gloomy, the only candles those in the chancel. This suits me; from my vantage point I scan the congregation, my eyes flitting over caps and coifs, the backs of restless heads. There is no sign of Pettifer. True, he did not say where he was going to pray, but this is the largest church in Plymouth, and Pettifer did not strike me as the sort of Christian who would prefer a small, humble chapel to a place where most of the town could witness him at his devotions and ask him about the fleet. Was he lying, then, about how he meant to spend his evening ashore? Some instinct had prompted me to follow him, something in his ostentatious piety that did not quite ring true. I determine to keep a closer eye on Pettifer in future.

Instead, to my surprise, I notice Gilbert Crosse, sitting in the back pew of the church, to my right. He has taken off his hat and hunches forwards, his arms wrapped tightly around his chest as if trying to make himself less visible. For a long while, he does not move, only sits with his head bowed, his hands motionless around his upper arms. I wonder what he prays for. He is a strange young man; obviously clever, and favoured by Walsingham for his abilities, yet apparently lacking in confidence. But I detect a fierce ambition beneath his timidity.

I shift from foot to foot as soundlessly as I can; the church is chilly and over the thin voices of the choir I hear rain slapping against the windows with each gust of wind, like a handful of gravel striking the glass. I am reminded again of how unmoved I always feel by the English church, though here it is generally assumed that if I am an enemy of the Inquisition I must, by definition, be a Protestant. Despite all the hypocrisy of the Church of Rome, they do at least have a sense of occasion. A Catholic Mass is a piece of theatre; this service is a

175

cold and soulless affair, and I can never escape the conviction that those attending feel the same.

When eventually the sparse congregation rise and shuffle forward to take the Eucharist, a man at the other end of Gilbert's pew slips out and disappears into the shadows of a side door. I watch him idly; I presume he wishes to avoid the communion. There are plenty of Englishmen who, while they attend church as the law demands, secretly consider the English Eucharist blasphemous and look for excuses not to take it. Gilbert himself remains in his seat, apparently still deep in prayer. I try to keep myself tucked away behind the pillar – I do not want him to think I am spying on him – but as he straightens up he glances towards the main door and catches sight of me. He has to squint to be sure, but it is too late for me to do anything other than raise a hand in greeting. He slides out of his seat and approaches, looking surprised, though not displeased to see me.

'Doctor Bruno. I did not realise you attended the English church. To be truthful,' he says, in a whisper, 'I was not sure of your religious leanings.'

'You are not alone in that,' I say, with a smile. I am often not sure myself. No wonder those around me are confused. 'I worship as Her Majesty commands,' I add. It is the sort of meaningless phrase people expect.

He nods. His eyes flit to the door.

'You do not take the Eucharist?' I ask.

He glances behind him to the congregation queuing at the altar and a look of guilt flashes across his face.

'Sometimes,' he murmurs, lowering his gaze. 'Though . . . May I confess something dreadful?'

'Please do.' I watch him, intrigued.

'I find the thought of it – all those people, drinking from the same cup. Their spit mixing in the wine – the idea turns my stomach. I look at it swirling in the cup and I cannot bring myself to put it to my lips. Is that a terrible sin?' He looks at me, anxious.

176

'I'm sure God understands. Personally, I have never understood why the Protestant faith bothers with the Eucharist. If there is no miracle involved, what's the point?' I say cheerfully. I wonder how long his fastidiousness will survive in the stinking confines of a ship for months on end.

A sexton standing nearby gestures for us to be quiet. Gilbert nods towards the door with a questioning look and I follow him out through the churchyard.

'Do you come to church every evening?' I ask, as we walk down the path to the lych-gate.

'I try. I find it helps to settle my thoughts. And it cannot hurt, can it – to offer up as many prayers as possible for such a voyage as this? We will have need of God's help against the Spanish.'

'Have you never sailed before?'

'Short journeys. Along the north coast of France and the Low Countries. Merchant ships around England. This will be something quite different.' He speaks with unexpected boldness, raising his face into the drizzle.

'You hold out great hopes for these maps of yours?' I say. He turns to me, his eyes blazing.

'Should a man not be ambitious for his work, Doctor Bruno? Are you not ambitious for your books? Well, then.' He offers an awkward smile. 'I know that pride is a sin. But my ambition is not for myself – or rather, not myself alone. To map the world accurately – think what that would do for the future of human endeavour! It has not been done yet – no, not even by Mercator. And for a nation that boasts some of the finest mariners and ships in the world, England is woefully deficient in the art of navigation. We make do with second-hand accounts by the French and Spanish, who were advancing this science half a century ago.' He shakes his head at the indignity. 'To think – Sir Francis Drake is the first man to have sailed the circumference of the globe, and still there is no English cartographer of any renown.'

'And you mean to change that?' I smile. I cannot help but admire anyone who is driven to break the limits of knowledge – precisely the kind of ambition Padre Pettifer decried to me earlier. And I know better than most how much determination is needed to try and change the way people view the world, or the universe.

Gilbert blushes. 'Yes. I do. Have you ever seen the *Theatrum Orbis Terrarum* of Abraham Ortelius?' he asks, as we turn down the hill into Nutt Street.

I nod. 'My friend John Dee had a copy in his library. It is a remarkable piece of work – the most expensive book ever produced, I am told.'

'And the first collection of maps all made by the same cartographer,' Gilbert enthuses. 'Well, I mean to make my own volume. The first English book of maps, detailing all the continents – yes, even Terra Australis, one day. It will be my life's work. I intend to follow Sir Francis Drake on his voyages, collaborate with his pilots and navigators, and create the most beautiful and the most advanced depiction of our world ever seen. As if you were looking down on the Earth from the heavens.'

'I would buy a copy of that,' I say, and he looks gratified. 'It is a great shame Sir Francis had no maps made of his circumnavigation,' I add, as we reach the entrance to the Star. Gilbert glances sidelong at me with a secretive smile.

'There were no charts published, by order of the Queen,' he whispers. 'That does not mean no maps were made.'

I give a low whistle. 'The Spanish would pay dearly for a sight of those.'

He grins. 'Indeed. But they will not get the chance.' Then his expression changes to one of alarm. 'Do not mention this, I pray you. Nor anything about the maps I am making for Walsingham. There are people on board that ship who are not to be trusted,' he adds, darkly.

178

'You can trust me,' I say.

'I know.' He fixes me with a solemn look. 'Captain Drake told me. And though I sometimes worry that his faith is too unquestioning when it comes to those closest to him, I am sure he is right about you.'

'I am flattered.' I want to ask him who he does not trust, since he must intend me to pick up the hint, but at that moment a group of men jostles past us through the front door, laughing loudly, and I am surprised to see Gilbert follow them inside.

'Do you come here to join the others for a drink?' I ask, stepping into the entrance hall.

'Oh, no.' He looks appalled at the idea. 'I call in after church each day to see if any correspondence has been delivered for Sir Francis. He has letters directed here while he is at anchor. Then I generally find a cheaper tavern for a hot meal before I return to the ship.'

'On your own?'

'Yes.' He looks defensive. 'I prefer my own company, Doctor Bruno. And there will be little enough chance of it once we are all cooped up on board. Though, if you . . .' He looks at me hopefully. 'I mean, I should be grateful for the conversation of a fellow scholar, if you have not already eaten?'

I hesitate, considering the invitation, before politely declining with the excuse of a prior engagement. I have the sense that there is more of interest to be drawn from Gilbert, and that I would not have to try very hard to prise it out of him, but I am tired and the prospect of an evening discussing meridian altitudes and the calculation of rhumb lines with this earnest, blinking boy does not raise my spirits. Given a choice, I would rather be looking at Lady Arden over the rim of a glass this evening. Yet, as I climb the stairs to our room, I find myself turning over Gilbert's words. He said Drake was too trusting

179

of those closest to him. He has already made clear that he harbours doubts about Jonas, but his choice of expression makes me wonder if he meant to direct my attention elsewhere. For who is closest to Sir Francis Drake in this fleet, if not his own brother?

TEN

When I unlock our chamber, I find it empty. I unbuckle my belt and fling it, with my dagger, on to the bed. Sidney must be in Lady Drake's chamber, no doubt entertaining the ladies with a sonnet, though he has left the fire burning low in the hearth. Beside it stands a silver tray with an open bottle of wine and one glass, an unusually thoughtful gesture on his part. My clothes are hung out on the fire screen; I pinch them between finger and thumb. They are stiff with sea water, mottled with white salt marks and still a little damp, and an unmistakable whiff of the harbour now clings to them, but all that will ease with wear, I reason. I tear off Sidney's embroidered doublet, fumbling with the buttons in my haste, and am unlacing my breeches when I hear a discreet cough from behind me. I whip around, conscious that my knife is out of reach, to see a figure in the shadows and a glint of light.

I let out an involuntary curse in Italian as my heart thumps like a blacksmith's hammer before slowing again. Lady Arden steps forward from the far end of the room, a glass in her hand. She smiles and takes a sip of wine.

'Forgive me – I didn't mean to frighten you. Sir Philip said you would be back soon and I thought it would be a good joke to catch you by surprise.'

181

'I could not be more amused.'

'Oh dear. You are angry with me. That is not a good start.'

'To what?' I catch the brusqueness in my voice and take a deep breath; she is not to know about the unseen presence in the shadows, the invisible man in black. I am more angry with myself for my own carelessness; if she can wait for me in my room without my noticing, who else might do the same?

She looks a little stung by my tone, but she pushes a loose tendril of hair from her eyes and tilts her chin up, determined. Her cheeks are flushed. 'I took the liberty of asking them to send up some wine. I'm afraid I had to make a start on it without you, though. Sir Philip said you had gone to church?' She raises a neatly plucked brow. 'You didn't strike me as the pious type.'

'Now and again the devotional urge overtakes me. Where is Sidney?'

'Playing cards with Lady Drake, I believe.' She lifts the glass to her lips and flashes a coquettish smile from behind it, as if inviting me to take my own meaning, then lowers her eyes.

'Cards?' Will Sidney never learn? Not content with writing endless poems to his childhood sweetheart Penelope Devereux, which he allows to be freely circulated around the court so that her husband, Lord Rich, cannot help but know of them, he now publicly courts the wife of another powerful man right under his nose – one whose patronage he depends on. If my fortunes were not so bound up with Sidney's – and if I didn't care for him as my friend – I might laugh at his audacity. As it is, he risks serious consequences; not least the damage to Lady Drake's honour and reputation in a town where she is well known. I lace my breeches again and make for the door.

'Wait, Bruno.' Lady Arden steps towards me, her hand outstretched. 'Are you Sir Philip's keeper?' Firelight dances on one side of her face, highlighting her fine bones and ivory skin. She is unquestionably a beautiful woman.

'I am the nearest he has to one,' I say, resting my hand on the latch.

Her voice softens. 'But does he need one? He is, after all, a grown man. And Lady Drake is likewise capable of making her own choices. You are not their chaperone, Bruno, though it is touching that you wish to play the part.'

'And Sir Francis, how would he feel? To be told that half of Plymouth has seen a man visiting his wife's chamber alone? Is he as broad-minded as you, I wonder?'

She laughs, a carefree, tinkling sound that implicitly reproaches me. 'Few men are, I find. There is a back staircase that comes out at the end of the corridor by our chamber. No one will see Sir Philip come or go, if that's what you are worried about. Besides, it is you who cast aspersions on the honour of your friend and mine. What harm if they are merely playing cards and talking?'

'The harm . . .' I pause, running a hand through my hair, 'the harm is all in what people perceive. Surely you, as a woman, can appreciate that?'

'Goodness, Bruno, you sound like one of the old beldames at court. "*As a woman?*"' She arches her brow again, pours a measure of wine into the second glass and moves towards me, holding it out, but just beyond my reach, as you might try to entice a dog with the promise of a treat. Against my better judgement, I let go of the door handle and step towards her.

'I would not like my friend to find himself on the wrong end of Captain Drake's cutlass,' I say, taking the glass. 'If they are only playing cards, why did you not join them?'

'I didn't want you to be lonely.' This time she holds my gaze and does not look away. I recall Sidney earlier, his blunt assertion that I would have her before I left Plymouth. I had assumed she made herself scarce as a favour to Sidney and Lady Drake, but perhaps it is they who believe they are bestowing the favour.

183

'Have no fear on that score, my lady. I am well practised at being in my own company. I have formidable inner resources.' But I hear my resolve falter, and so does she.

'I don't doubt it.' She smiles.

There is a long pause. I take a sip of the wine, keeping my eyes fixed on hers. I should go and save Sidney from his own folly. But I am not his keeper, as she says. Let him take responsibility for his own actions; it is all one to me if Drake refuses to take him on the voyage. It is another matter if Drake kills him a duel, persists the voice of reason. But Drake would not fight him, surely; or would he? Even if—

Lady Arden takes a step closer to me. I lower the glass slowly from my lips and experience a treacherous stirring in my groin. My heart may be firmly – uselessly – bound to a woman long vanished to France, but the body can be traitor to the heart. It is rare that such an opportunity presents itself, and rarer still the man who would turn it down out of some misplaced loyalty. And loyalty to someone, moreover, who gave me nothing in return but betrayal. Anger flashes through me at the memory; the colour in my face rises and, as if in direct response, I set the glass down on a table and move another step towards Lady Arden, who lifts her face expect-antly. That is when I hear it; the unmistakable sound of a board creaking outside the door.

She opens her mouth to ask what is the matter, but I hold up a hand to silence her as I stand, tensed, straining to hear more. I gesture Lady Arden to the far end of the room and lunge across to grab my knife from the bed. There it is again; a creak, a faint shuffling. Through the crack beneath the door I see the waver of a shadow. I draw the knife from its sheath, lower the latch as silently as I can, and in one sudden move-ment, I pull back the door to reveal the serving girl from this morning, her fist raised in the act of knocking. She lets out a piercing scream and I realise she has spotted the knife. I lay it carefully down on the floor and show her my empty hands,

184

shushing her as I do so. After the initial shock has passed, she stops the noise abruptly and stands there, staring at me, a sheet of paper rustling in her trembling hands.

'I'm sorry, sir, I wasn't eavesdropping, you startled me,' she mumbles. 'And the knife—'

'Hetty, isn't it? I didn't mean to frighten you. I thought you were someone else. That is to say . . . what do you want?'

She looks at the knife on the floor with a doubtful expression. 'I was just delivering this, sir.' She thrusts the paper at me and I have time to glimpse a red wax seal at the fold. 'Only, I wasn't sure if you had company and I didn't want to disturb—'

'No, just me,' I say, stepping into the doorway as she leans forward, her curious eyes flitting around as much of the room as she can see. 'Who gave you this?'

'A gentleman delivered it earlier. Because, you see, I thought I heard voices—'

'I was reading aloud.' I lift the paper to examine the seal. It bears the imprint of a shallow dish with a tongue of flame rising above it, just like the token hidden under Robert Dunne's bunk. My pulse quickens. The sacred flame. 'Who was he, this gentleman?'

'He didn't leave a name. Maybe it's on the letter.' She gives a little cough. 'Because Mistress Judith doesn't approve of gentlemen bringing company here, if you know what I mean,' she persists, nodding firmly to corroborate her own point. 'She says the Star is not that kind of house. She has asked guests to leave in the past for that sort of thing.'

'Do you come from Plymouth, Hetty?'

'Stonehouse, sir. The next village, across the headland.'

'Have you heard of a place called the House of Vesta?'

She looks at me with a superior smile. 'Everyone's heard of it, sir. But you don't want to go there, not if you value your purse.' She rubs her thumb and forefinger together.

'Is that so? And what do they offer there that is so costly?'

185

'Girls.' She says this as if it should be obvious.

'But those can be found all over Plymouth at a cheaper price, surely?'

She shrugs. 'The House of Vesta's for them with money to spare. The girls are young there. Clean, if you know what I mean. They say it's the one place in Plymouth you can be sure your parts won't drop off within the week. Sorry.' She claps a hand to her mouth and giggles. 'That's why only the better sort of gentlemen go there. Those that are willing to pay the price for peace of mind. The rest have to make do with it up against a wall by the dock and take their chances.' She sniffs.

'That is useful to know. And where is it?' I focus on the letter as I ask, turning it over to consider the seal as if it is the most interesting thing I have laid eyes on in many months, but my pretence at nonchalance quite rightly draws a derisory laugh from her.

'Well, now, sir. I don't know exactly. I believe it's kept secret.' The tilt of her head suggests it is a secret that might be available to interested buyers.

'Wait there.' I push the door ajar and grab my purse from the bed. Lady Arden sends me a complicit smile from the corner where she is lurking, out of sight. I motion to her to stay there.

'Here.' I draw out a groat for the serving girl and she looks at it, somewhat disappointed. 'It is all I have.'

'I heard the entrance is somewhere off Looe Street. Look for the apothecary's sign.'

'Thank you,' I say, closing the door. 'Good night.'

'You can't just walk in there off the street,' Hetty continues, tucking the coin somewhere in the folds of her skirts. 'You have to have an invitation. Know someone. Besides, it's a long way to walk this time of night.' She pauses for a beat. 'Mistress Judith understands that. She doesn't like to think of gentlemen being lonely of an evening.'

186

I pause at the half-closed door. 'Mistress Judith is a true Christian.'

'So, if you *do* want company, that is something she could arrange, if you'd like me to speak to her.'

'Ah. So it is not the morality she objects to, merely the revenue?'

'What?'

'Never mind. Thank you again.'

I close the door gently in her face and wait until I hear her footsteps padding down the corridor. Lady Arden watches me over the top of her glass, eyes alight with mischief.

'Everyone is concerned about you being lonely tonight, Bruno.'

'Yes, I am touched.'

'Is *she* the company, do you think?' She jerks her head at the door. 'She looks like she'd do it for a glass of porter. I wouldn't vouch for her cleanliness though.'

I respond with a brief, distracted smile; my attention is on the letter. *Fra Giordano Bruno*, it says on the front. I have not been addressed as Frater since I left holy orders; I glance at the door with a prickle of goosebumps on my arms. It is no secret that I was once a monk, but who here in Plymouth would know that, or address me as such? Only the men I have met aboard the *Elizabeth*. I turn the letter and break the plain red seal. There is just one line of text, written in block capitals in a neat, square hand.

I read it twice, pass a hand across my chin, blink hard and read it again to be sure I have understood the meaning, then snatch up my own black wool doublet from the rack in front of the fire, brush the salt from it, and open the door.

'Wait – where are you going?' Lady Arden cries as I rush out, almost slipping on the bare boards in my haste. 'Is it bad news?'

'Sorry,' I call over my shoulder on my way to the back staircase. 'Something urgent. No need to wait.'

187

One floor below, I crash into the room without knocking. As I guessed, Sidney is in full flow: back arched, chest forward, one hand flung out for dramatic effect. Lady Drake sits demurely on a stool by the fire, hands folded in her lap, gazing up at him with an expression somewhere between admiration and boredom as he declaims. He stops abruptly, mid-sonnet, and gives me a look that says he means to kill me later.

'Bruno! What are you thinking, man – do you not have the courtesy to knock?'

'I need to speak to you. Now – come with me. Forgive the intrusion, my lady.'

Elizabeth Drake regards my flustered appearance with equanimity. An amused smile hovers on her lips.

'Sir Philip was just reciting some of his poetry,' she says, though the explanation is hardly needed. 'I fear he had not quite finished.'

'My Lady Drake was kind enough to request it,' Sidney says, defensive.

'There are a hundred and eight sonnets in this sequence, my lady,' I say, turning to her. 'I can save you the trouble of hearing them: Stella rejects him and stays with her husband, Astrophel is sad, The End.'

She laughs. 'Is that it? No one dies?'

'They may yet,' Sidney mutters through clenched teeth, glaring at me. But he does not resist as I drag him to the door, where we collide with Lady Arden. I nod in passing as I push by her; Sidney pauses for a brief bow. She says nothing, only sends me a wounded look as she closes the chamber door behind her.

'You had better have good reason for this, Bruno,' Sidney says, as he thunders down the next flight of stairs to the entrance hall. 'She was—'

'What?' I pause in the curve of the stairwell and turn to him. 'About to fall into your arms? Was that your intention? Good work if so, Philip – write poems declaring your unrequited love for one man's wife and use them to seduce another's.'

'Keep your voice down! God, Bruno, your moralising grows tiresome – anyone would think you were still a monk.'

'If I were still a monk, I would have no moral scruple at all,' I say, but he is not listening.

'Seduce is an ugly word,' he continues, eyes bright with anger. 'You know nothing of courtly manners – why would you? It is not seduction to pay chaste court to a beautiful woman, it is an honourable tradition handed down from the time of King Arthur—'

'—yes, yes. But this is 1585 and you are not Sir Galahad. We have more important matters to occupy us. Look – this was just delivered to me by the serving girl.'

I hold out the paper. He reads both sides and looks at me. Below us, people mill about in the entrance hall on their way to the tap-room. I scan the shifting mass for a glimpse of a man in a black cap, but there is no sign.

'I don't understand,' Sidney says, turning the paper over twice more, as if this will help.

'It's Latin.'

He rolls his eyes. 'Yes, I can read the words, obviously. But not the meaning. Who would send you this? And why?'

'Look at the seal.'

He fits the broken halves together and frowns. 'The same image as that token we found in Dunne's cabin. What is it?'

'Do you recall what Savile said in the boat, when you asked him where to go in Plymouth? He made an allusion to the sacred flame – he meant the House of Vesta. I would wager anything this is its secret symbol. You said you'd heard Dunne was a regular.'

'The sacred fire of the goddess.' He nods, running his finger over the seal. 'But that still doesn't explain the message.'

I sigh, and continue on down the stairs. 'Come on. I'll explain on the way.'

'You want to go there now?' He stops again and lets out a short bark of laughter. 'You are extraordinary, Bruno. You upbraid me for merely reading poems to a woman of quality in her chamber, then merrily drag me off to a whorehouse instead?'

'Keep your voice down – do you want the whole inn to know where we are going?'

He makes an irritable noise and follows me down, the silk of his breeches rustling as he walks like the sighing of poets. 'Well, this is an odd turn of events. Who do you suppose sent the letter?'

'I don't know. But there is an obvious connection with Robert Dunne, which someone wants to bring to our attention. Do you still have that token with you?'

'In my purse.' He pats the bulge at his hip beneath his jacket. 'You realise it is likely a trap?'

'Most probably. But if so, there must be answers to be found. We will have to be on our guard, that's all.'

He exhales with an exasperated noise as we push our way through the main door and into the night air. I turn, checking the street in both directions, but see only the usual straggle of men, arms slung around one another's shoulders, singing sea shanties. But eyes are watching us from the shadows; I am sure of it.

The wind is still high; a thin mist of drizzle eddies about us, settling like a silver veil on our hair and clothes. Overhead the clouds chase each other across the sky and out to sea, brushstrokes of lead-grey against the darkening sky.

'The letter, then,' Sidney says, as we set off uphill between limewashed houses. 'What's the connection with Dunne?'

'You recognise the quotation?'

'"*Vexilla regis prodeunt Inferni.*"' He mouths the single line of the anonymous letter, enunciating each syllable as if this might render the author's meaning clearer. '"The banners of the King of Hell advance."' He considers for a

190

moment, screwing up his face as he ransacks his well-stocked memory.

'Come on, Philip, you are supposed to be versed in literature. One of the few Englishmen who claims to know the poetry of my country, at any rate.'

He turns to me, light dawning in his eyes. 'Dante! Is it?'

'Exactly. But do you remember where it comes from?'

He shakes his head, blank. 'From the *Inferno*, though I can't give you the Canto.'

'It is the opening line of Canto Thirty-Four,' I say, as we come to a fork in the roads. 'We're looking for Looe Street. Which way?'

'No idea.' He hails a brace of men, the worse for drink, weaving towards us, their lurching steps seemingly in perfect time with one another. 'I say, gentlemen – which way to Looe Street?'

The question is met with a chorus of guffaws and brutal upward gestures with their fists. 'Gentlemen!' squawks one, and his companion does a brief mime of what I can only guess is supposed to be copulation. But the first gives us broadly comprehensible directions while the second squints to eye Sidney in his finery with an appraising look I do not care for; almost certainly his befuddled brain is reckoning how much a man dressed like that might carry in his purse. Sidney evidently senses it too, because his hand strays to the hilt of his sword and the man takes a rolling step back as we continue down the street to our left, glancing behind us from time to time as we go. 'Good luck with it, mate,' one of the men calls out, when we are almost out of sight. 'You'll need it.'

'I can't say I like this, Bruno,' Sidney says in a low voice as the shadows between the houses grow denser. 'What did the fellow mean by that?'

'He meant nothing, except to set us on edge,' I say, striding on, determined not to be dissuaded.

There are fewer people in this side street; as it curves

191

around to the right it seems deserted, though the sound of voices and dogs barking carries through the damp air. We walk in the middle of the road, in case anyone is hovering in the shadows of doorways or the gaps between buildings. Sidney keeps his hand on his sword. Rivulets of filthy water trickle down the gutters at either side. The salt wind does not whip away the smell of refuse and rotting vegetables. 'Explain, then.'

'Canto Thirty-Four of Dante's *Inferno* is where he reaches the very centre of Hell. The circle of the Traitors, reserved for the worst sinners in all of history. And who does he find there?'

'Judas Iscariot,' Sidney whispers, his eyes widening in recognition. 'But why . . .?'

'I don't know. Whoever is sending these letters is taunting us – first Drake, now me – over the Judas book. It must be the same person.'

'But who would bother to taunt you? Unless he is someone who knows you and suspects you may be involved with the book.'

'Which brings us back to Rowland Jenkes. He sends me a quotation from an Italian poet, just to show he knows me. He is here, I am certain of it, watching us. Damn him!'

Sidney lays a warning hand on my arm; I have raised my voice without noticing. I look around, but there is no one to hear.

'We are certain of nothing yet, except that you have dragged me from a warm room and good company.' He straightens his hat and glances over his shoulder once more. 'So what do you propose? We march in and demand to know who has been sending anonymous letters?'

'I propose we do it a little more cleverly than that. The girls may know something. If Dunne was a regular he may have had a favourite. Men sometimes whisper their secrets into the pillow when their guard is down.'

192

Sidney regards me with a half-smile. 'What would you know of that? I don't believe you have ever let your guard down, Bruno, not even in the throes of it.'

He is wrong, but I say nothing.

'You do realise we'll have to pay, don't you?' he complains, a hand straying to his purse. 'You can't expect a whore to give up her time for nothing to answer questions, not even if you do your big melancholy eyes at her like a lost dog.'

'A lost dog?' I say, but he points ahead of us to a crooked timber-framed house of four storeys, each overhanging the one below as if it might topple forward under its own weight. Suspended over the front door from two creaking chains is a sign depicting the rod of Asclepius, the sign favoured by apothecaries. The shop on the ground floor is closed up for the night with thick shutters. I crane my neck to see the upper storeys. Splinters of light show through gaps in the curtained windows. Beside the apothecary's door is an archway leading to a dark passageway. Sidney steps closer and examines the posts on either side of the entrance. 'Look here! This must be it,' he whispers, indicating a small image carved into the wood. It shows a torch topped with a tongue of flame, identical to the seal.

I follow him along the passage. Even I have to stoop; it is an old house, built in an age when men were smaller, or hunchbacked. Sidney is bent almost double, cursing each time he knocks his head on a low beam. We straighten up into a small courtyard at the back of the house, sunk in shadow from the high buildings on all sides. Laughter erupts from somewhere overhead, sudden and staccato.

At the top of three worn steps is a door with a shuttered grille at head height and an iron knocker set above the latch. Sidney reaches towards it.

'Hold on.' I stop and draw back out of sight of the window, unbuckling my belt.

'Control yourself, Bruno – at least wait until we're inside.'

193

I ignore him. I remove my knife in its sheath and slip it into my boot before buckling the belt again. I gesture to his dagger. 'Conceal that if you can. They will have your sword from you at the door, but they are expecting us. We should be prepared.'

'It was her idea to leave,' he remarks, as he follows my example and tucks his short dagger inside his boot, leaving his sword buckled. 'Nell Arden, I mean. It was she who suggested she wait for you in our chamber. None of my doing.'

'And you didn't think to point out to her how that would look? For all of us?'

'I thought you might be grateful for the opportunity. It's been a while.' He lifts the iron ring on the door and bangs it three times, turning to smirk as he does so.

'How would you know? Don't imagine you are privy to every part of my life.' I push a hand through my hair.

'All right, don't bite. But hasn't it? You will not countenance another woman since *she* left, as far as I can see, and you say you don't visit whores, so I can't imagine where—'

'Perhaps you know nothing about it. Perhaps *I* consider some things to be private.' I hear the petulance in my voice. I am spiky because he is right, but I will not acknowledge this. Although his grin suggests he realises it already.

He breaks off his reply as the shutter behind the grille is drawn back and a woman's face appears in the opening.

'May I help you, gentlemen?' Her voice is unexpectedly refined. Sidney immediately sweeps off his hat and executes a professionally charming bow.

'Good evening, mistress. We were hoping for a drink and good company.'

The woman appears unmoved. 'Perhaps you have mistaken this house for some kind of inn, sir. I run a home for orphaned girls here.'

Sidney laughs. 'Is that so? But I do not believe I am mistaken. Are you, perhaps, the Vestalium Maxima? The high priestess

194

of the Vestals?' He offers another gracious smile, and she concedes the reference by returning it, briefly.

'Do I know you, sir?'

'Not yet.' He beams, and produces the silver token from his purse, holding it up to the light. She glances at it and nods.

'Where did you get that?'

'From a friend. He said we should—'

'Which friend?' Her sharp eyes flick from Sidney to me and back, sizing up our garments, our faces, the likely size of our purses.

'Robert Dunne,' I say, before Sidney can answer.

Her expression changes, though it is not clear whether my gamble has worked.

'I see.' She presses her red lips together. The bars of the grille divide her face into its constituent parts; it is hard to form an impression of the whole. 'What did you say your names were?'

'My name is Giordano Bruno,' I say, enunciating carefully, watching for a flicker of recognition from her. She studies me, impassive, before the shutter slides closed with a sharp crack of wood on wood.

Sidney curses through his teeth, but after a brief pause we hear a fumbling with the latch and the door opens to reveal a tall woman, elegantly dressed in a gown of green satin that is past its prime but was clearly once an arresting sight, much like the woman herself. She fingers a string of pearls at her throat.

'Well then. You had better come in. I would ask that you take off your weapons and leave them here. They will be quite safe.'

'But will we?' Sidney says, attempting a joke. She silences him with a glacial stare, and he meekly unbuckles his sword without another word. I hold out my hands, indicating my empty belt, though I see her practised eye travel over my body, pausing at my legs. For a moment I think she is going to demand that I be searched, but after a long look she gives me a curt nod.

'You can give me the token. And we take payment in advance,' she says, holding out a manicured hand with a smile which does not reach her eyes. 'A gold sovereign, if you please.'

'A gold *sovereign*?' Sidney stares at her, open-mouthed, waiting for her to laugh and tell him the real price. She continues to hold out her hand, the smile fixed in place.

'Twenty *shillings*?' Sidney repeats, still hoping he has misheard.

She looks at me. 'Each.'

'Christ and all his saints. What do I get for that?'

'A little taste of heaven.'

'A little taste? For a sovereign I expect a five-course banquet.'

'With respect, sir.' That same, smooth tone. 'As with so much in life, you get the quality you pay for. If you don't like our prices, there are plenty of places where you can pay a good deal less. Here you know what you are buying.' Her lips curve again into the ghost of a smile. We might be talking about any transaction, it is all so carefully couched in the language of business.

'I meant no offence, madam,' Sidney says, all gallantry once more. He takes a couple of coins from his purse, glaring at me as he does so; if we find nothing useful here, he will not easily let me forget the loss of two sovereigns. She glances at the money and regards us with the same inscrutable expression, before the reserved smile reappears and she nods towards a door.

'Follow me, then.'

I watch her with curiosity as she leads us through to a small parlour, the air over-warm and thick with the smell of good wax candles. She carries herself with a dignified bearing, as if she were a lady of quality. Perhaps she once was. I guess her to be nearer forty than thirty, though her figure is that of

196

a younger woman and she has clearly kept her pale skin away from the sun and wind. I am curious to know how a woman of evident breeding came by this trade, but her manner does not invite questions. Sidney flings himself into a chair with velvet cushions worn shiny with age and slides down, his long legs stretching out across a faded Turkish carpet. I stand by the hearth, where a neglected fire splutters and smokes in the grate.

'Well then – what is your taste, gentlemen?' She puts her head on one side and studies us. 'Tell me what is to your liking and I will see if we can oblige.' She makes it sound as if she is asking how we like our meat cooked.

'Robert Dunne told me I should ask for his favourite,' I say, before Sidney can answer. He glances at me.

'Did he now?' Her painted eyebrows arch; she seems almost interested. 'And what did he tell you about his favourite?'

I try to look nonchalant. 'Only that I would not be disappointed.'

She tilts her head. 'Well. I'll see what I can do. Wait here.' She leaves the parlour by a side door and we hear the sound of footsteps climbing stairs overhead. As soon as she is gone, I feel the clench of fear in my gut.

'She knows I am lying,' I hiss, when I am sure she is out of earshot.

'Not necessarily.' Sidney turns his hat in his hands and examines the feather. 'Do you think she knows anything about the letter?'

I shrug. 'I doubt it. The imprint in that seal came from one of those silver tokens. Anyone among her elite clientele could have used it. But whoever it was wanted to direct us here, there can be no question about that. All we can do now is tread carefully and hope to discover why.'

'And hope it was not for the purpose of running you through with a sword.' Sidney crosses and uncrosses his legs and turns his attention to a loose pearl on his sleeve. 'What do you suppose Dunne's tastes were? What if he was one of those who liked to be roughed up? Tied and whipped, that sort of thing. Then there are some who like hot candle wax—'

'She won't get anywhere near me with a candle, don't worry.' The fire spits a fat ember on to the carpet; I stretch out a foot and stamp it out. 'The girl will probably be so relieved to find that I only want to talk, she will be more than willing to help me.'

'Let us hope so,' he says. 'And what am I to do while you charm this vestal virgin into spilling Dunne's secrets?'

'Perhaps you could find someone to talk to. Ask a few questions.'

'I shall be badly out of pocket if I don't.' He offers a wry smile. At least the amusement is some compensation for being dragged away from Lady Drake. 'She intrigues me,' he says, *sotto voce*, gesturing to the ceiling, where creaking timbers and footsteps can be heard overhead. 'House of Vesta, indeed. Did she name the place herself, I wonder. She must be educated, if so. And she speaks like a gentlewoman.'

'The Vestal Virgins,' I muse, recalling my Roman history. 'Noble-born girls of Rome, sworn to celibacy in the service of the goddess. The penalty for defiling any of them was death, was it not? You have to admire her taste for irony.'

'What makes you think it is ironic?' We both start; the madam has appeared in the other doorway, soundless as a cat, a gleam in her eyes. 'Do not alarm yourself, sir, I am only teasing. You.' She points to me. 'Come with me. I will return for you, sir,' she adds, to Sidney. 'Meanwhile, I will have some wine brought to you.'

'Listen – don't go without me,' I say, turning back to him. 'Wait for me here, after . . .' I leave the sentence open, with a shrug. Something in the way the woman looks at us makes me uneasy, though perhaps it is just my anxious imagination.

'I'll be waiting here. Go and get your money's worth.' He mimes what I can only suppose is his version of a man

198

surprised by hot wax on his parts. I glare at him and turn back to the madam, who offers me her creamy smile and gestures to the second door.

She hitches her skirts and her narrow hips sway purposefully as she leads me up the stairs to a landing. From behind one of the doors comes the rumble of male voices and laughter; two or three men, it sounds like. There is a sudden outburst of cursing and cheering, as if a card game is in progress. I glance around, the fingers of my right hand flexing, ready to grab for my knife if I need to; I have not seen any armed men yet, but they will be here somewhere, lurking in the shadows, close enough to pounce at her signal on anyone who threatens trouble. Every brothel has them. I am beginning to question the wisdom of coming here.

'You know your Roman history then, sir,' the woman observes over her shoulder, in her precise accent, as she leads me past the door and up a further flight of stairs. Another staccato burst of laughter erupts from the room we have just passed. 'Perhaps you are a scholar?' The remark is innocent enough, but I am not inclined to give anything away.

'I have been many things,' I say.

'I do not doubt it. But you are not, at any rate, a sailor. Of that I am fairly certain.'

'How can you tell?'

'You are too courteous. You have none of that roughness that months in the company of men can breed, even in gentlemen.'

I incline my head with what I hope is an enigmatic smile. She laughs. 'So what brings you to Plymouth?'

'Business.'

'And you have seen Robert Dunne here?' She asks the question lightly. I meet her eye and look away. Neither of us has mentioned Dunne's death; I wonder if she is waiting for me to broach the subject.

'Yes.' I offer no more than that. She lowers her gaze and nods.

'Poor Robert,' she says. 'We heard the news, of course.'

'You knew him well?'

'As well as I ever know our visitors,' she replies evenly, looking at me from the corner of her eye. A politician's answer; I have underestimated her if I think I can trick her into giving anything away. A brothel-keeper – especially one who evidently counts men of influence among her clients – must be as practised in the art of discretion as any diplomat or spy. Down in Southwark, there are a couple of madams in Walsingham's pay; it is surprising how much a man will reveal when his breeches and his guard are down.

'Were you close friends?' she asks, as we reach a second landing.

'Close enough.' Like her, I would prefer to avoid questions about Dunne.

She touches the pearls at her throat and turns to regard me with a steady gaze. 'Yet he gave you his token. People usually come to us by personal invitation, you see. We pride ourselves on a certain . . .' she affects to search for the word '. . . exclusivity.'

I smile sadly, my eyes not wavering from hers. 'He gave it to my friend. Perhaps he had other things on his mind. But I'm sure you will find our money is as good as anyone's, Mistress . . .' I raise a questioning eyebrow.

'Grace.' She drops a half-curtsey, though I cannot tell if she is mocking me. 'They call me Mistress Grace. Well, I hope you will be satisfied, Doctor Bruno. I'll have wine sent up.'

Three doors lead off this landing. She moves to the one at the rear of the house, turns the handle and stands aside. She regards me for a moment longer, as if she is debating whether to add something further, but eventually she gives me a brief nod and turns away to the stairs. I breathe in, and push the door open. The sense of unease prickling in my stomach has intensified, though I cannot quite pinpoint the reason.

The room is small and dim; it seems to have been

partitioned from a larger room and through the thin plaster a series of unmistakable groans and creaks can be heard from next door. Two candles burn in a wall sconce and one on a small table. There is no other furniture except the bed with a nightstand beside it holding an earthenware jug and bowl for washing. A thin figure sits hunched on the bed, wearing a cotton shift. Her hands are clasped in her lap and her head droops down, lank hair obscuring her face. I can't help thinking that if I were a genuine customer I would want a slightly better show of enthusiasm, not this hangdog creature.

'Hello,' I say, as gently as I can.

She raises her head and with a sudden shock I understand. The figure before me is a boy, perhaps thirteen or fourteen years old, the skin of his face still downy, though the dead look in his eyes belongs to someone who has already lived too long.

'Ah,' I say, as I try to hide my reaction behind a blank expression. I back up against the door, scanning the room for hiding places of possible assailants. Either this is a trap, or Robert Dunne had more secrets than we have yet discovered.

'Do you want me as a boy or a girl, sir?' The child's voice is entirely empty of emotion. When I do not reply, he crosses his legs and the shift rides up towards his skinny thighs. A blue bruise stands out against the white skin. 'I have women's clothes I can put on, if that's your preference. As you like.' He shrugs, to show his compliance either way.

'Right.' I want to sit but there is no chair; instead I lean against the door and allow myself to sink down until I am sitting on the floor. 'I would like a drink, I think. What is your name?'

The boy tips his head back and looks down at me from under his hair, weighing me up. 'What do you want it to be?'

'The truth.'

An expression passes over his face that at first I do not

201

understand; he seems to shrink into himself and glances at the door, as if hoping for some kind of assistance. Then I realise he is afraid. And with good reason; sodomy is a hanging offence under English law, and the same goes for those who sell or procure it. No wonder he keeps his identity to himself.

'Give me whatever name pleases you, then,' I say, anxious that I have put him on his guard.

He relaxes a little. 'You can call me Toby.'

'Well then, Toby . . .' I am considering where to begin when there is a knock at the door. I jump up and fling it open, ready to reach for my knife, but there is only a pale girl with a low-cut bodice, who hands me two large pewter cups without once looking up to meet my eye. She is pretty, and very young – perhaps of an age with him. As soon as I have taken the cups she turns on her heel and stalks silently away. I close the door. Toby sits still on the bed, impassive.

'Wine?'

The boy nods, mutely watching me. He pulls his knees up under the shift and hugs them to him, an oddly touching gesture that makes him seem all the more childlike. Perhaps he knows something; my difficulty is how to win his trust without making him afraid.

I cross slowly, holding out the cups in front of me, as you might approach a nervous animal. He reaches out and takes one, large brown eyes fixed on me with no particular expression that I can discern. I sit beside him on the bed, though far enough away not to appear threatening. My nerves are taut, my senses alert for any indication of move-ment outside the chamber. The boy turns and looks at me, expectant.

'Should we begin, sir?' His small fingers tug at the collar of his shift. 'Tell me what you wish, and I—'

'Toby.' I adjust my position, tucking one leg under me, and take a gulp of wine, though not too much – I need to keep my wits sharp. I have found myself in some strange situations over the years, but nothing that quite compares to this. As I move, I feel a ridge jutting into my thigh. Lifting the bedsheet, I pull out a book, bound in calfskin, very new and expensive-looking. The boy lurches forward to grab it but I am too quick for him; I dart to my feet and hold it up, out of his reach, until he sinks back to the bed, glowering at me. I open the book to the frontispiece to find that it is a volume of Ovid's *Fables*. I note the printer's mark. The book was only printed last year. The front endpaper has been torn out.

'Is this yours?'

The boy looks stricken. 'I was given it. By a gentleman. I never stole it.' He holds out a hand for it, though half-heartedly.

'It is a generous gift,' I say, flicking through the pages. 'A book like this is worth a good deal of money, being so new. Although it is a shame this one has a page torn out – that might devalue it.'

His eyes flicker briefly to me, guilty. I decide to try another tack.

'Do you like the stories?'

His face brightens. 'Oh, yes. I like Perseus and the sea monster best, and Narcissus, who fell in love with himself.'

'Can you *read* them?'

He drops his gaze. 'Not really. He read them to me sometimes. He promised to teach me my letters from it if I was good.'

'If you were good and did as he asked?'

He does not reply, only bites his lower lip. When he looks up, he wears the expression of a child forced to confess he has been stealing from the larder. 'You won't tell Mistress Grace, will you? She would take it. And he would be angry.'

'I won't say a word.' I pass the book back to him; he immediately stuffs it under the mattress and sits on top. 'How would it be, Toby,' I say, leaning back, 'if we were to talk for a while?'

'Talk?' His brow creases and he glances to the door as if seeking approval for this unlikely suggestion. 'What for?'

I shrug, and take another sip. The wine is warm and aromatic and makes me think of Christmas; I feel it curl thickly through my blood and gently soothe my nerves. 'I am a stranger here, and I miss having someone to talk to. My friend Robert Dunne used to say you were a good listener.'

It is a gamble; I know this before I drop the name. No man with a predilection for illegal pursuits shares this information widely. The boy frowns, perplexed, and he glances again at the door.

'Robert Dunne?'

'Indeed so. He spoke highly of you.'

The boy only looks down at his hands, twisted in his lap, and murmurs something indistinct.

Perhaps this has been the wrong tack; for all I know, Robert Dunne was a violent pervert and the boy dreaded the sight of him and is glad he's dead. Perhaps he has never met Robert Dunne in his life. I try again.

'You heard what happened to him, I suppose?'

His head jerks up at this and his eyes briefly lock with mine; I read fear in them.

'What?' he whispers.

'He is dead. Did you not know?'

Confusion flits across his face. 'I . . .' He scratches the back of his neck, then reaches out and lays a hand on my thigh. 'Sir, do you want to undress?'

'No!' I say, with more alarm than I intended, jumping to my feet. I move purposefully to the window in case he tries to touch me again. The wind bangs the shutters softly against the glass. 'Not yet. Let us talk some more.'

'Then should I? I am sure you did not come here to talk.' He pulls again at the half-unlaced strings of his shift. The conversation is making him more uncomfortable than the prospect of whatever he thinks I have come for.

'No, really – we are both fine as we are. Forgive me, Toby – I am of a strange cast of mind tonight. I suppose I am in mourning for my friend Robert. You understand?'

He makes a movement with his head.

'Do you mourn him too?'

He shrugs, avoiding my eye.

'Did he visit you often?'

'Why do you ask me so many questions about him?'

'When someone you were close to dies, talking about them is a way of bringing them back. Making it seem as if they were still here. Do you not think? Have you never lost anyone you cared for?'

'My parents.' He doesn't lift his head.

'Is that how you came to be here?' I ask gently. He lifts his eyes and looks at me as if seeing me for the first time. When he speaks, it is a whisper so soft I can barely catch it.

'Mistress Grace brought me here to work in the kitchen when I was small. Now I am apprenticed to the apothecary downstairs, but she still gives me a room.'

'And she puts you to work like the girls?'

Again, the stubborn silence, lips pressed tight. He will not meet my eye. The candlelight seems to flicker and dance, so that at first I think there must be a draught in the room, but as I watch the flames I see that it is the wall itself that is undulating, as if ripples were spreading across its surface. Toby goes on looking at me, and I notice that his unhappy face has duplicated itself: two pale discs alongside one another, each blurring where they intersect. I take a step towards him and my legs feel strangely remote; I put a hand out to the wall to steady myself. Too late, I realise what has happened, and curse my own carelessness: I should have noticed that the boy did not touch his wine. In one lurching movement, I grab the bowl from the nightstand and force my fingers down my throat, gagging as bile rises in my stomach. I have the sense of being on board ship; the walls seem to pulse in time

205

with my head, but I persist, bending double as the sharp salt of saliva fills my mouth and my stomach heaves once, twice, before I retch violently and its contents erupt into the bowl and splash on to the bare boards.

Gasping, I wipe my mouth with my sleeve and lean against the wall. Toby watches me without moving, though there is fear in his eyes.

'What do they put in it?' I demand.

His voice almost disappears. 'Nutmeg.'

'Why?'

'It's what she does sometimes. It means she doesn't trust you. That's why she brought you here.'

I rub my forehead. I am still dizzy and off-balance; I can feel the heat of it working into my system, though I think I caught it in time to prevent worse damage. I wonder if they have done the same to Sidney, and if they mean to rob us. Padre Pettifer warned me; I should have listened. Then, through my muddied thoughts, there emerges a pinpoint of clarity: Mistress Grace addressed me as 'Doctor Bruno'. Yet I did not give her my title at the door, therefore: *she knows who I am*. She was waiting for me. Was it her that wrote the letter, then? But how could she know me, and why bring me here?

'Did Robert Dunne' – I speak slowly and deliberately, hearing my voice as if it comes from elsewhere – 'did he come to you as a client? Were you his favourite?'

He shakes his head. His outline is still blurry to me, but I see him dart another nervous glance at the door.

'Then why did she bring me to you? Is it a trap? What do they mean to do?'

When he does not reply, I take a step forward, my hand outstretched; he gives a little yelp, as if he expects to be struck. I grab the pitcher and pour its contents over my upturned face, then shake my head like a dog, scattering droplets.

'I don't know, sir,' he whimpers. 'I just do as I am asked.'

'Who sent the letter?' I wipe the water from my eyes and take another step forward, looming over him as he backs away with a whimper.

'I don't know about any letter, sir. I never even spoke to Robert Dunne. He didn't come here for me.' He presses up against the wall, trying to make himself smaller. 'You need to talk to Eve. She was his special one. I don't know anything.'

'And where is Eve?'

'She's gone.'

'Where? Where can I find her?' I kneel on the bed and grip his arm. 'Tell me – or shall I mention your book to Mistress Grace?'

'No!' He bites his lip. 'She sends them away when they get with child. They're no use to her here after that.'

'But *where*?'

'I don't know!' His voice is squeaky with panic; his eyes skitter to the door again, just as it is flung open and the figure of a man in black fills the space.

For the space of a heartbeat I freeze; Toby takes advantage of my confusion to slip from my grasp and dart for the open door, past the man, who gives him a cuff around the head as he ducks by. The door slams behind him. My vision is still slightly unfocused; all I can see is that he is tall, with a beard, and that he is holding something behind him.

I stand back, facing him, squinting to bring him into alignment. I can feel my head clearing, though my heart is galloping behind my ribs.

'So you are the famous Giordano Bruno?' he says, glancing around the room. He has a refined voice, much like Sidney's, but with an odd lisp. 'You know buying boys is against the law in this country? As well as against God's law, I hardly need add.'

'Who are you?' For one terrifying heartbeat I fear he is come from the authorities, that I have been set up to be caught with the boy. But that would make no sense; the madam and her entire business would be condemned with me.

His face splits into a knowing smile and I focus enough to see that he is missing most of his teeth.

'You don't know me, though I dare say you are familiar with my name. But I have a friend who is keen to acquaint himself with you. Or *re*-acquaint, I should say.'

My throat tightens. 'Did you send the letter?'

'That would have been my friend. I don't write so well any more. Not after what they did to me.' He holds up his right hand. It dangles at an unnatural angle from his wrist, twisted under. The tendons have clearly been damaged beyond repair. I have seen this before: in a man who was hung by the wrists for several hours during an unofficial interrogation. It is one of the Privy Council's preferred techniques in the Tower. A cold understanding begins to dawn.

'You are John Doughty.' My voice emerges as a croak.

He tilts his head and smiles, as if to imply that this is an interesting guess. At the same time he brings out his left hand from behind his back to show that he is holding a knife. I force myself to keep still. He believes I am unarmed; I will have only one chance to catch him while he thinks he has the advantage and I must time it exactly.

'What do you want of me, then?' I try to make my voice bolder, but it still sounds slurred.

'Why are you asking questions here about Robert Dunne?'

I stare at him. 'Why do you think?'

The smile disappears. 'I can only assume that Drake does not believe he died by his own hand. Is he right?'

'You tell me.'

'Ah.' He nods, his lips pressed together. 'Interesting. Well, it seems we are all looking for answers. For now, I want you to come with me. My friend is keen to see you. He has some questions for you too.'

'And if I refuse?'

He holds up the knife so that the candlelight catches the edge of the blade. 'That would be quite foolish on your part.'

208

I say nothing. Though my limbs still feel heavy, my head is clearing. I wait. When he sees that I do not mean to respond, he tilts his head, as if to say 'so be it', and steps forward, his blade pointed towards me. In one movement, I duck, seize the knife from my boot and lunge at him, catching him in the upper arm; he cries out and drops his weapon as he tries to grasp at my doublet. I shove him hard in the chest and half-slide, half-fall down the stairs, yelling for Sidney as I trip on the first landing and pull myself to my feet. I take the corner for the next flight of stairs as footsteps follow me from above; a couple of doors open a crack and I sense faces watching from the shadows, though no one moves to intervene. Curses rain down from the stairs above as the footsteps grow quicker in pursuit, but I reach the ground floor unhindered and find myself in a passageway with doors leading off it, all of them closed. My heart is racing; I begin to run, though my legs feel as if they are moving through liquid. I cast a quick look over my shoulder as Doughty reaches the foot of the stairs; he shouts something, though the sense of it is lost on me. I throw open the first door I see and plough through a bedchamber, where a white-skinned girl sits astride a man, tangled in sheets, riding him to a steady rhythm; I see nothing of their faces, though I hear their protests and call out an apology in Italian for the intrusion. On the far side of the room is a casement, unfastened; I fling back the shutter, push it open, and roll through just as Doughty appears in the doorway.

As the cold evening air hits my face, I barely have time to register that I was not on the ground floor, as I had thought, but only on the first, and that I am falling, and that in my semi-drugged state it is not an unpleasant sensation.

ELEVEN

My ribs hit a hard edge and I am sliding and falling again, until I come to land with a jolt in something soft. I put out a hand; it sinks down with a squelch and a foul smell rises around me. Looking up I can make out the jutting roof of a ground-floor room, which I must have hit on the way down, and above it, an open casement, from which a man's head is hurriedly withdrawn. I have landed, it seems, on the midden-heap in the House of Vesta's back yard; revolting as it is, it may have saved me from the broken bones I should have had from such a fall. The sound of shouting echoes from within; he will be out here any minute in pursuit. I push myself up from the mass of rotten vegetables and God knows what else and stagger towards the wall that borders the yard. I feel no pain yet in my side or my legs, but I am winded and my senses have been overtaken by a wild panic, my heart still hammering. Ahead of me in the wall is a gate, but it is fastened shut. Snatching quick, ragged breaths, I weave towards the far corner of the yard where a gnarled tree grows, some of its branches extending over the other side as if pointing the way. My legs feel unpredictable beneath me and I will myself to every step; looking back towards the house, I see a figure in the oblong of light from the open door. I pull myself up to the lower branches of the tree and scramble higher; as I throw myself over the wall I hear a loud cry. It is only when the noise stops abruptly as I hit the ground again that I realise the voice was my own.

Pushing myself up on my elbow, I glance around. I seem to have landed in a lane behind a row of houses. The light has drained almost completely from the sky overhead and the backs of the buildings either side cast the narrow street into deep gloom. I catch the sound of footsteps, running. A few yards ahead in the alley a squat man in a cloak is crouching, arms outstretched stiffly; I stifle a cry of alarm and skitter backwards away from him until I realise he is not moving a muscle. I squint at him suspiciously through the gloom, easing closer until he is revealed to be a handcart covered in sacking, of the kind a man might use to take vegetables to market. The footsteps draw near. I glance down the alley, but see only sliding, teasing shapes growing out of the dark. I climb into the cart and cover myself with the sacks. Curled up small, I can just fit. The wood reeks of manure. I hunker down and discover with a creeping dread that something is in the cart with me; I can hear it breathing, raw and ragged, close to my ear. I am on the point of leaping out when I realise the breathing is my own and the fierce war drum I hear is the sound of my blood pumping.

Running footsteps outside; they skid to a halt somewhere further down the lane. Voices carry through the dark.

'Well, he won't get far, not in that state.'

'I thought you said he brought it up.'

'The boy says he drank half a glass before he made himself sick. It must have done something.'

The second man curses. 'Then why wasn't he easier to deal with? You as good as had him by the collar, Devil take you! Did I not warn you about him?'

'He had a knife. She said she'd taken their weapons.'

'There you are, then. I told you not to underestimate him – he is a cunning dog. What else did you hear?'

'He was asking after Robert Dunne. It was all he wanted to talk about.'

Balled up in the cart, under my sackcloth, I cannot quite catch the murmured discussion that follows. My right hand strays down to my belt, and with a wash of relief I find that I must have sheathed my knife before I threw myself from the window, though I have no recollection of doing so. At least I will have some small defence if they should discover me. From the street there comes a cough, and a stamping of feet; I grip the cart's sides and concentrate on slowing my breathing. The side of my face feels wet.

'It would serve us better to watch and wait,' says the first voice. I would swear that I know it, though I do not dare look out to confirm. An attractive voice, if you did not have to look at the face it came from; educated, with a dark timbre. It is a voice I have not heard since I was in Oxford two years ago. 'We know where to find him.'

'But if he should discover—'

'Peace, John! We will find a better way. I have an idea.'

The first man makes some further protest, but it is brief, and the footsteps retreat. I remain still under the sacking, unsure whether they have really gone. Shouts and fragments of drunken catches float in from the street beyond the houses, but the two voices seem to have disappeared. I wait a few minutes longer before I risk peering out of the cart.

Though the lane is sunk further in shadow, it appears to be empty. With some effort I swing a stiff leg over the cart's side to climb out and tumble on to the ground, pulling myself to my feet to assess the damage. My right side burns with pain when I breathe; I suspect I have cracked my ribs on the way down. My legs are bruised and aching, but I must be grateful that the midden-heap saved me from breaking any limbs. My head throbs and my pulse is still racing, though my vision has

212

returned to normal and the strange sensations brought on by the nutmeg are receding. The night air feels cool on my face. As I stand there, taking shallow breaths so as not to strain my ribcage, I recall a young novice at San Domenico who claimed to have marvellous and terrible visions of angels and demons, after which he would often fall down as if in a dead faint; the other youths were enthralled by his tales and more learned monks than me declared him to have been touched by God and devoted themselves to interpreting his visions, until the novice master, a man of limited imagination but unrivalled common sense, discovered that the boy had been stealing nutmeg from the kitchen and consuming it, ground up, in copious quantities. I exclaim aloud and strike my forehead with the heel of my hand, amazed that I did not think of this sooner – the wine that smelled of spices in Dunne's cabin must surely have contained a heavy dose of nutmeg. That could explain the strange extremity of his drunkenness, the hallucinations, the irrational fear. Whoever gave it to him probably intended it to take effect over the course of the evening, leaving him confused and disconcerted, unable to defend himself from any attacker, just as the madam at the House of Vesta had intended for me. That was a curious coincidence too – had Dunne's drinking companion learned the trick at the House of Vesta? If so, then we need only establish who among the ship's company was also a regular visitor to the brothel. My thoughts flit immediately to Savile and his superior smile as he spoke of the sacred flame.

I emerge from the lane into a cobbled street lined with tall houses, the upper storeys leaning inwards. It is now fully dark, though here and there a candle burns in a window, and occasionally a wan moon peeks out through a gap in the clouds, allowing me enough light to see the curve of the street as it leads downhill. If I follow it, I reason, it must eventually lead me to the harbourside and from there to the Star. I pause to look behind me, wondering what to do about Sidney. I can

213

hardly risk returning to the House of Vesta in search of him; I am in no state to fight now, even if I could confront Doughty alone, and Mistress Grace is sure to have more armed men at her disposal.

I curse again and limp along the street, keeping close to the buildings on my left, neither seeing nor caring that I am stumbling through the gutter. I cannot think of going back to look for Sidney unarmed. Fear of what may have befallen him constricts my throat; if he has been drugged and attacked too, it is all my fault for thinking I could out-manoeuvre what was so clearly a trap. I have gained nothing by it, except a few bruises and the confirmation that John Doughty is in Plymouth and asking questions about Dunne's death. And the near-certainty that the man he was talking to as I hid in the alley, the 'friend' so keen to reacquaint himself with me, could be none other than the book dealer Rowland Jenkes.

At the Star, I let myself in through the yard, keeping to the shadows. The three sides of the building rise up in darkness; from the stalls come the soft stamps and snorts of horses, sunk in sleep. Groping my way around the walls to the door of the tap-room, I find it locked. I hesitate briefly, before deciding I am willing to pay the price of inconveniencing the servants for the sake of my bed and a bath. I hammer on the door and call out. There is no immediate response; I call again and somewhere overhead a casement opens and a voice advises me to shut my fucking noise, people are trying to sleep. I bang on the door one more time and stand back, wondering if I dare break a window. When I raise my voice again, I am surprised by a sudden loud splash from behind me; I realise, as the smell hits my nostrils, that the contents of a chamber pot have been flung from the casement above. I am fortunate that whoever threw it could not see to take aim; it missed only by a few feet. Next time I might not be so lucky. I lean against the door, trying to muster the will to find a storehouse or empty stable where I can sleep until the servants wake, when I hear the fumbling of a lock on the other side and the door creaks open. The maid Hetty stands on the step in a shapeless nightdress, a candle flame throwing shadows on her pale face. She pauses, taking in my bruises and my limp with a knowing glance, and smirks openly.

'Oh, it's you. Enjoy your evening at the House of Vesta, did you, sir?'

'A little too stimulating for my taste.' I am in no mood for her provocations, but recognise that it behoves me to show some humility here, since I am in the wrong. 'I am sorry to wake you.'

She waits until I am almost across the threshold. 'Looks like they know how to throw a punch, them virgins.'

The timing of this remark is impeccable; I cannot help laughing. 'What I would really like, Hetty,' I say, turning, 'is some hot water. As much of it as you can spare. Can that be arranged?'

'You'll have to wait till morning,' she says. 'And it'll cost extra. If you've any money left.'

'Put it on our account,' I say. Poor Sidney. He will need a hold full of Spanish treasure to meet the bill we are mounting up here.

She squints at my eye and hands me her stub of candle. 'Try not wake the other guests, won't you? I'll bring the water first thing. Watch you don't get blood on the sheets. Mistress Judith will have a fit.'

'I'll do my best. Thank you for your sympathy.' I touch a finger gingerly to the cut above my eye. It seems to have stopped bleeding for now. Hetty sniffs; it is clear she thinks I have only myself to blame. She is probably right. 'Do you not need the light to get back to bed, though?'

'Don't worry, sir – I know my way around this place at night better than the mice,' she says, and as if to prove it, disappears into the shadows, leaving me alone at the foot of the stairs. Somehow I find the thought of her scurrying silently around dark corridors disquieting.

I take two wrong turns before I identify the corridor that leads to our chamber, every creak of the boards seeming to echo through the whole building. I let myself in quietly. The window drapes are drawn, casting the room in hushed shadows. I ease off my boots and my stinking clothes, leaving them where they fall, and collapse on to the bed, and into oblivion.

I am jolted from a heavy dreamless sleep by the sound of someone entering the room. I try to sit up but my limbs feel inert and will not respond; it takes a few minutes before I can be certain of where I am. Memories of the night's events tumble through my sleep-fogged brain, even as the stiffness and pain in my body grow more insistent. Someone is moving softly around the room. My heart hammers; I am defenceless here, naked, unable to move. The footsteps come closer; there is a pause before the bed curtains are pulled back and I cry out, as the intruder also yells in surprise.

'Christ's bones, Bruno – are you trying to scare me to death?' Sidney yanks the curtain back fully and turns away just as fast. 'And put a shirt on, can't you – I don't want to see your wares on display.'

I reach out with some effort and pull a sheet over the lower half of my body. My head sinks into the pillow with relief.

'Thank God – I was worried about you,' I croak.

'Me? Bit late for that – I've been waiting for *you* half the bloody night. Eventually some girl turned up with your message to go on home without you – I must say, you could have let me know a little sooner.' He tosses his jacket on to one of the chairs and strides to the window.

'I never sent any message,' I begin, as he throws the shutters wide and a faint dawn light picks out the shapes of furniture. Sidney turns and makes another noise of shock.

'What happened to *you*?' He points to my torso. I look down and note the colourful map of cuts and bruises.

'I had to jump out of a window. I thought it was the ground floor, but I was mistaken.'

He cups a hand across his mouth. 'Sorry, I'm not laughing. Really.' He stands, yawns, stretches out his long arms above his head and plants himself in front of me, peering at my injuries, clutching his chin in imitation of a physician. 'At least you can still walk. So it *was* a trap. Did they rob you? Tell me what happened.'

I push myself up on to my elbows, wincing at the complex stabs and jolts of pain involved. He perches on the end of the bed while I recount the events of the previous night. He chuckles at the appearance of Toby, but when I mention the wine he slaps me on the leg – the nearest part he can reach – to show his irritation.

'You *never* touch the wine in a whorehouse, Bruno, certainly not on a first visit in a strange town – are you really so green? It's the oldest trick they know. You're damned lucky they didn't get your purse.'

'I realise that now,' I say, piqued. 'And I don't need you adding to my bruises. But the wine was spiced with nutmeg. And I'd wager that's what Dunne was given the night he was killed – the effects sound just the same. Wild drunkenness, hallucinations, morbid fear.'

Sidney scratches his chin. 'I didn't even know nutmeg could do that. Is it common knowledge?'

'To someone familiar with the properties of herbs, I'd say.'

We fall silent, both thinking of Jonas.

'But listen,' I say, 'that is not the biggest news.'

His eyes grow wide as I tell him about the appearance of John Doughty.

'Extraordinary. Drake said Doughty would not dare set foot anywhere near Plymouth. Just goes to show that Drake is not always right.' He evidently takes some satisfaction in this thought. 'But why was Doughty at the House of Vesta?'

'He was a sailor. They must know him there. The madam was obviously helping him – she took me to the boy, sent up the spiced wine—'

'Why the boy?' Sidney says, frowning. 'To test whether you were telling the truth about knowing Dunne?'

'Perhaps. Or because she suspected I was only there to ask unwelcome questions, and she wanted to learn what they were.'

'Either way, it seems beyond doubt that the place is somehow connected with Dunne's death. In which case – why deliberately lure you towards it?'

'He thought he was going to march me out of there at knife point, to wherever his mysterious friend was waiting.'

'The one you are persuaded is Rowland Jenkes.'

'You think I am mistaken?'

He rasps a hand across the stubble on his jaw and stands, stretching. 'I only say you are putting two and two together and making five, ever since you saw this man in black and decided he was watching you.'

'He was.' I struggle to sit up further. 'We know a book dealer with no ears has been interested in Drake's Judas book for months, with Dunne's agency. Who else could fit that description, who would also know me well enough to address me by name? Besides, I heard his voice.'

'It's two years since you last saw him, and you were under the influence of something that causes hallucinations.' He catches sight of my look and sighs. 'You are probably right. I just can't imagine what he's doing with John Doughty, though.'

'No more can I.'

He crosses the room to the other window and opens those shutters. Light spills across the floor. 'You've left this place in quite a state, too. I hope you're going to clear up after yourself.'

I ease myself horizontal. 'Sorry about the clothes. They'll have to be laundered again.'

'I'm not talking about the clothes. I mean your travel bag. Stuff everywhere.'

'What?' I jerk upright again, ignoring the spear of pain that shoots up my right side. He indicates the far end of the room, where my bag lies open, my few clean shirts tumbled out over the floor. I haul myself off the bed, wrapping the sheet around my waist, and kneel down.

'I didn't leave it like that. Someone has been through it.'

'What did they take?'

I pick up the discarded clothes, and search through the bag. My books are still there, but a sheaf of notes I had brought to work on appears to be missing. There was nothing incriminating that I can recall, just a few calculations and jotted ideas for a possible book . . . An idea occurs to me, making goosebumps stand up on my bare skin. I cross to the bed and look under it for the leather satchel I had brought back from the *Elizabeth* last night. I take it out and find it empty.

'My translation of the Judas book. It's gone.'

Sidney throws his hands up and spits out a curse. 'You left the room unlocked last night. I had the key. Damn it.' He glances around to his own trunk, which remains securely padlocked. 'Thank God they didn't take anything more valuable.'

'You don't think a lost gospel is valuable?' I shake my head. 'Drake will be livid. I assured him I would keep it safe.'

'Then you shouldn't have gone haring off to that bloody brothel without locking the room,' he exclaims.

'I realise that now.' We glare at one another until I punch my right fist into the palm of my left hand. 'Damn it! The letter was clearly a ruse to get us out of the way so that someone could go through the room looking for those writings.'

'But who would have known that you had it here?' He looks at me. 'No, don't tell me – Rowland Jenkes.'

219

'Do you have a better explanation?'

He opens his mouth to speak, but breaks off at the sound of a sharp knock on the door. Sidney opens it to find Hetty, pink-faced with the effort of carrying two pails of hot water, most of which she appears to have left along the floor to mark her progress. He takes one from her as she sets the other down. She wipes her hands on her apron, passes him the linen cloth she has draped over her shoulder and plants herself in the doorway, looking from one of us to the other. I gesture to the fact that I am wearing nothing but a sheet. Her eyes skim over the bruises on my chest with a look that says, I told you so. Reluctantly, Sidney reaches for his purse.

'You can take this laundry down while you're there,' he says, handing her a coin and indicating the pile of my soiled clothes. She regards them with distaste before scooping them up, making a face as she catches the smell of the midden. I am expecting a facetious comment about where I spent the night, but she seems cowed into grudging respect by Sidney's presence.

'Hetty, you keep your eyes and ears open around this place, don't you?' I ask, as she turns to leave.

'If it's worth my while,' she says.

'Yes, I understand that. Did you see anyone entering or leaving this room last night, after you brought me the letter?'

'What, apart from that woman?' she shoots back, without missing a beat. Her mouth curves into a knowing smile, pleased that she has hit the mark. But I am too distracted by the thought that Lady Arden was alone in this room after I ran out in search of Sidney. She also knew that I had been working on Drake's mysterious book. What possible use could she have for a half-finished translation of it? The idea is absurd, I tell myself, but my fists bunch at my sides; I have been burned before by a woman who stole from me when my guard was down.

'No one else?' Sidney asks, to cover the awkward pause.

220

'Well, I wasn't patrolling the corridor all night,' Hetty sniffs, shifting the bundle of laundry from one hip to the other.

'Never the less,' Sidney says, forcing a smile, 'if you do recall seeing anyone near this room, it would be enormously helpful.' His hand strays idly to his purse. Hetty's eyes dart after it like a cat watching a bird. 'A man in black, for instance?'

She affects to think about this. 'Can't say I did. Probably best to make sure your door's locked in future, though.' She gives him a firm nod, as if this is the final word, and stomps away, flat-footed, down the corridor.

'The very incarnation of charm,' Sidney remarks, closing the door. '*She* wouldn't cost you twenty shillings, that's for sure.'

'I hope you got your money's worth?' I ask, needled. I do not miss the implicit reproach.

'I?' He throws me the linen cloth and wanders over to the window as I kneel to wash the filth of the midden from my skin. 'Last night was your adventure, Bruno. I was only waiting for you to finish your business.'

'You waited a long time. The sun is almost up.'

A ghost of a smile hovers over his lips. 'See how dedicated I am.'

I acknowledge the evasion with a nod. If he enjoyed the House of Vesta's hospitality last night, he is not going to discuss it with me and I should know better than to ask.

'I could have broken my neck there,' I say, sounding like a petulant child. I twist to try and wash the scrapes on my back and yelp as white pain shoots through my ribcage.

'Idiot,' he says, but with affection. 'Here, give me that.' He strides over, takes the cloth from my hand and dabs it at the sore places between my shoulder blades, tender as a nurse.

TWELVE

I leave Sidney to rest and make my way to the tap-room in search of something to eat. While I am wolfing down some bread, cold eggs and small beer, avoiding the gaze of the handful of other guests who have risen early, Mistress Judith approaches, clearly flustered, a pitcher in each hand.

'I'm glad I've found you. Sir Francis Drake has just arrived and is looking for you, sir. In the front parlour.'

She bustles away towards the entrance hall without further explanation. I follow her through to see armed men standing outside a door opposite the staircase. I recognise them as Drake's guards from the ship; they stand aside to allow me through. Inside I find a curious tableau. At its centre, on a high-backed chair by the unlit fire, sits a woman of about thirty, dressed in mourning black, a veil thrown back over her hair. She is not an obvious beauty, but neither is she unattractive; if you had to sum up her thin face, you might call it resolute. She has the expression of one who has learned not to trust first impressions. Her pale eyes take the measure of me as I enter, though the set of her jaw does not reveal whether her judgement falls in my favour. Behind her stands an older woman in a plain grey dress, wearing the white coif of a servant, one hand resting on the back of the chair. Next

222

to her, like an anxious butler, the chaplain Pettifer hovers, canted over towards the seated woman with a solicitous air. Drake has planted himself in front of her, hands folded demurely at his belt, as if she is a ruler to whom he must show deference.

He turns when I enter, his look of relief followed swiftly by a frown and a brief raise of the eyebrows as he appraises my battered appearance, but he is too polite to remark on it. Earlier examination in the age-spotted glass propped above the mantel in our chamber revealed that, once I had cleaned the dried blood from my face, the damage is not as severe as it might have been; I am sporting a livid bruise on my forehead and a cut that looks worse than it is across my right eyebrow, but my features are more or less intact. Even so, I still have the air of a tavern-brawler.

Thomas Drake, present as always like his brother's shadow, leans against the window frame, arms folded. He registers my injuries with distaste. On a low day-bed opposite the window, Lady Drake and Lady Arden sit side by side, looking superfluous. Lady Drake has a cat on her lap. Lady Arden holds my gaze for an instant, her eyes stony, then turns pointedly away. Just as the silence begins to seem unbearable, Drake clears his throat and turns to the seated woman.

'Mistress Dunne, may I present to you Doctor Giordano Bruno of Nola? This is the man I was speaking of.' Drake holds a hand towards me; automatically I bow towards her chair, wincing as the movement crushes my ribs.

She regards me with no discernible emotion as I straighten up, forcing a smile.

'Is he going to *beat* the truth out of them?'

'Doctor Bruno rescued a small boy from drowning in the harbour yesterday,' Lady Arden interjects, in a matter-of-fact tone. 'The child would have died otherwise. But he was . . . dashed into the harbour wall as he tried to climb out.'

Her voice sounds unnaturally loud in the still air. Everyone swivels to look at her, then turns their gaze back to me. I think I see Mistress Dunne's features soften.

'I am sorry for your loss, madam,' I say, lowering my eyes. 'And how does your father?'

Her brow knits in confusion, or perhaps it is irritation.

'Forgive me, sir, but I do not think you are acquainted with my father?' She draws herself up as she says this, to match the slightly haughty tone; I presume I have breached some sacred English rule of etiquette, but this does not trouble me. I only want to hear her answer.

'No, I have not had the honour, but I heard he was unwell.'

The maid behind her inhales with audible disapproval. Mistress Dunne narrows her eyes at me and then glances at Drake, as if debating whether she is obliged to respond.

'Then the gossips, for once, report the truth – his health is failing badly,' she says. Her voice remains steady. 'His physicians fear he is dying.'

Small murmurs of sympathy emanate from the rest of the company at this revelation. I watch Mistress Dunne as she composes her face into the appropriate expression for a woman anticipating grief heaped upon grief.

'Again, I am most sorry.'

She acknowledges this empty courtesy with a small inclination of her head, though her eyes remain on me, still suspicious.

Drake coughs again, anxious to get to the point. 'Naturally, this is a difficult time for Mistress Dunne and her family,' he begins, twisting his big hands together. 'She has expressed some *concerns*.' He stops, as if unsure of the correct phrase for what he wants to say. It strikes me that this is the first time I have seen Drake appear at a disadvantage; it does not suit him. A pause elapses, as if he is hoping the sentence will complete itself. I look from one to the other, awaiting further explanation.

'My late husband was many things, Doctor Bruno—' Mistress Dunne stops and regards me with a tilt of her head. 'Are you a physician?'

'I am a doctor of theology.'

'I see.' She makes a dismissive noise through her nose.

Drake steps forward. 'Doctor Bruno, as I mentioned, is greatly skilled in this sort of matter,' he says quickly, as though someone has tried to argue otherwise. I say nothing. I have an inkling of where he is leading, and I do not like it.

'My late husband had many faults,' Mistress Dunne begins again, addressing me in the same level tone, 'but I do not believe that self-slaughter would have been among them.'

I glance at Drake; he is urging me to something with his eyes, but I have no idea what it might be.

'Do you have a particular reason for saying so, madam?'

'Because he was a coward,' she says, fixing me with a look that dares me to contradict her. Pettifer opens his mouth to speak, hesitates, then closes it again.

'I'm afraid I don't follow—'

'To end one's own life, if one felt it had become an insupportable burden to oneself and others – that is an act that requires a certain amount of courage, do you not think?' she asks, with the same direct gaze.

'One might argue the opposite,' I say. 'To shoulder one's burdens, to take responsibility for one's failings – surely that is the courageous course?'

Pettifer can no longer contain himself. 'Suicide is a grievous sin, Mistress Dunne, a violation of the sixth commandment. The Church makes that most clear. Man is the *imago dei* – to determine his own end is to usurp the prerogative of God, who alone knows the number of our days.' He shakes his head, as if to absolve her of such a heretical notion. 'Think of Judas Iscariot, who took his life through guilt and remorse after betraying Our Lord to death – you would not call him a model of courage, would you?'

Mistress Dunne turns to him, her smile fading. 'Perhaps each of us has our own definition of courage, Padre. But I hope you are not making a comparison between them?'

Flustered, Pettifer seems to realise he has tied himself in a knot; his round face flushes with his efforts to deny any intentional offence. I watch him, wondering why he was prompted to pluck that particular example.

'Mistress Dunne doubts the accuracy of my judgement regarding the manner of her husband's death,' Drake says, cutting across Pettifer's flapping apologies.

'I'm sure Captain Drake did his best in what must have been a very distressing situation,' she says, turning to me, the polite smile once more in place, 'but I fear he may have jumped to a hasty conclusion, not being in possession of certain facts.'

A tense silence unfolds. I look from her to Drake and back.

'I'm sorry, I don't quite—'

'Self-slaughter, as Padre Pettifer tells us, is a terrible stain on the soul,' Mistress Dunne continues. Her voice is firm, but I notice her fingers busily plucking at the cloth of her skirts, a sign that there is some emotion at work beneath the surface. 'Not to mention on a man's reputation and the fate of his family. I cannot accept that my husband died by his own hand. I intend to make the coroner investigate his death to my satisfaction, so that he can at least have Christian burial.'

On this last sentence, her composure falters and she presses a hand to her mouth. The maid passes her an embroidered handkerchief but she waves it away as she fights to bend her feelings to her will. Or so it seems. Asserting herself against the authority of Sir Francis Drake would be daunting for any woman, yet there is something in her demeanour that leaves room for a chink of doubt. It is true that the English like to keep their emotions buried so deep that an Italian could be forgiven for thinking they have never experienced any passion greater than mild irritation at the weather, but I cannot escape the sense that Mistress Dunne is playing a part here, and not playing it with total conviction. That little catch in the voice just now, the hand pressed to the lips: it is as if she has learned the expressions of grief from a book. Though I may be doing her a disservice; perhaps, as a well-born lady, this is as near as her breeding permits her to feeling.

My gaze flits again from her to Drake and back; I would not like to wager which of them will concede first.

'In the light of this,' Drake continues, clasping his hands behind him and pacing the floor as if he were giving a summary in court, 'I have persuaded Mistress Dunne to accept a temporary compromise. We will look into the circumstances of her husband's death more closely before the inquest, with all the discretion a matter of this nature requires. If we uncover nothing useful, she will formally object to the verdict of *felo de se* at the inquest and ask the coroner to investigate further.' He looks to Mistress Drake for confirmation; she gives a curt nod.

'I have told her you are the man for investigating this sort of business,' Drake continues, his voice bolder now, 'and she has agreed that you and I between us should do what we can to determine how Robert came by his untimely end.'

Every pair of eyes in the room is fixed on me – with the exception of Lady Arden, whose attention, I notice when I glance up, is studiously concentrated on the cat. I realise that I am expected to say something.

'But the inquest is tomorrow.' I say this half as a question, hoping that someone will contradict me; no one does.

'Then you will have to work quickly,' Mistress Dunne says, with a terse little smile that briefly shows her teeth.

I draw a deep breath. 'It is your belief, then, madam, that your husband was unlawfully killed?'

'If he did not take his own life – and I have already told you why that is impossible – then it follows that someone else must have taken it,' she says, impatience replacing the tremor in her voice.

'Forgive me,' I begin, with a nervous half-laugh to soften the blow, 'but you are implying that someone aboard Sir Francis's ship killed your husband?' I glance at Drake; he

227

has cupped a hand over his mouth and chin to disguise his reaction.

'That's what I wish to find out, Doctor Bruno.' She sighs, as if the detail tires her. 'You did not know Robert, but he had a particular gift for making enemies. One might say that is to be expected, given his pursuits. You cannot fail to have learned of his reputation, I'm sure.' She stands, brushes down her skirts and turns slowly to look at the rest of the company with a tight smile, to prove that she will not be shamed by whatever gossip followed her husband. The maid takes a step forward, her hand outstretched. Mistress Dunne neatly side-steps her and waves the hand away. Again I have the sense that she manages perfectly well without assistance from anyone.

'But you have reason to believe that these enemies are to be found among Captain Drake's crew?' I persist.

'No!' The denial is immediate; she flushes, apparently shocked by the suggestion. 'I say no such thing. I merely—'

She crosses the room and stops directly in front of me. She is tall for a woman; we are almost the same height.

'You have seen Plymouth, I suppose?' She flings an arm out in the direction of the window. 'Heaving with mercenaries – soldiers, sailors, foreigners – begging your pardon. Plenty of them more than willing to dispatch a man for a ready coin. If my husband's enemies wanted him dead, they would not be short of willing hands. And they would have known exactly where to find him.'

'I assure you once again, Mistress, that no assassin could possibly have boarded my ship, that night or any other,' Drake says. The conversation appears to be taxing his diplomatic skills. 'I have more than enough reason to be scrupulous about the security of my vessel. No one could have found his way past my watchmen.'

'Sir Francis, if you are determined from the beginning that there is no murderer to be apprehended, then our agreement would seem redundant.' Her smile suggests this is meant half in jest, but her eyes say otherwise. I think I understand Drake's reasoning: by nominating someone outside his own circle to satisfy Mistress Dunne's thirst for enquiries, he can distance himself from me if I fail. On the other hand, I am a stranger in this city; it may be that I can move among the crowds, asking questions, slipping obscurely into places where the famous Sir Francis Drake could not hope to pass unnoticed.

Drake bows his head. 'You are right, madam. I will do my best to keep an open mind.'

'I hope so, Sir Francis. There is a great deal at stake here, for both of us. I only want to make sure the truth is served.' She juts her chin upwards and keeps her eyes on him for a moment, to let him know she is not someone he can hood-wink. 'Come, Agnes.' She flicks a hand at the maid, who scuttles to follow her. On her way past me, Mistress Dunne stops. 'I am going to break my fast now, Doctor Bruno, and then I wish to view my husband's body. Perhaps you would like to accompany me?'

'Is that wise?' Drake cuts in.

'If he is to reconsider the cause of my husband's death, would it not make sense for him to examine the body? Perhaps all his theological training may help him to notice some symptom that escaped your attention,' she adds pointedly, drawing her veil down over her face.

'I meant rather, is it wise for you to go?' Drake pulls at the point of his beard. 'Robert has been dead three days, madam, and it was not a sight for ladies even when he was fresh.'

I notice Lady Drake flinch slightly at her husband's choice of words; fame and wealth have not taught him to be more delicate with his language. No wonder she is susceptible to a sonnet or two. I try to catch Lady Arden's eye, but she keeps her head turned towards the window.

'I was raised in the country, Sir Francis,' Mistress Dunne replies, extending a hand, palm upwards. The maidservant lays a pair of kidskin gloves across it. 'I have seen both my brothers and my sister in their coffins, and one of my brothers was kicked in the head by a horse – that was not pretty, I promise you. I will not faint at the sight of a corpse. I feel it proper that I should see him before he is buried – wherever that may be.' She pulls on her gloves carefully, her slender fingers extended.

'So, you are the last surviving child of your family?' I ask.

She gives me a sharp look. 'Yes. Why do you ask?'

I shake my head. 'I was only thinking it is hard you should have to bear so much loss.' I assume a sympathetic expression. She narrows her eyes.

'Even so,' Drake says, still rubbing at his beard, 'I fear the sight may distress you.'

'What *distresses* me, Sir Francis,' she says, shaping the words clearly and precisely, 'is the thought that my husband may be wrongly declared a suicide while his murderer escapes justice.' With this, she sets her shoulders back and sweeps from the room, her maid scurrying in her wake. At the door she turns to me. 'Meet me here in the entrance hall in half an hour.'

Pettifer makes as if to follow her. 'Would you like me to pray with you, madam, before you address yourself to this sad task?' He knots his fingers together in supplication, his round cheeks flushed. Priests never feel a greater sense of their own importance than around the dying and the newly bereaved, I have noticed.

A spasm of irritation twitches Mistress Dunne's face, but she masters it.

'Thank you, Padre, that is kind – perhaps when I return I shall have greater need of comfort.'

'As you wish, madam. Just send me word here – I am at your disposal.' He bows his head and follows her out.

Drake closes the door behind them and exhales with some force. 'Elizabeth, I have told Mistress Dunne you and

230

Lady Arden will dine with her today. We must show her Christian compassion, and she may be glad of female company.' He pushes both hands through his hair and walks to the window.

'She didn't look as if she was much interested in any company.' Lady Drake clutches the protesting cat, who appears to be making a bid for freedom. 'She was quite rude when you introduced me and my lady cousin – she barely acknowledged us at all.'

'Well, you must allow that she is in the first shock of grief, my dear,' Drake says, still looking out at the street. 'She is perhaps not herself.'

'I might want to hang myself if I'd married her,' Lady Arden remarks, to no one in particular. Drake and his brother turn and stare at her. I catch her eye and grin; she allows a brief smile, which she hides behind her hand. Perhaps she has forgiven me after all.

The ladies stand and stretch delicately; the cat seizes his chance and darts under the day-bed. As they leave, Lady Arden glances over her shoulder at me, but she is gone before I can convey anything with my eyes alone.

'Bruno – a word.' Drake beckons me towards the window. We look out through the small diamond panes of glass, the street outside distorted by their warps and bubbles. He lays a hand on my shoulder. 'I'm sorry to have sprung this on you. Especially when . . .' he indicates my injuries. 'What *happened* to you?'

I hesitate. 'I visited the House of Vesta last night.'

'Ah.' A brief frown crosses his brow. 'Someone should have warned you about that place. They don't tend to welcome strangers who arrive unannounced.'

'That is the complicated part. I was not unannounced – I was lured there by an anonymous letter that made reference to the Judas gospel. I believe it came from Rowland Jenkes – the book dealer with no ears that Dunne took you to.'

231

Drake looks even more bemused. 'What has he to do with the House of Vesta?'

'I don't know. But Dunne was a regular there. I thought someone might recall something, but when I started asking questions about him, I was cornered and set upon by a man I am certain was John Doughty.'

'Doughty? Good God.' Drake rubs his temple with the flat of his hand as he processes all this. 'So he *is* in Plymouth. What would he want with you?'

I shake my head. 'I didn't stay to find out.' I point to the cut on my face. 'I jumped out of a window. Unfortunately, it was on the first floor.'

Drake smiles, despite himself.

'What I do know is that they were waiting for me. The madam was part of it – she led me into a trap, ready for Doughty. So perhaps she could be questioned, if you want to find him.'

Drake nods slowly, his face grim. 'I will make some discreet enquiries. The difficulty with the House of Vesta, Bruno, is that it is not an ordinary brothel. It operates by discretion and exclusivity. Customers come to her by introduction only. She takes the girls very young, so she can guarantee to her clients that they are clean. Some as young as eleven, and you won't find any over fifteen. They say it's the one place in Plymouth you can be sure you won't get the pox, and there are plenty willing to pay her prices for the peace of mind.'

'So she attracts the wealthiest men in the area,' I say, beginning to understand.

'It has grown into a sort of meeting place for men of influence in the town,' he says. 'They go there to dine, smoke, play cards, talk business – not just for the girls. Any man with ambition wants to be included in that company, and the benefits far outweigh the moral objections. Makes it very difficult for anyone in authority who tries to have the place investigated or shut down – as I found out when I was mayor.' His jaw tightens at the memory.

'Which is why that woman – Mistress Grace – believes she is above the law?' I finish the thought for him. 'She has the most powerful men in the town by the balls.'

'They say you can get whatever you want at the House of Vesta with no questions asked, as long as you are willing to pay.' He gives a meaningful nod. I consider telling him about Toby, but decide against it; if Drake does persuade the authorities to investigate, it would be the boy who was punished for his sins, not the people who forced him to it.

'Nevertheless,' Drake says, brisker this time, 'there are certain pressures that can be brought. If she is hiding John Doughty, I want to know about it.'

I turn to leave, but he lays a hand on my sleeve. 'One more thing, Bruno. In your nocturnal wanderings, did you see anything of Jonas last night?'

'Last night? No, not after we came ashore.'

'Hm.' He takes a deep breath. There are shadows under his eyes; it looks as if he has not slept. 'Jonas did not come back to the ship all night. No one has seen him. Plymouth is full of thugs who would lay into a man because they didn't like his complexion, and believe they are defending England that way.' He grimaces. 'I hope Jonas has not fallen foul of that sort.'

He lets his hand fall from my arm and continues to stare out of the window, as if the answer might present itself if he waits long enough.

'I hope not,' I say, though another explanation occurs to me. 'I'm sure he will turn up. Perhaps he drank too much and ended up spending the night in the arms of some Plymouth maiden.'

'He'd be lucky to find a maiden in Plymouth, even at the House of Vesta.' Drake tries to summon a smile. 'I dare say Jonas enjoyed the same pastimes as any other sailor on shore leave, but he never neglected his duty. He was supposed to take the middle watch last night, after midnight. That's not something he would have forgotten. I hope to God he is back by tomorrow, at any rate – he must be the principal witness at the inquest. It was he who found Dunne hanging.'

Perhaps Jonas had good reason to make himself scarce before the inquest, I think. Or perhaps there is someone else who does not want him to testify.

'Why did you ask Mistress Dunne about her father?' asks Drake, abruptly changing the subject.

'It was Lady Drake who mentioned to me that Mistress Dunne is an heiress. Robert had told Gilbert that he expected to come into some money soon. I wondered if he might have meant his wife's inheritance.'

He nods, understanding. 'A good thought. And she would hardly want a gambling husband getting his hands on her father's fortune too.'

'In fact,' Thomas says, 'it is difficult to imagine anyone with as much reason to want him dead as his wife.'

There is a silence as we all consider this.

'Even so, I cannot see how she could have engineered this particular outcome,' I say, eventually. 'Assuming she wanted him murdered, she would have done better to poison his dinner at home, or have someone attack him on the road. A death that looks like a suicide is not to her advantage – quite the reverse.'

'As she is at pains to make clear,' Drake says. 'We must find this killer before the inquest. I will see that you are amply rewarded, of course,' he adds, seeing my expression. 'That is not in doubt.'

'That is generous of you, Sir Francis, but—'

His brow darkens. 'But what?'

'I only wonder – why me?'

'Ah.' He moves closer, drops his voice. 'Sir Philip has told me a little more about your work.'

I look at him, perplexed, thinking he means my books.

'For Walsingham,' Drake whispers, to clarify. 'Any man who has earned Master Secretary's trust and respect also has mine. My brother and I were most impressed, weren't we, Thomas?'

Thomas Drake makes a noise that could mean anything, and folds his arms across his chest. I have rarely seen anyone look less impressed.

I give a little cough and try to look humble. 'I may need resources, Sir Francis. Information is not cheap in this town. People keep their eyes and ears open, but they sometimes need encouragement.'

Drake nods, murmuring assent. 'I will arrange a purse for you when you return from your excursion with Mistress Dunne.' At the door he pauses. 'Watch her closely, Bruno. She is determined to make trouble. She could ruin me.'

It is tempting to observe that, if the verdict goes his way, it could ruin her, but I appear to be in Drake's pay now, so I say nothing.

'What about the book?' I ask, as I am leaving.

'I suppose it will have to wait.' He rubs his beard and looks gloomy. 'I will pay you for your work there, too, do not fear.'

'Where is it?'

'Safe under lock and key in my cabin aboard the *Elizabeth*.' He glances around the room as if he might have left it lying unguarded somewhere.

I consider whether to mention the pages stolen from my room, but decide it would not help matters if I were to damage his new faith in me. I may yet find the thief without Drake needing to know of my folly. 'If I were you, sir, I would keep it with you, where you can see it.'

'Why? The ship is safe enough, is it not?' His brow creases and he glances across at Thomas.

That's what Robert Dunne thought. I decide not to say this aloud.

In the entrance hall I find Sir William Savile loitering, a leather travelling bag at his feet.

'Ah, Bruno!' he says, unexpectedly animated. 'Have you heard about this oath? Damned impertinence, if you ask me.

Not sure I like the precedent either. Instinct tells me it goes against the proper order of things. What does Sir Philip say? I suppose he has sworn it readily, being desperate for a berth.'

I wait until he stops for breath. 'What oath?'

'Oh, Pettifer the chaplain, you know, is going about this morning with great pomp and ceremony, announcing that every man who means to sail with the fleet must swear an oath of loyalty to the Queen and to Captain Drake as supreme commander of the enterprise before we set sail.'

'Is that a problem?' I wonder what has prompted this; does Drake sense stirrings of unrest, or is this a pre-emptive measure, to try and flush out the killer?

'Not in theory, but' – he glances about, then leans in – 'it does rather give a mandate to any course of action that takes his fancy, don't you think? It robs one of any capacity to challenge him once at sea – he can simply say, "But you were sworn, my masters, and to break your oath is as good as treason." I mean, it's all very well for the crew, you know, but for a gentleman . . .' He regards me down the length of his nose. 'That's why I wondered if Sir Philip meant to swear.'

'You had better ask him, I have not heard him mention it,' I say. I like Savile less every time I speak to him. I glance down at the buttons on his green silk doublet; disappointingly, they are flat, silver and all present. 'Are you going somewhere, Sir William?' I ask, indicating his bag.

'Decided to take a room here until we sail,' he says, tapping the bag with his foot. 'I reasoned I'd be spending time enough in that poky cabin once we leave, and since no one seems to know the day nor the hour at present, why should I not sleep in a feather bed while I can?'

'Cabin fever already?' I say. His eyes narrow; before he can reply there is a commotion behind us and a woman's voice, low and cultured, cuts across him.

236

'There you are, Doctor Bruno. Shall we get this over with?'

I turn to see Mistress Dunne, pulling on a pair of gloves, the granite-faced servant scowling at her elbow. But Dunne's widow is not looking at me; her gaze is fixed over my shoulder, on Savile, with an expression that appears more than anything like irritation. While this is likely the response Savile provokes in many people, it takes me by surprise because I had no inkling that they knew one another.

Savile crosses the hall in two strides and sweeps off his hat, bowing low.

'Sir William Savile, Mistress Dunne. You may not remember, we met once, at court I believe. Please accept my sincere condolences for your loss.' He raises his eyes, looking suitably regretful. At least he has the decorum not to mention the money Dunne owed him, I think. Not yet, anyway.

'At court. Yes, I suppose it was.' Mistress Dunne sounds vague; she concentrates on her gloves. 'I thank you. Please excuse us. I am going to view my husband's body.' She looks up sharply as she says this; Savile seems to flinch.

'A distressing task, madam. God be with you,' he adds, hesitantly, as if he is uncertain of the protocol.

'Well, I shall have Doctor Bruno with me, which is the next best thing,' she responds in a clipped voice. 'One never knows when one might need a theologian on hand. A pleasure to meet you again, Sir William.'

Savile is still muttering something about sad circumstances as she is halfway through the door, though I notice she casts a glance back at him before she leaves, and it is not a friendly one. It does not require any great genius to see that this exchange is not all it appears; even Savile's personality cannot account for Mistress Dunne's hostility towards him. What history is there, I wonder, as I limp to catch up with her outside the inn.

'I am not, strictly speaking, a theologian, madam,' I say, as we make our way along the narrow street towards the centre of the town, since she appears to have no intention of

237

beginning a conversation. The skies are clearer today, the sun hazy behind a threadbare gauze of white cloud that shows patches of blue as pale and fragile as eggshells. But the air is still cool; a sharp wind gusts in from the sea, stinging the cut on my face. Last's night rain lies puddled between cobbles.

'I am not, strictly speaking, interested.' She looks straight ahead as she walks. She has a long stride for a woman and my bruised legs and ribs pain me as I work to keep up. 'We both know this is no more than a gesture to placate me. But we shall play along until the inquest. No doubt Drake is paying you well to conclude whatever best suits his purposes.'

I subside into silence. After a few more yards she turns to me and sighs, impatient.

'Well – what are you, then?'

'I am . . .' I hesitate. What am I, exactly, at this point in my life? This August morning of 1585, at the age of thirty-seven, how do I explain myself, to her or to anyone? I am, variously, a heretic, an ex-Dominican, a philosopher, a spy, a poet of sorts, a teacher, an exile. A lover – once perhaps, though that seems distant. A necromancer, if you believe my detractors in Paris. A traitor, if you ask the Baron de Châteauneuf. A hunter of murderers, if you ask Walsingham. I shift shape, like Proteus, according to necessity; so much so that I am in danger of losing my original form altogether.

'I am a philosopher, if you like. I write books.'

Her glance flits sideways beneath her veil to take me in. 'It would appear philosophy is a dangerous sport.'

'That is just the way I practise it.'

We walk in silence, through narrow streets I am gradually coming to recognise. Just behind my shoulder I can hear the steady wheezing of Mistress Dunne's maidservant, laboured as bellows.

'You are acquainted with Sir William Savile, then, madam?' I say, after a while. She seems irked by the interruption.

'Hardly acquainted. I believe I may have met him at court,

with my husband. I barely recall, but one doesn't wish to look rude. One meets so many people.' She trails off, distracted.

'Are you often at court?' I keep my voice light, as if making conversation, but I sense she is wary of my questions.

'Not these days, no.' She presses her lips together; behind her veil, her face is closed. 'We used to be,' she says, in a softer tone, just when I think she will not discuss the matter further. 'When Sir Francis first returned from his voyage around the world, he and the gentlemen who travelled with him were much celebrated. That was when I married Robert. He came home a rich man, and for a while it pleased Her Majesty to keep her gallant gentlemen sailors about the place. But . . .' She gives a small shake of the head and rubs a thumb along her brow, through the veil. 'Things change. I suppose that is the nature of life, is it not? And our task is to look on good fortune or ill with equanimity.' She says this as if she holds the idea in contempt.

'What changed?' I ask gently.

'Oh, you will have heard, no doubt.' Her voice is brisk again; she picks up her pace to match it. 'Robert grew restless. He said he missed the adventure.' She laughs, short and bitter. 'How strange you men are. For a woman there is risk enough in the day to day – just the getting of children is a roll of the dice with Providence. But no – you men must seek it by circling the Earth in a tub of wood. Or throwing away all you have on a hand of cards.' Her tone is like the edge of a knife; I glimpse the naked fury she harbours for her husband. 'After a while he took to avoiding the court. Too many creditors. We came back to Devonshire, leased a manor near Dartington, but even then he was hardly at home. He spent most of his time in Plymouth, where he could still trade on his reputation as one of Drake's famous crew. But there's only so many times men will stand you a drink and waive your debts in return for a tale about the Straits of Magellan. The credit notes began piling up again, and still the damned fool thought he could mend it all with one lucky night at the card table. But there never is a lucky night for men like Robert.' She stops and turns to me, so abruptly that the maidservant collides with my back. 'No doubt you think me an unnatural wife, Doctor Bruno, to speak so ill of a man who has suffered a cruel death not three days since.'

'I can see nothing more natural than to be angry when someone you care for persists in wilfully destroying himself and those around him, against all advice,' I say.

'Exactly!' she exclaims. 'Robert was not a bad man, but he was unhappy. Since he returned from that first voyage with Drake, something was tormenting him. It wore away the good side of his character, little by little. If there had been children, it might have been different. But . . .' She turns away, adjusts her veil.

I let this comment disappear into the sounds of the street, the raucous Plymouth goodwives and gulls vying to drown each other out. So they had no children; his fault or hers, I wonder. If she is about to come into a significant inheritance from her father, that would make her an attractive prospect to new suitors, who might give her children where Robert had failed. Sidney's comment about rich widows comes to mind.

We have emerged into the square around the Market Cross, lively at this hour with traders and stallholders, shouting their wares from beneath coloured awnings that snap in the breeze like sailcloth. Raw-faced women with vast baskets balanced on their hips tout bread, fish, strawberries, fresh-cut reeds, and more pies; others, in cheap, bright gowns, move among the crowds, touting themselves. It is never too early for commerce, it seems. Ragged children chase one another through the throng, laughing and dodging fists and kicks as their keen eyes scour the ground for any fallen food that can be salvaged before the dogs grab it. Mistress Dunne lifts her skirts to avoid the fresh piles of horse dung and presses

240

onward, her mouth set in a determined line, towards the ancient-timbered Guildhall, which overlooks the square, leaning forward on its row of wooden columns like a grandfather on a stick.

'So, these creditors Robert trailed after him,' I say, hurrying to keep up, 'these are the enemies you spoke of?'

She purses her lips. 'They were certainly not his friends, put it that way – although some started out as such. But I did not mean them – they were ordinary, workaday enemies. They were not the ones that frightened him.'

'Then, who?'

She glances about and lowers her voice. 'My husband was involved in something – I hardly like to—'

'Sir!' A hand tugs at my sleeve and I look down to see the boy Sam hopping from one foot to the other, his eyes lit up with delight at finding me again.

'Good day, Sam.' I make him a little bow and his whole face scrunches up with laughter. 'What are you doing here?'

'Looking for something to eat.' He draws a hand across his nose.

'Did you find anything?'

He shakes his head and his lip juts out. 'I picked up a bit of bread but my brother robbed it off me.'

He is a scrawny thing; I wonder if anyone feeds him at home.

'Well, then.' I slip a hand into my purse and bring out a penny. I indicate a girl standing nearby with a tray of fresh pies. 'Get yourself a pie, and make sure you hide it from your brother.'

His solemn eyes widen and he regards the coin as if he has just witnessed a miracle.

'I am going to find someone from the coroner's office, Doctor Bruno,' Mistress Dunne announces, with a dismissive glance at the boy. 'You can stay here.' She gestures to the maidservant to follow, puts her shoulders back and disappears through the main

241

door of the Guildhall. Sam stands close to my side, turning his penny over and over in his hand as if he is afraid it might vanish. As I am gazing at the top of his head, an idea occurs.

'Sam, you and your friends must know everyone in Plymouth, I think?' I crouch to look him in the eye.

He bites his lip, torn between his desire to be truthful and his fear of disappointing me. 'Not everyone who comes in off the ships. But the townsfolk, mostly I do.'

'Good. I need to find someone. A girl. All I know is her name is Eve, and she probably works . . .' I hesitate, seeing his earnest expression. How much do children understand at his age? 'She might be one of the girls who works along by the harbour. One of the ladies who paint themselves.'

'A whore?' he says brightly. What is he – six years old, seven? I wonder if he has any concept of what a whore is. Growing up by the docks, they are as common a sight to him as fishermen or gulls, I suppose.

'I think so. She used to work at a place called the House of Vesta until recently. I need to find out where she's gone. It's important,' I add in a whisper, and pat my doublet where he knows my purse is stashed. He nods again. 'Perhaps you could ask around. You can start now, if you like.'

He looks doubtful. 'Can I have my pie first?'

I laugh. 'Of course.'

'Can I share it with my dog?'

I look around. The only dogs to be seen are mangy street scavengers. 'You can share it with whomever you like. Just don't let anyone take it from you.'

He grins, and scampers away, lightfooted, until he is lost behind barrows and swirls of bright skirts. I turn to see Mistress Dunne approaching with a gaunt young man in the robes of a clerk.

We turn a corner to find ourselves at the lych-gate of the church I visited the night before. The sun slides behind a cloud. A plump verger in a black cassock and violet chimere appears from the church door, exchanges a few private words with the clerk and greets Mistress Dunne with solemn murmurs of condolence, though his distaste for the task is evident in his jowly face. He is carrying an unlit lantern.

'The coroner asked us to keep the body in the crypt until the . . .' he hesitates, selecting his words carefully '. . . the manner of burial is settled upon. It's the coolest place, you see. We are fortunate that the weather has been unseasonably cold for August, else the body would be corrupted worse than it is.' He cannot quite disguise the wrinkling of his nose. It is clear that he would prefer not to have the corpse of a suspected suicide contaminating his church. He gives the impression that he would gladly drag the dead man to a crossroads and drive the stake through his heart himself, given the chance.

Mistress Dunne draws herself up, lifts her veil and looks him directly in the eye.

'My husband will be given Christian burial as soon as the inquest is over tomorrow,' she announces, in a tone that admits no contradiction. 'Agnes!' she snaps her fingers towards the maid. 'See that this gentleman is recompensed for the trouble he has been put to.'

Agnes dutifully rummages in her skirts and draws out a purse. I cannot help feeling impressed by Mistress Dunne's composure in facing down the censure of the Church; whatever she felt for her late husband, she seems determined to defend his name in death while she still can.

The verger immediately finds a more charitable spirit. 'That is most generous, madam. If you would just follow me . . .' He gives me a curious look, his small eyes resting on me in passing, trying to calculate my connection to the widow. He shepherds us along a narrow path around the north transept of the church until we reach a low doorway, which he unlocks with a key from his belt. As he opens it, he turns back to us.

'Are you quite certain, madam, that you wish to proceed? The sight, you know – for a lady . . .' He makes a little moue with his mouth.

'Of course I wish to proceed, I have ridden from Dartington for the purpose. I do not expect it to be pleasant, but it is my duty.' Mistress Dunne straightens up again and the verger shrinks under her gaze. He holds the door open.

'You will forgive me if I remain here – we have incense burning, but . . .' He does not need to elaborate. Mistress Dunne draws a handkerchief from her sleeve and presses it over her nose and mouth. I cover my lower face with my sleeve. The verger takes out a tinder-box and lights the lantern, handing it to the clerk and murmuring a few words as he does so. The clerk nods and, with his light aloft, enters a small vestibule and almost immediately turns right down a flight of stone steps. At the bottom he pushes open another door and the smell of putrefaction gusts out, thick as fog. I hear the clerk gagging, though he presses on, the small circle of light wavering forwards.

The crypt is low-roofed, supported by plain stone columns. It is true that the air is cold and damp down here, but evidently not enough to protect Robert Dunne from corruption, despite the incense burners set into niches in the walls. My stomach clenches and my heart is racing; the sepulchre stench takes me back to Canterbury the previous summer and the grisly discovery I made there in an underground tomb. My old dread of confined spaces rises up; I attempt a breath through my mouth but the air tastes metallic and sickly-sweet. I have to stop and lean against a pillar until I am sure I will not faint. Mistress Dunne walks on, her face set in that same resolute expression; if she is affected, you would not know it. In the wavering light of the lantern, I see that the clerk has turned slightly green.

At the far end of the crypt a makeshift bier has been created from wooden trestles and planks. On top lies a shapeless mound wrapped in a shroud. The smell of decaying flesh grows stronger as we approach. The clerk holds up his light and indicates the body, his face buried in the crook of his arm. Mistress Dunne looks at me. Since it appears no one else is willing, I step forward to draw back the winding sheet and force myself to look.

Mistress Dunne gives a little cry, muffled by her handkerchief, and clutches at her maid's arm to steady herself. I do not blame her; no effort has been made to lay out the body with any humanity. The eyes stare out of the blackening face at some nameless horror on the ceiling, a vision granted only to the dead; the jaw has not been tied, and hangs slack in a hideous grimace, teeth bared and tongue lolling. Some unspeakable fluid seeps in a glistening trickle from the nostrils and the corners of the eyes. The clerk has turned from green to grey and is swaying slightly, the cone of light from his lantern sliding back and forth up the wall.

'For the love of God, man, could you not have laid him out better, knowing his widow was coming? Bound the jaw and closed his eyes, at least,' I say, angry not just that Mistress Dunne should have to see her husband like this, but also at the lack of feeling or respect for a fellow creature. She looks up at me, surprised.

'Coroner said the body was not to be interfered with,' the clerk mutters, defensive, barely opening his lips.

'Would it have hurt to lay him out properly for burial?'

The young man's mouth curls into a sneer. 'With the burial he'll have—'

'The manner of my husband's burial has yet to be determined,' Mistress Dunne says, mustering her dignity. 'Kindly leave us. I would like to pay my last respects.'

'I'm not to leave the body unattended,' the clerk says, trying to breathe through his mouth.

'Why, do you think these ladies will tuck him under their arm and make off with him?' His attitude is beginning to irk me.

245

'You may jest, sir, but it wouldn't be the first time a body's been stolen,' he says, pompously.

'Well, then – you won't mind if I just take a closer look? Hold the light nearer, would you?'

The clerk hesitates, but moves the barest step forward and lifts the lantern. Steeling myself, I wrap the end of the shroud around my fingers and tilt the corpse's slack chin. A pale fat maggot falls out of the mouth. Mistress Dunne cries out. The clerk makes a violent retching sound and dashes for the door, dropping the lantern. With great presence of mind, Agnes grabs it; fortunately the glass has only cracked, not smashed, and the flame is still intact. From outside we hear the sound of copious retching.

Mistress Dunne has turned away, but she maintains an admirable self-control. Coroner be damned, I think; grasping the linen shroud firmly, I tear off a long strip and tie it around the corpse's head so that the mouth no longer hangs so hideously. My stomach heaves as if on a strong ocean swell as I touch the fine hair, but when the band is knotted the poor man looks a little more presentable. I consider closing those dreadful staring eyes, but the thought of whatever is seeping from the eyeballs causes me to draw back, too squeamish to do him this final courtesy. I look down at his face in the candlelight. Robert Dunne was a broad-faced man with a heavy brow and strong, square jaw. His hair was thinning, though he kept it long on top. Although the face is mottled and bloated, I have some sense now of what he looked like in life. He has become a man, like me, like any other, rather than merely an inconvenience.

'If they have their way,' Mistress Dunne says, her voice muffled by her handkerchief, 'he will be buried in this sheet and nothing more, tumbled into an unmarked grave at a crossroads out of town with a stake through his heart.'

'It seems cruel to punish a man further when he has already dealt himself the ultimate punishment,' I murmur. I have

246

difficulty regarding self-slaughter as a sin of the same magnitude as murder; often I question whether it can be a sin at all. If a man's temperament inclines him to melancholy, can he really be blamed if that melancholy overwhelms him? There have been times in my life, especially since I have been living in exile, when I have known the black glitter of despair, and understood all too well the lure of oblivion, the promise of an end to the constant battle of being. Of course, the scriptures tell us it is no end at all, only the beginning, but I have my own views on that. Sometimes only my belief that I have not yet given the world all that I am capable of offering has stayed my hand; this is a kind of arrogance, perhaps, but it serves.

'My husband did not kill himself, Doctor Bruno,' she announces firmly, through her handkerchief. 'Let us keep that in mind. Though I agree with you in principle. And harsher still to punish the kin he leaves behind.' She nods towards the body. 'Can you tell anything from looking at him?'

I glance at her. She is clearly an intelligent woman; the least I can do, it seems, is refuse to treat her like a child.

'If a man has died of slow strangulation, such as hanging by the neck,' I say, indicating Dunne's face, 'the pressure causes the veins in his face and eyes to break, so you see crimson marks on the skin. And the eyes would protrude more, the tongue too.'

She nods, thoughtfully. 'Yes, I once saw a woman hanged for a witch where she could not afford someone to pull on her legs. And if he had died some other way – could you not tell?' Her eyes stray uncertainly back to her husband.

'It might have been possible to tell when he was first found. But by the time a body has lain two or three days the blood drains away to the lower extremities and the flesh starts to darken. Your husband has already passed through rigor mortis and out the other side – the face is beginning to lose its shape.' I shake my head. 'It is impossible to say for certain. A physician might cut him open for signs of poison, though even that might be difficult at this stage.'

She keeps her eyes fixed on the body and says nothing. Her expression is hidden behind the handkerchief still clasped over her mouth and nose.

'They do say if a body is murdered, the image of the murderer can be seen fixed in the eyes,' the servant Agnes says, unexpectedly, making us both start. 'Though I'm sure I don't know how that would work if it was self-slaughter.'

Mistress Dunne turns and looks at her with undisguised scorn.

'Well, you are welcome to take a closer look, Agnes. It would make things a great deal easier for all of us if you could tell us whose image you see.'

Agnes shrinks back, perhaps wishing she had kept this wisdom to herself. A silence falls, broken only by the sleepy buzzing of flies. I try not to think about where they are coming from.

'Would you like me to leave you to pay your respects?' I say, when I can stand it no longer. Robert Dunne's body has nothing to tell me, and I am in urgent need of air.

Mistress Dunne appears to wake from a reverie; she gives herself a little shake and turns to me.

'No. Let us leave.' She glances back for a last look at her husband. 'Poor Robert,' she says, and her tone is not without pity. 'While I do not accept that he died by his own hand, Doctor Bruno, I do not doubt that he courted his death. One way or another, he himself was the instrument of it.'

We emerge into the churchyard and I am so grateful for the salt air that I gulp great lungfuls until I begin to feel lightheaded and have to steady myself against the wall. The clerk is hovering by the door, shame-faced, his shoes spattered with vomit. At the smell of it, I feel my own gorge rising again. Only when we have returned the lantern to the clerk and left him to lock up does Mistress Dunne remove the handkerchief from her face and breathe tentatively, as if she doesn't trust the air. Her face is pale, and after a few faltering steps she stumbles; I catch her arm and guide her to a flat stone tomb, where she sits gratefully.

'He courted his own death?' I ask, once she has recovered a little colour in her cheeks. 'I need to know what he was involved in, if I am to help you.'

She gives me a long look and reaches up to fiddle with her veil.

'You know the story of Thomas Doughty, I suppose?'

'I know the bald facts.'

She narrows her eyes.

'You mean, you know Sir Francis Drake's version. He made Robert one of the jury that convicted Thomas Doughty of treason. Robert was haunted by guilt for his part in it.' She lowers her voice. 'He said barely a man present, saving Drake's closest supporters, truly believed Drake had the authority to execute a gentleman like Doughty. Many of them, even the jurymen, believed his death was tantamount to murder, but they were afraid to cross Drake out there, on the edge of the world. Doughty's brother John nearly lost his wits over it, Robert said, and called down curses on the voyage and every man he held to blame for his brother's death.'

'But your husband returned to England safely, which would seem to argue against the power of John Doughty's curses,' I say.

She purses her lips. 'You tell that to a sailor. Other ships were lost. After we married and moved to Dartington, John Doughty started writing to my husband. He was in prison by then. I don't know what the letters said, but Robert was sorely troubled by them.'

'Threats, you think?'

'He would not tell me, but I believe so. Robert was a superstitious man. He had the house blessed by a priest, but he also sent Agnes to see a wise woman, and had the place hung all about with charms to ward off witchcraft.'

'John Doughty claimed to practise witchcraft.'

249

She nods. 'Oh, I know. This year my husband had news that two of his fellow jurymen from the voyage had met untimely deaths. Then he learned this had happened since John Doughty was released from prison. He grew obsessed with the idea that Doughty had killed them with magic. In April this year we were invited up to court and spent a few weeks in London. Two men turned up at our lodgings there, unannounced. Robert went out to supper with them, though I could tell it was against his will. One of them was John Doughty.'

'And the other – let me guess – was a man with no ears?'

Her eyes widen. 'You know him?'

'Pox scars, and very blue eyes?'

She nods, still bemused.

'I believe so. His name is Rowland Jenkes.'

'He gave Robert a French name, apparently, though he didn't sound French to me. My husband never told me what passed at that meeting, but the next day I found him packing his bags, saying he had to go to Plymouth on business. I barely saw him after that.' She pauses, looks down at her gloved hands folded in her lap. The maid Agnes gives a little cough. 'I mean to say' – Mistress Dunne jerks her head up, suddenly discomfited – 'he came home from time to time, to visit, you know. He was last home perhaps three months ago.' She says this with a peculiar emphasis, as if she has been caught out in a lie. I try not to show that I have noticed.

'But he was living in Plymouth almost permanently?'

'He took lodgings here. He wrote to say he had found a way to clear his debts and he intended to join Sir Francis on another voyage to the New World, which he believed would restore his fortunes.'

'Not a word of Doughty or the false Frenchman with no ears?'

'He didn't mention them again. But he sounded more optimistic than he had for some time. I believed the voyage would do him good. A man like Robert was always more at home out at sea.'

'You did not fear for his life, making another such voyage? Or feel that you would miss him, perhaps?'

Her expression hardens. 'I trusted God to bring my husband safely home, if it was His will, just as He did before. As for whether I would miss him . . .' she pauses, considering her answer. 'You are evidently a clever man, Doctor Bruno, and so I doubt it has escaped your notice that I am not over-whelmed by grief. I married Robert in too much haste and God has granted me ample time to repent it since. I had no objection to a prolonged absence, especially if it resulted in my husband's debts being cleared.'

Looking at her stern profile, her severely parted hair pulled back under her veiled hood, I find it hard to imagine her making any kind of reckless or impulsive gesture.

'You can have no idea what it is like – little by little, to watch his estate and my dowry trickle through his hands like water. To let the servants go, one by one, until the only maid I have left is Agnes, who stays out of loyalty and not because I can pay her what she deserves. To turn down invitations, pretending I am ill, because I cannot afford a gown to wear.' Her voice has grown tight; this is the nearest I have seen her to tears. 'Because my husband' – she fairly spits the word – 'has thrown everything away on the roll of a die. But this does not mean' – she holds my gaze, steady and earnest, as if she were on the witness stand – 'that I am glad he is dead. Especially like this.' She breaks off, pressing the balled-up handkerchief to her lips again.

Like this? In a manner so inconvenient for her, does she mean?

I hesitate before I speak, unsure whether it is wise to tell her what I know. I decide that it is best to be open with her, in the hope that she will be so with me.

'I believe that John Doughty is here in Plymouth.'

She turns slowly to stare at me, lowering the handkerchief.

'If that is true, then there can be no doubt my husband was murdered.'

'Sir Francis says it would have been impossible for him to board the ship unnoticed.'

She makes a dismissive little noise through her nose. 'Sir Francis will say whatever is expedient. Doughty could have had an ally on board. I suggest you turn your enquiries in that direction.' She reaches up to settle her veil over her face once more. 'I think I am recovered enough to return. Shall we?'

I offer her my arm, but she ignores it. We walk back towards the market cross in silence, sunk in our own thoughts, Agnes a disapproving presence at our shoulder. As we make our way down the hill into the warren of streets that lead to the quayside, I turn to Mistress Dunne.

'These lodgings your husband took in Plymouth, where were they?'

'I don't know. I didn't visit. Somewhere cheap, I would suppose. He was hardly in a position to be extravagant. Why – do you think there is something to be found there?'

'I don't know. He had very few possessions with him aboard the ship. Perhaps he left some clue in his lodgings.'

'Sir Francis returned to me what was found in his cabin. Some curious effects . . .' She pulls the kid leather at the ends of her fingers. 'A richly ornamented prayer book, for one.'

'I saw it. A beautiful piece of work.'

'It was not Robert's. Nor, I suspect, was the purse hidden inside it.'

'How can you be sure?'

'If my husband had owned a book that valuable, he would have sold it long ago for ready cash, or used it as a wager.' The wind threatens to lift her veil; she reaches up to tug it into place. 'As for the five gold angels – Robert never had that kind of money in his hand for longer than a day.'

'Could he have won it?'

She gives a cynical laugh. 'More chance of Hell freezing over.'

'A payment, perhaps?'

She appears to give this some thought. 'I don't know. But I fear my husband had been pressured into dealings with John Doughty and the fellow with no ears, something outside the law. The few times I saw him after he left for Plymouth, he seemed troubled.'

'But not troubled enough to take his own life. Of that you are certain.'

She darts a sidelong glance at me. 'No. Not as troubled as that.'

'It is supposed that John Doughty means to assassinate Drake and claim a reward from the King of Spain. You don't imagine . . .?' I leave her to fill in the rest. She stops and lifts her veil to look at me.

'Robert? You think he was mixed up in that?' She shakes her head as if the force of this action will make it untrue. 'No. That can't be. He worshipped Sir Francis. He would have died rather than harm a hair of his head.'

'Perhaps he did.'

As we approach the front door of the Star, a small shape detaches itself from the wall and comes bowling along the street towards us, shouting.

Sam skids to a halt at my side, his face shining with fresh triumph. 'Sir! I have found that whore you wanted!'

'Ah – thank you, Sam. You were very quick.' I turn to Mistress Dunne, who is looking at me with a raised eyebrow and a hint of amusement. I briefly consider offering a justification, but there is none that does not involve the revelation that her late husband was a regular visitor to a brothel; she may or may not know this already, but it would show a distinct lack of feeling to confront her with it minutes after she has paid her last respects to his corpse. So I merely shrug and offer her a helpless smile.

'I can take you there now, if we hurry,' Sam says, clamping his hand around my wrist, his face concentrated with the effort of pulling me. For a small boy, he exerts considerable force.

'Don't let us keep you,' Mistress Dunne says, in a light tone. Behind me, a loud tutting from Agnes.

'It's not what—' I begin, but she makes a dismissive gesture.

'I have no wish to interfere in your business, Doctor Bruno. Thank you for your company this morning. I expect we will see you at supper.' She cannot quite keep the smirk from her face as I bob her a little bow.

'Your timing is impeccable, Sam,' I mutter, allowing myself to be towed after him as the women open the door. He blinks up at me.

'Was that your wife, sir?'

'My *wife*? God, no!' I say, with more force than necessary.

'That's good. She looks like one of them is all smiles then – bam! – she'd box your ears out of nowhere,' he says, nodding firmly. He sounds as if he speaks from experience.

'You might be right. But we should be kind, Sam – that lady has just lost her husband. She is grieving.'

'She don't look like it,' he says, with a robust sniff. The child is no fool.

THIRTEEN

On the far side of Sutton Pool, at the extremity of the harbour, the streets reek of poverty and neglect. Houses that look beyond repair crowd together in dark, narrow lanes, leaning crookedly against one another like rotten teeth. The windows have sacking nailed up in place of glass; it flaps a melancholy rhythm in the wind. Sam skips nimbly over the rutted ground; more than once I have to tell him to slow down, as I must pick my way carefully to avoid the slops that run from over-flowing gutters. All around I am aware of eyes watching me from doorways and the mouths of alleys, the shadow of derelict buildings. Wild hollow eyes in starving faces, following every step as if they could burn through my doublet and see the purse hidden there. In Italy, men like this would put a blade in you for half a loaf, never mind a purse that would feed their family or keep them in drink for a month. My hand stays firmly on the hilt of my knife. But to my surprise no one steps forward, no weapon flashes in the gloom; they barely stir as I pass, motionless except for the gleam of their watchful eyes. Perhaps they lack the will for the effort it would take to bring me down. Even the gulls here sound as if they have given up.

'You don't want to come down here by yourself, sir,' Sam

calls knowledgably over his shoulder. Perhaps it is his presence that is protecting me.

'That is good advice,' I say, sidestepping a huge mound of fresh shit that might belong to one of the gaunt dogs that patter along the streets, or might not.

'Lots of the whores live down here though,' he says, cheerfully. 'Can't move for 'em, my uncle says. This is where the sailors come when they're down to their last groat, before they go back on their ships. Take home more than they bargain for, my uncle says. Not much further now, sir.'

He stops at a low doorway and pushes it open. Inside is a small, dingy room, stinking of urine and ale. The walls look as if they have scrofula, patches of damp plaster bulging and flaking away to reveal the horsehair and rubble stuffed in the cavities. A handful of men slump on stools around a table, sleeping off the effects of drink, while women in filthy clothes, their breasts hanging over their bodices, drape themselves over the men's shoulders, their eyes clouded. One of these creatures rouses herself as we come in, and makes a pathetic attempt to smooth her skirts.

'Is that you, Sam? What have you brought me, my darling?'

I fight not to let my reaction to this woman show on my face, but her appearance would provoke horror and pity in anyone with a grain of human feeling. She is bone-thin and the skin of her face and chest shows the red weals that proclaim to the world she is in the early stages of the pox. Her hair is lank and scabbed bald patches show through her scalp in places where it has been pulled or fallen out. Is this really the whore Robert Dunne so recently favoured? It can't be possible. I dart a sharp glance at Sam; perhaps he has tricked me, luring me here to the mercies of these desperate people, knowing I have money to spare.

'Eve?' I ask, tentatively.

'If you like,' she says. Her eyes are barely focused on me; she says it as a reflex. 'Where have you sailed in from, darling?'

256

she asks, languidly rearranging herself over the table. Her breasts are shrivelled and shapeless with her lack of flesh. 'Don't matter – I'll take whatever coin you have. Do you want it here or in the street?'

I look again at Sam, more urgently this time. He grins.

'This is the gentleman wants to know about Eve,' he says, holding on to my sleeve.

The girl's eyes open a fraction wider and she appears to register me for the first time.

'What you want with Eve then?' She pushes a strand of hair behind her ear; there is still some vestige of coquetry in the gesture. 'I promise you, darling, there's nothing she can offer you that I can't.' She gives a cracked laugh. 'En't that right? Oi.' She kicks the nearest man in the ankle; he lifts his head an inch from the table and mumbles something before sinking back again.

I don't doubt her word; this woman looks as if she could give you everything under the sun, I think, trying not to stare at the pox welts on her face.

'I want information,' I say. She blinks and sits upright, frowning in concentration. 'Where would I find her?'

'Eve . . . She's most likely been sent to Goodwife Mullen,' she says, surprisingly lucid. 'That's where she sends them as are stupid enough to get their belly filled. She can still squeeze a few pennies out of them.' She raises a hand and rubs thumb and forefinger together, the universal sign for avarice.

'She? You mean Mistress Grace?'

She produces the dirty cackle again; it collapses into a hacking cough. 'Mistress Grace. Like a mother to us all, she is.' She spits a gob of phlegm on to the floor. 'Not that I ever had a mother I remember. Can't have been any better.'

'Were you one of . . .' One of the Vestal Virgins, I had been going to say. It seems almost insulting. I could not begin to guess this girl's age – she could be anywhere from sixteen to forty – but I suspect she barely remembers her maidenhead either.

'One of her girls, her Vestal Virgins. Oh, I was, sir. And look at me now – aren't I the very model of purity?' She lifts the ends of her hair, twirls them around her fingers in a parody of flirtation, then lets her hand drop limply to her side.

'What happened to you?' I ask, more gently. 'Did you have a child?'

'No, sir. I had the other sort of ill luck, the one with no reward.' She points to her face. 'I conceived *this* from some generous gentleman. And this gives her nothing to sell. So.' She shrugs. 'If you can't earn your keep, there's no place for you. I had to find a new home, as you see.' She gestures around the room.

'What do you mean, "sell"?' I ask, trying to piece together her explanations.

She rolls her eyes. 'What I said. If any of the girls get with child, she sends them to Goodwife Mullen soon as their belly starts to show. She's a wet-nurse who keeps her mouth shut for money. They wait out their confinement, then if the child is healthy, Mistress Grace finds a home for it. Not out of the goodness of her heart, mind.' She makes the money sign again.

'She *sells* the babies?'

'You'd be surprised, sir, how many folk have uses for a healthy infant,' the girl says, leaning forward as if imparting a confidence. 'Gentlewomen, as can't have their own. She does the deal in advance, so the lady can pad herself out with cushions, pretend to go into her confinement, if she wants to pass it off as her own. They usually only want boys, though.'

'And if it's a girl?'

'Mistress Grace has people who'll raise them for her till they're old enough to be useful. For profit, naturally.'

'Until they can work in the brothel, you mean?' I shake my head. I thought I had seen most of the corruption known to humankind, but this is new. 'She is breeding her own stable. *Dio porco.* She must have been at this business a while. What age does she start them?'

The girl shrugs. 'Soon as they start to bud. Eleven, twelve. There's plenty of customers would take 'em younger, but Mistress Grace says it wears 'em out too soon.'

'She is all compassion.' I picture barren gentlewomen stuffing their bodices with cushions while they wait to buy a whore's bastard. My thoughts flit by association to Mistress Dunne and the sadness in her voice when she mentioned that her marriage had produced no children. 'And Eve? This is what happened to her?'

'Ah, Eve – she was a sweet one.' The girl's eyes glaze over and she slumps forward, resting on her elbows. Just as I think she has forgotten me and drifted into some reverie, she flashes a sudden grin. Most of her teeth are missing. 'She had what you might call a natural modesty. Wasn't hard to believe she was a blushing maid. I almost believed it, and I knew what she was up to every night. The gentlemen loved little Eve.' She laughs again and spits out whatever it has dislodged. 'But I suppose even her luck ran out,' she adds, sombre again.

'Where will I find Goodwife Mullen's?' I ask.

She sits up straight, focusing her gaze on me with disconcerting suddenness.

'She won't admit you. She keeps the girls out of sight. It's not strictly legal, see, but they turn a blind eye. What's it worth to me?' She sticks out a filthy hand. Her palm is blistered with marks of the pox. Her deflated breasts rest on the table top.

I reach into my purse and throw a penny on to the table. Almost before I can blink she has closed it in her fist and spirited it away somewhere inside her rags.

'Out in Stonehouse. On the waterfront, the white house at the end. Like I say, wait till she's gone out. She has a manservant guards the front door. Some of the girls try to run, see. But she has a yard out the back they can take the air. You might see Eve there.'

I thank her and beckon to Sam, who has stood patiently

259

against the wall through this exchange, watching the passed-out men with the same fascination you might save for rare animals in a menagerie.

'Don't want nothing else from me, darling, while you're here?' the girl says, without enthusiasm, jutting out a hip and planting a hand on it as if to show off the figure she might once have had. 'I mean, since you've paid.' She gives a hollow laugh; she knows very well how she looks. I glance around at the drunks half-lying across the table. Do men still pay her? Perhaps in the dark she can hide what she is becoming, poor creature.

I smile. 'No, you take the day off.'

'Thank you, sir – I'll spend it in prayer.' She grins, and ducks in a half-curtsey.

I fish inside my doublet and draw out another groat. 'And buy yourself a hot meal – what *is* your name?'

'Hardly matters, does it? Not like anyone's going to carve a headstone for me.' She lurches forward and snatches the coin; I flinch from her breath. 'I like you, darling. I'd have taken you for nothing, just for your pretty smile. I wasn't always this way, you know,' she adds, with unexpected ferocity. 'If you'd seen me back when I was worth something . . .' She looks down at the coin in her hand; her shoulders slump.

'One last thing,' I say, at the door. 'At the House of Vesta, did you ever know a man called Robert Dunne? Or John Doughty?'

'Oh, probably,' she says, and laughs until the coughing threatens to overwhelm her. 'Probably both at once. They never give their real names, unless they're fools and fancy themselves in love.'

'Of course.' I realise I have not thought of this. Even if I find this Eve, how can I be sure she will tell me anything about Robert Dunne? She may not know him by that name, and I can hardly describe him; I have only seen the man three days dead.

260

As I leave she says, 'Send Eve my good wishes, won't you.'
I turn. 'I still don't know your name.'
She pauses, looks down. 'Sara. That's how she knew me.'
'I will, Sara.' I nod. 'It means "princess", you know.'
'Really?' She considers this. 'And aren't I fucking just?' With a toothless grin she lifts her skirts, ducks a curtsey and blows me a kiss. At least she can still smile. I have seen the pox take hold; the best she can hope for is that the insanity comes quickly.

I have rarely been more relieved to step into air that I can breathe; even the lanes around the tenements are an improvement on the fetid air of that hovel. The stench of it is so thick in my nostrils that I could almost believe I have caught the contagion without so much as touching the girl. Sam and I stand on the harbourfront, feeling the wind in our faces, letting it sweep away every foul odour. My bruises ache and throb, and my eyes are heavy; I would like nothing more than to return to the Star and fall into my bed. I would also like to know if Jonas has been seen yet; his disappearance makes me uneasy. But the sun is high overhead, though still webbed with cloud; the day is moving towards noon and I am no closer to finding any answers. If I am to learn anything useful before tomorrow, I must chase every scent, however faint. Like a pig after truffles, as Sidney put it. I consider asking him to come with me to find the house of this Goodwife Mullen, who stables pregnant young girls as if they were brood mares, but reason that if I must gain access by stealth, it will be easier alone.

'Are we off to Stonehouse, then?' Sam asks, as if reading my thoughts.

'Won't your mother be expecting you?'

He shakes his head. 'She'll be out.'

'Who gives you your dinner then?'

He frowns, as if he doesn't understand the question. 'We just see what falls off the stalls.'

I smile. 'Do many things fall off?'

'They do if people bump into them. It's not stealing,' he adds, hotly, 'if you knock it by accident. Any case,' he says, 'you don't know the way to Stonehouse. I know the house she meant. You need me to show you.' He tucks his small hand under my arm as if the deal is settled. To Sam, I realise, I am some kind of guardian angel, dropped from heaven with a bottomless purse. But more than that, I make him feel that he is useful to me, and this in turn makes him feel important. It is the relationship of patronage in microcosm, I think, putting an arm around his shoulder; a reflection of my present situation with Sir Francis Drake.

'Come, then,' I say. 'Show me the way to Stonehouse. But first we're going to stop at a decent tavern for some hot dinner.'

His eyes light up, amazed. 'With meat?'

'With meat. And we are not going to knock anything off tables by accident while we are there, are we?'

He beams; you would think I had promised him fireworks and a sugar castle. 'No, sir.' He lays a solemn hand over his heart. 'Not even if it's *very* near the edge.'

FOURTEEN

A sullen bank of cloud has mooched in off the bay and blocked out the sun by the time we limp into Stonehouse, a small village of squat cottages that straddles a promontory on the other side of the headland. For most of the walk Sam has been clinging to my back like a monkey, his skinny arms tight around my neck; though he never complained, I could tell the distance was hurting his feet, bound up as they are with nothing but rags, so I offered to carry him over a stony patch of ground. When I asked about shoes, he claimed he's never had any and looked at me as if I had asked whether he owns a carriage. He weighs no more than my travel bag, but with each step his knees thud into my bruised ribs. After half a mile I am regretting having begun this journey.

A chill wind slices across the cliffs; the clouds have turned the landscape grey, green and brown. 'Call this a summer?' I say to Sam. 'Where I come from, it's warmer than this in mid-winter.' To lift our spirits I tell him about Italian summers, the riot of colour around the Bay of Naples: the shocking blue of sky and sea, the violent sunlight, the little white houses and churches with their red and purple explosions of bougainvillea, the sunsets so wild and vivid you fear the sea is aflame, as in the end of days. The fat lemons that hang from the trees, dark glossy grapes you can eat straight from the vines. Then I grow a little carried away and tell him Pliny the Younger's story about the boy who befriends the dolphin and rides on his back across the bay, and when he asks if I ever did this I tell him all Neapolitan boys ride on dolphins to school, and the mermaids wave at them as they plait their golden hair.

'Oh, we have them,' he says, unimpressed.

'What, mermaids?'

'Yes. They lie out on the rocks when it's sunny. Ours don't have golden hair though. They have whiskers. They look more like dogs.'

'Those are *seals*,' I say. 'Italian mermaids are the most beautiful in the world. They can't live in English waters because it's too damned cold.'

'Why did you come here, then?' He waves a hand at the murky estuary stretching out before us as the road slopes down towards the cluster of houses.

'Some men wanted to kill me,' I say. There seems no point lying to a child.

'Oh.' He thinks about this. 'Why?'

'I provoke people. Sometimes on purpose. Other times, I don't even realise I'm doing it. Just something about my face.'

He nods gravely. 'Sometimes my uncle gives me a slap for nothing. Just for being there.'

'Then you understand.'

'When I'm grown,' he announces, 'I am going to have a ship like Sir Francis Drake, and fight the Spanish, and bring home treasure, and my uncle will never dare clout me then, and my brother won't push me in the water or throw stones at me with his slingshot.'

'Quite right,' I say. 'They will all have to call you captain. Now – let's find this house.'

He laughs and hugs his arms closer around my neck. We walk on a few more yards. At the outskirts of the village I swing him down to the ground, gasping at the pain in my side.

I recognise the place by the girl Sara's description: a lime-washed cottage set apart from the rest at the end of the street that faces the estuary. An expanse of silted sand stretches from the far side of the road down to the mud-coloured water. Gulls patrol the beach, standing sentinel on the overturned hulls of fishing boats. I squint up at the house. All the windows are shuttered.

'I suppose we just wait for the goodwife to go out,' I say, casting around for somewhere to keep our vigil. A few yards along the beach is a small boat that will serve.

'She might be out already,' Sam observes.

'You are sharper than me today,' I say. 'How will we find out?'

He thinks about this. 'I could knock on the door and ask for her.'

'What if she answers it?'

'Then I just say I got a message for Jem. And they say there's no Jem here, get on your way, and then we'll go round the back.'

'Good work,' I say. 'You are earning your keep today, Sam. Wait for me to hide in that boat. And if she's there, walk away so she doesn't get suspicious.'

He scampers off and I hunker down inside the boat, watching the door. At length it is opened by a short, broad woman in an apron, her hair scraped back under a white coif. She shakes her head and points up the street, then slams the door in Sam's face. He saunters away in the direction of the promontory, then hops down the low sea wall and sits himself down on the sand to wait. I pass the time by trying to organise the facts of Dunne's death in my mind according to the memory system I developed for King Henri in Paris, but they refuse to fit in neat concentric circles; instead they fly up and scatter like a flock of starlings. There is a splat against the boards of the boat as a seagull shits an inch from my shoulder; I flinch away and the movement sends shivers of pain through

265

my ribs. My eyelids grow heavy; I let them drop and picture the Bay of Naples, blue and silver, shimmering tails of dolphins and mermaids arcing over the surface.

A moment later I snap them open again; Sam is standing over me, poking my shoulder.

'You were asleep,' he says, mildly reproachful.

'I was not. I was thinking. What's happened?'

He points to the street in front of us; the stout woman, a shawl wrapped around her shoulders, is waddling off towards the village, a large reed basket hooked over her arm. When she has turned a corner, out of sight, we dash across the damp sand to the cottage.

A path runs around to the rear of the house, past a garden enclosed by a wall not much higher than a man. A wooden door is set into it at the very back but this is firmly locked. From behind the wall comes the sound of women's voices, subdued. Trees grow at the edge of the garden, branches snaking over the wall.

'Shin up there and see if you can see anyone,' I say to Sam, pointing to an apple tree. 'If there is a man there watching the girls, jump down straight away. If not, try to catch their eye. We are looking for the one called Eve.'

I hoist him on to my shoulders and he grabs the lowest branch and pulls himself up, agile as a cat. He feels his way along until he is sitting in a fork of the tree, well inside the garden, his little legs swinging. From below comes a girlish exclamation.

'You're early for scrumping apples, little master,' says a voice.

'I'm not stealing,' Sam says. 'I'm looking for a girl.'

Ribald giggles from within. 'Come back in ten years, sweetheart, when you've money in your hand,' one of them says.

'My master has money.' Sam kicks his legs, nonchalant. 'He wants a girl called Eve. He needs to talk to her.'

My master, I think. There is something oddly touching about this.

'Your master?' another girl asks, her voice anxious. 'Is he a sailor?'

'He's off Captain Drake's ship,' Sam says.

There follows some discussion between the women that I cannot catch; their words come in short, excited bursts. 'I am called Eve,' says the same voice. 'When can I see him?' She sounds breathless; I already know she is going to be disappointed.

'Now,' Sam says, pointing down. 'He's right here.'

'Tell him I am locked in, we can't leave. He'll have to climb up where you are.'

I curse inwardly. Sam shins obligingly along the branch and perches on the wall, motioning for me to join him. I grip the wall with both hands and pull myself up, white-hot needles of pain spearing my right side. As I emerge on to the top, steadying myself with the branches, I hear the girl say, her voice bright with hope, 'Robert?'

Below me is a neatly kept garden, the lower part given over to orchard, the end nearest the cottage planted with box hedges and herb beds. It is large enough that here, at the wilder end, we could not be overheard from the house. Frowning up at me is a young woman, barely more than a girl, with a round, pretty face, her hair tied back in a white coif. She wears a grey smock that hangs shapelessly from thin shoulders. Though there is no sun, she lifts a hand to shade her eyes and squints hard at me. Her expression, as I predicted, is crushed.

'Who are you?'

'My name is Giordano.'

'What?'

'Never mind. Are you Eve?'

She nods, then casts a nervous glance back at the cottage. Blank windows stare over the garden. Hanging not far behind Eve is another girl, a little older, dressed in the same clothes.

'Is someone watching you?'

She jerks her thumb at the house. 'He's asleep inside the

back door. But he might wake. There's a maid in the kitchen too, but she's on our side. Only if the goodwife finds out we've talked to you we'll all be punished.'

'How will she punish you?' I ask. My mind conjures images of pregnant young girls savagely beaten, a punishment I have brought on them through my interference.

'Lock us in our rooms,' she says, with a little shrug. 'That's all they can do here. She can't lay a hand on us in case it hurts the babby, see.' Her fingers stray protectively to her belly. She is barely more than a child herself.

'Will it fall out if she beats you?' Sam asks with relish, kicking his heels against the brick wall as if he is the spectator at an interlude.

'Sam – I need you to keep watch at the front for me. Tell us when the goodwife is coming back. Quick, now.'

He nods, eager to obey his orders, then jumps down and scurries down the path to the street. Eve turns and whispers something to her friend; the other girl skips away closer to the house, evidently to keep watch from her side.

'Have you come from Robert?' Eve asks, when they are out of earshot, with the same eager smile. 'Can he not come himself? I've been waiting for days and heard nothing.'

I watch her carefully, wondering what answer will best serve my purpose.

'You were waiting for Robert to come?'

She clicks her tongue, impatient. 'Of course. As soon as he had made arrangements, he said.' Her face clouds with suspicion. 'Why, what is the matter?'

'Did you know that he was planning to sail for Spain with Sir Francis Drake any day?'

Her brow knots in confusion. 'But that was before. He said—'

'Before what?'

She pulls the material of her dress tight to reveal a tiny swollen stomach. She smooths a hand across it reverently. 'Before *this*.'

'Eve,' I say, and my tone causes the colour to drain from her face. 'Robert will not come to you again.'

She shakes her head, takes a step back as if to distance herself from the news. I see her eyes are brimming with tears. 'You're lying,' she hisses, but there is fear in her face.

'Listen, Eve . . .' I edge my way along the branch to the fork in the tree where Sam had sat. I am closer to her now; I do not quite dare to jump down into the garden in case this guard appears, but I hardly like to shout the news I have to break from on high, like a messenger from the gods in an inn-yard play. She steps further away.

'If you come down here I'll scream and that brute will come out with his crossbow,' she says. I glance at the cottage in alarm, unsure whether she is bluffing. 'Why should I believe you? What do you know of it?' Without waiting for an answer, she wraps her skinny arms around her chest and pouts. 'Robert will come for me. I know he will.'

'Eve, I need you to trust me. I have to speak with you, with no threats of screaming or crossbows, and it must be done quickly, before the goodwife returns.' At the mention of her keeper, Eve makes a face. 'Oh, I almost forgot,' I add, 'Sara sends you her good wishes.'

'Sara? Where is she?' She scans the wall as if I might have brought her with me. 'Do you know her?'

'I saw her just this morning. It was she who told me where to find you.'

'Oh. And how does she?' She looks down as she asks this, twisting the fabric of her dress between her fingers, fearful of the answer.

'As you would expect,' I say. I may as well give her the truth in everything.

She nods. 'She will die, won't she?'

'Eventually. But it is an unpredictable disease, it can run fast or slow.'

'I should like to see her again.' She heaves a sigh that shakes her whole frame. Her hand returns absently to her belly. After a long silence, she moves closer to the tree. 'Will you tell her so, if you see her? She was always kind. Poor Sara.'

'I will.' I wait. She rubs at her eye with the heel of her hand. Eventually she looks up.

'Tell me, then. Where is Robert?'

I try to banish the image of Robert Dunne lying cold in his shroud, the stench of his flesh rotting unburied in the crypt.

'Robert Dunne is dead, mistress. I'm sorry.'

'No!' She cries out, clasps a hand to her mouth and sinks to the ground, her skirts puddling around her. The other girl, stationed near the box hedges, snaps her head up and makes as if to come over; I hold up a hand in warning and swing down into the soft grass. It is a drop of little more than six feet, but it jars all my bruises and I have to keep myself from crying out. I kneel beside Eve and offer her a handkerchief. She balls it in her fist and presses it to her mouth. 'Who killed him?' she croaks, barely audible.

'Why do you say he was killed?'

She blinks at me.

'Because he was afraid.'

'Of whom? Did someone want him dead?'

A huge sob seems to well up from the core of her being and explode noiselessly as she covers her face with her hands and her whole body shakes. I lay a reassuring hand on her shoulder and wait for the waves of grief to subside, though not without a degree of impatience.

'Mistress Grace,' she says, peeling her hands away to reveal red, brimming eyes. 'Or his wife, I suppose, though she would not have known we planned to run away. He hasn't seen her for months, not since he came to Plymouth in the spring. In any case, she is sick and like to die very soon, he says, so I doubt it was her.'

Not the last time I saw her, I think. Robert Dunne evidently knew how to please his young mistress. 'Tell me about your plan,' I say, gently. 'It might help.'

'He never meant to go with Captain Drake,' she whispers, between ragged gulps. 'He said he had some business to finish here with the fleet and then he would come into money and take me away, and we would raise the child as a family. Somewhere far from Plymouth,' she adds, with vehemence. 'And once his wife was in her grave, we would be properly married.'

I watch her: the clenched fists, the flushed cheeks, the determination. Did she really believe this would happen?

'Did Mistress Grace know of this plan?'

'No, but . . .' She scrubs at her wet cheek with her knuckles. 'I told someone there. The House of Vesta, I mean. She might have forced it out of them. She can do that.'

'The boy Toby?'

She looks at me, surprised. 'You know him?' Her eyes narrow. 'I never saw you there. Does she let you have Toby as well? I thought it was just—' She bites her tongue.

'No,' I say, quickly. 'I only spoke to him once. So you think Mistress Grace may have uncovered your plan and tried to prevent it?'

'She'd have done anything to stop us if she knew,' the girl says, lowering her voice further. 'She wants to take the baby, see. All our babies. She thinks we don't know, but the girls talk.' She gestures towards the house. 'Robert said he wouldn't let that happen.' She stops, swallows hard, and a fresh wave of sobbing breaks over her. 'What am I to do now?'

'Eve, listen to me.' The seriousness of my tone causes her to break off her crying and sit up. 'Something may be done for you, but you have to help me find out what happened to Robert. Do you understand?'

She gives a mute nod, her face puffy with misery.

'Good girl. Robert died in his cabin on Captain Drake's ship the *Elizabeth Bonaventure*. So even if Mistress Grace or his wife had reason to want him dead, they must have had help from someone on board. Did he ever mention any of his fellow crewmen who wished him ill?'

She blinks back tears and considers. 'He didn't like Captain Drake's brother. Said he was too keen to throw his weight around, you'd think him the Captain-General. Robert said he had respect for Captain Drake but not for the brother – thinking he could speak to gentlemen as if he was their better, and him only the son of a farmer.'

I suppress a smile; I have heard this sentiment before. 'But you don't know of any particular quarrel?'

She shakes her head. 'There was another man, Sorrell, Sewell, something like that? Robert owed him money. He said he was afraid this man would send someone to collect it before he'd had a chance to finish his business here in Plymouth.'

'Savile, perhaps?'

'Might have been. He was always complaining about someone. Robert felt life had not given him his dues. That's what he said to me. He said he had no one else to talk to. His wife never listened.'

They never do, these wives.

'Did he ever mention a man called John Doughty?'

She gives me a quizzical look. 'No. But there's a Master Doughty who's been coming to the House of Vesta the last few months. I heard Mistress Grace address him so as she was showing him into her private rooms. He even came to me on occasion,' she adds, with a hint of regret.

There is a silence, filled by the screeching of gulls. 'Eve,' I say eventually, 'given that you were . . .' I pause, considering how to put this delicately. 'Given that you entertained a number of men at the House of Vesta, how can you be so sure the child is Robert Dunne's?'

She looks at me as if I am stupid. 'Because Robert was the only one I loved,' she says firmly. 'And there must be love, to conceive a child.' Clearly she believes this brooks no argument. I wonder who has put such fantasies in her head, and how she has sustained them against all the evidence that living in a whorehouse must have provided. I decide to change tack.

'Did Robert ever explain this business that he had to finish in Plymouth?'

'No. Only . . .' she hesitates and falls silent, twisting the handkerchief between her fingers.

'Please, Eve. Anything Robert told you might help to find out who killed him.' I lower my voice. 'If we can't find out, he will be buried as a suicide, and all his goods will be taken. If that happens, we will never know if he left provision for your child in his last testament.'

Hope flickers in her eyes. 'Do you think he did?'

'I suppose it is possible. If he meant to take care of you.' I feel low for deceiving her, though it is no more than Dunne himself had done. 'But it will do him no good for you to protect his secrets now, if he shared any.' I nod encouragement; she opens out the handkerchief, smooths it on her lap, weighing up the idea.

'He had grown troubled in the last few weeks,' she says, eventually. 'I was only brought here a fortnight ago, when Mistress Grace discovered about the child. I'd been faking my courses the past two times with pig's blood from the kitchen, but she caught me.'

'Resourceful of you.'

'It's an old trick.' She sounds scornful. 'But before that Robert still came to the House of Vesta as often as he could. He talked about God and Hell a lot. Asked me if I thought it could ever be right to take a life.'

'Did he? And what did you answer?' I make my voice as gentle as I can. I sense I am nearing something important and I must tread carefully, as one would approaching a deer on a hunt; softly, softly, lest she take fright and bolt.

'I said in a war, if someone was going to kill you otherwise,

I was sure God would not punish a man who killed to protect himself or his kin.'

'And what did Robert say to that?'

'He seemed pleased. I think it's what he wanted to hear.'

I nod slowly, and wait. There must be more.

'Another time,' she says, in a reflective tone, 'he asked if I thought a man could be forgiven for betraying a friend, if it was to save a life. I said I could not see how such a situation could come about and he said I was probably right.'

'He didn't elaborate?'

'No.' She rubs her nose with the handkerchief. 'But he often used to ask me what I thought it was like in Hell. Would it be burning flames or cold like a sea of ice? For some say one and some the other. I would tell him not to think of such things, and he would answer that he was afraid his soul was already damned.' She shudders. 'I hated it when he talked like that. I tried to change the subject, to make him talk about the home we would have with the baby when we were married, and he said it would have to be far away from England.'

There is more I would ask her, but we are interrupted by a scrabbling on the other side of the wall as Sam's mop of hair appears over the top. 'The old woman's coming,' he yells, with as much urgency as if he were announcing the sighting of a Spanish fleet off the coast. 'She's at the top of the street.'

I push myself to my feet, wincing, and brush the grass off my breeches. 'One more thing, Eve. Robert had lodgings in town – do you know where they were?'

She purses her lips. 'Rag Street, he said. By the sign of the Bear. I never went there.' She holds the handkerchief out to me.

'Keep it.'

She shakes her head. 'I cannot, sir. She'll know it's not mine.'

'Take this instead, then.' I find a penny from the purse inside my doublet. Whatever I lay out now will be Drake's to reimburse. I move to the tree.

'One more thing, sir – I've just recalled.'

274

'Yes?' I wait, my hand resting against the trunk.

'The last week or so that I saw him, before I came here, he was very pleased about something. It was to do with the ship, the *Elizabeth*.' She stands up, shaking out her skirts. 'He said he'd found out something about one of the people on board, someone he was to sail with.'

'And . . .?' I try not to show my impatience.

'He said he'd learned that someone on that ship had a wicked secret, one that was going to cost them dear. And he rubbed his hands together like this.' She demonstrates, looking like the figure of Avarice in a morality play.

I think of the purse hidden inside the prayer book, fat with five gold angels. Was Dunne blackmailing one of his fellow sailors?

'Did he tell you a name?' I ask. The hairs on the back of my hands and arms are prickling with anticipation. 'Or any details?'

She frowns. 'I am trying to remember.'

Suddenly there is a cry from the girl keeping watch by the cottage; I jerk my head up to see the back door opening and a bulky figure filling the doorway.

'Quick!' I hiss, grabbing the lowest branch of the tree and hauling myself up.

A shout comes from the far side of the garden; some crude English oath. Eve cries out; I hear a sharp whistling and a thud as the bolt of a crossbow buries itself in the tree trunk where my leg had been a moment earlier. I scramble along the branch as far as the wall; one quick glance shows me the man is striding across the grass towards us, reloading as he goes. I yell to Sam to get down. Just as I swing myself down to the other side, I hear the scrape of iron on brick as a second bolt narrowly misses, striking the wall and showering us with fragments of mortar.

Sam has already started running towards the street; I call him back and instead drag him up the bank behind the houses, into a scrubby clump of trees. 'He will chase us out into the

275

street if we go that way, it is too exposed,' I explain. Without argument, he slips his hand into mine and allows me to lead him through untended gardens and along unfamiliar streets, glancing over our shoulders at every turn, until I am sure the man with the crossbow must have given up.

'Can you get us back from here?' I ask Sam, when we finally stop to rest by a drinking trough at the junction of three streets. The ground is higher here and I have a view over both the Sound and the estuary below us; the great ships sit stately as castles in the distance. He nods and we trudge back towards Plymouth together, footsore and weary. As we walk, I look down at him and consider what it might be like to have a son; exhausting, is my conclusion. For all the tenderness of this small hand clinging to mine, there is something terrifying about the enormity of a child's trust, their faith in your power to make the world right. Since I fled from San Domenico – and even before that – I have had enough to do keeping myself out of trouble; the prospect of taking responsibility for another person's welfare seems beyond my capabilities. But perhaps every man feels that before he becomes a father. Not that this is an immediate problem; I have no means to raise a child, nor any woman to carry it, yet.

Lost in these thoughts, I am not paying attention to Sam's chatter. We have taken the path along the headland and he is pointing out to sea, yapping around my feet like a small dog, something about tunnels.

'What tunnels?'

'In the cliffs,' he says, still pointing. I follow the direction of his finger across the flat grey water to the small rocky island that sits in the centre of the Sound like a sentry-post. 'People call it Drake's Island now,' he says proudly. 'All through the cliffs, my uncle says, there are old tunnels made years ago for hiding places.'

'Smugglers, I suppose.' I squint out towards the island. It

looks an ideal staging post for dropping off illegal shipments from larger ships, any goods you might want to bypass the customs men; hide them in the tunnels and ferry them back to the mainland under cover of darkness. 'Is it manned now, the fort?'

Sam doesn't know. I peer harder, but it is impossible to see at this distance if there is any human activity. What a miracle it would be, I have often thought, if someone could devise a lens, such as the kind old men use for reading fine print, that would enable you to see distant objects closer. My friend John Dee had experimented with such a device, combining convex and concave lenses in various arrangements, but with no great success. It is the kind of instrument I feel certain the Arabs must have invented; perhaps there might have been some record of such a device, if Christendom had not been so arrogantly blind to science and destroyed so much of their great knowledge. In all its history, I wonder, has the Christian church ever brought anything but strife and bloodshed, either to those who embraced it or those who refused it? The thought leads me back to the brittle manuscript locked away in Drake's cabin.

'Are we going to see any more whores today?' Sam asks, jolting me back to more prosaic matters as we reach the end of Castle Street.

'No, Sam – I think I am done for the day.'

'Where shall we go instead then, sir?' he persists, valiantly trying to disguise his own tiredness.

'I am going to the Star to rest. And you should go home to your mother. Here. You have been a great help to me today.' I fish out the penny he has been waiting for. He looks disappointed at being sent on his way, and hovers at my side until I reach the entrance to the inn.

'I could help more, sir,' he says, beaming up at me. 'I know my way all around Plymouth.'

'I don't doubt it. But I have no more need of help today.'

'Tomorrow, then?' He is tenacious, I will give him that.

'Maybe. There is one thing you could do for me, Sam.'

'Yes, sir?'

'Keep a lookout for a man who dresses all in black. He has no ears, a pocked face and very blue eyes. He will probably be wearing a hat to hide his lack of ears, but you are clever enough to spot him.'

'Are you going to kill him?' Sam asks, interested.

'Of course not.' Not unless he tries to kill me. 'I just want to know where he is lodging.' But I recall what the girl Eve told me of the questions haunting Robert Dunne: can a man be damned if he kills another to save his own life? I must hope for my own sake that the answer is no. Though, as Sidney likes to point out, the charges against my soul are weighty enough already; one more murder would hardly tip the scales.

The entrance hall of the Star is bustling as usual; guests in fine clothes milling about, wanting to be noticed, while porters heft trunks and bags into service corridors as Mistress Judith sails here and there like a mighty barge, greeting paying customers in honeyed tones and berating servants like a banshee, often in the space of the same breath. At the foot of the great staircase is a little knot of ladies I cannot avoid: Lady Drake, Lady Arden and Mistress Dunne, with the chaplain Pettifer in attendance, red-faced and fretting. Lady Arden casts a long, cool look in my direction, but her face gives away nothing. A flicker of amusement relieves the solemnity of Mistress Dunne's expression.

'Did you have a profitable day, sir?' She turns to the other ladies. 'Doctor Bruno has been visiting whores since dinner time.'

'I hear it is one of his preferred pastimes,' Lady Arden says drily, 'though by the state of him I cannot think it is good for his health. Your sleeve is torn, Doctor Bruno.'

So that is why she is so frosty with me today; she must

have heard about our expedition last night. But how? A serving girl edges past us carrying a large pitcher of water; immediately I think of Hetty. Nothing is private in this inn. I glance at my sleeve with a soft curse; there is a tear almost a foot long in the seam.

'Perhaps I should leave off climbing apple trees at my age,' I say, poking a finger through the material. Lady Arden shakes her head and turns away to hide a smile.

'Sir Philip will be glad to see you,' says Lady Drake; already I detect a warmth in her tone when she mentions his name. The sooner I can get Sidney out of temptation's way, the safer he will be. 'He has been stamping about here this past hour looking for you. I believe he went to wait in the tap-room.'

'Perhaps I had better go and find him,' I say, bowing as I back away to make my exit.

'We are all in a state of great excitement,' Lady Drake continues, then remembers herself and casts an anxious glance at Mistress Dunne. 'Saving your presence, mistress. Sir Francis has had a message to say that Dom Antonio travels with a French merchantman that is about to dock in the Sound, and will be with us before sundown. My husband will hold a supper here tonight to welcome him.'

Mistress Dunne makes a contemptuous noise. Lady Drake turns, her cheeks colouring. 'We are all most sorry for your loss, madam,' she says, sounding anything but. 'However, Dom Antonio of Portugal is a royal visitor, expected these past weeks, and Her Majesty expects us to show him a fitting welcome.'

Mistress Dunne looks away, her mouth tight. 'I ask you how you would take it, my lady, if your husband had been murdered and his fellow officers were out carousing while he lay unburied?'

'Is my husband to neglect his duties because yours put a rope around his own neck? Do you not think his death has caused my husband enough trouble already?'

Lady Drake has raised her voice more than she meant to; other guests have stopped to listen. Lady Arden lays a hand on her cousin's arm to restrain her. Mistress Dunne turns pale; her lips are compressed so hard they disappear into a white line. For a moment I think she might slap Lady Drake, but in the next instant her legs appear to buckle and she flails a hand, looking for support; the maid Agnes steps silently out of the shadows and helps her to a bench by the wall. A space clears around her. Into this shocked silence ambles Savile, fresh from the tap-room, whistling a catch.

'What's all the fuss here?' he says, looking around the company with a hearty grin. No one answers. Then he catches sight of Mistress Dunne, limp as a cloth doll, with Agnes fussing by her side. With one stride he is across the hall.

'What ails you, madam? Do you need a drink? A physician?'

Mistress Dunne swats him away, seeming to resent his attentions. 'I am perfectly well, thank you, sir.' She leans on Agnes and with some effort pushes herself to her feet. 'I am just a little tired, that is all. It has been a difficult day and I am not quite recovered from the journey. Perhaps I am out of temper.' She fires a furious look at Lady Drake. 'I think I will retire to my chamber, if you will excuse me.' Still supported by her maid's arm, she moves gingerly towards the stairs.

Savile looks as if he means to follow them, but thinks better of it. Instead he watches the ladies climb the stairs and turns to me, disgruntled.

'Women, eh? You show them a courtesy, they'll none of it. Then if you don't offer to assist them, they complain there are no true gentlemen left. Can't win. Do you think she's all right?' He jerks his head towards the stairs where Mistress Dunne has disappeared around a corner. He looks genuinely concerned.

'I should think she is tired, as she says.' I glance around and catch Lady Arden's eye. She relents and allows me a half-smile. I wonder if I might take the chance to explain to her

280

about last night, but Lady Drake is upset by her outburst; she whispers something and Lady Arden nods, slipping her arm through her cousin's and leading her towards the parlour, though she pauses to glance back at me over her shoulder. Savile harrumphs and stamps away out of the front door, banging it behind him.

'Doctor Bruno, may I speak with you?' Pettifer is at my elbow, knotting his fingers together, his smooth pink face creased in concern. 'Mistress Dunne tells me you accompanied her this morning to view her husband's body. I have been praying with her this afternoon.'

'I'm sure that is a great comfort to her.'

He narrows his eyes, uncertain whether I am being sincere. 'Well, it is part of my office, to comfort those who mourn.' He looks uneasy. 'Though in such circumstances as these, it is difficult. I cannot reassure the poor lady that her husband's soul is with God when we do not know that for certain.'

'We shall have to wait until the coroner decides tomorrow where his soul has gone.'

'I see you are determined to be flippant, Doctor Bruno. I suppose it is to be expected of one who has abandoned religion.' He sounds disappointed rather than accusatory. 'I only wanted to ask if you noticed anything about the body that might be of use to the inquest?'

'To determine his manner of death, you mean?' I wish he would stop his endless fidgeting; if he were a priest in my country, I think, he would at least have a rosary to play with. 'But you saw him shortly after he died, Father. You prayed over him, did you not?' He acknowledges this with a nod. 'If you and the others noted nothing then, it is unlikely that I would have a clearer picture after three days.'

'True, true. I only wondered. Hoped, I suppose, that you might have some insight denied the rest of us. They say you are very knowledgeable in these matters – though it is a

281

curious expertise for a theologian.' He raises an eyebrow, to let me know he does not entirely trust me.

'I try to broaden my knowledge as much as possible. You can never tell when it might come in useful. Speaking of theology, Padre, may I ask you a question?'

He clasps his hands together and adopts a pious expression, but his small eyes grow wary. 'Of course.'

'Did Robert Dunne ever talk to you about Hell? Or judgement? Did you sense that something was troubling his conscience in that regard?'

'His conscience?' The chaplain frowns. 'He seemed anxious, as I said, and he spoke of himself as a sinner, but then should not we all? He said nothing specific, that I recall.'

But I sense a hesitation in his answers, as if he doesn't like the way this is tending. I stroke a finger along the stubble on my jaw. 'Nothing, for example, about whether a man is always damned for taking a life, even if it is to save his own?'

'No!' He looks horrified. 'No, indeed. He never asked any such question of me. What on earth has put that in your mind?' His tongue flicks nervously around his dry lips.

'Something his widow mentioned. I am sure it is of no importance. After all, if he had spiritual concerns, he would have expressed them to you before anyone, would he not?'

'I would certainly have hoped so.' He smiles, though it looks strained at the edges. 'Well, his soul is in God's hands now, and his body in the coroner's. Will we have the pleasure of your company at the dinner tonight for Dom Antonio?'

'I have not yet been formally invited. But I am sure Sir Philip will be present.'

'Indeed.' He gives a little bow and turns to leave. 'Dom Antonio. Formerly Prior of Crato, you know. He is another who has exchanged religion for politics – and much good it has brought him.'

'It must be a great relief to the Lord Almighty to know that he can count on such true servants as yourself. Men undistracted by things of the world.' I smile pleasantly. 'Tell me, did you say you were at Cambridge, Padre?'

He stops, halfway to the door. 'Yes. Why do you ask?'

'Just curious. It is a university I should like to visit.'

He blinks rapidly. It is plain by now that my questions unsettle him, though courtesy obliges him to disguise it. An idea is beginning to form like a tight bud in the back of my mind. I return his bow and leave him staring after me, still cat's cradling his fingers as if the agitation of his thoughts must find an outlet somewhere.

FIFTEEN

Sidney is not in the tap-room. Instead I find him in our chamber, writing a letter to his wife.

'Where the Devil have you been?' he cries, leaping up from the table. 'Your little friend has been up here looking for you.'

'Sam?'

'Who's Sam?' He casts around for his pipe. 'The fisherman's boy? No, I mean the pudgy maid who likes to get into everyone's business. She seemed particularly anxious to find you. I'm afraid I was rather short with her.' He packs tobacco leaf into the bowl and presses it down. 'Lady Drake has been quite chilly with me today. I'd wager anything that maid told her where we went last night. Women don't take it kindly, you know – the idea that a gentleman might pass up their company for that of a whore. They don't like the idea of whores in general. For the sake of propriety, we are all supposed to collude in the pretence that the business doesn't exist.'

'I don't know what they are so exercised about. We are all selling ourselves one way or another.'

He sighs, and sparks a tinder-box into life. 'Isn't that the truth. Well then, tell me what progress you have made today.'

So, while he leans back in his chair, stretching out his long limbs and puffing small gusts of blue smoke into the air, I recount for him my first sight of Robert Dunne and what I learned from Sara and Eve.

'She *sells* babies?' Sidney looks aghast.

I shrug. 'That is hardly a new trade. Children are a commodity like anything else, for as long as there are some with too many and others without. The point is, if Mistress Grace seriously believed Dunne meant to run off with the girl, that would give her reason to get rid of him. And she is obviously connected to John Doughty.'

Sidney takes his pipe out of his mouth and studies the end of it, considering. 'What man would be such a fool as to believe a whore who tells him she is carrying his child? He can't seriously have planned to elope with her. Not with his wife about to come into her inheritance.'

'He probably said it to keep her sweet. But the girl evidently believed it – perhaps sincerely enough to persuade Mistress Grace it was a danger.'

'So we stumble again on this problem of who actually strung him up.'

I cross to the window and lean both elbows on the sill, pushing my hands through my hair. 'I think I should speak to the watchmen on the *Elizabeth*. I know they have sworn to Drake that no one boarded that night, but of course they would say that if they had been bribed.' Below me in the inn yard, I see a stable boy loading saddle bags on to a horse. The sky is still banked with cloud, though lanced in places with spears of gold light. 'Everything points back to John Doughty having an accomplice on board.'

Sidney rises and taps his pipe out in the fireplace. 'Yes, but *who*?'

I throw my hands up. 'Well, if I knew that . . .' I catch sight of his face. 'Go on then – what is your solution?'

'You know the Spaniard has still not returned?'

'You take his disappearance as a confession?'

'Don't you? It makes sense. He knows he was seen in Dunne's

cabin that night. He has knowledge of medicinal herbs – he could have given Dunne the nutmeg. Perhaps he feared the investigation was coming too near him, so he decided to cut and run.'

'But why? What could be his motive?'

'Is it not obvious?'

'Not to me,' I say, but I already know what he is going to say and I feel my jaw tighten.

'The man is Spanish,' he says, simply. 'Our enemy by birth. It is unnatural that he should have pledged allegiance to Drake, given that the purpose of the voyage was to plunder Spanish ports. Come on, Bruno – consider the likelihood that he was sending intelligence to his countrymen. I'd wager Dunne found him out and meant to tell Drake.'

'So every man who is not a native Englishman is suspect? Not to be trusted?' I turn to face the room, leaning against the window ledge with my arms folded. The implication makes me angry, though I recall the girl Eve's words about Dunne having discovered that someone on board had a secret that would cost them. Could he have found out that Jonas was leaking information?

'I do not say that. But think about it – to betray Drake's mission from the inside, even to assassinate him with one of those potions, would be his passport back home. What better way to earn the gratitude of his sovereign and his compatriots, not to mention a substantial reward?'

'It is a neat theory,' I say. I cannot keep the coldness from my voice. 'But I offer you another – suppose he has vanished because he knew who killed Dunne?'

'Murdered, you mean?'

I shrug. 'If Dunne's killer is still in Plymouth, why not?'

He considers this. 'It's possible. Though until he turns up alive or dead, it is useless to speculate. Let us concentrate on what we have in our hand.'

'And what is that?' I kick a heel against the panelling,

frustrated with myself, with him, with Robert Dunne and whoever killed him. 'A clutch of useless hypotheses, with no proof save the testimony of a frightened whore. And a lot of bruises and a lighter purse to show for it.'

He laughs. 'Poor Bruno. The things you do for me. But we have one more thing up our sleeve that you forgot to mention.'

'What is that?' I extricate myself from his grip and rub my ribs.

'The address of Dunne's lodgings. We should go there before we are expected at this supper.' He makes a face. 'Drake has gone out to the ship this afternoon to meet Dom Antonio. He wanted me to go with him but I excused myself. Said I had to write my report to Walsingham. He grew anxious then and asked that I convey nothing of our present troubles.'

'Are you trying to avoid Dom Antonio?'

'Until I know what is happening with the voyage I must keep up this pretence that we are returning to London with him. He can't continue his journey until my armed men arrive, and Drake feels he is one more liability here, if there is a killer at large. You know Philip of Spain has offered a reward for his death too.'

'Dom Antonio's? I am feeling left out.'

'Don't worry, I'm sure Pope Gregory would like you dead, if he could reach you. It is quite the badge of honour, it seems, to have a head of state seeking your assassination. The only person who wants my hide is my wife, most of the time.'

'And the Queen, when she learns you have taken off for the New World without her permission.'

'Ah, yes. And her. Do you know' – he spins around to face me, eyes blazing – 'Drake actually suggested I should take Dom Antonio and the women and return to Buckland Abbey for a few days? Keep them out of all this, as he put it. What in God's name does he think I am?'

'Oh, I don't know – Dom Antonio's official escort, perhaps?'

He glares. 'I will not be dismissed by Drake again. Come

287

on. We cannot be the only ones who know about Dunne's lodgings here. If he left behind anything useful, let us make sure no one else finds it first.'

Rag Street is a steep, cobbled lane uphill from the harbourside. The sign of the Bear can be seen swinging from a three-storey house halfway along. There is no entrance except the low door to the tavern, so I push it open and Sidney follows me in, ducking his head to avoid the beam. This part of town looks as if it might once have known better fortunes than it enjoys now; though the houses are large, it is evidently a neighbourhood where a room and a meal could be got cheaply, and without anyone asking too many questions.

A few groups of drinkers, largely sailors by the look of them, sit around the benches by the fireplace with leather tankards between them; I feel their gaze slide over me and Sidney as we enter, but they soon return to their talk. We make straight for the harassed-looking woman who comes out from behind the serving hatch, wiping her hands on her apron and pushing her hair out of her eyes where it is coming loose from her cap. She stares at Sidney with naked amazement; it would seem she is not used to so much finery all in one place. He sweeps off his hat and makes a bow.

'Mistress,' he begins, with aplomb, then leans in and lowers his voice. 'We are looking for the lodgings of one Robert Dunne. We believe he stayed here?'

Immediately her face hardens. 'Friends of his, are you?'

'In a manner of speaking.'

'Well, I en't seen him for a good few days. I started to think he might have run out without paying what I'm due. Over a month's rent, he owes me.' She balls her hands into fists on her hips and glares from Sidney to me, as if expecting one of us to answer for him.

'I'm afraid, good madam, that Robert Dunne is dead.' Sidney adopts a sorrowful expression.

The woman puffs up her cheeks and blows the air out forcefully through pursed lips. 'Well, that explains it. I've been knocking on that door for days with no reply. Someone said there was a smell. How shall I get my money now?'

'He's not in the room,' Sidney says, sending me a quizzical glance. 'There is to be an inquest into his death tomorrow. I'm sure his debts will be taken care of once his estate is settled. We come at the request of his widow to look through his effects.'

'Widow?' She raises her eyebrows. 'Now there's a thing. I always thought he was a bachelor. Never mentioned no wife to me.'

'He didn't go home to visit her?' I ask.

'Not since he's been here, and that was just after May Day. This last week is the longest he's been away, that's why I thought something might have happened. There were those two men came here a couple of times looking for him – they haven't been back either. I wondered if he was in trouble.'

'What were they like, the two men?' I ask.

She shrugs. 'Well spoken, both of 'em. Not dressed up so fine as your friend here, but they had the look of gentlemen. At least the one with the beard did, for all he had so many teeth missing. The other spoke nice, but was obviously a wrong 'un – missing both ears, he was, though he tried to hide it under his hat. Eyes blue as cornflowers. Wasted in that ugly face. Not that I spoke to 'em much, mind. They didn't stop to chat.'

Sidney and I exchange a look.

'Can we see the room?' I ask.

'If you can get through a keyhole. Or under the door. Whoreson's locked it and taken the key with him, hasn't he? I want that back off him and all, 'fore he's buried. God rest him,' she adds, just in case.

'You don't have a spare?' Sidney frowns.

'I dare say there's one somewhere, but damned if I can find

it. My husband used to do all that. I haven't got round to it since he's been gone.'

'I'm sorry for your loss,' Sidney says, with a pious expression.

'Not as sorry as that bastard'll be when he gets tired of his whore and tries to come home,' she says, pressing her lips together. Sidney, for once, is lost for a reply.

'I can get through a keyhole,' I say. She looks at me.

'Come on, then.'

She leads us through a door at the back of the tavern into a small, dingy courtyard that smells as if all the residents empty their pisspots into it. At the back there is an archway with a door leading off it and another at the far end.

'That's the street entrance,' she says, indicating. She pushes open the first door, set into the wall. 'Second floor, the room at the front, facing inwards. If you do any damage forcing the door, I want paying for it.'

To my relief, she doesn't offer to accompany us. The stair-well is so quiet you can almost hear the dust swirling. From behind a door on the first floor comes a faint sound of moaning.

'Nice digs,' Sidney says. 'Imagine a gentleman, coming to this.'

'A lesson to stay away from the card table.'

'Some of us are luckier than others.'

'Robert Dunne probably thought that once. Lady Luck is more fickle than a street whore.'

The smell of piss is even stronger on the stairs, but there is something else too, a whiff of corruption that intensifies the higher we climb. Light is sieved through slats in the shut-ters; we feel our way, and the boards seem brittle and rotten beneath our feet. As we reach the second-floor landing, we disturb a cat from its slumber on a window seat; it snarls and darts away through our legs, making us both start and cry out, and then laugh with relief. The smell is worse here.

Sidney tries the catch of the door and gives it a little shake, just to be sure. 'Dear God, she is not mistaken. It smells as if something died in here.'

'Well, we know it wasn't Robert Dunne,' I say, moving him aside and kneeling to insert the blade of my knife into the keyhole. I work it for a few minutes, until the knife slips and nicks the edge of my finger. Cursing, I suck the blood away and return to the task.

Sidney leans against the wall, arms folded, watching.

'It is a fascinating trick, this. Are all Dominicans taught it?'

'Yes. We learn it as novices, along with our Aquinas. So that we can let ourselves into nuns' bedchambers with minimum fuss. Give me your hat pin.'

'What?'

'The one holding your feather in.' I look up. 'There are always sacrifices in the line of duty, Philip.'

He sighs, and passes the pin. I bend it into shape, then slide it into the lock alongside the blade of my knife. After a little effort I feel rather than hear the click, that perfect moment of alignment when everything fits into place and the shaft turns, drawing back the bolt.

'I will teach you one day,' I say, handing him the pin.

'Hardly an appropriate skill for the Countess of Pembroke's brother.'

'But a very apt one for Sir Francis Walsingham's son-in-law. Well, then.' I push the door open a crack, feeling my stomach contract as the smell worsens. 'Let us see what secrets Dunne left behind.'

The room is dark as a crypt, and smells as bad. The shutters are pulled tight across the window and blades of light slice through the darkness from the cracks between them. Taking a deep breath, I cross to the window, feeling a crunching beneath my boots as I do so. I lift the wooden bar that holds the shutters in place and pull them open; a forlorn light filters through the cracked glass.

'Christ and all His saints! Look at that!' Sidney jumps back as if he has stepped on hot coals, pointing at the boards; the floor of Dunne's room is writhing with white maggots, hundreds of them, like a living carpet. 'Where are they coming from?'

'There.' I point to a ragged blanket in one corner of the room, where fat sated flies circle lazily around whatever is concealed beneath. Sidney retreats to the doorway, gagging. I am almost inured to the smell of death after the church this morning, though I fear what we may find under the blanket. Before I have the stomach to lift it, I wrestle with the catch of the window; it sticks, but I shake it with greater urgency until something snaps and the casement creaks open, allowing a gust of air into the foul room. One or two flies make their escape. I exhale, gasping, and suck in a gulp of clean air.

'Sword,' I say, stretching out my hand to Sidney.

Reluctantly he unsheaths it and takes one step into the room, holding it, hilt-first, towards me. 'Try to keep it clean,' he says as I take it. 'It's mostly ornamental.' I give him a look and return to the pile of rags. Gingerly spearing one corner of the blanket with the point of the sword, I brace myself and whip it away, my left hand over my mouth. More flies, dislodged, swarm angrily upwards, as I stare at what lies beneath.

Behind me, I hear Sidney laughing. It sounds slightly hysterical.

'Poor fellow,' he says. His voice comes out strangled. 'Poor old boy. What have they done to you, eh?'

The corpse of a dog is slumped on its side in the corner, so heaving with flies and grubs that it almost seems to be moving. It looks to have been some kind of terrier, a ratting dog. Brown and white fur sticks up in tufts from the decaying flesh.

'Must have been Dunne's,' Sidney says, peering at it from a safe distance. 'I suppose it starved after he didn't come back for it.'

'In three days?' I shake my head. 'This dog has been dead longer than that. But look at all this.' I sweep a hand around the room. I am not sure what I had been expecting to find in Dunne's lodgings, but it was not a miniature apothecary's shop.

The room is L-shaped, with the shorter arm to the left of the door, where a pallet with a straw mattress leans against the wall. The only other furniture is a table strewn with dried leaves and flowers, sheets of paper, a metal bowl and tripod, a pestle and mortar and several glass bottles stoppered with corks. Beside these lies a pair of leather gloves.

'Come in, Philip, for God's sake, and close the door. They're only maggots, they won't bite. Do you know what this is?'

He sheaths his sword, pulling the door to behind him and gagging again as he does so. He picks his way across the maggots to look where I am pointing. As he reaches out to pick up one of the dark green leaves, I grab his wrist. 'Don't touch it. It is so deadly the poison can be absorbed through the skin. First your arm is paralysed, then your heart stops.'

'Monkshood?' he asks.

'Without a doubt.' I pull one of the gloves on to my right hand and pick up an elongated blue flower. 'One of the deadliest toxins known to man. Or beast,' I add, nodding towards the dog. 'It looks as if Robert Dunne had his own little poison laboratory here.' At the back of the table is a small vial of dark green glass with a silver stopper. I lift it; it is three-quarters full of a clear liquid.

'Intended for Drake, you think?' Sidney says, peering closer.

'He certainly meant it for someone – you don't make a tincture like this to cure stomach ache. It only takes a small dose – this could easily be smuggled on board and slipped into a glass. The effects are fatal almost immediately. As I suspect our four-legged friend there found out.'

The papers piled up on the table and beneath it bear witness to a disturbed mind; Dunne appeared to have been scribbling

293

in a frenzy and scattering the pages around him. Some look like recipes, listing measurements of leaves, seeds, roots and aqua vitae, with manic crossings-out and demonic faces scrawled in the margins. Others are the beginnings of letters never sent; these are more interesting. I shake a maggot off one of the sheets on the floor and begin to read aloud.

Dearest Martha,

I beg you to consider that God in His wisdom sometimes sees fit to answer our prayers in roundabout ways, by degrees and in unexpected guises. God He knows how long we have prayed for a child and here is an answer, though perhaps not the one you looked for. But this child we can raise as our own and keep the girl as nursemaid, and who will be any the wiser. I pray you do not dismiss it out of hand, wife, for sooner than you think I shall be a rich man, God willing, and we shall begin a clean page as I know you have long desired. I will no longer be the man I have been

The ink fades here and the letter ends, unsigned. I give a low whistle. Sidney shakes his head, incredulous.

'Did you ever hear such a thing? Perhaps that whore wasn't so foolish as she seemed – it was Dunne himself who was deluded. Did he seriously think to persuade his wife to take in his whore's child? And the girl too, under her roof?'

'Stranger things have happened.'

'You have met Martha Dunne. I should quake to serve her a dish she didn't like at supper, never mind cross her in this way. It seems the man's misplaced optimism extended beyond the card table.'

'Except where his immortal soul was concerned, apparently.' I unfold another balled-up page from under the table. Nothing of any real significance, nor the next. Then I smooth out a third, and my pulse quickens as my eyes skim it. 'Listen to this, Philip.'

Do you think your deeds will not find you out? You may be sure they will be judged by God and man. As for God's judgement, I leave that to your conscience, but if you wish to escape the censure of your fellow man, and most especially your captain on whose goodwill all our fortunes depend, you know my price. Another five will seal my lips for good.

'Blackmail?' Sidney looks at me, eyes wide. 'Who is it addressed to?'

I turn the paper over and back. 'No name. Damn it. So it was true – the girl Eve said Dunne had found out a wicked secret about one of his fellow sailors, one he said would cost the man dear, but she could tell me no name either. He was evidently threatening to inform Drake.'

'That explains the five gold angels.' He moves over to the window, sticks his head out and breathes deeply.

'It looks as if the fellow did pay up. Dunne must have been so pleased with his success he thought he'd try again.'

'But his lips *were* sealed for good,' Sidney says, grim-faced.

'What we don't know is whether these are drafts of letters he subsequently sent, or just idle scribblings,' I say. 'I wonder if his wife knew he had cooked up this plan with the girl.'

'One more reason for her to be rid of him,' he observes.

'And yet we stumble every time on the fact that his wife was a day's ride away at Dartington. So if she was behind it – who did the job for her?'

Sidney wanders back to the table; the crunching of maggots under the soles of his boots sets my teeth on edge.

'I cannot think clearly in this foul air,' he says. 'Let us bundle up these papers and read them somewhere else – I don't think I can bear another minute. You can take contagion from the dead, can you not?'

'If you get too close,' I say. 'Let us just be sure we have not missed anything.'

I stand in the middle of the room and allow my gaze to travel slowly around every corner, lifting my hand occasionally to swat away the flies.

'Do you suppose—' Sidney begins, but I hold up a hand to silence him as I freeze, alert to a sudden disturbance in the air, an interruption of the stillness. I turn slowly, straining my ears; the door I told him to close is only pushed to, a foot or so ajar, and now I hear it, an unmistakable creak on the boards outside.

'Who's there?'

There is no reply; only a taut silence, like the intake of breath. I gesture to Sidney; his hand is moving to his sword when there comes a noise – a soft whistle, a rush of air quicker than a heartbeat – then the thud of a blade hitting the cracked plaster behind me. Sidney yelps, a delayed reaction, and I stand, immobile, unsure which way to turn. After what feels like an eternity, but can only be a fraction of a heartbeat, I whip around, thinking he has been hit, but he is unharmed though white with shock, staring at the knife embedded in the wall.

In an instant I stir into action, hurl myself through the door and on to the landing, closely followed by Sidney; footsteps clatter on the stairs, two floors below by now. We give chase immediately; I almost lose my footing on the worn treads of the steps but by the time we reach the courtyard it is empty, the only sound the banging of the street door as it slams behind our mysterious assailant. With a hail of inventive curses, I wrench it open and see a figure fleeing around the corner. I make to run after him but the pain in my ribs becomes too much to bear and I have to slow down, gasping for breath; as I lean against a wall, doubled over, I see Sidney overtake me, nimble and long-limbed, right hand clasped around the hilt of his sword. When I have recovered my breath, I set off again in pursuit, rounding the corner into the next street to see Sidney gaining on the man and finally, in one impressive burst of speed, diving at his back and bringing him crashing to the ground. I catch up with them just in time to see the man struggle to his hands and knees, with Sidney standing over him, sword drawn. The man lifts his head and wipes away a trickle of blood from his nose.

'Good God,' Sidney says, as if he had run into an old acquaintance. 'Thomas Drake.'

SIXTEEN

Thomas looks equally amazed to see us; he rises slowly, brushing the filth of the street off his clothes and looking from Sidney to me, his face drained of colour.

'I thought . . .' he begins, but then his mouth keeps working, his jaw shaping words without sound. I know that I must look equally witless as I stare at him, but I cannot will myself to any sensible response. Sidney recovers faster; the blood rises back into his cheeks and it is as if the fury of the shock boils up and erupts in one motion, as he strides out and seizes Thomas's doublet by the buttons, bunching the cloth in his fist and pushing him up against the wall of a house.

'Christ in heaven – you tried to kill us!' he splutters, scrabbling to articulate his disbelief. 'You will answer for this, Thomas Drake. Who sent you?'

Drake's brother shakes his head like an agitated dog. His bravado has been punctured; his face is still pale as milk and he appears genuinely frightened.

'No one. That is to say – I came of my own accord. I didn't know it was you in there.'

'Really?' Sidney's voice drips with scorn, but he lets go of Thomas's clothes and allows him to slump against the wall. 'It was just coincidence, then, that you show up with a knife at Dunne's lodgings at the very time we are searching them? Something you didn't want us to find, is that it? Something that might incriminate you?' He wipes away flecks of spittle with the back of his hand; he is so angry I can see him shaking. His other hand is still on the pommel of his sword. 'Was it you he was blackmailing?'

'What?' Thomas Drake tugs his shirt and doublet into place and draws himself up a little; now that the immediate danger is over, the old hostility creeps back over his face. 'What are you talking about? How was I to know you would be there? I only found out this afternoon that Dunne had this lodging house. I thought—' He breaks off again and stares at Sidney, eyes lit with fury. 'What blackmail? Did you just accuse me of murder, Sir Philip?'

Sidney does not answer immediately; I see a muscle twitching in his cheek as he works to master himself. 'No, Thomas Drake,' he says, eventually. 'I asked if Robert Dunne had been blackmailing you.'

'And you implied thereby that I might have had reason to kill him. God's death!' He runs his hand through his hair and looks around, as if he is considering bolting up or down the street. Instead, he takes a deep breath and addresses himself to me, presumably to slight Sidney. 'I depend on my brother's success, as I am sure is painfully obvious to everyone. I am nothing without him. So you can see that I am the last person who would want to jeopardise this voyage, knowing how much he stands to lose. Do you not think' – here he turns to Sidney, raising his voice – 'that if I had wanted to be rid of Robert Dunne, I would have waited until we were out at sea and found some better means to contrive his end?'

'Like executing him for mutiny, you mean?' Sidney says, arching an eyebrow. 'That has proved an effective way for men like you to be rid of gentlemen, I believe.'

'Be careful, Philip Sidney,' Thomas says, in a voice that could cut through glass. He leans back against the wall. 'You are talking of matters about which you know nothing. That business with Thomas Doughty is long buried.'

Sidney opens his mouth to reply, then closes it again, but I see his knuckles whiten around the hilt of his sword.

'It's not buried very deep, though, is it?' I say. 'You don't believe that. The curse of John Doughty lives on.'

'No curse about it,' he says. 'John Doughty means to destroy my brother, or die in the attempt.' He glances along the street again and lowers his voice. 'When I came up those stairs today and heard voices in Dunne's room, I thought it must be him. That's why I threw the knife.'

Sidney gives me a sidelong look to see whether I believe this.

'Why did you assume it would be Doughty?' I try to ask this lightly, but it sounds like an accusation all the same.

He hesitates, then appears to relent.

'A fortnight ago, Jonas the Spaniard told me he had seen Dunne with a man he believed was John Doughty here in Plymouth.' He pauses, checking for passers-by. There is only one old woman, further up the street, sweeping her front step. 'I confronted Dunne in private. He denied it in the strongest terms, said he had not seen Doughty in years. He became agitated at the accusation, but anyone would. I did not take that as proof.'

'You did not tell Sir Francis this?'

Thomas makes a face. 'My brother is already obsessed with John Doughty, as you have seen.'

'With reason,' I murmur.

'I did not want to add fuel to his fears while he was occupied in preparations for such a complex enterprise,' Thomas continues, giving me a hard look. 'And I confess I was reluctant to take the Spaniard's word at face value. He is forever trying to ingratiate himself with my brother, perhaps because he knows his fellow sailors doubt him. I suspected this was one more such ploy. None of us had laid eyes on John Doughty for years, and Jonas admitted he had not seen the man close-to. To be frank, I supposed he was inventing it to make himself important, or to satisfy some grudge against Dunne. It was only when you said John Doughty had attacked you at the House of Vesta that I realised he could have been telling the truth.'

'And now Jonas is missing,' Sidney says.

'I don't trust him an inch,' he continues, when Thomas Drake has left us, clearly reluctant to let him off so easily.

'I know you don't. But he seemed honestly nonplussed at the mention of blackmail. I don't think he can be the one with the secret. I would swear he wasn't acting.'

'They are all acting,' Sidney says, grimly, as we head down-hill towards the harbour. 'One way or another.'

For a while we walk in silence, each turned inward to our own thoughts. 'What if Jonas killed Robert Dunne?' Sidney says, as we reach the door of the Star. 'No, hear me out – what if he killed him out of loyalty to Drake?'

'That is certainly a new twist on the business. Explain?'

'Think of the way Dunne was found,' he persists. 'Hanged by the neck. Then that verse sent to Drake from the Gospel of Matthew. Suppose *Jonas* sent it? To draw attention to the fact that Dunne died like Judas Iscariot, the very incarnation of treachery. What if the Spaniard did it to save Drake's life, because he saw Dunne plotting with John Doughty and feared Dunne meant to harm the Captain-General, but knew, after Thomas Drake's response, that his superior officers would not listen?'

'Then where is Jonas now?' I say, pausing in the entrance hall to look at him. 'Why did he not stay to receive a pat on the back from Drake for saving his life? Why dress it up as suicide, then send a hint that it was not?'

He gives me a scornful look. 'He could not expect Drake to reward him for killing a gentleman on a suspicion. It is my belief that he has run away to save Drake any scandal, like a loyal servant. The letter was meant as a clue to the truth.'

'This morning you were convinced Jonas was a traitor.'

'Well, I have thought further on the matter,' he says, with a touch of loftiness. 'And now I am persuaded it is the only plausible explanation. I would wager you a hundred pounds.'

'Let us not bet on it,' I say, at the turn of the stairs. 'Look where that led Robert Dunne.'

I lack the energy to argue, but I am not persuaded by his theory. Quite the contrary: a knot of apprehension tightens in my gut every time I think about Jonas and his unexplained disappearance. 'If we only knew who Dunne was blackmailing. I begin to feel the answer lies there. Five gold angels is a lot of money – how many men aboard the *Elizabeth* would be able to pay that?'

'Thomas Drake, for one,' Sidney says, aggrieved. He looks down at his hose where he fell in pursuit. 'Look at that. Horse shit all over me. I shall have to change before supper.'

We round the corner to our corridor to find Hetty lurking outside the door, making a desultory show of sweeping.

'Your sweetheart is back,' Sidney murmurs, taking out the key. Hetty leans on her broom and stares us down as we approach. I wonder how long she has been waiting.

'Do you want to know what I know?' she says, without preamble.

'How can I possibly know that until you tell me?' I say, though I am careful not to sound too impatient. Hetty's eyes and ears can venture places in this inn where I could never go.

She pouts. 'No point me telling you unless it's worth something to you to know,' she says, and resumes her half-hearted efforts with the broom.

Sidney unlocks the door, winks at me and closes it behind him, leaving me alone with her.

'How about you tell me what it is, and if I judge it to be valuable information, I make recompense accordingly?' I offer.

She looks at me, nonplussed.

'You got such a funny way of talking.' She sniffs. 'All right, then. That widow, the one you went out with this morning.'

'Mistress Dunne?'

'Her, yes. I seen her maid delivering a message. Want to know who to?'

'Of course.'

She is buoyant with the triumph of her knowledge; she looks as if she is in danger of exploding. 'That gentleman who came in this morning. Took a room upstairs for a few days.'

I frown, trying to work out who she means. She makes an impatient noise.

'*You* know him. He's with Captain Drake. Bald. Fine clothes. Feather in his hat. Talks to everyone like he's telling his dog not to shit in the hall.'

'You mean Sir William Savile?' I stare at her.

'Is that his name?' She looks uninterested in the finer details. 'Him, anyway. You were talking to him this morning downstairs, when the Captain was here,' she adds, to clarify.

'Yes, that's him.' I nod. 'And Mistress Dunne's servant was delivering a message to him? Are you sure?'

'Course I'm sure. She went to his room and put it under the door, I seen her. And about a half-hour later he delivered a reply. Want to know what it said?'

'How would you know that?' I ask, though I can already guess. By way of an answer, she reaches into the pocket of her apron and brandishes aloft a folded sheet of paper.

I cannot help laughing; she grins from ear to ear and holds out a grubby palm. I concede defeat and reach for my purse.

'And *that* is worth a penny at least,' she says sternly, in case I should think of cheating her.

'You can have a groat. But how did you come by it?' I ask, searching for a coin.

'He didn't know the two ladies had gone out. He slipped it under the door. But not quite far enough.' She takes the coin I offer between finger and thumb and regards it with considerable satisfaction. Whoever else may have benefitted, Robert Dunne's death is proving extremely profitable for Hetty.

'Thank you, Hetty,' I say, opening the door to my room. 'You have excelled yourself.'

'You can't take it away, sir,' she says, looking at me as if I am simple. 'Or they'll know. You'll have to read it quick and I'll slip it back before anyone knows it's missing. Won't take you long to read, it's only short.'

I open the paper. It says, simply,

Here. During supper.

I look up at Hetty. 'What does he mean by this? Where?'

She drops her gaze and twists the broom between her feet. 'Don't ask me, sir. I can't read it. I never learned.' She looks oddly vulnerable as she says this, and will not meet my eye.

I read the note aloud. She shrugs again. 'They're arranging to meet, I suppose. "Here" must mean in her chamber.' She sniffs. 'She don't waste time, eh? Husband not even cold and she's lined up another one to warm her bed.'

'And which is her chamber?'

She gives me a cool look, one eyebrow raised. 'Not sure I rightly remember.'

'Oh, for the love of God.' I reach into my purse and bring out another groat. 'Will this help, do you think?'

'It might.' The coin vanishes inside her apron. 'Second floor, end of the corridor. Looks out over the courtyard.'

'Don't mention this to anybody, Hetty,' I tell her, handing the paper back. 'Keep your mouth shut and your eyes and ears open and there could be more where that came from.' I pat my purse and her face lights up with a slow, greedy smile, though I don't trust her not to gossip the moment she is out of sight.

'I shall miss you, sir, when you have to go,' she remarks, as she picks up her broom. 'We've not had so much to-do here since the company of players came by in June.'

'Glad we are keeping you entertained,' I say, with a tight smile.

'By the way,' she adds, turning as she reaches the stairs, 'that other lady was looking for you earlier.'

'Which other lady?'

She pauses for effect. '*You* know. The one what was in your chamber last night.'

Before I can reply, she gives me a lascivious grin, hoists up her skirts and scurries away downstairs to her next intrigue.

SEVENTEEN

Drake's armed men are everywhere, positioned around the entrance hall and outside the door to the private dining room. They lend the place an air of unease, weapons bristling in their hands, light glinting off the edges of steel blades. People do not like their presence, you can tell; the atmosphere is subdued, the drinkers on their way to the tap-room keep their heads down and avoid conversation. It is almost as if we are already at war. Drake stands by the dining-room door, deep in conversation with one of the soldiers; when he sees Sidney and me coming down the stairs he beckons us to him with a nod. He does not smile.

'A word, if I may, gentlemen, before we dine.' He steers us into a window embrasure. 'Have you made any progress today?'

I watch him closely. Studying his broad, tanned face, I think of what this man has faced and lived to recount: day after day of looking death in the eye, of staring down tempests and waves higher than churches, together with all the fury of the elements, and learning to hold that implacable expression in place, his most important task as captain to keep panic at bay. On a ship of screaming, babbling men, terrified for their lives, he is the one man who must not show fear, or all is lost. It is this determinedly calm face that he presents to us now, but I can read the strain in his eyes. At sea, the forces arrayed against you are at least straightforward. Here, his enemy could be anywhere – including at his dining table tonight.

I give a brief account of my investigations, concluding with the discovery at Robert Dunne's lodgings. I do not mention Thomas and his knife. When Drake hears about the monks-hood and the dead dog, he cups a hand across his mouth and chin and nods silently.

'So it is true,' he says, just when I think he does not mean to speak at all. 'Or partly true.'

'It seems beyond doubt that Robert Dunne was experimenting with some kind of poison. It is hard to imagine for what purpose, if not to use against you, Sir Francis.'

Drake rubs his beard and his gaze wanders away to the window.

'I need you to read something for me,' he says, after a long pause, drawing out a letter from inside his doublet. Sidney holds out his hand but Drake hands the paper to me. 'In confidence,' he adds. His lips are pressed together and his jaw taut.

I unfold the paper, with Sidney reading over my shoulder.

'*Muy estimado Señor Capitan*,' it begins. The whole letter is in Castilian, written in a neat, slanting hand, though the ink is smudged along the left-hand margin.

'*Into your hands, my captain and friend, I place my true written confession, to which I swear before Almighty God . . .*'

The letter is signed Jonas Solon. It lays out his own account of how he suspected Robert Dunne of plotting against Drake and how, in defence of his captain, he gave the traitor a fatal draught and hung him from a beam to give the appearance of a suicide. Belatedly, he says, he realised that his action had only brought more grief to the expedition; to spare his beloved captain further trouble, he was leaving for destinations

307

unknown, his guilt and his fear of being discovered proving greater than his courage. He humbly hoped Drake and God (in that order) could forgive him. By the time you read this, he concludes, I will be far away. He is sorry not to have the chance to say farewell. Everything he did was done for love of his captain. He commends the voyage to God, etcetera, etcetera.

'You owe me a hundred pounds,' Sidney murmurs in my ear.

I look up from the page to meet Drake's expectant look. It is unclear whether or not he already knows its contents.

'You read Spanish?' I ask.

'I recognise some words. But I need to know precisely what this says. I was going to ask Gilbert to translate it, but on reflection I thought it best as few people as possible knew of it. Read it to me, would you?'

Keeping my voice low, I translate for Drake as closely as I can the text of Jonas's letter. His face remains drawn but impassive throughout. When I have done he rubs his forefinger along the edge of his beard and nods.

'So Jonas has decided to confess,' he says, after a long pause.

'And you do not believe it.'

He watches my face, his expression intent.

'Interesting. What makes you say that?'

I tap the paper. 'Because I don't believe Jonas wrote this either. The Spanish is not quite – how would you say it? It doesn't ring true. It's very good, no doubt about that, but there is the occasional construction, a turn of phrase now and again that strikes a false note. A native speaker would not express himself so.'

Drake nods again. 'I'm sure you are right. But I will give you an even more compelling case for its falsehood.' He pauses, his eyes flitting quickly from right to left, and lowers his voice. 'Jonas Solon is illiterate. He could not write so much as his own name.'

'Ah.' There is an eloquent silence, during which I make a commiserating face at Sidney. 'Unfortunate that whoever wrote this did not think to check on that fact first.'

'Yes,' Drake agrees. 'But it is not common knowledge. Jonas is ashamed. He makes every effort to conceal the fact. I was perhaps the only man aboard who knew, aside from my brother. So . . .' His eyes stray back to the letter in my hand with a significant expression.

'So someone else wrote this to incriminate him,' Sidney says, stating the obvious.

'But there would be no one to contradict this account,' I say, finishing Drake's thought for him. 'If it were read before the coroner's court tomorrow.'

Drake looks at me with appreciation. 'Once again, you see the situation clearly, Bruno. On the one hand, this could resolve my immediate problem. We have here a signed confession of murder. No need for a verdict of *felo de se* nor a lengthy investigation.'

'On the other, it rather raises the question of what has happened to Jonas,' Sidney cuts in. 'They will put out the hue and cry for him if they believe he is guilty of murder.'

'It would seem likely,' I say slowly, 'that whoever wrote this is fairly confident that Jonas will not appear to contradict it.'

'Truly, I fear the worst.' Drake sighs, and it seems to shake his whole frame. 'I have sent out four discreet men to search. I almost wish I could believe this,' he says, taking the letter back. 'It would be preferable to the alternative.'

'Take courage, Sir Francis – he may yet be found alive and well,' Sidney says, though he doesn't sound convinced.

'And if he is, he will be wanted for murder.' Drake stares out of the window, his face sunk in gloom.

'His illiteracy would then be evidence in his favour,' I point out. 'And besides, we will have found the real killer by then.'

'I wish I had your confidence, Bruno,' Drake says. And I wish I were sincere in it.

'Who else knows about this letter?'

'Only my brother. And my wife, though she does not know its contents – the letter was put under the door of her chamber this afternoon, addressed to me. I have asked the servants, of course, but no one saw anything.'

I would bet Sidney's hundred pounds I can find one who did.

'Who else on your ship speaks Spanish?'

'A few of my men can make themselves understood, I know that much, but well enough to write a letter like this?' He shakes his head. 'Only the educated ones, and even then I could not swear to it – I have never seen them write in Spanish.'

He tucks the letter inside his doublet, takes a breath and rolls his shoulders back. 'Let us go in. Say nothing to the others of this confession, but keep your eyes and ears open. Dom Antonio is expecting lively company and good cheer tonight. I am doing my best to hide this trouble from him. But the sooner he is away from Plymouth, the easier I will feel.' I note that he does not look at Sidney as he says this. 'In any case,' he continues, 'my wife is uneasy. She would be safer at Buckland, I feel.'

'Naturally,' Sidney says.

'So I have decided to stay ashore for tonight. To reassure her, you understand.' This time he does fix his eyes on Sidney, whose expression does not falter.

'A very sensible idea, Sir Francis,' he says, in a tone that belies the thoughts that must be running through his head. I find myself wondering about Lady Arden. Where will she be, in this new arrangement? On a mattress at the foot of their bed? Or will she move to a room of her own and, if so, who will be reassuring her tonight? Then I remember that Lady Arden still thinks I rejected her company last night in favour of a whorehouse; unless I correct this misunderstanding, she will want no reassurance from this quarter.

310

Gathered around the table in the wood-panelled dining room are the most favoured of Drake's captains, the men he keeps closest. Knollys is here, and Carleill, Walsingham's stepson; Captain Fenner and the others who dined with Drake that first evening. Sidney whispers the names of those he recognises. Here too are Pettifer the chaplain and Sir William Savile, who I notice has positioned himself close to the door. I am surprised to see Lady Drake and her cousin present. Lady Arden makes a point of busying herself with a piece of bread, but eventually she lifts her eyes and meets my gaze, holding it steady, her expression neither hostile nor particularly inviting. Then, when she is sure I am still watching, her attention slides away and fixes on Savile, whom she favours with a warm smile. She only spoils the effect of this by glancing quickly back to check that I have noticed.

At the head of the table, in the place of honour, is the man I must assume is Dom Antonio, Prior of Crato, once and future King of Portugal. Perhaps. He is a small, nervy man, with large sad eyes and a curling moustache that might once have been jaunty but now appears out of place and sorry for itself, much like its owner. He does not look like a king. He looks like a dog that expects to be kicked. That is what being hounded from your throne by Philip of Spain would do to you, I suppose. Yet he is nicknamed 'The Determined', and he must have at his core some undaunted flame of hope, or misplaced confidence; why else would he be back in England, soliciting Queen Elizabeth to raise another force on his behalf and end his exile?

Dom Antonio rises as we enter. Drake introduces Sidney and the Portuguese gives an elaborate bow.

'I can hardly find the words to express my gratitude to Her Majesty,' he says, clasping his hands to his chest, 'that she does me the honour of sending so great a courtier as you are known to be, sir, to escort me to her presence.'

He has at least perfected the art of flattering those whose help he depends on, I think, watching him; a trick I have not yet acquired, despite all my years in exile. I could learn from this man.

'The honour is mine, sir,' Sidney says, returning the bow, and once again I am impressed by his mastery of diplomacy. You would never guess from his smooth smile that he intends to leave Dom Antonio to the care of four rough soldiers while he himself absconds across an ocean.

Drake takes his place at Dom Antonio's right hand and waves Sidney to a seat next to him. I find a chair next to Pettifer, who greets me with reserved politeness and enquires after my day's labours. I have just embarked on a potted version when the door is flung open again and Gilbert Crosse appears, breathless and blinking rapidly, his glasses sliding to the end of his nose, apologising so earnestly for his lateness that he trips on all his words, which only makes him more awkward. Drake, laughing, waves away his apology and presents him to Dom Antonio. The Portuguese evidently thinks the newcomer's status does not warrant him rising from his chair, but then he leans forward, both hands on the edge of the table, and frowns.

'I have seen you before, sir, have I not?'

'*Before?*' Gilbert seems bewildered by the question; his face grows even more strained and anxious as he looks around the other guests as if one of us might know the correct answer. 'No, I don't think so, my lord. Begging your pardon,' he adds, bobbing his head meekly. He makes as if to sit down next to me, then stops, perhaps afraid that he is not supposed to sit in the presence of dignitaries without their express permission. It is the kind of detail I worried about when I first came to the French court.

'But I am sure – oh, if my memory were not so poor!' Dom Antonio laments, with a laconic wave that Gilbert interprets as leave to take his seat. 'So many countries I have visited

312

these past few years, so many houses, so many good Christian souls willing to take me in, and others not so good, all too ready to sell me for a handful of silver. Too many faces – they all begin to – how does one say? To blur.'

'Have you been to Antwerp, my lord?' Gilbert asks.

'Not recently.' Dom Antonio considers. 'No, I don't think it was in Antwerp.'

'Then I fear you may have confused me with someone else,' Gilbert stammers, blushing from his neck to the tips of his ears at having told a prince he is wrong.

'Perhaps,' Dom Antonio concedes, reluctantly, leaning back in his chair and fixing Gilbert with his melancholy eyes. 'Perhaps it will come back to me.'

Gilbert gives a polite little laugh and lowers his head, clearly hoping not to draw any further attention. 'I fear so many years of living in hiding have addled his wits,' he whispers to me. 'I have never seen the man before in my life.'

The first course passes without incident. Despite the presence of the ladies, the conversation among the men around me is all of arms and strategy, firepower and tonnage. No one mentions Dunne's death nor the disappearance of Jonas, as if by prior agreement. Maybe Drake has convinced these men that it will all be over by tomorrow. I try to keep up with the nautical talk but I do not understand many of the terms and soon my mind turns inward, sifting through the day's revelations in the hope that some meaning will emerge. At my side, Gilbert is listening earnestly and nodding, occasionally attempting to join a conversation by offering some insight from his calculations. I notice the captains for the most part ignore him. Perhaps they do not take him seriously – a navigator whose knowledge is all based on mathematical theory no doubt seems of little consequence to these hardened explorers.

All the while we are eating, I keep my eyes on Sir William Savile. The cut on his lip is healing, I notice. Drake said he had an altercation with Robert Dunne the evening he died, a tavern brawl that Savile did not want to discuss because he thought it beneath a gentleman's dignity. Dunne had set on him unprovoked, he said. That begins to look rather different in the light of the message Hetty showed me. As I study him, I am struck by a sudden memory of my conversation with Jonas in the rowing boat ashore last night, before he disappeared. We had been speaking in Spanish, and Savile joined in. Though he addressed us in English, he had clearly been following the conversation. So he speaks Spanish too. He glances up, catches me watching him and raises his glass with a merry grin. I return it, and lift my own towards him. I can match him for nonchalance; let him go to his rendezvous, thinking he is unobserved. In the meantime, I remind myself to make my attention less evident.

I do not have too long to wait. As soon as the serving boys return to carry out the dishes, Savile stands, stretches and announces with unnecessary volume that he has an appointment with the close stool. Beside me, Pettifer makes a prissy little tutting noise.

'I have sometimes observed,' he whispers, from the corner of his mouth, 'have not you, that men of breeding often display no evidence of it. Whereas men not gifted with the advantage of noble blood, but who have availed themselves of the benefits of scholarship, do often show more refined manners to the world, since they are more conscious of being judged. Men like you and me,' he adds, in case the point was not clear.

'Mm,' I say, watching the door as Savile slips out. 'Would you excuse me for a moment? I'm afraid I too must – you know.'

'Well, of course.' He looks put out; he had condescended to draw a parallel between us and I rebuffed him. But offending Pettifer is the least of my concerns at present. I excuse myself and squeeze past the seated guests and the serving boys to the door. Sidney gives me a questioning look as I leave; I gesture with my eyes to Savile's empty chair.

The entrance hall is quieter now; perhaps everyone is in the tap-room for supper. I take the stairs to the second floor and tread as quietly as I can along the creaking corridor, following the directions Hetty gave me to Mistress Dunne's chamber. Wan evening light falls, slanted, across the bare boards. All the doors along the passageway are shut, but I hear the murmur of voices, muted, from one at the end, on the side that faces the courtyard. I slow my steps, keeping against the wall, where the boards make less noise under my weight.

'But how did you allow this to happen?' A woman's voice, tight with anger.

'If you would let me explain . . .' Savile's voice, placatory, wheedling. 'Fate was against me—'

'Fate! Do not talk to me of fate, William – you have marred everything, you alone.'

'How many times must I say it – there was nothing I could do, the priest was with him.' Savile's voice rises, growing defensive. 'Besides, it is done now. You have the end you wanted, one way or another.'

'You think *this* was what I wanted?' She makes an explosive sound through her lips. 'God preserve me from foolish men. How does any of this serve us?'

'Martha, you know I did not intend—'

This is where I make an error of judgement. I am too anxious to see how they interact with one another, the subtle cues of gesture and touch that often express better than words the relationship of one person to another. I want to ascertain the degree of intimacy between these people who claim to have barely met. As I move closer and crouch to put my eye to the keyhole, the floor betrays me with a loud groan and Savile breaks off without finishing his sentence; I can almost hear the tension bristling as he strains to listen. The rustle of

315

frantic whispering rises inside the room; Savile hisses, '*You go – I cannot be seen coming out of your chamber.*'

I hear movement; if they find me here, any advantage I have will be lost. I try the next door along the passage; to my surprise, it opens and I find myself in an empty bed-chamber. I slip the pin under the latch, just in case.

There follows the sound of a door opening, the creak of boards in the corridor, some scuffling, more hurried whispering, then the click of a door closing again and footsteps outside, fading towards the stairs. From Mistress Dunne's room comes a sound like a muffled sob, but which might just as well be laughter.

When I am sure that no one is stirring outside, I leave the room as quietly as possible and pick my way towards the stairs. As I round the corner I collide with Hetty, a leather jug in her hand. Liquid slops over the rim and splashes both of us; she swears colourfully, though I am relieved to find it is only water.

'You're in a hurry, sir,' she observes, wiping herself down with a sly smile. 'Looking for something?'

'The gentleman you mentioned earlier, the bald one who left the message – did you see him?'

'Just this second pushed past me. Went down to the dining room, he did.'

'Thank you.' I hesitate. 'Where would I find his chamber, if I wanted to leave him a message?'

'Why would you need to do that, sir? You're having supper with him, as I recall.'

She feigns an uncomprehending look; I give her a stern glare.

'I do not have my purse on me. Just tell me, will you?'

She gives me a pitying look, as if this lie is so feeble it hardly bears the telling.

'I'm afraid I don't recall which room he has, sir.'

I suck in my cheeks, but I reach inside my doublet for my purse just the same.

'By Christ, Hetty, you should be a usurer, you would bleed a man dry in no time.'

'God helps those as help themselves, Mistress Judith says.'

'I'm sure she does. A groat, no more. It is all I can spare. Tell me something else, since you know everything – did you notice anyone leaving a message at Lady Drake's door this afternoon?'

'Lady Drake? Why, has she got a secret sweetheart too?'

'No,' I say firmly, before she can run with any rumours. 'Someone left a letter for Sir Francis. He is particularly keen to find out who it was.'

She pockets the money with a serene smile. 'I was washing the floor in the tap-room this afternoon. Never went near Lady Drake's chamber. Sorry.'

'And you didn't notice anyone behaving oddly? No one hanging about who should not have been?'

She makes a derisive noise through her nose. 'Everyone behaves oddly round here, sir. How would I know the difference?' She tucks her pitcher into the crook of her arm. 'First floor, you want – turn right at the stairs, third door along. Facing the yard.'

'Thank you. And it is a private message, so . . .' I mime sealing my lips. She merely arches an eyebrow and continues on her way. She would lie to me as soon as look at me, I have no doubt of it, though for as long as I have an open purse she has decided to favour me, it seems.

Luck is on my side; the first-floor corridor is empty. I could have made use of Sidney's hat pin, but he is not here; I must do my best with the thin blade of my knife. Though I nick my fingers several times in the process, the lock eventually yields and I open Savile's room.

There is nothing here except a short cloak laid out on the bed and his leather bag. I lift the flap and begin to look through the contents. Nothing of any special interest; only a few clothes, hastily packed, which should make it less obvious that I have been rummaging through his belongings. Like Sidney, Savile is fond of his fine clothes, and appears not to have considered how much use these silk and brocade doublets will be in the middle of the Atlantic. I curse softly, striking my knee with my fist; there is nothing conclusive here, nothing to prove the exact meaning of Savile's elliptical conversation with Mistress Dunne. If only I had stayed quiet and heard more. What does she think he has marred? What did he mean by 'the end you wanted' – surely a reference to her husband's death?

At the bottom of the bag I draw out a pair of sleeves of fawn-coloured silk; I give them a cursory glance and am about to fold and replace them when I notice that the cuffs are decorated with tiny mother-of-pearl buttons in the shape of a flower, a line of four on each. Except that on one sleeve, there are only three. I hold it up to examine it more closely. There is a brownish stain near the lace trim; I rub it with my thumb and a powdery substance adheres to my skin. I sniff it just to be sure, but I already know what I have found. The sleeve with the missing button smells of nutmeg.

EIGHTEEN

I pause outside the dining room to lean against the wall, slow my breathing and compose my expression. Savile must not suspect anything until I have had a chance to speak to Drake and let him decide how to proceed, though Savile is sharp enough to mark my empty place at the table and perhaps connect it with the sounds he heard upstairs. If not, he will certainly notice something amiss when he realises his room has been left unlocked. It is one thing to pick a lock, another altogether to close it again, and I gave up for fear of breaking the mechanism. After some deliberation, I left the sleeves in the bag; though I would have liked to show Drake the evidence, I reasoned that Savile must be unaware that he has lost a button, or that it could incriminate him.

I wait until I am sure I can enter the room with a neutral expression. It is a talent of sorts, this ability to keep my most turbulent thoughts from being read in my face. It would have served me well in the politics of religious life, but it is useful enough in this strange existence I ended up with instead. Savile turns his head briefly as I take my seat, his glance mildly curious, though he quickly returns to his audience; he is regaling Dom Antonio and Drake with some tale that involves exuberant arm gestures. The Portuguese is laughing politely.

Drake wears a fixed smile, but he is looking past Savile to the panelling on the wall, his thoughts elsewhere.

I spear a piece of pork on my knife and when I look up again Savile has reached the climax of his tale; the men around him are laughing, though none so heartily as the teller himself. I lay the knife down and cast my gaze around the table. The drone of conversation begins to sound distant, like a swarm of bees on the other side of a window; I seem to see their mouths moving – talking, chewing, laughing – as if time had slowed and I was standing outside, looking on. The whole atmosphere here feels infected with suspicion, bluff and counter-bluff, falsehood and fear, as if we are all of us engaged in some grand card game where the stakes are men's lives and the winner will be the one with the greatest skill at lying. And the men who are dealing the cards are somewhere out of sight, still hiding in the shadows.

Gilbert does not speak much for the rest of the meal, except to remark on the appetites of others, though I see his eyes flit from one speaker to another, always attentive to the conversations around him. A great wave of tiredness breaks over me. I find myself longing to leave this company and fall on my bed, close my eyes, embrace oblivion. Though this is wishful thinking; my mind will be too busy turning over the day's revelations for sleep to come. I may as well make use of the time by working.

When the board has been cleared the ladies announce that they are retiring; we all stand as they leave and wish them a good night. Lady Arden looks back over her shoulder at me as she reaches the door and briefly smiles. After they have gone, there is a general stirring; some go out to piss in the inn yard, others take the opportunity to stretch and move around the table, others take out clay pipes and tobacco pouches. I excuse myself from my dining companions and ease my way around to Drake, who stands to greet me.

'Sir Francis, may I take the book tonight?' I ask, in a whisper. He frowns, glancing towards his brother.

'What for?'

'To continue working. I could finish the translation by morning, if I put my mind to it.' If I set to work now, I may just be able to rewrite the pages that were taken from my room, and I need not confess the theft to Drake.

A smile briefly creases the corners of his eyes. 'I can't help thinking you would do better to get some sleep, Bruno. Take a look at yourself.'

'I would sleep easier, sir, if there was a complete copy of that book. For safekeeping.'

'You really think someone will attempt to steal it?'

'I think that bookseller you met wants it very badly. He is a ruthless man with no scruples.'

He considers, glancing back at his brother. 'Well . . . Thomas will not like it. He already thinks you mean to use the copy for your own profit – he will be even less keen to trust you with the original. Padre Pettifer has warned me in the strongest terms against making the translation – he says no good can come of spreading heresy and I would be calling God's curse down on the voyage.' He shakes his head. 'I begin to think I have done so already.'

'Do not say so, sir. None of this is your doing. Nor is it God's displeasure. We are close to finding the man responsible for Dunne's death, I am sure of it.'

'I wish I were. I cannot tell you how sick I am at heart when I think of Jonas. Every moment I expect a messenger to tell me they have found him.' He heaves a sigh and lays a hand on my shoulder. 'Take the book for tonight, then. I would offer you one of my armed men, but I have promised them to Dom Antonio. Besides' – he looks me up and down – 'I'd wager you can take care of yourself if anyone comes knocking. Come and collect it now – I mean to retire early tonight.'

'Quite right too, Sir Francis – if I had a beautiful wife in town I would do the same.' Savile appears behind me, throwing an easy arm around my shoulder the way Sidney does. I try not to tense. I wonder how much he has overheard. 'Meanwhile, we lonely bachelors must seek solace in the bottle and the card table. Will you join us, Bruno? You seem like a man who has a face for gambling.'

'You think?' I say, with a perfectly blank expression.

'There, what did I tell you – you are doing it now!' He claps me on the back as if I have performed a trick. 'You are adept at hiding your true self. An invaluable skill for the card table. One poor Robert Dunne never mastered, alas.'

'The same may be said of most of us, do you not think, Sir William?' I say, with a pleasant smile. 'But I'm afraid I must decline. I have no taste for risk.'

'You surprise me,' he says, and I detect an edge to his voice, but perhaps I imagine it.

It takes Drake some time to extricate himself from the lengthy farewells, especially with Dom Antonio, who has become quite emotional with all the wine, and embraces Drake several times over, brushing tears from the corners of his eyes as his speeches grow more effusive and less coherent. Sidney tells me he plans to join the card game; I wish him luck and tell him to keep an eye on Savile, note if he does or says anything unusual. Sidney gives me a quizzical look, but Drake gestures for me to follow him and I have no chance to elaborate.

One of the armed guards accompanies us up the stairs to the first floor. Another is already stationed outside the door of Lady Drake's chamber. Drake nods to him and pauses, his hand on the latch, as if gathering his thoughts before going in to his wife. I almost speak, thinking I should tell him what I have discovered about Savile. Instinct checks me; Savile will not run anywhere tonight. He has the arrogance to believe he is above suspicion and I would need stronger proof before I accuse him outright.

A small fire has been lit in Drake's chamber and the air is warm and smells of woodsmoke. Lady Drake sits close to the hearth, her maidservant is perched on the window seat, sewing. Lady Arden stands by the fireplace, a small bag at her feet.

'Ladies.' Drake sweeps across the room and unlocks a wooden chest placed beside the bed. 'I hope you are not too fatigued by this evening.' He withdraws from the chest the leather satchel containing the book.

'Not at all, Francis,' Lady Drake says. 'Dom Antonio is quite the storyteller, is he not? So very many tales of escape and subterfuge, one could listen to him all night. And indeed, I feel I have.'

'I feel I have lived through every minute of his adventures with him,' Lady Arden says, with a wicked grin.

'Now, now, ladies – be kind. Dom Antonio is a good man who has suffered a great deal at the hands of Spain. Besides, he is our ally.'

'Not in any useful sense,' Lady Arden says, with a snort. 'He lacks the support for a successful uprising in his own country. Queen Elizabeth may offer Dom Antonio hospitality because she pities him, but she is too prudent to throw good money after a hopeless cause.'

Drake looks at her as if he has just witnessed a talking dog.

'You are very well informed, my lady,' I say, impressed.

'Did I not tell you I had plenty of opinions to share?' she says, with an impish smile.

'Here.' Drake pushes the bag into my hands, but does not let go of it. 'You are sure you can keep it safe?' He looks as if he is wavering; perhaps he is picturing his brother's response if Thomas were to discover that I had taken the book unsupervised.

'I will guard it with my life, Sir Francis.' It may yet come to that, I think. If he knew I had allowed the copy to be stolen, he would not let me within a mile of it. I notice Lady Arden's eyes rest on the bag with interest.

Drake nods and slowly releases it into my hands.

'Return it to me here first thing tomorrow,' he says. 'Keep your room locked tonight. And perhaps when this inquest is over we will have more leisure to discuss what to do with it, once we know its contents.'

I nod, and turn to leave.

'Lady Arden,' Drake says, 'let me call for a servant to take your bag up for you.'

'Oh, please do not trouble yourself, Sir Francis,' she says quickly, 'I thought perhaps Doctor Bruno might carry it for me.'

I look at her; she meets my gaze with innocent eyes.

'Doctor Bruno is not a porter,' Drake says, a little embarrassed.

'But it is on his way – I'm sure it would be no trouble,' she persists. 'My maidservant is waiting for me in the room.'

'I am happy to help,' I say, not wishing to appear over-eager.

'Well, if you don't mind . . .' Drake looks doubtful, but he opens the door for me. I pick up Lady Arden's bag and gesture to her to lead the way, with a bow to Lady Drake as I take my leave.

'I have been banished to a room of my own while Sir Francis is ashore, you see,' Lady Arden explains, when the door has closed behind us.

'You are not afraid to stay on your own?' I follow her to the stairs.

She laughs. 'What should I be afraid of?'

'This present business. The letter left under Lady Drake's door earlier. Your cousin was anxious, Sir Francis said.'

'*He* was anxious, you mean. But I am not sure it is mysterious correspondents that concern him so much. I think rather he means to deter any visitors.'

'Ah. No sonnets for Lady Drake tonight, then.'

'Alas, no. And do you and Sir Philip intend to sample the diversions of Plymouth again tonight?' she asks sweetly, as we reach the second-floor landing.

'My lady – I was not – my aim last night was to find out some information that might help Sir Francis.'

She turns to me and raises an eyebrow.

'That is to say – in the matter of this death. Nothing more.' I sound unusually incoherent.

She gives a light laugh. 'You do not have to justify yourself to me, Doctor Bruno. You are free to visit all the whores you want. Here, this is my chamber for tonight.' She stops in front of a door and I realise it is the chamber next to Mistress Dunne's, where I hid earlier. I put down her bag at my feet and pause, listening for any sound from the neighbouring room. There is only the low murmur of women's voices.

'Even so. I would like you to know I do not make a habit of visiting whorehouses.'

She looks up at me. A faint smile plays about her lips; I suspect it is at my expense.

'Unlike my cousin, I find I am at liberty to hear sonnets this evening. Sir Philip mentioned that you are something of a poet.' Her gaze is direct now; it would be hard to misinterpret her meaning. The leather bag containing the Judas book hangs across my shoulder; it seems I have a stark choice.

'My poems are all in Italian,' I say softly.

'So much the better.' She smiles. 'I shall be spared the awkwardness of judging whether they are any good or not.'

She lays a hand on my sleeve as she pushes open the door, but even now I hang back, feeling the weight of the book around my neck. She senses my hesitation. 'Besides,' she says, 'I know something that may be of interest to you in *this present business*, as you call it. And I'll wager no one else has noted it.'

'Really? And what is that?'

She adopts a coquettish smile. 'I will tell you in return for a poem.'

Everyone here is bartering information, it seems. I glance up the corridor towards the stairs. For a moment I think I

325

see a stirring in the shadows, the outline of a figure, but when I look again there is nothing.

'Your maidservant,' I whisper, indicating the door.

'I have given her the evening off. I dare say she is amusing herself somewhere, gossiping, or flirting with sailors. You might carry my bag in for me, at least.'

What would Sidney say if he could see me, I wonder as I follow her over the threshold and hear the door close behind me. He would tell me I needed to live a little; to forego the rigours of books occasionally for the solace of a warm, willing body. He would tell me bluntly that it is fruitless to stay true to the memory of a woman who is long gone, over the sea; he would say that I am a fool to deny myself pleasure, or even the chance of love, for the sake of someone who, in any case, left me without compunction. But perhaps he would not understand the melancholy that steals over me every time I consider the possibility of transferring my affection to another woman. Of course, he would counter that you don't need affection for a woman to lie down with her, though as I grow older, I find that an empty kind of solace without it.

'There is no fire here,' she says. 'I can have one lit, if you prefer.'

'I am warm enough, thank you.'

'Yes, you look a little flushed.' She smiles. 'Do I frighten you, Doctor Bruno?' I shake my head. She seems disappointed. 'I thought perhaps you might find me too bold.'

I do not tell her that I encountered plenty of bold women at the court of King Henri in Paris; young wives bored by their ageing, impotent husbands, all too willing to throw themselves into the path of any young man at court for the fleeting excitement of a little intrigue, especially if he was exotic-looking and trailed a dangerous reputation. I was an object of fascination to them because I seemed immune to their charms. In truth, their heads were so empty of any thoughts beyond court gossip and their own appearance, I

326

grew weary of their company before they had even finished saying *Bonjour*. Besides, a man of low birth promoted beyond his station must be careful where he makes enemies. But there are no such considerations to stop me here. I look at Lady Arden. Her room faces west; evening light falls on her face, gilding the soft skin of her cheek and the curls of dark hair across it. Holding my gaze, she reaches up and unpins her hood.

'I find you refreshingly free of false coyness,' I say, after a long pause.

She laughs again, shaking her head so that a glossy fall of hair tumbles down her back. 'That is a diplomatic answer, if ever I heard one. Well, then – let me hear a sonnet and in return I shall tell you a secret that is not mine to tell.'

So I recite from memory a sonnet I wrote years ago. I close my eyes as I speak and the words jolt me back to a different time, to snowy peaks against high blue mountain skies; to narrow passes, freezing nights, hunger and exhaustion; the fear of going forward vying with the impossibility of going back. When I have finished she exhales slowly, as if she has been holding her breath.

'That sounded beautiful. What is it about?'

'It . . .' I falter, unsure how to explain words that flow so naturally in my own tongue, fearing the poem will seem lumpen and unnatural in English. 'It is addressed to a lonely sparrow. It tells the bird to fly away and be reborn, to find a nobler destiny. It's an allegory,' I add, feeling wrong-footed. She is still looking at me intently, a small furrow between her brows.

'Of what?'

I shrug. 'Of the soul. And of letting go of what you love.'

'Say the last line again.'

'"*E non tornar a me, se non sei mio*."'

'What does it mean?'

'And don't come back to me, unless you're mine.'

She nods, slowly. 'Did you write it for a woman?'

'No. I wrote it eight years ago, when I was crossing the Alps from Geneva into France, and I understood clearly that I would never see my home or my family again.' But poems change their meaning, even those you write yourself; they fit themselves to your understanding of your own life over time. When I say that final line now, I think of a woman, and it is as if I wrote it for her, long before the fact.

Lady Arden crosses the room and stands in front of me.

'Are you lonely?'

'Sometimes,' I say. My voice catches in my throat. 'Often.'

'As am I.' She reaches out and places her hands gently on my shoulders. My hands move instinctively to her waist. We stand like this for what seems a long time, listening to the stillness and the soft rhythm of our breath.

'You promised me a secret,' I whisper, my lips against her brow.

'Later,' she says. Her hand strays across my chest to the opening at the neck of my shirt and slips inside, her fingers cool on my skin. She moves closer, and her lips part slightly as she presses her hip against me and feels my arousal. Her mouth hovers over mine, so near I can taste her breath, as she continues to unlace my shirt. Her fingers reach my belly and she tugs at the leather strap of the satchel I still carry slung across my shoulder. 'You may have to put this down,' she murmurs.

'Lock the door,' I say, lifting the bag over my head, and she obeys, then takes me by the hand and leads me to the narrow bed as she loosens her bodice. She undresses herself with a sense of urgency, her bright eyes fixed on me all the while, gauging my response; there is an efficiency in the way she goes about it that eliminates any need for the usual dance of seduction, the importuning on my part and feigned resistance on hers. Lady Arden, I conclude as she pushes me on to my back and takes me in her hand with a practised movement, is used to getting what she wants, once she has decided on it. I recall what Sidney said about widows: they are dangerous because they don't need you. But they still need you for this, I think, closing my eyes.

She kisses me hard, taking her pleasure hungrily as she slips out of her skirts and sits astride me, forcing me to move to her rhythm, and if the thought crosses my mind that perhaps she would have chosen anyone so long as his face and manner pleased her, and that I just happened to be convenient, it hardly matters. This is no more than a fleeting pleasure, and there is no reason on either side to pretend otherwise; no one is being deceived here, and there is something simple and liberating about this fact. We are two strangers attracted to each other, and will likely not meet again after this brief interlude; we expect nothing of one another. Sidney is right: simple pleasure is one thing I allow myself too little of. And so I abandon myself to it: I slide my hands around her small waist and arch my hips further into her, and when she cries out softly amid snatched breaths, her eyes gleaming, lips parted, I roll her carefully on to her back and she lifts her legs to wrap her thighs around my sides, crushing my bruised ribs so hard that I cry out, and she giggles, pressing her hand to my mouth as I move slowly towards my own crescendo. But when I close my eyes and gasp my release, it is not her I am thinking of.

Afterwards, she lies with her head on my shoulder, her hair fanning out over the pillow, her left hand stroking my chest in abstract patterns. She props herself up on one elbow, a provocative smile twitching at the corners of her mouth.

'How did that compare with last night?'

I smile.

'Well – considering that last night I was drugged, attacked and jumped out of a first-floor window, I would say quite favourably.'

She gives me a light slap on the arm. 'I meant, the girl you had last night.'

'I did not have a girl last night, I told you. I have not had a girl for a long time.' I turn my face away as I say this. 'Tell me this secret you promised, then.'

I feel her tense against me and her hand falls still. I realise I should have waited; I have implied that what we have just done was mere prologue to the real object of my interest.

'Mistress Martha Dunne is with child,' she says idly, looking at the ceiling.

'What?' I sit up, staring down at her. She sprawls on her back, coiling a twist of hair around one finger, and gives me a lazy smile. 'How can you be sure?'

'I told you, my sister has four. It's early still, but once you know the signs, they are easy to spot. Small wonder she is so keen to contest a verdict of suicide – she won't want to lose her husband's property if she has a child to raise.' She stretches her arms above her head and traces a finger down my spine, though I am too busy fitting this new revelation into the picture to pay much attention.

'She did not tell you this directly, though?'

'Oh, no. She was hardly likely to confide anything in us – I think she resented having to speak to my cousin and me at all, but Sir Francis seemed determined she should have the company of women. I thought you might be interested precisely because she seems to be at pains to conceal the fact.'

'You cannot account for people's behaviour when they are grieving.' I pull the sheet around my knees and hug them to my chest, my thoughts still racing, tripping over one another. She gives a little snort.

'I have never seen any widow look less grief-stricken,' she says. 'Unless perhaps myself.'

She laughs, and her fingers flutter up and down my back again. I shiver, and swing my legs over the side on to the floor.

'Where are you going?' she asks. An injured note has crept into her voice.

'I'm afraid I have work to do.' I smile, to take the sting from my hasty departure.

'Not so soon.' She pouts, rolls over on to her front and reaches for my hand. 'You can work later, surely?'

'The night is short and I must finish this before tomorrow. Besides, my lady, your maid will want her bed and I cannot be seen coming from your room in the morning. I could not risk the damage to your honour.'

She rests her chin on her hands, regarding me with her head on one side.

'"My lady", is it, still?' She laughs. There is a resigned note to it. 'You have better manners than many a nobleman I have met, Bruno.'

I step back, out of her reach, and search for my shirt. 'Is that my appeal?'

She looks hurt. 'Is that what you think? That I was curious to try someone who was not of noble blood – what, for variety? For comparison?' She gives me a long look. 'Your appeal, Bruno, is who you are. All of you. I am not indulging some taste for low-born men, if that is what you suppose. This is not a habit for me either, you know.' She sounds – understandably – offended.

'I apologise, my lady.' I pull my shirt over my head.

'Perhaps, in future, you might leave "my lady" at the bed-chamber door,' she says.

In future? 'You know I have nothing to offer you,' I say simply, and hold my hands out, empty.

She lowers her lashes and gives me a sly smile. 'Well, I would not say that.' She sits up straighter. 'Listen, Bruno – I do not need a man to bring me land and titles. I have those already. I am fortunate in having the freedom to choose someone who can hold my interest purely for his own qualities.'

'Then I am flattered.' Perhaps I should say more, but I am unfamiliar with the etiquette of such encounters. I hurry into

331

the rest of my clothes and pick up the bag with the manuscript. At the door she calls me back.

'I think you have forgotten something.'

I look down at myself; I am fairly sure I have all my clothes, though they are somewhat disarrayed. More importantly, I have the book. She kneels up on the bed, the sheet held loosely against her so it barely covers her small, neat breasts. She tilts her chin expectantly and I am upbraided again by my own lack of gallantry; I cross the room, sweep her up in a dramatic gesture and crush her mouth with mine. She tries to pull me back to the bed but I extricate myself and blow her a final kiss from the door.

As it closes behind me, I pause in the dim corridor to catch my breath. I feel unexpectedly exhilarated, though it is also a relief to be returning to my own room. I am still smiling to myself when I round the corner by the stairs and walk straight into William Savile.

'Doctor Bruno!' he exclaims, as if he could not be more delighted to run into me. I have to admire the way he manages to look completely unruffled. 'But your chamber is not on this floor, is it?'

'Neither is yours,' I say. His smile fades. He watches me for a moment, then lets out a hearty guffaw and slaps me on the shoulder.

'I do believe you are right. What is this – the second floor? God's bones – a few too many glasses of Rhenish and I can't even find my way back to my room. What a fool! You too, eh?' The smile remains fixed, but his eyes narrow.

'Me too,' I say, moving past him. I see his eyes drop to the bag. 'Give you good night, sir.'

'Give you good night.' He hesitates, then retraces his steps behind me, but very slowly.

'You smell of quim,' Sidney says, as I enter our chamber. He is lying on the bed, fully clothed, his hands folded behind his head.

'I am amazed you can smell anything through the fog of wine around you.' I lock the door and sit down on a cushion by the hearth, the bag in my lap.

'Well, at least one of us has had some satisfaction tonight,' he grumbles. 'I lost five shillings to that preening fool Savile.'

'Not such a fool, then. The man is certainly skilled at deception, I will grant him that. Listen to this.'

He sits up and listens, cross-legged on the bed, as I unfold everything I have learned today about Savile and Mistress Dunne. His eyes grow wider and he whistles when I come to the part about searching Savile's room, the missing button and the scent of nutmeg.

'Well, that certainly throws a different light on matters.' He stands, stretching his arms out.

'We have been looking in the wrong place all this time,' I say. 'We assumed Dunne's death was linked to his association with John Doughty and Rowland Jenkes – we didn't consider the possibility that he might have been killed for another reason altogether.'

'Did we not say his wife had the most to gain from his murder, but not the means? But if she and Savile are involved they could have planned it together.' His face is bright with excitement.

'Wait until you hear the strangest of all. Lady Arden is convinced Mistress Dunne is with child.'

He frowns. 'Is that so outlandish?'

'It is if she has not seen her husband for months.'

'Well I never. But what did she mean when she said he had marred all? Marred what, I wonder?'

'Presumably it was not part of the plan to dress up his murder as a suicide – she gains nothing from that, as we have seen. But perhaps they had to rush the business if she found she was with child.' I cross to the window and open the casement, lifting my face to the chill evening air. 'Neither the girl Eve nor Dunne's landlady seemed to think he had left Plymouth since he arrived. But Mistress Dunne made very sure to mention to me that he had visited her around three months ago. She wanted to avert suspicion, in case her condition came to light, I suppose.' I turn back to face him. 'Perhaps the original plan was for Savile to kill Dunne discreetly during the voyage. Then Martha Dunne would come into her inheritance, a wealthy widow with no feckless husband to gamble it all away. And Savile could come back and offer to marry her.'

'But the child must have thrown that plan into disarray – it meant they had to get rid of Dunne sooner, because he would have known for certain her pregnancy was none of his doing.' He slams his fist into the palm of his hand. 'By God, I think we have it! And Dunne had begun to suspect – that must be why he threw a punch at Savile that night.' He jumps to his feet. 'What are we waiting for? We should take this to Drake immediately and he can go straight to Savile's room with his armed men and confront him.'

'I don't think Savile is in his room. I caught him prowling about the second floor – on his way to her, I imagine. He pretended he was lost. As did I.'

Sidney grins. 'Am I the only one not roaming the corridors of this inn with a cockstand? So much the better if he is with her – we will catch them *in flagrante*. They can hardly deny it then. Let us go and find Drake at once, before the gallant Sir William slips back to his own room.' He moves to the door.

I step in front of him, holding up a hand.

'Drake will be in bed with his wife now. You disturb them if you wish, for I will not. Savile is going nowhere tonight, and I must finish this translation. I will speak to Drake first thing in the morning.'

Sidney's expression darkens. 'Poor Elizabeth. It galls me to think of it – a fresh young woman like that being pawed by those barnacled old hands of his.'

'Don't think of it, then. Now, if you'll excuse me, I have work to catch up on.'

I take the book from the bag and unwrap its oilskin covers as tenderly as if I were handling a new-born infant. On the writing desk in the corner I set out my inkhorn, a quill and a pen-knife, a pot of sand for blotting and a supply of candles.

The Coptic script is faint and worn in places but still my heart beats faster against my ribs as I return to the beginning and once again tease out, with painful slowness, the meaning of the words. As I ease each sentence from the obscurity of its ancient Biblical language into the clear light of Latin and watch the paragraphs take shape, I wonder with every line if I am transcribing the true words of history's greatest traitor. So absorbed am I that I am only dimly aware of Sidney moving about in the background: undressing, putting on his nightshirt, wandering around the room, closing the window, peering over my shoulder.

'Do you suppose he killed the Spaniard too?' he says, breaking into my thoughts.

I turn, irritated. 'What?'

'Savile. Perhaps the Spaniard found him out and Savile had to silence him. Then he could have written that false confession letter to throw the blame. Although,' he continues, as if debating with himself, 'that presents a difficulty. If Jonas knew enough to accuse Savile, why did he not tell Drake immediately?'

'Philip,' I say, returning my attention to the manuscript, 'I will speculate with you in the morning. Get some sleep or I will never finish this.'

He looks piqued. 'Bruno – we have a murderer within our grasp. If we apprehend him and turn him in to Drake, the fleet can leave and our places with it are secure. If we delay, we may miss the chance.'

I do not reply. My thoughts have already run ahead to Drake's possible responses. To have a man of Savile's status arrested and tried for murder, with the evidence so scant, would be no small task. How would anyone prove that Mistress Dunne's child was not her husband's, now that he is not here to deny it, unless by waiting until it is born to see who it looks

335

like? Savile would have London lawyers involved, and interventions from influential friends; the charges would be dismissed in no time. From the little I know of Drake, he will not want to entangle himself in a legal case that could take months. Might he not rather set sail with Savile on board, and make his own arrangements for justice once they are far from English shores? I dip my pen in the inkwell and return to the page. What Drake decides to do with the information tomorrow is his business, I remind myself, though it sits uneasily with me.

Eventually, when Sidney realises he will have no more of my attention tonight, he lies down and pulls the sheet over himself. Before long, I hear him lightly snoring. I light another candle and force my eyes back to the page in front of me.

Dawn light is already seeping along the horizon, edging the rooftops through the window in faint gold, when I lay down my pen and press the heels of my hands against my eyelids. Judas Iscariot – if he is truly the author – ends his gospel with an eyewitness account of how the friends and disciples of Christ took his corpse from the sepulchre under cover of night and buried it secretly in an unmarked grave, for fear his tomb would be desecrated by his enemies. This grave robbery gave rise to the myth that Christ in his mortal body had walked free from the tomb, defeating death – a myth his followers were happy to bolster with their own claims of meetings, sightings, conversations with the dead man. A myth that has persisted down the centuries, shored up with hundreds of thousands of lives. I rest my elbows on the table and push my hands through my hair, squinting through gritty eyes at what I have just written. Sixty-seven pages that could destroy the Christian Church. This book unwrites the doctrine of salvation. Sixteen hundred years' worth of theology: it is as if every book ever written since the gospels themselves is erased at a stroke. I close my eyes and I can almost see it: all the lines of ink of all the pages of all the books, disappearing, unravelling, running backwards, back into the pens that wrote them, back to the inkpot, the pages left pristine and white, ready for a new theology. I lay my fingertips reverently on the pages of the Judas manuscript. But this must be a forgery, says the rational voice in my head; it cannot be otherwise. Then why did the Vatican library have it under lock and key? Why did the young Jesuit steal it and try to run to the other side of the world, if not because he believed it was potentially devastating? And it would only be that dangerous if it were true.

I throw a dusting of fine sand over my pages to dry the ink and wrap the original book carefully in its protective covers. On the bed, Sidney lies half in, half out of the sheets, one hand curled loosely by his mouth, his face flushed in sleep like a child. I watch him for a moment with an affection that is almost paternal, though he is only seven years my junior. The Queen was right not to let him go to war, however much he may resent it. He is not made for fighting; he is a poet and a scholar who belongs among books, not the blood and dust of battle. But I fear for him; this determination to prove himself in the field will hurt him.

I bunch my pages together and tap the pile on the table to straighten the edges. I must protect this copy at all costs. If Rowland Jenkes somehow stole my first translation of the early pages, it can only have whetted his appetite for the rest. My eyelids droop and I seem to see his face looking right at me: his strange aquamarine eyes; his lofty, knowing smirk. The image looms, growing and shrinking as if in a candle flame, and I imagine I hear him laughing; a knot of dread slowly tightens under my ribs and I remember how, in Oxford, he promised to return and kill me.

NINETEEN

I jolt awake and cry out as I open my eyes to see Sidney's face inches from mine as he shakes me by the shoulder.

'Calm down,' he says, straightening up. 'Captain Drake is here.'

I blink and lift my head slowly from my arms; the room is full of blank light and my neck is stiff. I have fallen asleep at the table, hands spread protectively over my pages. I ease myself round, rubbing my neck and shoulders, and see Drake standing in the doorway. He shuts the door behind him and perches on the end of the bed. Sidney is already dressed, I notice. I have no idea what the time is.

'Is it done?' Drake asks. 'I want to lock that book away before we leave for the inquest. Thomas would never forgive me if he knew I'd let it out of my hands.'

I pass him the bag with the manuscript. 'I have finished the translation.'

'Anything of interest?'

I hesitate. Where to begin? If I were caught in a tempest in the Straits of Magellan there is no one I would rather at the helm, but Drake is not the man I would choose to analyse a lost Gnostic gospel – particularly not one as explosive as this. 'Interesting, yes. Perhaps we can discuss it when you are less preoccupied with Dunne.'

'If that day ever comes,' Drake says, in a voice of infinite weariness. 'I used to thrive on little sleep. I was famed for it. But these past few days . . .' He shakes his head. 'I begin to feel sleep will elude me for ever. Sir Philip says you have something to tell me about the Dunne business?'

I tell Drake all that happened the day before concerning Savile and Mistress Dunne, including my discovery of the sleeves with the missing button and the traces of nutmeg, and my conclusion that Dunne must have been given the spice in his wine the night he died. I finish with Lady Arden's observation about Martha Dunne's pregnancy. He does not interrupt, but the creases between his eyebrows grow deeper as I speak.

'Savile?' he says, eventually. He looks as if he has been slapped. 'But he has put up a good deal of his own money for this venture. And I heard good reports of him, from men I trust. He fought in Ireland as a youth, I believe.' He passes a hand across his mouth and chin. 'It may be true that he is involved with Martha Dunne – they would have met at court, I suppose. It may even be true that she is carrying his child. But there is one flaw in your theory – if Savile killed Dunne so that Martha would be free to marry him, why is she making such a fuss about proving it to be murder, not suicide? She must realise that any attempt to investigate could throw an unwelcome light on them.' He purses his lips and shakes his head again. 'It makes no sense.'

'I thought the same,' I say. 'But I can only conclude that she is trying to divert attention away from herself and Savile.'

'But why dress the murder up as suicide in the first place?' Drake asks. 'If he went to the trouble of drugging him with nutmeg, why not give him something that would finish him off?'

'Perhaps he thought it would look too obvious if Dunne

died by poisoning aboard the ship. He might have meant only to make sure Dunne was not in his right mind, and deal with him later. The plan must have gone awry somehow.' I shift my gaze to the window; it is clear that Drake is not convinced. 'Savile said "the priest was with him". Either he meant in his cabin or on the walk back to the harbour that night, when Padre Pettifer found Dunne wandering drunk in the street and brought him back to the ship. Perhaps Savile intended to attack him in the town, but was forced to carry out the murder by a different means and tried to disguise it as suicide as a last resort.' I end with an apologetic shrug. 'I don't have all the answers, I'm afraid.'

'That is the difficulty,' Drake says, still frowning. 'Nothing is clear enough for me to come out and accuse a man like Sir William of murder.'

'It is clear he was drinking with Dunne in his cabin that night,' Sidney says, quick to support me. 'We have his pearl button as evidence.'

'That is no proof that he murdered Dunne,' Drake says. 'He could easily deny the nutmeg. Listen.' He sighs. 'I don't have to like or admire a man to value him as an investor. I would have to see the blood on his hands before I risk an accusation of that kind. I could not replace him or his money at this stage.'

'You could ask him where Jonas is,' I say. His expression changes and I know I have touched a nerve. 'My guess is that Jonas suspected the killer – let us say it is Savile. Perhaps the Spaniard confronted him. So he had to be silenced – and the killer decided to try and tie up the whole business neatly with the false confession, knowing there was already some doubt over the suicide and fearing there would be an investigation. Whoever killed Dunne knows what happened to Jonas, I am certain of it. There is even a chance he may yet be alive somewhere. And Savile speaks Spanish,' I add.

Drake sucks in his cheeks and gives me a long look. 'Very

well, then. I will speak to Savile after the inquest. He is due to give testimony as a witness. Meanwhile, if we are to pursue this, you must bring me better evidence. Talk to Dunne's widow again – see if your honeyed Italian tongue can trick her into giving anything away. You have a gift for charming the ladies, I understand.' He almost smiles, and there is the hint of a twinkle in his eye. I feel the colour rising in my face, though I keep my expression steady.

'It would seem Mistress Dunne has been charmed quite successfully already,' Sidney observes.

Drake picks up the bag with the manuscript and crosses to the door. 'The inquest starts at nine. I am going to break my fast and gather the men I need. It might be useful for you to be there, both of you, to hear all the witnesses' versions of events in one place. Perhaps it would be wise to keep an open mind, at least for now.'

'He does not want to confront Savile.' I wait until the door has closed behind Drake before voicing the obvious.

'Understandably,' Sidney says. 'Murder is a grave accusation – he doesn't want to risk Savile taking offence and withdrawing his stake in the expedition at this stage.'

'I could understand that, were it not for the disappearance of Jonas.' I rise from the desk and stretch to ease my back. 'Drake claims affection for the Spaniard. You would think he'd take the chance to question someone who might be able to account for him.'

'Perhaps he means to present that forged confession to the inquest after all,' Sidney says. 'It would make his life easier. Then maybe he'll just cut off William Savile's head once we are west of the Azores,' he adds cheerfully. 'I'm going downstairs for some food. You should clean yourself up, Bruno.'

I change my shirt, wash my face and attempt to impose some order on my hair. Before I leave the room, I hide my new translation of the Judas Gospel under the mattress and make sure the room is locked.

Downstairs, I take a piece of bread from the tap-room and wander out into the inn yard, feeling the need for some air. The morning is chilly, the sky blank and grey, with rows of cloud stacked to the horizon. The gulls sound more mournful than ever. I shiver; summer seems to have given up on England, or vice versa. The serving girl Hetty appears around a corner, carrying two full pails of water, and gives me a knowing look. I try not to read too much into this; she always has a knowing look, though I cannot help wondering if it was her scuffling about in the shadows when I visited Lady Arden's room last night. At the memory of Lady Arden I experience a quick stab of guilt; I have barely given her a thought since I left her. I picture her sleeping, dark hair spread over the white pillow, breathing softly through parted lips. The image prompts me to smile to myself as I hurry back inside before Hetty can catch me out with any insinuating comments.

In the entrance hall, Sidney stands talking to Pettifer. The chaplain wears his black clerical robes and tugs repeatedly at the ribbon tying his neck-bands, as if it restricts his breathing. Sidney catches sight of me and beckons me over.

'Drake has gone on ahead with his brother, he asked for us to follow.'

'I bid you farewell, gentlemen,' Pettifer says, clasping his hands together. 'I must get to the Guildhall on time.'

'You are a principal witness, are you not?' I ask.

He frowns. 'I suppose I am. Being one of the last to have seen him.'

'But you will not tell the coroner's court what Dunne wanted to pray about on that last night?'

'You know I cannot.' He draws himself up, his cheeks flushing. 'That is to say – I will mention that he seemed distressed. But not so much that anyone could have predicted the consequences.' He lowers his eyes. 'It will be a sad business for all of us, I fear. Those who knew him.'

'Most especially for his widow,' Sidney says.

'At least when this is done she will be able to bury him,' I remark.

'Yes, but where?' Pettifer says ominously.

Sidney nudges me; Savile is springing down the stairs, spry and hearty as ever and dressed in his usual finery: a doublet of grey-green silk with knee-length breeches to match and soft leather shoes better fitted for dancing on fine Turkish carpets than crossing the cobbled streets of Plymouth with their open gutters.

'Give you good morrow, gentlemen,' he says, rubbing his hands as if anticipating some great sport. He turns to me with a roguish smile. 'Find your room in the end, Doctor Bruno?'

'Yes, thank you. And you?'

'I did. But I tell you – I fear the security at this inn. I am fairly certain someone broke into my room yesterday, though I cannot say when. The lock had been tampered with. You have observed nothing suspicious since you arrived?'

'That is worrying,' Sidney says, his face a picture of concern. 'Was anything taken?'

'Not that I could see. But I think someone had been through my bag. It is my good fortune that there was nothing of any great value there for them to find.' He looks at me as he says this and I return his gaze, unblinking, until he looks away. 'I think I shall move back to the ship tonight – I feel safer there, for all the sailors' talk of Dunne's unquiet soul keening around the decks. It can't be moaning any more than he did in life.'

Pettifer tuts quietly at the lack of respect. I exchange a glance with Sidney.

'In any case,' Savile adds, in a breezier tone, 'once we have this business out of the way, the fleet will be free to sail.'

'I for one shall be glad to haul anchor,' Pettifer observes, nodding solemnly. 'I think we would all like to leave this unfortunate tragedy behind us and look ahead to our mission.'

We all concur with sympathetic murmurs, though I feel

Savile's eyes on me again. Does he suspect something? In any case, he has been put on his guard now; it will be harder to catch him out.

Sidney elbows me as we emerge from the Star's main door into the street and I look up to find the boy Sam lolling against the wall of a house opposite. His dirt-streaked face lights up when he sees me. He wipes his nose on his hand and skips across, nimbly dodging a pile of horse dung, to clutch at my sleeve.

'What are we doing today, sir?'

I smile down at him and ruffle his hair, thinking as I do so that he almost certainly has lice. 'Well, I don't know about you, Sam, but I am going to an inquest at the Guildhall. It will be very dull and I'm afraid I won't need any assistance.'

His face falls, but only briefly. 'I seen that man you said. With no ears.'

I stop dead. 'Where? When?'

He points down the street. 'Early today. At the end of Hoe Lane. He was talking to a girl.'

'What girl? What did she look like? Did you know her?'

He nods vigorously and points back to the Star. 'She's from there. She has brown hair and small eyes. The fat one.'

My heart turns over. Hetty. *Dio porco.* 'What did they do? Did you hear anything they said?' I grip him by the shoulder.

'He gave her money. And a letter.'

'And then what? Did you see where he went?'

'I followed him to the Market Square, but then my brother came running to tell me about the body so I went with him to see it.' He grows more animated. 'My brother says drowned men come out the sea at night and steal children from their beds but he's a liar.'

'What body? Philip, wait.' Sidney has gone on ahead; he turns and frowns, questioning. I beckon him back.

'They found him in the Sound early this morning,' Sam says, proud to be the bearer of such significant news. 'The

344

fishermen found him. Washed up on the rocks by the Hoe. My uncle helped pull him into the boat and they rowed him round to the wharf. His head was all bashed in.' He looks delighted with this detail.

'Where is the body now?' I crouch so that I can look him in the face.

'They put it in a shed. It was all swelled up and it stank worse'n a dead dog,' he says, with relish.

'Has the coroner examined it yet?'

'Who?'

'Never mind. Sam, you must take me there. I need to see this body.'

'Whose body?' Sidney strides up, impatient. 'Come, Bruno, we shall be late for this inquest.'

'A body has been washed ashore this morning. I want to see if it is – you know. You go on to the Guildhall. Take note of the testimonies, look out for discrepancies, or those witnesses who seem unsure of their story. Or those who seem too sure.'

His jaw twitches. 'I am not your clerk, Bruno.'

'I thought you wanted to help Drake?'

He rolls his eyes. 'I will save a space for you. Come as soon as you can.'

I nod and allow Sam to lead me by the hand towards the harbour.

A row of wooden huts stands along the north-east wharf of Sutton Pool, many with doors barely attached to their hinges. Those that stand open disgorge fishing nets, oak barrels cracked with age, iron buckets, coils of rope and rusted chains over the quayside. Outside one I see Sam's uncle Amos with a group of other men, conferring in low voices. One carries a sword buckled around his waist and talks louder than the others.

Amos greets me with a curt nod.

345

'Is the body in there?' I ask, though the question is redundant; you could smell it from the other side of the Pool if you were downwind.

'What is it to you?' says the loud man, swinging around to face me. 'Who are you?'

I suspect he is a parish constable; I have come across his kind before. 'My name is Giordano Bruno of Nola.'

'I hope you don't expect me to repeat that,' he says, glancing around at the fishermen, who respond with a smattering of laughter. 'What's your business with this? How did you know about it?'

'The boy told me,' I say, indicating Sam. 'I am with Captain Drake's party. A man went missing from his flagship the night before last. I have been sent to enquire about this body.'

A shadow of suspicion passes over the man's face, but he takes a step back, and when he speaks again his tone is markedly less aggressive.

'You can look if you want, but I doubt it's one of Drake's crew. This one looks foreign. Like you.'

'Spanish?'

'How should I know? He hasn't been saying much.' The fishermen cackle again. I give the constable a sardonic smile.

'That's my shed,' Amos says, as I stand on the threshold. 'If it's your man, can you ask Captain Drake to send someone for him? I've had to take all my gear out and it looks like rain later. And there's the smell to think of.'

'I will. If you could stand back – there is not much light in here.'

Amos obliges, clearing his colleagues out of the way. I step into the narrow hut and once again find myself looking down at a bloated body. The man has been laid out on a piece of canvas sailcloth, presumably used to carry him ashore. Tangled black hair falls across his face. Gingerly I pull it back to reveal the swollen features of Jonas Solon. His eyes stare up at me, wide and glassy. The tongue protrudes slightly. The face and

346

head are badly bruised and the clothes are torn in several places; it is impossible to tell whether this is the result of being pounded against rocks by the tide, or if he was attacked before he ended up in the water.

I sit back on my haunches, looking at the body. When a man has drowned while conscious, the hands are often clenched in fists near the mouth, as if he had tried to keep the water out. Jonas's limbs are relaxed, suggesting he did not fight his drowning. Because he was intoxicated or knocked out? Perhaps Savile used the nutmeg on him. But Jonas was a skilled herbalist; he would have been too cautious to fall for that.

'You've seen his head?' Amos says, breaking into my thoughts.

'No.' I look up at him, questioning, and he indicates that I should turn the body over. With a deep breath, I place a hand on the chilly flesh and roll him towards me. At the side of his skull, close to the temple, a bloodless wound gapes; he has been struck with a heavy object, or else fallen hard on his head. Overcoming my distaste, I part the hair near the wound and see that bruising is still visible under the skin. I press the wound with my fingertips; the bone is intact. This blow did not kill him, but it could well have rendered him unconscious, to make certain he would drown.

'Was it you who found him?' I ask Amos.

'Christopher here,' he says, jabbing his thumb towards the group of men standing outside. 'Saw him floating. Called me over and between us we hauled him into the boat.'

'Down by the Hoe, Sam said?'

'Foot of the cliffs down there. There's a path leads down to a jetty. It's quite steep around the west side. It's my guess he fell from the top and landed on the rocks before he went in the water, poor bastard. Must have been drinking.'

He didn't fall without help, I think as I stand, wincing as my knees click. 'This man is a friend of Captain Drake's,' I say, raising my voice for the men outside, with as much authority as I can muster. 'The body must not be touched until the coroner sends someone to fetch it. His death will need to be investigated. Anyone interfering with the body could be implicated.'

'And that will be my business, thank you,' says the man with the sword, stepping very close to me. 'I am a constable of this parish. So you can leave off giving orders as if you owned the place.'

I point the tip of a forefinger to the centre of his chest and step towards him; he looks so surprised that he backs up, despite himself. 'Not orders. Just friendly advice,' I say, with a terse smile. I take a last look at Jonas's battered body, spread out on the sailcloth, and silently pay my respects.

I can feel their eyes on me as I walk away around the quayside; I hear the tenor of their muttering, if not the actual words. Fucking foreigners, cause more trouble than they're worth, is the gist of it. As I turn up one of the little cobbled streets that leads towards the Market Square, Sam comes trotting after me like an obedient pup.

'Leave the gentleman alone, Sam,' Amos calls. 'He has business to attend to, I'm sure.' Sam looks crestfallen, but he allows his uncle to lead him away.

A crowd has gathered outside the Guildhall, largely in the hope of catching a glimpse of Drake himself, or so I gather from the snatches of conversation that brush past me as I push through, provoking angry shouts as I do so. Armed men in the livery of the Plymouth Town Corporation stand each side of the door, barring it with their staffs; I explain my business and, though it takes some persuasion, they finally step aside to let me pass. Inside I find a large room with a high beamed ceiling and clean, stone-flagged floor, laid out with benches to either side and a long trestle table on a dais at the far end, where three men in the black robes of lawyers are perched like rooks, shuffling their papers and murmuring among themselves. Mistress Dunne sits to their right, a handkerchief pressed to her lips; the very picture of dignified grief. Arrayed along the benches I recognise a number of sailors from the *Elizabeth*, including Gilbert Crosse, Thomas Drake, Padre Pettifer and William Savile, who looks straight ahead with perfect composure. He does not once glance at Martha Dunne. I think of the wrecked body I have just seen at the wharf, and a knot of anger tightens in my stomach as I watch Savile lean across to Gilbert and make some disparaging comment about the lawyers, which makes both men laugh. Let him laugh for now; the joke will lose its shine soon enough. Sir Francis Drake sits opposite Mistress Dunne, his mouth set in a hard line. Sidney stands at the back with other onlookers and briefly raises a hand in greeting when he spots me in the doorway.

I have to rest a hand on the door post to steady myself; the scene recalls so sharply my previous experience of English justice, in a courtroom in Canterbury. It is an experience I had hoped not to revisit.

'Well then, Captain Drake,' says the lawyer sitting in the centre, a man with a severe stare and bristling eyebrows whom I presume to be the coroner. 'You say you have no reason to believe that Robert Dunne's death was anything other than it appeared – a clear case of self-slaughter by hanging.'

Drake inclines his head by way of affirmation, his expression inscrutable.

'And yet,' the coroner continues, 'we have heard the testimony of Master . . .' He consults his notes. '. . . Master Gilbert Crosse, who saw the Spaniard Jonas Solon entering Dunne's cabin that night with a draught of something. It is known that he is a skilled herbalist. This same Jonas has now absconded, which might be seen to support Mistress Dunne's contention that her husband was unlawfully killed by person or persons unknown aboard the *Elizabeth Bonaventure*.'

Mistress Dunne evinces a muffled sob here; it is expertly done.

'However . . .' The coroner sifts his papers and allows his gaze to travel ponderously around the assembly. 'I do not think we can infer proof of guilt merely from a man's absence. Is there any further evidence, Sir Francis, anything at all, that might assist me in my conclusion? Anything you might add concerning this Spaniard?'

Drake stands, straightens his doublet and clears his throat. I fix my eyes on those gathered on the benches: if one among them forged that confession from Jonas, he must be expecting Drake to present it to the coroner at this point. I watch Savile in particular.

'Nothing else, Master Coroner,' Drake says. 'Whatever the reason for Jonas's absence, I am certain it has no connection with the suicide of Robert Dunne.'

He sits down. Martha Dunne narrows her eyes. Savile's gaze flits briefly to her before he fixes it steadily on his folded hands before him. Gilbert blinks at Drake, his expression somewhat chastened; perhaps he is disappointed that his testimony is apparently being disregarded. Pettifer appears more interested in watching the rest of the assembly; as his gaze travels around the room his eyes meet mine and he looks quickly away, as if embarrassed. Thomas Drake sits with his arms folded tightly across his chest, watching his brother. He can be discounted, I think; he knew Jonas was illiterate. Not one of the others has reacted in a way that suggests they were hoping for a mention of the letter, but then they would be obliged to dissemble, or else give themselves away.

'Very well,' the coroner says, suppressing a small sigh. 'It is a pity we cannot hear a first-hand testimony from this Jonas Solon.'

'That would be difficult,' I say, stepping forward and raising my voice. All eyes turn to look at me. 'Jonas Solon is dead.'

TWENTY

There is a rush of whispering around the courtroom. I see Drake lower his eyes, as if he is turning his feelings inward. He cannot be surprised by the news, but perhaps until now he still harboured some hope. The coroner lays down his papers and peers forward over the edge of the table, frowning.

'Who are you, sir, to interrupt my court?'

'Dr Giordano Bruno of Nola, sir,' I reply.

'This man travels with Sir Philip Sidney,' Drake adds, validating my presence.

The coroner studies me a moment longer, then gestures for me to continue.

'Jonas Solon was pulled out of the water this morning,' I say, loud enough for the room to hear. 'It seems he fell from the cliffs of the Hoe and was washed up on the rocks. His body is at the wharf by Sutton Pool awaiting your attention, sir.'

The coroner nods slowly, but his expression suggests he is taking a while to catch up with these developments.

'He must have thrown himself from the cliff in remorse for what he did,' Mistress Dunne says, her voice strident over the urgent, muttered speculations. If she and Savile did not produce that confession letter, she is certainly quick to seize the advantage.

'It is equally possible that his death was a terrible accident,' Drake says, his voice composed.

The coroner inhales, takes his papers in both hands and examines them in silence as if hoping to find the correct answer written down somewhere. At length he looks up, clears his throat and addresses the room.

'It would appear that this business is more complex than was originally thought. I suggest that we adjourn this inquest until the circumstances of this new death have been properly examined and taken into account. Therefore, I would ask both parties—'

At this, Mistress Dunne rises to her feet to protest. I do not stay for the summary. Instead I fight my way back through the crowd to the market place, ignored by the people pressing towards the doorway for a sight of Plymouth's most famous citizen. I sit down on the base of the market cross and rest my head in my hands, suddenly overcome by weariness and a sense of defeat. How can anything be proved? If Savile pushed Jonas to his death, there can be no evidence for it, unless someone saw him. And if it was not Savile, then who? Mistress Dunne too: her face was tight with anger at the adjournment. She had the perfect solution within her grasp, if she could persuade the coroner to see it her way: a murderer who apparently threw himself from a cliff in a fit of remorse, and moreover a foreigner, whom everyone would be willing to believe guilty. Everyone, that is, except Drake. There would have been no verdict of *felo de se*, no prolonged investigation; she would have been free of her husband, free of his accusations about the provenance of her child, free to inherit her father's estate and share it, in due course, with the man she chose to remarry. The more I consider it, the more certain it seems that Savile and Martha Dunne engineered Dunne's death between them. The others may be behaving oddly, though perhaps that is to be expected, with the tension affecting the crew. But I have no idea how to prove Savile killed him, unless it be with a forced confession – and that I leave to Drake's discretion. I hang my head between my knees and punch one fist into the palm of my other hand, cursing softly in my own language until I become aware of a shadow looming over me. I look up and see Sidney outlined against the sky, peacock feather bouncing in his cap.

'There is no more we can do now. Come back to the Star and get some dinner.'

I haul myself to my feet and we trudge through the market in the direction of the inn, each sunk in our own thoughts.

'Do you suppose Savile killed Jonas, then?' Sidney says, after a while.

'He must have done. We know he speaks Spanish – he could have written the letter. It would have worked out very neatly for him and Martha Dunne if Jonas could be made to take the blame.'

'Drake will have to confront Savile now,' he says. 'It will all come out. The child and all.'

I shake my head. 'I don't know. There is still no real evidence for any of it, except for a button and the smell of nutmeg – not unless one of them breaks down and confesses. And I would not put money on Mistress Dunne wavering. That woman could lead a battle charge without flinching.'

'We should have done what I suggested last night,' Sidney says, irritated. 'Burst in on them in the act. Then they could not have denied their liaison, at least.'

'I was busy last night.'

'So you were.' He slaps me on the back and grins. 'Will you visit Lady Arden again tonight? Was she sufficiently gratified by your performance to warrant a reprise?'

'*Vaffanculo*, with respect, Sir Philip,' I murmur, but I cannot keep from smiling; if I close my eyes, the image of Lady Arden's flushed, eager face briefly displaces the thoughts of battered corpses.

As we enter the Star, we find Lady Drake descending the

353

main staircase, attended by her lady's maid and one of Drake's armed men. Sidney greets her with an elegant bow but she barely acknowledges him; her attention is all on me, with a questioning look.

'Where is she?' she asks, in a low voice, as she approaches. 'We are supposed to be dining with the Mayor and his wife today. I had not thought you would keep her so long.'

'Who?'

She gives me a reproving look and I realise her meaning.

'I don't know, my lady.' I can feel the blush stealing up my neck; I, who pride myself on my ability to give away nothing in my face, colouring like a schoolboy. 'I have not seen her – this morning.'

Lady Drake frowns. 'But – you have just been with her, have you not? Walking on the Hoe?'

'No.' I look at her, puzzled. 'I have been at the Guildhall, at the inquest. And before that – on another matter, down at the wharf. I have not seen Lady Arden since, ah . . .' I scratch the back of my neck and look down. 'Since I helped her with her bag last evening.'

'Her *bag*,' Sidney says, with a meaningful nod.

Lady Drake ignores him; anxiety flits across her face. 'But – what are you saying, Doctor Bruno? You wanted to meet her this morning at the Hoe. You sent her a note.' She rests a hand on my arm, nodding, as if this will encourage me to agree. A slow coldness begins to spread through my gut. With the discovery of Jonas's body, I hardly paid attention to the boy Sam's news that he had seen a man with no ears handing a note to the maid from the Star. I glance up to the first-floor gallery, half expecting to see Hetty peering over, looking pleased with herself.

'I sent no note,' I say quietly. Lady Drake covers her mouth with a hand. 'Did she go out alone?'

She nods. 'To the old castle.' There is a tremor in her voice. 'I warned her, but she is so headstrong – she really believes she can go about with the same liberty as a man. I told her she should not go alone and she rolled her eyes at me. She said she had no need of a chaperone at her age.'

'I would never have asked her to meet me anywhere so remote,' I say, subdued. 'She should have realised that.'

'She thought it was some game of yours,' Lady Drake says. 'She was excited by the prospect. She likes to push the bounds of propriety – it is the sort of thing she would consider daring.' She looks at me as if this is my fault. 'Oh God. Is she in danger?'

'I don't know.' I attempt to sound reassuring, but my stomach is knotted with dread. 'I think we should find her as quickly as possible.'

'But whoever would want to harm Lady Arden?' Lady Drake presses her hand to her mouth again; her eyes are wide and threatening tears.

I glance at Sidney. 'I think it more likely that someone is trying to get to your husband. A woman alone is an easier target – and you are usually surrounded by armed men, my lady.'

Her eyes widen further. 'You think someone meant to harm me as well?' She flinches and looks about wildly, as if expecting to see an assassin running at her with a sword.

'I think, my lady,' Sidney says, stepping forward and taking her gently by the arm, 'that you would be advised to go directly to the Mayor's house and stay there until your cousin is found safe and well. Keep your husband's armed men close about you.'

'But I cannot wait there, making polite conversation, not knowing what is happening,' she cries, clutching at my sleeve. 'I had rather wait here for Sir Francis, he will know what to do.'

'Your husband will be occupied with all that is going on here, my lady,' Sidney says. 'Better he knows you are out of harm's way with the Mayor while he searches for Lady Arden.

Come – I will walk you there myself.' He offers his arm; after a brief hesitation, she takes it.

At the door, she turns and pins me with a fierce look. 'Find her, Bruno. Since you are partly to blame.' She sweeps out, towing Sidney in her wake. He grimaces at me over her head on his way out.

I throw open the door to the tap-room, where Mistress Judith is wiping down the tables.

'Where is Hetty?' I demand. She snaps her head up, alarmed at my tone.

'What has that slattern done now?' She straightens, hands on her hips. 'She has been slow doing her rounds this morning, I know – I had another guest complain his chamber pot had not been emptied since last night. I do apologise, sir – I'll send her up when I find her, useless wench.'

'No – I need to speak to her urgently.'

She stares at me for a moment, then appears to think better of arguing. She points to the yard. 'I sent her out to the pump for some water – that was a good half-hour ago. I dare say she is idling with the stable boys, though I have warned her against it. "Listen up, my little madam," I told her . . .'

She is still talking as I stride out into the yard. I doubt the stable boys are of much interest to Hetty – not unless they have pockets full of coins they will trade in return for spying on the guests. Around the corner of a stable block I find her, a wooden pail by her feet, giggling with a gawky lad in a rough canvas jerkin. She glances up and at the sight of me the laughter dies on her lips.

'Do you know what they do in my country to people who spy?' I roar, bearing down on her with a hand to the hilt of my knife. 'Gouge their eyes out with the point of a dagger, that's what.' She gives a yelp and stumbles backwards, kicking over the pail. Water spreads in a pool around her feet.

'Now, look here, mate,' the youth begins, stepping towards me, 'you can't just talk to people—'

356

'If you want to keep your balls, my friend, make yourself scarce before I lose my temper,' I say, facing him down with a stare that could melt lead. The force of this anger is invigorating, and I am only partly putting it on. The weight of my earlier weariness has evaporated, burned up in my fury; I feel every inch alive, coiled, every nerve ending charged. The boy pauses briefly to consider his options, then scrambles around the corner, scattering gravel under his boots in his haste.

'You are going to tell me everything,' I say to Hetty when he is gone, circling around so that I have her backed up against the wall of the stable. My hand still hovers over my knife but I keep it sheathed; let no one say I drew a knife on a young woman. But at least the sight of it has wiped that infuriating smirk from her face. 'It was you in the corridor last night, wasn't it? Hiding in the shadows, spying on me?'

'I just go about my jobs, cleaning and that,' she says, with that same sulky defiance. 'Can't help it if you happen to be where you should not. *Sir*,' she adds, with a sarcasm that would wither the leaves on the trees.

'The man who has had you spying on me,' I say, taking a slow breath to keep me from losing my temper and slapping her, 'he gave you a letter this morning. What did it say?'

She glares at me with pure loathing. 'I can't read. I told you that already.'

'Oh, come on. You expect me to believe that? When you have been deceiving me from the beginning?'

'It's true!' She looks indignant. 'All I know's he gave me that letter and said I was to wait till you'd gone out, then take it to that woman you been with last night.'

'Has he been paying you well for spying on me? Bringing me letters?'

'Better'n you,' she retorts. The smirk reappears. I raise my hand in a flash of rage; she cowers and I lower it, trembling, shocked at myself. I have never struck a woman in my life, and some have given me better reason than this.

357

'That lady you delivered the letter to,' I say, through my teeth, 'may die because of it. I hope you think that was worth the few pennies he threw you for your trouble.'

'What?' The colour drains from her face; her mouth hangs open and she stares at me in horror. 'But he's a respectable gentleman. Least, he talks like one.'

'Do you think? Did you never question why he has no ears?'

'He said you cut them off him in a duel. He said he had to fight you because you wronged him, and you cut his ears off, and he has been looking for you ever since.'

'*Dio porco* – Hetty, will you believe anything? What kind of a duel would that be?' I throw my hands up. 'What else did he tell you?'

'That you are a dangerous man and you go by several names because you are wanted for murder in three countries.' She sounds as if she is quite impressed by these credentials.

Despite myself, I cannot help a brief, incredulous laugh. 'I am only dangerous if you cross me. So you must know where to find this man. You have been his messenger long enough.'

'I don't, sir, I swear it.' Her bravado quickly deflates. 'I would meet him at the back door of the yard. He used to come into the tap-room, that's how he knew to find me. But he doesn't come in any more.'

Not since he saw Sidney and me and thought we recognised him, I think. I grab her by the upper arm and she makes a strangled squeak. 'Listen to me. If you know anything more about this business that you have not told me, now is the time to spill it. That lady is a relative of Sir Francis Drake. If any harm comes to her because of that letter, I will make sure he and all of Plymouth know of your part in it. Understand?'

Her round face crumples and she nods mutely, tears springing to her eyes. 'I never meant harm to no one, sir, on my life. Carrying letters is not a sin, last I heard.'

I let her go with a sigh. 'No. But lying is. And so is abetting a murderer.'

She looks stricken, but she volunteers nothing further. Either she is as ignorant as she says, or Jenkes frightens her more than I do. Suddenly her expression changes as her eyes dart past me; her mouth curves into a malicious little smile. I whip round to see the stable lad reappear with a solid-looking man from the kitchen.

'You all right, love?' he asks her, balling his big hands into fists at his side in readiness. I fix Hetty with a hard look; I see her calculating the opposing risks. Finally she picks up her pail and nods.

'Fine, Harry. Just getting the water.' She shoots me a resentful glance.

'Excuse me, gentlemen,' I say, with more self-possession than I feel, as I walk calmly between them towards the gates of the inn yard. I keep a hand to my knife, half expecting them to hurl themselves after me as soon as my back is turned, but they content themselves with a few muttered curses.

I turn in the direction of the Hoegate at a half-run, forcing myself to believe that there is still a chance of catching Lady Arden before Jenkes finds her. It is broad daylight, the streets are far from deserted, the castle itself is garrisoned: what can they do, in such a public place? They can hardly attack her right there. In any case, that will not be their intention; Lady Arden is of no use to them except to bargain with Drake. At least, I must hope that is true.

I quicken my pace as I reach the open ground of the headland. A sharp salt breeze chafes at my face. The air carries the promise of rain. Ahead, the castle looms on the promontory, its four round towers planted like sentries, keeping watch out to sea and over the harbour mouth.

I follow the path that skirts the walls of the castle on the seaward side, but there is no sign of a woman alone. A few people are out walking, though most hurry purposefully with

359

packs or baskets, shawls or caps pulled tight against the wind. I make my way between the scrubby trees, searching to either side, until I emerge to the east of the castle, where a footpath runs down to a row of houses that line the harbour wall. Directly ahead of me is a kind of gatehouse, built around an archway with three exits. One, to my right, leads out to another path that runs along the edge of the Hoe, at the top of the cliffs where Jonas must have been pushed to his death. The archway to the left leads out to the road around the harbour, and the one straight ahead opens on to a steep flight of stone steps down to the water, where iron rings are set into the wall for mooring. I take the first couple of steps, but there are no boats tied up. I turn instead to the right, out towards the Hoe. The gatehouse gives on to a square battery jutting out into the harbour, with four cannon arrayed along it. A bored young man wearing the town livery and holding a pikestaff stands by the wall, keeping a cursory watch out to sea. A scrawny dog sits by his feet.

'Have you seen anyone come by here?' I ask him, urgently.

'Have I seen anyone?' He screws up his face and looks at me. 'Like who?'

'I'm looking for a woman.'

'En't we all.'

I make an impatient noise. 'Have you seen a woman come by here, on her own? Well dressed? She might have met a man, or two men. Somewhere near here, by the castle?'

'I'm paid to watch out there,' he says, pointing to the bay. 'I en't got time to be worrying about who's meeting who behind me. There's guards on the castle walls, ask them.'

'This woman might have been kidnapped,' I say, my eyes still darting about at any sign of movement on the path. The soldier's face registers a flicker of interest at this news.

'Really? What, here?'

'You haven't seen anyone get into a boat here? Or walk off that way, along the cliff?'

He considers the question. 'There've been boats coming and going by the steps. Now I think of it – there was a group got into a small boat a while back. One of them might have been a woman, but they had cloaks on so you couldn't exactly see. I only took notice because they was completely silent. All of them – never spoke a word to one another. Two of them kept very close, like they was almost joined together. The third was waiting in the boat, he was at the oars.' He shakes his head. 'I didn't really pay them any mind though. It wasn't anything too far out of the ordinary.'

'But did you see where they went?' My thoughts are racing ahead, a dozen terrible tableaux forming one after another in quick succession in my mind's eye.

'Out there,' he says, pointing vaguely at the ships rocking at anchor in the Sound. I follow the direction of his finger. The majestic ships of Drake's fleet dominate the horizon, pennants snapping in the wind. Among them, smaller merchantmen showing the colours of France, the Netherlands or the Baltic states and between all these great hulls, the rowing boats bob back and forth, ferrying men and goods in and out of the harbour, the lifeline between the big ships and the town. This boat the soldier saw could be anywhere by now – if it was even them.

'Keep your eyes open, will you? In case you should see those men again, or anything unusual. One of them has no ears – if you see him, apprehend him at once.'

The youth looks amused. 'Who do you think you are, Spaniard – my commanding officer?'

'A woman's life could be in danger. A wealthy woman,' I add, and he registers this with interest, calculating the potential advantage to helping. 'You can get word to me at the Star on Nutt Street. Ask for the *Italian*,' I say, over my shoulder.

I cast a last glance at the bay under its swiftly moving canopy of clouds. The gulls scream and circle ceaselessly around the ships. There is nothing I can usefully do here on my own, with no idea even of which direction to pursue them. My best course of action is to return to the Star and find Drake; with all the companies of armed men at his command, he will surely be able to organise search parties along the roads and out into the Sound. But they will have to hurry, I think, as I step back into the shadow of the gatehouse; if Jenkes and Doughty have taken Lady Arden by boat, they could easily have reached one of the ships by now. Who knows what contacts they might have on these merchant vessels – they could be out into the English Sea by dusk, and Drake would surely need some greater authority than his own name to board and search foreign vessels.

I pause by the archway that leads to the water stairs, peering out at the harbour, my chest constricted with guilt over Lady Arden. I am about to take the path back up past the castle when I notice something white on the floor in the corner. Bending closer, I see that it is a piece of paper, balled up, as if it has been tossed aside by someone coming in or out. I crouch by the top of the stairs and unfold it; as my eyes skim the neat, sloping hand to the bottom of the page, a chill washes over me. The signature is my own.

Except that, of course, it is not: the letter is signed in my name, and ripe with full-throated declarations of passion. It begins 'Carissima' and asks the recipient to meet me by the castle gatehouse, where I would have a surprise for her. Gesu Cristo. She would have been surprised all right, to find – what? Rowland Jenkes with a knife, I imagine; it would have been a simple matter to press a blade to her ribs from under the cover of a cloak, without anyone noticing. To make her walk the short distance to the river stairs, keeping as close as a lover, the point still pressed against her skin, and force her into a boat. Why did she not scream for help? I did not understand that – but she must have dropped the letter before she was made to walk down the steps to the water, in the hope that someone would find it and make the connection.

Carissima. Dear God – and she believed I wrote this. Are women so easily deceived by a little gilded flattery? I crumple it in my fist, my face burning with anger; I feel implicated, as if the blame is partly mine as Lady Drake said. If I had not gone to Lady Arden's room last night, if I had not been seen, I would not have handed them a weakness to exploit. If that damned maid had not been so greedy for a few pennies . . . But this game of *what if* achieves nothing.

Despite the pain in my ribs, I run the distance back to the Star, the letter clutched in my fist. I can only cling to the hope that Lady Arden will be safe until Doughty and Jenkes can play her as their trump card against Drake. The next move will be his to make.

Mistress Judith is waiting for me in the entrance hall and is upon me almost before I am in the door. 'Sir Francis wants you.' She clutches at my sleeve. 'He is in his wife's chamber, with others of his men. I have the sense something bad has happened, but no one will tell me anything. Nothing concerning the inn, I hope?'

'Nothing for you to worry about, mistress,' I say, but I can see that my distracted manner and drawn face do not reassure her.

It is Thomas Drake who opens the door to me, his expression forbidding. Without a word he gestures me inside. Lady Drake is folded into a window seat, a handkerchief pressed to her mouth. She springs up as I enter, her eyes questioning. I answer with a taut shake of my head and fresh tears well up and spill down her cheeks as she sinks back down.

'You found nothing, I suppose?' Drake stands by the fireplace. His mouth is set in a grim line. To his left, Carleill and Sidney sit at the writing table, as if waiting to take dictation.

I hand Drake the crumpled letter. 'I found this down by the gatehouse to the castle steps.'

He runs his eyes over it and looks up at me, accusing.

'I did not write it,' I feel compelled to say. Still he holds me in that long, level stare.

'Even so,' he says eventually, 'someone must have known that such a message would have the desired effect.'

I look at the floor. 'The maid here has been spying on us – all of us – since we first arrived. I believe she is being paid by Jenkes the book dealer and John Doughty.'

Drake's jaw tightens. 'Get her in here. Thomas, go and find her.' He turns back to me as his brother slips out. 'The castle steps, you say? So you think they have taken a boat?'

'That is my guess. A soldier on the battery there thought he saw a man and a woman boarding a small boat, rowed by a second man. She must have dropped the letter in the hope that someone would see it.'

'Or else it is a trick on their part, to distract us.' He rubs his beard. 'Carleill, I still want men sent out by land to search. A party on every road out of the town. And if they have left by water, they will not have got far in a small boat. The Sound is full of my ships – we will question all those keeping watch, and on the foreign merchantmen too. Someone must have seen them if they boarded a ship.' He snaps his head around at a stifled sob from Lady Drake. 'Do not disturb yourself, my dear. We will find her safe and well, I promise.'

Privately I think this promise may be a little rash, but I say nothing. The door opens and Thomas marches Hetty in with a tight grip on her arm. She pulls away from him with a black look, but her face is puffy. Despite such intimidating company, she still struggles to keep up her defiant manner.

'Let me go! I en't done nothing,' she says, addressing Drake. 'I know no more'n I told him.' She points at me.

He crosses to her with one stride and stands very close, bearing down on her. I can imagine grown men quaking before that glare, but Hetty merely stares back.

'Those men you have been working for – where are they?' he barks.

'I don't know. He only ever gave me letters to deliver. He didn't tell me all their comings and goings.'

'Well, we shall soon see if you are telling the truth,' Drake says, as if it doesn't matter to him either way. 'I shall have your room and your belongings searched. Any money you had from them, you earned by abetting kidnappers. I'm sure you know the penalty for such a crime and I shall personally see that you are arrested for it if there is anything you are keeping back that could help to find Lady Arden. So if you want to save yourself, you'd better start talking, girl. Thomas, ask Mistress Judith to come here, would you?'

'No!'

Thomas Drake already has the door open when Hetty's strangled cry stops him. He closes it softly. Everyone is looking at her. A sob rises in her throat and slowly she reaches into her apron. When she draws her hand out, holding another folded and sealed letter, it is clear that she is shaking.

'This is meant for you, sir.' She holds it out to Drake, her eyes downcast, her voice no more than a whisper. 'The man with no ears – he said I was to give it you at sunset. No earlier. And if I broke my word, he would send someone to kill me in my bed. The way he said it, sir – I didn't doubt he meant it. He has these blue eyes that would burn you up, like the Devil, sir, and he speaks like icy water down your back.' She shivers and two fat tears roll down her cheeks. For all Hetty's posturing, this fear looks genuine. It is a striking description of Rowland Jenkes.

'All right.' Drake takes the letter and breaks the seal. He reads it in silence. We all watch as his face grows slowly darker. A muscle jumps in his cheek. For a long time he does not speak. Then he looks back to Hetty. 'Is he expecting you to take a reply?'

She shakes her head. 'No, sir. He said that was the last one for now. That was why it was important you didn't have it too early.'

He nods. 'Get back to your business. I shall tell Mistress Judith you are to be watched at every turn. If he gets in touch with you again, by any means, you come straight to me. Understood?'

Hetty nods; when Drake turns away, she scurries to the door.

'Wait!' Drake calls, as she is about to open it, and she jumps as if she has been stung. 'That letter you left under the door of this chamber last night – who did that come from? Not the same man, surely?'

Confusion chases across her swollen face.

'What letter?'

Drake takes a step closer, his jaw set tight, and she cowers against the door.

'Addressed to me. Come now – you will do yourself no favours. Who sent the letter last night?'

'I – I don't know what letter you mean, sir,' she says, looking genuinely fearful. 'I never left no letter at this room last night, I swear it. Only the one this morning.'

'God help you if you are lying, child,' Drake begins, and she shakes her head frantically.

'I'm not, sir, it's God's honest truth. If you had a letter last night, it didn't come by my hand.'

Drake clicks his tongue. 'Get out. What would you know of God's truth?' He makes an impatient gesture with his hand, like someone shooing away a dog; Hetty is out of the door in an instant. I have never seen her move so fast.

'That girl should be under lock and key, brother,' Thomas says, anger in his voice. 'Even now she is not telling all.'

'That is precisely why it would not help to lock her up,' Drake replies. 'These men may use her to make contact again. She is an easy conduit to me. If they do, we will have a better chance of finding them.'

Carleill gives a discreet cough. 'The letter, sir?'

Drake holds it at arm's length. 'Listen to this.

366

Fair exchange is no robbery, as people like to say. One item of value in exchange for another. You have something of value to us, and vice versa. Bring it to the chapel on St Nicholas Island after sundown and we will make an exchange I believe will be satisfactory to both parties. Do not be deceived, Captain Drake – I speak of a fair deal. You are to come alone, without your armed men, carrying only the Coptic book. Moor your boat at the northern jetty and approach by the path that leads up the cliff. If you do not abide by these conditions, I fear it will be too late to effect any exchange.

I look forward to our transaction.

He pauses, sucks in his cheeks, looks around the room.

'Is it signed?' Carleill asks.

'No. But we hardly need doubt who wrote it. This book dealer with no ears, Devil take him.'

'Well, you shall not go,' Thomas says, as if the decision rests with him. 'Anyone can see it is a trap. Does he really think you would be such a fool?' He snorts in disdain. Drake passes a hand across his brow, frowning.

'Too late for an exchange means he will kill her if you do not do as he says, does it not?' Lady Drake asks, from the window, fighting to keep her voice steady.

'Noisy threats only, my dear,' her husband says. 'He would not harm her – she is all he has to bargain with.' He does not sound as if he believes this.

'Let us not forget there are two of them,' I say. 'They have devised this between them. Jenkes will get the book he covets, and John Doughty will get you, Sir Francis, alone and unarmed, where you cannot escape.'

'Except that it is they who will be undefended,' Thomas says, animated. 'We have a fleet full of armed men at our disposal – why do we not simply surround the island, now that we know where they are, and blast the devils out?'

'Because they would kill Lady Arden, fool,' says Lady Drake. 'Either those men will, or your soldiers. Francis would never risk her life.'

'Sometimes there must be casualties in any conflict, my lady,' Thomas replies, turning to her.

'Casualties?' Lady Drake stands, indignant. 'What war are you fighting, Thomas Drake, against a book dealer and a traitor who has long carried a grudge against my husband? You think a woman's life a fair price to pay for such a victory?'

'My lady, John Doughty will not rest until your husband – my brother – is dead,' Thomas says, trying to keep his tone respectful. 'Would you have Sir Francis walk willingly to his execution? Because know this, my lady – they will not hand back your cousin, and I'm afraid you are the fool if you believe they would ever keep to such a deal. They will simply kill them both. Better we take the island by force—'

Lady Drake chokes down a sob.

'Peace, both of you, I cannot think,' Drake says, holding up a hand for silence. 'There is only one landing stage on the island,' he continues, as his wife and brother glare at one another, 'and that is the one facing the Hoe. The Sound is full of my ships – how do they imagine they will escape, even supposing they keep their word? Do they not think my guns would fire on them before they had even cast off? They must have some other plan.'

'Their plan is to kill you,' Thomas says.

'Is the island fortified?' Carleill asks, rising. There is something immediately calming about his presence; he is the sort of man you would be glad to have in command in the heat of battle.

Drake shakes his head, his expression rueful. 'Work was begun on defences nearly forty years ago, in King Edward's time, but they were never finished. Two years ago the town corporation petitioned the government to make me military governor of the island. I offered a hundred pounds of my own towards building a fort, but the Privy Council did not believe the threat justified the cost, so the funds were never released. The town corporation maintains two gunners stationed there, to keep the smugglers off, but aside from the beginnings of the fort, the old chapel and four cannon on the south-east side, there's nothing out there.'

'In any event,' Thomas says, 'by the time they took to their boat, you would be dead, brother. It would be small comfort to fire on them then.'

'I will go,' I say. A long silence unfolds while everyone turns to stare at me.

'But they will see you are not my husband from a mile off,' Elizabeth Drake says. 'And then they will kill Nell before you even reach them.'

'I am not so sure,' I say, turning to her. 'For one thing, if the light is fading they will not see who is approaching, especially if he has a hooded cloak. And besides – I cannot vouch for John Doughty, but I suspect Rowland Jenkes is canny enough to have set this as a double trap. They will know, surely, that Sir Francis would not simply come unarmed to their summons. They will expect someone to take his place. And Jenkes will expect that person to be me.'

'Why you?' Thomas narrows his eyes.

'Because he knows that I have a connection with both the book and with, erm, Lady Arden,' I say, not meeting his eye.

'Lady Arden? You?' Thomas looks incredulous. 'What connection could you possibly have with her?' But I see understanding slowly dawning on his face even before he has finished the sentence.

'Oh, be quiet, Thomas,' Elizabeth says. 'I think Bruno is right. If my husband is not there, they have no reason to kill anyone. It is the book this Jenkes wants, after all. Perhaps they will let Nell go once he has it.'

'And what of John Doughty?' Thomas chips in again, belligerent. 'What does he get, if Francis does not come? Will he not want to keep Lady Arden to barter with?'

'Besides, Rowland Jenkes has wanted to kill Bruno for two years,' Sidney says, in a low voice. He has been unusually quiet, though I have observed him paying sharp attention from his seat in the corner. 'Either way, one of them will have his revenge. Let *me* take the book. Neither has any vested interest in killing me. And let a boatload of armed men follow me and land out of sight, concealing themselves. I will hand over the book, escort Lady Arden to safety and then the armed men can show themselves. We can stop them before they make their escape.'

'What a neat solution, Sir Philip,' Thomas says. 'I wonder that my brother did not think of it, with all his experience of combat.'

Drake shoots an irritated glance at Thomas. 'It is a noble gesture, Sir Philip, and I am grateful for it. But we would do well not to underestimate these men. They will be prepared for any such stratagem, I am certain. Besides – I cannot possibly permit you to put your life in danger on my behalf. How could I excuse myself to the Queen and your family if anything should happen to you?' He says this with an apologetic, paternal smile, but Sidney bristles and turns away. Once again he has been denied an opportunity for heroism because he is viewed as the Queen's pet. Looking at him, I cannot help but be moved by the fact that he offered to go in my place, to save me.

'If no one went tonight,' Carleill says, carefully, 'if we simply refused to play their game – what would they do then? They will not harm Lady Arden, surely, for then they would have nothing left to bargain with.'

'We cannot take that risk,' Drake says. 'They may not kill her immediately but they will keep her and try the same trick again, I am sure. And who knows how they may be using her in the meantime?'

Elizabeth gives a cry and presses her knuckles to her mouth.

'Rowland Jenkes is a devout Catholic,' I say, trying to reassure her. 'He will kill in the name of his religion, because he believes it is God's work, but I do not believe he would ill-use a woman.'

'Whereas I would not have the same faith in John Doughty,' Thomas says, with a sour face. 'He would do anything in his power to hurt my brother, even by association.'

Elizabeth begins to cry again. Drake puts an arm around her shoulders, sending his brother a black look.

'We can debate this all day, but they are expecting someone after sundown,' I say, eventually, 'and I think it must be me.'

'Bruno is right,' Carleill says, in that soft, assertive voice. 'But perhaps Sir Philip is right, too. We should have armed men at the ready, set in small boats offshore, to prevent them escaping.'

'Exactly. Carleill, you and Thomas will return to the ships to muster the men. The finest marksmen of the fleet. My wife will stay here with armed guards.'

Elizabeth looks stricken. 'I do not want to be left alone, Francis,' she says. 'What if they come for me next?'

'No one will harm you, my dear,' he says, patting her hand. 'Sir Philip can stay with you if you are afraid.'

Sidney nods, his jaw clamped tight. Only I know how furious he is, and what an effort it is costing him to hide it.

'Bruno,' Drake says, turning to me. 'You and I will discuss our strategy. We must equip you with a boat – a light craft, something you can manage alone. And a pistol. Perhaps a pair would be better.'

'No. I cannot conceal a pistol about my person. If they see I am armed, they will kill me and Lady Arden without hesitation. Let me take only my knife, hidden away. Jenkes will want to prolong this,' I explain, seeing his doubtful expression. 'He will not kill either of us straight away if he can help it. There would be no satisfaction in that for him. My best hope of getting us both out alive is to play along with him.'

'But this is not a game, Bruno.' He lays a hand on my shoulder. 'I know you are a brave man, but the consequences . . .' He trails off, shaking his head, as if unwilling to elaborate.

'It is not the first time I have faced death,' I say, trying to sound as if I take it in my stride. 'Someone must go, or Lady Arden has little hope. And we have established it cannot be you, sir. There is no choice. It is part of their design.'

He gives me a long look in silence, weighing me up. Whatever happens, the responsibility will ultimately fall on his shoulders. Elizabeth breaks away from him suddenly and throws her arms around my neck.

'Bring her back, Bruno, and you will have whatever reward you ask.'

'To return with our lives will be all the reward I need, my lady,' I say, detaching her, conscious of her husband looking on. In his face I see only regret. I glance at Sidney and he looks away. I know what he is thinking: I am stealing the glory he dreams of. But Drake is right; there is no guarantee either I or Lady Arden will come out of this alive. Even so, I have no choice but to try.

TWENTY-ONE

The last streaks of light outline the horizon as I stand with Drake and his brother on a landing platform by the artillery tower on the headland at Millbay. The clouds are violet and indigo against the darkening sky; out in the Sound, the masts of the fleet seem picked out in black ink. Directly ahead is the dark hump of St Nicholas Island. A determined wind blows in from the sea, stinging my eyes.

Drake rests a hand on my shoulder. 'Are you sure you are ready to face this, Bruno?'

I take a deep breath and exhale with a curt nod. I am dressed head to foot in black, and beneath my doublet I wear my belt, shortened across my chest and over my shoulder, with my knife attached in its sheath. Over this I have tied a dark travelling cloak with a hood. The manuscript, tightly wrapped in its oilskins inside the leather satchel, hangs at my side.

'I should go,' I say quietly. 'They will be waiting.'

'There are rowboats full of armed men stationed between the fleet and the island, and between the north shore and the harbour,' he says. 'If you manage to get back to your boat with Lady Arden, signal with your lantern so they do not fire on you by mistake.'

'That would be unfortunate.' I laugh; it comes out tense and high-pitched. I do not miss the fact that he says 'if' I return. It is obvious that, one way or another, I am walking into a trap. Lady Arden may be dead already, for all we know. I cannot allow that thought to settle for even an instant; it makes my heart trip.

Sidney has stayed behind, at Lady Drake's insistence. The disappearance of her cousin has overturned her blithe disregard for her husband's fears and she is terrified to be left alone, despite the guards Drake has assigned to her; if her husband cannot be at her side, she wants the reassurance of some other competent gentleman. What comfort Sidney may attempt to offer Lady Drake is hardly my greatest concern at present. I took an awkward leave of him at the Star. Both of us knew what I was facing; I could not tell if he still envied me this chance for solitary glory, or if he was now feeling the guilt of relief that he had once again been left to take care of the women. Although only one woman, now.

'I should never have brought you here, Bruno,' he had said, sombre. 'I cannot help the feeling that this is all my fault.' He had seemed unsure of himself for the first time, undecided between an embrace, a handshake or a punch on the shoulder.

'I would only have got myself into some other trouble in London,' I said, trying to keep my voice light. 'It is my fault they took Lady Arden, none of yours.'

'True,' he said, gloomily. 'At least I won that wager, eh? I said you would have her. Oh Christ.' He tried to laugh but it fell away into silence.

'*Madonna porca*. Come here, man, don't be so English.' I grabbed him by the shoulders and hugged him tight. After the initial surprise, he threw his arms around me, thumping me on the back all the while as if this would make the act more manly. Sometimes I wonder how he ever survived travelling through Italy.

'For God's sake, take care of yourself, Bruno,' he said

fiercely, turning away. 'Give those whoreson dogs a blade in the gut from me. And make damned sure you come back, do you hear?'

'You know I will.'

I had given him a mock salute. And then Drake had arrived, and I was bundled away in a whirl of instructions and timings and defensive strategies. I had glanced over my shoulder at Sidney as I left, but he was leaning with one hand pressed against the door frame, looking at his feet, like someone trying to catch his breath after a long climb.

I think of this now as Drake peers out over the murky water.

'I see no lights from the island,' he says, frowning. 'That is worrying – the gunners ought to have a lamp lit by this hour.'

'The gunners are almost certainly not in a position to light lamps, if Doughty and his friend have got to them,' Thomas says, grim-faced.

I step into the boat, pausing to find my balance, the bag with the book held tight against my chest. Drake is explaining about tides and currents and drift, how I need to point the prow west of the jetty to compensate, but not much of it registers. I feel cold, and oddly numb.

'Let them have the book, naturally,' Drake says, crouching on the lowest step above the waterline. The sea laps at his boots each time the level undulates; my little boat bumps against the wall. 'Don't try to fight them for it. Get yourselves out – that's all that matters.'

I look up into his brown eyes and read there a reflection of my own thoughts: that my chances of coming back safely with Lady Arden are almost nil. Only a hopeless innocent would expect an honourable exchange from the likes of Jenkes and John Doughty. Drake and I are far from naïve. Jenkes wants the book, certainly, but once he has it in his hands he has no reason to let me or Lady Arden walk away. Especially not me. She will be a casualty of that vendetta.

'Keep an eye on Savile,' I say. 'He may seize the chance to slip away while you are distracted.'

'Leave him to me,' Drake says, as I settle myself on the narrow plank seat and take the oars. He reaches down to untie the mooring rope. 'I will not forget your courage, my friend.'

'God go with you, Bruno,' Thomas says, unexpectedly.

I scan his face for traces of sarcasm, but find none. I nod, and cast off.

Spray surges up and hits my face, stinging the open cuts, each time the prow slices through a small wave. The wind has made the surface choppy, white crests gleaming under the last light of the day, but there is not much of a swell. Even so, my shoulders ache with each heave of the oars and the island appears to float out there in the gathering dark, seeming further away with every stroke, as if it is toying with me.

After some time, I settle into a rhythm with the oars and my thoughts are free to fly ahead to the ridge of land on the horizon. The wind whips salty strands of hair into my eyes. I know that I may be rowing towards my death, though my rational mind refuses to accept the truth of this. My pulse beats fast but my thoughts remain oddly calm. Eight years ago, I climbed out of the window of my monastery to save myself from death at the hands of the Roman Inquisition. I have looked death in the eye many times since, and each time he has shaken his head and dismissed me, until the next time. Tonight he may not be so generous. But if I bolt now, if I turn back to shore as every sinew in my body urges me to do, Lady Arden will almost certainly suffer a cruel end. I do not love her – I barely know her – but I feel a responsibility towards her. I am, after all, implicated in what has happened to her, and I could not abandon her to those men, not while I have a conscience and my strength.

Sounds drift across the water from the great ships of the fleet, but they are snatched away by the wind. For me there is only the plashing of the oars through the waves, the keening of the gulls overhead, the forward motion of the boat and the rocky haunch of the cliffs on St Nicholas Island that now, finally, veer up ahead of me. As I squint towards it, I catch the flash of a lantern at the top. It hangs for a moment, apparently suspended in mid-air, then is extinguished. Somewhere out there, beyond the island, Carleill's men wait in their boats, ready to fire on Jenkes and Doughty as they make their escape. I did not feel it my place to contradict Drake or his military commander, but I cannot believe the kidnappers would not have pre-empted this. I feel certain Jenkes and Doughty would not create so elaborate a strategy and then row straight into the path of Drake's fleet on their way out. They must have another plan. A plume of spray slaps me in the face again and I recall my walk along the Hoe with Sam. He had talked about a network of secret tunnels used by those who bring in contraband. But if these were still in use, Drake would surely have mentioned them.

The water eddies faster around the foot of the rocks and I have to fight to heave the craft level with the landing stage, which has been built out from the shallow beach on the north side of the island. The current pulls me hard to the west and the wind drives me backwards, away from the shore; I feel my shoulders may be wrenched out of their sockets in the effort to maintain a straight course. After wrestling with the weather for so long that I fear I may never make it ashore, a fortuitous wave bumps my boat against the wooden pillars of the landing stage and I grab for the iron ladder that hangs from it, slippery with tendrils of weed. Once the boat is secured, I gather my equipment: the bag containing the book and an unlit lantern. A tinder-box, tucked away inside my doublet. I check that my knife is in place. As I climb the ladder, my arms shake with fatigue and it is a struggle to bear my own weight. Another sharp ploy by Jenkes and Doughty, to ensure whoever comes to meet their challenge will be exhausted by the journey. I could have asked someone to row for me, but the light I saw suggests they were watching my approach from the high point of the island. If they had seen two people in the boat, they might have considered the deal broken already.

I pull up the hood of my cloak and leave the lantern unlit. The wind has driven the clouds inland and clear patches of sky are widening over the water, fading to violet, the first faint glimmer of stars visible. A bright gibbous moon hangs overhead, giving some light to the uneven path that curves ahead up the cliff. I breathe deeply and begin to climb, keeping close to the rock, my ears straining for any sound that would betray an ambush. But there is no sign of life here except the gulls.

Fear holds all my nerves taut. The hairs on my body bristle. At any moment I expect to hear the whistle of a crossbow bolt, or feel a cold edge of steel against my neck, but I reach the top of the cliff path without hindrance, which only makes my fear all the greater. Ahead I see a clump of scrubby trees and my heart lodges in my throat; surely here, in their shadow, is where they will take me, unguarded as I am? But all I can hear is my own ragged breathing and the moans of the wind. I whip around at every creak of a branch, every snapping of a twig. As I follow the path through, there is a sudden flapping of wings and a crashing of leaves as I startle some bird out of its roost; I smother my instinct to cry out, but by the time I emerge from the trees on to a wide grassy expanse at the summit of the island my whole body is trembling.

In the moonlight I can make out the form of a small chapel. To the south and east of it, the outline of ramparts, the half-finished fort Drake had mentioned. The place is entirely still; there is no sign of any movement save the branches of the trees and the scudding clouds above me. If there were soldiers stationed here, I fear Thomas Drake was right; the men waiting for me will have made sure they could not interfere.

I walk towards the chapel, slowly, one cautious step after another. As I draw closer I can make out its narrow pointed windows, black slits along the side, and a low arched door at one end. It has no tower, just a gabled roof that looks in need of repair. There are no lights anywhere. This is where they want me, I think to myself as I approach the door. This is where they will be waiting. Jenkes will appreciate this setting; Jenkes the faithful son of Rome, who hates all heretics with a holy fury and regards their murder as an act of piety. Will he shed my blood in a holy place? The chapel is exposed on all sides here, the wind cutting across the clifftop, scything at the hood of my cloak. I pull it tighter around me and walk up to the door, my tread as silent as I can make it.

I exhale slowly, trying to calm my pulse. My palms prickle with sweat. This is where it will come, I fear: the killer blow, out of the darkness behind the door. I can almost feel them waiting for me. The wind drops suddenly, as if holding its breath. I set down my unused lantern and undo the top buttons of my doublet, loosening my knife in its sheath so that I can draw it in one movement when I need to. I place a hand on the latch, and turn it. The door creaks open an inch.

In case anyone is hiding behind it, I kick the door hard so that it smashes against the wall behind and judders on its hinges. Nothing moves inside. I peer into the black maw of the chapel. After a long pause, I step forward on to the threshold.

Faint light from the windows slants across the worn flag-stones. All else is smothered in a thick, velvet darkness. I breathe in the mineral smell of old stone. Then I hear it, or perhaps I sense it, the sound is so insubstantial, but it is there – a muffled, shallow breathing, quick and panicked, like a cornered animal. I take another step inside, slipping the knife silently from its cover. The sound grows stronger; I am not mistaken. I lower my hood, not wanting my vision obscured, and advance another two paces, blade held out before me. I jolt as I hear the swift creak and slam of the chapel door. I should have expected that: now I am trapped. Blackness closes around me; from somewhere there comes a brief, muffled cry, or perhaps a sob. I wheel around in the dark, pointing my knife this way and that, jabbing it from side to side, but it only slices through chill air. I can feel the fear rising in my chest, the dread that threatens to overtake my reason; with all the force of my will I fight it down and concentrate on straining my ears through the dark for any tell-tale sound.

In the silence, I catch the rasp of a flint striking; at the far end of the chapel, the small glow of a tinder-box sparking. I keep absolutely still. So one of them is directly ahead of me, but that leaves one to creep up from behind. The spark catches and a candle flame wavers into life. It moves, not towards me but to the side, and another orange petal of light blooms from it, followed by another, and another, until there is enough light to make out a figure passing down the side of the chapel, lighting the stubs of candles in wall sconces. Finally he turns to me and takes a step closer. I hear a soft movement from my left and jerk around, hearing myself gasp aloud at the sight that greets me. In the dim, flickering light I see Lady Arden, her hands tied in front of her, a cloth bound over her mouth and a noose around her neck. The rope attached to it is slung over a beam in the rafters. Her feet rest precariously on a rickety wooden trestle. There is barely any slack in the rope. If she lost her balance, or if the bench were to be kicked from under her, she would begin to choke immediately. Her eyes bulge with terror; she makes a whimpering noise, stifled by her gag.

The figure with the candle makes his way towards me, though he stops a good few feet from the range of my blade and fixes me with a knowing smile. He is instantly recognisable. Rowland Jenkes must have suffered the pox badly as a young man; his face is pitted with the marks of it. Livid scar tissue swells around the holes where he cut off his own ears after he was nailed to the pillory in Oxford. Despite all this, England's most notorious dealer in forbidden books must once have been a handsome man; above his high, sharp cheekbones, those extraordinary eyes still exert a strange pull. Warm, dancing eyes that invite you to fall into them, so at odds with the ravaged landscape of his face. But the warmth is deceptive, as I learned two years ago.

Jenkes shakes his head in slow disbelief, still smiling, looking me up and down as if I am a long-lost brother, thought missing or dead. He does not appear to be armed, though this too may be a deception.

'Well – you are not Sir Francis Drake, but what an unexpected pleasure.' His droll tone tells me it is anything but. His voice, like his eyes, does not belong with his alarming appearance; it is refined, cultured, soothing. 'Welcome to the chapel of St Michael, Giordano Bruno.' He sweeps a hand around. 'Of all the places we could choose to be reunited. Who would have thought? The Lord's design truly is a mystery, don't you think? I was just saying to Lady Arden here,' he continues, conversationally, never taking his eyes from mine, 'how we go back, you and I. Some might call it coincidence, but I say it is the working of Providence.' The smile fades a touch. 'It was impossible for me to return to Oxford, after your visit. I had to leave behind a lucrative business. I resented that.'

'Please accept my apologies,' I say, in a voice like ice.

'Oh, that is gracious of you. Well, no matter. I am used to moving on. As are you. We have that in common too – neither of us welcome in our own countries for our beliefs. I spent a year in France, making myself useful, buying and selling books, keeping my eyes open. Until one day I heard rumours of a very special volume. One that I had been told did not exist. Do you recall, Bruno, you came to me in Oxford looking for a book that was supposed not to exist?' The smile peels back; his teeth glint in the light. 'Well, here was another. One of the English recusants had been imprisoned in the Marshalsea with a gentleman sailor, a man who had travelled around the world with Sir Francis Drake and as his reward found himself charged with treason, though he was innocent of any offence save pursuing justice for his murdered brother.' He shakes his head again, in exaggerated sorrow. 'In prison, this desperate sailor told stories of his travels. One of those stories concerned a Coptic manuscript and a murdered Jesuit.' His eyes flit to the bag under my arm; his tongue darts quickly over his thin lips in anticipation. 'Most of the other prisoners thought he was raving, but one, this Catholic recusant, believed him. On his release, this man fled to join the English Catholics in Paris, where he told the sailor's story. When the rumour reached my ears – no, I never find that any less funny – I returned to London to seek out this gentleman sailor. But I forget – you have already met.' I see his gaze move beyond my shoulder. From behind me comes the unmistakable click of metal on metal. Another stifled squeal from Lady Arden. I turn slowly to see a figure step out of the shadows, and recognise immediately the man who had burst in on me at the House of Vesta.

Doughty plants himself between me and the chapel door. He is holding over his arm an ornately carved wheel-lock pistol. Its muzzle points directly at me. No wonder Jenkes appeared so at ease in the face of my knife.

'A pleasure to meet you again, Doctor Bruno. You left without saying goodbye the last time. I only wanted to talk.' Doughty offers a cold smile, showing the gaps in his mouth. 'Look at all the trouble you could have saved us if you hadn't run off like a skittish hind.' He gestures towards Lady Arden.

I hold his gaze as steadily as I can, to show that I will not be intimidated by him this time, though it is difficult to ignore the pistol. He has an intelligent face, but he wears a hunted look, the eyes deep-set in shadowed sockets and always flickering away from me, as if waiting for a blow to fall from some unexpected quarter.

'John and I found we had common cause,' Jenkes continues, moving around to the edge of my line of sight.

'You are Catholic, then?' I ask Doughty, turning back to him. My voice sounds less steady than I would have liked.

He shakes his head. 'I care nothing for any prelate in Rome. I never betrayed my country, whatever they said – it was England betrayed me. All I desire now is to see Francis Drake suffer as my family has suffered. If that means siding with the French or Spanish, well – I have already been punished for that before the fact.' He smiles, stretching his mouth back to show off the price he paid.

I have had enough of them amusing themselves at my expense. I swing the bag with the book around to my front and lift the flap. 'Shall we make this fair exchange you speak of, Jenkes? Then we can all be on our way.'

He responds with a thin smile. 'Put the knife down first, Bruno, there's a good boy, you'll have someone's eye out.' When he sees me hesitate, he strolls casually across to the bench where Lady Arden balances, rests one foot on it and gives it a little nudge as if testing its solidity. I see her raise her eyes to heaven as tears spill down her cheeks. I drop the knife; it clatters to the stone floor and Jenkes removes his foot, nodding approval at me. He saunters back, picks it up and studies the carved bone handle. 'Nice craftsmanship. They know how to fashion a weapon, your countrymen.' He runs a forefinger appreciatively along its length and tests the point of the blade against the tip of his finger. A wash of cold courses through me. Now I am naked, with no defence except my wit, and I do not know how that will fare against a knife and a pistol. 'I worry, you see, Bruno,' Jenkes says, looking up, in the manner of one making small talk. 'I worry that Francis Drake does not understand the concept of a fair exchange. Even now, I fear that he has surrounded the island with armed men waiting to fire on us as soon as we show our faces.'

He watches me closely for a reaction. I guard my expression.

'Sir Francis will keep to the terms of your proposal,' I say, evenly.

'Evidently he will not,' Doughty says, indignant. 'We stated clearly he was to come in person.'

'You must have known Drake would not come here alone.' I turn to him, fighting to keep my voice calm. I pat the bag. 'I have what you want here, Jenkes. Let the agreement stand.' I look across at the book dealer, knowing my fear is visible but clinging to the absurd hope that he can be reasoned with. He assumes a thoughtful expression, pretending to consider this, as he moves back towards Lady Arden. My throat constricts.

'I'm afraid John is right, Bruno – strictly speaking, Drake has already broken faith with us.' He pauses to look regretful, then with one swift motion he kicks his heel back and knocks the bench from under her.

The rope jerks taut; a hideous choking sound explodes from her throat. In the space of a breath I hurl myself towards Lady Arden and grab her just below the knees, using all the strength left in my arms to lift her upwards to restore some slack in the rope. I struggle until she gets her knees on to my shoulder and hangs there, still choking, her bound hands clawing at the noose. I close my eyes, expecting at any moment to hear the explosion, smell the cordite, a heartbeat before the shot enters my brain. Instead, all I hear is Jenkes's laughter.

'Very quick reaction, Bruno,' he says, tipping the bench upright again and indicating that I should set Lady Arden's feet back on it. 'Impressive. Just a little test for you.'

Her weight falls against me as I balance her. I glance up; her breathing is laboured and her face puce, her eyes unfocused. I fear that if I let go she will faint and her feet will slip again, until she is spinning slowly from the end of the rope.

'I recall another woman you got yourself mixed up with, in Oxford,' he muses. 'Risked your life to save her too, didn't you? You belong in an ancient tale of chivalry, Bruno. It quite breaks my heart to think of you wasting so many years in a monastery, denying womankind such gallantry.' His attention is concentrated on scraping dirt from under his fingernails with the tip of my knife. From the corner of my eye, I see Doughty move around to my right, a cold gleam where the pistol is still levelled at me. Jenkes snaps his head up suddenly. 'Give me the manuscript.' He holds a hand out and clicks his fingers impatiently.

Gingerly, I let go of Lady Arden's legs; she sways unnervingly, but seems to have recovered enough to find her footing, at least for now. I reach into the satchel and draw out the manuscript in its wrappings. Jenkes's eyes glitter; he licks his lips again and holds his hand out. I hold it close against my chest; I will not put it into his hands, if I can help it, until I see Lady Arden cut down, or I have no means left to bargain.

'As soon as I saw you at the Star that night I knew Drake must have brought you here to evaluate this. He proved particularly stubborn about selling it, though I offered a good price. I realised I would have to find another way.' He steps closer, left hand outstretched, the knife still clutched in his right, though he lowers it to his side. His eyes are fixed on the manuscript with a wolfish greed. 'When that helpful little maid at the Star brought me the translation you had been working on, I knew immediately that this was the real thing. The lost Gospel of Judas. Did you make another, by the way?'

I do not reply.

'Well, I don't suppose it matters,' he continues. 'A translation is worth nothing without the original to validate it. Though the Vatican will not like the idea of an unauthorised copy circulating.'

'So that is your customer?'

He looks up to meet my eye and laughs. 'Why, would you not have come if you had known? Would you have left her to swing rather than concede anything to your enemy? Do you still hate Rome so much?' He does not wait for me to answer. Instead he tilts his head to one side, pats the manuscript and regards me with an eager curiosity. 'Tell me, then, as one scholar to another – is it authentic?'

I hesitate barely the space of a breath before replying. 'Almost certainly not. Second century, the usual gnostic teachings. Nothing the Church has not seen and put down a hundred times. It was not written by Judas Iscariot, if that is what you mean.'

Jenkes tips his head back and lets out that cracked laugh again; it echoes around the roof like flames on dry wood. 'You are a good liar, Bruno, like all Dominicans, but not quite good enough. That you should feel the need to lie tells me all I need to know. Hand it over.'

He steps closer, nodding towards the package. The hand holding the knife hangs loosely at his side; his desire for the book has caused him to relax his guard. I calculate the action, the distance; bruised and aching as I am, I could kick him in the groin and have him on his back, pinned to the ground, a foot on his neck and the knife off him before he had time to react. It could be done. But not with John Doughty standing behind me, his pistol cocked; I would be dead in an instant, and Lady Arden would drop to a slow strangulation.

I nod towards her. 'Cut her down first.'

'Do you really believe you are in a position to negotiate, Bruno? First I want to see that you have not brought us some forgery or substitute. Although that would be very foolish indeed on your part and Drake's, and whatever else you may be, I do not take either of you for a fool. Show me the book. John!' He gestures Doughty across the room to Lady Arden. Doughty rests a foot on the bench, his gun still pointed at me.

'Do as you are asked, Bruno, and no one will be hurt.' Jenkes lifts the knife to the side of my head and holds it against my ear. 'Though it is tempting, to show you first-hand what I endured. Handsome fellow like you – how would you like to look like me?' He presses the knife a little harder. A warm trickle runs down my neck. I clamp my jaw tight and keep my eyes fixed on his. 'You would find ladies of quality like this one here less eager for your company, I fear.'

Keeping my head as still as I can, I unwrap the manuscript from its protective oilcloth and open it to the first page, willing my fingers not to tremble. Jenkes bends towards it, almost salivating. He lowers the knife, lifts the book from my hands and turns a few pages, his attention wholly absorbed. I look across at Doughty. His foot rocks the bench a fraction, to show me I should not think of moving. I press my sleeve to my ear and it comes away spotted with blood, though the cut is only small, just enough to give me a taste of what might come next. We are entirely at their mercy; if it pleased them to make us suffer before death, we would be powerless to stop them. I try to push the thought away, but the fear of torture sits like a stone in my throat.

Jenkes turns another page. A slow, triumphant smile curves over his face.

'The hour grows late, Rowland,' Doughty says, impatient. 'The boat will be waiting. Let us get this over with.'

I sneak a quick look at him. This is welcome news; if they are in a hurry to leave, perhaps they will not have time to indulge any drawn-out toying with their prey.

Jenkes snaps his head up and for an instant his face glows, as if he were experiencing his own private rapture. 'This is the book,' he says, jolting back to himself. 'Cut her down.'

I stare at him. My legs almost fold under me and I have to concentrate on standing, the wave of relief is so great it threatens to knock me off balance. Does he really mean to keep to the bargain? Even John Doughty looks sceptical, though after an exchange of glances with Jenkes he steps up on to the bench, takes a knife from his belt and, tucking the pistol under his arm, proceeds to sever the rope above Lady Arden's head. She slumps into his arms, knocking them both off balance; Doughty falls backwards and just manages to catch her as she topples from the bench. She can hardly stand, she collapses into him and he lets her slide to the floor. I take a step towards them to find the point of my own knife inches from my eye.

'Stay where you are, Bruno.' Jenkes holds the blade steady in front of me until Doughty has righted himself and aimed the pistol at me once more. When he is sure that I cannot afford to move, he wraps the manuscript again and motions to me to pass him the bag, where he tucks it safely away. 'Thank you. Not the sort of thing we want falling into any old hands, is it? Best it is kept secure where it can do no harm.'

I do not reply. I have long ceased to care about the book; all I want now is to be allowed to leave with Lady Arden. He slings the bag over his shoulder and pauses to study me.

'This chapel was completed in the twelfth century. They were most ingenious with their building works, those monks.' He gestures to the crumbling walls. 'It doesn't look much from here, I grant you, but it does hold a few surprises. Chapels built in remote high places are often dedicated to Saint Michael – patron saint of those who suffer. How apt.' He smiles, showing his teeth. 'Even you might find yourself offering a prayer to him, Bruno.' He picks up an empty lantern and takes one of the lit candles from a wall sconce to fit inside it.

I realise now, with a flat sense of inevitability, that my brief flicker of hope was a delusion. We are to die here, and cruelly, if Jenkes has his way. Doughty heaves Lady Arden to her feet, hooks her limp arms around his neck and half-hauls, half-forces her over to where we stand.

'You had better take her,' he says, pushing her roughly towards me. 'She is your whore, is she not?' I brace myself to support her weight, hooking an arm around her waist to keep her on her feet. Her eyes are glazed, as if she is drugged, perhaps the effect of being partially choked. She slumps into me.

'I found her not especially pleasing,' Doughty adds, lightly. 'Though I imagine one gets more out of it when she shows some enthusiasm? She seemed unwilling to give me her best efforts, I must say.' He laughs, a low taunting snigger. His words rouse Lady Arden from her stupor; anger surges through her, sparking in her eyes as she spits a curse at him, though it is muffled by her gag. I feel all her muscles tensed against me and I am seized by the urge to rush at John Doughty and crush his head into the wall. As if reading my thoughts, he lifts the pistol again and levels it at my face. I find myself hoping, absurdly, that he will shoot Lady Arden first; at least that way I would not feel I was leaving her for them to torture further after my death. A great tremor travels across her shoulders; after it has passed she seems to subside. She closes her eyes. I keep mine open, fixed on Doughty. I will die looking him in the face, so he remembers that look for the rest of his sorry days.

But he does not pull the trigger. Instead he glances over to Jenkes, who walks purposefully to the east end of the chapel, where a small stone altar stands bare under the narrow window. Setting his lantern on the altar, he crouches behind it, busy with something on the floor, out of view. After a short while, I hear a strained grunt accompanied by the grating of stone and Jenkes reappears, beckoning us. Doughty makes a brusque gesture with the gun, so I shuffle forward, pulling Lady Arden with me as best I can. She seems better able to move her feet as we approach Jenkes, though it is I who falter as I feel the cold muzzle prodding between my shoulder blades. There is less light here; the sconces Jenkes lit are at the other end of the chapel and are already burning down. The semi-circular chancel behind the altar is sunk in near-darkness; an orange glow licks up and down the stone as the candle dances wildly in a draught. Jenkes indicates the floor; he lifts the lantern and holds it closer so that I can see where he is pointing.

He has removed one of the carved memorial stones set into the floor to reveal a rectangular space. I can see nothing but two worn stairs, leading down into black. A stale, dank smell drifts upwards.

'Down you go,' Jenkes says pleasantly.

Sweat prickles on my palms and my brow. I hesitate, unable to move my feet. Does he mean to incarcerate us underground? My heart skitters like a terrified creature; since I was a youth I have had a horror of confined spaces, of airless darkness. I have a recurring nightmare of being buried alive. I would rather he shot me here and now, and have it all over in an instant; I almost say so. But there is Lady Arden to think of.

'Don't take all night about it, Bruno, we have a pressing appointment with a French merchant ship,' Jenkes says, pointing to the maw of the crypt. 'We're coming with you, don't worry.' The enigmatic smile again; he is enjoying himself.

I try to close my mind to thoughts of what awaits us down there and concentrate on each step, each breath. The opening is only wide enough for one person at a time. I let go of Lady Arden, wait until I am sure she is able to stand, then turn my back on the stairs and begin to descend backwards into that dark space, holding both her hands with mine and leading her down, one at a time, until I can see nothing. I have no idea how far down the stairs will lead, but I count about a dozen before I reach a solid brick floor. I guide her down the last step; she stumbles and falls against me, and I pull her close to shield us both from the cold. All around us is thick darkness and the smell of damp stone.

Lady Arden shivers in my arms. I unfasten the cloak at my

neck and wrap it around her shoulders, but she goes on shaking violently. A faint light hovers at the top of the steps; I fully expect to hear the stone grind into place over us. But, true to his word, Doughty begins to descend with the lantern in one hand, the pistol in the other. Halfway down he pauses, waiting for Jenkes, but there is light enough to see that we are in a vaulted undercroft, lined in aged brick. Crates and barrels are stacked around the walls. Jenkes eventually appears on the steps and reaches up, pulling the memorial stone overhead until it falls into place with a heavy crash. He is holding another lantern. Coiled over his arm is a length of rope – presumably that which had suspended Lady Arden from the beam.

Now the four of us are seemingly trapped down here. My mind is a riot of unformed terrors, though for Lady Arden's sake I fight to keep my breathing steady and my face composed. Jenkes walks slowly towards us, rope in hand.

'I hope you won't make this difficult, Bruno,' he says. His eyes shine in the semi-darkness. 'Just remember, any attempt to cause trouble on your part and you will have a shot between the eyes before you can blink. Then you wouldn't be here to protect the lady, would you? Not that your protection is worth much, but it allows you to maintain the illusion of control, does it not? Now – this will interest you. Come and look.'

At the far end of the undercroft, three barrels are piled up in a corner. All around them, on the ground, are fragments of broken brick. Jenkes sets down the lantern cautiously, some distance from us, takes hold of a barrel and heaves it out of the way, then does the same with the others. Behind us, Doughty prowls, silent as a wildcat, only the swinging cone of light tracing his movements. Jenkes holds up his lantern to illuminate a patch of loose bricks set into the floor.

'I told you these monks were ingenious,' he says, squatting to prise one brick out with his fingers. It scrapes away easily and he tosses it to one side. 'This is hard labour – why don't you do it for me, Bruno?'

Unwillingly, I release Lady Arden, who leans back against a pillar, and crouch at Jenkes's feet. I lift out another brick, and a gust of chill, damp air causes goosebumps to rise on my skin.

'That's it, keep going,' Jenkes says, 'all the loose ones. The chapel was intended partly as place of worship, partly as vantage point. This undercroft is built into the very rock of the island. But they were afraid that if the enemy invaded – France, as it was then – the island would be taken first. They built into their chapel a means of escape.'

'A secret tunnel?' So that was why the two of them were so untroubled by the prospect of Drake's waiting fleet.

He looks almost disappointed. 'You know of it?'

'Drake knows of it – they will be waiting for you at the other end.'

A brief shadow of doubt crosses his face. 'Where is the other end, then?' When I do not reply, he laughs. 'You are bluffing. Good try, Bruno. There are plenty of legends about the tunnels, but very few people know of their existence. The customs men had this entrance bricked up years ago, but the smugglers are enterprising fellows, and there is more than one exit, to foil the authorities. The tunnel itself is in a poor state of repair, but it is still passable. Drake's men will be waiting till dawn to catch us leaving by sea. By which time we will be long gone.' He pats the bag at his side.

'They will catch you one way or another,' I say, trying to sound as if I believe it. 'Drake already has the hue and cry out for you.'

Jenkes shakes his head and tuts, as if he is disappointed in my efforts. 'You know very well that is not true, Bruno. Drake would not do anything that would risk Lady Arden's life. It was a gamble, I'll admit, but Doughty seemed sure of it.'

'What about Robert Dunne?' I say, turning to John Doughty. 'Was he a gamble too?'

He gives a baffled laugh. 'Dunne? Yes, I suppose he was.

392

A gamble I lost, in the end, which I should have foreseen. Poor Dunne was cursed by ill luck. Worse even than mine, so it seems.'

'So what do you get out of this charade?' If I can at least keep them talking, I give myself time to think. Unfortunately I cannot fathom any way out that will not leave Lady Arden or me, or more likely both of us, dead. 'You didn't really believe Drake would come here in person?'

Doughty considers the question. 'No, I suppose in my heart I did not. But this will do almost as well for now. I will leave her head in the church for him to find.'

Lady Arden makes a frantic noise through her gag. She sinks to the floor, tears streaming down her face. She is so pale I fear she may vomit; with her mouth bound, she would choke immediately.

'By rights I should leave it on the cliff for the sea birds to peck out her eyes, like he did with my poor brother's,' Doughty continues matter-of-factly. 'See how he likes that. Show him a prelude to his own death.'

'You really think you will kill Drake one day?' I ask.

He does not miss the scorn in my voice. His expression hardens as he steps closer.

'I must believe it,' he says, through his remaining teeth, and in those words I hear the force of the man's despair. 'The only thing that stops me following Robert Dunne's example is the oath I swore to my brother, that I will see Francis Drake in his grave before I go to mine. That man took everything from me.' He is so close I can feel his breath on my face. The muzzle of the gun presses against my breastbone. I hear the blood thudding in my ears. 'My brother, my money, my reputation. My patriotism. Even my fucking teeth,' he adds, with a sour laugh. 'And I had good teeth. While he collects land, titles, fame, royal favour, a beautiful young wife.' He casts a glance at Lady Arden. 'I would have preferred to have taken his wife, of course – saving your presence, my lady – but Elizabeth

393

Drake is too closely watched. This bitch will have to do. I will take his spoils from him, one by one, until he knows how it feels to lose everything. England will never give me justice, so I must make my own.'

'Or persuade a desperate man like Robert Dunne to do it for you,' I say, though I did not miss his reference to 'Dunne's example'.

A thin smile. 'Persuade . . . yes, it sounds better when you put it like that. Robert Dunne was a despicable coward. You can make a coward do anything if he thinks he will save his own skin. Especially a coward in debt. I settled his debts at the House of Vesta, you know. After that he was my creature.'

'But he wasn't, was he?' I say. 'He didn't do what you wanted, in the end.'

'True.' He sounds regretful. 'I thought he was desperate enough to do it for the money. A small dose of monkshood in Drake's wine would have done it – hardly a problem once they're out at sea. I even showed Dunne how the poison was distilled. He seemed so willing at first.' He makes a sharp, wincing motion and clicks his tongue. 'I should have realised he had that pathetic filial loyalty some men develop towards Drake. In the end his conscience weighed heavier than his fear. He took the coward's way out.'

So he really believes Dunne killed himself? I recall the letter Drake received the day after Dunne's death with the verse from Matthew's gospel, with its reference to Judas's remorseful suicide.

'Is that why you sent that letter?' I ask. 'So that Drake would think Dunne's death was connected with the Judas book?'

A small crease appears between his brows; he darts a glance at Jenkes. 'Which letter?'

'The one with the Bible verse: Matthew 27 verse 5.'

Doughty only looks more confused; the crease in his forehead deepens. '*Matthew?*'

'Judas went from that place and hanged himself,' Jenkes says, smoothly.

'You see? He knows it word for word.'

'My dear Bruno – I know most of the scriptures word for word. As do you. But why would anyone send such a letter?' He arches an eyebrow.

'You tell me. To imply that Dunne hanged himself out of remorse for his treachery, just like Judas? To serve as a warning to Drake, that the Judas Gospel brings nothing but harm?' I suggest. 'Or simply to frighten him. To show him once again that you know everything that touches him, even on his ship.'

Doughty lets out a bark of laughter. 'Frighten him? It would take more than a letter with a line of scripture to frighten El Draco.'

'Really? What would it take – a letter threatening the curse of the Devil? No, that did not work. One telling him you are watching his wife, perhaps?'

John Doughty looks abashed, but only briefly. 'I was not quite myself when I sent those. Prison can turn a man's wits, you know. But I never sent him any Bible verse.'

'No more did I,' Jenkes says, with a shrug. 'The others, yes, via the girl to you and this lady here. But no verses.'

'We are wasting time,' Doughty says, impatient. 'The ship sails on the evening tide and we must be on it, or risk being found by the hue and cry. What does it matter who sent the letter?'

'It matters,' I begin, 'because . . .' But I find I cannot answer the question. All along we have believed that the letter was sent either by Dunne's killer, or someone who knew his identity and wanted to toy with Drake. The other letters had led me to assume that they were connected with the first one. But the recent discoveries about Savile and Martha Dunne have thrown all those theories into confusion.

'Do you know who killed Robert Dunne?' I ask. 'Indulge me – it is not as if I can tell anyone now. Satisfy my curiosity.'

'Is that your last request, Bruno?' Jenkes cocks his head to one side, but Doughty holds a hand up to silence him, still frowning at me.

'Does Francis Drake truly believe Dunne did not kill himself?' He shakes his head, looking perplexed. 'I knew there was an inquest, but I thought that was the widow's doing, it was to be expected. Who would want Dunne dead?' He appears disconcerted.

'Other than you?' I say.

'He was no use to me dead. Not yet, at least. Not until he had served his purpose. Dunne knew I had marked him for his part in the jury that falsely convicted my brother. But as I told you, he was a coward. I convinced him that by killing Drake for me, he had a chance to save himself and his women.' He lets out a sharp laugh. 'I even promised him a share of the price on Drake's head. I thought that would swing the balance.'

'The twenty thousand ducats,' I murmur. 'You meant to claim that from Spain?'

'Of course.' He says this in a clipped, businesslike tone. 'But I suspected Dunne was not such a fool as to believe I would let him live. I had supposed he decided it was better to damn his soul with suicide than with murder.' He purses his lips and his brow creases again. 'But you seriously think someone else killed him?' He glances at Jenkes. 'Someone who guessed what he planned and wanted to save Drake, I suppose?' He smacks a fist into his palm. 'So he must have confessed his purpose to someone else on board. Who?'

Now it is the book dealer's turn to look impatient. 'What does it matter? The man is dead and it has nothing to do with us. Enough talking – it is time to go.'

He gestures to me to turn around, and wrenches my arms back, binding my wrists behind me. My knees crack against the floor as he pushes me down and drags me across to the pillar where Lady Arden lies curled up and whimpering, her face buried in her knees, as if she could make herself so small she might escape their notice. Jenkes sits me upright, my back against the pillar. He does the same with Lady Arden on the other side, then takes the remaining length of rope and wraps it around the two of us, binding us fast to the pillar, so tight I can feel the cord cutting into my chest each time I expand my lungs to breathe. Lady Arden makes the occasional hiccupping sob, though subdued, like a child whose tantrum has subsided. It is a defeated sound. I hope that she is only semi-conscious; I wish I were in that state myself, but my awareness seems heightened by the nearness of my death, as if everything is picked out in perfect clarity. I see the black hairs on the back of Jenkes's hands as he moves the lantern some distance away and begins to shift one of the barrels towards us; I hear the scrape of the wood over the brick floor. I notice how the veins bulge at his temple with the effort of moving it. He does the same with the other two, positioning them around us. When he has arranged them to his satisfaction, he dusts off his hands and smiles, as if pleased with his handiwork.

'In the time of the heretic queen's father and grandfather, this undercroft was used as a munitions store,' he says, in a conversational tone. 'Some supplies were left, in anticipation of the new fort.' He takes out my knife and uses it to prise open the bung in the top of one barrel, then calls Doughty to help him lift it. Now I understand why he moved the lantern to a safe distance. He indicates the far side of the undercroft and they carry the barrel between them, tipping it up to release its contents as they move backwards towards me and Lady Arden. A trail of fine black powder snakes behind them; they scatter it liberally around us before wedging the barrel into place next to me. Then they cross the room again and lay a second trail.

When they have done, Doughty surveys the tableau before him and curls his lip. He seems displeased with the result.

'I would still rather Drake found her head on the altar,' he says. 'There should be some poetic justice to this.'

'Do you know how long it would take to sever a head with a knife like this?' Jenkes snaps. 'And how would we walk away, covered head to foot in blood? No, this is the practical solution. The fuse is long enough to give us time to get some way into the passage. The explosion will seal off the entrance here, and will be large enough to attract attention. While Drake's men are busy trying to dig out what's left of the gallant Bruno and his lady, we will be long gone. Come – take this lantern.'

'Should we not at least make sure they are dead first?' Doughty says, crouching to our level and cocking the gun towards me.

'Do not waste good shot. We will have need of that. You think three barrels of gunpowder will not suffice? Besides,' Jenkes looks at me and smiles his lazy, reptilian smile, 'I want to give Bruno time to repent. To count the minutes as he sees his death stealing towards him. I have often observed that heretics lose their defiance when they realise they will shortly face their Maker. You are a man with a ready wit, Bruno, but I fear it will not hold up when you have to stand before the throne of judgement.'

I say nothing. He looks disappointed, as if I have deliberately spoiled his game.

'Come, then,' he says to Doughty, who disables the pistol, tucking it into his belt, then takes one of the lanterns and lowers himself cautiously into the hole. Jenkes sets the other lantern down by the entrance to the tunnel shaft, slips the satchel over his head and traces his path back to the beginnings of the gunpowder trail.

'At least take the gag from her mouth,' I say, my voice shrill with panic. I have escaped Jenkes before; I could do so again, if only my thoughts would stop jostling one another long enough for me to see a clear path. I try to move my wrists behind my back but the cords are so tight there is barely any give; I succeed only in making them cut deeper into my flesh.

'So you can whisper your enduring love to one another as you die?' Jenkes says, amused. 'Very well. Never let it be said I am not merciful.' He breaks into that dry cackle again.

I see a flash of steel by my right eye; for a dreadful moment I wonder if I have provoked him by asking a favour. Perhaps he will do something worse to Lady Arden. But I hear the swift tear of cloth, followed by a soft sigh and a choking cough. The pillar is narrow but I am tied so tight I cannot turn my head to see her. Jenkes drops the severed gag on the floor and returns to the gunpowder fuse he has laid. He readies a taper and turns back to judge the distance between himself and the entrance to the tunnel, then concentrates on tidying his thin black powder ropes with the tip of his boot, making sure there are no breaks in the trail, nothing which might cause the flame to falter and die before it reaches its goal. When he is satisfied that everything is ready, he strikes his tinder-box carefully, his eyes meeting mine with a black glitter as he lights the taper from its spark. Then, in one practised movement, he lowers the taper to the end of one fuse, waits until he is certain it has taken, repeats the movement with the other, then scuttles across the floor, snatches up the bag and the lantern and disappears into the hole in the corner. When only his head is visible, he pauses.

'Goodbye, Bruno,' he says. 'My lady. I hope Saint Michael hears you.'

His laugh echoes up the shaft as he descends, like some diabolical figure vanishing through the stage in an inn-yard theatre show. The pool of light wavers and diminishes with him.

'Bruno?' Lady Arden's voice emerges harsh and guttural, as if she is unused to using it. I think of her bruised and swollen throat and the rope that almost choked the breath from her – the same rope that now holds us fast to this pillar. Would it have been kinder to let her die there, in the church? Or will it be quicker this way? Would you lose consciousness in an instant, I wonder, or would you be aware of the force ripping through your frame as you were blasted in all directions?

'I'm here,' I say, knowing that my tone can convey no reassurance. I cannot even reach for her hand.

'Will we die?' she croaks.

There is no light now in the undercroft save the two little blue-gold dancing flames sizzling steadily towards us in a pincer movement. I stretch my legs as far forward as I can, sweeping my left foot and then my right in wide, desperate circles, hoping to disrupt the line of gunpowder, though I cannot see where I am kicking and I know that Jenkes has laid the trail in a loop out of my reach. The flames grow as they eat their way relentlessly along the line of the fuse, as if their progress only makes them hungrier.

'See if you can kick the powder away,' I say in desperation. The silence is filled by the short, frantic scratches of our heels in the dust.

'I can't see where it is,' she whispers. 'And I can't move my legs much anyway.'

'Never mind.' I do not know what else to say. She begins to murmur something soft and urgent under her breath, the cadence rising and falling. I strain to catch the words, but her voice goes on in the same chant, faster and faster, like the senseless babbling of a lunatic and I think the fear has turned her wits, until I catch *now and at the hour of our death, Amen.*

'Nell?' I say. The frenzied muttering continues. *Holy Mary, Mother of God, pray for us sinners, now and at the hour of our death, Amen.* 'I am so sorry,' I say, raising my voice over her manic repetitions. 'This is my fault. If it were not for me, you would not be mixed up in this.'

She pauses, mid-prayer. 'Not true,' she says. 'They took me because of Sir Francis, because they could not get to Elizabeth. You heard him. And in any case,' she adds, her breathing

400

growing fast and shallow, 'even if it were because of you, I cannot regret it. I would not undo that night with you.'

'Really?' I turn my head as far as I can, but all I can see is the twin flames advancing on us. The air is thick with smoke; tears spring to my eyes and I struggle to catch my breath through the acrid smell. I know that her declaration is of a piece with the frantic Hail Mary, a clutching at anything that will make her feel less alone as she waits for death, now moments away, yet it catches at my heart. I wish I could reach her, at least take her hand as we brace ourselves for the impact.

'Do you love me, Bruno?' she asks. I can hear the spike of terror in her voice. 'Do you? Oh, God have mercy on us.' She starts up a low moan which threatens to break into uncontrolled screaming. I feel I must soothe her, if only to prevent that being the last noise I hear.

'Yes,' I reply, surprised at how calm I sound.

'Then say it,' she demands, though it emerges as a harsh croak.

'I love you.' The words hang in the air with the smell of burning powder. A harmless lie to ease her last minutes; no one is hurt.

I feel oddly empty, as if watching this scene from outside. The flames have sucked their way along the trail and almost reached us, though they loop away on their detour, just out of reach. By the time they have burned around this last curve, they will touch the powder scattered all around us and finally ignite the barrels.

Behind me, in the darkness, Nell gives a choking sob. 'And I you,' she croaks. 'In another life—'

I make a gentle shushing sound, but it seems to me as if the noise comes from some other person. As the flames crackle the last few inches, I muster a final surge of energy and wrench my arms back, struggling with all my remaining strength against the rope that holds me to the pillar. I escaped Rowland Jenkes once; perhaps that gave me a false confidence, the belief that I could do it a second time. The rope bites into my flesh, rubbing it raw, but he has made it secure; I cannot save myself this time. Nell has taken up her prayers again. I think of the woman I did once love, and perhaps still do, far away; would she ever hear of my death, or care one way or another? Perhaps she is dead herself by now; I will never know.

The flame nearest me touches the powder around my feet and flares up; I writhe away as a sudden shock of heat scorches the left side of my body. There is no time to think; I pull my knees in, turn my face away from the flames and brace myself for the grand conflagration. In the thick darkness Nell screams, one long, piercing note, and the last thought that passes through my smoke-dazed mind is that at least the explosion will make that stop.

TWENTY-TWO

But the scream continues, boring through my skull, insistent and drawn out, until she runs out of breath and the note collapses into a protracted fit of coughing. I remain still, curled tight away from the kegs, every muscle tensed, awaiting the white-hot blast. After a long pause, I lift my head. Smoke grates against my throat, my eyes. There is nothing but blackness and the curtains of smoke. I let out a sudden, amazed bark of laughter.

'Bruno?'

'It didn't happen,' I say, jubilant. My own voice is harsh now from the fumes. 'The powder must have been too damp. It didn't take. Thank *God*.' I almost mean it. I laugh aloud again, my eyes streaming with tears.

'So – we are safe?' she asks, her voice small and shaky.

'Safe?' My euphoria quickly subsides; we still have no way of freeing ourselves and there is precious little air in this undercroft. Already I can feel my head swimming from breathing in the smoke. And what of Jenkes and Doughty? They cannot be too far along the tunnel. They will be expecting an explosion; when it does not come, will they return and silence us some other way, or are they in too much of a hurry to escape? 'We are in better shape than we would have been if these barrels had ignited, that much is certain,' I say.

403

'I feel dizzy,' she says. 'My throat hurts.'

'Take short breaths. We're going to get out soon,' I say, trying to sound convincing. 'Can you move your hands at all?' Unlike me, her hands are bound in front; she has a better chance of wriggling free. My throat is also scorched and my mouth dry and cracked; I would give anything for a sip of water. Drake's men will come eventually when they realise that no one has left the island, but they might wait hours, by which time we could have been poisoned by the smoke, or slaughtered like animals by Jenkes and Doughty, if they return.

'I can move them a little.' Her voice floats, disembodied, through the darkness. 'But I haven't the strength.'

'Try,' I say, with more force than I intend. 'If you can free your hands, you can untie us. It's our only chance – they have bound me too tight to move.'

She does not reply. I am afraid she has passed out, until I hear a scuffling noise, accompanied by a series of grunts and hard breathing, the sound of exertion. After a few moments she gives a sharp cry that might be pain or triumph, or both.

'I have one hand free!' she exclaims.

'Quick, then – untie us.'

There is a longer delay; she must first free her other hand, then find the knots that hold the rope binding us to the pillar. I curse again the loss of my knife. I listen to her scrabbling fingers, biting my tongue against my impatience, reminding myself of all she has been through. I make reassuring noises as she swears an oath, then half-sobs in frustration; when at last she falls still, I fear she has given up or collapsed, until I feel the rope around my chest slacken and I am able to lean forward, away from the pillar. She crawls through the smoke, trailing coils of rope, and hurls herself into me, burying her face in my neck, gasping or sobbing. I remind her gently that my wrists are still bound behind me. With shaking hands she unties them and finally I can stretch my stiff arms and

404

shoulders, though I am encumbered by Nell clinging to me like an infant.

I prise her away as gently as I can.

'We need to get out,' I say, trying to impart a sense of urgency without alarming her further. 'Are you burned?'

'Scorched a little on one side, but not badly,' she says. 'But it's hard to breathe in here. My throat . . .'

'Don't speak, then.' I hold her by the arms until I am sure she can stand alone. Inside my doublet I find my tinder-box and the candle I saved from the lantern. I can see nothing but smoke and blackness in the undercroft, so I place my hand on the rough surface of the pillar and take a few steps to my left, to be certain I am away from the gunpowder. We were remarkably fortunate – the barrels must have grown damp from being stored underground too long – but I do not want to take any chances. The flint strikes sparks and after a couple of attempts the candle lights, a feeble glow in the smoke.

'Stay there,' I instruct her. I grope my way fruitlessly along the walls until I reach the stone stairs we descended from the church. Relief ripples through my chest, allowing me briefly to forget my aches and pains. Shielding the candle, I climb until I can push against the stone over the entrance. It does not move. Cursing, I climb a few steps higher so that I can wedge my shoulder under the slab and use the whole weight of my body to force it upwards. I groan with the effort, all my muscles straining. Again, nothing. Jenkes has sealed it somehow. I run my fingers all around the edge, but I cannot make out any bolt or padlock. It must have some secret locking mechanism impossible to see in this light. After one last push, I concede defeat.

Holding my candle carefully behind my hand, I climb down and call to Nell. It is difficult to tell whether the smoke is beginning to subside, but my breathing seems fractionally less effortful. Through the haze I see her figure emerging, tentative, towards me. I reach for her hand.

'The entrance is sealed,' I explain. 'We have no choice but to use the tunnel.'

'But – those men are down there!' The whites of her eyes flash at me in the darkness, rolling like a spooked horse. 'They'll kill us if they find us following them.'

'They'll be long gone by now,' I say, with a firmness I do not feel.

'Can't we just wait here? Drake will come for us eventually, won't he?' She grips my arm, her face close to mine.

'Eventually is no good. This air will poison us if we go on breathing it for much longer. You said you felt dizzy – that's the smoke. I feel it too. If we pass out here we may not wake again. We have to take our chances. Come.'

I lead her towards the entrance to the tunnel, feeling my way with my feet so that we do not fall down it. The candle flame is no more than a fuzzy halo, barely penetrating the smoke. A loose brick skids as I kick it, then another, until I can feel a welcome breath of cool, damp air drifting up from the open shaft.

'I will go first,' I say. If Jenkes and Doughty are down there waiting, better I come upon them; I will at least put up a fight. 'Watch your step – come right to the edge of the hole – that's it. There – you see those rungs?' The mouth of the tunnel gapes, a bottomless pit in the faint light. Attached to one side I can see iron staples set into the wall. From here I can only make out the first two, but I have to assume they continue all the way down. 'Climb down on those. Tie the bottom of the cloak around your waist. We'll be doing it blind, though. I'll have to put the candle out as we climb.'

I sit among the loose bricks, my legs dangling over into the empty space. She moves alongside me and I hand her the candle.

'Take this. When I have gone down a few rungs, use it to find your footing, then blow it out and tuck it in your bodice.

Keep it secure – we will need it. You will have to feel your way down. Can you do that?'

She looks up, biting her lip, gives me one miserable nod. I position myself on my knees, facing the wall of the shaft, then lower my foot to the first iron bracket and the other foot further still, to the next. Groping in the thin light, I step down another, and another, amazed each time that they hold my weight. The metal feels ancient; rusted and grainy, gnawed by age and damp. But five rungs in, the air is clearer. I look up and see Nell's foot casting about for the first rung; she finds it and makes her footing secure, then extinguishes the light with a sharp puff. Darkness covers us.

I lose track of how far we descend, or how long it takes. The air grows colder the further down we climb and soon I am shivering, despite my wool doublet; I can hear the scrape of my breathing, my chest burning with each lungful. Moisture trickles down the walls of the shaft; in places the iron rungs are slippery with moss or weed. Stepping to the next rung, and the next, becomes an act of pure will. It feels as if we are descending to the frozen depths of the earth where Dante found the Devil himself devouring Judas Iscariot. At any moment I expect Nell to give up, to let go her hold on the rungs and tumble on to me, dragging me down with her to the bottom of the pit, but she keeps a tenacious grip and a steady pace. I dare not call out to her, in case Jenkes and Doughty are anywhere within earshot; though I can hear her laboured breaths, she makes no complaint.

At length, just as the muscles in my arms are about to mutiny, I put my foot down to find there are no more iron rungs, only an uneven rock floor sloping gently downwards. I step off to find myself in a tunnel, just high enough for me to stand, if I hunch over, and wide enough that I can touch the sides with my arms outstretched. There would be a limit to how much contraband you could smuggle through a tunnel this small, I think, peering ahead into the blackness. A whole cargo might take several journeys. God, a man would have to be determined – or desperate – to make a living this way. I whisper to Nell to watch her step. She arrives beside me, flexes her arms, and hands me the candle. I pause, straining to hear anything beyond the constant drip of water. When I am as satisfied as I can be that there is no movement ahead of us, I strike the tinder-box; the flame takes several attempts to catch, and gutters dangerously, but it holds and we are able to press on with its weak cone of light showing the path.

The tunnel is rough-hewn, rudimentary and in poor repair; fissures gape in the walls and roof and the water seeps in relentlessly, in some places no more than a trickle, but elsewhere a steady stream, pouring down the rock and along the floor. I think of those monks five hundred years earlier and the force it must have taken to hew this escape route out of the living rock. Here and there the passage is scattered with rubble where parts of the tunnel have subsided; I try not to think about the weight of the sea above us, the walls pressing in, the fact that I have no idea how far we have come or how much longer we must continue in this dank, subterranean trough. Instead I keep my breathing steady and concentrate on each step, guarding the candle flame and keeping alert for any sound that would betray the presence of another human. I can feel the pressure of Nell's hand on my back, her fingers clutching at my shirt as if she fears I would leave her behind.

'Who was the woman?' she says, out of nowhere.

'What?' I almost miss my footing and stumble, then turn, holding the candle up to look at her. Her hair hangs loose, the ends scorched a little on one side; her face is smeared with soot but her eyes have regained some of their fire.

'Which woman?'

'The woman in Oxford. The man with no ears said you risked your life for her once.'

'More than once,' I say, without thinking.

'Did you love her?' Her tone is accusing.

'It was a long time ago.' I turn back to the path ahead and continue walking, partly to hide the smile. Of all the things she could choose to worry about at present, it is the thought of another woman that preoccupies her. I find this oddly endearing. A woman's mind is a strange thing indeed.

I have barely taken five steps when I freeze, and the smile dies on my lips. A distant rumble reaches us from somewhere up ahead. I have been half-expecting this since we entered the tunnel; I did not believe that Jenkes and Doughty would leave anything to chance. Perhaps they took more explosives with them to seal off the tunnel once they reached the end. That rumble, I realise with a sickening certainty, is the sound of the rock collapsing, trapping us down here – or, worse, cracking open the roof of the tunnel to let the thousand tons of water above us surge in. I hesitate, stiff with fear, heart racing, awaiting the great onrush of the sea through the darkness. Moments pass; the water does not come. At length I allow myself to exhale and motion for Nell to continue.

Some yards further on, I find the source of the sound: a section of the wall has fallen, almost blocking the tunnel with debris. Water is gushing through the crack; not fast enough yet to cause a problem, but the fissure is a deep one and the pressure of the water could burst the wall open further. I wedge the candle into a crevice in the rock wall, where it flickers precariously, and begin to pull the fallen rocks away with both hands.

'We need to hurry,' I say, hurling lumps of stone behind me; more tumble into the gaps I have made as fast as I can clear them.

'Are we in danger?' she asks, crouching alongside me and grabbing at a rock.

I glance sideways at the water coursing through the cleft in the tunnel wall. 'Until we get out, we cannot assume ourselves safe. Help me here.'

We work in silence until we have cleared a gap large enough to crawl over. The candle gutters out as she tries to pass it through to me on the other side and it takes some time to spark the tinder-box into life again. The tunnel is pitched into blackness and I have the uneasy sensation that I can hear someone breathing close by. I reach up to help Nell through the gap; she hauls herself down, slipping on loose rocks, wincing as she turns her ankle upon landing beside me, but without complaint. She stands unsteadily, resting a hand on my shoulder, her breath coming in ragged gasps, and I see that she is weak. Her treatment at the hands of Jenkes and Doughty has injured her, perhaps more than I can see, and though she pushes on valiantly, I realise she is in pain. I can only hope she will be strong enough to reach the end of the tunnel – though I have no idea where the end of the tunnel might be, or what awaits us there.

'Lean on me if you are tired,' I instruct her. 'I must keep my hand around the candle flame or we will lose it.' But the candle is burning down fast; we will lose it soon in any case. I have to keep shifting it from hand to hand as the hot wax drips on to my fingers. I have lost all sense of time; it seems as if we have been down here for days. 'I feel like Orpheus,' I say, taking a step forward as the light flickers and dims.

'Don't look back, then,' she says, with a small laugh, 'or I shall be left down here for ever.'

The tunnel roof is lower now; we have to stoop to continue, making progress all the harder.

'He was lying, you know,' she says, out of the darkness behind me. 'The man called Doughty. He did not violate me. He wanted to taunt you.'

'It would be no dishonour on your part if he did, my lady,' I say, keeping my eyes fixed on the candle. I wonder if she feels obliged to deny it for my benefit, in case I should consider her compromised.

'But it is true,' she insists. 'He would have, but the other onc stopped him. The man with no ears. They argued about it – No-Ears said it would be a sinful act that would taint them both. And yet he would have been quite happy to kill us.'

'Rowland Jenkes has his own moral code,' I say. 'Sins of the flesh bring no glory to God. I think he prides himself on his asceticism.'

'You called me "my lady" again,' she says softly.

'I'm sorry. It is a hard habit to break for a man of my birth.'

'Are we going to die, Bruno?' she asks suddenly, as if reading my thoughts.

'Yes,' I say. 'Some day. But not down here, if I can help it.' On impulse, I turn, cup her bruised face in my hand and press my mouth to her scorched lips, because I have just realised that the tunnel has begun to slope unmistakably upwards.

TWENTY-THREE

The tunnel ends abruptly, emerging into a round shaft lined with brick that appears to be a dry well, the bottom covered with a mulch of dead leaves. The candle is burned down to a stub, but in its faint glow I can make out iron treads hammered into the wall at ascending intervals, just as there were in the shaft we climbed down. The air smells less dank here, but when I crane my neck upwards, I see only darkness. I reason that it must be the middle of the night, but even so, you would expect some glimmer of natural light at the entrance. As I consider this, my heart lurches so violently that I stagger and have to hold myself up against the slimy wall: perhaps Jenkes and Doughty have sealed the entrance to this end of the tunnel, as a last bitter joke on us? I do not know where the tunnel emerges – whether near the city, where we might hope to be heard, or in some remote spot along the coast, where no one sets foot except those smuggling in contraband. There is nothing for it but to try.

'Can you climb?' I ask. She raises her eyes to the blackness above us.

'I don't think I have a choice,' she says, forcing a smile.

'Good. Wait until I call you, though – no point wasting your energy if we can't get out at the top.'

'What?' Her face twists with alarm and she clutches at my sleeve. 'I can't go back, Bruno. I don't have the strength. I would rather just . . .' Her eyes fill with tears; her resolve visibly drains from her face as she slumps against me. I wish I could take the words back.

'We will find a way,' I say, squeezing her arm. 'Come – hold this while I climb.' I hand her the last of the candle. She shivers, flinching as the hot wax touches her skin. I place my foot on the first of the iron rungs and begin to pull myself up, dread sitting heavy in my stomach.

The shaft must be at least a hundred feet deep, perhaps more. Shadows close around me as I climb, until the candle is no more than a pinprick of light far below. As I make my slow way upwards, I recall what Jenkes had said about giving me the chance to repent. Another man might start praying now, indeed would have been praying fervently to every saint he could name for the past few hours, but I find I cannot, even in what may well be the hour of my death. Ironic, that for thirteen years of my life I spent most of my waking hours in prayer, only to find that prayer eludes me when I truly need it. Experience has taught me that the only one I can depend on to save me is myself.

At the top of the shaft my fingers brush against a rough surface; holding tight with my left hand, I extend my right and tentatively feel the shape of a wooden cover. I flatten my palm against it and push. It does not budge. As I am straining against its resistance, the iron staple under my left hand slips. I cry out as my knuckles scrape hard over the brick; one side has come loose in its fittings, but for now it holds. If it should come away altogether, I will fall back into the darkness. Gripping it hard, I gather all my remaining strength and heave my shoulder against the wooden cover. With a groan, it moves and through the crack I taste a breath of fresh, salt air. I brace myself, push again and climb another step as I do so, lifting the heavy cover with me until I can move it far enough to

413

one side to grasp the stone lip of the well and pull myself up through the opening.

I collapse sprawling on to a dry dirt floor, sucking in great gasping lungfuls of air, cold and sharp as a blade to my raw throat. I lean over the rim of the well and call down into the darkness to Nell that it is safe for her to climb, though all I hear is my own voice spiralling down into the hole and the patter of a few loose stones I knock over the edge. There is no longer any sign of light from the candle.

While I wait for her to appear, I try to ascertain some sense of my surroundings. As my eyes adjust, I can see that some kind of shelter has been built over the mouth of the well, simple but substantial, with stone walls on three sides, the fourth open to the elements. I struggle to my feet and stand fully upright for the first time since I was tied up, stretching out my aching limbs and back. At the open side of the shelter, I venture to poke my head outside, conscious that Jenkes and Doughty may yet be waiting for us. My hand moves instinctively to my belt, only to find my knife gone. I curse under my breath; I have only my fists and my feet now to defend myself, and I feel so weak I would like just to lie down inside the shelter and sleep for days.

Outside there is only silence – but it is a silence alive with the sounds of the night: a brisk wind soughing in the leaves, the groan of branches, the low rumble of the sea close by and, far off, the barking of dogs. Feeling bolder, I step out and look up into dense woodland. The moon is high overhead in a cloudless sky, a silver coin glimpsed through the trees. The pale light filtering through would be sufficient for us to make our way through the woods, if Nell is strong enough – though I have no idea which way we should go. Perhaps it would be better to rest in the shelter until dawn so that we can take our bearings – or would we be more vulnerable at first light? I rub my forehead; my brain is so fogged by pain and the bone-deep exhaustion that follows prolonged terror that I cannot make any useful decision. I listen again to the night around me and hear the pull and slap of waves; we have evidently come out close to the shore. I decide we should wait until morning so that we can see where we are, and make our way back to Plymouth as best we can.

I peer into the shadows between the trunks ahead and wonder which route Jenkes and Doughty have taken. Their boat must have waiting somewhere further along the coast, out of sight of the fleet in Plymouth Sound. Drake does not have enough men to watch the coastline; they could be out to sea in the time it takes Drake's armed patrols to realise no one is leaving the island by boat. They could be in France by dinner time tomorrow. For now, I feel nothing but weariness at the thought. I am too numb with relief that we have both escaped with our lives even to summon any anger towards Jenkes for the loss of the book.

I return to the stone hut and push the wooden cover further over to widen the entrance to the well shaft. I strain my eyes peering into the dark hole, but there is no sign of Nell.

'Are you there?' I call down. My voice bounces off the stones and is lost in the blackness. 'Keep climbing. Don't think about it – just put one hand over the other. Come on – I can almost see you.' I continue talking to her, repeating similar sentiments, the way you might try to calm a skittish horse, until the top of her head appears out of the gloom. 'That's it,' I say, encouraging, reaching out a hand towards her. She twists to look up at me, a pained smile breaking over her face. She reaches up with her left hand for the final rung, the one that had begun to tear loose when I put my weight on it. Before I can warn her, she grips it to pull herself up and lets out a wild scream as it wrenches free from the wall and she loses her balance, falling back. I grab at her and manage to catch a handful of her sleeve; for a moment she hangs there, her whole weight suspended from that scrap of fabric over the well shaft. I hear the stitches rip where the sleeve is attached to her bodice; I lean further over, jam my knees against the stone rim of the well and clutch with my other hand at her wrist just as the stitches give way. She is a slight woman, but her whole weight is now suspended from my two hands, and my arms feel as if they might pull out of their sockets. Worse still, her hand is clammy with fear and I can feel her fingers beginning to slip from my grasp.

'Get your feet back on the rungs,' I instruct, through gritted teeth, struggling for a firmer grip of her wrist with my left hand. My palms are sweating now and if she does not soon support her own weight, I will be helpless to stop her falling. The screaming stops abruptly; I hear her breathing hard as she flails around, searching for the iron staples in the wall. A sound from outside distracts me; I jerk my head up and realise that the barking of the dogs is getting closer. My concentration wavers in the face of this new threat; just as I am about to lose my grip on her hand, the strain suddenly eases and I almost fall forward. She has managed to place her feet back on one of the rungs. Clasping her hand tight, I guide her upwards the last few steps, past the missing rung, until I am able to drag her over the rim of the well. She collapses into my arms on the floor, shaking violently like someone in the grip of fever. I hold her, stroking her hair gently as her breathing calms, but my nerves are tight as catgut as I listen for sounds outside. The dogs are closer still. Through the slit windows in the wall I can make out dancing flames, the flickering light of torches approaching. There are footsteps, and raised voices. Nell tenses against me, looking up, her eyes wide, questioning. I am frozen in position, unable to move.

'Holy fuck!' exclaims a man's voice, not far from our hiding place. A chorus of cries erupts; it is hard to discern how many men are outside, but they appear to have discovered something shocking. I motion to Nell to keep quiet while their animated debate continues; just then, a great snarl erupts in front of us and she screams again. In the doorway to our shelter stands

416

a huge dog, snapping its jaws, eyes and teeth gleaming out of the night. It is too dark to see what kind of dog it is – perhaps a mastiff. It is an angry one, that much is certain; the fur on its neck bristles and its hackles are raised, its hindquarters coiled to pounce, though it holds back and lets out a furious volley of barks to attract attention. It appears to be waiting for a command to attack.

Sweat springs out in beads along my hairline as the dog and I continue to stare one another down. Once, in Oxford, I saw a man who had been savaged by a dog; I try to push the thought from my mind, but the image of his corpse, lying in wet grass with its throat torn out, remains stubbornly vivid. Nell scrambles around behind me and the movement makes the dog start and snarl again, but it has evidently been well trained; it maintains its position, muscular shoulders filling the narrow doorway. It seems it will not go for the kill until it is commanded.

'Throw the gun outside and come out with your hands on your head, or I will set the dogs on you,' calls a stern voice. It takes me a moment to realise he is talking to us.

'I have no gun,' I shout back. 'There is a woman here, badly injured. We are unarmed.'

This is met with a hasty conference among the men, during which I clearly catch the words 'fucking Spanish'.

'Show yourselves, then,' comes the response.

'Call the dog off first,' I say. There is a further outbreak of indignant muttering, but after a pause I hear a low whistle. The dog snaps its head round, gives me a disappointed look and trots reluctantly away. I heave myself up, hoist Nell to her feet and half-carry her out of the shelter, hoping that my legs will not buckle under me.

We emerge into a circle of torchlight to find four halberds pointed in our faces. The men holding them are wearing a livery I cannot make out, but beneath their tunics they are wearing quilted arming doublets – they have come dressed

417

for a fight. A second dog crouches at their feet, showing its teeth.

'Poaching, is it?' says the man who ordered us out. He is in his fifties, with a grizzled grey beard and narrow eyes.

I shake my head, trying to muster the energy to speak.

'Where is the gun? Throw it down where I can see it,' he says again.

'I told you, I have no gun.'

'Then how did you kill them?' He steps aside and motions to one of his men to hold up the torch. On the path ahead of us I see two dark mounds. I do not need to step closer to see that they are the bodies of a man and a dog.

'I didn't. We have only just now climbed up out of the well.' I gesture to the stone building behind us. 'We were taken hostage on St Nicholas Island, but we escaped through the tunnel that comes out at the bottom of the well shaft. The men who took us captive came this way some time before us. One of them had a pistol.'

The men look at each other. 'Likely story,' one mutters, and I have to agree; my tale is so preposterous I would not believe it if I were him. Though from the glances they exchange I suspect the tunnel is not news to them.

'Stand apart from one another,' orders the grey-bearded man. 'Search them,' he says to one of his troupe. 'If you are not poachers, you are smugglers, I reckon. Either way, Sir Peter will see you hang.'

'Who is Sir Peter?' asks Nell, letting go of my shoulder. It is the first time she has spoken since she emerged from the well shaft.

'Sir Peter Edgecumbe,' the man says. 'These are his lands you're trespassing on and his gamekeeper you've murdered, and rest assured you will swing for it. Both of you.'

'Then we are in Mount Edgecumbe park?' she says, with an incredulous laugh. 'But I know Sir Peter Edgecumbe.' She draws herself up, wincing, to her usual posture and tilts her chin. 'I am Lady Eleanor Arden, widow of Sir Richard Arden of Beauchamp Hall in Somerset. My late husband was well acquainted with Sir Peter. Take me to him immediately – he will be able to help us.'

'Oh, I'm sure you're a fine lady all right, sweetheart.' He points at me and laughs. 'And who's this – the fucking King of Cockaigne?'

Nell puts a hand on her hip. 'This is the renowned Italian scholar Giordano Bruno.'

'Oh, well that makes all the difference,' says the bearded man, and his subordinates laugh openly. 'Listen, you insolent strumpet. I lead Sir Peter's household guard, and I have the power to arrest the both of you for trespass, poaching and murder. You don't look like you're in much of a state to put up a fight, but if you want one, we can oblige.'

She steps forward until she is no more than a foot away from him and pushes the shaft of his halberd to one side, eyes flashing defiance, her jaw set firm. He seems too surprised to stop her.

'*You* listen, arrogant churl. I am the cousin of Lady Drake, and Doctor Bruno travels with Sir Philip Sidney, Master of the Queen's Ordnance. Do you see this?' She tilts her head back and points to her throat. 'Yesterday I was taken captive by two wanted criminals who tried to hang me by the neck – the same men, by the way, who killed your gamekeeper and are quite possibly still at large on your master's estate. Doctor Bruno rescued me. We have escaped death at least three times tonight and we are damned exhausted by it. Even now, Sir Francis Drake has his men out searching for us, and if he should find that we have suffered further ill-treatment, then by God, I swear you will answer to your master for it. Take us to the house this instant and let me speak to Sir Peter's steward, if you will not take my word.'

The bearded man glances uneasily at his colleagues; clearly he fears she may be telling the truth. She has the bearing and the imperious tone that belong to the high-born, honed over a lifetime of expecting the world to obey you. I watch her with growing admiration. She turns to me and squeezes my hand, flashing a triumphant smile, despite all her pain and weariness. Sidney was right; she is a woman who is used to commanding. Jenkes and Doughty, with their threats of rape and murder, stripped the protection of rank from her; they reduced her to the unwelcome truth of her physical weakness and made her vulnerable. By asserting her status again over this guard, she can begin to repair the damage to her pride. It is impressive to watch her assume this hauteur as easily as slipping on a cloak.

'Bring them up to the house then,' the bearded man snaps at the others, turning away. Nell leans into me and I feel her body go slack with relief.

'Everything will be all right now, Bruno,' she says. 'You'll see.'

TWENTY-FOUR

'You were fortunate that the household guard gave you the benefit of the doubt,' Drake murmurs. He faces away from me, still looking out of the chamber window with his hands clasped behind his back. 'He could have accused you of murder and thrown you in a cell right there. We might not have found you for days.'

'Lady Arden is quite formidable when she decides to assert herself.' I take another sip of wine.

'I know it,' Drake says, with a grimace.

'We were fortunate too that Sir Peter Edgecumbe's steward was accommodating. He woke his master in the middle of the night for two strangers who looked like vagabonds or cutpurses. Thank God Sir Peter recognised Lady Arden, in spite of everything.'

I close my eyes briefly, recalling what had followed. The cool ale to soothe our throats, warm water to bathe, maidservants to dress our wounds, the soft feather beds, the bread and meat in the morning and clean clothes given by Sir Peter and his wife, all of which Nell had promised to repay when she returned home. Drake's men had finally landed on the island a couple of hours after we escaped, and valiantly followed us through the tunnel and out to Sir Peter Edgecumbe's estate on the promontory facing Plymouth on the west side of the Sound. Sir Peter sent his own men to accompany me back to the town after I had broken my fast; Nell's injuries were not as bad as I had feared, but she was weakened by shock and exhaustion and the effects of breathing so much smoke, and needed to rest before she could consider riding back. I had sustained some minor burns along my left arm and my eyes and throat were still dry and painful from the smoke, but when I considered the events of the night, I could only marvel that we had escaped with so little damage.

Drake observes me with curiosity for a while, then resumes his brisk manner. 'In any case, God granted you His protection. But above all my wife's cousin owes her life to your courage, Bruno. I am in your debt, and I will not forget it.' He passes a hand across his beard. 'And now that she is safe, I must decide what is to be done about the rest of this affair. Then perhaps I can get back to my fleet.'

He does not even try to disguise the impatience in his voice. This whole business with Jenkes and Doughty has been an inconvenient distraction for him – one that would not have come about if the fleet had not been delayed by Dunne's death, or if Sidney and I had not turned up in Plymouth. I understand his feelings, but I suppose I had hoped for a slightly fuller expression of gratitude after the night's ordeal. But Drake has a fleet of ships and hundreds of men dependent on his decisions, and he is keen to press on.

We are gathered in his chamber at the Star, the room once occupied by Lady Drake, who is now a guest of the Mayor and guarded by six of Drake's stoutest soldiers. Sidney and I are shortly to dine with Dom Antonio and his attendants, but first Drake wants to brief me on all that has happened since I left for St Nicholas Island the night before.

'My men and Sir Peter's searched the entire estate last night and into the morning but found no trace of Jenkes or Doughty,' he says, standing with his back to the fireplace. 'I have sent out boats to board and search ships leaving the Sound, though I do not strictly have the authority to do this. But my guess is that they will have set out from further along the coast, in Cornwall. Perhaps they joined a ship from a different harbour. In any case, they have had a significant start.'

'Rowland Jenkes has a great many contacts in France,' I say. 'He will have taken the book to Paris, no doubt, where there will be Vatican agents willing to pay dearly for it.'

Drake makes a dismissive gesture. 'I care little for the book now. It angers me that this Jenkes should profit from it, naturally, but not so much that I am willing to devote men and resources to pursuing it. It seems a small price to pay, given that you and Lady Arden have escaped with your lives.'

I say nothing. The book is of no consequence to Drake because he is not a scholar and cannot imagine its significance; he regards it merely for how much coin it would fetch. I can think only of the fat, self-serving cardinals in Rome locking it away in some dark vault in the Vatican, burying its extraordinary revelation for ever. At least I still have my translation.

'My concern,' Drake continues, 'is what has become of John Doughty. This business has not served his purpose at all, except to show me how near he can come to my family. And your report troubles me greatly. I have long suspected he would set his sights on Elizabeth, to hurt me where I am most vulnerable.' He pulls at the point of his beard. 'I have decided that she should go to her family in Somerset while I am at sea. When Lady Arden is well enough to travel, I will send them both back to Buckland with an armed guard to make their preparations. I think it best that Dom Antonio goes with them. Your men can accompany him, Sir Philip, and travel on to London from there. I cannot prepare for this expedition if I am worrying constantly about his safety and that of the women.'

Sidney looks up from his position by the window and nods.

His armed men arrived this morning and he has lodged them at a hostelry outside the town walls out of his own pocket; the sooner they are on the road to London with Dom Antonio, or staying at Buckland Abbey at Drake's expense, the better for him. I feel a pang at the thought of the women leaving; the prospect of remaining in Plymouth with my own plans still uncertain seems far less attractive in Nell's absence.

'At least we know that Doughty had nothing to do with Dunne's death,' I say. 'I am certain he was telling the truth when he said he believed Dunne took his own life.'

Drake and Sidney exchange a glance.

'We have some news there,' Drake says.

Sidney crosses the room to lean on the mantel. 'You have missed all the excitement,' he says.

I look at him. 'You are right – all the time I was tied up waiting for a barrel of gunpowder to blast my head off, and crawling through a tunnel under the sea and climbing a well shaft to be set upon by a pack of dogs and armed men, I was thinking to myself, how I wish I were not missing all the excitement.'

Drake smiles.

'Savile has confessed,' Sidney announces, with an expression that suggests he claims the credit.

'Well – not quite,' Drake says. 'He has confessed to everything except the murder. That is our sticking point.'

'Then – what has he confessed to?' I look from one to the other, confused. 'What happened?'

'Sir Philip caught them in the act,' Drake says. It is difficult to tell from his expression whether he approves of Sidney's actions or not.

Sidney shrugs. 'I did what I said we should do the other day. I had come back here yesterday evening to fetch some belongings for Lady Drake, while you were all occupied with the rescue attempt.' His voice is light as he says this, but I hear the implicit reproach; I wonder if Drake does.

Sidney had embraced me with obvious relief when I returned to the Star, but the pleasure of seeing me alive seems to have been shortlived and quickly tarnished by his usual resentment at being left behind with the women and denied a chance to prove himself. He has not asked me anything about my experiences last night. I know him too well to be wounded by his apparent dismissal; all the same, I find I am gritting my teeth as he embarks on an account of his own heroics.

'I happened to see Savile heading for the stairs to the second floor,' he continues, with evident relish. 'I took it upon myself to follow him. I thought if he was cornered and could no longer deny his relationship with Martha Dunne, he would be compelled to admit to the murder in the face of all the other evidence. The button, the nutmeg and so on.'

'So you just walked into their bedchamber?' I say, amazed.

'Yes.' He grins. 'I gave them a little time to get warmed up. They had stationed that bovine maidservant outside the door to keep watch. She tried to tell me her mistress was indisposed. I said, I'm sure she is, and strode right past her. They hadn't even locked the door.' He shakes his head, as if he pitied anyone foolish enough to make such a simple mistake.

'And you found them *in media res*?'

'Not exactly. They were still clothed, thank God,' he adds. 'But I caught them in a close embrace – enough to make it difficult to explain away. I confronted them then and there with everything we had guessed about their affair and the pregnancy.'

'That was dangerous,' I say, and have the satisfaction of seeing Drake nod in vigorous agreement. 'What was to stop them simply denying it all?'

'They did at first. At least, she did.' He makes a face. 'That woman is hard as flint. God knows what Savile sees in her.'

'The prospect of her imminent inheritance, perhaps?'

'Huh. Well, they tried to deny it, of course. She conceded that she was pregnant but said the child was her husband's and that she would have me arrested for slander if I dared to suggest otherwise. Sir William was an old friend of the family, she claimed, who was comforting her in her grief. With his breeches unlaced? I asked.' He folds his arms across his chest, clearly delighted with himself. 'Pair of fools. Then I delivered the *coup de grâce*. I said we had sufficient evidence to have Savile arrested for the murder of Robert Dunne.'

'But we don't,' I say, glancing at Drake. His lips are pressed together.

'They weren't to know that,' Sidney says, defensive. 'Savile proved the weaker, in the end. He was already rattled by the fact that we had uncovered their little secret – when he thought he was to be accused of murder, he caved in altogether.'

'Not altogether,' Drake corrects quietly.

Sidney glances at him, irritated. 'He said he would only explain himself to Captain Drake. So I insisted he come to my chamber where I could keep an eye on him while I sent a messenger to fetch Sir Francis from the Hoe – I told Savile he could not be trusted not to flee. He was scornful then – an innocent man had no reason to flee, he said, and in any case he would not go anywhere while his funds were tied up in this expedition. But he gave in and came with me nonetheless.'

'Funds he had a good mind to withdraw, he said, if this was how he was respected by other gentlemen,' Drake adds, giving Sidney a pointed look. I understand his anger; Sidney had gone against his express wishes and accused an important investor of committing murder, without any conclusive proof, and in the process had drawn Drake away from the operation to save the life of his wife's cousin. While Drake is too much of a diplomat to reprimand a man of Sidney's status, he clearly resents having been forced into this position. 'By the time Sir Philip's messenger arrived, there was little more I could usefully do to help you, Bruno,' Drake continues, turning to me. 'The armed men were under Carleill's command, so I returned to the Star to deal with this development. It was fortunate that

426

the accusation of murder, though rash, had shaken Savile. He had not realised we knew so much already – he was willing to admit his guilt in some parts, the better to insist on his innocence of the main charge.'

'Then he still maintains he did not murder Dunne?'

Drake nods. 'He conceded this much – that he and Martha Dunne were lovers, and had been for the best part of a year. He had promised to help her.' He stops and purses his lips. 'He assured me he would give up the whole truth, provided I did not report it to the authorities.'

'And what was his version of the truth?' I ask.

Drake looks weary. 'Best you hear it from his own lips. I should like your view on whether or not he is lying.'

An armed guard stands by the door to Savile's room, lolling against the wall. He jerks quickly to attention as Drake approaches.

'I asked Sir William to remain here until I decided what to do about the situation,' Drake tells me, in a low voice. 'He is not happy about it, as you may imagine. He feels he is as good as under arrest.'

'Then why has he agreed to it?'

'Because he has the wit to realise that, if the inquest accepts Dunne's death as murder, there is sufficient evidence to make him the principal suspect.'

'Though probably not to convict him.'

'Well, exactly – that is our problem. I could call in the coroner and the town authorities, but with a man of his status it would not be a simple matter. If I take that course, he will send for a lawyer from London. We could be delayed weeks.' He stops outside the door and pins me with a frank look. 'And of course he will withdraw from the voyage, along with his investment. He has made that clear. You will appreciate that Sir Philip has put me in a very difficult position. I cannot help wishing he had consulted me first.'

427

Sidney has declined to accompany us; he says he has heard Savile's version of events already and in Sidney's view it wouldn't fool a child. Drake wisely ignored the remark, but that had not diffused the tension between them. Sidney is bristling with resentment; he thought he would have all the credit for catching the murderer and, though he will never admit it, he wants Drake's praise as well. But taking matters into his own hands without asking the Captain-General has worked against him. I sigh. If the story of Thomas Doughty and its repercussions has taught us anything, it is that Drake will not tolerate any challenge to his authority. You'd think Sidney would have realised that by now.

Drake knocks sharply on the door. Despite the circumstances, he is evidently determined to treat Savile with courtesy. The question of degree is part of what makes this situation so fraught, and Drake knows it; though Drake is also a knight, Savile is a gentleman born, like Sidney, and almost certainly does not regard the Captain-General as his equal in status.

'Yes?' says an imperious voice from within.

Drake opens the door to a small though comfortably appointed chamber. Savile is seated at a table, writing a letter. He looks up as we enter and his expression hardens when he sees me.

'What, Francis – have you brought this *monk* to hear my confession?'

'In a sense,' Drake says, ignoring his tone. 'I want you to tell Doctor Bruno your account, as you told it to me.'

'Why? What authority has he to judge me?'

'None. But it was he who gathered the evidence against you, and so he would be called to testify, if it comes to that. Besides, I want a witness, in case you should try to deny your story.'

A muscle twitches in Savile's jaw.

'I thought we had reached an agreement?'

'This is part of the agreement,' Drake says calmly. He takes

428

up a place on the window seat. I remain standing. Savile turns his chair around to face us.

'Well, now. Where would you like me to begin?' he says.

'All the evidence suggests that you intended to kill Robert Dunne so that you could marry his wife, who is carrying your child,' I say. 'Begin with that.'

'And I challenge you to prove any of it,' he says, with a self-satisfied smile. If he had been shaken by the accusations the night before, he shows no sign of it now. He carries himself like a man who has already won.

'Robert Dunne had not seen his wife for four months,' I say. 'His landlady will testify that he had not left Plymouth since April. And they were never able to conceive together before.'

Savile looks as if he is formulating another lawyer's argument to this point, but Drake cuts in.

'Just give your account, Sir William. And keep it brief.'

Savile hesitates, then turns to me.

'Very well. I tell you this in confidence,' he says. 'Sir Francis has agreed to that. And I tell you only because what you already know looks bad for me. But I did not kill Robert Dunne that night.' He crosses and uncrosses his legs and stares at his folded hands for a long time, as if deciding where to begin.

'Martha Dunne wanted to be free of her marriage, it is true. She had suggested an annulment, but her husband would not hear of it,' he says eventually, looking up. 'There was no affection involved, of course – the grasping dog was clinging on because he knew she would inherit from her father. Martha could only be rid of him if he died, but she was afraid that people would suspect her if anything happened to him. As you know, a woman who kills her husband is guilty of treason, and would be burned.' He pauses, rubbing a thumb along his lower lip. 'She was unwilling to take the risk. But she could not stand the thought of Robert laying hold of her inheritance, so she knew she would be forced to act sooner or later. When he announced his plan to come on this expedition with Sir Francis, she hoped he might meet with an accident at sea. Sadly, he had proved remarkably resilient in the past.'

'Were you and she already . . .?'

'I was fascinated by Martha the first time I met her,' he says, with emphasis, as if I have called the strength of his feeling into question. 'We were introduced at court last year when she attended with her husband.' He gives a wry laugh. 'She is a formidable woman, Martha. Well, you have spent time with her, you must realise that.' A distant expression drifts over his face and I see that he is genuinely captivated by the woman. I cannot begin to imagine bedding Martha Dunne; her flintiness shrivels me completely. There is no logic to desire, I suppose. Although the attraction of her father's money must also have been formidable.

'So she persuaded you to help her with her difficulty,' I say, trying to shake the image of Savile and Martha Dunne in the act.

He sucks in his cheeks. 'I knew I would be at sea with Robert for many months together. There are ample opportunities aboard ship for a man to meet with an accident.'

'But Dunne was an experienced sailor, and you are not,' I point out. 'Was that why you took the nutmeg – so that you could make him disorientated and push him overboard?'

'I had no plan so clearly devised as that,' Savile says, examining his nails. 'In the event, there was a more pressing problem.'

'She found herself pregnant.'

He gives a barely perceptible nod. 'I hear it was you who noticed that. Surprisingly sharp eye you have, Bruno – most unmarried men would not be able to spot the signs for another few months. But then, you were a monk, of course – I imagine you and your brothers knocked up countless serving girls down there in Rome, didn't you?'

'Naples,' I say drily. 'Hundreds of them.'

'Go on, Sir William,' Drake says from the window.

'At first she thought she could keep it a secret,' Savile says, 'so that her husband would not learn of it before he set sail. He was the only one in a position to deny the child was his, and if all went well, he would not return to do so. But Martha was very ill with the child in the first weeks, and though she only confided in her maid Agnes, one of the other servants had eyes as sharp as yours in these matters, Bruno. Rumours began among their household in Dartington. Their steward still had some loyalty to his master, for all his faults, and sent word to Robert in Plymouth that his wife may be with child – knowing, of course, that Robert had not seen her for weeks. This steward also told Robert that I had stopped at the house as a guest on my way to Plymouth.'

'So Robert could be in little doubt as to the father,' I say. 'And he tried to blackmail you?'

'*Blackmail?*' He frowns, as if he does not understand.

'For five gold angels. Did he write you letters threatening to expose you?'

Savile looks bemused. 'What a strange question. Of course not. He did what any self-respecting man would do on learning he has been cuckolded. He punched me in the face.' He rubs the cut on his lip, now pulling tight into a scab.

'But he was already under the influence of the nutmeg by then, according to those who saw him,' I say. 'Why did you give it to him that night? Had he confronted you earlier?'

'That evening, before the party was due to go ashore, he asked me to take a drink with him in his cabin. I was apprehensive, of course. I took some spiced wine, as a precaution. I thought if I could dose him with nutmeg, he would grow incoherent – that way, if he made any wild claims, I could always claim it was the drink talking.'

'And he accused you?'

'At that point he was not unreasonable,' Savile says. 'He

431

only told me that he had received this letter and wanted to know if there was truth in it. I said we should discuss it in private, over a drink.' He flexes his fingers and glances at Drake. 'I denied everything, of course. I said I had called in at his house looking for him, and had ridden on to Plymouth when I found he was not at home. Told him the steward was probably just trying to make trouble, undermine Martha and assert his own authority in Robert's absence, the way servants will.' He gives a lofty wave of the hand, as if we all sympathise with the devious ways of servants. 'I said it would be pure folly to repeat any such unfounded rumours, especially in the hearing of others – he would only dishonour himself and his wife. He wanted to believe it. He grasped me by the wrists and apologised for having impugned my reputation.'

So that was where the button was torn off, I think.

'But you had to make sure he didn't repeat the accusations in public.'

'Well, you see my predicament, surely,' Savile says, as if his actions were perfectly sensible to any reasonable person. He stands, crosses to the hearth and turns to face me. 'He agreed that I was probably right about the steward. He promised to say nothing until he had heard from Martha. But I was not convinced – he was not known as a discreet man and I knew he often confided in the Spaniard, Jonas. I didn't want my name associated with rumours of that nature. Certainly not in the hearing of anyone in the fleet.'

'Yes, that might have made the accident you were planning for him seem a little less convincing,' I say. 'Especially if you were hoping to marry his widow eventually.'

'Obviously.' He appears unabashed. I wonder why he is being so frank with us. Perhaps because he suspects we have guessed all this already.

'So you decided this accident needed to be brought forward?'

'Who is telling this story, Bruno – me or you?' He smiles,

flashing his teeth, but there is an edge to his voice. I make a gesture of concession – I want to hear his version to the end.

'I thought I had contained the problem for the time being, but I knew he would not keep it to himself for long. I intended to follow him that evening. He often went to the House of Vesta, but lately he had been seen meeting strangers in less salubrious parts of town – connected with his gambling debts, I supposed. But that suited me well – a gentleman attacked in a back street would be thought the victim of robbers. If he was found dead like that, it would raise few questions – everyone knew Dunne had creditors after him.' He shrugs. 'I thought the nutmeg would make it easier to overpower him.'

'But it took effect quicker than you expected.' I indicate his lip.

'Yes.' He touches the cut, with feeling. 'That was unforeseen. He went to the Star with the others for a drink first, so I had to go along too. He was already beginning to grow wild by then. He repeated his earlier words, more aggressively this time. I tried to draw him away from the group, afraid they would hear, but he resisted, and lashed out. Fortunately for me, the inn threw him out before he could start a brawl, or draw further attention to the cause of it.' He spreads his hands wide, as if to say, what else could I do? 'I followed him to the House of Vesta, thinking I would contrive to meet him on the way out and lead him somewhere more remote. But I never got the chance. When he left, he was accompanied by Padre Pettifer.'

'The chaplain?' I stare at him, amazed – the pious padre at a notorious whorehouse? 'What was he doing there?'

Savile gives me a look that suggests this is a stupid question, but it is Drake who answers.

'Praying for their souls, I should think.'

Savile laughs. I turn to Drake to see if he is joking, but his expression is perfectly serious.

'I believe it is part of his charitable work in the town,' he says. 'Some of the priests take very seriously the example of

Our Lord in spreading the word of God among prostitutes and publicans.'

Savile snorts again. 'I doubt that's the only thing he was—' He breaks off at a look from Drake and turns back to me. 'So now, Bruno, you know as much as Sir Francis, and as much as I am able to tell. Because whatever happened to Robert Dunne after he returned to the *Elizabeth*, it was none of my doing.' He ends with a shrug, as if challenging me to contradict him.

'How does that follow?' I say, angered by his confidence. 'You have just admitted that you intended to kill Dunne that night.'

He shakes his head. 'You have sufficient proof to know that I had reason to want him dead. After Sidney burst into Martha's chamber all puffed up with his own cleverness, I could hardly deny that part of it. So I am cooperating, by telling you the truth.'

'That is very sharp of you,' I say. 'You confess to every accusation but the most significant, then you try to negotiate.'

He clicks his tongue, impatient. 'I do not deny I would have gained from Dunne's death. But not if it were taken for suicide – and there is my whole defence. That was self-evidently not in Martha's interest – she stands to lose everything. So the fact that whoever killed him tried their best to make it look like self-slaughter should be proof enough that it was not me.'

'But you needed to silence Dunne quickly, before he could tell anyone else about the steward's letter. Besides, Mistress Dunne stood to gain a great deal once her father died. Perhaps you decided it was expedient to change your plan once more.'

'You are wandering into the realm of speculation now, Bruno. I do not expect a man like you to understand the concept of honour,' he adds, curling his lip, 'but Martha would lose more than her property if the coroner gave a verdict of *felo de se*. The stain of suicide on her family's reputation would last a lifetime. I would never have put her in that position. A gentleman would know such things instinctively.'

434

'You get a child on another man's wife and scheme with her to murder him, and you dare talk to me of honour?' I step forward, jabbing a finger in his face.

'Keep your voice down, Bruno, there's a good chap,' he says, arching an eyebrow.

I catch Drake's warning glance and bite down my next retort.

'Well, Sir Francis,' Savile says, folding his arms, 'for myself, I am not sure what this has achieved, other than allowing this *Catholic* to imagine he can take the moral high ground, but I have nothing more to add. Except that I would like you to take your guard away from my chamber. In England a man is innocent until his guilt is proved, as I recall. And since I am not going to be tried for this, my innocence endures indefinitely.'

Drake rises to face Savile, though he does not reply immediately. His quick eyes flicker over Savile's face as he calculates.

'God's blood, man, I have already assured you I will not take flight,' Savile snaps.

'It would look like an admission of guilt if you did,' Drake says mildly. He presses his fingertips together and steeples his hands under his chin. 'I think the matter might be resolved if you were to return to your cabin aboard the *Elizabeth*, Sir William,' he says eventually, with impeccable courtesy. 'If you are still intending to travel with us, that is. I have hopes of a fair wind soon enough.'

Savile gives him a long look, his eyes suspicious, as if he fears he might be tricked. 'That is another way of keeping me informally under guard, I suppose.'

'Not at all. It is a way of demonstrating that I agree with the principle of your presumed innocence.'

'I would be free to come ashore when I choose?'

'Of course. Though it would be in your interests to keep a discreet distance from Mistress Dunne until the inquest is concluded.'

Savile falls silent, considering, then nods. 'And I have your word of honour that neither of you will mention any of this to the coroner or the town authorities?' There is a note of warning in his voice. He is hinting at the agreement he mentioned earlier; the price of his continued involvement with the fleet is Drake's silence.

Drake inclines his head, and stands to take his leave. It appears that he considers this price reasonable. I watch Savile, trying not to react to the self-congratulating smile that creeps slowly over his face as he looks at me. There is something in his manner that makes me inclined to believe his account, but this bargain infuriates me nonetheless; Savile wears the complacent expression of a rich man confident that he can buy his way out of any trouble. I clench and unclench my fists, and say nothing. He is right that I have no authority, and Drake appears to consider the matter settled.

'Let us go, Doctor Bruno,' the Captain-General says, gesturing towards the door. As he reaches it, I turn back to Savile.

'And what about Jonas Solon?'

Savile looks startled. 'What about him?'

'You said you feared Dunne would confide in him about the steward's letter and the pregnancy.'

'I feared Dunne telling anyone,' Savile says, defensive. 'I only mentioned the Spaniard because I knew they were friends.' There is alarm in his eyes.

'I think you suspected that Dunne had already told Jonas,' I say, warming to the idea. 'Was that why you had to silence him too? Did he accuse you?'

Savile flicks his head as if trying to shake off a persistent fly. 'No, and no. The Spaniard never spoke a word to me about the business. I have no idea if Dunne confided in him, but I certainly never laid a finger on Jonas. It's impossible.'

'Not at all. You speak Spanish,' I say, in the same defiant tone. From the corner of my eye, I catch Drake's expression.

With every word, I am undoing his neat arrangement with Savile. 'When I was speaking to Jonas in the rowing boat, you understood our conversation.'

'I understand a little,' Savile says, with a shrug. 'What has that to do with anything?'

I glance at Drake. He gives a short nod.

'You wrote a letter to Captain Drake, purporting to be from Jonas. Explaining his absence.'

'I did no such thing,' Savile snaps, colour rising in his cheeks. 'I understand Spanish, but not well enough to write it. But in any case, I have a better defence.'

'Let us hear it, then.'

'I was nowhere near Jonas the night he died. I was at the House of Vesta all evening. A number of people can testify to that.'

I am tempted to repeat my point about honour, but I bite my tongue; where he puts his cock is none of my business. I am only interested in whether he is trying to negotiate his way out of two murders. 'You had to walk there and back from the quayside,' I say. 'You could have gone via the Hoe and found him up there.'

'Perhaps I could, if I had been alone,' Savile says, in a smooth voice. 'But I walked to the House of Vesta and back in company. I was not on my own all evening.'

'Will your companion swear to that?' I ask, growing more aggressive as I feel my conviction wavering.

'Oh, I should think so,' he says, cheerfully. 'Sir Francis could ask him. My companion was Thomas Drake.'

'Thomas?' Drake looks startled, then shakes his head. 'But Thomas does not go to the House of Vesta. He would not.'

'That may be what he tells you.' There is a vindictive gleam in his eye. 'Go and ask him.' He spreads his hands wide again. 'There you have it – I cannot write a word of Spanish, and I was in company the whole evening when Jonas fell over the cliff, or was pushed, or whatever it may be. So you and Sidney will have to go back to your room and cook up another half-baked theory, Bruno. And now,' he adds, 'if you don't mind, *gentlemen*, I should like to finish this letter to my lawyer.'

Outside the room, Drake exchanges a few words with the armed guard, who nods and slips quietly away. The Captain-General's face is tight with anger, though I cannot tell if it is directed at me. I wait for him to speak.

'Do you believe him?' he says, in a low voice, when we are far enough away from Savile's door. 'About Dunne, I mean?'

I look at him. I had been expecting a reprimand for my hasty accusations about Jonas; he was obviously embarrassed by Savile's revelation about his brother.

'I think I do.' I speak slowly; my judgement only really begins to crystallise as I form the sentence. 'I don't doubt he can be a very persuasive liar. But he was thrown by my question about the blackmail – that seemed to me an honest response. He didn't know what I was talking about.'

Drake nods. We reach the end of the passage in silence.

'And you, Sir Francis?' I ask, emboldened. 'Do you believe him?'

'I am inclined to accept his version,' he says, carefully. That is not the same thing, I think, but I say nothing. 'Though I will have to speak to my brother now.' His jaw tenses again.

'I'm sorry – I did not realise Thomas would be dragged into it,' I begin, but he waves the apology aside.

'All the years I was mayor of Plymouth, I tried to do something about that place, as I told you,' he says, his words coming quick and sharp. 'It is despicable, in a community of civilised, Christian folk, to have young girls traded like so much horseflesh.'

'And thrown on the street when they are considered broken jades,' I say.

'Exactly.' He shakes his head. 'You may imagine the

opposition I encountered. It was my belief that some of the aldermen were taking bribes in order to block any attempt to close it.'

'I suppose they claim that where there are sailors, there will always be whores,' I say.

'Yes. Though you know the Queen's father, King Henry, shut down all the brothels in Southwark for a time. So it can be done.'

'He was king of England, though.'

He gives a tired smile, and claps me on the shoulder. 'True. The mayor of Plymouth does not have quite the same reach. In the end I had to settle for trying to improve the conditions of the girls. I pressured the churches to get involved, as a matter of conscience and charity. Padre Pettifer was an enormous help – he has tried to liaise with the madam about placing the unwanted babies with Christian families, and finding honest work for the girls when they are no longer required.'

'I admit I was surprised to hear that he visited. It is the sort of place I imagined he would make a point of denouncing.'

Drake smiles. 'Yes, Pettifer can appear a little pompous. But beneath the bluster he is a good priest, or I would not take him on the voyage. He is not afraid to get his hands dirty.'

Perhaps it appeals to his sense of moral superiority, I think, uncharitably. Then I recall the brothel-keeper's illicit trade in unwanted babies and a shadow of a suspicion flickers through my mind. 'I imagine the madam was delighted by his intervention.'

'Oh, she was furious, of course,' Drake says. 'But at the time it was a compromise we both accepted – she found it preferable to the prospect of any other measures I might take against her enterprise. Though that was four years ago now. I do not think the present mayor is so troubled by what goes on.' He purses his lips. 'But I never imagined Thomas would be seen there, knowing how I feel about the place.'

'And Padre Pettifer continues his charity work with them?' I ask, keeping my voice carefully neutral. Drake looks at me from the tail of his eye.

'So it seems, though I have not discussed it with him for a long time. He said he found the girls remarkably receptive.'

'Did he.'

We look at one another for a moment and burst out laughing. It shifts the tension that has built up since Savile's confession. I feel my shoulders relax; I had been bracing myself for Drake's reprimand.

'To the message of Christ, I mean, of course,' he says, still smiling. 'He said the girls took readily to the idea of a churchman coming to pray with them. According to the madam, it improved their morale, so she was not inclined to object. I think he hears their confessions too, though he would not say as much.'

'*Dio porco*. What confessions those must be. No wonder he always wears that expression.'

'What expression?'

'As if someone has pushed a cork up his arsehole and he might explode from the pressure.'

Drake attempts to suppress his smile. 'That is a very wicked way to describe one of God's servants, Bruno. I will never be able to look at him again without that coming to mind.' He pauses at the top of the stairs. 'I hope you and Sir Philip will not object to dining with Dom Antonio today, if you are feeling well enough? Poor fellow, he is desperate for some intelligent company, but I cannot entertain him every hour of the day. I am anxious to return to my ship. I have been absent more than I would wish over the past couple of days.'

'Of course. There is one matter, though.' I glance around in case Hetty or anyone else is lurking in the shadows. 'If we are agreed that Sir William is telling the truth, then . . .'

'Then there is still a murderer at large,' he says softly.

'So we are still hunting.'

He puts his head on one side and gives me a long look. 'I am reluctant to ask any more of you, Bruno. After all you have been through. If you do not wish to go on with this, you need only say so.'

'I have given you my word that I would help you, Sir Francis,' I say. 'I do not like to give up on a task before it is finished.'

'Good man.' He pats me on the shoulder. 'Enjoy your dinner. And keep an eye on Sidney. See if you can rein him in. I know he means to help, but . . .' He shakes his head and leaves the thought unspoken.

I nod. 'It will make for a difficult atmosphere on board, will it not – now that Sidney has confronted Savile with these accusations?'

'Yes,' he says. His face is grave once more. 'Exactly what I have been thinking.'

TWENTY-FIVE

The tap-room downstairs is bustling; despite Drake's best efforts at discretion, talk has seeped out quickly into the town and the stories have grown in the telling. Two deaths among Drake's own crew were a source of interest and speculation, a lively subject for the town gossips, but the killing of the two guards on St Nicholas Island has provoked fury since the bodies were brought ashore earlier. Both were local men with families; according to Mistress Judith, there would be a fierce appetite to see someone brought to justice for their murder. Sharp-eyed observers had noted the movement of Drake's small boats around the island the previous night and connected the two, giving birth to rumours that an advance party of Spanish invaders had landed on the island and escaped to Plymouth. More impressionable citizens are packing their belongings, ready to flee the town. Some are saying Drake's voyage is cursed and has brought the wrath of God, or the Devil, on Plymouth; they predict the deaths will continue until the ships set sail.

'Won't make life any easier for the likes of you,' she says, looking at me with a sigh. 'Or any of the foreign merchants, for that matter. Can't deny it's good for business though.' She waves a hand around the crowded entrance hall. 'They're all here for a glimpse of Drake and his captains.'

Outside the tap-room, I run into Gilbert Crosse, a roll of papers bunched in his fist.

'Afternoon, Gilbert. You are in a hurry.'

'Ah, Doctor Bruno.' He blinks rapidly and glances behind me to the stairs, looking harassed. 'You are not going up to see Sir Francis, by any chance? Some messages have arrived for him and I am just on my way to the stationer's up the street for more paper and ink before he closes business for the day. With all the recent dramas, Sir Francis has had a great deal of correspondence and we are eating through our supplies. At this rate, we shall have none for the voyage. If it ever happens,' he finishes, with a defeated expression.

'I have just left him,' I say, half-turning. 'I think he intends to return to the ship soon. Do you want me to take them up to him?'

'No, no, don't worry,' he says, edging past me. 'You look as if you have had enough exertions.' He nods to my bruises. 'I am glad to see you safe,' he adds, lowering his voice. 'There was a lot of talk among the men last night about what was going on with all the small boats around St Nicholas Island. I didn't pick up the details – just enough to know that Lady Drake was in danger and you were helping Sir Francis. Was it connected with Robert Dunne or Jonas? Is there a threat to the fleet?' He looks at me expectantly, blinking behind his glasses.

I smile. 'Lady Drake was never in any danger, I assure you. Nor is the fleet. I had better let you take your letters up.'

'Yes.' He sighs. 'I ought really to put every letter into his hands myself. I would be the one blamed if any correspondence went missing. Can you imagine? Give you good day, Doctor Bruno.'

He is past me and almost at the turn in the stairs when a thought occurs to me.

'Gilbert!' I hurry up after him until we are level. 'Do you always give Sir Francis his letters directly, or would you sometimes ask others to take them in to his cabin, if they are on their way there?'

He frowns. 'Almost always I make sure I put them into his hands, but there are occasions, of course – if I am in a hurry, and some trusted person is on his way in to see the Captain-General, I might ask him to pass them on. Why?' He sounds defensive, as if he fears I might accuse him of failing in his duty.

'The day Robert Dunne was found dead,' I say, lowering my voice, 'did you ask anyone to take Captain Drake's letters in to him?'

He screws up his face. 'I'm not sure I recall – everyone was in such a state that day. I came ashore early to find the coroner, and I remember I collected some letters for Captain Drake at the Star as usual. But I didn't return to the ship until much later.'

'Try to recall, if you can. Captain Drake received an unusual letter that day. I wonder if it was among those you picked up from the Star?'

'I'm afraid I didn't look at them in any detail,' he says, biting his lip. 'But – wait – I came back to the ship just before dinner. I was on my way up to the captain's cabin when I bumped into – yes, it's coming back to me now! You're right – I *did* entrust the letters to someone else that day.'

'And who was that?'

He murmurs a name. I nod, understanding, as a number of pieces seem to fall into place.

TWENTY-SIX

I find Sidney in the private dining room with Dom Antonio and his attendants. Two armed men flank the door. Sidney raises his eyebrows in a question; I give a minute shake of my head.

Dom Antonio glances up and his funereal expression brightens a fraction. 'Ah! And here is our Italian hero. Saviour of women, avenger of wrongs.'

I wave this away, embarrassed. 'Not a very efficient avenger, I fear. The wrongdoers fled.'

'Nonetheless, my friend, you saved a young woman's life. Not many of us can make that claim. Am I not right, Sir Philip?'

Sidney makes a polite noise and looks at me with a stiff smile. I gesture towards the door.

'Forgive me, Dom Antonio, gentlemen, but may I borrow Sir Philip? I'm afraid it is a matter of urgency.'

The Portuguese holds out his hands in a gesture of surrender. Sidney scrapes his chair back and follows me out, his face eager.

'Well?' he says, when we are out of the guards' hearing.

'I think I know who the killer is. Come with me.'

'What are you talking about? Come *where*?'

I turn to see him standing, hands on hips.

'You have told me nothing about Savile,' he hisses. 'I thought we had all agreed he was the killer? He has as good as confessed – don't tell me you found his denials plausible? And now what – you have cooked up some new theory?'

'I don't believe it was Savile. Neither does Drake. He admitted to plotting Dunne's death – he would not have said so much if he didn't think the confession absolved him of the actual murder.'

'He is a clever man. He thinks he can deceive us by parsing out the truth. And you have apparently fallen for it. Are you trying to make me look a fool, is that it?'

I hear the frustration in his voice. I sigh.

'It's not about you, Philip. Savile could not have killed Jonas – Thomas Drake can vouch for his whereabouts all night.'

Sidney's face falls. 'Are you sure? Savile is nothing if not cunning, he could have slipped away.'

'Drake is checking that with his brother. But I have at least discovered where the Judas letter came from.'

'Really?' He looks sceptical.

I glance around the entrance hall. A steady press of people are pushing their way through to the tap-room, though some are hovering at the foot of the stairs, perhaps hoping, as Mistress Judith suggested, for a glimpse of Drake.

'We should not talk here. Come with me and I will explain on the way.'

He gives a theatrical sigh. 'Oh, very well. Where are we going?'

'The House of Vesta.'

'For the love of God – I cannot afford any more visits there.' He rolls his eyes. 'Besides, it is broad daylight – they won't be open, will they?'

'I am hoping I can find what I need nonetheless.'

'Huh.' He cracks his knuckles. 'Promise me no jumping out of windows this time?'

I grin. 'I will do my best. Another night like that would destroy me.'

'Nothing could do that, Bruno, you are indestructible. God knows what you are made of, but it is not ordinary flesh and blood, I swear.'

'We have assumed that whoever sent Drake the Matthew letter left it at the Star to be collected by Gilbert along with the rest of his correspondence,' I say, when we are outside. 'Slow down, will you?' I have trouble keeping up with Sidney's loping strides even without my current injuries. My body aches in unexpected places and I find myself walking with a limp to compensate. 'And that was puzzling me, because it meant the killer must have left it the previous evening, before Dunne was murdered. But no one at the Star remembered a letter being delivered that night, and it didn't come from Jenkes.'

'But Drake said Gilbert brought that letter to him from the Star along with the others,' he says, slowing until I have caught up with him.

'The letter was delivered to him along with the others, that's why it looked as if it had come from the Star,' I say. 'But Gilbert was in a hurry that day, dealing with all the arrangements. He handed the letters over to someone he trusted, someone who was on his way in to see Drake.'

'And you think that person slipped the letter into the pile as if it had come with the rest?' His eyes widen. 'Who was it?'

'Someone who is a frequent visitor to the House of Vesta, though you wouldn't think it. But I need proof before I confront him.'

Though he presses me, I will say no more until we reach Looe Street and see the sign of the apothecary.

Sidney clutches my arm. 'What are you going to do? She will not let us in, you know, not after last time. She will probably call her thugs to make sure we never come back.'

'I am not calling on her directly,' I say, pushing open the apothecary's door.

I have always liked the atmosphere of an apothecary's shop: the sharp, bitter vegetable scents hanging in the air, the steam from the distilling apparatus misting the windows, the neat array of bottles and jars of curiosities ranged along the shelves, the knowledgeable air of the apothecaries themselves, who in some rare instances could be as experienced and well informed as a physician about the workings of the human body, but were more often affable fraudsters, selling garden herbs and sugar-water with extravagant claims of long life and immunity from disease. On entering this one, though, I am reminded of my experiences in Canterbury the summer before, and shudder. Sidney glances at me, and closes the door behind him.

The apothecary, a small, clean-shaven man with anxious eyes and receding hair, is busy at his ware-bench, shredding leaves into a white marble mortar with quick, slender fingers.

'Gentlemen,' he says, acknowledging us with a nod, still intent on his task. When he has finished he looks up and stares without restraint at my appearance. 'By heaven, sir – I hardly know where to begin!' I detect a gleam in his eye as he comes out from behind his counter to examine me more closely; he smells good business here. 'A salve for those burns, I think – they do not look too severe, but often surface burns can be the most painful. And a tincture of arnica for the bruises. I see by the way you are standing that you have a pain in your side – ribs or muscles? I can make you up a poultice for either—'

I hold my hand up to stop him. 'I was looking for your boy.'

His expression hardens. 'What boy?'

'Toby. Your apprentice.'

'There's no Toby here.' His face is guarded now, his eager salesman's patter dropped.

'Whatever he calls himself, then. I will not detain him long – I only wish to speak to him.'

His glance flickers over his shoulder towards the back room, where someone can be heard moving around. 'Whatever your business with him, you can go about it when his day's work's done,' he says. His tone is firm but his eyes are still nervous; I wonder if he knows or suspects what Toby gets up to at the house next door and wants to make sure it is kept far from his own premises.

I am thinking of a convincing argument when Toby himself appears from the door to the back room, wearing an apron made of sacking and wiping his hands on a cloth. He flinches when he sees me and seems frozen, unsure whether to turn and run or pretend he does not know me.

'Hello, Toby,' I say, smiling.

He stammers something, giving his employer a frightened look.

'I won't keep you from your work,' I say, as gently as I can. 'I just had a quick question. It's about Ovid.'

His face is already flushed from the steam of the distilling apparatus in the back; now his colour deepens from his neck to his hairline as he opens his mouth to speak and finds no words.

'I wonder, my good fellow,' Sidney says, in his best aristocratic voice, stepping forward to address the apothecary, 'I have long searched for some remedy that would counter the effects of too much wine. If any man could find me some such compound, I would owe him my eternal gratitude.' He taps the purse at his belt lightly. 'Would *you* know of any such thing?' He follows this up with a dazzling smile and the apothecary finds his attention torn. He makes a fierce gesture to the boy, who beckons me towards a door at the side of the shop.

While Sidney charms the apothecary, I follow Toby through into the passage that runs along the side of the building. The sun does not penetrate here, between the houses, but I recognise this alley as the one that leads to the courtyard and the entrance to the House of Vesta behind the apothecary's. The boy seems to read my fears, for he glances towards the end of the passage and bends his head to talk, as if this will make him harder to see.

'We must make haste,' he whispers. 'I shall have such a beating for this already. My master fears for his reputation, see. He probably thinks . . .' He gives me a meaningful look and leaves the sentence unfinished. I decide to come straight to the point.

'That book you have in your chamber, the one you said a gentleman gave you.'

His whole body tenses. 'What of it?'

'I need it.'

'Why?'

'It might help me to catch a murderer.'

His eyes grow wide, but he shakes his head. 'I don't have it.'

Disappointment drops like a stone in my gut. 'You sold it?'

'Of course not.' He looks briefly affronted, then lowers his gaze. 'Mistress Grace found it. She didn't believe it was a gift.'

'Toby, no one believes that.'

He squirms his shoulders, then raises his eyes to give me an accusing stare. 'Did *you* tell her?'

'No, I swear. She and I did not have much time for conversation after I had to flee your room.'

'Keep your voice down!' He looks around, but the alley is empty. He points at my injuries. 'I heard you jumped out a window. Did you get a beating? I am sorry for it. I've seen men leave the House with worse, mind.'

'They didn't touch me. Listen,' I say, leaning in, 'if you no longer have the book, do you at least have the page you tore from it?' He hesitates, long enough for me to take it as an affirmative. 'The page you tore out because it had an inscription to its owner, yes? Or else he had written his own name in it. You have kept it, haven't you?'

He looks at his feet again and gives one guilty nod. 'I liked the picture.' His colour deepens.

450

'Toby,' I say, making my voice as gentle as I can, 'I really need that page. I can't explain fully but it could be vital evidence.'

'Then you will know his name, and he will accuse me of stealing it,' the boy says, miserably.

'I know his name already,' I say quietly. His mouth falls open. 'And he won't dare accuse you of anything,' I continue. 'He will be too busy defending himself.'

He shakes his head again. 'Mistress Grace has threatened to throw me on the street already for thieving from a customer.'

'If you get me that page, I will tell Mistress Grace that I gave you the book. Without that page, she can't prove it was not mine to give. But if she finds it, she has all the proof she needs against you.'

He looks doubtful.

'They cut off your hands for stealing,' I add casually. His gaze shifts to his blistered fingers with their chewed nails then back to me, terror in his eyes. 'Though for an item of that value, it would probably be hanging.'

'All right, I will get it,' he says, so soft I can barely hear him. 'But I can't go yet – you'll have to wait till I finish for the day.'

'I need it now. Besides, what if she shows him the book and he confirms that you stole it from him before I have a chance to speak to her?'

His face creases with the weight of his dilemma. 'But my master won't allow . . .' He points to the shop.

'My friend is keeping your master busy spending good money in there,' I say. 'It will only take you a few moments to run upstairs. Hurry now.'

He hesitates, then scuttles along the alley to the far end and disappears around the corner.

Minutes pass, and after five I begin to worry: perhaps he has forgotten where he hid the page, or perhaps the madam has caught him. I glance back to the door into the apothecary's;

451

the boy's master will come out if we don't return soon, wondering why I have dragged his apprentice away from his work for so long and fearing what depraved scenes he may discover in the alley. At least I can rely on Sidney to keep him talking. He is probably inventing an entire textbook's worth of maladies.

My relief on hearing footsteps from the end of the alleyway is shortlived when I realise they are accompanied by a woman's voice, followed by a man's muttered response. I dive back inside the shop, where the apothecary and Sidney raise their heads together from the scrutiny of some greenish powder and look at me as if I am interrupting something intimate.

'Where is my apprentice?' the apothecary demands, as if I might have buried him in the alley.

'I think he had to go and relieve himself,' I say pleasantly. He scowls.

'You were saying?' Sidney indicates the substance laid out on a square of waxed paper on the ware-bench.

But we never hear the apothecary's exposition of whatever miracle cure he is offering, because the front door opens and Mistress Grace enters, plucking off her gloves, borne along on wafts of lavender perfume, her bearing as haughty and composed as any court lady. Over one arm she carries a velvet pouch on a slim gold chain, and in her hands a woven basket. She raises her carefully plucked brows in surprise on seeing us.

'Well, if it isn't our friends . . .' She twirls her fingers in a searching gesture. 'I'm sorry, I have forgotten your name.'

'I think you know my name, mistress,' I say, unsmiling. She allows her sharp gaze to travel up and down me.

'You do not look well, sir. Perhaps the rigours of Plymouth life do not agree with you.' She turns to Sidney with an elegant curtsey. 'Good day, Sir Philip. I trust you are in better health.' Her face is impassive, but there is no doubt that she is mocking him. Nonetheless, the apothecary stares and stands up a little straighter, realising he is in the presence of a knight. Perhaps he is wishing he had thought to charge more.

'I am glad to have seen you again, mistress,' I say, matching her smoothness. 'I wanted to ask you about a friend of yours. Master John Doughty.'

She turns pale under her paint but maintains her composure. 'You are mistaken, sir – I do not know anyone of that name.'

'Really? That is curious – he distinctly said he knew you. Perhaps you knew him by a different name. In any case, he is wanted for murder, so it is as well you are not acquainted. His close friends and associates would certainly be questioned, under suspicion of hiding him, or helping him escape.' I smile through my teeth.

She looks towards the street window, where the shadow of her broad-shouldered bodyservant can be seen loitering outside, cleaning his ear with his finger.

'It is indeed fortunate, then, that I do not associate with people of that sort,' she says sweetly, and turns to the apothecary as if to show that the subject is closed and I am of no further interest.

He holds out to her a selection of packets wrapped in paper. 'Here you are, Mistress Grace – common rue, mugwort and pennyroyal. I was a bit short on the rue this week but I can make it up when the next batch comes in. I will adjust your account, of course.'

'Those are all abortifacients, are they not?' I pick up a jar from the ware-bench and sniff it. The apothecary gives me a hard look.

'They are herbs with a variety of medicinal purposes, sir, for those with the knowledge to use them,' he says.

'But principally known for prompting miscarriage,' I say. 'Though not always successfully, from what I hear. Of course there are other ways of dealing with unwanted children.'

Mistress Grace gives no sign of having heard this; she is engaged in checking her packages, weighing them in her hand before opening each one, lifting it to her nose and delicately sniffing the contents. Each time she pauses after smelling them and her eyes wander, unfocused, to the shelves on the wall as if she is deep in contemplation, while the little apothecary twists his hands and fidgets behind his bench, nervously awaiting her verdict. It would be a foolish man who tried to cheat her, I reflect. Sidney gives me a warning look.

The door to the alleyway opens at that moment and Toby reappears, breathless. He freezes in the doorway at the sight of Mistress Grace and looks wildly from me to his master.

'Where've you been?' the little man says, though I suspect his show of anger is more for Mistress Grace's benefit. 'Empty your bowels in your own time, boy, not mine. And it would make everyone's life easier if you didn't have strange men coming in this shop asking after you.' He glares at me and Mistress Grace finally turns around with a sweet smile.

'Pengilly, I find I could use more nutmeg,' she says to the apothecary. I snort, but she ignores it. 'I'm sure you have some in the back you could look for.'

He takes the hint, and with a small bow, leaves us alone in the shop. Mistress Grace places her packets carefully in the basket, shifting its weight on her arm.

'Gentlemen,' she says, still smiling, 'I fear you did not receive the best of our hospitality on your first visit to my house. Especially you, sir.' She tilts her head towards me with a look of sympathy. 'I feel we should make it up to you. Come and take a drink with us this evening, as my guests.' She looks up from under her lashes and her eyes glitter in a way that must once have been devastating.

'I have seen how you treat your guests, madam,' I say, avoiding her eye. 'I would rather not repeat the experience.'

She lays a white hand on my arm. 'That was an unfortunate misunderstanding. I should be glad to speak to you. But I would ask you not to bother this boy while he is at his work. Master Pengilly and I have an agreement. And this boy talks too much nonsense as it is.' Her eyes flit again to the tall shape of her servant outside the door. Toby flinches as surely as if she had struck him.

'I thank you, mistress,' Sidney says, before I can reply, 'but we dine with Captain Drake this evening so I fear we must refuse your invitation.'

'I would gladly talk with you though, mistress,' I say, 'if you would give me a minute of your time without the company of your friend outside.' I nod to the door. 'I am unarmed,' I add, holding up my hands to show her the absence of any weapon at my belt.

'That's what you said last time,' she says tartly.

'Fortunate that I lied, then. Since I was almost attacked by your friend John Doughty.'

She laughs. 'I have no friend of that name, as I said. You were very drunk that night, sir. I fear you were imagining things.'

We stare at one another for a moment longer. She makes a point of turning away first.

'Do you have that nutmeg, Pengilly?' she calls. 'I am ready to leave now.'

I plant myself in front of her, blocking her way to the door.

'How much do you get for them? The babies,' I ask, riled by her supercilious stare. 'Sir Francis Drake thought he had reformed that practice, but you found a way round it, didn't you? You and your collaborator. Did you fear Robert Dunne would try to stop you, was that it?'

For the first time, her composure is disturbed; she falters, looking to the street door, then to the back room of the shop. I glance at Toby; he is cowering by the door to the alley, trying to make himself invisible. I notice his right hand is balled into a fist.

'I don't know what you are talking about, sir,' she says, pulling herself up with a little shake of her shoulders. 'But it sounds like malicious slander, which in this country is punishable by law.'

'Accuse me before the Sheriff, then,' I say. 'I will repeat it for his benefit. And the Mayor, and anyone you care to name.'

She gives a low, tinkling laugh, tinged with pity. 'I don't think that will be necessary. I fear you would not find them sympathetic, however.'

'Oh, that's right – you believe you have them all by the balls,' I say, taking a step towards her. 'We could take the matter to the Star Chamber, if you prefer. We might find an impartial judge there.'

'The Star Chamber would not concern themselves with provincial matters such as this,' she says, but the laughter sounds forced this time.

'They would concern themselves with the murder of a gentleman,' I say, folding my arms.

'I fear you must be confused, sir. No gentleman has been murdered on or near my premises, nor any other sort of man.'

'One may have been murdered at your behest, by someone close to you. Someone who also had a vested interest in silencing him.'

'I think you have said enough, sir. Pengilly!'

The apothecary appears instantly from the back room; he has evidently been skulking just out of sight, eavesdropping.

'Ah, good,' Sidney says, rubbing his hands cheerfully to dispel the atmosphere. 'We should be on our way too – I will take the dandelion infusion and whatever you said the other thing was, for stomach ache. And the salve for my friend. How much?'

He lays his coins out on the ware-bench. While the apothecary's attention is held by the glint of silver, I cross the room to Toby, who looks stricken.

'Goodbye,' I say, holding out my hand for him to shake. He stares at it, then understanding dawns and he grasps it tight. I palm the wad of paper between my fingers. 'Take care of yourself now, and work hard for your master,' I say, nodding to the apothecary, who looks up briefly and snorts. Toby's

456

eyes are full of panicked questions; I answer with a brief shake of my head. Mistress Grace is watching us. I realise that, for now, she does not know whether I have any proof for my accusations; if I mention the book, I lose that advantage. I have no choice but to break my promise to Toby.

'And you be sure to take care of yourself too, Doctor Bruno,' she says, with an icy smile. 'The streets of Plymouth can be dangerous for foreigners.' With a last piercing glance at me, she sweeps out.

The apothecary pushes Toby towards the room at the back and points a finger at me. 'Your friend here is a good customer, so I'll hold my tongue this time. But if you want the boy in future, master, you find him outside my shop. I'm a God-fearing man. You hear?'

God-fearing enough to make your living selling quack remedies for pox and miscarriage to prostitutes, I almost say, but I too hold my tongue. Instead I incline my head to show my remorse, and take my leave.

'You bloody fool,' Sidney says, when we are outside the shop. His right hand grips the hilt of his sword; we scan the street in both directions for any sign of Mistress Grace and her muscled servant. 'You think you can accuse a woman like that of murder to her face? If you're right, she'll want to cut out your tongue before you can repeat it to anyone. We'll be lucky if we make it back to the Star in one piece. Especially now that only one of us is armed.' He casts another furtive glance behind him and quickens his pace.

'That's not my fault. And we are not going back to the Star – we're going to the *Elizabeth*. At least, I am,' I say, limping after him. 'I need to get there before she has a chance to send a message out. I don't want our man forewarned.'

'Come on, then,' he says, as we hurry towards the quayside, keeping well away from the mouths of alleys and side streets where anyone might be lurking. 'Make your grand revelation.

Though I think I have guessed,' he adds, eagerly. He seems to have forgotten his earlier pique at being robbed of his prize in Savile.

'Why does a man kill?' I say.

He falls back to walk beside me. 'Money? Jealousy? Revenge? Power?'

'All of those. Or to silence someone who knows a secret about him. Something that could destroy his position and his prospects.'

'Stop your games now and tell me.'

I pull him into a doorway, checking to see that no one is following us, and unfold the paper Toby pressed into my hand. There is an engraving of the nymph Daphne metamorphosing into a tree, her young breasts peeking boldly through the leaves – I see why poor Toby wanted to keep the picture – but it is the name inscribed in ink at the top of the page that interests me. I feel my chest expand with relief. It would have been better to have the whole book, but this will serve. Sidney stares at it without speaking, then whistles softly and nods, as if conceding victory.

TWENTY-SEVEN

'Bruno! Sir Philip – come in, I had not expected you. Take a seat.' Drake opens the door to his cabin and waves us towards his vast table, now overlaid with piles of papers covered with figures. Thomas Drake sits behind it, quill in hand, his back to the long window. He appears even more irritated than usual at the sight of us.

'My brother has told me of your courage last night, Doctor Bruno,' he says, inclining his head. 'It is a shame those rogues escaped – and with the book, too. But it seems God protected you.' It is difficult to read whether this is sincere or another jibe.

'It was the book or our lives,' I murmur. 'It would have taken a miracle to get out of there with both.'

'My family is indebted to you,' Drake says, with a stern look at Thomas. 'Now – what brings you out here?'

'Bruno has something to tell you,' Sidney says, in a conspiratorial tone.

'To do with Dunne?' Drake almost pounces on me.

'There is a matter I wish to discuss, Sir Francis,' I say. 'But could you first send for Padre Pettifer? And ask him to bring a notebook. Don't mention that Sidney and I are here.'

Drake frowns, but he opens the door and exchanges a few words with one of the guards outside the door.

'What is this about, Bruno?' he says, closing the door as the man's footsteps can be heard descending the stairs. 'Is it to do with Savile's testimony? He is back on board and as good as confined to his cabin, but I'm afraid my brother has confirmed his story. They went to and from the House of Vesta in company that night and spent at least half the time there playing cards together, along with several other gentlemen.' He shoots a fierce glance at Thomas. 'So it seems unlikely that Savile could have slipped away to meet Jonas.'

Thomas Drake skewers first me and then Sidney with a black look. Our hasty confrontation of Savile has laid bare his secret and exposed him to his brother's judgement; clearly he does not thank us for it.

'Let us hear what the chaplain has to say.' I turn away from Thomas's glare; I have no wish to provoke him further.

'What has he to do with it?' Drake asks, faintly impatient.

'It may be that he has some information.' I think it best to keep vague for now.

'God's blood – if he knows something about the business, why would he not have told me?' Drake paces the room, fists clenched at his side. 'Must everyone on this ship hold on to his secrets, at the expense of my voyage?' He directs this last at his brother; Thomas shrinks into the seat and lowers his eyes.

There is a light knock on the door. Drake barks a command and Pettifer appears tentatively on the threshold, a notebook tucked under his arm. Sweat prickles on my back; I only hope I am not wrong this time. At Drake's gesture, Pettifer closes the door and stands before his captain with an expectant look, hands clasped before him.

'Sir Francis?'

Drake waves him to a seat at the table. 'It was Doctor Bruno who wanted to speak to you.'

Pettifer's head snaps round, his eyes immediately wary. He lays his notebook on the table and cocks his head to one side, raising his eyebrows in an unspoken question, still that look of slight superiority on his face; he believes he is above being summoned by the likes of me.

'I wanted to ask you a couple more questions about your conversation with Robert Dunne the night he died, Padre,' I say, in as friendly a manner as I can assume.

'Really – must we go through this again? I have told all I know to Captain Drake long before you arrived.' He turns to Drake in appeal.

'Hear him out, Ambrose,' Drake says, waving for me to continue.

'It would help me to take some notes. I wonder – could I have a page of your notebook?' I nod towards the book on the table. It is a plain notebook, bound in cloth and board; not obviously handsome or costly.

'Well, really,' Pettifer blusters, but his grip tightens around the book. 'Paper is expensive, you know. Surely you have your own? Or perhaps Captain Drake?' He indicates the pile of papers on the table in front of Thomas.

'I'm afraid I have left all my writing things at the inn,' I say, with regret.

'I don't like to tear the book,' he says, though half-heartedly, as though he knows how feeble it sounds.

'Give him some paper – I will have the book replaced for you before we leave, if the cost is an issue.' Drake snaps his fingers, though he gives me a hard stare. I hope this will be worth it, he seems to be saying.

Reluctantly, Pettifer opens the book at the back and carefully tears out a blank page, which he slides across the table to me. I perch on the edge of the bench opposite him and pick up one of the quills that lies on its stand in front of Thomas, but I do not dip it in the inkwell.

'You said you were a Cambridge man, Padre Pettifer,' I

461

say, studying the nib of the quill. 'Do you go back there often?'

He looks startled by the change of tone. 'Not often. Why?'

'But you have friends there still?'

'Naturally, a few. Look, what has this—'

'Do they send you books, these friends? As gifts, perhaps, on occasion.'

'Books?' He affects puzzlement, but I see the pinpoint of understanding in his eyes as his thoughts rush ahead of one another, wondering where I will go next. Good, I think. I have him worried. Everything he says from now on will be an attempt to dodge the truth.

'Books,' I repeat, smiling.

'No,' he says, though he is twisting his fingers together. 'Not that it is any business of yours who sends me books,' he adds in a lofty tone.

'I was only concerned,' I continue, 'because I came across a book recently which I supposed to be yours, and I was afraid it had been stolen from you.'

'What book?' he snaps. The colour is slipping from his cheeks as his tone grows more aggressive. 'Where? I have had no books stolen. Why would you suppose it to be mine?'

'One question at a time, Padre. This book was printed by the new university press at Cambridge, which was founded last year. They have produced only a few books so far. This one is a volume of Ovid's fables – did I say? – which is one of their newer works. Printed this year, and hard to get hold of, unless in Cambridge itself, for I hear the London booksellers are boycotting the new presses.' I lay down the quill and keep my eyes fixed on his.

'No one sent me any such book,' he says, but his voice sounds more subdued.

'But you did go to Cambridge this year, Ambrose – I recall you telling me,' Drake says, softly. 'When I approached you

462

in the spring about this voyage, you had just returned. You were visiting your old tutor, I think.'

He swivels to look at his captain with alarm. 'Well, yes, that is true, but I do not have the kind of money to spare for brand-new books.'

'What is your tutor's name?' I ask.

He narrows his eyes. 'I don't see what that—'

'Is it Roger?' I draw from inside my doublet the page young Toby had torn from the book, with the woodcut of Daphne. At this, Pettifer clasps his hands tighter together to keep them from trembling. 'You see, this endpaper was torn from the volume of Ovid I found, printed by the Cambridge University Press. It is inscribed, "To dear Ambrose, with fond memories, Roger, 1585."' I hold it up so that he can see I am not bluffing. 'It would be an extraordinary coincidence if there was another Ambrose in Plymouth who had the same tutor at Cambridge.'

He says nothing, but his face is blanched of colour and his lips pressed tight.

'What is this about, Bruno? Come to the point, for God's sake, if there is one,' Thomas Drake says, irritated.

Sir Francis lifts a hand to silence him and motions for me to continue.

'I will, Thomas, for it concerns a place you know well,' I say, smiling at him. 'You asked me where I came across this book, Padre. But I think you already know. I found it in the possession of a young boy at the brothel known as the House of Vesta.'

'Ah.' Pettifer flicks his head, dismissive. 'Yes. Very well then – it was stolen from me.'

Drake raises an eyebrow. 'You denied that a moment ago.'

'I did not want to get the poor boy in trouble,' he says. Two pink spots are rising in his cheeks now; he speaks fast, as if his lies must sustain themselves on their own momentum or risk falling apart. 'God knows those youngsters are desperate enough. And Sir Francis is well aware that if I set foot in such a place, it is for God's purposes, to try and bring some salvation out of such grievous sin. So yes, I lost the book there, but I did not report it for fear the boy would suffer.' He looks from me to Drake, his defiance returned. 'Have you written everything down to your satisfaction, Doctor Bruno?' he adds, with venom. 'For there is nothing more to tell.'

'I'm afraid that is not quite all, Padre,' I say, looking apologetic. 'Your visits to the House of Vesta were in part concerned with the placement of unwanted children with Christian families, am I right?'

Pettifer half rises from his chair and places his hands flat on the table. 'Sir Francis, I must protest! Such matters should not be discussed with the likes of—'

'Let him ask his questions, Ambrose,' Drake says, in that same gentle tone that will brook no argument. 'I am interested in your answers.'

I take a deep breath. 'The boy said you sometimes read to him from the Ovid book.'

'I thought to improve his education, poor creature.' He slips a finger inside his collar and loosens it away from his throat.

'And that was why you visited him alone?'

'*What?*' He splutters. 'One might better ask what *you* were doing in the boy's chamber?'

'I was trying to find out who killed Robert Dunne.'

He opens his mouth to speak but blinks at me instead, wrong-footed.

'You see,' I continue, leaning forward across the table, 'Dunne had recently found out a terrible secret about someone on board this ship. Something which, if made public, would destroy that person's reputation and their chances of sailing with Captain Drake, now or in the future.'

Pettifer runs his tongue around his mouth. Sweat glistens along his upper lip. He shakes his head.

'I believe,' I say slowly, 'that Robert Dunne had found

464

out you did not visit that boy to save him from his sins. In fact, you added to them.'

Silence hangs over the table as Drake stares at Pettifer.

'That is slander,' the chaplain says. His voice emerges high-pitched and squeaking. 'Of the most damnable kind. You had better retract it immediately, sir.'

'Was the boy part of your pay-off from Mistress Grace?' I persist. 'For allowing her to continue the practice of selling the unwanted children got on the girls in her house, before she threw them on the street? I assume you took a cut of the profits, too. Did Dunne know about that? He certainly knew you were well able to pay his blackmail demands.'

He jolts with surprise at this, and frowns. 'What demands?'

'Dunne was blackmailing you, wasn't he? Five gold angels is a lot to lose, and you feared there would be more such letters. You knew he could destroy your standing by telling Captain Drake about your arrangements with the House of Vesta. You were in fear of him.'

'No – no, you have it all wrong,' he bleats, flapping his hands. 'I never paid Dunne any money. He never asked me for any. I don't know anything about five gold angels.'

I stand up, for better effect, so that I am looking down on him. Drake, Thomas and Sidney watch like spectators at a dog-fight, rapt. 'You saw the state he was in when he left the House of Vesta that night. Did you know he had been drugged with nutmeg, or did you think he was just drunk? No matter' – I press on, before he can object – 'either way, you got him back to the ship and, with help from Thomas Drake, carried him to his cabin. Thomas went to find the Spaniard, to bring Dunne a cure. You were left alone with Dunne, who was as good as helpless, and you saw a chance to silence your tormentor for good. What did you do, press his face into the pillow? He must have been so confused in his senses he did not put up a fight. You crushed the life out of him and left him there. When Jonas looked in, he thought Dunne had passed out from drink and went away again.'

'No – no, I swear that is a lie!' Pettifer cries. He is growing flustered, his eyes darting from me to Drake, pleading.

'Ambrose,' Drake says, faintly, as if he does not want to believe what he is hearing.

'But you must have been terrified that Jonas had realised the truth. When nothing was said, you decided to make sure. You went back to Dunne's cabin on the pretext of praying with him, and strung him up to look like a suicide. Then you locked his room and threw the key overboard, I imagine.'

'This is pure fabrication. You must believe me, Sir Francis – we know each other, you and I—'

'The next day,' I continue, relentless, 'you saw a chance to link Dunne's death to the Judas book you believed to be heretical, to deter Captain Drake from having it read. You wrote a verse from Matthew's Gospel, making it look as if Dunne's death was somehow a result of the book's dangerous influence. And implying too that Dunne himself was a traitor. Perhaps he had confessed to you his plans to assassinate Sir Francis on the voyage?'

Pettifer leaps to his feet, his face scarlet. 'Assassinate – I do not know what you are talking of, sir, but I refute all of it! If you believe for a moment that I could hear of a plot to harm the Captain-General and not tell him of it immediately, you are more lacking in your wits than I first believed. Sir Francis, you know me,' he says again, wheedling, his eyes shining with unshed tears. 'Would you hear the lies of a stranger and a foreigner against my word?' He knits his fingers together as if in prayer, raising them towards Drake.

I push the page from the notebook across the table to Pettifer. 'If you did not kill Dunne, testify to it by signing this paper.'

'What right have you—'

'Will you sign your name here? To attest that what you say is true?'

466

'You are trying to trap me,' he blusters, hesitating. He raises his eyes and looks around the company for support, but finds only stony faces. I dip the quill into the ink and hold it out to him. He glances at Drake, who nods towards the paper. Pettifer takes the quill from me with a look of pure hatred and scrawls his name across the page. 'And what do you propose to do with this?' he asks. His voice shakes, but with anger now.

'Nothing,' I say. 'Except compare it. Do you have the letter with the Bible verse, Sir Francis?'

'Of course.' Drake looks at me, uncertain.

'May we see it?'

He nods, and unlocks the cupboard in the corner. He unfolds the Matthew letter and holds it out. I hold up the page Pettifer has just signed beside it. They are the same size. There is an identical water stain across the lower right corner of both. 'And look, here,' I say, pointing to the writing. There has been some attempt to disguise the hand in Drake's letter, but way the double T in 'Matthew' is crossed is identical to the double T in 'Pettifer': a broad cross stroke that does not quite meet the first T. It would be hard to doubt that these pages, and the writing on them, came from the same source. For further confirmation, we pass them over to Thomas and Sidney, who bend their heads over the papers and lift them after close scrutiny, with a nod of agreement.

'Did you write that letter, Ambrose?' It is the quiet sorrow in Drake's voice that finally undoes Pettifer. He sinks back to his seat and presses his face into his hands.

'Yes. God forgive me.' It comes as a muffled whisper. His shoulders are shaking. 'The letter, yes. But the rest is lies.'

'The Ovid book?' Drake says, in that same disappointed tone.

Pettifer looks up. 'I do not see any book.'

I click my tongue, impatient. 'The book is in the possession of your friend Mistress Grace at the House of Vesta. But you recognise this endpaper, do you not?'

He nods, miserably. No one speaks; there is only the sound of the ship's timbers creaking, the water lapping outside, and the chorus of the gulls. After a while, Pettifer seems to gather his thoughts. He lifts his head and addresses himself to Drake. When he speaks, he has almost mastered the tremor in his voice.

'I confess I lost the book at the whorehouse, Sir Francis, yes. You know it was my habit to pray with those poor sinners there, as Our Lord did. It seemed to bring some comfort to them. A book like that is costly, so I do not blame a desperate boy for taking it. I had only thought to brighten their lives with stories. Mostly from the Scriptures, of course,' he adds, hastily, 'but I believed they might enjoy the classics, too. I'm afraid I was there the night Robert Dunne came in, reeling with drink. When he learned that the whore he favoured had been sent away, he threatened in his anger to become violent. It seemed to me that it would be in everyone's best interests if I helped him back to the ship. I left him in his cabin to sleep it off, and later I went back to see if he was all right. He had woken, but he seemed unusually troubled and asked if I would pray with him, as I told you. Afterwards, I bade him good night and went to my own quarters. That was the last time I saw him, and I assure you he was very much alive.' He pauses for breath, and wipes his mouth with his hand. 'And he never confessed any intention of harm towards you, Sir Francis, or I would have spoken immediately.'

'No one saw him but you after Jonas looked in and believed he was asleep,' I say. 'When you learned I had been to view Dunne's body, you were very anxious to know if I had been able to tell anything about his death from looking at him.'

'I only wished to know if the matter could be resolved quickly, like everyone else.'

'Really? You weren't afraid that an experienced eye would be able to tell from the body that he had not died by hanging?'

Pettifer does not reply, though he gives me a very unchristian look.

'Explain the letter, then,' Thomas Drake says, brusquely. He has no love for the chaplain, but he must weigh this against his dislike of me, and his evident desire that I should be proved wrong.

'The letter . . .' Pettifer lowers his eyes to the table in a show of contrition. 'I admit that it was an act of folly on my part. When I learned the details of Dunne's death I was distraught, naturally. But I thought the symbolism too important to ignore. I sincerely believed he had taken his own life, you see, and what I knew from praying with him the night before – well, it was clear that something was weighing on his conscience. It seemed to me that he must have been overcome with remorse, though I swear I did not know for what. He had only talked to me of sin in general, and a fear for his soul.' He stops and swallows hard. A muscle has begun to twitch under his right eye. 'A death on board is a bad omen for a voyage, everyone knows. I thought if I could convince you, Sir Francis, that it was connected with the Judas book, you would be fearful enough to abandon the translation. It was wrong, I see that now. But I acted in good faith – I wanted to protect us all from the consequences of dabbling in matters that so clearly violate God's law.'

'Whereas indulging your desire for young boys,' I say, my voice tight, 'God smiles on that, does He?'

Pettifer rises, his face swollen with rage as he plants himself squarely in front of me, eyes burning. 'Repeat that slander again, Italian, and I will—'

'What will you do? Call the Constable? The Sheriff? Or will you just push me off a cliff, like you did with Jonas Solon?'

'More lies! I never laid a finger on the Spaniard. How do you reason that?'

'I think you were afraid Jonas had realised Dunne was

already dead when he took him the draught. He may have thought he was passed out at first, but given all the speculation, he had time to rethink. He would have known you were alone with Dunne when you returned to the ship. Did he voice his suspicions to you? Did you see your chance to silence him and incriminate him at the same time?' I pause for breath; Pettifer is staring at me as if he thinks I have lost my wits. He turns to Drake, holding out his hands in appeal.

'Sir Francis, will you let this man stand here and abuse me in front of you? I have no idea what he is talking about, you must believe me.'

'You speak Spanish, don't you? And you have already admitted to one letter – will you deny that you wrote the other, the supposed confession from Jonas?'

Pettifer's eyes threaten to bulge out of his head. 'Everything you have said to me from the moment I walked in is the grossest insult, and I will see you pay for it. I should expect no less from a Dominican—'

'Gentlemen.' Drake's voice cuts across us, and immediately we fall silent, like chastened children. He fixes the chaplain with a steady look. 'Did you see Jonas the night he died, Ambrose?'

'Of course not,' Pettifer snaps, then remembers to whom he is talking, and modifies his tone. 'I was nowhere near the Hoe, Sir Francis.'

'Where were you, then? And can anyone testify to it?'

Pettifer takes a deep breath and exhales slowly. When he speaks again his voice is calmer. 'I was at the House of Vesta,' he says. 'Mistress Grace will vouch for me.'

Sidney gives a loud snort. Pettifer glares at him.

'Seems half my crew was there that night,' Drake says, sounding tired.

'Did you walk there and back alone?' Thomas asks the chaplain.

'Yes.' He eyes the floor and his voice grows quieter. 'I prefer not to be seen entering the place. They let me in a side door. You understand – though the Lord knows my conscience is clear, I think it best not to give others the opportunity for gossip.'

'And you went directly back to the ship?' Thomas persists.

Pettifer hesitates. 'Actually, I stopped by the church to pray first.'

'What time was this?' Drake asks. There is a sharpness to his tone that suggests he is growing impatient with Pettifer.

'I don't know,' Pettifer says, looking uncomfortable. 'It was already near dark. I didn't stay long.'

'Can anyone vouch for this, Ambrose? Did others see you at church?'

'The sexton was still there, I'm sure he would remember. But when I reached the quayside to take a boat back to the *Elizabeth*, I ran into your secretary, Sir Francis. He was returning at the same time.'

Drake frowns. 'Gilbert? That was late for him to be ashore. Did he say where he'd been?'

Pettifer looks blank. 'No. And I didn't ask. I believe we would all have more peace if everyone minded his own business more often.' He spears me with a glare.

'Not when two of my men have died,' Drake says. There is a new hardness in his voice. He gathers up the letters without looking at Pettifer. 'I think you had better stay aboard the ship for now, Ambrose, until these allegations have been proved true or false.'

'Sir Francis, you cannot possibly think—'

Drake holds a hand up for silence. 'I will reserve judgement until I hear this boy's testimony. It should be a simple matter to tell whether or not he is lying for gain. Bruno, I want you and Sir Philip to fetch the boy and bring him to the Mayor's house. Let's keep this away from that muttering rabble at the Star. Take Sir Philip's armed men – if your suppositions are correct, the Grace woman may be keen to prevent you.'

'I would feel better if I were armed myself, Sir Francis,' I say. 'I lost my knife to Doughty and Jenkes last night and I am not in the best state to fight without one.'

'Was the weapon valuable?'

'Not greatly, in itself. But it had value for me. It was all I had of my old life.'

He nods, understanding. Then he crosses to the locked cupboard in the corner of the cabin. While he rattles his keys and rummages inside, Pettifer's eyes bore into me with a look of such fierce hatred that I know I have made an enemy for life, regardless of whether he is innocent or guilty. I look away, but the force of his stare continues to burn me. If I were a more superstitious man, I would fear I was being cursed.

'Here,' Drake says, returning with a weapon laid across his open palms. He draws it from its sheath to reveal a dagger of burnished steel, its blade tapering to a point as fine as the nib of a quill. The metal is dark and has only a dull gleam, but on closer inspection this is because the surface is mottled with patterns like the grain of wood. The grip is wrapped with bronze thread and the pommel and guard embellished with decorations of vines and flowers. It is an exquisite piece of work.

'Damascus steel,' Drake says, pleased by my look of amazement. 'We took it from an officer on a Spanish ship off Nicaragua. Beautiful, isn't it? Valuable, too. The patterning on the blade is unique. Damascus steel beats anything that comes out of Toledo. They say you can drop a hair across the edge and it will be cut cleanly in two. I have never tried that trick, but you are welcome to experiment. Go on, take it.' He holds the knife out, pommel towards me.

'I cannot keep this, Sir Francis – it must be worth a fortune,' I say, weighing it in my hand. It is so light and perfectly balanced it seems to slice the air with a sigh as I curve my arm. I notice Pettifer takes a step back.

'The debt I owe you is greater,' Drake says. 'As for this

business . . .' He waves a hand around the cabin to encompass Pettifer, me, the letters, and shakes his head as if in despair. 'We had best move quickly. Ambrose, you will wait here with Thomas until we have some answers.'

'Sir Francis,' Pettifer says, in a small voice, as Drake reaches for the latch. 'May I speak to you in private? There is one thing I need to explain, away from these mad accusations.'

Drake nods at me and Sidney to let us know we are dismissed, and closes the door behind us.

'Drake should have his cabin searched,' Sidney says, in a low voice, as we wait on the lower deck. 'It may be that he kept the blackmail demand from Dunne somewhere.'

'I doubt it. Whatever else he may be, Pettifer is a clever man.' I clench my jaw. 'I'm sure he would not have held on to anything that could incriminate him. My fear is that there will be nothing but the boy's testimony against him. And how will that look – an uneducated apprentice accusing a well-respected parson of sodomy?'

'Surely girls can be found who will testify against Mistress Grace, at least?'

I think of the girl Sara in the slums, her mind and body eaten away by the pox. 'There are witnesses, but I'm not sure how much credibility they'd have.'

'Huh. From what I've seen, you'd be lucky if you found a man of authority in this town willing to bring Mistress Grace before a judge,' Sidney says, with a sniff. 'Her trade is too much to their advantage. Pray God the boy's testimony will be sufficient, because—' He breaks off when he sees Gilbert Crosse hovering on the main deck, a leather portfolio clutched to his breast.

'Is everything all right, Sir Philip?' Gilbert hops from foot to foot and chews his lip in that way that makes him look like a schoolboy. 'Have you two been with Sir Francis? I came up just now to ask him to sign these letters but I heard voices so I thought it best not to interrupt. I know he has so much to worry about at the moment.' He ducks his head and offers a sheepish smile.

'I'm sure he will be out soon,' I say, feigning not to notice his fishing for news. Sidney has adopted a policy of ignoring him altogether. Gilbert's faux-humble manner grates on him. I wonder how long the young cartographer hung about outside Drake's cabin, and how much he might have overheard.

'Ah, here he is,' Gilbert says, holding out his folder as Drake appears from the quarterdeck. 'I have made fair copies of those letters, Sir Francis – do you want to sign them now?'

Drake stops and regards him with a strange expression, as if trying to remember what he is for. 'Later, Gilbert. I must go ashore now and see my wife. Leave them in my cabin – you will find my brother there.'

'It's just that I too am going ashore, to church,' he persists, still fidgeting, 'and I thought if they were signed and sealed I could take them to the messenger and have them on the road tonight. Else they will have to wait until the morning.'

Drake sighs. 'Then let them wait. I must not delay this evening. Go and call one of the men to row us, would you? And tell Captain Fenner I will be gone until later tonight. I leave him in charge.'

'If I might beg you to wait while I fetch my cloak and bag, perhaps I could come with you now, to save taking another boat?' Gilbert says, with hopeful eyes.

Drake hesitates. 'No, this boat will be full. I will send it back for you.'

Gilbert looks disappointed, but he nods without complaint and scurries away to his tasks.

'No word of these suspicions must escape to anyone for the time being,' Drake whispers, once we are in the boat. 'Until we have some verification. These crimes Pettifer is accused of would be monstrous in any man, but in a priest . . .' He shakes his head. 'If the men see corruption in those who have spiritual authority over them, what example do they have? There would be chaos. A ship's chaplain's job is to put the fear of God into the crew.'

'I thought it was to console?' Sidney says.

'At sea, the fear comes first,' Drake replies, grim-faced.

A messenger is sent for Sidney's armed men to join us at the quayside. Drake goes on ahead to the Mayor's house with his own bodyservants. I feel a faint flutter of nerves as I watch him go, and find my eyes darting along the busy wharves, scouring the crowds for anyone who might be watching us too closely, keeping his head down or his hands inside his cloak. Mistress Grace's tart warning comes back to me; she will not allow her enterprise to be threatened without a fight. The hulls of the fishing boats crack together as they rock on the swell; their owners stack up pots and untangle nets ready for the night's work. On the quayside, the fishwomen have gone home for the day, but there are others with wide baskets slung across their hips, selling strawberries or pies to anyone disembarking. The street whores will not come out in force until dusk, but already a few hopeful early arrivals loiter on corners where the steep cobbled streets open on to the quay, their painted faces garish in the flat light. A couple try to catch our eye; I turn away. We cannot afford to be distracted. Sidney keeps a hand on the pommel of his sword; he too scans the faces that pass by, alert for any sign of trouble.

'That weapon he gave you is worth a king's ransom, you know,' he remarks, after a while, stealing an envious glance at the dagger now strapped to my side. It is larger than my old knife and harder to conceal, though it does look more imposing. 'He obviously regards you highly.'

I shrug. 'I have been useful to him. But I fear his regard will diminish very quickly, if we cannot find sufficient evidence against Pettifer.'

Sidney sucks in his breath through his teeth. 'It is infuriating

– everything you said back there fits, everything points to the chaplain. It is just a matter of proving it.'

'That is what we said about Savile.' In truth, I have begun to admit a sliver of doubt over confronting Pettifer so publicly with such stark accusations.

'The boy's testimony will be good enough, won't it?' He sounds as if he wants reassurance.

'He will be afraid, though. He may feel it is in his best interest to hold his tongue.'

Sidney's armed escorts are broad-shouldered, solid young men with rough, good-natured faces. They clatter up to us, looking hastily assembled and a little awkward; they had not expected to be called upon this evening and there is a faint smell of the ale-house about them, though they all seem sufficiently alert and clear-eyed to do their job. Just the sight of them, big and confident, surrounding us with their bright liveried tunics and swords at their belts, would be enough to deter all but the most determined assailant, I think, as we set out together up the hill towards the House of Vesta. Groups of bystanders part before us, pointing and muttering. I am not used to feeling so conspicuous, though there is a curious satisfaction in being taken for a man of status.

When we reach the apothecary's shop, I motion for Sidney and the guards to stay outside, but I leave the door open so they can be seen. The little man is standing on a stool taking an inventory of his shelves when I enter; his expectant look withers immediately when he recognises me.

'Oh. It is you,' he says.

'Where is the boy? I need to see him urgently.'

Pengilly curls his lip in disgust. 'I thought I made myself clear to you. In any case, he is not here.'

'Then where is he?'

'What business is it of yours?'

'My friends would like to know,' I say, gesturing to the open door. He catches sight of the men, who grin at him but stand so their swords are visible. He swallows.

476

'She called him back to the house. I expect you'll find him there. And you can find him there in future, as I told you.'

I nod and turn towards the door.

'Sir,' he calls out, as I reach the threshold. He gestures to the armed men. 'You won't hurt him, will you? He's a good lad.'

'He will be fine, I assure you.'

Sidney and I run up the alleyway beside the shop into the rear courtyard, followed by the men. There is no sign of life in the windows above us. I bang on the House of Vesta's door and do not let up until I hear footsteps approaching.

'For the love of God,' comes a female voice from inside, 'we are resting. Come back later.'

'Open this door now, or we will open it for you,' Sidney shouts, in his most commanding tone.

There is a short pause, and the panel behind the iron grille is slid back. A woman's face appears. It is not Mistress Grace.

'What do you want?' She looks frightened. 'We are not open yet.'

'I want to see the boy,' I say.

'He is unwell,' she says, but there is a small hesitation that gives her away. She reaches to close the panel.

'Go on, lads,' I say, standing aside. 'Get this door open.'

It is an empty threat; the door looks solid enough to withstand cannon fire, but the woman gives a little cry and a moment later I hear the click of a lock and the door opens a fraction.

'Do not hurt anyone,' she pleads, crossing herself as I push past her and take the stairs two at a time to the second landing, closely followed by Sidney and his men. Women's screams echo through the house at the sound of our invasion. I fling open the door to Toby's room to see him lying on the bed in his shirt and breeches, convulsing. Mistress Grace stands by the window looking on, her slender silhouette framed against the light. She regains her composure remarkably quickly after the shock of my arrival and arranges her expression into a sad smile.

'Poor boy,' she says, in a tone whose sincerity would fool no one. 'I fear he has eaten something that disagreed with him.'

I rush to the bedside. Toby's breathing is laboured and his skin has a greenish hue. There is a thin trickle of blood-flecked vomit running from the corner of his mouth. All around his head on the sheet are spots of dark red. I curse my stupidity; I have been so concerned about Mistress Grace wanting to silence me that I missed the far more obvious danger. I lean close to the boy's face. His breath smells foul and his eyes are clouded. His muscles spasm again and he gives a plaintive cry.

'Toby.' I give his shoulders a little shake. 'Toby, can you hear me?'

He stares at me, but his eyes register nothing. 'This boy needs a physician,' I bark at her, 'you must send for one right away. And he must be made to vomit immediately.'

'I think you are overreacting,' she says, smoothly. 'It was probably some bad shellfish. But I have sent for a physician nonetheless.'

I look at him. His ribcage hardly moves and he exhales with a strained croak, as if the act becomes harder with each breath. I grab his shoulders and haul him into a sitting position. He is barely conscious. Supporting his bony shoulders with my left arm, I push two fingers of my right hand into his slack mouth and press down until he starts to gag. His chest heaves a few times; I push him forward until a thin yellow slurry dribbles down his chin. Mistress Grace simply stands there watching. It is not enough, and we both know it.

'What did you give him?' I demand.

She opens her eyes very wide, as if to say she has no idea what I could mean, and shakes her head. Toby makes a small

478

noise; at the same time, I feel his fingers scrabble weakly at the back of my hand. He is trying to speak. I put my ear to his mouth and hear the word 'drink'.

'He wants a drink,' I say. 'Get him water.'

She doesn't move. It is only then that I see the empty cup on the floor. The stains around his head and on his smock are not blood but wine; he must have been force-fed some draught of poison in a cup of wine, that is what he was trying to tell me. His limbs shoot out in different directions and his body bucks under another violent spasm, until he falls horribly limp in my arms. His eyelids twitch faintly.

'Send one of your men down to the apothecary now, ask for some potion that will induce vomiting, or any antidote to poison,' I say, turning to Sidney in desperation, but it is clear that we are too late. Whatever Toby has ingested has already done its work. I squeeze the boy's hand, but though his fingers are still warm, there is no response.

'The physician will be here soon enough,' Mistress Grace says, her tone consoling. 'I'm sure he will know what to do for the best.'

'The boy will be dead by then, and you know it,' I say. I lay Toby down again on the narrow bed. His long hair sticks to his forehead and his mouth is half open as he fights for breath, but with less conviction each time. He looks no more than a child. Caught by a great wave of pity and anger, I raise my head and look at Mistress Grace; her complacent expression as she stands there watching a young boy die fills me with rage. I spring across the room and catch her by the upper arm, pushing her against the wall so fast that she hardly has time to flinch. 'The physician will see what has happened here, and we will have the Sheriff out before you have time to hide the body. You will hang for murder, *mistress.*'

She makes a little moue with her painted lips and leans her face away, as if she finds it indelicate to be so close to a man.

Hypocritical witch, I think, though I let go of her in disgust. There is nothing to be gained from threatening her.

She rubs her arm and moves away to the window. 'You should never have come here. You should have heeded the warning and stopped prying into matters that are no business of yours. See what your meddling has achieved.' She jerks her head towards the boy on the bed. My fury seems to swell and burst in my chest, so that I can hardly speak.

'You dare to blame *me* for this? It was a pitiful scrap of a life this boy had, but it was not yours to throw away when it no longer suited you. None of these children are your property to dispose of. And you will hang for this, I will make sure of it.'

'Will you?' she says, a ghost of a smile hovering at her lips. 'You, Doctor Bruno, with all your influence in this town? You are fond of the boy, I see. And after only one night.'

'Have you no pity?' I shout, taking a step towards her. My hand flies to the unfamiliar knife at my belt and I am gratified to see that she looks genuinely frightened. 'He is a child,' I say, more quietly, letting my hands fall to my sides. 'A child.'

'Bruno,' Sidney says gently, from the doorway. 'There is nothing we can do here. Let us go.'

'Listen to your friend, Bruno,' Mistress Grace says, folding her arms, though her gaze strays warily to the dagger. 'I have no doubt the physician will find that the boy died of some sudden seizure. It happens all too frequently.'

'I'm sure it does, in this place.' Even as I spit the words at her, I feel the weight of hopelessness settle in my chest. The physician will be part of her circle too, as will the magistrate, the Sheriff, the constables. There will be no justice for one orphan boy. And no one now to testify that anything illegal went on at the House of Vesta between him and Ambrose Pettifer. My accusations will look like no more than malicious slander. 'We should leave two of your men here to make sure she does not run,' I say, turning to Sidney. 'Sir Francis Drake wants her questioned.'

'I have no intention of running anywhere, but I will not have your men in my house,' she says, narrowing her eyes. 'You have no grounds for it. And Sir Francis Drake would do well to remember he is no longer mayor of this town.' She says this with a hint of satisfaction. We both know any threats I can make are empty. She is entirely confident of her immunity here and not even Drake's influence can touch it.

I give her a last, hard stare, to let her know I have not surrendered, then cross to the bed and look down at Toby. His eyelid is still twitching and his limp hand jerks involuntarily, but his face has grown a waxy grey, his eyes sunk into shadow. He is halfway across the threshold of death already; if a physician really has been called, he would need a miracle to bring the boy back now. I reach out and take his hand; his fingers are cold and clammy. I wonder what she gave him; with the arsenal of ingredients she keeps to poison infants in the womb, she would not be short of possibilities. I murmur a benediction over him in my own language; it is many years since I last administered any sacraments of the church, and I never will again, yet in this moment I feel there is nothing else I can offer him. The words form as easily as if I had been repeating them every day, and there is a strange comfort in the old familiar expressions, though only for me – Toby cannot hear me now, and would not understand if he could.

'*By the sacred mysteries of mankind's restoration, may Almighty God remit for you the punishment of the present life and of the life to come, and may He open to you the gates of Paradise and admit you to everlasting happiness.*' The way I say it, the sentiment sounds more like a challenge than a prayer. Yet there is a sense of reverence in the room; when I turn back to the door, Sidney and his armed men are standing with their heads bowed. I shoulder past them to the stairs with my eyes to the ground, so they will not see my face. She is right – I caused his death. I failed to save him. And for what?

TWENTY-EIGHT

'You cannot blame yourself, Bruno. Who was to know she was so ruthless? Here, this way.'

I have not spoken as Sidney leads us back towards the Mayor's house. His pace hurts my legs and my ribs but I do not complain; what have I to complain about? A churchbell peals insistently from somewhere beyond the rooftop, summoning the town to Evensong.

'*I* should have known. A woman who throws young girls into the gutter once they have borne her a child to sell? Look at us – walking the streets with armed guards. We were so busy worrying about our own safety that we did not see the real danger. So much easier for her just to silence the boy. God damn her!' I burst out, stopping at the corner of a side street to catch my breath. 'We should have taken him with us this afternoon. He would still be alive.'

'You could not have known,' Sidney says again, laying a hand on my arm.

I retreat into silence; he does not know, because I never speak of it, how heavy the dead weigh on my conscience. In the turbulent years since I left San Domenico Maggiore, there have been others whose lives I feel I could have saved if I had been quicker to recognise a killer – even those who became victims precisely because they tried to help me. Some nights, their faces appear to me in the mist of sleep, quietly accusing. Sidney takes the view that regret is the most pointless of all sentiments, since the past cannot be changed, but he is young still; I am finding that the more years I accumulate, the closer my regrets shadow me.

'I wonder if your inamorata is back from Mount Edgecumbe,' Sidney says, casually, turning up a small side street. 'She will want to express her gratitude to you, no doubt.'

'She is hardly my inamorata.'

He only raises an eyebrow and makes a show of suppressing a smirk.

The Mayor's house is the grandest in the street: a fine four-storey double-gabled building of white stone, with vast windows that stretch almost the entire width of the façade on the first three floors, their expanse an imposing display of wealth for anyone who knows the cost of glass.

We are shown into a spacious parlour on the ground floor by a liveried servant. Drake is seated behind a table at the far end of the room, poring over papers. His head snaps up as we enter, his eyes questioning.

Lady Drake sits in the window, her auburn hair bound up in a gold caul. She is deep in conversation with a portly older man who wears a fine wool doublet and leather boots, his fingers studded with gold rings. He offers a bow to Sidney and introduces himself to me as the Mayor; as I shake his hand, I recall Mistress Grace's loaded remark about how Drake should remember he is no longer mayor of Plymouth. Did she mean to imply that she need fear no reprisal from the current mayor? The suspicion colours my impression of the man; there is something unctuous about his manner, and I must force myself to accept his welcome with a smile. But he barely has a chance to speak before Lady Drake launches herself at us and clasps both my hands.

'Doctor Bruno, I am forever in your debt. I never believed I would see my cousin Nell alive again.'

'Is she here?' Though it is true that I have given Nell little thought since I left her this morning, now that I am here, I realise how much I want to see her, to be assured that she is recovering.

'They brought her back after dinner – in a carriage! Was that not kind of Sir Peter? All she could talk of was how she owes you her life.' I fear she might weep, but she gathers herself and presses my hands firmly as she fixes me with a new, more knowing expression. 'She will want to reward you.'

'Your gratitude and your husband's is all the reward I need, my lady,' I mumble. The Mayor stares at me as you might an exotic animal. Sidney is pointedly looking out of the window. 'Besides,' I say, extracting my hands and tapping the dagger at my belt, 'Sir Francis has already made me a handsome present.'

'My cousin is resting,' she says, 'but I will tell her you are here. I'm sure that will do more than any physician's draught to restore her spirits.'

'Elizabeth, my Lord Mayor,' Drake says, rising from his seat, 'I must speak with these gentlemen in private.'

'Of course, of course. I will have some refreshment brought. It is dusty in the streets today, is it not?' The Mayor bustles towards the door with officious politeness. 'My Lady Drake, would you like to take a turn in the garden?'

'Thank you, your worship, but I think I shall see how my cousin is recovering,' Elizabeth says, smiling sweetly. 'And whether she is ready to receive visitors.'

'Well?' Drake says, impatient, when the three of us are left. 'Where is the boy?'

'Dead,' Sidney says bluntly.

'What?'

'Mistress Grace poisoned him. She must have done it as soon as we turned our backs this afternoon.' I shake my head bitterly. 'I should never have left him.'

'I will have a messenger send the constable there directly,' Drake says, his voice hard with anger. 'But this is bad for us. Without the boy, there is no witness to this crime you accuse Pettifer of. And if you cannot prove the crime, you cannot prove there were ever any grounds for blackmail, and the murder charge falls apart.' He looks at me steadily as he says this. I do not miss the emphasis on 'you'.

'You think I am mistaken?' I ask quietly.

'Not entirely,' he says. 'Pettifer will never admit to what you accuse him of with the boy. And though it pains me to say so, I acknowledge there could be truth in that. As for the trade in babies – I can well believe it. But I think our chances of holding them to account for it are small, when the most powerful men in the town will not move against Mistress Grace. I have sent men to fetch the pregnant girl from Stonehouse, though I imagine they will have thought of that and moved her elsewhere. I only hope she is safe.'

'Then we cannot prove that Pettifer committed the murders?' I hear my voice faltering.

'Unless there is some evidence that Dunne's blackmail demands were addressed to him, it remains your word against his. And he is well connected in the town.'

'Whereas I am a foreigner and a Catholic, as far as everyone here is concerned,' I say, finishing the thought for him.

Drake holds his hands out, as if to show he is helpless to deny it. 'Pettifer would use that against you. No jury in the county would consider a case against him, I can promise you that now.'

'Then what?' I look from him to Sidney, waiting for one of them to make a suggestion. To have found the killer – to have directly caused a boy's death in pursuit of him – only to watch him slip effortlessly out from every accusation, would be a bitter defeat. 'Will you take him on the voyage, Sir Francis, suspecting him to be a murderer?'

'There is something I wish you to see, Bruno. Come and

'look.' He beckons us over to the table where he has a number of papers spread out. He picks up a sheet and hands it to me.

I skim the contents briefly. It is a short letter addressed to Captain Drake, dated some months ago, executed in a neat, sloping hand; the writer is putting his arguments for a greater degree of responsibility on the voyage, with a commensurate fee, on account of his wide experience of the Spanish coastline and ports, and in acknowledgement of his unofficial role as ship's physician. He also asks for a better berth. Though the letter is written in English, it is signed by Jonas Solon. I look up from the paper and stare at Drake, bewildered. His jaw is clenched tight.

'I don't understand – so Jonas could write after all?' I falter.

'No. He asked someone to write this for him. He thought I would be more inclined to consider his request if he made it formally, in a letter, like an educated man.' He pauses to master whatever emotion this memory of Jonas has stirred in him. 'I had forgotten all about it, until I was reminded. Bruno – Ambrose Pettifer wrote it for him. That's what he wanted to tell me.'

I look down, half expecting the floor to give way beneath me. A long silence follows. I cannot think what to say – my only thought is of the apology I will have to make to Pettifer, and how it will stick in my throat.

'This letter was among my correspondence,' Drake says. 'I had to dig it out when Ambrose mentioned it. But what interests me is this. Look – here is the forged confession letter, supposedly from Jonas. I have been comparing them while I waited for you. The hand is quite similar in places, do you not think? It looks as if whoever wrote the confession letter had tried to imitate the writing in this letter here' – he points to the paper in my hand – 'not realising it was not written by Jonas himself.'

'Which means someone would have had to find it among

486

'your papers,' I say, slowly, almost to myself. Someone with access to Drake's private letters.

'But,' Sidney jumps in, 'surely it could be a double bluff? Pettifer could claim someone tried to copy his hand, whereas in fact he wrote both—'

'Philip,' I say, with quiet despair, 'it means that Pettifer already knew Jonas was illiterate. He would not have written the confession letter.'

'He could still have killed Dunne, just as you described it,' Sidney says, trying to sound encouraging. 'The blackmail makes that plausible.'

'Perhaps,' Drake says, again, in that slow, thoughtful way that clearly means he disagrees. 'But something about this confession letter sits uncomfortably with me, and I cannot quite put my finger on it.'

'Whereas the writer has put his fingers all over it,' Sidney says, examining the paper. 'He is not a neat draughtsman, whoever he is trying to imitate. Look here, at the left margin, where the words are smudged and blotched all the way down. I recall a chap at Oxford who did the same – he wrote with his left hand, and would not learn with his right, so that every time he copied a line he would blot the first part as he went along. His tutor refused to read it, so he—'

'Give me that.' I snatch the letter from his hand, tilting it to the light. Sidney is right; I have failed to see what was in front of me all along. Drake is staring at the paper; he too has begun to understand.

'No. No – it is not possible. But why?' He raises his eyes to me. 'I have had him under my nose all this time. I can hardly—'

'*Who?*' Sidney says, turning from me to Drake, aggrieved at being left in the dark. 'What have you found?'

'Gilbert Crosse is left-handed,' I say, tapping the letter. 'The first time we met him he offered me the wrong hand to shake and corrected himself. I thought he was having a joke at the expense of a foreigner – we laughed about it, remember?'

'Gilbert? You think he wrote this? Then – he killed Dunne?' Sidney stares at me, disbelief etched in the lines on his forehead. 'Why?'

'Because Dunne knew what he was up to,' I say. 'And was making him pay for it.'

'And what *was* he up to?'

I glance at Drake. 'That time I saw Gilbert at church – the man who had been sitting beside him slipped out halfway through the service. He was wearing riding clothes. I would bet that Gilbert's very public show of piety has provided him with a useful meeting place that no one suspected.'

'Passing secret letters, you mean?' Sidney's eyes grow wide. Drake presses his fingers to his temples. 'To whom?'

'Jonas as good as told me, though I didn't realise it at the time,' I say. 'He said, "if anyone is spying on this ship, it is not me". I just supposed he meant it as a figure of speech, to emphasise his innocence. But I think he suspected that there really *was* a spy. And think how keen Gilbert was to point our suspicions towards Jonas from the beginning.'

'Gilbert has been acting as my clerk since the first days of planning this voyage.' Drake speaks quietly, still holding his head as if it hurts him to speak. 'He has seen all the navigational charts – he knows each nautical mile of our proposed route and has every coordinate plotted in his logs. What do you imagine the Spanish would pay for that information? It would lead our entire fleet directly into a trap.'

'Robert Dunne must have guessed at it somehow,' I say.

'Instead of warning me, he used the knowledge to try and squeeze some money out of Gilbert – guessing he could afford it with Spanish gold in his purse.' Drake bunches his hands into fists by his sides and his jaw tightens.

'But we now know that Dunne was planning to poison you somewhere along the way – his loyalty no longer lay with the voyage. He was more interested in what he could gain from threatening Gilbert in the short term.'

'That doesn't explain Gilbert's betrayal.' Sidney looks incredulous. 'Why would he spy for the Spanish? Risk the safety of the whole fleet, when he was travelling with it? It can't just be the money, surely?'

'Only Gilbert can answer that,' Drake says, his voice thick with sorrow, or anger, or both. I look at him.

'We must find him. He said he was going to church, did he not? Quick – if we get there in time, we may even catch him passing a letter to his contact. We could take them both at once, and have evidence in our hands.' I am halfway to the door, a hand on my knife, when Drake speaks.

'Wait, Bruno. Gilbert is not at church. He meant to go, but I had forgotten I promised Dom Antonio a tour of the *Elizabeth Bonaventure* – he has been pestering me to look around since he arrived. He was keen to see the charts of our voyage – I sent a message asking Gilbert to look after him aboard since I was coming ashore to see my wife and check on Lady Arden.'

'Well, if Gilbert is still on board, what are we waiting for?' Sidney says. 'He can't go anywhere. Let us hurry back to the ship and arrest him.'

'Oh, God,' I say, staring at Drake.

'What is it, Bruno?' He catches the alarm in my tone.

'The other night – Dom Antonio recognised Gilbert. He knew they had met before. Gilbert denied it, quite fiercely – said Dom Antonio must be confused by all his travels. In the end Dom Antonio couldn't be certain and conceded he must be mistaken.'

'I remember that,' Drake says, anxiety flaring in his eyes.

'What if Dom Antonio was right? Why would Gilbert deny it, unless they had met somewhere that would give away details he didn't want people to know?'

Drake's brow creases. 'Gilbert has worked and studied in Europe, I know that much. He was clerk to the English Ambassador in Paris for a time last year – perhaps they met there.'

'Wherever it was, there's a reason Gilbert denied it. And he has already silenced two other people who could have exposed his secret.'

'God's blood. You think Dom Antonio is in danger?' Drake's face freezes. 'But he has my own armed men with him.'

'You said he wanted to look at the maps. If Gilbert has a key to your cabin, he might argue that they should leave the guards outside, for privacy. They could be alone there together. Gilbert would have his opportunity.'

Drake pauses while the possible scenarios play out behind his eyes. Then he gathers himself, breathes out – one short, sharp breath – and assumes the stance of a commander.

'We must get back to the ship with all haste. Sir Philip – since Gilbert's original plan was to go to church this evening, it may be that he had a meeting arranged. Take your armed men and hurry there – see if you can find anyone who might be a courier, expecting to meet him. Bring him for questioning if you do. Bruno – you and I will leave immediately.'

Lady Drake is just coming down the stairs as we hurtle along the passageway towards the front door.

'Doctor Bruno! Marvellous news,' she calls down, clapping her hands together. 'Lady Arden is much recovered and is longing to see you.'

'Not now, Elizabeth,' Drake shouts, flinging the door open. 'Stay here until we return.'

'Excellent – give her my good wishes,' I call back, without stopping, but it comes out as a croak. My throat is dry with fear; I can only hope we are not too late.

TWENTY-NINE

'I do not want to believe it, Bruno, and yet it seems I must.' The rowboat crests another wave and drops, flinging spray into our faces. Drake turns to the man at the oars. 'Damn it, man, can you not go any faster?'

'I'm sorry, Sir Francis, I'm doing my best – the wind's against us this evening.'

'Forgive me – I know.' Drake leans forward over the prow of the boat, as if this might help him arrive sooner. 'It's just that I must reach my ship urgently. Keep at it – I will see you rewarded.'

The man grunts and lowers his head, his muscled shoulders straining into each stroke of the blades.

'I know I have been wrong with the others, sir,' I say, 'but everything adds up now. I only pray that we reach the ship in time.'

He beckons me closer and I shift up on the seat to hear him better as he lowers his voice so the boatman cannot hear.

'But Gilbert could not kill Dom Antonio in my cabin and make it look like anything but murder, and himself the killer?' he asks. 'He has been so careful to try and disguise the other deaths. Surely he would not risk giving himself away now.'

'It depends how desperate he is,' I say. The wind whips my

words away and Drake has to lean in to hear me, so close that I feel his hair brush my forehead. 'And where they met – if he fears Dom Antonio could incriminate him, he may grow reckless, especially if he thinks this is his one chance to be alone with him, away from the guards. As for the means . . .' I pause to push my hair out of my eyes, though the wind snaps it straight back. 'I don't suppose he intends to cut Dom Antonio's throat in your cabin. But something in a glass of wine – some slow-acting poison, that would take effect later? That could easily be done. Dom Antonio would not suspect a thing.'

'Where would Gilbert get any such poison at short notice?'

I shrug. 'No one has cleared out Jonas's quarters, I imagine? There is a whole trunk of potential poisons on board. Gilbert is an educated man – I would not put it past him to have read up on physick.'

Drake nods, taking it in.

'And you gave him a key to your cabin?' I ask.

'He had one already, so that he can work there if I am occupied elsewhere. He can only open the main door and the chest where my papers and charts are kept – everything else of value is locked away. I saw no harm in it.' He rubs his knuckles into the hollow between his eyes. 'I trusted him, God damn it!' He lifts his head and looks at me. 'My brother berates me for investing my faith too quickly in my men. He begs me to remember the price on my head. But I pride myself on being a good judge of character. Pride that comes before a fall, it seems.' He presses his lips together. 'Dom Antonio and I fought together, some years ago. I led a force that was supposed to help him recapture the Portuguese throne. Philip of Spain was too strong – all we managed to take were the Azores. That poor man has been running from Spanish assassins for as long as I have – if anything should happen to him aboard my ship, at the hands of my own clerk, Her Majesty would—' He breaks off; perhaps he cannot even imagine how the Queen would respond. 'Gilbert came to me from Walsingham, you know. I thought I could trust him.' He turns to me, his expression somewhere between pleading and outrage. It is not clear if he means Gilbert or Walsingham.

'Walsingham has been wrong before,' I say, quietly, tucking my chin down into my collar. I will not forget my own experience at the hands of a man Walsingham had also trusted, mistakenly.

Drake shakes his head and sinks into silence. I count every wave, every slice of the blades through the water, every breath, every heartbeat. The boatman is clearly working at the limit of his strength, and still the journey seems to take half a lifetime. By the time we bump up against the hull of the *Elizabeth* and Drake shouts for a ladder, I begin to dread every buffet of the waves, every moment's delay.

Captain Fenner hurries across the main deck as soon as he sees Drake climbing aboard.

'Captain-General – we did not expect you back so soon. Is everything all right?'

'Where is Dom Antonio?' Once again, I admire Drake's ability not to let his fear show in his demeanour. His voice is brusque, but you would never suspect him of panicking.

'In your cabin, with young Gilbert,' Fenner says. 'I showed him all the munitions when he arrived, then he said he wanted to look at the charts. They went off together and I went back to my duties. Shall I fetch—'

'Thank you, Fenner.' Drake places a hand on the captain's arm. 'Come, Bruno. You too, Fenner – we may have need of you.'

A suspicion of alarm crosses Fenner's grizzled face, but he merely nods.

I follow Drake up the stairs to the captain's cabin. Two armed guards flank the door. Drake greets them quietly.

'Is the Portuguese inside?'

One of the guards nods. 'With your clerk, sir. They told us to keep watch out here.'

Drake turns to me, dropping his voice. 'We must proceed carefully. We do not want to startle him – he may do something rash if he thinks he is cornered.'

'Does Gilbert carry a weapon?' I ask.

'Not to my knowledge.' Drake grimaces. 'But then it appears he does a great many things outside my knowledge, so that is no guarantee.'

He turns the door handle. It is locked. He takes the key from the ring at his belt, and slides it quietly into the lock, but it meets with resistance halfway. The Captain-General curses under his breath.

'He has left the key in the lock on the inside, so that it cannot be opened,' he mouths.

'Must we break it down, sir?' Fenner asks.

Drake shakes his head. 'No. Let us avoid force unless it proves necessary.'

'Can we get in from the other side?' I whisper. 'From the quarter gallery?'

Drake frowns. 'It could be done, if the rear door or a window was open. You would have to climb down a rope from the poop deck, though – it would be dangerous.' He gives me an appraising look. 'You are injured, Bruno – better one of my men tries it.'

I shake my head. 'I am fit enough. Let me do it while you remain here – we will trap him from two sides.'

Drake considers this and gives a curt nod. 'Very well. Fenner – take him up and see that he is safe. Hurry – they will be aware that we are out here by now. And, Fenner' – he drops his voice to a whisper – 'when you are done up there, I want you to go down and search Master Crosse's quarters. Bring me any papers, money – anything you find of interest. Search thoroughly.' He turns back to the cabin door. 'Gilbert! Are you in there? I cannot open the door – could you unlock it?'

494

'Just coming, Captain.' Gilbert's voice sounds bright and easy from inside. I hesitate, half-expecting him to throw the door wide to reveal Dom Antonio peacefully poring over navigational charts, no harm done, just to prove me wrong. But the door does not open. Drake rattles the handle.

'Gilbert – let me in! That is an order.'

'I am trying, Sir Francis – there seems to be a problem with the lock.' His tone is still cheerful; it is clear from the acoustics that he is not speaking from close to the door.

'He's playing for time,' I whisper. Drake makes a savage gesture with his head as he lifts his hand to bang on the door. Fenner and I hurry up to the poop deck on the level above.

The old captain does not waste any time with questions about what is happening below; he wordlessly gestures over the wooden guardrail on the starboard side. I lean down and see where the rigging of the mizzenmast is secured to the sides of the sterncastle; it looks straightforward to shin down one of these ropes and drop on to the quarter gallery below.

'You all right?' Fenner says. I nod, hoisting myself over the rail, so that I am clinging to it on the other side. Below me is a sheer drop to the water. I shudder, and concentrate my attention on the side of the hull immediately before me. I shuffle along until I can grip the taut rope of the rigging, leaning out, pushing with my feet against the wood as I pass one hand over the other, finding footholds where I can, keeping the tension in my arms though I can feel the rough rope burning the palms of my hands. Once my foot slips against the hull as the ship rocks on a sudden swell; my shoulder wrenches sharply as my full weight hangs from my arms, some thirty or so feet above the sea, but I scrabble with my feet and find my balance again, until I can stretch out my left leg and gain a foothold on the rail of the gallery.

I drop as quietly as I can on to the wooden planks and crouch below the level of the wide casement that runs around three sides of the cabin. The door into the captain's quarters is directly in front of me; I consider trying it, but if it is locked, Gilbert will hear and we will have lost the element of surprise. I ease myself along until I can raise my head enough to peer through the window.

Dom Antonio is closest to me, seated at the bench behind the captain's wide table, his back to the window, a series of papers spread before him. His right hand toys with the stem of a wine glass; it is full of a deep-red liquid. My heart lurches, but the Portuguese seems distracted; he is watching Gilbert, who stands behind the inner door. He appears to be fiddling with the key, or at least, he is making a show of doing so. From my vantage point it does not appear that he has any kind of weapon in his hands, though I cannot take that for granted – Gilbert is nothing if not resourceful. Glancing across the cabin, I see that one of the casements on the other side is open a fraction, just enough for me to ease my hand inside. I do not want to alert Gilbert to my presence until I am able to get inside the cabin with my knife, in case he should lunge for Dom Antonio.

'What is the matter?' I hear Dom Antonio ask, anxiety in his voice.

'Nothing to worry about – I think the lock is a little stiff,' Gilbert replies. 'Is the wine good?'

Dom Antonio looks at the glass in his hand as if he had forgotten it was there. Drake is hammering impatiently on the door. I have no time to lose. Crouching lower, I scuttle around the gallery until I am under the open casement. I draw my dagger silently, clamp the handle between my teeth; in one movement I reach up, grip the lintel above the window and swing myself through the gap to land on the table. The gust of air sends all the papers flapping to the floor. Dom Antonio jumps back, pressing himself against the seat and making the sign of the cross. Gilbert spins around, staring at me.

'What—'

'Jesu, Mary and Joseph – he has come to murder me!' Dom Antonio cries out. I take the knife from my teeth and point it towards him; he cowers behind the table.

'Don't touch that wine,' I bark. 'Put it down. Have you drunk any?'

The Portuguese shakes his head and does as he is told.

'You,' I say to Gilbert, turning the point of my dagger towards him and jumping down from the table. 'Get away from that door. And keep your hands where I can see them.'

The young cartographer blinks rapidly behind his eye-glasses and edges across the room, holding his hands up before him, palms outwards, as if to ward off the madman. His tongue darts nervously around his lips. 'Doctor Bruno, have you quite lost your wits?'

I hold the dagger out, keeping it level and my eyes fixed on him while I cross to the door and, feeling behind me, turn the key with one smooth movement. 'Nothing wrong with that lock as far as I can see,' I say, as Drake bursts in, followed by his two armed guards. Gilbert backs towards the table, staring from me to Drake in amazement.

'Dom Antonio – are you all right?' Drake says, unsure who to address first.

'I am quite well, thank you. I was just taking a look through your charts here, when – what is happening, Francis? Is this man dangerous?' He gestures to me.

'This one, no,' Drake says, his shoulders settling now that he has regained control of the situation. 'Gilbert – I see you are giving Dom Antonio my good wine?'

Gilbert colours. 'I – yes, I thought, in your absence, Sir Francis, you would have wanted me to show your guest the proper hospitality—'

'Most thoughtful of you,' Drake says, taking a step closer to the table. There is an edge to his voice that Gilbert cannot fail to have noticed. 'But he does not appear to be thirsty. Why don't you drink it instead?' Drake swipes up the glass from under Dom Antonio's nose and holds it out to Gilbert.

The young cartographer shakes his head urgently. 'I can't, Sir Francis – you know I do not touch strong liquor. I have a weak constitution.' He breaks into a nervous laugh.

'Nonsense – this is excellent stuff. It'll put fire in your belly. Drink it down.'

Gilbert opens and closes his mouth again, blinks hard and appears to decide he has no choice. He reaches out a hand for the glass, but as he takes it from Drake, he allows it to slip through his fingers. The fine Venetian crystal shatters against the boards, the wine splashing in an arc like blood. Gilbert cries out and presses his fingers to his lips.

'Forgive my clumsiness, Sir Francis – I did not mean . . .' He swallows hard. 'I will repay the damage, of course.'

'Will you?' Drake raises an eyebrow. 'Do you know how much Venetian glass costs, Gilbert? Where will you come by that kind of money?'

Gilbert swallows. The puddle of wine seeps into the wood at his feet. So we will never know now whether it was poisoned, though Gilbert's reluctance to drink it himself does not argue in his favour. I watch him closely; if he is acting, it is skilfully done. He has said nothing so far to give himself away, despite being caught off guard.

'Dom Antonio,' I say, turning to the Portuguese, who looks entirely confused by the intrusion, 'the other night you thought you recognised this man.' I jerk my dagger in Gilbert's direction.

'Yes, but it seems I was mistaken.' Dom Antonio gives a theatrical sigh. 'I lose track, you see, in all my travels. Faces seem familiar, even when they are not.'

'Yes, yes,' I struggle to keep the impatience from my voice, 'but where did you think you knew him from? You must have an idea.'

'Well, yes.' Dom Antonio looks at me, mildly bewildered. 'It seemed to me that we had met before in Paris. Not more than a year ago, certainly. This young man had a beard then, but it didn't suit him.'

'I have told Dom Antonio, with the greatest respect, that he is mistaken,' Gilbert cuts in. 'We have never met before. Nor have I grown a beard, not since I tried at twenty.' Again, the self-deprecating laugh.

Dom Antonio holds out his hands, palms up. 'There you are,' he says. 'An old man gets confused.'

'Where in Paris?' I demand.

'If I had to pin it down,' the Portuguese says, creasing his face in concentration until his brows knit together, 'I would say I had seen him at the Spanish embassy. I was there trying to negotiate terms of an accord with Spain through the Ambassador—'

'Bernadino de Mendoza.'

'I see by your face that you have met him. Yes – a duplici-tous fellow. They offered talks, but it all came to nothing. As always, with King Philip.' His mouth turns down.

'And Master Crosse here?' I say, cutting off any further lament.

Dom Antonio narrows his eyes to peer at Gilbert. 'I would swear that I saw this young man at Mendoza's residence, being shown in as I was shown out. But if he says it is impos-sible . . .' He shrugs again.

'Now that I think of it,' Gilbert says carefully, 'it is possible that I was delivering a letter to the Ambassador. That was sometimes part of my duties when I was in Paris.'

'Was that where you cultivated the habit of passing letters to the Spanish?' I say. My dagger is held level, pointed towards him. Light glints dully off its blade. Gilbert jerks his head up and stares at me.

'What?' The colour drains from his face. His gaze swings wildly to Drake, who holds up a hand to silence me.

'Put away your weapon, Bruno, we are only talking,' he says, with quiet authority. Gilbert's face visibly smooths out as he watches me sheath the dagger. 'Speaking of letters – I received a very distressing letter from Jonas Solon shortly before his body was found at the foot of the cliffs. In it he confessed to the murder of Robert Dunne.'

He allows this to hang in the air as we both watch Gilbert's reaction. For a moment he works to master his expression, then he looks at Drake as if confused.

'Then – why did you not mention it at the inquest, Sir Francis, if you knew he had confessed?'

He is good, I will grant him that. He blinks in innocent confusion behind his glasses, holding his master's gaze steady. I could almost believe him.

'Because I knew the letter to be a forgery,' Drake says, looking calmly at Gilbert. 'Jonas Solon could not read or write. That letter could only have come from someone trying to cast the blame elsewhere. Presumably the man who killed both Dunne and Jonas.'

'But—' Gilbert is staring at him, shaking his head, though it is hard to tell whether the frozen expression in his eyes is fear or disbelief. 'That can't be, there was—'

'A letter among my papers, signed by Jonas?' Drake almost smiles. 'Yes. It was written for him. But someone with access to my personal correspondence might have seen it and not realised.'

Gilbert shakes his head; he moves back against the table as if it might offer some protection.

'Did they recruit you at the Spanish embassy?' I ask, in a conversational tone. 'You were afraid that Dom Antonio would identify you, weren't you? What did you put in the wine you gave him?'

'There was nothing in the wine. I don't know what you are talking about. I wrote no letters from Jonas – my Castilian is not good enough. You must be mistaken, both of you . . .' His words tumble over one another, until he falters.

'Who told you the letter from Jonas was in Castilian?' I

ask. Gilbert's mouth falls open; his Adam's apple bounces in his throat as he tries to swallow.

'I have not shown that letter to anyone except Bruno,' Drake says. 'Though I almost asked you to translate it. You were counting on that, I suppose?'

'No – I – there are others on this ship who speak Spanish – why do you not ask them?' he blurts.

'Because they are not left-handed,' I say. He seems to crumple at this; the fight goes out of him and he slumps against the edge of the table so that he is half sitting on it.

Drake holds his hands wide. 'Why, Gilbert?' He sounds like a disappointed father. Gilbert raises his eyes briefly to his captain, then drops his gaze to the floor. He does not answer.

'Robert Dunne found out what you were up to, didn't he?' I say. 'And he tried to use it to his own advantage. Five gold angels is a lot of money, whatever the Spaniards are paying you. And then he asked for more. I'd have been angry too. And afraid that the money would not buy his discretion for long. Better to silence him permanently.'

Gilbert still does not speak, nor look up.

'And even then you realised you weren't safe,' I continue. 'Sir Francis was not convinced by the suicide, so you decided to make Jonas your scapegoat.'

Still nothing. I catch Drake's eye; he gives a minute shake of the head. After some moments, Gilbert looks up.

'You cannot prove any of this.' His voice sounds dull, as if he does not believe it.

'I have asked Captain Fenner to search your quarters,' Drake says. 'If you have any correspondence hidden there, we will bring it to light.'

'You cannot do that.' He looks indignant. 'Not my private things—'

'Nothing is private on my ship,' Drake snaps.

'You will find nothing,' Gilbert says, though he sounds afraid.

'Wait,' I say. 'He thought he was going to church this evening, before you asked him to stay and show Dom Antonio the maps. Perhaps you should search his person. You hide the letters inside your shirt, don't you?' I take a step closer to Gilbert. 'When you fell against me in the boat that first night, you were afraid I had dislodged them.'

In this instant, I know we have him. Gilbert's face grows white and rigid; his left hand closes instinctively over his breast, as if to protect whatever is hidden there. Drake glances at me, nods approval; the brief hesitation is enough for Gilbert. He swings his legs over the table and lunges for Dom Antonio. The Portuguese, who has been watching all this time with a face of growing incredulity, is caught unawares; before he can react, Gilbert has whipped Dom Antonio's ornamental dagger from its sheath at his belt and is holding it to the Portuguese's throat.

'Gilbert, let him go. What good will it do you now?' Drake fights to keep his voice reassuring. Dom Antonio lets out a strangled whimper.

'It is all lies,' Gilbert says, through his teeth. 'But you will not listen. You will have me arrested with your lies. You know nothing about it.'

'Let Dom Antonio go, and I am willing to discuss anything you wish,' Drake says.

Gilbert shakes his head. He sits upright, the knife still held in place. 'You are lying.' He turns to me, desperation in his face. 'This is all your doing. If you had not come here, inter-fering in matters that were not your business—' He breaks off. 'I thought we had some affinity, you and I, as fellow scholars?'

I look at him, at his strangely earnest, self-righteous expres-sion. We have more affinity than he knows; I have done the same undercover work, betrayed the trust of others and coded my betrayal into secret messages, delivered by fast riders in the dead of night. I have done it for the money, but also because I believe in the freedom of this realm of England, however imperfect, and I want to defend it, even though it is not in my blood. I wonder what lured Gilbert into his spying. Sidney is right; I do not believe it was merely the money. Gilbert is too complex for that.

'Put the knife down, and we will talk,' Drake says, in that same, steady tone. 'If you are innocent of all these charges, I want to hear you answer them, believe me – I would like nothing more than to hear your defence. But you cannot help yourself by harming anyone else.' He holds a hand out for the knife, nodding encouragement.

Gilbert darts a quick glance over his shoulder, at the casement I left open when I entered. 'Let me leave the ship,' he says. 'Give me your word that I can leave the ship unhindered.'

'Where would you go?' Drake says. He is beginning to sound weary.

'To your Spanish friends?' I ask, moving a step closer. Gilbert flinches as if he has been struck. I can read the fear in his eyes; he is like a cornered animal, unsure whether to fight or run. But the hand holding the knife is trembling violently; he is not a born killer. I would wager he has never stuck a blade in anyone, nor has any desire to, but panic is making him desperate. Drake puts out a hand to stop me. Without taking his eyes off us, or the point of the knife from Dom Antonio's neck, Gilbert eases himself up on to his haunches on the bench. At the last moment, he pulls the casement towards him and swings his torso through the gap, shoving Dom Antonio aside as he disappears through the window to the gallery. I throw myself across the table after him, as Drake rushes for the main door that opens on to the quarter deck. If he tries to climb to an upper deck, we will have him trapped.

By the time I have hauled myself through the open window, Gilbert has already pulled himself up on the wooden rail and is leaning out to grab at the lower part of the rigging. I reach for his leg and almost catch him, but he is young and nimble, and not injured as I am, and he jerks his foot out of my grasp, pulling himself further along the hull of the ship by means of the outer rigging, though he is encumbered by the knife that he clutches in his right hand. The wind tugs at my hair; the ship's timbers creak as it rolls gently, though here, suspended above the water, every slight movement feels as if it might throw me off balance. I swing myself up to the ropes after him, when I see him hesitate. He has reached the end of the rigging; he must climb up to the deck of the ship or try to reach across to the rigging of the mainmast some feet away. He looks up, to see Drake and Fenner, with several more of the crew and the armed guards, staring down at him from the rail of the quarterdeck above. He glances down, at the dark green water below. I watch him coil himself; he means to jump across to the next web of rigging, but that brief pause has allowed me a couple of feet closer. Just as he gathers his forces to spring, I let go with my left hand, swing my body out from the ship and lunge at him. He flails with the knife, grazing my hand before I grasp the sleeve of his doublet around his right wrist. I tighten my grip; he can't move his hand to wield the blade and his balance is thrown; he teeters backwards and his spectacles fall but he regains control. I am gratified to find that, though he is nimble, I am the stronger; I pull his hand back and smash the inside of his wrist hard against the hull. Something cracks as his bones make contact; he yelps in pain, but still he holds tight to the knife. He tries to wrestle his arm out of my grip but I draw his hand back and crunch it against the side a second time; this time he cries out and drops the knife. I do not bother to watch it fall and disappear with barely a splash into the water below.

But I cannot draw my own knife without letting go of the rigging with my right hand. Instead I release Gilbert's wrist with my left and grab him instead by the hair, pulling his

504

head back and ignoring his cries as I manoeuvre myself around behind him, hooking my left leg around his knee and pressing him against the ropes from behind. He tries to lash out, but I slip my right arm under one of the ropes and catch his wrist again, holding myself to the rigging by keeping the rope in the crook of my arm.

'Are you going to give me that letter, Gilbert, or must we fight over it?' I hiss in his ear, my breath coming in jagged gasps. He struggles against me, but I am pinning him to the ropes with my bodyweight now, and I feel him weakening.

'There is nowhere left for you to run, Gilbert.' I spit the words at him through the bite of the wind. The swell seems greater up here, the gusts fiercer. 'Surrender now, give me the letter, and he may yet treat you with clemency.'

He makes a noise that might be a hollow laugh. Then he makes a sudden stab backwards with his elbow. I grit my teeth.

'I don't want to do this, you know,' I say, as I grab him by the hair again, drag his head back and smash it forwards again between the ropes into the wooden side of the ship. The blow was not as hard as I could have made it, but there is a nasty crunch and he lets out a howl. His head drops forward, limp, and I feel the resistance subside in his body. I reach around under his left arm, pull at the front of his doublet until I hear a button rip, and fumble around inside until my fingertips make contact with paper and I draw out a folded letter. 'Thank you,' I mutter. 'You could have made that easier on yourself. You might as well climb up to Drake now,' I add, prodding him in the back. His head still droops forward and I wonder if the blow could have knocked him out. If so, Drake will need to lower a rope and haul him up. I glance up, about to call up to Drake, when Gilbert suddenly jerks his head backwards, as hard as he can, slamming the back of his skull into the bridge of my nose. I cry out in pain and shock; caught off balance, I let go of the rope with my left hand, though I keep hold of the letter. Blood drips down my lip and over my chin. Gilbert gives me a strange, fleeting smile, clasps a hand around my wrist and flings himself out into the air, tumbling backwards like a jongleur, dragging me with him.

I feel the pull of his weight; my right arm is wrenched out from behind the rope and I catch one dizzying glimpse of the sheer wall of wood at my back and the distance down to the sea. But my leg is still hooked inside one of the ropes; I jolt to a sudden stop and an excruciating pain shoots up my arm as my shoulder jars with all the force of Gilbert's trajectory halted as he dangles there, gripping my left sleeve. My leg is bent back; something tears in my knee as I swing back against the ship, hanging upside down as Gilbert swings wildly with his free hand, trying to get a better purchase on me. I close my eyes; only two things matter now – holding on to the rope with my leg, and not letting go of the letter. I can feel my leg slipping; above us, Drake is barking orders, but there is no chance of him reaching us in time. Just as I fear my arm can no longer take the strain, I hear a tearing sound; I glance down and see the cuff of my shirt rip away from the sleeve. Gilbert sees what is happening; he claws the air with his free hand but the last stitches give way and I watch him plummet, almost gracefully, to the sea. He hits the water in a plume of white spray. Almost immediately, a longboat is lowered over the side from the main deck, men shouting to one another as it descends. I fix my eyes on the frothing water below; is Gilbert trying to make his escape, or knowingly taking his secrets to the bottom of the Sound? As I go on squinting at the shifting patterns of light on the surface, a dark shape bobs up and strikes out through the waves, away from the ship. So Gilbert can swim: there is my answer. The longboat has almost reached the water. He will not get far.

'Give us your hand then, mate,' says a voice, very close to me. I jerk my head up, spluttering through the blood filling my nose. A burly man, one of Drake's crew, has climbed down the rigging over the side of the ship and is holding out an arm the size of a thick branch. He slips it under mine, pulls me upright against the rigging and half carries me to the top, where Drake's face peers over the rail. With the last of my strength, I manage to raise my arm and hold out to him a blood-spattered letter, sealed in crimson wax. As they lift me on to the deck, I look back to see two men hauling a dripping figure out of the waves and into the longboat.

THIRTY

'Drake will have to reconfigure his entire route now.' Sidney pulls back the drapes at the chamber window and throws wide the shutters. If I open one eye, I can just glimpse a pale blue sky washed with early morning sun.

'He may even ask us to help him,' he continues, lacing his breeches. 'You know a little of navigation, and he is now without a cartographer, after all. There is no possible way he can refuse us a place on the voyage, after what we have done. That courier fellow did not come without a fight, I can tell you.'

'Uh-huh.' I ease myself up on one elbow. Every movement of my left shoulder is jagged with pain. The bruise across the bridge of my nose throbs gently. Sidney has already told me of his encounter with Gilbert's contact in the church, embellishing his own heroics with each retelling. I let this pass; I am only glad he can finally feel he has played a part in resolving Drake's troubles.

'He was there in that back pew right enough,' Sidney says, shrugging on his doublet. I make an encouraging noise and swing my legs gingerly over the side of the bed, testing the damage after a night's rest has allowed my torn muscles to stiffen. Everything hurts.

'I stationed my armed men at either end of the pew, then

I slipped in beside him. He was pretending to pray. I leaned over and whispered, "Gilbert's not coming tonight, my friend." You should have seen his face.' He pauses, halfway through fastening his buttons, smiling to himself as he recalls. 'Of course, he tried to claim he didn't know any Gilbert, didn't know what I was talking about. But when I told him Gilbert had been arrested and told us everything, and he could tell us his side the easy way or the hard way, he couldn't be helpful enough.'

'That was cleverly done,' I say, as I have said at this point during all the previous accounts.

'It was a gamble, I'll admit,' he says, straightening his ruff and checking his reflection in the spotted glass. 'But it paid off. He was terrified as soon as I suggested he could be questioned in the Tower. He's only a small fish – a French merchant who lives here in Plymouth, has some arrangement with agents of the Catholic League to pass letters to couriers on French ships. He had no idea what was in them – just a bit of easy money for him.'

'So Gilbert's letters were going direct to the Spanish Embassy in Paris,' I murmur, pulling myself up to standing on the carved bedpost.

'Straight into the hands of Mendoza,' Sidney says. 'If we hadn't found out in time, Drake's entire fleet would have been sailing right into a Spanish ambush.' He shakes his head. 'I still don't understand it. Gilbert Crosse never seemed like a man to be excited by money – you only have to look at his clothes to see that. And there's no evidence that he was driven by religious conviction – he comes from a good Protestant family. So if it wasn't for money or faith, then what?'

I shrug my less painful shoulder. 'Perhaps the letter will give us some clue. It's encrypted, of course, but Drake will have sent a copy to Walsingham by now. His cryptographers will make short work of it.'

'They will have its meaning unravelled by the time Gilbert

arrives at the Tower,' he says, running a tortoiseshell comb through his hair. 'Then he can explain himself in person.' He sounds unconcerned. I try not to think of how Gilbert might be encouraged to explain himself in the Tower.

'By then, Bruno, you and I will be out to sea,' Sidney continues. 'Just think of it – the wind in our hair, this town and all its vices far behind us, the open horizon and adventure ahead.' His face is alight with the prospect of it.

'Pettifer and Savile just waiting to give us an accidental nudge overboard any time the sea is rough,' I say. He turns and glares at me.

'You had better stop your naysaying in Drake's hearing,' he says, pointing his comb at me.

So it seems there is no way of deferring this choice any longer. At present, all I wish for is more time to rest. I am prevented from replying by an urgent hammering on the door.

'Get that, would you, Bruno?' Sidney says, strapping on his sword. 'It will be Drake's messenger, I'll wager. I wonder if he will give us Dunne's cabin? You wouldn't be superstitious about sleeping in a dead man's bed, would you? Personally I don't care for that sort of nonsense, but I know most mariners would – oh, for the love of Christ, we're coming!'

The knocking grows more insistent. I pull the door open to find Hetty standing there wearing her usual expression of sullen resentment. I am surprised she is still employed; perhaps Mistress Judith has yet to hire a replacement. Hetty does at least have the grace to look slightly sheepish in my presence.

'Near wore my knuckles to the bone there,' she mutters. 'Someone downstairs to see you. *Sir.* Says it's urgent.'

'Who is it?' I am wearing only my shirt and underhose. I cast around for my breeches.

'Not you. *Him.*' She points through the open door at Sidney. 'I dunno but he looks important.'

'Well, let us not keep him waiting, then,' Sidney says,

brushing past me, beaming magnanimously at the girl and puffing out his chest as he strides towards the stairs. He looks like a man who expects at long last to be rewarded.

I throw on my clothes, tame my hair as best I can, and follow Sidney down to the entrance hall a few moments later. Over the banister I can see him talking to a man who wears the green and white Tudor livery, though he is spattered head to foot with mud. His coat is sewn with a gold badge which I recognise, as I draw closer, as the crest of Queen Elizabeth. Sidney, when he turns to me, is as pale as if he were seasick.

'This messenger has come from the court. Ridden almost without stopping, he says. To give me this.' He holds up a letter on creamy paper, sealed in thick crimson wax. The messenger stands patiently, eyes lowered and hands folded, while Sidney rips it open. I watch his gaze travel over the lines inside, his face growing taut with fury as he comprehends its meaning. He turns to me, his eyes burning.

'Duplicitous bastard!' he spits, turning on the unfortunate messenger, who takes a step back.

'What is it, Philip?' I ask, though I think I can guess.

'See for yourself,' he snaps, thrusting the letter into my hand and storming out of the door, leaving it banging in his wake.

I know where I will find him. I limp after him along Nutt Street but his anger has driven him faster than I can walk with my present injuries; he is already far ahead of me by the time I have skimmed the letter, tipped the poor messenger and asked Mistress Judith to give him something to eat and drink. I understand my friend's fury, but not his surprise. Did he really believe the Captain-General would take him to the other side of the world, knowing he did not have the Queen's permission to leave England? Drake must have dispatched a messenger the day we arrived; he realised immediately that no amount of Spanish gold would compensate Queen Elizabeth for such flagrant disobedience. From the minute Sidney announced his intention to travel with the fleet, he was a liability to Drake. I have to admire the smoothness of the Captain-General's deception; the promises he has held out to us over these past days – promises that ensured our ongoing help with his situation – all the while knowing his messenger was tearing up the road towards the court, ready to unleash the Queen's fury.

I glance down at the letter in my hand as I approach the Mayor's front door. It is curious to think of Elizabeth Tudor writing this in her own hand, barely able to contain her indignation as she dips her quill. The writing is bold and swooping, with long tails and loops, the signature underscored with curlicues. It is a confident hand, but the quill has been pressed so hard to the page that the ink has spattered and blotched in places. This is a letter that expresses its depth of feeling in its imperfections, a letter written in the heat of sovereign anger. She absolutely forbids Sidney to sail with Drake, on pain of withdrawing patronage from both of them. If he leaves court now, she tells him, he had better not bother to return. He is to be on the road the day he receives this letter, without delay, and bring Dom Antonio directly to court as promised. She is calling her puppy to heel, snapping her fingers to watch him come running. And he has no choice. No wonder he is boiling. I only hope I have arrived in time to stop him throwing a punch at Drake; I have a feeling Sidney would come off worse.

I might be entitled to feel deceived too, I think, as I wait for my knock to be answered. I have put my life in danger to help Drake this past week, for a promised reward that he knew all along he had no intention of giving. True, I did it for Sidney's sake, and for Lady Arden's, but it is hard to escape the feeling that Drake has made use of us.

I can hear raised voices as I am shown along a passage to the parlour we visited yesterday. But before the maid reaches the door, we are intercepted by Lady Drake, who puts a finger to her lips, slips her arm through mine and leads me through the house to the garden door, despite my protests.

'Better you leave them to sort out their differences,' she whispers, nodding back to the parlour, where Sidney's aggrieved tone competes with Drake's lower, mollifying cadences. I cannot make out their words, but I hardly need to. 'Sir Philip is very angry, isn't he?' she adds. 'Poor thing. I know how much he wanted this adventure. But on the whole, my husband does better to upset him than the Queen, don't you think? Besides, he may not be so furious when he hears what my husband proposes instead.' She leans closer, as if to impart a great secret, and giggles, a hand pressed to her lips. There is a girlish quality about Lady Drake, I think, as I bend my head to play along, which some men would find alluring, though I have always preferred the sort of woman who is unafraid to look a man in the eye as one adult to another. 'He thinks you and Sir Philip and Dom Antonio should be our guests for a few days at Buckland Abbey, before you leave for London.'

'Sir Francis is not staying in Plymouth?'

She shakes her head, impatient. 'Of course he is. Once he has seen Jonas buried, he is anxious to set sail as soon as possible, but first he wants me and my cousin away from Plymouth. We are to return home tomorrow, in your company, if Sir Philip is agreeable. I think we could make your stay a pleasant one.' She pauses for a knowing smile. 'But for now, Bruno, I think it would do you good to take the air,' she adds, propelling me out into the courtyard.

I see Nell sitting on a bench in the shade of an apple tree, affecting to read a book. She does not raise her eyes until the last moment, when she feigns surprise and shyness at my arrival. Her hair is bound up and dressed in a narrow French hood to disguise the damage done by the fire, and she wears a silk scarf around her throat to cover the bruises left by the rope. Though she is pale, the cuts on her face are less prominent and her eyes have regained something of their sparkle. There is a new awkwardness between us as she places her book carefully beside her and offers me a tentative smile, though her eyes grow wide at the sight of my new injuries.

I make a small bow. 'My lady. You are looking rested. How are you feeling?'

'I look hideous, Bruno, there is no need to lie about it,' she says, gingerly touching the cut on her cheek. 'And you have looked better yourself, if we are being truthful. But bruises will mend, and we are alive, thank God.' She laughs, though I can see it still pains her to swallow. 'Sir Francis says you were extremely brave and caught the killer.'

I offer a modest shrug. 'He gave himself away, really. Poor boy.'

She arches an eyebrow. 'How can you pity him? He will be executed as a traitor, Sir Francis says.' She gives a delicate shudder. I have the impression she rather relishes the prospect. I can only assume she has never witnessed a traitor's execution.

'He will probably die of fright before they get him near the Tower.' I take a seat on the bench beside her. Gilbert knew that what he did was treason, even before he committed murder for it, and he would have understood the penalty: the slow journey to Tyburn on the hurdle, the sight of the gallows and, beside it, the scaffold with the butcher's block and the brazier, where you would be laid after choking a few minutes at the end of the rope, to have your genitals cut off, your torso slit open from throat to navel, your entrails unwound on a stick before your eyes and your heart cut out and thrown into the fire. Anyone who has watched such an execution can never scrub those images from his memory; with that end in mind, you would need a compelling reason to betray your country.

I still do not understand what drove Gilbert. He had none of the traits of a religious fanatic, that I could see. Quite the opposite: he considered himself a man of science, so I thought, but some of these young converts learn to hide it well. Perhaps we would never know, unless he spoke up in the Tower. I wince at the thought.

Nell reaches over and eases her hand across mine. I find myself twining my fingers with hers, though it is hard to drag my mind away from images of what awaits Gilbert once he is taken to London.

'But you are not too distraught at being forbidden to sail with Sir Francis?' She says this with a knowing look.

'I can stomach the disappointment. But Sidney is livid. He is young – he longs for adventure.'

'And you?'

'Not so young any more. As for adventure – I do not seek it out, but it seems to follow me regardless. I don't need to cross an ocean to find it.'

'So I have learned,' she says, touching the scarf at her throat. She traces small patterns on the back of my hand with her fingertips. Goosebumps rise on my skin. 'Bruno . . .' she begins, hesitant. 'There in the crypt, when we thought . . . I spoke a little recklessly, I fear. I pushed you to say something you did not mean.'

'My lady, Nell . . .' I say, though I am not sure how to continue.

'Come, Bruno, let us at least be frank with one another. You do not love me – you barely know me, nor I you. I like your company, better than I have any man's for a long while. That night, I imagined that if we survived I might be bold enough to defy every convention, but—' She breaks off and squeezes my arm, her expression full of regret. 'I am not so green that I can forget the distance between us.'

I nod. An unexpected sadness swells in my throat; not at the loss of her so much as at the reminder that this is how it will always turn out for me. I have learned, to my cost, that to love someone means lowering my defences, and in a life like mine I cannot afford to do that.

She leans her head against my shoulder. 'I wish it could be otherwise, Bruno. I curse the obligations of rank sometimes, but there it is. In another life, you would have been the sort of man I looked for. But since I am not free to choose, I think for the present I am happier with no husband. Perhaps neither one of us is made for marriage, eh?' She smiles. 'Though I must confess I would have loved to see my family's faces if I introduced you as my betrothed. Especially Cousin Edgar the boar. They would be lost for words.'

'I think,' I say carefully, 'that if I were ever to marry, I would want it to be for a more substantial reason than to scandalise someone's relatives.'

'True,' she says, with a sigh. 'Although it would have been fun.' She runs a hand along my thigh. I glance up at the house, conscious that the Mayor's household may well be watching from the windows. Taking her hand, I raise it softly to my lips and replace it in her lap, though more in a spirit of regret than desire.

'I had better see if Sidney has settled his differences with Sir Francis,' I say, as I stand. 'And then we must pack our bags.'

'But Elizabeth has told you of our plan to go to Buckland?' she says, rising and tucking a loose curl of hair into her hood. 'Those few days, before we each go back to our own lives – perhaps there we might briefly forget the differences that separate us?' She offers me a sly smile, a look from under her lashes that tells me exactly what she means.

'I hope we might,' I say, relieved. I have a sudden urge to take her in my arms and crush her mouth to mine right there, but instead I bend and place another chaste kiss on her hand. Sidney may scorn the company of women, but I have not known enough of it in my life to tire of it. A few days of softness before I must return to face my future would not hurt. As long as I remember to guard my heart.

'I am truly sorry to see you leave, Bruno.' Drake shields his eyes and scans the view from the Hoe. The evening sun is beginning its slow slide towards the horizon, leaving a wash of coral and gold in the sky. Over the surface of the water, bands of shadow shift with the movement of the clouds, changing its colour in a restless patchwork. Small waves crest in white flecks around the great ships. Music drifts across the open water from their decks, the lilt of flutes and viols. On St Nicholas Island, all is still and quiet. Drake breathes deeply and rolls his shoulders back. I steal a glance at him while his attention is fixed on the horizon. The strained expression that had haunted him since we arrived has melted away; he carries himself with a new lightness, as if he has taken off a lead cloak. When he smiles, you see the genial man under the ruthless commander. I begin to feel that it would have been a worthwhile experience to sail with him.

'As am I. When do you plan to leave?'

'As soon as possible. I will see poor Jonas buried and Gilbert and his courier put on the road to London under armed guard. I have already sent a fast rider to Walsingham with the coded letter – he will have plenty of warning.' He turns to me, suddenly sombre. 'I do this with a heavy heart. People think me unfeeling, because I value discipline. A captain who does not is no captain at all, and the same goes for a ruler. But I know what awaits Gilbert, and I don't send him to it lightly.'

'Unsentimental is not the same as unfeeling,' I murmur.

'Quite. You express it better than I could.' He sighs, and returns his gaze to the water. 'Sir William Savile has decided not to sail with us, you know,' he says, after a long silence.

'He has not withdrawn his money?'

'No, God be thanked. But now that Robert Dunne is to be buried like a Christian and his wife will be a respectable widow, he reasons it is easier to let us do the work while he stays here and bides his time until he can marry her without scandal and I bring home a healthy return on his investment. The child will be christened as Dunne's and Savile will legally adopt it as his heir once he marries Martha. Very neat.' He folds his arms and smiles into his chest. 'God knows I have no great admiration for William Savile, but it may be he makes the woman a better husband than her first. Poor Robert. God rest him.'

'And Pettifer?' I do not quite meet his eye as I ask this.

'Pettifer travels with me as our ship's chaplain.' He glances sideways at me. 'Does that surprise you?'

'I was mistaken in accusing him of the murders, and I am sorry for it, but everything else I told you, Sir Francis – I am convinced it is the truth. If you had seen that poor boy's face, you would not doubt it.'

Drake holds up a hand to stop me. 'I can believe it, Bruno – all of it. Pettifer may rail against your accusations until he is hoarse, but it is plain to see that the shock of near-discovery has frightened him. He is very contrite, and I like to think he will change his ways.' He clasps his hands behind his back. 'Besides, he will do less harm out to sea, away from temptation, than left here to collude with that woman. As for the House of Vesta . . .' He curls his lip. 'I have spoken at length to the Mayor about cleaning up that nest of vermin. They cannot go on believing they are above the law. I have also written to the Sheriff.'

'What if the Mayor and the Sheriff are among her clientele? Nothing will be done. That is what she stakes her whole business on.'

'*If* they are, Bruno' – and he lays heavy emphasis on caution – 'they will have to think carefully about which side of the law they wish to be found on. I hinted at the possibility of a Royal Commissioner coming from London to investigate if that place carries on unchecked. That ought to frighten them sufficiently. I have every confidence that by the time I return from this voyage, the House of Vesta will be no more than an old wives' tale in Plymouth.' He flashes me a quick smile, his gold tooth winking in the light.

I nod. No one could argue with his course of action, but I cannot help wondering what will become of those young girls if the House of Vesta closes down. Will they just find themselves selling their wares down at the docks, without even the security of food and shelter, ending their days like that poor pox-blighted girl Sara? I bite my lip; there is nothing I can do about it either way, and at least Mistress Grace would no longer profit from them.

'So you have a few empty berths aboard the *Elizabeth*,' I remark, after a while.

'I'm afraid so. Which makes it all the greater pity that you cannot come with us. I would have liked a man of your abilities with me on the voyage.' Drake pauses, still squinting out to sea. 'You must feel that I have deceived you.'

'I knew from the start that you had no intention of taking us. I tried to disabuse Sidney of the idea several times, but he would not listen. He had his mind made up.'

'Yes, he is still not speaking to me,' Drake says, pulling at his beard. 'But he knows better than I how dangerous it would be to defy the Queen. He will thank me for it one day.'

'His wife will thank you for it now. As will Walsingham.' I hesitate, unsure how he will respond to my next question. 'Have you spoken to Gilbert since he was arrested?'

'No.' His face tenses again and his voice grows hard. 'I considered it, but I cannot bring myself to look him in the eye. Loyalty, Bruno.' He turns to me with a grave expression. 'For a man in my position, it's the prince of all virtues. All those ships, all those lives, are in my care,' he says, pointing to the fleet peacefully dominating the Sound, the vast ships bright against the glinting water. 'That's why treachery like his is the hardest thing for a captain to forgive. Harder even than the murders. To think he sat at my table, eating my food, sketching our plans as I talked with my captains, and then sent every word off to the Spanish – it curdles my blood.' He bunches his fists, then slowly releases his hands to hang at his sides. 'It was disloyalty that brought me all the problems with the Doughty brothers, and look where that has ended.'

'Is there any news of John Doughty and Jenkes?'

'None yet.' He presses his lips together. 'I have put messengers on every vessel leaving for the French ports along this stretch of coast, warning the customs men to look out for them. Jenkes at least is conspicuous, you would hope. But if they have made it to France they will disappear like rats into the sewers, to pop up again somewhere else. John Doughty will pursue me until one of us is in our grave, I have no doubt of it.'

'And yet, if Gilbert had not murdered Robert Dunne, then Dunne might have carried out his plan to kill you before you were even across the Bay of Biscay.'

He nods, reflective. 'There is truth in that, I suppose. But do not ask me to be grateful to Gilbert yet.'

'I thought I might speak to him before I leave,' I say, quietly.

'What for?' His eyes narrow.

'I want to understand why.' And – because I know what they will do to him before he dies – to make sure he knows better than to try and hold on to his secrets.

Drake makes a non-committal noise and returns his gaze to the sea. 'I have always loved this view,' he says, after a while. 'But that is nothing to how much I love to see it from the other direction, sailing back into Plymouth after months at sea.' He raises his head and the salt breeze lifts his hair. 'Of all the sights I have seen in the world, there is none I love so much as the sight of home.'

I do not speak, because at his words my throat constricts and tears prickle at the back of my eyes. I blink them away. Nothing so painful to an exile as the dream of homecoming.

I allow myself to imagine I am gazing out across the peacock-blue waters of the Bay of Naples, and I wonder if I will ever see that view again.

Drake points to the horizon, where a scalloped band of cloud glides up towards the land, edged with lilac and gold. 'If the Spanish ever do raise a fleet to invade this island, I believe this is where we will sight them first. Sometimes I fancy I see them – ranks of galleons appearing along the skyline. Then I blink and they are just clouds. But the image of it chills me to the bone.'

'Pray God that day never comes,' I say. 'But if it did, I cannot think of anyone I would rather have commanding England's defences.'

He smiles then, and the creases appear at the corners of his eyes. He rests a hand on my shoulder. 'God go with you, Bruno. It may be that this voyage owes its success to you. If you had not discovered Gilbert, we would have been sailing straight towards a Spanish ambush. I will see you well rewarded, do not fear. And Sir Philip too, for his part.'

I incline my head in a gesture of deference. 'God speed you, Sir Francis, and bring you safe home.'

'I pray we meet again.' He steps forward and embraces me, his strong hands crushing my bruised shoulders. When he releases me, I bow low and leave him standing there on the clifftop, lit by the evening sun, arms folded across his chest as he surveys his ships, his sea, his horizon. Every age produces only a handful of truly great men, and I have a feeling that I have been fortunate enough to earn the admiration of one of them.

The town gaol stands behind the Guildhall, an ugly building of dirty white stone with rows of mean barred windows squinting at the alley in front like narrowed eyes. I brace myself before entering and press a handkerchief over my nose and mouth, trying to push away the memories of my own experience in an English prison as the foul smells bring them rushing back. I hand over the fee to the turnkey, who unlocks a door and leads me along a filthy passage. A thin, high-pitched wailing seeps out from behind a side door, while someone pounds on another as we pass.

'In there,' the turnkey says, unlocking a door at the end of the passage. He rummages in one ear with a forefinger and regards his findings. 'You got ten minutes. He can't touch you, he's chained up, but shout for me if you want to come out sooner.'

I blink, accustoming my eyes to the gloom as I hear the door locked behind me. The animal stink of excrement and urine is fierce here, but the straw beneath my feet looks relatively fresh. Gilbert is huddled in a corner. His face is bruised from his fall into the sea, and his hair hangs in matted rats' tails, thick with salt. He screws up his eyes to peer at me, looking like some nocturnal creature without his eye-glasses. As I take a step closer he realises who I am and turns to the wall.

'Are they feeding you?' I say, to break the silence.

'If you can call it that,' he mutters.

'Then Drake must be paying for it. Otherwise you would have nothing.'

'Please convey my humble gratitude to him,' he says, lifting his head and spitting the words at me. 'They wouldn't dare let me starve anyway – I'm expected at the Tower any day, didn't you know?'

There is nothing I can say to that. I wrap my arms around my chest and keep my eyes to the floor. Perhaps it was a mistake to come here.

'What have they done with the letter?' he asks, after a while. He sounds as if he does not care.

'Sent it to London.' I crouch down so that I can look him in the eye without quite sitting on the floor. 'You would save yourself a lot of trouble by just telling them the cipher. They will have it out of you one way or another.'

522

He shrugs. 'Let them decipher it in London. Then they will see.'

'What will they see?'

'That I am not a traitor.'

I breathe in and out carefully through my cloth, and still the air makes me retch a little. 'You will have a hard time persuading Captain Drake of that.'

'He would understand if he read the letter.'

'He can't, it's written in code. You are speaking in riddles, Gilbert. What would he understand?' I try to keep my patience, reminding myself that I am at liberty to leave at any time.

'That I did not betray him. Those letters I sent to the Spanish envoys – I never told them Drake's true plans. I changed the details, the coordinates, each time so it was plausible enough to fool them, but not enough to jeopardise the voyage.' He shifts his weight on to one side and stretches his legs out before him, wincing as he does so. 'There was never any danger to the fleet, I made sure of that. But Robert Dunne took against me from the beginning – I once criticised his judgement in front of Drake. He was looking for ways to discredit me. One evening he followed me to church and saw me hand over a letter. He thought he could turn it to his own profit. If he had kept out of it, none of this would have happened.' His voice quivers with anger as he speaks, and he draws a fist across his mouth to wipe away spittle.

'But you must have known five gold angels would not keep Dunne quiet for long,' I say. 'So, what happened – you decided to silence him?'

'I didn't *decide* it, the way you make it sound,' he says. He slumps back against the wall. 'I didn't know what to do.' I catch a tremor of desperation in his voice. He looks very young. 'Then I was out on deck that night the chaplain brought Dunne back drunk out of his wits.'

'You saw your opportunity?'

'I watched. No one paid me any attention – they had all

523

grown used to the sight of me out there with my instruments. Dunne was in a terrible state. He vomited all over the deck. Padre Pettifer helped him to his cabin. I saw him leave and the Spaniard arrive with one of his potions. After he left, I stayed there on deck, trying to summon up the courage. I thought he'd probably be asleep. I hadn't planned to do anything like that, but—'

'You had no choice, is that it?'

'I thought it was my one chance. I waited until everyone had gone but the watch, and they were too busy playing cards up on the foredeck to worry about me. I tried the door of Dunne's cabin and it opened. He was lying face down on the bunk. I knew all I had to do was push his face into the pillow and hold him there – if I could do that, people would think he suffocated in his sleep with the drink – but he was beginning to stir and I was afraid he'd wake before I was done. He was stronger than me, I could not have managed it if he tried to fight back. I suddenly lost my nerve and was about to run when I heard was a knock at the door. I panicked. There was a cavity under Dunne's bunk – all the officers' cabins have them, for storage. I could hear the chaplain calling out, asking Dunne if he was awake. I curled up under the bunk and shut the door. Just in time – Pettifer came into the room and woke Dunne.'

'Why did he do that?'

Gilbert shrugs. This part of the puzzle has no meaning for him any more. 'I didn't understand what he was saying. He kept telling Dunne that he should have no regard for the lies of a common whore, and if he ever repeated them things would only be worse for the girl. I don't know what girl he was talking about.'

'What did Dunne say to that?'

'He was only half-conscious. He didn't really listen. He just started babbling to Pettifer about hell and the Devil, and whether God could ever forgive sins as black as his. Pettifer

524

said he would assure Dunne of absolution, as long as he didn't go about repeating slanders.'

I nod to myself. Pettifer certainly knew how to use his position to guard his own dirty secrets. 'Was Dunne reassured?'

'I don't think he was listening. It was clear he wasn't in his right mind – he just kept moaning about how his soul was damned and he deserved to die for what he had done. I thought he was consumed with guilt over blackmailing me.'

'Not quite,' I say. 'Did that make it easier?'

'Not really.' He picks at the quick of his fingernails. 'Eventually Pettifer gave up. He said they'd talk again when Dunne was sober. I heard the door close behind him but I had to stay under the bunk until I was sure Dunne was asleep. I found a length of rope in the cavity. I guessed Dunne had used it to tie his trunks together when they were brought aboard. But it gave me an idea.'

'String him up and make it look like he did it himself.'

'If you'd heard him – I knew the chaplain would confirm that he had been in a state of despair. He would believe Dunne was overcome by his demons some time after they had spoken, so the rest would accept it too. It seemed like the perfect solution. Except that he was so heavy.'

'You smothered him first?'

He nods, staring at the wall, his eyes unfocused. 'I locked the cabin. He was sleeping face down. I sat astride him, kept my knees on his arms and pressed his face into the pillow. He was too deep in drink to fight much. It was moving him off the bed was the hard part. I was amazed no one heard us.'

'You did not think that a man who dies by hanging looks different from one who was smothered? That it might arouse suspicion?'

He pushes a clump of hair out of his eyes. 'I didn't think of that, no. Not till afterwards – I overheard Drake discussing it with his brother the next day. At the time all I wanted was to get out. I locked the cabin behind me to delay anyone finding him and threw the key into the water.'

'No one saw you leave?'

'No. But the Spaniard was awake when I went below decks. He asked where I'd been. I said measuring the stars and he left it at that. But it didn't take long the next day before I realised Drake was not convinced by the appearance of suicide. I thought, if that gets out, Jonas will mention me.'

'So you saw a way to silence him and clear up any doubt about Dunne's death at one stroke.' It is not even a question any more.

'I knew Jonas would not say anything to Drake until he was certain,' Gilbert says. His voice has grown flat and emotionless; he is no longer justifying himself, merely recounting a series of events that already seem like the distant past. 'I asked him if I could speak to him in private, away from the others, that night we all went ashore. I led him up on to the Hoe cliffs.' He gives a weary shrug, as if the rest is hardly worth the telling.

'If only he had not been illiterate, you would have been safe,' I say.

'Perhaps.' His chin drops to his chest; he appears to have lost interest in me. We sit in silence for a few minutes. I can feel the smell seeping into my clothes, my hair, my skin.

'Have you told Drake that you were giving false information to the Spanish?' I ask eventually.

He looks at me as if I have lost my wits. 'You imagine he would credit that? He would accuse me of lying. In any case, he will not lower himself to ask me. He will leave that job to Walsingham and his friends.' A shiver jars his thin frame at the prospect.

'Tell them everything,' I say quickly. 'That is what I came to advise you – do not try to hold anything back out of some misplaced loyalty to your Spanish paymasters. You will talk one way or another, and it were better you do it willingly.'

'Do you think I don't know that? I know Walsingham. I know what he does.' He swallows hard. 'But I have no loyalty to the Spanish. If I had, I would not have lied to them, would I?'

'Then why do it at all?'

He makes a small noise of contempt through his nose. 'Money – why else? They paid me well for what they thought were Drake's plans. Of course they did.' He gives a rueful laugh that teeters on the edge of tears.

'But you worked for Walsingham – for the Queen. They would have paid you handsomely, surely? You were going to be England's first renowned cartographer, you told me.'

He looks up at me and fixes me with his pale, urgent stare. 'That was the problem.'

'I don't understand.'

'They informed me, after I had agreed to the voyage, that the maps I made for Queen Elizabeth would never be published. That was part of my commission. They were supposed to be kept secret to preserve England's advantage over the Spanish.' He swipes the back of his knuckles across his eyes and the chains clank ominously as he moves. 'The thought of all that work, locked away in the dark, seen by no one but a handful of naval captains. I could not let that happen, don't you see? Maps should not be tools of war, kept close by one country to gain power over another. I wanted my maps published and read. How else are we supposed to advance our knowledge of the world? The Spanish Ambassador offered me a great deal of money. But he also promised that, when I returned, he would have my work published in the Low Countries at his own expense.'

'And afterwards? How did you imagine you would return to England, once you had published maps that were supposed to be state secrets?'

'I did not intend to return. The Spanish Ambassador promised me a pension for life.' He lowers his voice. 'You only have to look how things are tending. Drake is brave, certainly, but there will be war with the Spanish soon and we do not have a hope of defending ourselves against invasion, not with all Spain's power. I thought a clever man was one with a view to his own future.' He chews his bottom lip and falls silent.

'It didn't occur to you that the Spanish might be less friendly when they realised all your information had been false?'

'They would just have assumed Drake had changed his plans.'

He is naïve if he thinks the Spanish Ambassador would be so easily fooled, but then he has been naïve all along; it is no help to him to point it out now.

'You almost got away with it.' I rise painfully to my feet. 'And now your maps will never be made. By God, Gilbert – you risked your life and took others for the sake of your own ambition? Was it worth it?'

His lips curve into a painful smile. 'I thought it worth the gamble. History remembers the men who dare greatly in the pursuit of knowledge, Bruno. Without them, there would be no progress. To be one of those men who changed the course of the world – that is what I dreamed of. I would have thought you of all people would understand that. Have you not also risked your life to publish your books?'

I meet his eye. He is right; I recognise the desire that burns in him. The ferocity of a scholar's ambition for his work can rival that of a father for his child. I have been guilty of it myself, but enough to betray my country? I never had a chance to consider that – my country rejected me first. I chose a life of exile for the sake of my books. And if I had to kill to give them life, or die for them, would I do it? I could not entirely discount the idea.

'Tell Walsingham you sold false information to mislead the Spanish. He may show you mercy,' I say, turning to leave.

He laughs: a dry, brittle sound, like the crackle of kindling. 'No, he won't.' He shakes his head. 'There will be no mercy for that. Walsingham would send his own grandchildren to Tyburn if he thought they had betrayed England.'

I can say nothing to this – I know it to be true. Queen Elizabeth's spymaster is unbending when it comes to protecting the realm, and just as ruthless as Drake. Perhaps this is part of what makes him a great man, too.

'I will die as a traitor.' He seems to shrink even further inside himself as he says this. His voice is hollow, as empty of self-pity as it is of hope. I can offer him no comfort on this score.

'Your time's up, Spaniard.' The key rattles in the lock and the door creaks open. 'Out you get. Leave this filth to rot.' Now that I have had my money's worth, the gaoler evidently feels no further need to waste his efforts on courtesy.

'Remember what I said, Gilbert. Answer their questions and you may yet be saved the worst.'

The gaoler cackles. 'Not bloody likely. This one's going to the Tower tomorrow. And the French bastard next door. It'll make this place seem like a fucking palace.'

'Doctor Bruno,' Gilbert calls, as the door is closing. His formality sounds strange in this pit. He struggles to his knees, the chains striking the stone. 'Will you tell Drake I did not betray him? I want him to know that, at least, even if he does not believe me.'

I am still not sure if I believe him, but I nod anyway, snatching a last look at him through the tiny grille in the door before I blunder out into the air and sunlight, thinking about the risks a man will take to make his mark on the world. For Drake, this means pitting himself against the elements and the might of Spain to cross the ocean, not for the treasure, but simply to say that he has done it. For Sidney, it means leaving a wife and new-born child and a comfortable life of poetry and politics for the blood and dust of battle. For Gilbert, it meant gambling a traitor's death against the chance to see his maps famed throughout Europe and his name spoken in the same breath as Mercator and Ortelius. And for me – a life in exile, chased from one court to another, knowing that I will never see my homeland again without facing death, all because I refused to keep my ideas to myself, because I too knew that I *had* to put my books out in the world, even if the act of doing so cost me my life. I believed Gilbert when he said his ambition was more than vanity. He wanted nothing less than to change the way men think about the world, and he was right: this I do understand.

EPILOGUE

'Burn it.' Sir Francis Walsingham pushes the bundle of papers across the table towards me. They have been rolled together and bound with a black ribbon. I reach out and lay a protective hand on them.

'But, the Queen—'

He shakes his head. 'She wants no knowledge of it, Bruno. Without the original, this is no more than an extremely dangerous fiction.' He regards me with a grave expression.

'But surely, if the Vatican are trying to conceal a text of this significance from all of Christendom, that is a matter to concern her?' Sidney lays his palms flat on the table and leans forward, giving his father-in-law a defiant look. Walsingham remains silent, his attention fixed on his clasped hands in front of him. The candles have burned low in the wall sconces and in the silver candlesticks on the dining table, gilding the edges of our wine glasses and casting leaping shadows along the linenfold panelling. Dusk falls earlier, now that September is almost out, and the evening air is sharp with the chill of autumn.

The soft light catches the lines on Walsingham's face: the shadows under his eyes from all the nights when England's business keeps him from sleep; the furrows in his high forehead from frowning over encoded dispatches from all over the realm and the rest of Europe; the sombre downturn of his mouth beneath the fine moustaches. You do not often see Walsingham laugh; his is not a job that allows much room for frivolity. He is over fifty now, and though he appears to have the stamina of a man half his age, the strain of defending England and her queen is beginning to show.

'The Vatican may have all manner of heretical writings locked away in its archives,' he says, raising his head. 'They have spent centuries trying to suppress the Gnostic sects.'

'Perhaps because they were afraid,' I say quietly. 'Perhaps they needed to protect their own advantage, because they feared one of those Gnostic gospels contained the truth?'

'That is not Queen Elizabeth's fight, Bruno,' Walsingham says. He sounds tired. 'Look how Christendom is tearing itself apart over differences in interpreting the scriptures we already have. And you bring her a book that is not concerned with the finer details of the composition of bread and wine, but one which purports to overturn the entire doctrine of salvation and denies the resurrection.' He spreads his hands wide to illustrate the enormity of my folly. 'No possible advantage could come to her from making public such a book as this, and every possible harm. As soon as she understood its contents, she wanted no part of it. And she advised me that if anyone printed or distributed copies of it, they would be punished as heretics.'

'But what if it should be *true*?' I persist.

'Do *you* think it is true?' he asks, after a pause.

I look at him, finding no clue in his unfathomable dark eyes as to how I should weigh my answer. Walsingham is unswervingly devout in his Protestant faith, and conservative with it; for all his seeming mildness, he will have men racked or disembowelled sooner than see it threatened. Do I believe the Gospel of Judas? It is not a straightforward question, as he well knows. For all their errors, I believe the Gnostics were groping their way towards the truth. We humans are more than flawed clay, born stained by sin, worthless without redemption, as it has suited the Church to tell us all these hundreds of years. That spark of divinity the Gnostics recognised, that potential to create, to invent, to comprehend the universe and, in doing so, to become god-like – that lies dormant in all of us. We deserve better than an eternity spent struggling out of Purgatory, or consigned to Hell by some arbitrary predestined salvation, depending on your preferred doctrine. Or so I believe. I am not sure this is what Walsingham wishes to hear.

'There are elements that I find plausible,' I say carefully.

He allows a small smile. 'A diplomat as ever, Bruno. It is certainly an intriguing document. But still, best destroyed. For all our sakes.'

I draw the papers towards me and nod, lowering my eyes with appropriate deference. But I do not make him a promise.

'And Her Majesty?' I ask, hardly daring to voice the rest of the question.

Walsingham does not reply immediately, but when I look up and meet his steady gaze, I already know his answer and my hopes plummet like an anchor.

'I have spoken to the Queen about your situation, Bruno, but . . .' He purses his lips and shakes his head. 'There is little she can do. Your ideas are too controversial. She finds your books thought-provoking, she told me so, but she cannot be seen to endorse them publicly. It would be impossible for her to give you any kind of official role at court, especially after she was forced to banish John Dee.'

I nod, though I feel numb. John Dee was the nearest Queen Elizabeth ever came to appointing a court philosopher, but his knowledge of astrology and his alchemical experiments made him a figure of suspicion to the more extreme Puritans among her advisers, who began to attack him subtly with rumours of black magic and all kinds of immorality, even to cast sly aspersions on the Queen herself for listening to his counsel. Eventually, to spare his reputation and hers, she paid him to travel in Europe, furthering his studies, though Dee and all his friends knew this amounted to banishment. He has been gone two years now, with no prospect of being recalled. So there was little chance that she would willingly become the patron of another philosopher whose knowledge of occult sciences made him just as dangerous, and who was not even a native Englishman. But still, I had dared to hope.

'I understand.'

'After all Bruno has done for her, you'd think she could find something,' Sidney bursts out, rising to his feet. 'If it were not for Bruno, she might be a prisoner of the Queen of Scots and her French allies by now. We all might.' He looks aggrieved. 'Why, if he hadn't come to Plymouth with me, Drake might never have found out his clerk was selling advance notice of his route to the Spanish – she would have lost her entire investment, not to mention hundreds of English lives, and been humiliated at the hands of King Philip. If that is not worth a reward, I don't know what is.'

Walsingham inclines his head. 'Her Majesty knows well what efforts Bruno has made in her service. Though you may be interested to learn, it turned out young Master Crosse was not lying.'

'Really?' Sidney frowns. 'But I thought he confessed to the murders?'

'The murders, yes. But we had the letter decoded and all the details he had sent to the Spanish Ambassador were incorrect. I forwarded it to Drake just before he set sail and he sent back confirmation. If all Gilbert's communications followed that pattern, the fleet would not have been in any more danger than it was already, in Drake's view.'

'He is still a killer,' Sidney says, in case this should undermine our achievements.

'And he will die for it,' Walsingham says mildly. 'That is

the law. The one concession, since it appears that his treason was only partial, is that he will be hanged until dead before he is put to the knife. I gave him my word.'

We sit in silence, each of us picturing a traitor's end.

'Her Majesty will reward you, she promised,' he adds, turning to me. 'As will Drake, and Dom Antonio, who cannot sing your praises highly enough, it seems. You will be well provided for, Bruno. For a while, at least.'

'That is very gracious of them,' I say, trying to sound as if I mean it. A gift of money is never unwelcome, but it would buy me only a few months' grace. I do not need a purse so much as I need a job – some official position that will allow me to stay in England and write my books, and confer some status on them when they are published. A teaching post at one of the universities would have been useful, a position at court even better. Now it looks as though there is no place for me at either. I was never truly a part of this court circle, though they opened their door to me for a time. But I could not belong among men like Sidney and his uncle the Earl of Leicester, or even Walsingham, all of them bound together by blood, marriage and politics over the best part of three decades. My face, my voice, my ideas mark me as different. Perhaps, as I have often feared, a man like me belongs everywhere and nowhere.

I try to harden my expression, so that my face will not betray the disappointment I am battling. Instead, I reach for the jug and pour another glass of wine.

'Her Majesty was pleased to support you while she could do so covertly,' Walsingham continues, his tone gentle, 'and after some discussion we feel there is a way she could do so again.' He notes the light in my eyes and holds up a hand, as if warning me not to let my hopes race ahead of his words. 'Intelligence from Paris suggests that Mary Stuart's supporters there are still fomenting their conspiracies against the Queen, and that their plots grow more ambitious by the day. If we had a man in Paris able to watch them and report on their movements, that would be worth a good deal to Her Majesty, and of course to me.' He gives me a long look.

'But Your Honour, my earnest desire is to stay in London,' I say, trying not sound as if I am begging. I do not need to spell out to him the dangers that would wait for me at the French court.

'I know that, Bruno.' He exhales and shakes his head. 'And it grieves me that I cannot give you what you want. But I am offering you a chance to do Her Majesty further service. Who knows – perhaps in a couple of years things might be different.' He holds out his hands, palms up, to show that this is the best he can do.

'Thank you, Master Secretary,' I say, forcing a smile, though my heart feels dragged down by its own weight. 'I will think on it.' In a couple of years, King Henri of France might be pushed off his throne by the Catholic League, who would tear me to pieces quicker than you could say a novena. In a couple of years, Spain might invade England. These are volatile times: in a couple of years, we might none of us be where we are now. Besides, we all know it is an empty promise, held out only to soften the blow. If Queen Elizabeth can find no place for me now, while my service to her is fresh in her mind, she is unlikely to be any better disposed towards me two years hence.

'You might catch up with Rowland Jenkes in Paris, Bruno,' Sidney says, leaning back, his hands behind his head. 'Have a little word with him about his manners in Plymouth. You might even get to track down the original of that book.' He nods to the papers on the table. Walsingham frowns.

'I have seen enough of Jenkes for several lifetimes,' I say. The thought of him at large in Paris only adds to my reluctance.

There is a timid knock at the door. Walsingham calls to enter, and it opens wide enough to admit the hesitant figure of Sidney's wife Frances. She slips in and stands behind her husband's chair; Sidney turns and rests a hand on the mound of her belly. Walsingham's face visibly softens.

'What is it, daughter?' he asks.

'A messenger has arrived from Lord Burghley, Father,' she says, with as near to a curtsey as her advanced pregnancy will allow. 'He has come by river from Whitehall and says it is urgent.'

'Very well. Would you excuse me, gentlemen?'

We all stand as Walsingham pushes back his chair. He seems relieved at the interruption.

When the door closes behind him, Sidney puts his arm around his wife and pulls the fabric of her dress tight over her belly.

'What do you think, Bruno – does this not look like a strapping son in there? To judge by the bloody size of it.'

'I think Lady Sidney looks in fine health, and I'm sure the child is too,' I say, seeing how the poor girl blushes. She raises her eyes and gives me a grateful smile. She is only nineteen, pale and pretty, though she looks exhausted. After a few days of living with Sidney, I can appreciate why – and I am not even with child.

'He is a fighter too,' Sidney says, prodding her abdomen. 'Kicking and pummelling his way out, is he not, my dear? Going to be a soldier like his father,' he adds, expanding his chest with pride.

Frances gives a weak smile and bites her lip. 'Not if I can help it,' she murmurs.

'Get along, then – you should be resting, not running errands for your father,' he says, patting her absently. 'Bruno and I have business to discuss.'

I bow as she leaves, though I note how she lingers at the door, her gaze resting briefly on her husband. I can only guess what she must be feeling.

'So you are really going?' I ask, when the door is closed behind her.

'I am. Thanks be to God, the Queen relented. I had an audience with her at the end of last week, and she confirmed my posting.' His face is alight with excitement. He looks like a man in love, I reflect, except that the object of his desire is the command of a garrison in Flushing.

'So she has forgiven you for attempting to run away to the New World?'

'It seems so. At least, I had the impression she feels a small degree of guilt in driving me to such desperate measures. The governorship of Flushing is her way of making amends. She has even offered to stand god-mother to the child. But *he* has not forgiven me,' he adds, darkly, jabbing his thumb towards the door where Walsingham left. 'Firstly for trying to join Drake's voyage without telling him, and now for going to war just as the child is about to be born.'

'I can see his point of view.'

'It's not as if I'm its wet-nurse.'

'What does Lady Sidney feel?' I hardly need ask this; her thoughts were plain enough on her face.

'Oh, she is furious. Won't let me near her bed since I told her the news. But you know how *wives* are,' he says, making a face.

'No, I don't.'

He straightens his chair and sits up, his expression apologetic. 'No – forgive me. Thoughtless.' He pauses, weighing his next words. 'It must have been hard, saying goodbye to Lady Arden.'

I shrug the question away. 'It was what it was. A dalliance, nothing more. It's not as if either of us was deceived about that.'

'Even so,' he says. 'I think she was growing fond of you.' He does not ask directly whether I felt anything for her. Perhaps he thinks that would be overstepping the bounds of friendship.

'Perhaps.'

During those few days at Drake's country estate, the sun had made a last, brave attempt at summer, and we had spent evenings walking the long sloping lawns in golden light while swallows looped and skittered overhead. It was a brief, happy interlude, made all the sweeter by the knowledge that it could not last.

'Still, I don't doubt there will be a great many beauties at the French court delighted to see you return,' he says, catching my faraway look.

'They will be far outnumbered by the Catholic Leaguers who are horrified to see me,' I say, my spirits sinking again at the thought of Paris. 'Besides, I have no interest in French courtesans.'

'No. I know you too well. You still hold out hopes of catching up with Sophia, am I not right? It is the only thing that makes the prospect of France bearable to you.'

I look away to the window. I did not realise I was so easy to read.

'You need to forget her, Bruno,' he says, gently. 'Find someone else.'

'The way you have forgotten Penelope Devereux?' I turn back to him, raising an eyebrow. 'At least I have not written her a hundred sonnets.'

'A hundred and eight, actually,' he corrects. We look at each other and burst out laughing.

'I wish you were not going,' he says, when the laughter subsides.

'What difference will it make to you where I am? You will be busy defending Flushing.' I stop abruptly; I had not intended to sound quite so piqued. Deep down, a part of me still feels that he and Walsingham could have tried harder to find a way for me to stay. Sidney looks surprised.

'But you would have been here when I came back,' he says, his face suddenly sincere.

I look at him. How young he looks in the candlelight, his

eyes bright with anticipation of his great adventure. But you cannot guarantee that you will come back, I think, though I do not say it. I am seized by a sudden urge to plead with him not to go to war, to spell out the odds of a victory against the Spanish, but he is a grown man, and he wants his chance to prove it.

He pours more wine for us both.

'On reflection, I'm quite glad we're not halfway across the Atlantic, you know. I don't think I could have suffered Drake ordering me to swab out latrines for months on end. And think of the *damp*.'

'And the piss-drinking and weevils.' I laugh. 'I did tell you.'

'Besides, I would have missed the chance to go to Flushing.'

'Quite right. Because a military camp, by contrast, will be just like Whitehall Palace. Turkish carpets and feather beds all round – no lice or scurvy there.'

'Shut up, Bruno,' he says, with affection. 'You will not deter me, whatever you say. It's all I've wanted, to be a military commander. And when I come home, it will be to a hero's welcome. Let them call me a lapdog then.' He grins as he stands, raising his glass. It glows a deep crimson in the candlelight, rich and warm as blood. 'To us, Bruno. To our futures. To freedom and glory and poetry. And to seeing you again very soon, with great tales to tell.'

I stand and chime my glass with his. 'To all those things,' I say. 'Especially the last.' But as I drink, I feel a shiver pass through me, as if a cloud has crossed the sun. As if someone has walked over my grave, my mother would have said. I do not believe in premonitions, I tell myself. The candles have almost burned down to ashes. *To our futures*, I murmur again, as if, with enough conviction, I can will it to be true.

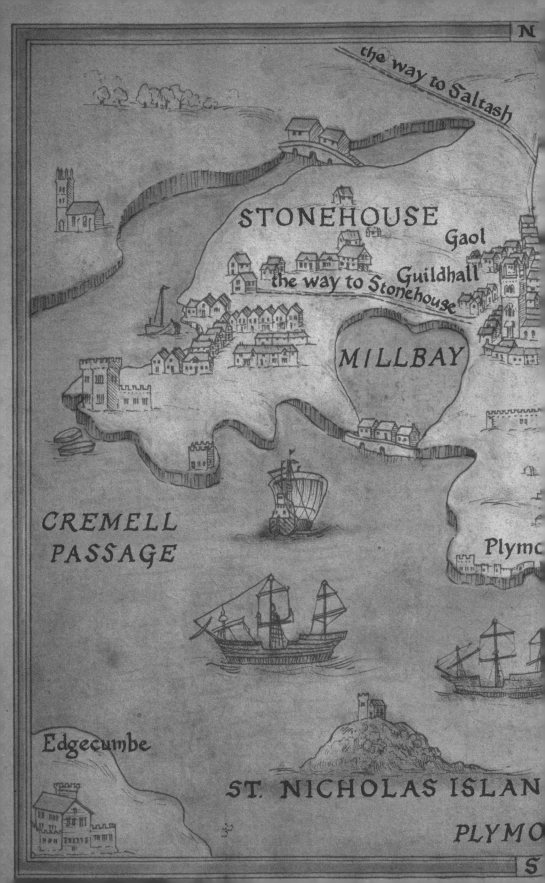

the way to Saltash

STONEHOUSE

Gaol

Guildhall

the way to Stonehouse

MILLBAY

CREMELL
PASSAGE

Plym

Edgecumbe

ST. NICHOLAS ISLAN

PLYMO

EDWARD
HEATH

EDWARD HEATH

A Singular Life

MICHAEL McMANUS

First published 2016 by
Elliott and Thompson Limited
27 John Street, London WC1N 2BX
www.eandtbooks.com

ISBN: 978-1-78396-264-8

For David and Paddy Hunt,
with the greatest affection, respect and gratitude

Contents

Introduction

During its eighteen-month gestation period, this book has been through a considerable metamorphosis. It has always been envisaged as a serious publication, its principal purpose being to mark the centenary of the birth, on 9 July 1916, of Edward Richard George Heath – privy counsellor and Knight of the Garter, wartime soldier and peacetime statesman, competitive sailor and talented amateur musician, and one of the most controversial politicians of the post-war era – but the proposal I originally had in mind was for a form of 'Festschrift'. A collection of essays collected in accordance with such a solidly European tradition would have appealed to its subject, but the quality and volume of material generously submitted by so many friends and colleagues necessitated a fundamental rethink. So the book you hold is rather different from the one originally intended.

The consistent, unyielding vision motivating all the hard work – the driving purpose, if you will – has not been an aspiration to detail, yet again, the already well-documented career of Ted Heath, but rather to capture and vividly evoke the complex, multi-faceted essence of the man – his relentless sense of purpose, his idiosyncratic (and often highly counter-productive) sense of humour, his strengths, quirks, weaknesses and foibles. In short, I wanted to explain what 'made him tick'.

Peter Walker was a protégé of Sir Edward's who ran his leadership election campaign in 1965 and stuck by him through thick and thin, willingly accepting the consequent opprobrium as a price worth paying. Even he once said, 'In the years I have known him, there have been only four or five occasions when I have penetrated his deepest thoughts. He is a very self-contained person and also a fairly shy one.' So Ted Heath is not the easiest subject for a historian or biographer – even one who knew him well and worked closely with him for five years, as I did.

Around sixty-five people who knew him personally have contributed to this book, each in his or her distinctive voice. The intention behind presenting so much primary material is to enable readers to form their own opinions of Heath, digesting and assimilating the evidence and unlocking the conundrum for themselves.

While this book is not a biography, it certainly does cover all the main stations of his life. Where the contributions of others do not join up neatly, or require illumination or counterpoint, I have filled in the gaps. I have also written a full, first-hand account of my own five-year period running the private office of Sir Edward, or 'The Boss', as we called him – including the unforgettable experience of running through his entire life with him, for the purposes of producing his 1998 memoir, *The Course of My Life*.

I have also, reluctantly and with no little sense of distaste, sought to address the nebulous and, to me, incredible allegations that have been made against Heath in 2015 and 2016, in connection with the supposed abuse of under-age male persons. As I shall make clear, I personally do not believe Heath ever had sexual relations with anyone – and I cannot imagine ever being persuaded otherwise. He seems to have decided, early in life, that he would manage independently and on his own in his personal life – a vow he never appears to have broken.

As this book reveals, in his political life Edward Heath sought always to be analytical and rational; and he possessed a rare gift for cutting incisively through copious briefings and masses of information, to the very heart of the matter. He could therefore appear cold and, to the less thick-skinned of those around him, positively rude. Certainly he struggled to express the softer emotions, but he was capable of great generosity and also of expressing affection to those he loved.

So, here he is – for fans and critics alike – that 'great lighthouse' in Roy Jenkins's memorable phrase – summoned back to life by the recollections of those who knew him best.

Chapter One

Early life (1916–1950)

The life of Edward Richard George Heath was remarkable by any standards, but it began unremarkably. He was born in Broadstairs on the Isle of Thanet. His father William was a jobbing builder who became a small businessman and his mother Edith had been a lady's maid. William was a fairly laid-back character with an eye for the ladies, whereas Edith was fiercely ambitious and determined that Edward should want for nothing.

With the recent death of Denis Healey, there is no one left who knew the young 'Teddy' Heath but, fortunately, many interviews exist with those who did. They give a consistent flavour of a serious and ambitious young man who drove himself very hard indeed; and who was generously supported by his parents, who denied themselves many aspects of material comfort in order to provide for him as he progressed through grammar school and university.

Heath and his younger brother John were very different, but remained close until John died, in his early sixties, in 1982. Their father William once said: 'Johnny would no sooner get to the bottom of the street than he fell into a tar barrel or something. Teddy could be out for hours and hours, and still come home as bright as a new pin.' In another interview he said: 'Teddy has a will of iron. He read and read about politics. His bedroom was like a library. When he was reading – or for that matter playing music – to try to talk to him was like speaking to a brick wall. Then suddenly he would stop what he was doing and say, "Let's go for a walk, mummy." And the rest of us would have to stop what we were doing and go out with him.'[1]

One of Heath's school friends from Thanet days, **Ronald Whittell**, had this to say about young Teddy and the household in which he grew up:

'Mrs Heath . . . was one of the most determined women I've ever known. She used to complain about Teddy sitting up in his bedroom reading instead of spending more time in boyish pursuits. It was a decided shock to both his parents when he turned out the way he did – they hadn't expected such a brilliant child . . . He never tried for popularity. He wasn't actively liked or actively disliked. He was respected and accepted, though a little bit intoler-ant . . . He seemed to achieve maturity of character earlier than others.'[2]

The only time I saw tears in Heath's eyes was when Michael Cockerell, that brilliant BBC film-maker, showed him a montage of images of his mother. 'Yes, so beautiful,' he murmured gently (Michael also asked him whether he had ever changed a nappy, which elicited a far less revealing – indeed rather nonplussed – response). Edith Heath drove herself very hard, not least to provide for her beloved elder son, and when her terminal cancer manifested itself while Heath was on a trip to the US as a newly-elected Member of Parliament, she could hardly bring herself to reveal her condition to her family. William Heath remarried twice – and all three of his wives were 'Mummy' to him and to his sons, but Edith was irreplaceable to Heath. Although he was clearly delighted his father lived to see him become Prime Minister, we all knew it was his mother who made him the man he was.

John Heath married twice and his first (by this point ex-) wife, Marian Evans, wrote a book in 1970 entitled *Ted Heath – A Family Portrait*. Heath thought the book meretricious and opportunistic; and he deeply resented the impression it gave of him having been over-indulged as a child and a young man. Indeed, he was highly sensitive to any charge that he was spoiled, or favoured over his brother John, four years his junior, but there's no doubt he was the beneficiary of disproportionate financial support from both par-ents and also of love, affection and attention from his mother in particular. Especially when considered in light of the genuinely virulent attacks to which Heath was subsequently subjected, the book in fact reads rather well, even favourably. What really upset Heath – that shy and private man – was surely that his family and its internal affairs had been brought into the public domain in this fashion, purely because of their connection with him. This is what **Heath** said, in an interview for his memoirs, about his family background, his upbringing and, in particular, his relationship with his brother:

'Our sporting interests were different, because I never played soccer. Our father was a very good soccer player, but refused to allow me to play soccer, because, he said, it would interfere with musical activities and getting down to the homework, which he was always very insistent upon. My brother, who wasn't so concerned with homework, did play soccer. In the summer I was swimming and played tennis; and in the winter I did cross-country running. [John's] first marriage just didn't come off – and he allowed her to divorce him, by going off with some woman for the night. Nothing happened, but it was good enough grounds for divorce. She then married a journalist in Broadstairs and wrote the book about me, to make some money. In that, she says that I was always the favourite of the family and he was ill treated. There's no truth in that at all, because my parents went to great lengths to ensure that we were similarly treated. The examples are that I got the scholarship to Chatham House but he couldn't get a scholarship, so they paid for him to go to Chatham House; and another example was that I learned the piano, so they insisted on him learning the violin. He didn't follow it up after he left school because he went to the war, but afterwards he did become very interested in music and he and his second wife spent a lot of time going to concerts in London and so on. So we had that interest in common.'

Heath was certainly a smart and mature child and, whilst he was no boy genius, he was a diligent student and, for much of his schooling, was accelerated into a class where the other pupils were a year or two older than he was. One of his former teachers, **Dr E. A. Woolf**, who travelled with Heath on his first overseas trip – to Paris when Heath was thirteen – said this in a newspaper interview many years later:

'I dare to say if Heath had applied his mind to it, he could have been academically brilliant, but he would only bite on the subjects that really interested him. For the rest, a broad outline satisfied him. We were a very lively school under a great headmaster. I was a Liberal – I stood as a Liberal candidate – but I don't think any of my current affairs class became

Liberals. I didn't mind what point of view the boys put forward, so long as they supported it with reasoned argument. Heath could certainly argue.'[3]

When Heath was in his seventies, a mischievous journalist good-naturedly tried to tease out of him whether his reading ever veered into the traditional areas of interest for an adolescent boy. Did he, she asked, pore through books to 'find the rude bits'? At first he deflected the question: 'Of course they talk about all these things and it is ridiculous to try and censor them . . . I think there is a stage in life that most people go through, when they want to find out about these things.' Did he? she asked. 'Oh yes . . . people behave like that when they are in that stage of youth.'[4]

He enjoyed precocious conversations with adults, about music, history and current affairs. Through his father (who looked after the weekend homes of a number of successful and high-profile London personalities) he became acquainted with Alec Martin of Christie's and also a leading London solicitor, Royalton Kisch, who made a big impact on him. **Arnold Goodman** (later Lord Goodman) was, at that time, a young solicitor in Kisch's office and became a lifelong friend of Heath:

> 'I remember him as an alert young man. I think of him then as an eager, questing person who was looking for founts of experience, founts of sophistication, founts of knowledge. I think perhaps he was looking for these outside his own world and often from people older than himself. He was very genuine. He was not at all a young man on the make.'[5]

As he considered his options upon leaving grammar school, Heath fixed his sights not only on the ancient university of Oxford, but specifically upon the college that he believed would lend the greatest prestige to him in future life – Balliol. He would later claim: 'Balliol helped me. It really ironed out all the class distinctions, and then so did the army.'[6] He won his place, but not, to his chagrin, an academic entrance award to smooth his path. Financing his life at Oxford was therefore a challenge. He received a loan of £90 a year from the Kent Education Committee, but his family had to make sacrifices to ensure he was able to pay his way as he sought to impress under the shadows of the 'dreaming spires', topping his funds up to around £220 per year. They evidently did so willingly. William Heath later explained that Mr Norman, the headmaster at Chatham House, sent for him when Teddy won his place, to persuade him he must take it up: 'He told me that Teddy might be Prime Minister. So his mother and I decided that he should go. It would have broken his heart had we refused. I had to work damned hard though.'[7]

It is hard to avoid concluding that, to the young Heath, everything and even every*one* was, in a sense, a potentially helpful means to an end – grammar school, university, his various foreign trips, the interim jobs he took, even the Second World War – and, from an early age, the end he had in mind was a successful political career. He took every opportunity, seized upon every introduction and missed no chance to widen his circle of acquaintances, his contacts or his personal horizons.

In his early days at Oxford, Heath had to survive on a very restricted budget, but still he threw himself with gusto into the activities that fascinated him. He joined the Oxford Union Debating Society and, whilst he joined all the political societies, he was already a Conservative. He also founded the Balliol choir, composed incidental music for the university dramatic society and helped to reconstruct the chapel organ. Indeed, he soon won the three-year organ scholarship at Balliol, worth £100 a year, which enabled him both to live less frugally and also to add a fourth year in Oxford to the usual three. His discipline and determination to succeed had again won through. When a future parliamentary colleague, Julian Amery, arrived at Balliol two years after Heath, he found him well established: 'Impeccable in dress and precise in speech, Ted was already a leading figure in the Oxford University Conservative Association and would soon become President of the Union. He laughed easily, seemed to be everywhere and yet somehow remained a man apart.'[8]

Heath's academic work generally took second place to his other, more career-orientated endeavours but to his credit, as one of his tutors from his time at Balliol cheerfully attested some years later, he never sought to conceal this fact. **Charles Morris** (later Lord Morris of Grasmere) was a fellow and tutor in philosophy at Balliol:

'When he was seeking a place at the college, straight from school, I asked him what he wanted to do in life after leaving Oxford, and he replied that he wanted to be "a professional politician". I do not think I ever heard any other schoolboy answer a similar question in these terms.'[9]

[5]

Heath used his long vacations to travel; and a European continent in ferment with conflict and political extremism was the crucible in which his lifelong political convictions were formed and hardened. His first big trip was to the Nuremberg rallies in September 1937, when he was introduced to several senior members of the Nazi hierarchy. He returned home convinced war could not be far off – and utterly opposed to the policy of appeasement. The following summer he visited the Republican side in Spain during the civil war. This is a first-hand account from **Heath** of how he diced with death:

'My sympathies were firmly with the elected government of the Spanish Republic simply because it was not a dictatorship. The base for our visit was Barcelona, and we travelled there via Calais, Paris and Perpignan. Instructions in our rooms told us to go down to the basement in the event of an air-raid alarm. It was just as well that we did not heed those instructions, opting instead for the excitement of watching the bombers flying past. During one raid, a bomb went straight down the hotel lift shaft, killing all those who had rushed down to the basement shelter. A few days later, we set out to drive south to Tarragona and, when we were nearly halfway there, a single aeroplane flying low along the road spotted our procession of cars and machine-gunned us. His aim was poor and we were able to stop the cars, dive into the ditch alongside the road and crawl along it away from our vehicles.'

Academically Heath never quite dazzled, but he certainly made a name for himself in political circles, not least when, having seen the preparations for a European war which were underway in both Germany and Spain, he supported the Master of Balliol, Sandy Lindsay, in the 'Munich' by-election in the autumn of 1938, against the pro-Chamberlain official Tory candidate Quintin Hogg (later Lord Hailsham). He was ambitious, but also highly principled. His opposition to appeasement was also fiercely expressed in the Union chamber.

When the Union debated the motion 'That this House disapproves of the policy of Peace without Honour', Heath 'attacked the muddled policy of the Government, which had been largely responsible for bringing us to the verge of disaster', according to the report in the university newspaper *Isis*: 'He maintained that the original Chamberlain declaration was indecisive . . . He had no faith in a lasting peace, but foresaw further trouble – in Switzerland, Holland, and elsewhere. Had we won Hitler's goodwill? Hitler could not be trusted: that was clear to everyone save Mr Chamberlain. He was prepared to give justice, but not sympathy, to Nazi Germany, for Nazism was essentially incompatible with Democracy. Finally, our defences were in a sorry state. This speech was competent if a little too long and, as a Conservative, Mr Heath must have astonished some of his confrères by his bitter attack.'

Heath assailed Chamberlain more fiercely still when the Union Society was invited to express 'No confidence in the National Government as at present constituted' in November 1938 (carried by 203 to 163). As *Isis* reported, Heath said that 'everywhere there was the greatest distrust of the Government. It was nothing more nor less than an organised hypocrisy, composed of Conservatives with nothing to conserve and Liberals with a hatred of liberty . . . As for Mr Chamberlain's foreign policy, it could only be described in the maxim, "If at first you don't concede, fly, fly, fly, again" . . . He quoted an American journalist's opinion that, in the next crisis, Mr Chamberlain would again turn all four cheeks at once.'

Heath soon caught the eye (and earned the admiration and friendship) of **Philip Kaiser**, an Oxford contemporary and friend with a great future ahead of him as a US diplomat:

'You got the impression of a guy who was highly intelligent, well motivated, not a glad-hander but agreeable and congenial. Retrospectively, perhaps, looking back, there was a little bit of a quality which comes out more prominently in the person presented today – essentially self-protective, a certain obliqueness about him which came through in a rather charming way in those days. Now that characteristic is, I think, part of his image problem today – it's come through rather strongly in the public man.'[10]

By the time he left Oxford in the summer of 1939, Heath had been President of the Oxford Union and also of the Balliol Junior Common Room; and he had also headed the university's Conservative Association. He and Madron Seligman, who would become his lifelong best friend, planned a trip to Franco's Spain, but Heath was denied a visa, so they decided instead to travel to the disputed city of Danzig, via Berlin. **Heath** recounts again:

'When we arrived in Berlin, we looked at the grotesque new Chancellery and then went for a full briefing from Anthony Mann, the *Daily Telegraph* correspondent there. His warnings had filled us thoroughly with foreboding by the time we caught the night train to Danzig. The atmosphere was very tense, and both Madron and I were acutely aware of how the attitude towards the British had changed among the German population. Then we decided to go by boat up-river to Warsaw, at that time still a lovely, sophisticated city and one very much under French influence. Its softness of style, welcoming atmosphere and easy pace of living were reminiscent of Paris. We reported to the British embassy, where the ambassador and his staff were horrified to see us. Having heard their forecast, we decided to start on the long hitch-hike back home.

'We saw massive German forces in tanks and trucks moving towards the Polish border. As if we did not already have enough problems, Madron insisted upon pulling out his penny whistle, playing once again the same old tunes I had heard incessantly for the past three weeks — all slightly out of tune. I had come to dislike these dirges intensely, and had already lost my temper with him after his umpteenth rendition of "Colonel Bogey" on the platform of Leipzig station. Now, as we tried to escape Germany on this ghastly train, out came the wretched penny whistle again. We had another flaming row, but at least I won and we had some peace afterwards.

'Once we reached the border, we walked across the bridge to safety in France. Late that night, we arrived to find a blacked-out Paris, dropped off the car and spent the night in a small hotel. The next day, we reported to the British embassy. "Unless you get out now," was the simple advice, "you will never get out at all." So full was the cross-Channel boat that, as it pulled away from the quay, it seemed about to capsize, taking all those waving goodbye down with it. My parents met me at Dover a week before Poland was invaded. It had not been possible for me to get in touch with them while we were away. They must have had some anxious moments, but they never mentioned them, and never complained. We had cut things pretty fine.'

Heath volunteered for the Army as soon as war was declared, but his services were not immediately required, so he was able to go on a lengthy debating tour of the US with a Liberal colleague, speaking at twenty-six universities right

across the country. When he was called up, in August 1940, he was soon recommended for a commission in the Royal Artillery. He was posted as a second
lieutenant to 107 Heavy Anti-Aircraft Regiment, just as it was being formed,
and helped to lead the anti-aircraft defence of Liverpool, which was under
fierce attack by the Luftwaffe. The CO, Lieutenant-Colonel Richard Barrow,
was looking for an adjutant and interviewed half a dozen candidates with the
assistance of the regimental quarter-master, **Major William Harrington**:

> 'Afterwards the CO told me that he thought one of them stood head and
> shoulders above the others. I agreed with him. We each took a piece of
> paper and wrote down the name of the one we thought the best. We found
> we had both written the same name – Heath . . . He didn't know much at
> first, but if Teddy didn't understand something, he would ask how to do
> it, rather than make a mess of it. When he had been told once, he never
> needed to ask again . . . I used to tell him that he worked too hard, but he
> took no notice. He got down in black and white what everyone was sup-
> posed to do. There was no room for mistakes.'[11]

Another of Heath's commanding officers, **George Chadd**, would become
a lifelong friend and confidant. In later years Chadd would speak warmly of
Heath's 'industry and devotion to duty and attention to detail':

> 'We had four guns, heavy ack ack, plus a hundred and twenty men – it
> was a bit of a responsibility for a chap of twenty-four and I had a sleepless
> night wondering whether Heath would make a site commander. Then I
> found out he had sat up all night writing orders for the site.'[12]
>
> 'I've never seen him put a foot wrong . . . He was always meticulously
> correct in his conduct and behaviour. The men liked him. He was never
> impatient with dullards or arrogant to people not so bright as himself. He
> drank a glass of beer in the mess and he read a lot . . . but he didn't go
> out much except with his band . . . He was the perfectly behaved officer.'[13]

Like his famous namesake, Heath was an enthusiastic bandleader and was
not above commandeering medical transport for his battery band. Once he
was caught and, as George Chadd later recalled, 'got a real rocket over that

ambulance!' Heath was soon promoted from Second Lieutenant to Captain and became adjutant of his regiment. During the gruelling campaign to liberate the Low Countries and France, Heath distinguished himself again. **James Hyde** was the orderly room sergeant of 334 Battery of the 107th Regiment:

> 'We were all wondering what sort of person he would turn out to be, and we were none too happy. Up to then he hadn't done any fighting worth speaking of. I was suspicious of him, but within a fortnight or three weeks he exercised such a persuading influence that one found Heath was first-class. So far as administration was concerned, he was perfect . . . [and] he rapidly understood men and their reactions. The men liked him because they thought he was a fair man . . . He was a tough skipper. If he said the battery was going to do it this way, that was it.'[14]

It is a cliché – but true – that war often inspires ordinary people to do extraordinary things. It didn't necessarily do that to Heath, but he did rise to the challenge and served his country admirably. The gentle, thoughtful, music-loving, somewhat soft-edged Oxford undergraduate had become a man. He was mentioned in despatches and awarded a military MBE. He didn't enjoy the war as such, but he did like the camaraderie and classless, meritocratic and democratic atmosphere of the Army – so much that he later became a Lieutenant-Colonel in the Territorial Army and CO of the 2nd Regiment of the Honourable Artillery Company. He also spent three years as a Master Gunner of the Tower of London, which may sound arcane, but is, in fact, a considerable honour.

Back on 'Civvy Street', Heath had to decide what to do next. He was attracted to a career as an orchestral conductor, but a conversation with Sir Hugh Allen, Professor of Music at Oxford, was sufficient to put him off. 'To get to the top,' Sir Hugh had warned, 'you have to be as big a shit as Malcolm Sargent.' He had a scholarship offer of £100 from Gray's Inn (awarded on 'testimonial and qualifications') but, whilst law and music sang their siren songs to him, it was politics that beckoned. He took the civil service exams and came joint top, with his Oxford friend Ashley Raeburn. He was allocated to the Ministry of Civil Aviation, under **Peter Masefield**, later chairman of the British Airports Authority. Heath gamely admitted to Masefield that he had no ambition to forge a long-term career as a civil servant, but wished merely 'to gain experience of the workings of the Civil Service machine from the inside'. Nonetheless, his new boss enjoyed working with him:

'A pleasant, sound, and highly intelligent ex-President of the Oxford Union and Colonel in the H.A.C. who clearly gets on well with people, regards our more dyed-in-the-wool civil servant colleagues with amused detachment, is first-class on paper and potentially an excellent administrator . . . When you get to know him (which isn't easy) he is a sensitive and warm-hearted chap who has a direct approach and an endearing sense of the ridiculous.'[15]

After a couple of near misses, at Ashford and Sevenoaks, Heath was soon selected for a constituency – the suburban seat of Bexley, which Labour had won by almost 12,000 votes in 1945 but retained in a by-election just a year later by only 1,851 votes. The selection committee consisted of six men and two women, one of whom was **Gladys Whittaker**, who gave this account of her first, fateful meeting with the thirty-one-year-old Heath:

'That half-smile of his is what I will always remember . . . Of course he was good on policy. We put him through the mill – I asked some sharp questions myself – but it is the smile that sticks in my mind. It was not the broad grin which we are used to from him now, but a shy kind of half-smile.'[16]

Heath had no option but to resign from the civil service forthwith – with some sadness, for he had discovered an aptitude for the work and enjoyed his time under Peter – and took an unlikely job as a news reporter at the *Church Times* under its left-leaning editor Humphry Beevor, as he began to nurse Bexley in earnest. He once told me that he knocked on every door in the constituency at least twice between his adoption in 1947 and the general election in 1950. Heath told some tales of his time as a candidate – all of which amused him greatly but seem rather tame today. For instance, when asked whether he intended to marry, he deflected the question by saying this was 'not something to be rushed'. In fact, Heath had been in a serious relationship with a girl from his home town of Broadstairs but it had not worked out. Kay Raven was a teacher in a preparatory school and daughter of a local doctor. She and Heath played tennis together as teenagers and she was secretary of the carol concerts. When

I worked for Heath he was still in regular and warm correspondence with her sister Margaret, who lived in Zimbabwe.

He rarely spoke about this relationship, but was coaxed into doing so by **Michael Cockerell** for a television profile recorded in 1998:

> 'He told me about Kay Raven, his Broadstairs girlfriend, who had waited patiently for him throughout the war against Hitler. His friends expected them to marry. But Colonel Heath never got round to proposing to her. "She decided she would marry someone else, but I don't discuss these things," said Heath. "Did you get over it?" "Yes." "It was said you kept her photograph by your bed?" "Yes." "Did you?" "Yes." And he looked away, as if close to tears.
>
> 'Heath of course never did marry. He told me that he felt that in some ways that had been a political advantage for him, "because instead of having to spend time with one's family – or not spending time and being divorced, it means I have just been free to use my time in the world of politics".'

Marian Evans also referred to Kay Raven in her book about Heath and his family:

> 'In the early 1950s when Teddy's girl friend of long standing decided to get married, it came as a surprise to the family. Mummy burst into tears when I spoke of it so. It would seem the girl had met someone else and felt she couldn't think only of Teddy. We all clubbed together later to buy her a wedding present and I've no doubt she lived happily ever after.'[17]

Anthony Staddon, who worked with me on Heath's memoirs, similarly recalls how reluctant Heath was to elaborate on this topic, or on any of his close relationships, even for the book:

> 'It was not easy when working on his memoirs to coax him to talk about those areas which were of obvious interest to the general reader, such as his relationships (particularly with his mother and Kay Raven). He would often complain, "Why do people want to know about that?" and start to narrate a story about a meeting at the British Museum instead. There is no doubt that the death of his mother hit him hard: one of the few times

when he spoke quite movingly was when he recounted how he broke off the 1951 election campaign to nurse her when she was dying. That was probably the most emotional I ever saw him. While he did open up and talk about his mother, we were unsuccessful, by and large, in persuading him to talk about Kay Raven, other than to say that, after he returned from the War, she married someone else and "that was that" . . .

'He found it very hard to demonstrate his emotions unless perhaps through music. I don't think we will ever know whether this was in response to his upbringing and his mother's devotion to him (reciprocated), or his failed relationship with Kay Raven or simply an unwillingness to do so. His troubled relationship with women has been well documented and there is no doubt that he could find friendship with some women difficult and he preferred the company of men. Part of the reason was his upbringing; few women would have been prepared to dote on him like his mother reportedly did.'

In a perfect illustration of how politics diverted and occupied his energies, during his first election campaign, **Heath** relished an occasion when the banter got a bit lively:

'I arrived at one [evening meeting], the last in the evening, at a school in Welling to find an orgy of rowdy exchanges, with many of the people present, including the chairman, on their feet. No one took any notice of me as I crept along the wall to the table at the top where I sat down. Even then I had to tug at the chairman's coat to attract his attention. Holding up his notes in an attempt to gain silence, he proclaimed: "The candidate's arrived. Let us hear what he has to say." As an uneasy quiet descended upon the meeting, he declared: "I will tell you about him." He then attempted to impress my local credentials upon the audience. "He was born in Kent," he began. This provoked no response from the onlookers. He went on rather more loudly: "He was educated in Kent." Still there was no response. Finally, he concluded: "And he lives in Kent." To this, a man at the back shouted: "And for all I bloody well care, he can die in Kent!"'

Heath's job at the *Church Times* was in no sense a career move. As he nursed Bexley and played a time-consuming role in the Territorial Army, he was astonished that, for his colleagues, writing for the paper seemed to be a full-time and exclusive occupation. 'Is this the only job you've got, then?' he once asked a work-mate. 'I mean, aren't you writing a novel or something?' Two of his colleagues at the *Church Times* later shared their memories of Heath. **John Trevisick** worked with Heath at the paper and later became its news editor:

> 'Beevor took endless delight in trying to catch Heath out, and Heath would stall on abstruse questions – a damned good training for him, of course . . . Heath shook with laughter like a jelly when he heard of a colleague's misfortunes – like being bitten by a dog when on a fruitless assignment, or losing oneself in a fog when on the way to a fourth-rate religious play at Walthamstow . . . It was a bizarre appointment, for which Heath had no qualifications either as a journalist or a theologian.'[18]

Another colleague in those days, **Rosamund Essex**, later became editor:

> 'Details were inclined to go wrong under EH – not through neglect but through his strange working environment . . . Ecclesiastical words and institutions meant little to him . . . He never mastered the word "schism" (which he pronounced "skism") though I am sure he must later have learnt its meaning in politics . . . But I liked him enormously. He was fun and he was friendly . . . Standing in his shirt-sleeves and running with perspiration he would let his rumbustious laugh echo around the linotypes.'[19]

After two years, Heath moved on to a role that suited him better, becoming a trainee at Brown, Shipley, a merchant bank in the City of London. This somewhat mature trainee – he was now thirty-three years old – moved from desk to desk and enjoyed himself very much indeed. The role was a means to an end, but he knew his chances at Bexley were evens at best and his toehold in banking was a handy each-way bet: if he lost at Bexley, he had a job; if he won, he had a handy source of additional experience and income that would be perfectly compatible with the requirements of a newly-elected, back-bench MP. All he had to do now was to win at Bexley. That was his overriding ambition – and he was well used, by now, to achieving everything upon which his heart was set.

CHAPTER TWO

Rise through the ranks
(1950–1959)

From the outset, Heath's drive and ambition impressed his supporters in Bexley, but there were serious problems that needed to be urgently addressed. The first (and most pressing) was the dire financial situation of the association. Traditionally, Tory MPs and even candidates had been expected to make a substantial personal donation each year to their local association, but the more egalitarian ethos of the post-war era had swept that away. Heath did, however, prevail upon five of his friends to make a contribution of £50 each – contributions that were more than matched by wealthy local supporters. He recruited a full-time agent, Reg Pye, who rapidly became an indispensable ally and friend, addressed every possible meeting and knocked on every possible door. He sensed every vote might count and, when the election came, on 23 February 1950, he was proven right. After a recount (and the collapse in a swoon of the returning officer), Heath won by 133 votes – a victory he would always attribute to the intervention of a Communist candidate, appropriately named Mr Job, who won three-and-a-half times that many votes. Heath would later joke: 'I told Mr Job that he was welcome to stand again at any other general election at Bexley and that, if he found it difficult to put up the £150 deposit, to come and see me for help.'

Heath never moved into a home in the constituency. He would say, perhaps only half-jokingly, that this was because he didn't wish to become embroiled in 'difficult questions about which butcher to use and which pub to frequent'. When he finally had the wherewithal to buy a home of his own, in the mid-1980s, he was in no mood to change his policy, as one of his staff from that time, **Nick Rundle**, vividly recalls:

'I was round at Wilton Street one evening in the early 1980s, having carried out some menial piece of research. The Boss was surrounded by estate agents' bumf. "None of these houses are remotely suitable," he sighed. Foolishly, and perhaps emboldened by a couple of very sizeable whiskies, I let slip the comment, "What about any nice houses in the constituency?" The steely eyes flashed. "There *are* no nice houses in the constituency."'

It did not take long for Heath to make his mark in the Commons. With a group of nine other first-time MPs, including Iain Macleod, Robert Carr and Enoch Powell, he formed the One Nation Group and nominally co-authored the Group's first publication, which set out a potential political trajectory subtly different from that of Churchill and his team. The 'One Nation' concept is still important today – claimed by Labour politicians as well as Tories – and it was a wise decision to join up, especially in the early days. It demonstrated fresh thinking without carrying any taint of disloyalty. A significant advantage for Heath was the fact the more intellectual members of the Group could be relied upon to do the thinking, the researching and the drafting. He was more than happy to bask in the reflected – or refracted – glory that resulted from their cerebral endeavours.

Heath wisely waited a few months before making his maiden speech, which, unsurprisingly perhaps, was on the subject of the Schuman Plan and early moves to develop closer political cooperation in Europe – a process in which the Attlee government had refused to engage:

'Anyone going to Germany today is bound to be impressed by the fact that the German dynamic has returned; that Germany is once again working hard and producing hard, and that therefore Germany will become a major factor in Europe. I suggest that there are only two ways of dealing with that situation. One is to attempt to prolong control, which the Chancellor has already dismissed as being undesirable and impracticable.

The only other way is to lead Germany into the one way we want her to go, and I believe that these discussions would give us a chance of leading Germany into the way we want her to go.

'After the First World War we all thought it would be extremely easy to secure peace and prosperity in Europe. After the Second World War we all realised that it was going to be extremely difficult; and it will be extremely difficult to make a plan of this kind succeed. What I think worries many of us on this side of the House is that, even if the arguments put forward by the Government are correct, we do not feel that behind those arguments is really the will to succeed, and it is that will which we most want to see. It was said long ago in this House that magnanimity in politics is not seldom the truest wisdom. I appeal tonight to the Government to follow that dictum, and to go into the Schuman Plan to develop Europe and to co-ordinate it in the way suggested.'[1]

In the summer recess of 1950, Heath went on holiday with fellow 'new boy' **John Rodgers**, MP for Sevenoaks. At one point on that trip, Heath confided in Rodgers that 'I owe everything to my mother, really'. **John Rodgers** recounted the trip:

'He was an agreeable companion, with an eye for the good things – the interiors and exteriors of churches – but he could go very silent, rather distressingly so on drives. There would be just a grunt. He was really rather suspicious when someone else drove. He was very keen on keeping fit, and liked to go to bed early – about ten or eleven at night. He has an iron self-control which is really almost frightening.'[2]

Heath always had a natural and precocious gift for identifying and recruiting mentors; and, as an ambitious young man, he naturally had at the top of his list the party leader himself, Winston Churchill, who, after five years as Leader of His Majesty's Loyal Opposition, was now facing relishing the imminent prospect of returning to office as a peacetime Prime Minister. The young Heath's courageous stand over appeasement now stood him in good stead both with Churchill himself, and also with those around him, most notably Anthony Eden, widely assumed to be Churchill's likeliest successor.

In less than a year, Heath was a junior opposition whip. He was in two minds about the role, because whips are denied the right to speak in the House of Commons – except in very rare circumstances – and he was concerned the voters of Bexley might mistake this self-denying ordnance for indolence on his part. Nonetheless he took the job. He knew every existing whip had a veto over new appointments to the office, so the offer proved he had already made a favourable impact. Turning down the job might blunt that.

Heath remained with Brown, Shipley after his election and, during the summer recess in 1951, he travelled to America and Canada for the bank. He was in Ottawa when Attlee called an election for 25 October and travelled back to the UK on the *Queen Mary*, with Labour's Manny Shinwell for company.

His first re-election campaign was to be marked by personal anguish. His mother had lived to see him elected to the House of Commons, but when he returned home from the US, he was informed that she was terminally ill with cancer. Here is one of the few passages in Heath's memoirs that shows genuine emotion:

'My political optimism . . . was completely overshadowed by news of my mother's illness . . . I rushed down to see her and was appalled by her condition. I wanted to put off my visit to America, but my father strongly urged me to go. Upon my return, I found that her health had taken a serious turn for the worse. She had been moved back home and was obviously dying. I fought the election campaign in Bexley with this shadow hanging over me. I drove home to the coast every night and then back to Bexley again the following morning to continue canvassing. Each evening I played the piano in the sitting room under her bedroom, all the pieces I knew she loved most. My mother died in the early hours of 15 October 1951. It was a devastating blow for me, the first I had sustained in my family life and one that I hardly knew how to handle. My father always believed the diagnosis should have been made much earlier, and her life might then have been saved.'

Two weeks before polling day, Edith Heath succumbed. Her son told almost no one in Bexley what had occurred and retained his seat by 1,639 votes.

Nationally, Labour won a record number of votes, but the Tories had a narrow majority in the Commons. Elected as Prime Minister by the people for the first time, albeit without even a plurality of the vote, Churchill appointed Anthony Eden to his old job as Foreign Secretary. The two of them believed the Parliament had, at most, six months to run. Heath became a junior government whip, as a Lord Commissioner of the Treasury, under chief whip Patrick Buchan-Hepburn and had to resign from Brown, Shipley. The Conservatives had a majority of just sixteen seats and, in such circumstances, the Whips' Office acquires great importance; Anthony Eden later wrote: 'Though Mr Heath's service in Parliament had been short at that time, I have never known a better equipped Chief Whip. A ready smile concealed a firm mind.'[3]

Heath rose rapidly as well as steadily, becoming joint deputy chief whip, then deputy chief whip and then, once Eden had won his own mandate in the 1955 general election, chief whip. **Patrick Buchan-Hepburn** (later Lord Hailes) would later recall:

'I didn't even know how he would turn out when he came in . . . but he dedicated himself, as he does to whatever he does, and didn't look miserable the whole time because he couldn't make speeches. He was soon made Deputy Chief Whip . . . With Winston I couldn't get what a Chief Whip usually has – regular appointments in the mornings – but, whenever I was called, [Heath] could carry on, and I could be absolutely certain everything would be all right. He's absolutely reliable. He had more self-assurance as time went on . . . Many people who don't know it under-rate what the Whips' Office can be – what a lot you can learn about politics and people, particularly if you are not very expansive. He did know about people. He took great trouble to know about them, and their backgrounds, and what they wanted . . . he enjoys people, but I don't know that he needs them – he's extraordinarily self-sufficient . . .'[4]

The Hon. Ned Carson was MP for the Isle of Thanet – including the Heaths' Broadstairs home – between 1945 and 1953. He divided MPs up between tea-room types and smoke (or smoking) room types, and, according to him, 'Ted was one of the smoke room set from the beginning. A real

House of Commons man.'* After one very late division, Carson went to the whips' office and demanded of Heath: 'Why don't you get married and go home and let me get to bed?' Heath looked up slowly, with 'a very blank face', and answered him simply: 'I don't want to get married.'[5] **Carson** provided Heath's former sister-in-law, Marian Evans, with a helpful portrait of Heath as a young whip:

'Ted Heath would use more of a "soft sell" to get his way. If I had shown signs of not voting with the party, he would walk up casually and say something on the lines of, "Now be a good chap. It's not really a matter of your conscience this time, is it? Do come into the lobby with us. There's no point in abstaining." I remember, however, one occasion when he was very stern in a tactful way and I was so surprised at this I went into the lobby at his bidding.'[6]

Heath's appointment as Government chief whip to Anthony Eden after the 1955 general election must have seemed like paradise on earth to him. He had held Eden in the highest esteem since rallying to his anti-appeasement banner in the 1930s and the 1955 election result – an increased majority for an incumbent government – seemed almost too good to be true; a genuine, fresh mandate for an optimistic new era. Far more than under Churchill, who was always a mentor rather than a friend and evidently treated him more as a protégé than as a necessary ally, Heath now regarded himself as part of the indispensable inner circle of the Prime Minister. However, it was not long before he realised that he wasn't – quite – in the innermost of the many concentric circles that surrounded a well-regarded man who promised much but delivered so little.

Shortly after the 1955 general election, Heath spoke in support of the young prospective candidate in his neighbouring constituency of Dartford, **Peter Walker**:

* The tea-room set would regard the smoke-room set as somewhat boorish; the smoke-room types would regard the tea-room set as rather effete.

'My first meeting with Ted was when he came to my constituency (Dartford), where there was some displeasure that they had adopted someone quite as young as 22. Ted as the then Chief Whip of the party came and addressed a public meeting. "I know some of you are concerned about the age of this candidate," he said, "but have no worries – as chief whip I can assure you, when he reaches the House of Commons, I shall tell him how to speak and how to vote."'[7]

In his memoirs, **Heath** wrote about the role he held between 1955 and 1959:

'When I accepted this position, I was fully aware that few Chief Whips had gone on to hold a Cabinet post, and none had ever reached the summit. It is essential to have an immensely strong personal bond of trust with the leader of the party, and I was very fortunate indeed to work in this capacity with two men whom I had always respected, Anthony Eden and Harold Macmillan. But a particularly unhappy episode, perhaps the unhappiest of Britain's entire post-war history, tested my loyalty to breaking point, and I was forced to take the hardest decision of all. In doing so, I subjugated my own views and doubts to the overriding need to hold the Conservative Party together at a time of crisis – not for my benefit alone, nor even for that of the party but, I profoundly believe, for the long-term benefit of the country.'

The history of the Suez Crisis has been chronicled elsewhere, in great detail and, in several instances, with peerless historical authority. I hope readers will forgive me citing the brief explanation that Heath and we, his team, crafted together for *The Course of My Life*. He took great care over this section of the book, so it carries his personal authority to an unusual degree:

'The Suez crisis began with the nationalisation of the Suez Canal by Egypt's militant nationalist leader, President Gamal Abdel Nasser, on 26 July 1956. I heard about Nasser's seizure of the Canal late at night just after the House of Commons had risen. The Prime Minister . . . had gathered together the members of the Cabinet . . . to discuss the situation. He had also called an emergency Cabinet meeting for the next morning.

At that meeting, it became clear that we were hopelessly ill prepared for any firm and immediate action, despite the fact we had only recently left the area. Lord Mountbatten, Chief of the Defence Staff, stated that there were no plans to deal with this eventuality at the Canal. We all sat in silence for a few moments before the meeting broke up. The Chiefs of Staff went on talking about an invasion plan and the rest of us followed the Prime Minister into the Chamber to hear his first public statement on the crisis . . .'

As that brief account makes plain, Heath was in the thick of the crisis from the beginning – and with good reason. Whilst the bulk of the Conservative parliamentary party remained loyal throughout the crisis, on both wings there were rebels. The 'Suez Group', led by Julian Amery, Fitzroy Maclean and Charles Waterhouse, were outraged by Nasser's actions and extremely bellicose, favouring robust military action by Britain to reassert her role in the Middle East. A very different group – one more positively disposed towards Eden – of around twenty to thirty MPs, organised by Sir Alec Spearman, were opposed to any military intervention and were joined, in due course, by Edward Boyle and Anthony Nutting, both of whom resigned as ministers over Suez.

The Suez Crisis not only marked the end of Britain's post-imperial pre-tensions in the Middle East; it also destroyed Anthony Eden, both politically and physically. With the full connivance of his chief whip and a tiny cadre of senior colleagues, Eden knowingly misled the House of Commons over Suez. Again, **Heath**'s own first-hand account is vivid and indispensable:

'Secret discussions on the possibility of an invasion between the British, French and Israelis were carried out in Paris in the latter part of October. I was first told of these discussions after a meeting of the inner circle of Ministers and officials held at Chequers on 21 October. I was alarmed, but far from surprised, that a plan was being hatched to circumvent the negotiations in New York. Four days later, I went into the Cabinet Room as usual shortly before Cabinet was due to start, and I found the Prime Minister standing by his chair holding a piece of paper. He was bright-eyed and full of life. The tiredness seemed suddenly to have disappeared.

"We've got an agreement!" he exclaimed. "Israel has agreed to invade Egypt. We shall then send in our own forces, backed up by the French, to separate the contestants and regain the Canal." The Americans would not be told about the plan. He concluded, somewhat unnervingly, that "this is the highest form of statesmanship".

'The Sèvres Protocol, as it became known, had been signed the day before, in a suburb of Paris. Sir Patrick Dean had signed on behalf of the Foreign Secretary, Selwyn Lloyd, and Christian Pineau and David Ben-Gurion had signed, respectively, on behalf of France and Israel. Only Lloyd, Macmillan, Butler and myself were to know about it. I did my utmost to change Eden's mind, warning him it was unlikely that people would believe him – and that, even if the Protocol remained a secret and people accepted the official reason for going in, the very act of doing so was likely to split the country. Eden did not dispute any of this advice, but simply reiterated that he could not let Nasser get away with it.'

Less than a week later, on 30 October, **Eden** informed the House of Commons that 'Israel forces had crossed the frontier and had penetrated deep into Egyptian territory'. In response:

'Her Majesty's Government and the French Government have accordingly agreed that everything possible should be done to bring hostilities to an end as soon as possible . . . We have called upon both sides to stop all warlike action by land, sea and air forthwith . . . Further, in order to separate the belligerents and to guarantee freedom of transit through the Canal by the ships of all nations, we have asked the Egyptian Government to agree that Anglo-French forces should move temporarily – I repeat, temporarily – into key positions at Port Said, Ismailia and Suez. The Governments of Egypt and Israel have been asked to answer this communication within 12 hours.'[8]

The emergency debate that followed grew more and more fierce. The following day, British and French planes bombed airfields in Northern Egypt and, at the United Nations, the UK and France vetoed US and Soviet calls for a ceasefire.

Despite all the secrecy, many people were already suspicious. **William Yates**, newly elected as MP for The Wrekin in 1955, had served with the 8th Army and he said what all too many people were now beginning to think. On a spurious point of order, he stated that, 'I have been to France and I have come to the conclusion that Her Majesty's Government have been involved in an international conspiracy' and asked the Speaker, somewhat disingenuously it must be assumed:

> 'I want to know whether it would be considered right and patriotic for a person deliberately to try to bring down Her Majesty's Government in those circumstances?'[9]

Heath and his team were struggling to control their flock. On 3 November, the House of Commons met on a Saturday for the first time since the 1940s. The military news from the Canal Zone was encouraging, but there was a potentially catastrophic run on sterling and the Americans were strongly disinclined to help. On 8 November there was a confidence vote in the House of Commons. In his memoirs, **Heath** recounted one terse and revealing anecdote from that evening:

> 'A message was brought in to me that some Members wished to see me outside. I found Captain Charles Waterhouse, the leader of the Suez Group, and Julian Amery, one of the strongest and most effective advocates of its policies. Waterhouse told me he could ensure that all the members of the group would vote with the government in the division that night, provided I would give an undertaking to bring about Eden's downfall as leader of the Conservative Party. I told him to go to hell and, without further discussion, went back to finish my dinner.'

In that confidence vote, not a single Tory MP opposed the Government and only six abstained. One of the six was Nigel Nicolson, whom **Heath** had known since Balliol days:

> 'He said he would support the government if I could assure him that there had been no secret plot to carry out the invasion. In my position, there

was no way that I could deny or confirm this. I looked Nigel straight in the eyes and said nothing. He understood completely.'

The story thereafter was one of national humiliation and personal decline for the Prime Minister. Almost inconceivably, on the advice of his personal physician, Sir Horace Evans, almost as soon as the Suez expedition had ignominiously failed, Eden went to the West Indies to recuperate. Heath and Macmillan warned him against absenting himself, but his mind was made up. It was the second disastrous expedition he authorised that year. When he returned, speculation about his likely successor was rife. Then, in a debate in the House of Commons on 20 December 1956, he said this:

'We have been accused of being, ever since the Israeli attack on Egypt, and indeed long before that, in collusion with the Israelis . . . Her Majesty's Government have been asked to prove that they had no foreknowledge of the Israeli attack . . . We warned the Israeli Government of the consequences of an attack on Jordan, and we gave a number of other warnings . . . But to say that Her Majesty's Government were engaged in some dishonourable conspiracy is completely untrue, and I most emphatically deny it . . . So of course we discussed every possible hypothesis. But I repeat that there was no agreement arrived at until I informed the House about it.'[10]

Heath sat listening to his erstwhile hero being untruthful in the House of Commons. Then he went to No. 10 Downing Street, where a fateful meeting occurred:

'I went along from my room . . . to have a word with Freddie Bishop, the Prime Minister's principal private secretary, about the general outlook. As we were chatting, Sir Norman Brook, the Cabinet secretary, came through the door from the Cabinet Room, where he had been seeing the Prime Minister, looking like an old Samurai who had just been asked to fall on his sword. We paused, as Brook said, "He's told me to destroy all the relevant documents. I must go and get it done." With that, Sir Norman, loyal as always to his Prime Minister, went off to destroy the Sèvres Protocol and other documents which confirmed the collusion between Britain, France and Israel over Suez.'

It would be difficult to overstate the extraordinary degree of care and attention that Heath devoted to this section of his memoirs. There had been almost universal acknowledgement amongst historians of the period of the skills he displayed – holding the party together during the crisis, not only mollifying the loyalist majority but also keeping in close touch with the two wings of the argument – but he made it very plain to the book team in the late 1990s that his conscience was still troubled. So we pressed him: would resignation not have been the *right* thing to do, the honourable thing to do? Reluctantly he assented. This was indeed his view and part of him still regretted his decision not to resign. A Prime Minister deliberately and knowingly misleading the House of Commons was, to his mind, more or less an act of treachery against the Crown, the people and the state. That momentous thought went into an early draft of the book.

For precious weeks, other sections of the draft memoirs were almost or totally neglected by him as he agonised over this. Eventually he called me in for a private word. He had always admired Eden and he still felt considerable gratitude and loyalty towards him. Furthermore, Eden's widow, his second wife Clarissa, was still alive (at the time of writing, she still is) and it would cause her immense pain and embarrassment if, after all these years, he were to denounce his one-time idol, mentor and friend. Could I therefore craft a form of words that would recapture the spirit of that fateful conversation with Nigel Nicolson: not defending Eden's judgement or actions, but also not condemning him out of hand? In other words, could we make sense of his decision to carry on as chief whip in 1956, a decision over which he had evidently agonised at the time. We shall never know if sparing Clarissa Avon's feelings was his real motive, but the fact is, his decision to stick with Eden and tide the party through the aftermath of Suez did weigh heavily upon his conscience until the end. This is an edited version of what was published:

'Some may ask why, given my doubts about Suez, I did not resign as Chief Whip. There was one overriding reason. When you accept that position, you do so knowing that it demands service in all conditions. The Chief Whip is not called upon, indeed is not expected, to speak in the House of Commons or make publicly known his views on matters of government policy. He and his colleagues in the Whips' Office are expected to keep in the closest touch with the views and feelings of government backbenchers, to report them faithfully to the Prime Minister and his senior colleagues, and to ensure that the government's business is sustained by them in the House of Commons. It is also his responsibility to make the best possible arrangements with the Chief Whips of the opposition parties for the sensible management of business in the House. As this crisis developed, the feeling between the two sides of the House became so bitter that only the two Chief Whips were on speaking terms with each other. If that bond were ever to be broken, the parliamentary system would collapse.

'The Chief Whip's relationship with the Prime Minister is a special and personal one. He owes his complete loyalty to the Prime Minister, who is entitled to count upon it. Any doubts or reservations should be expressed completely privately, one to one – which I did. For a government Chief Whip to resign as a consequence of disagreement on a matter of Cabinet policy is unknown . . . To my mind it is no exaggeration to say that the resignation of a government Chief Whip on a major issue of policy would be a mortal blow to the government. Certainly a Prime Minister could hardly survive it. For a Chief Whip to resign, particularly during a national crisis such as Suez, would be an act not only of utter disloyalty, but of wilful destruction.

'I thought that the situation did not call for or justify an act of such devastating disloyalty to the Prime Minister as my resignation would have been . . . A further consideration in my mind was that there might be a useful part for me, as Chief Whip, to play in rebuilding morale and self-confidence in the parliamentary party in the coming months. The crisis was bad enough already, and my task was to try and hold the party, and the government, together. If I could do that, I knew that the more sensible elements within it would be able to protect the party from complete disaster. So I just got on with doing my job.'

Michael Hughes-Young MC, MP for Wandsworth Central 1955–1964 – who served as a government whip between 1956–1964 and later became Lord St Helens – talked about Heath as chief whip some years later:

> 'Ted would chew a subject over and over and over again, not saying much himself. I would guess he loathed having to make his mind up on his own. He took the most extraordinary amount of trouble over things and people – over anybody or anything . . . Where he was frightfully good was after Suez, when Anthony went off to the West Indies . . . Ted had immense influence then. Ted was the chief of staff. The party would almost certainly have fallen apart but for him. He was immensely approachable to the back-benchers, reassuring. In a different way he was very good vis-à-vis Ministers. He was the one very tangible link between the party and the Government.'[11]

Subsequent events arguably vindicated Heath's decision, in terms of party management at least; and Anthony Eden was certainly grateful to him, writing in his memoirs: 'Though Mr Heath's service in Parliament had been short at that time, I have never known a better equipped Chief Whip. A ready smile concealed a firm mind.'[12] Heath had long admired – and also been close to – Eden's eventual successor, Harold Macmillan; and it was he whom Macmillan chose as a dining partner on the evening of the succession, gleefully telling reporters, as they left the Turf Club after an agreeable dinner, that they had simply been discussing 'the future'. Heath was now serving under a third leader in succession who had played a role in inspiring him to join the Conservative Party – and who had also encouraged and nurtured his talents. Heath spent two more years running the Whips' Office, as Macmillan steadied both the party and the ship of state; and he continued to flourish. Memories of Suez lingered, but economic development began to have an impact on the people of Britain; and not before time.

At the beginning of 1959, it was reported that Heath was suffering from gastroenteritis. He was extremely physically robust and proud of his stamina, right into his seventies, so the public announcement of an illness must have grieved him considerably. In fact, what he had contracted was jaundice – hepatitis. He could drink no alcohol for six months – and celebrated the end of the ordeal with champagne, which remained a firm favourite. He recovered in good time to play his part in securing Macmillan's triumph in the general election on 8 October. In a clear signal that he was set to emerge from the cloistered obscurity of the Whips' Office, Heath played a role in the national campaign, speaking in support of colleagues in seats more marginal than his own. Consequently, arrangements had to be made to ensure Bexley was not neglected, as **John MacGregor** recalls:

'My mother took a telephone call one morning from Central Office. Mr Heath wanted to "look after his ladies" in Bexley at the general election. I jumped at the chance and went to No. 12 Downing Street to talk it over with Ted. I was very impressed by watching Ted addressing big audiences in Bexley – a hundred at least – and answering questions, all off the cuff. He knew everything that was going on in the constituency. He was very convivial there and he would deal with endless notes from Rosemary Bushe, his constituency secretary. He ran a very active door-to-door operation and he wanted me to handle that. He then introduced me to his other secretary, Jean Dungey, and told me "You'll be seeing a lot of each other". He was right. There was a film we wanted to see together and, very sweetly, Ted told us both that we should take some time off and drove us to the cinema himself. We are still married and owe him a great debt.'

After that victory, Heath was at last granted the front-line role he craved, as Minister of Labour, in those days a senior cabinet position. He informed Macmillan he wanted a full term in the post and rapidly set about pioneering the kind of high-level interaction and cooperation between the 'two sides of industry' that he had seen work to such good effect in continental Europe, most notably West Germany. Critics would subsequently say this was the first manifestation of his 'corporatist tendencies'. Kinder historians might argue he was ahead of his time. He had success in averting a strike on the railways, oversaw the end of National Service and established a good relationship with many trade unionists, including Victor Feather, but he was not destined to have the full term he sought.

In the reshuffle in spring 1960, Macmillan appointed Alec Home – then in the Lords – as Foreign Secretary, which necessitated appointing a senior figure to handle foreign affairs in the elected chamber. Heath became Lord Privy Seal at the Foreign Office. He had wide-ranging responsibilities in the post, but Macmillan had one particular, historic task in mind for him – a task that would change the destiny of the nation, as well as dominate Heath's life and shape his reputation for all time and also, over a period of decades, open up and entrench a bitter rift in the Conservative Party.

Great Britain had played a full part in the establishment of the European Free Trade Area (EFTA), a free-trade organisation open to European nations with qualms about signing up to the 'ever-closer union' in the Treaty of Rome – the foundation document of the then European Economic Community (EEC). There were feelings of loyalty across parties to our partners in EFTA, but they were as nothing compared to the political support for the so-called 'white Commonwealth'. Although opinion within the Conservative Party was moving strongly and decisively towards Britain finding its place within an expanded EEC, there was an almost universal view that this should be allowed to happen only if the Commonwealth could be protected – in particular so-called 'Commonwealth Preference', the favourable terms upon which the nation used to trade with Commonwealth nations.

Geoffrey Adams was Heath's private secretary when he became Lord Privy Seal in 1960, taking over from John Profumo, who was promoted to become Secretary of State for War:

'Jack Profumo was a smooth operator, who relied on getting his way by exercising large quantities of charm (and, occasionally, with the help of a visit to the office of his glamorous wife, the actress Valerie Hobson). Ted was no less forceful a personality, but expected to win arguments through rational discussion of the options. He could generally be counted on to follow the advice of his officials, which made working for him relatively stress-free.

'When things went wrong, a rebuke could (naturally) be expected, but usually delivered calmly, if firmly. I remember one occasion, early on in his incumbency, when I was required to organise a rail journey for him to attend the 1960 Conservative Party Conference, in Scarborough. I obtained the tickets and made a reservation in first class, only to discover, too late, that Cabinet Ministers travelling by train were entitled to a complete compartment (when such things existed) to themselves. We in his office were not used to dealing with Cabinet Ministers and no-one had briefed us appropriately. Although I was duly chastised, I do not recall the incident having any lasting ill-effects when I had to visit Scarborough myself later in the week with a Ministerial red box.

'Ted's principal task was to be conducting the first set of negotiations for Britain's entry into the Common Market (subsequently vetoed by General de Gaulle). His remit accordingly covered the whole of Europe. The only overseas visit on which I accompanied him was to Paris for a meeting of the Western European Union in November 1960. We flew over the evening before, fortified by BEA's champagne ("we should do this more often," he suggested) and were accommodated at the Embassy. The following morning there was no sign of him when I reckoned we should be leaving for the meeting. I eventually found him still in bed, surrounded by the English newspapers and the remains of his breakfast. We somehow made it to the conference in reasonable time, but I do recall him being quite relaxed about time-keeping.'

Alec Home and Heath were soon engaged in a considerable amount of preparatory work with the governments of 'the Six' – as the founding members of the EEC were known. Chancellor Adenauer of Germany was particularly supportive of the British aspiration to join the EEC, but from the outset it was evident French President Charles de Gaulle was going to be the problem. On 17 May 1961, **Heath** reported to the House of Commons on the progress made to date. He radiated optimism about the prospects for the UK being accepted into full membership of the still relatively new EEC:

'One of the major political achievements of the Six has been to create a Franco–German rapprochement which is invaluable. Our presence would undoubtedly consolidate this and contribute towards the balanced development of the Community. These, then, are most powerful reasons why we should use all our strength and energy to find a solution to the problem of a closer relationship between ourselves and our partners and the European Economic Community. It is against these political factors that we should place the very real difficulties of finding a solution in the economic and commercial field.

'Above all, I think that the technical and commercial matters I have mentioned must be . . . set in the context of the unity of Europe and the contribution they can make towards the freedom of Europe, of the unity and freedom on which peace depends.'[13]

This speech was followed by a punchy contribution from Denis Healey, who criticised Heath and the Government generally both for a lack of clarity so far as policy towards the Treaty of Rome was concerned – and also for dwelling on the subject to so pronounced a degree. It is extraordinary to be reminded just how pro-EEC the leadership of the Conservative Party was becoming – and how lukewarm or even hostile Labour would be, from the mid-1940s until the mid-1980s. Nonetheless, Government papers reveal just how precarious the situation did become at times. In the summer of 1961, Heath's successor as chief whip, Martin Redmayne, was strongly urging caution; and **officials at the Foreign Office** (on 5 July 1961) warned that the French were spoiling for a fight:

'General de Gaulle . . . believes that if, improbably, the UK did apply to join the EEC, it would be difficult to fit her in to it, because of the difference between her national and imperial traditions and that of the other member states. On the other hand, General de Gaulle does want the UK, still at the centre of her Commonwealth, to be associated in some way with the achievement of his primary objective, which is to build a West European confederation under French influence, strong enough to pursue a world-wide policy largely independent of the vagaries of American policy, and, if need be, to stand up against Soviet pressure with only intermittent American support. The more distressed he becomes by manifestations of American "immaturity" the more anxious he is to secure British cooperation and consequently the more ready he is to contemplate British membership of the EEC, if this is the only way in which it can be secured . . . The most unexpected advocates of British accession are the federalists led by M Monnet . . . [who] believes that although British participation might alter the character of the European Community, the UK, once in, would want to make a success of it and would be a positive element. He probably overestimates the extent to which his own federalist ideas might take root here . . . We have to remember the element of arrogance in General de Gaulle himself: there is nothing to be lost and something possibly to be gained by giving him advance warning of our decision to apply for membership, as long as we confine ourselves to telling him what we propose to do and do not invite him to declare his attitude in advance.'[14]

Macmillan decided it was time for formal negotiations to begin and 'Grocer' Heath – the man who impressed and depressed simultaneously with his grasp of the details – was born.

Over a year of hard negotiating began. Heath was supported by the so-called 'Flying Knights' – senior officials Sir Eric Roll and Sir Pierson Dixon – as he sought to grind away opposition to British accession, both at home and also amongst sceptics in the Six. Publicly as well as privately, **Heath** sought to reassure prospective European partners that the application was being made with serious and constructive intent, for instance in an important address to Ministers from the Six in Paris on 10 October 1961, given just as the negotiations began:

'We shall be anxious, once we are members of the Community, to work with you in a positive spirit to reinforce the unity which you have already achieved . . . The British Government and the British people have been through a searching debate during the last few years on the subject of their relations with Europe . . . In saying that we wish to join the E.E.C., we mean that we desire to become full, whole-hearted and active members of the European Community in its widest sense and to go forward with you in the building of a new Europe. . . In a world where political and economic power is becoming concentrated to such a great extent, a larger European unity has become essential. Faced with the threats which we can all see, Europe must unite or perish. The United Kingdom, being part of Europe, must not stand aside.'

Just two days later, **Heath** was at the Conservative party conference in Brighton, as delegates debated 'The European Common Market and the

Commonwealth'. Although in much of his speech he sought to reassure delegates about the position of the Commonwealth, on the subject of sovereignty and the political aspects of the EEC he did not mince his words:

> 'We have to form a judgment on events in the future, for the next 15 years or 25 years or 50 years, in order to judge correctly how to form our path . . . If the final decision is not to enter Europe, it will be impossible to reverse that decision for many, many years to come . . .The best way to maintain our freedom and independence . . . is, in fact, in unity with other countries in a free Western world . . . This group of nations in Europe is going to have a great influence on political affairs . . . I am not one who has an inferiority complex about our ability to influence the Community when we play our full part in it. Our voice will be heard and our voice will be welcomed . . . In every international organisation to which we belong we have given up a degree of sovereignty . . . We are going to these negotiations in a genuine attempt to reach agreement over suitable arrangements for our Commonwealth, our agriculture and our EFTA partners . . . Let us go into them with your backing, to achieve success.'

The policy of Her Majesty's Government received an overwhelming endorsement from the rank and file. Three months later, on 21 January 1962, **Heath** drafted a magisterial, fourteen-page, Top Secret note to the Prime Minister. It was deeply personal and revealed his steely determination to do everything he possibly could to bring the intricate negotiations to a successful conclusion, outflanking and out-arguing the French, without ever seeking to isolate or humiliate them:

> 'The British Delegation feels frustrated at the leisurely pace of the negotiations so far. . . . I detect myself a growing feeling among the other Delegations in the EEC that, after a bold start in Paris, we have not in fact pressed our case as hard as they had expected . . . I also believe that these other Delegations looked forward to our presence at the negotiating table because they had expected us to be able to do what none of them had successfully done, namely to be able to stand up to the French and to

outwit and outmanoeuvre them. They are beginning to feel disappointed in us in this respect . . . We . . . suspect the EEC, and the French in particular, of wanting to carry on the process of negotiating by watering down our proposals, by exacting concessions without reciprocating them, and by making the UK fit into a Community of the Six rather than by co-operating in the creation of an enlarged Community of Ten . . . Taking the negotiations as a whole, my general conclusion is that our object should be both to speed them up and to bring the greatest possible pressure to bear on the EEC. We should do this . . . by being firmly and persistently but politely aggressive . . .'[15]

Whilst **Heath** remained hopeful and his remarkable energies never dipped, he had become aware of a difference in outlook between the UK and even the more favourably inclined nations of the Six:

'It has now become clear that we and the Six approach these negotiations from two basically differing standpoints. The Six are expecting the UK and other applicants to adapt themselves to fit into the pattern of the already existing Community of Six. We on the other hand are approaching the negotiations with a view to arranging appropriate alterations to the existing framework which would suit the enlarged Community. The Six have so far shown themselves to be rigid in their position and in order to make any progress it is we who have had to make all the concessions to break the log jam. If the negotiations are to succeed it will be necessary at some point to have this out with the Six and make it clear that some concessions must come also from their side.'

In late February 1962 there was talk of a 'grand remonstrance' – and possibly a daunting month of continuous negotiations. **Heath** again wrote confidentially to senior colleagues, in terms that still carry formidable power and relevance today, especially in the year of a hotly contested referendum on the UK's membership of the European Union:

'On the continent of Europe support for the idea of European integration comes from all sections of political opinion – except the two extremes. In several countries it has been the principal bond between the parties of the centre: and it has been a sufficiently effective bond to ensure that the great divide in politics has come not down the middle, but on either side of the centre.

'There are widespread misconceptions on the political obligations which we would have to accept if we join the EEC. Many people suppose that we should be entering a federal super state in which our national sovereignty would be swallowed up and which would result even in the disappearance of the British monarchy. These misconceptions thrive because of uncertainty as to the exact political content of the European communities . . . The Treaty of Rome has no political provisions, though an eventual political objective is implicit. In the absence of any explicit definition of political aims it is probable that in the course of time the process of economic integration would have led to a corresponding process of political integration along the same lines.

'Before this political process could begin, however, the French Government, which combines an extreme jealousness of its national sovereignty with a desire to create a powerful European grouping, came forward with proposals for a separate political organisation to complement the existing economic organisations.'

One French proposal now was to institute regular meetings of Heads of Government to discuss foreign affairs – with all and any binding decisions to be taken only by unanimity. This was an early iteration of what would later become the so-called 'Foreign Affairs Pillar' of the European Union. In light of the seeming guarantee for a national veto, **Heath** felt able to write:

'There is nothing here to cause us any misgivings . . . It is true that when General de Gaulle disappears from the scene the pressures in Europe to advance towards federalism will build up again. But if we are members by that time we can effectively prevent this advance if we want to do so . . . In short a European Political Treaty gives us a guarantee that the processes of economic integration contained in the Treaty of Rome cannot drag us into a federalist super state against our will.'

On 10 April 1962, **Heath** was in reassuring and expansive mood when he addressed the Ministerial Council of the Western European Union in London:

'You yourselves have decided that those who want to join the Economic Communities as full members must also join the Political Union. I am sure that this was the right decision. If this European Union is going to achieve the great things which we confidently expect of it, then, in our view, it must be political as well as economic. As members we should want to strengthen its political development . . . We have all along recognised that the Treaties of Rome and Paris had a political as well as an economic objective. It therefore came as no surprise to us when the six Governments, having successfully established the foundations of their economic co-operation, began to consider how they could develop and define the conditions for closer political unity . . . We are looking forward to joining you as soon as possible in constructing a Europe united politically as well as economically.'

This speech – amongst many others of a similar tenor, all made publicly and on the record – makes a total nonsense of claims that Heath played a leading part – or even the leading part – in a conspiracy to conceal, or even understate, the political significance of joining the EEC. If anything, he was a cheerleader from the outset for the concept of political integration. In his speech to the party conference in Llandudno on 11 October 1962, **Heath** adumbrated themes that would remain close to his heart and to his thinking until his dying day:

'We have seen two great groups develop since the end of the last war – the United States, the Soviet Union. Now a third group, of the countries of Europe, is growing stronger – economically stronger, and with that a political cohesion [is] developing . . . What is our attitude? It is that we welcome these developments in Europe. We welcome the abolition of old rivalries . . . Europe is incomplete without Britain and we in Britain are incomplete without Europe. Therefore we wish to play our full part in this great development . . . Never at any time have we hidden the fact that these political issues loom foremost in these decisions . . . If we are going to face up to the fundamental problem of the political relationship of Britain with Europe, we must also face up to these other questions being openly discussed of the use of sovereignty and the best use to which we can devote it in the modern world . . . We are not being asked to go into a Federation, but we . . . want to play our part in devising these new arrangements in Europe itself to give us yet greater political cohesion.'

By the end of 1962, however, even Heath was struggling to remain positive. Every indication was that, despite the months of gruelling negotiation – and the remarkable consensus that had been established between the British Government and its equivalents in West Germany, Italy and the Benelux countries (or, as Heath would argue subsequently, precisely because of that consensus, which threatened French hegemony in Western Europe) – France almost certainly intended to veto British accession on any terms. Macmillan's burgeoning (and somewhat surprising) relationship of warmth and trust with President Kennedy was not helping matters. Successive summits at Rambouillet and then Nassau left de Gaulle with a grievance, persuading him that the task of weaning the British off their preferential (and, as he saw it, deferential) relationship with the US and turning them towards Europe was all but impossible. These manoeuvres served only to foster even greater French paranoia about the supposed dominance of the Anglo-Saxon nations – and **Macmillan** wrote a private note to Heath on Boxing Day 1962:

> 'I only trust nothing I have done at Rambouillet or Nassau has increased your difficulties. My impression of de Gaulle is that he is friendly to me personally, not unfriendly to Britain (always remembering the insults which he conceives were put upon him by Churchill during the war), wants friendly relations with Britain, but does not want us now in the Community because he is in a mood of sulks about the future of Europe politically and would like to stay where he is with France dominating the Five.'[16]

Macmillan's sense of foreboding was not misplaced. In January 1963, de Gaulle did indeed veto British accession to the EEC. For **Heath** this was a bitter reverse and one he found hard to forgive. He wrote warm letters to senior figures in the other five national governments of the Six, demonstrating that, for him at least, this was definitely unfinished business:

'It is difficult to express one's feelings on occasions such as this . . . but I wanted to say that I am very conscious of the special debt of gratitude which we owe you for everything you have done over the long months of the negotiations . . . I need hardly add that we do not regard the suspension of the negotiations as the final word. We shall do everything we can to continue our work for true European unity.'

On 4 February 1963, **Sir Evelyn Shuckburgh**, who headed the UK delegation to NATO, sent Heath a veritable paean of praise for his Herculean efforts:

'Of course there are a good many consolations and I may say that the greatest of all to my mind is the fact that you personally have emerged from the whole affair with such a tremendous reputation and, indeed, with a position in Europe and at home which is in many ways unique . . . It means that you will be able to continue with full power and effect to press the policies in which you believe. All of us who think it necessary for Britain to get closer to Europe pin our hopes on you . . . There is little doubt that de Gaulle is determined on bolder strokes still and that keeping Britain out of the Common Market was a necessary part of his main programme. This probably involves . . . getting the Americans out of Europe . . . with a view to a deal with the Soviet Union . . . The only thing to do is to oppose [these ambitions] and, as we did over the Common Market, mobilise all the contrary forces that are available to thwart and contradict this megalomaniac idea.'

Heath scrawled across the top of this missive just three words: 'an excellent letter'. A considered account of Heath's performance during those negotiations came two decades later from **Eric Roll**:

'Heath proved to be an outstanding leader. He combined in a unique way the qualities of a first-rate official having complete mastery of complex technical details with the necessary political touch in his contacts with Ministers and officials of other countries, with the press, and with London. He was the sort of Minister British senior civil servants particularly admire and like to work with, always ready to listen to advice yet quite clear in the end as to what ought to be said and done.

'Heath was equally good in small encounters, often over lunch or dinner, with one or two of the other delegations as he was in larger, more formal meetings, including the plenary ones . . . He is, to be sure, a very reserved man, but he is entirely capable of the warmest and friendliest feelings and of great personal kindnesses. He is also quite capable of losing his temper, though in my experience this was more likely to happen with his own ministerial colleagues than with officials . . . As far as the delegation itself was concerned, any internal differences of opinion that appeared as the negotiations progressed were due to the difficulty of the situation itself and to the problem of keeping closely in step with Ministers in London but in no way to clashes with the leader who won his team's complete respect and affection.'[17]

No one blamed Heath for the de Gaulle veto, though his diplomacy did fail him once, when he likened de Gaulle's petulant outbursts to '*cris de perro-quet*'. Although Heath was enhancing his reputation both inside and outside Parliament, when Harold Macmillan succumbed to anxieties about his health in autumn 1963 and announced he was calling time on his premiership, it was still, just, too soon for him to put himself forward as a compelling candidate for the leadership. It was therefore very much in his interest that someone from an older generation, rather than one of his contemporaries, should 'emerge' to succeed his mentor. This 'young cardinal' was strongly in favour of an 'old Pope'.

Patrick Jenkin (Lord Jenkin of Roding) was born in 1926 and became an active Conservative in his early twenties, joining the Bow Group in 1951. He was first elected to Parliament in 1964, for Winston Churchill's former seat of Woodford. He recalls a turbulent time in the history of the Conservative Party:

'Even with his now impressive record, Ted was not yet seen as a credible future leader of the Party . . . I was not yet an MP, but I was at the Party

Conference in Blackpool . . . and well remember the turmoil about who should take Macmillan's place if he had to resign; it absolutely dominated the Conference. RA Butler ("RAB"), Deputy Prime Minister, was assumed by many to be the natural successor and he had many supporters.

'What was not generally known then was that Macmillan was determined that RAB must definitely not succeed; or that, even from his sick-bed in King Edward VII Hospital, he was plotting to ensure he got his way. The other potential candidates were Lord Hailsham and Reggie Maudling, with a couple of outsiders, Iain Macleod and Ted Heath. Butler had to deputise for the Leader's speech, and made a very uninspiring speech. Hailsham destroyed his own chances by unashamedly engaging in populist propaganda on his own behalf; and Maudling made a very lacklustre speech which ruled him out in the minds of many people.

'Macleod realised that his earlier controversial spell as Colonial Secretary had made him pretty unpopular with many on the right wing of the Party – Lord Salisbury's jibe "Too clever by half!" had stuck. I was quite close to Iain at that time, and I and others begged him to see that he would be the right man to lead the Party into the next election, due in 1964. Curiously, Ted Heath's name was scarcely being mentioned; indeed, at that stage he does not appear even to have been involved in any of the informal meetings of the candidates.

'At the outset, Lord Home had firmly declined to put himself forward as a candidate, but, as support for the other candidates fell and the pressure for him to lead the Party grew, he began to be persuaded that he should reconsider. At the 1963 Conference, I have a very clear recollection of senior MPs going round telling anyone who would listen: "It's got to be Alec, it's got to be Alec!"

'Once Macmillan realised Lord Home was the only serious candidate who could unite the Party, he announced his resignation; and, when Her Majesty the Queen visited him in hospital, he duly advised her to send for Lord Home. When Alec Home was summoned to the Palace, he made it clear that, if appointed, he would disclaim his peerage and, as Sir Alec Douglas-Home, fight a by-election. After consultations, he was able to assure Her Majesty that he would, if appointed, be able to form a Government, so he kissed hands and became party leader and Prime Minister.

'The appointment of a major Scottish landowner and patrician was very controversial. Indeed, several Cabinet Ministers had already announced that they would be unable to serve under Sir Alec Douglas-Home's leadership and resigned. This included Macleod and Enoch Powell. Heath had of course considered whether he should join them but, wisely, put loyalty to the Party before his personal views. Macleod later realised that his resignation was a grave mistake; it effectively ended his chance of ever becoming leader.'

When Alec Home replaced Harold Macmillan as Prime Minister, he naturally wanted his own team around him. Heath had supported Home in the poll of ministers taken by the Lord Chancellor, Lord Dilhorne; and his reward came in the shape of one of the longest titles in government, as Secretary of State for Industry, Trade and Regional Development and President of the Board of Trade. So far as regional development was concerned, **Heath** explained his philosophy in an article in January 1965 for the *Crossbow* magazine:

'To develop the resources of a region whilst maintaining its own characteristics; second, to secure a more even spread of the economy over the whole country in order to enable it to operate at a higher level without strain in any particular area; third, to create a way of life appropriate to each region so that those born there would prefer to work and live there rather than emigrate, and others would be prepared to go there with their families, build up their businesses, and spend their lives there.'

It was not for regional policy that his tenure was noteworthy, however, but for his doggedness as a self-styled 'moderniser' in driving through the abolition of Resale Price Maintenance (RPM), a practice in which a manufacturer could fix the price at which goods could be resold, preventing larger or more efficient retailers from undercutting more expensive (and usually smaller) rivals. This system was estimated to cover as much as 40 per cent of consumer expenditure on goods. There was widespread resistance to abolition of RPM and small shopkeepers – often regarded as the backbone of Tory support in the country – were in uproar. The party machine, already nervous with an election approaching, actively discouraged him from pursuing the reform, as did many faint hearts around the Cabinet table, but Heath's nerve held steady, as did support from the new Prime Minister. George Hutchinson, then in charge of the party's publicity, later wrote: 'I have never myself heard a Cabinet Minister so much abused by his colleagues, so badly spoken of and so widely condemned in the party.'[18]

In the autumn of 1963, Heath flew to Scotland, accompanied by his Parliamentary Private Secretary, **Anthony Kershaw**, the MP for Stroud – and told him about his plan to abolish RPM:

'I said, "It's fine, but there'll be a hell of a row." He wouldn't reply to that sort of observation – he never would, he just docketed it away in his mind. Then he worked on it and didn't give an inch. The document I saw in the aeroplane two or three months before it was introduced was substantially the law which he backed through. He wouldn't take anything from the Cabinet or anyone. He takes a long time to make [his mind] up and he talks to an awful lot of people, but after he's made it up you might as well talk to yourself.'[19]

In the same interview, **Kershaw** made the following, highly insightful, remarks about Heath:

'We had some quarrels about his lateness. One gets the impression he's not always alert to what's going on about him. On the contrary, he's got an extraordinarily quick eye. I remember one day he had his hair cut in a slightly different way. I looked him up and down as usual and turned away slightly – and he said, "Too short?" I didn't think I had given anything away at all. He's got an unsettling habit of reading and signing letters while he talks to you, and you can't believe that he's concentrating on what you're saying: yet he is really doing the two things at the same time. It's an amazing trick . . .'[20]

In his opening speech at Second Reading, **Heath** presented the abolition of RPM as part of a wider, modern Conservative approach to economic philosophy, grounded in rigour and free enterprise. He also made it very plain that this was the agreed policy of the entire Government, not just a quixotic, personal campaign:

'If we are to obtain a sustained and steady rate of growth, undoubtedly we must make the most efficient use of all our resources. This, in my view and the view of the Government, can best be obtained by increasing competition over a wide field. This is why it is essential now, at a time of expanding economy where the level of incomes is all-important and where industry should be cost-conscious, that prices need to be kept down.

'The Government have given very careful consideration to this matter and have decided, in the context of modernisation and the essential development of a competitive economy, that the arguments in favour of ending resale price maintenance, with the safeguards set out in the Bill, are conclusive. At a time when our effort is being devoted to getting goods to the ultimate purchaser as economically and as cheaply as possible, how can we continue to sanction a system under which a man can be taken to court for lowering his prices?

'I know that many of the anxieties about the Bill centre on the small trader, and I . . . regard these fears to be exaggerated. The experience in other countries has shown this to be so. The small retailer, because of his characteristics, is an essential part of the distributive system – indeed, more than that, he is an integral part of our national life. There have been times in the past when people have said that the small trader was going under – it happened when the multiples came into the retail distributive trade. But it has never happened . . . and it will not happen now. The reason is that the efficient small shopkeeper is flexible, and adapts himself to the needs of the consumer. As a result, he prospers, and deserves to do so.'[21]

In one division, the Government's majority fell to just a single vote. Heath was unmoved and as far from panic as a recumbent statue. He merely quoted Churchill: 'One vote is enough.' Despite all the uproar, the Bill made it onto the statute book as a market liberalisation measure of some note. 'After the RPM fight he was emotionally exhausted,' Madron Seligman later recalled. 'You can see it from a photograph: his eyes are all screwed up. But he said that three or four Presidents of the Board of Trade had funked it and it had to be done.'[22] **Patrick Jenkin** believes Heath's hard-won victory over RPM consolidated his reputation as a moderniser in Tory ranks:

> 'Heath was convinced that this modernisation measure was essential to strengthen retail competition in the interest of consumers. So, despite the fierce opposition, he persuaded Parliament to pass the Bill. MPs and the wider public recognised his determination to achieve his objectives, and the wisdom of his policy; nobody has ever sought to reverse it.'

Heath had held Bexley by over 8,000 votes in 1959, but he knew things would be tighter in the forthcoming election, for no one could be wholly immune to the national tide, which was clearly away from the Tories and towards Labour. He therefore supplemented his team, bringing in two ambitious young Tories to 'hold the fort' for him when necessary. One happened to be the grandson of his hero and mentor Sir Winston Churchill – 'Young Winston', who went on to be MP for Daveyhulme in Greater Manchester. The other was **Hugh Dykes**, now Lord Dykes:

> 'I recall going down to Bexley for Ted Heath to show me around and was much amused by his rather scathing comments about some of the local people he pointed out to me in the distance. . . I did the mundane side of the constituency visiting programme whereas Winston was more elusive and metropolitan, I noticed. Every day Ted Heath could get down to the seat for the campaign, where we had a team parading around visiting the usual places from residential streets to institutions and shopping areas, with Ted at the front. He was very impatient if there were any delays, partly as he had to go back to London regularly as Secretary of State.
>
> 'I recall once he was annoyed at being delayed by awkward members of the public as he spluttered to me, "Come on, Hugh, this isn't a Sunday School outing!" I also did a number of warm-up speeches if Ted was delayed or late. These were clumsy and inept, but he was always extremely generous in praising me and thanking me afterwards which made me feel very guilty. Although Ted was a shy personality, when meeting newcomers he was always very kind – and generous towards his staffers, so far as I could tell.'

On 15 October 1964, Heath retained Bexley by 4,589 votes but Labour, led by Harold Wilson, won nationally by just three seats and the Liberals, led by Jo Grimond, made their first net gains since before the Second World War. The general election was a shattering experience for the Conservative Party, but the defeat was not unalloyed bad news for Heath. He spent the weekend after the election with the Seligmans and, browsing around bookshops with them, he remarked, 'Isn't it lovely to be free?'[23] Within a week he was a director, as well as a substantial shareholder, at Brown, Shipley; he would soon be lunching in the City most weekdays and he evidently 'put in a shift' for the bank. Alec Home put Heath in charge of policy and asked him to put together and then lead a dynamic, new shadow treasury team. It was in the latter role that Heath excelled and established himself as a credible candidate for leader.

Michael Heseltine was not yet in the House of Commons, but he soon would be; and he was developing a very clear idea of where the future for the party lay:

'The emergence of Alec Douglas Home, I felt, failed to capture the changing conditions of the time. For the previous couple of years, as a member of the Bow Group and as a Conservative candidate in both 1959 and 1964, people like me were looking for a much more modern, technocratic leader. And I vividly remember, in that context, saying to my then fiancée Anne, you must come to this dinner at the Coningsby Club, where Ted Heath is speaking. This is the future of our party. Looking back, I think it's probably unrealistic to explain in social terms why one felt that, but his role in Britain's attempt to join the European Community seemed to reflect the very changed conditions in this country in the adjustments of the post-war world. There was nothing inherited about Ted Heath. He had come a long way, entirely on his own merits. There was no golden circlet or silver spoon – all of which had a positive message for people like me – and his views were very radical.'

David Howell had a traditional – if unusually impressive – CV by the time he became MP for Guildford in March 1966. After taking a First at Cambridge he worked briefly at HM Treasury, then worked as a journalist and became chairman of the Bow Group. He was Director of the Conservative Political Centre from 1964 until 1966:

'After the 1964 Election, although the much underrated Sir Alec Douglas-Home had lost only narrowly, the Conservative leadership clearly had to change and Sir Alec had anyway had enough. Harold Wilson with his promise of a revolution spurred by "the white heat of technology" was raising the stakes and another election plainly lay not far ahead. The Conservatives, in unfamiliar opposition, also wanted change. We *all* wanted change and Heath was clearly the coming man – or in practice not quite so clearly since there was the genial, clever Reggie Maudling waiting just there on the side lines as well.

'Because Wilson and Labour had won so narrowly, we all knew another election could come at any time. Alec gave Ted Heath responsibility for policy development and Ted rang (while I was in the bath) and asked me to go with him to Alec's home, the Hirsel, for an overnight visit to receive various papers from the defeated leader and discuss strategy and policy for a possibly imminent election. The expedition was much publicised, with photographers both at Euston as we climbed into our sleepers and also at Edinburgh Waverley as we decanted, slightly dishevelled, early the next morning. Sir Alec came to meet us and drive us home.

'I have described elsewhere this rather odd occasion, at which, to my certain knowledge, nothing in the way of strategy or policy was in fact discussed; and how, when it came to running through all those papers, Ted immediately dozed off (as was his habit) while Sir Alec was trying to hand him documents. I had to reach over and take them. A front-page photo in the *Sunday Times* almost captured the precise moment. Ted then asked me to write up the conclusions from this most non-conclusive meeting, which I did with gusto. Such opportunities are gold for advisers, who can, of course, put down anything they like in pursuance of their favourite causes, of which I had plenty.'

Patrick Jenkin became an MP for the first time at the 1964 election. He watched from the ringside as the party leadership tried to restore morale:

'Wilson appointed Jim Callaghan as Chancellor and Sir Alec decided that he needed a new face as Shadow Chancellor. Ted Heath got the job. Labour had come into office committed to major tax reforms: the reform of Corporation Tax involving a new Profits Tax on Companies, plus a further tax on dividends, which is to say, the double taxation of distributed corporate profits; a harsh new system of taxing 'Close Companies' (small unquoted companies), which were to be taxed as if they were individuals, making them liable to steeply graduated tax rates; and much higher rates of income tax, including treating married couples as 'common spending units'. All this was in Callaghan's first Finance Bill in 1965.

'It fell to Ted Heath to lead the battle against the Bill and, with the whole Committee Stage taken on the floor of the House as was then the convention, he was on his feet day after day, and night after night, leading the Opposition's fight to secure amendments. I, though a new back-bencher, took a full part in these debates with the advantage that, while we all had started from scratch to learn the details of Labour's new taxes, I had spent some time in tax chambers at the Bar and was familiar with the legal jargon of the tax system.

'Ted Heath had been in his element throughout this long, debilitating battle: already known as a man for mastering detail, his skill and determination in debate attracted much admiration. Though the frequent votes were almost all lost, Conservative back-benchers realised that here was a man who, in debate, could dominate the House of Commons. In my view, it was this battle that led to his being seen as a potential future leader.'

Heath did indeed assemble a formidable team to contest Labour's Finance Bill at every possible step of the way and, given the Government's precarious majority in low, single figures, the chances of causing mayhem were promising. Amongst the established and future 'big names' involved in this effort were the likes of Keith Joseph, Tony Barber, Martin Redmayne, Peter Walker and Edward Boyle. Heath's group met on a daily basis, whenever the Finance Bill was in play, either for breakfast at Heath's home in the Albany apartment complex in Piccadilly or else in Westminster. Their stamina would be tested as much as their intellectual capacity. After ten heavy sessions in May and early June, Heath took a break in France and returned fully recharged, with renewed energy for the struggle. One of the specialists supporting his important and demanding work was the young accountant and tax expert **John Cope** (later Lord Cope of Berkeley):

'Ted Heath recruited a large team of MPs to help him deal with the Bill. Each was given a section of the Bill to study, consult and speak on. A selection of advisers from the Law, Accountancy and so on fed advice in to the team. He masterminded the whole team brilliantly. He worked all hours and was on top of the detail and intervened whenever necessary. Mark Schreiber, now Lord Marlesford, and I acted as secretaries to the team with support from other colleagues in CRD [the Conservative Research Department], particularly Tony Newton, later Lord Newton of Braintree, who was Head of the Economic Section.

'The Bill was debated in full for three and four days a week over five weeks in May and June in Committee of the Whole House as was then the rule for Finance Bills. It was "exempted business" not subject to the normal 10 pm cut-off and the debates went to midnight and sometimes to 3, 4 or 5 am night after night. It was a hot summer and the debates were often highly technical. Ted Heath drove it all personally whatever the hour and then chaired meetings of advisers from 8 am.

'Then in July the Report Stage took another five days until the small hours. One night an ambush was carefully planned by Ted Heath with all his old Chief Whip's skills. Conservative MPs were invited to dinner in groups nearby and once at dinner were told the plan. The chamber was empty and some Labour MPs had drifted away. Then at 1 o'clock a vote was called, all the pent up Conservatives arrived at once and the Government was defeated three times over the rate of Capital Gains Tax for Unit and Investment Trusts. That change was later accepted by the Government as were many other points. In all the Government amended its own Bill 440 times including rewriting whole sections. That showed the folly of trying to undertake major tax changes without careful planning and consultation, as well as the effectiveness of the Opposition.

'My experience of working closely for Ted Heath at that time made me realise his exceptional intellectual energy, stamina and powers of sustained concentration. I later realised that this applied to everything he did. Music and sailing were not just hobbies. He relaxed by studying them assiduously to a very high level. He was a very experienced and efficient organiser who got results. He could also be a considerate boss, although sometimes his concentration on the matter in hand meant that he forgot everything else. He was concerned to use every minute positively and was easily bored at functions.'

As Cope mentions, at the Report Stage of the Bill, in the small hours of Wednesday 7 July 1965, with support from the Liberals, Heath and his team delivered three successive victories over the Government on Unit and Investment Trusts, all in double figures. It was an ambush in a guerrilla war of attrition that could never bring ultimate victory, but the effect on an otherwise demoralised parliamentary party was remarkable. Heath enjoyed his triumph: 'The lesson for the Government is plain: it should resign and resign quickly!' In the end Heath and his eager young team managed to spin out the debate to 21 and a half days (211 hours), with six all-night sittings and 680 Conservative Opposition Amendments. Although Labour did 'get its Bill' in the end, Heath was now unquestionably a man to watch. Despite decent local election results in May 1965 Alec Home was widely regarded as a liability to his party, as **William Whitelaw**, the then chief whip, wrote in his memoirs: '[Tory MPs] continued to harp on the need for a younger man and, indeed, the more successful Ted Heath was in his conduct of the Finance Bill that summer, the more the critics felt that someone of his generation would be more suitable than Alec Douglas-Home as the Leader.'[24]

The more impact Heath made as shadow chancellor, the more he was baited by Labour MPs, who accused him of blatantly lining himself up for a leadership challenge. As journalist **Nora Beloff** wrote in early June: 'He has been bitterly hurt by incessant jibes from the Prime Minister and others that his every remark or joke is inspired by his secret aim to oust his leader . . . He has developed a loathing for Mr Wilson that goes far beyond the play-acting antagonisms normal in politics.'[25] Heath even went to see Alec Home in person, specifically to reassure him he remained loyal. Home never doubted him. Nora Beloff's remark about Heath's growing distaste for Harold Wilson was well observed and prescient. Wilson genuinely aggravated

Heath and seemed to possess all the easy self-confidence and populist flair that he himself lacked. Worse was soon to come.

Anthony Kershaw later recalled how scrupulously Heath conducted himself, despite all the speculation:

'He would never do anything underhand – this was terribly clear when Alec was elected leader of the party and a number of people declared themselves, or let it be known that they would be available. The one person who was in that category who didn't move or do anything at all was Ted.'[26]

As speculation over the leadership intensified, there were reports that an over-eager group of Heath's supporters, without his knowledge, had sought to destabilise Home, but there was never any clear evidence. No one ever suggested Heath was involved in any way. In the *Daily Mail*, **Walter Terry** expressed his fears that Heath might never truly win the party over:

'His charm, assisted at suitable moments by jelly-shaking laughter, is distilled by the cautious skill of his intellect. But is Mr Heath loved and adored in the constituencies? Maybe by some. One of his problems, politically, is his bachelordom: in logic it is absurd and in fairness it is outrageous, but many in the Conservative Party hesitate before giving their overwhelming support to an unmarried leader.'[27]

On 22 July 1965, just a fortnight after Heath's triumphs in the division lobbies, Alec Home informed the 1922 Committee that he had decided to step down as leader. Heath – far from plotting busily at Westminster – went to Glyndebourne, for a performance (perhaps appropriately) of Verdi's *Macbeth*.

Alec Home's legacy to the party included a new set of rules for the party's MPs to elect their leader, not by a clear majority of votes, but through a series of rounds with a notional requirement of a 15 per cent margin of victory. Willie Whitelaw was keen the contest should be clean – and quick. It was both: it was over in five days, without acrimony. There were three candidates. The assumed (albeit narrow) favourite was Reggie Maudling, with his wealth of experience and emollient style. Thought of as being to the right of him – and more inclined to stir up trouble, promote modernity and challenge vested interests – was Heath. In its editorial on the eve of the ballot, the *Daily Mail* would endorse him as 'the man for all our seasons'. Reassuringly for the party's grandees, most MPs were fairly happy about the thought of either of them as leader; neither man was particularly ideological or inclined to make enemies. On the margins, Enoch Powell also contested this election.

Michael Heseltine, still outside the Commons, but now an adopted candidate looking confidently forward to a long parliamentary career, was a frustrated onlooker in the contest that followed:

'I was candidate for a safe Tory seat at Tavistock and it was as sure as anything is in life that I would become a Member of Parliament within a matter of months. I undoubtedly broke all the social conventions, by ringing Sir Henry Studholme, the MP, and saying, as courteously as possible, "Look I know it's your job and not mine, but because I'm going to be there and you are not, I thought you might like to know my views." I don't think he was in the least bit interested in my views, to be honest, but nonetheless, I told him I thought Ted Heath would be the man. He didn't agree or disagree and the matter was left. I felt the need to ring, to convey that message.'

In 1965 Heath was widely regarded not as what one might today term 'Heathite', but as an energetic radical and moderniser and, compared with Reggie Maudling on the centre-left of the party, very much the candidate of its centre-right. His leadership campaign was a well-run, even slick, undertaking and with his characteristic attention to detail Heath put Robin Chichester-Clark in charge of winning votes from his Unionist colleagues from Northern Ireland, which he did with notable success, delivering a clear winning margin (8–3) for his man in a close contest overall. One of those Ulstermen was **Stratton Mills**, who had become Ulster Unionist MP for North Belfast in 1959, at the age of just twenty-seven, remaining in the Commons until he stood down in February 1974. He is one of the old breed of liberal unionists, who felt comfortable engaging fully with the British Conservative Party. He strongly backed Heath in 1965 and would, in due course, become a full-hearted supporter of power sharing in Northern Ireland:

'The leadership campaign lasted for less than a week and I recall the first meeting at Peter Walker's flat, with around fifteen of us in the room. Ted and Tony Barber had to climb in over the roof from the adjoining street, so no one saw them arriving. Peter had a list of all the Conservative and Unionist MPs who had a vote and he was going through that list. Heath would comment on each one individually as they were called out – "Not sure about him, but he is going to have a number of high-profile approaches in his constituency, which he won't know were instigated by me . . ." or "Can't remember why, but I fell out with him – total waste of time" or "So-and-so – who's close to him?". Each name was dissected by Heath, with Peter Walker writing up the notes. We foot soldiers were then given the task of getting in touch with certain people and hanging around in the lobby and the smoking rooms, picking up intelligence and passing it back to Peter Walker.'

Peter Walker's account of the leadership election is invaluable:

'When Home did resign, I asked Ted at once, "Are you running?" He replied: "Yes – and you must run my campaign." I accepted, but only if he agreed to listen to – and take – advice. "OK," he said, "so long as I agree with it!" Charlie Morrison, Ian Gilmour and I quickly set up an office at 12 Gayfere Street and installed a researcher there. Each solid pro-Heath member was sought out and asked to lobby his or her friends. There was an enormous amount of cross-checking, as people were canvassed and re-canvassed. Keith Joseph was canvassing for Ted and it was he who delivered Margaret Thatcher's vote for him. Ted had one-to-one meetings with all the doubtful.

'Reggie Maudling was ahead in the public polls, but I assured Ted he would win. Reggie's cause wasn't helped by some curious advisers – such as Lord Lambton and William Clark. Our prediction was dead-on for Ted's vote and we were two out as between Reggie and Powell. I let the Whips know Ted and I were at Gayfere Street and we waited for an hour and a half before Reggie conceded.'[28]

Heath received 150 votes to Maudling's 133 and Powell's 15. He had not, technically, won by a sufficient margin, but Maudling and Powell stepped aside and Heath became the youngest Tory leader since Disraeli. Liberal leader Jo Grimond, who had revived his party not so much on its deathbed as back off the undertaker's slab, severely damaging the Conservative vote between 1959 and 1964 and effectively giving Wilson his victory, publicly recognised that Heath might halt that revival in its tracks. A gnomic quotation from Charles de Gaulle was revived in the press, in which he forecast Heath supplanting Wilson as Prime Minister and bringing the UK triumphantly into the EEC. Party morale improved and it was perhaps Michael Heseltine who captured the moment most eloquently: 'Heath is like a gale of fresh air. Everyman is in charge now.'

During the brief leadership election campaign, Maudling had run slightly ahead of Heath in the public opinion polls, but Heath received rather more editorial support from the newspapers. After his victory, 'informed opinion' was that the party had chosen a path of radicalism and modernisation, in preference to the relatively laid-back style of Maudling. The first Gallup poll after Heath's coronation suggested that 66 per cent of voters thought the party had improved its chances of victory by choosing him as leader; only a nugatory 4 per cent thought its chances were now worse.[29] Maudling was no anti-European, but everyone knew Heath would work far harder to ensure the UK joined the EEC; he also had formidable pro-market credentials in the economic sphere after his battles over RPM.

Patrick Jenkin was one of the first generation of Tory MPs to have a vote in the election of their party leader:

'Ted Heath made history in at least two notable respects when he became leader of the Conservative Party. He was the first leader who was elected, rather than "emerging" from the counsels of the higher echelons of the Party; he was also the first leader to come from an ordinary, working-class background. The significance of this was not lost on the country – or the media. Here was, as the *Sunday Mirror* put it, "a new kind of Tory Leader – a classless, professional politician who has fought his way to the top with guts, ability and political skill". Heath was, moreover, unequivocally committed to the modernisation of both party and country; and to renewing the case for Britain joining the EEC.'

Contributions to this book from a wide range of Heath's associates have referred to the formidable carapace this shy and sensitive man developed, equipping him to go into public life without risking either his sanity or his physical health. It was given to few to find a way through that defensive shell – to wound Heath or even to wind him up. Harold Wilson was undoubtedly one of that small number. Early on in my time working for Heath, I saw in Salisbury a note to Heath from one of his staff at No. 10. Evidently, Heath, riled by the frequent references to Wilson's glittering academic record, had asked someone to obtain his own Finals results from Oxford and also those of Wilson. The comparison was not at all favourable and, there in his unmistakeable hand, was simply 'NFA' (No Further Action). How feeling it necessary to write those three letters must have hurt him. I often wondered what happened to that: I could not find it when I worked on Heath's memoirs some time later. Heath was equally jealous of Wilson's easy, pseudo-patrician manner and once said to me of Wilson's pipe, 'he never smoked the damned thing'. I think he did in fact smoke it, but that was hardly germane: it was an obvious part of the Wilson 'act' and that act, that *schtick*, endowed Wilson with the power to rile Heath, usually with minimal effort. Two days after Heath was elected leader, he opted not to speak in an opposition-led debate in which the Tories attacked Labour's alleged failure to honour election promises, but that did not inhibit **Wilson** from goading him with a line of attack that he knew would palpably hit:

> 'My first task, an agreeable one, is to compliment [Mr Heath] on his election as leader of his party. I am not going to inflict on him the traditional courtesy of saying that I hope he will be there a long time and have a long and happy life on that Bench. We always say this on these occasions. I am sure he will . . . The Leader of the Opposition distinguished himself with a sustained attack on the [Finance] Bill for 23 days; perhaps his motives were not exclusively fiscal in character, but they seem to have paid off . . .'[30]

Iain Macleod wound up for the opposition, witheringly describing Wilson as 'an essentially trivial man'. On television the same night, Wilson proclaimed: 'I am supremely indifferent to whom the Conservatives choose as their leader.'[31] That debate was a rehearsal of sorts for the following Monday,

2 August, when Heath moved a formal motion of censure in the House of Commons against the Government, just four hours after his formal installation as leader. The Liberals put down their own amendment and refused to support the Tory motion, which guaranteed it would fail (by 303 votes to 290) – but the occasion was really all about Heath taking the opportunity to impress his own MPs. He did not. His speech brought disappointment: it was turgid, long-winded and, in places, surprisingly anodyne and lacking in fervour. Critics also drew attention to the fact he deemed it appropriate just to attack the Government, rather than putting forward alternative proposals of his own.

Nonetheless, in one short passage **Heath** did touch upon a more personal vein, hinting at the kind of philosophy, policies and practices he intended to promulgate:

'The first thing that it is essential to do in the present situation is to stop trying to "kid" the people that everything can be done easily by gimmicks, by new Ministries, or merely by new and meaningless phrases. I believe that the impetus for change must come from individuals themselves, from men and women. That is the basis of our policy, because it leads to the encouragement of individuals.'[32]

John MacGregor was Heath's choice to run his private office after he became leader:

'Every day was packed and Ted was exceptionally hard working; he got through his boxes, churning out work. He was meticulous in getting all the arguments, all the facts, before making up his mind. He had a huge command of the facts – and expected the same thoroughness and dedication of others. He was always regarded as a dry person, but in fact he had an extremely dry sense of humour. His wit could be piercing, but there was never any malice. He had immense compassion. He did all the little personal touches – for instance inviting my daughter (who is his god-daughter) and her fiancé to Glyndebourne as a wedding present. I organised a big Far East tour in 1965 1966, using a creaking old Britannia plane. We took a lot of journalists, plus Tony Barber and Chris Chataway. I lost him for a time in Singapore and subsequently discovered he had slipped away to order some huge orchids for my wife Jean.

'There were endless weekends of work. Once we went to Bristol and had a reserved first-class carriage on the train back to London. "Good," I thought. "Thank goodness. At last I can go through all these boxes of work with him." Then a pretty young Canadian woman, a journalist, stuck her head into the carriage and Ted gave her all his attention. He flirted with her really – not sexually – but he was flirting, and they went on for ages, with him talking very freely. He was moody at times, but that's the problem about being lonely. I often wondered, when I left Albany late at night, and there he was, wondering how he was going to make this breakthrough. I think he played the piano for comfort.

'In his memoirs, Ted refers to "the champagne quality of New York". That reminds me of a discussion we had rather late on one of the drafts for a Party Conference speech. The draft, referring I think, to what he wanted to achieve for Britain and its citizens, talked about building in marble rather than stone. I remember Ted recoiling from this as being too "fanciful" and wanted to be more prosaic. I think I persuaded him to keep it in as it was a good aspiration for the country but also brought out his own aspirations in his life. He did like the good things in life too, including as a collector; and he often brought things back for the Albany from overseas trips.'

Heath moved quickly to appoint **Jim Prior**, the MP for Lowestoft who had only recently been made a vice-chairman of the party organisation, as his new PPS:

'I was a bridge to the people who had voted for Maudling and to the rural side of the party. But I had voted for him myself . . . It takes a good many years to get a really close relationship with him – much longer than with most men. And he was never really happy while working with the Shadow Cabinet in 1965 and 1966 – he was determined to try and cut the size because he always felt much happier working with a small group.'[33]

Perhaps the most notable appointment was that of Iain Macleod as principal spokesman on Treasury and economic affairs. Macleod had taken himself into internal exile during the Home years, but he was now propelled back into the second most important job in the party, after that of leader, despite the sensible appointment of Reggie Maudling as Deputy Leader. Alec Home was given the new post of 'External Affairs and Elder Statesman' and Christopher Soames took on Maudling's former foreign affairs role. Tony Barber was promoted to the trade brief. The party enjoyed a 'bounce' in the opinion polls – moving into a 7.5 per cent lead over Labour – and Tory MPs went off on their holidays in good spirits after Heath also bounced back to give a punchy performance on ITV's *This Week* programme. Heath – again – resigned from Brown, Shipley, and went off on holiday to the south of France.

David Howell remembers that summer well:

'Almost immediately, with congratulations pouring in, Ted decided to go to France to stay with his oldest friends, the Seligmans, and he asked me (again) to accompany him. In his memoirs, and with hindsight, Ted thought this visit was a mistake. The media were all over him and his sometime bête noire, Edward du Cann, happened to be staying at a nearby hotel in Villefranche. A meeting was arranged – I am not sure at whose instigation – but the feelings of distrust and dislike were mutual and visible too.

'After some confusion over my arrival at Nice airport, when I was mistakenly swept up with a team of top Treasury officials who had been summoned by George Brown to a nearby villa where he was holidaying, Ted Heath arrived to pick me up. There was no room for me at the Seligmans' quite modest villa, so he drove me up to a nearby glittering establishment owned by the Necchi family (sewing machines I think), where a room was found for me of considerably greater luxury than my boss's room chez Seligman. Ronnie Grierson, who knew everybody even then, appeared on the scene and swept Ted off, with me in tow, to meet the great, the good and the not so good on various yachts and palace-like villas along the Riviera. Gianni Agnelli, Dru Heinz and others were on his list.

'A significant worry amongst the Conservative faithful and grassroots membership was that their leader was not married. The word was that he had had an early but unhappy love affair but the lady had turned him down. The story went that he had vowed never to commit himself again, never to let himself be vulnerable, or succumb to weakening passion. The message went around that the leader must be introduced to suitable partners. With a youthful sense of duty I felt I should take some action and brought round to dinner at his Albany flat one of my most dazzling and charm-laden girlfriends – ready to make any sacrifice in the interests of the Party. It was a hopeless mission. She sat down very close to Ted on his black leather sofa, whereupon he immediately rose, patted the cushion and went to stand behind the sofa, well out of her aura. There was no interest and there was to be no sacrifice. Contrary to some assertions, however, Ted did like accomplished women and had several close female friends, but none close enough for partnership or marriage to be in the frame. So the Tory faithful would just have to lump it.'

The first few months of Heath's leadership were testing for him and the first crisis originated not at home, but in Southern Africa. The white minority still controlled the reins of power in Rhodesia and neither a Labour nor a Tory government was willing to contemplate giving the country its independence without majority rule. On 11 November 1965, Rhodesian leader Ian Smith illegally declared independence. Within the party rank and file, this post-Imperial entanglement retained the power to stir up strong passions, in both directions. Heath saw little viable alternative to offering broad support to Harold Wilson, but, when the Labour Government proposed an oil embargo, in a division on 21 December 1965 Tory MPs split three ways: most joined their leader in abstaining, but thirty voted for the embargo and eighty against it.

From the beginning of their close working relationship, **Jim Prior** was impressed by Heath's resilience: 'He comes through it all with tremendous courage – he is absolutely determined to do things well.'[34] He was concerned, however, by the extent to which problems could weigh upon Heath's mind, causing him to brood and isolate himself, even when in company, for instance when he hosted a meal for a group from Bexley, just as the Rhodesia storm was breaking over his head:

'He had his constituents into lunch. My wife had to sit next to him. She'd met him three or four times by that time, but he sat through nearly the whole of lunch without saying a word to anyone – to his constituents, to my wife, to anyone. He seemed incapable of radiating any warmth at all, at that time. He had to learn how to do that.'[35]

Heath's first major speech as leader, in Inverness in September, fell flat – and the legendary journalist **George Gale** had no doubt why. After listening to his leaden speech about the state of the nation, which had been prepared by a crowd of advisers, he watched Heath come to life on the plane home, as soon as he went off book and started to talk about music, paintings and how he believed 'people should be able to live in the communities where they were born': 'Heath should get a new speech-maker, who knows him as Sorensen knows Kennedy; or write his own speeches; or even throw away his script and speak out unrehearsed and unscripted, and show himself, and not his image.'[36] Sadly for Heath, it would be decades before he did that, many storms, four general elections and much heartbreak later.

Heath's challenge throughout his period as leader was not only to dent the dominance of Harold Wilson, but also to stifle the recovery of the Liberals, which had begun, almost imperceptibly, in the late 1950s, but acquired considerable momentum in the first half of the 1960s, under the mercurial but charismatic (and, importantly, TV-friendly) leadership of Jo Grimond. Conservative historian **Robert Blake** believed Heath was the ideal candidate to head off the Liberal revival:

'What Mr Grimond has to show is that he stands for something distinct not merely from the extremes of the other parties, but from the middle ground which is increasingly occupied by the moderate and majority elements in both the big parties . . . In this respect Mr Heath's election may be particularly damaging . . . He is precisely the sort of man who Mr Grimond must least like to see as leader of the Conservative party.'[37]

One big change in Heath's life after 1965 was taking up competitive sailing, which certainly served to undermine any perception that he was in any way effete, lethargic or physically unfit. **Brendon Sewill** ran the Conservative Research Department in the 1960s and later worked for Tony Barber, when he was Chancellor of the Exchequer. Here, he recalls the difference between

Heath in public and in private, and the way in which sailing became just another separate compartment of his life:

'Unlike Iain Macleod, Ted Heath did not have a natural flair with words. My first contact with him was when I had responsibility for the content of the party political broadcasts in the October 1964 election. Those programmes were more important in those days, and involved a good deal of speaking from a script straight to camera. Ted would sit for what felt like hour after hour, sucking the end of a pencil, rejecting draft after draft, crossing out any purple phrase, determined to get it right but ending up appearing wooden and without humour.

'It was the same with his speeches at the Party Conferences, where drafts were discarded through the early hours and a team of loyal secretaries frantically re-typed the final version on the morning of the speech. I remember one conference, at Blackpool, where the re-typing was not finished when the time came to depart from hotel to the conference. The second half of the speech had to follow in a taxi and get hastily reconnected with the first half on the platform as he waited for the call to give the rousing call to arms. Not surprisingly it wasn't all that rousing.

'But that is not entirely true. When relaxed with a small group of intelligent people, a group of businessmen or an academic audience he was fluent and brilliant. The eulogies he gave at a few memorial services, most memorably that of Michael Wolff in 1976, when he spoke from the heart, were the best I have ever heard.

'His difficulty with speeches came because he was determined to get the facts right, to present a clear, concise, factual argument. He despised attempts to turn politics into emotional appeals. Harold Wilson was anathema because of his verbal tricks, and his ability almost always to get the better of Heath at the then twice weekly PMQs by turning a serious point into a joke at Ted's expense.

'For Ted if something went mildly wrong it was a sign of inefficiency to be deprecated, not to be laughed at. I recall going to see him in the Albany before he was due to speak in a debate on defence, and was due to bring with me our expert on defence, Brigadier John Corbyn. When I told Ted that I had just heard that he had been taken seriously ill, Ted's reply was one word: "Why?" It was typical of his sense of humour but also reflected his attitude to minor emergencies.

'His sense of humour was an acquired taste: it consisted of making a provocative, almost offensive remark, and then waiting for an adroit reply. But more often the recipient was just left puzzled at his rudeness. I only recall one example. In January 1965, Rab Butler had just been demoted after making some indiscreet remarks and Heath had been appointed in his place in charge of Tory policy making. As the young and nervous new director of the Conservative Research Department, I met him at the door and took him in our antiquated lift up to what had always been reverently known as "Rab's room". Seeing a photo of Rab on the wall, Heath said to me: "What's he doing here?" I quailed. But I soon learnt the technique: I should have replied: "We have another space on the wall for your photo when you get the sack!" He would have loved that repartee and his shoulders would have shaken with mirth.

'Ted Heath kept his life in three separate compartments: politics, music and sailing. I was in the politics compartment: when I tried to amuse him by recounting my own minor nautical mishaps – running aground in the Solent or getting lost in a fog off Brittany – he showed no interest. In the sailing compartment he talked to the crew of *Morning Cloud* about how to win the next race, but I guess never asked them about politics. So far as I was aware there was no compartment for women, no compartment for sex or for jokes about sex – he just found all that boring and irrelevant, like my fog story.

'He tolerated Mervyn Pike as a member of his Shadow Cabinet because she was a quiet sensible woman, but I recall that, when Margaret Thatcher replaced her, she frequently annoyed him. He placed her at the far end of the long table, on his right (I used to sit immediately opposite him, behind Iain Macleod). After Heath had given all the main shadow ministers a chance to speak, and was on the point of summing up, Margaret had the habit of raising (in her then somewhat shrill tones) a fundamental point of principle which would have meant starting the discussion again. She was thanked curtly and then ignored. That was the start of the unhappy relationship.'

Patrick Jenkin recalls the early days of Heath's leadership of the party:

'He began well: he appointed Iain Macleod as the new Shadow Chancellor; he strengthened the Front Bench by appointing a number of newer younger MPs (I became a junior spokesman on Treasury matters; and I have always recognised that it was Ted to whom I owe this important first step up the greasy pole). He also set about reforming the party machine, realising that poor organisation had contributed to our losing the 1964 election; and he accelerated the review of policy. He was acutely aware the Party was likely to face another early election and had to be better prepared than it had been in 1964.

'Heath was also the first Conservative Leader to be elected in Opposition since Bonar Law in 1911, which made the task of establishing his authority over his MPs and the Party much more difficult than if he had held the office of Prime Minister. As well as attracting far more intrusive scrutiny by the media, and having to face a Prime Minister with the skills and ruthlessness of Harold Wilson, he quickly found that his own style – marshalling evidence, listing strings of facts, deploying arguments and so on – however successful it may have been as Shadow Chancellor, was far less effective for an Opposition Leader dealing with Wilson (for whom he had already developed a profound contempt, bordering on loathing).

'Uncharacteristically, he turned to using the weekly Prime Minister's Question Time as an opportunity to trade insults with insults in a way that grew more and more bitter with every occasion. While this was often greeted with delighted cheers from his supporters on the benches behind him, it has to be recognised that he soon began to lose the respect of commentators that his previous Parliamentary work had attracted. Week after week, as *The Times* put it describing an early clash, the drubbing Mr Wilson handed out to his new rival, "pulled the rug from under Mr Heath and left him gasping on the floor". Andrew Roth described it as "more like a Sicilian vendetta than the normal Parliamentary pillow fights".

'As the media criticisms increased, they really upset Ted Heath. I believe they were part of the reason why, in contrast to his earlier character as a friendly, convivial and popular new MP in the years following his 1950 election, he became more and more withdrawn and "buttoned up". When his advisers tried to improve his public image, making various suggestions as to how this could be done, he refused to heed their advice: he despised the manner in which Harold Wilson engaged in stunts to catch the eye of the media, and point-blank refused to do anything of the sort himself. He spent less time frequenting the tea room and chatting informally to other members, and he rarely stopped people in the corridors to congratulate them on a good speech or a good question. Indeed, his abrupt, almost unfriendly, behaviour upset more and more of those on whose support he depended.

'When Sir Alec had become Leader, he had appointed Heath to be the Chairman of the Party's Advisory Committee on Policy; and, from the start, the review was entirely dominated by the imminent prospect of another election. He told the National Union Executive in 1965 that he was concentrating on "particular sections of the electorate whose previous support had been lost at the General Election". This approach imported flaws into the whole process. Previous reviews had always started from a review of the philosophical basis of the Party's policies with the details then being fitted into a coherent framework. With Heath in charge, it really did go into detail. He simply assumed the Party's broad philosophy was well known, and that broader themes would emerge as the detailed work was done. He told one ACP member: "We have to find new practical ways in which to apply our principles to current problems that are worrying the electorate."

'When Ted became Leader, the same approach was pursued, but with even greater urgency. As the detailed work progressed, it became clearer and clearer that Heath disliked being confronted with arguments on basic philosophy, often refusing to reopen issues which he claimed "had already been decided": he upset former Ministers whose own policies from their time in Government were being summarily rejected without any philosophical explanation; and his reluctance to debate concepts gave rise to difficulties in distinguishing Conservative policy from that of their opponents. "Which twin is the Tory?" was a Liberal poster taunt at one point. One former adviser was asked to write to Heath to tell him: "The public wants to know where he wants to go as much as how he aims to get there."'

Heath didn't much care for the party chairman he inherited, Edward du Cann, who had worked with him at the Board of Trade, but an election was due and he did not feel able to replace him. He also fell out with Angus Maude, a one-time comrade from One Nation days, after Maude wrote a piece in the *Spectator*, in which he lamented a 'Tory Winter of Discontent':

'It is obvious that the Conservative Party has completely lost effective political initiative. Its own supporters in the country are divided and deeply worried by this failure, while to the electorate at large the Opposition has become a meaningless irrelevance . . . For Tories simply to talk like technocrats will get them nowhere.'[38]

Heath was understandably offended by this and Maude resigned as spokesman on colonial affairs within days. Meanwhile Labour remained comfortably ahead in the polls and everybody expected an early election. After Labour increased its majority in the Hull North by-election (having just announced a new bridge over the Humber), the Parliament's days were evidently numbered. At the end of February, Wilson announced a general election for 31 March 1966. Despite Heath's best efforts, the campaign was largely uneventful and the conclusion always seemed foregone. Heath made one gaffe, which still made him wince years later, when, in a clumsy attempt to satirise the gimmickry of Harold Wilson mid-campaign, he failed to deploy the subjunctive: 'No doubt it will be only another month now before we read of Mr Wilson having tea at No. 10 Downing Street with a pregnant panda.' More cynical commentators felt he was implicitly, or possibly subconsciously, conceding the election. In general he acquitted himself well rather than spectacularly, putting industrial relations reform at the centre of his appeal to the nation, but Labour increased its majority to almost 100 seats. No one blamed Heath, although it was no auspicious experience for him. He remained upbeat. Now, he felt, at last, he really had a period of four or five years in which to knock the Conservative Party properly into shape.

What came next was a very distinctive phase in the life and development of Edward Heath. It was time for Heath the moderniser; Heath the radical; and Heath the man of action. He set about sorting out the party machine but he made a mistake by not moving Edward du Cann, the party chairman, whilst also making it obvious he didn't think he was the right man for the job.* Heath had initiated a process of policy overhaul before becoming leader and now he intensified it dramatically. He also went out amongst the people in an attempt to appear energetic and down to earth. It didn't persuade. Even as Wilson lost his sheen and sense of indomitability, with a series of economic mini-crises, Heath consistently ran behind his party in the polls. The party membership in the country remained loyal to its leader – as it generally does – but his MPs were dismayed by his inability to better Wilson in debate, by his failure to project successfully through the by now almost ubiquitous medium of television and also by the lapses in personal charm – sometimes, but not always, excusable as clumsy attempts at humour – which he displayed towards colleagues.

Patrick Jenkin recalls:

'Despite Heath's difficulties in communicating, the Conservatives were soon leading in the opinion polls. This came to a head with the 1967 devaluation of the pound sterling, which was seen as a disaster for Labour. It was absolutely typical of Wilson to say in a broadcast on the devaluation: "From now the pound abroad is worth 14 per cent or so less in terms of other currencies. It does not mean, of course, that the pound here in Britain, in your pocket or purse or in your bank, has been devalued. What it does mean is that we shall now be able to sell more goods abroad on a competitive basis." This went beyond even Wilson's usual legerdemain and Ted Heath won much deserved praise for his trenchant attacks on the Government's failure and Wilson's deceit. It showed that, given the right context, he could perform as effectively as he ever had.

'Sadly these occasional successes for Ted could not overcome the difficulties he had in making himself an effective communicator with either the public or even his own backbenchers. Reading the accounts of the period between the 1966 and 1970 elections, I have been struck by the constant references to these difficulties. I believe that the heart of the problem lay in that it was impossible to fit him into any familiar pigeonhole. As one

---

* In 1967, du Cann did quit, supposedly of his own accord, but with a parting shot that screamed 'bruised ego'.

prominent MP put it: "He still seemed vaguely alien, one of them, yet not one of them." A BBC *Panorama* film described him, at a series of informal public events, "pasting on a grin". By 1968, an NOP poll reported that only two-thirds of even Conservative voters wanted Heath to stay on as party leader. Curiously, he was much more effective in small informal meetings and answering questions than in larger set-piece meetings which tended to be those reported by the media. He made little attempt to cultivate journalists; one otherwise very pro-Conservative commentator wrote privately to the Chairman of the Party: "Something drastic needs to be done about his speeches or he will soon end up being totally ignored." Another described his style as being "addicted, perhaps by now incurably, to the factual statement, the plain exposition, marshalling and enumerating his policies like a laundry list".

'What is extraordinary is that, despite Ted Heath's communication problems, the Party's fortunes did improve. During most of this period, the Labour Government became increasingly discredited and the polls showed consistent majorities for the Conservatives.'

The policy review that ran during these years was, to modern sensibilities, surprisingly secretive. Many of those involved were from outside the world of Westminster politics and, perhaps understandably, given Labour's seemingly unbreakable hegemony in national power, they did not wish their names to be made public. Rumours did, however, leak out of radical plans to change the machinery of government and reform trade union legislation (which was largely generic and founded in case law). **David Howell** became an MP at the 1966 general election, but retained his involvement in the policy review:

'In the Opposition years that followed the 1966 defeat, Mark Schreiber (now Lord Marlesford) and I set up a break-away research group from the official Research Department, toured America and Canada and began importing radical ideas for change in machinery and policies. Amongst our innovations, in which Heath in Opposition took a strong interest and which he would adopt when he did eventually become Prime Minister, albeit in somewhat diluted form, were Policy and Programme Budgeting

Systems (PPBS), Programme Analysis and Review (PAR) and a new central government capability for giving strategic shape to all Government
programmes and expenditure – the so-called Central Policy Review Staff.
This we intended to be located in No. 10 alongside the Prime Minister,
but the mandarins had other ideas and it would end up under the wing of
the Cabinet Office and under the control of the Cabinet Secretary and
the Head of the Home Civil Service.'

As the fruits of the policy review were revealed, Heath's already iron-
clad confidence grew. In 1968, **Douglas Hurd** was headhunted from the
Conservative Research Department to become Heath's political secretary
and head of his private office – making him to all intents and purposes, in
the absence of a wife and children, the most important person in his life:

'My father, who was a backbench MP*, knew Ted slightly. As a young
diplomat, I might have met him once or twice when he was in charge of
negotiations to join the EEC. I also remember hearing him play the organ
in Moscow in 1963, when he signed the partial test-ban treaty between
Britain, the United States and the Soviet Union. At the age of 36, when
I was in the Rome embassy, I wanted a change of career and wrote to six
or seven people I knew in different professions – including Ted – to see
if I could be of use to them, or whether they had any ideas about what
I should do. Typically, Ted sent a telegram saying, "Come back at once
to meet Sir Michael Fraser, at Central Office". Michael was then deputy
chairman of the Conservative Party Organisation.

'Ted is very decisive. I spent two years organising his life as Leader of
the Opposition. It was a difficult but fascinating job. I learnt a lot about
government and about the whole of Britain. Nowadays, everybody in politics preparing for government meticulously plans campaigns which take
them all over the country. In Ted's day it was a very new idea. Ted has
always been highly professional in whatever he does and fairly displeased
when things go wrong, although it's not easy to have a row with him
because he just retreats into monosyllables. He simply isn't interested in

---

* Sir Anthony Hurd (1901–66), MP for Newbury 1945–64.

amateurs. That's one of the reasons why he never particularly bothered to talk to me about his music. I'm not a musician and wouldn't have had anything interesting to add to a conversation. To him, sailing and music were the other compartments in his life. They were different challenges – other mountains to climb.

'Ted has never been any good at small talk, which undoubtedly did a lot of harm and often sent me into despair. I've lost count of the times I've had to watch him sitting at the top table in between two important ladies, usually the wives of Tory grandees. These women, always desperately interested in Ted, tried talking to him about music and sailing because they thought that's what he would want to discuss. Naturally, they had nothing of interest to say and so communication was impossible.'[39]

Few people have given greater service to the Conservative Party than **Roger Boaden**. He worked closely with Heath when he was leader:

'In February 1968, EH was the main guest at the Young Conservative Conference in Bournemouth, which I was organising. Before he was due to arrive we experienced a heavy snowfall, so heavy, there was snow lying on the beach. I received a message to say EH would be late. He had been in Broadstairs attending a music event, and had been stuck in the snow. Many of those driving down to attend the conference were stuck overnight in snowdrifts.

'We were using what was then the Palace Court Hotel as our head-quarters, and the manager had re-decorated a two-bedroomed suite for his important guest. The manager went to a lot of trouble, arranging the décor of one room as art deco, and the other in a more traditional pattern, and he had laid on a range of drinks he believed would please his guest.

'Other Party and YC VIPs who would normally want to be around when the Party Leader arrived, gave up and went to bed, but I stayed up with the manager to await EH's arrival. Prior to that conference a colleague working closely with EH, asked me if I could describe my relationship with EH. I told him I felt it was a bit cold and distant, he told me it will change, but you may never know how and when.

'Eventually EH did arrive; he was cold and fussing about the bad weather. The manager greeted him, explained about the two bedrooms, and we took him up to the suite. EH looked at both rooms and decided on the traditional room, whilst I stood in the lounge holding his bag. The manager left, and EH turned to me. "Throw the bag in that room, and kick off your shoes, sit down and have a drink," he said. "You look knackered. Do you like a good malt?" I explained I had never had a malt, and he proceeded to pour two glasses from The Glenlivet bottle, which we had set up for him. We chatted for quite a long time. That was an important moment for me. It marked a distinctive change in the way he treated and addressed me. As my colleague had described, it was hard to define, but it was different. It was no longer cold and distant. I felt I had been accepted.

'Thereafter, whenever we met, EH greeted me with "Oh it's you", or "Ah it's Boaden". As a footnote: Throughout the three Election campaign tours I organised for EH, I always carried a hip flask of The Glenlivet, and on several occasions he made good use of it!'

At Easter 1968, Heath went for a break at Aviemore. As so often was the case, it was a working holiday, with Douglas Hurd also invited. There was a cold snap and, when he wanted to swim before breakfast, he had to walk through snow in his trunks and dressing gown to get to the swimming pool. He also tried curling, watched some skating and read the lessons at Aviemore church. 'Some electors like to see us working flat out all the time,' he told a journalist who seemed critical of him taking time out in this fashion. 'Then we get tired and the result is bad laws and bad decisions. Then the citizens suffer.' Trips such as this had a lasting effect on him, as **Douglas Hurd** recalls:

'I remember going with him to Aviemore, the Scottish ski resort, in its early days. He watched these people whose parents, living in the mid twentieth century, would never have dreamed of skiing, or of having a family who skied, and yet here they were skiing, and enjoying it. Ted remarked upon that, and said that was just the sort of thing for which he was aiming. Being part of Europe was part of that but it wasn't the whole of it, it was just part of it.

'We fought the 1970 election on the slogan "A Better Tomorrow", which was the key to the thing and arose because of a conversation he had in Australia when he won the Sydney–Hobart race in 1969. He was being driven by a man who had emigrated and settled in Australia. Ted was cross-examining him and he said: "Well, Sir, the thing really is, in this country, tomorrow is always better than today." That phrase stuck in Ted's mind and that was really what he was aiming at – that people with his sort of modest background should be able to get an organ scholarship, should be able to do those kinds of things, should be able to ski. Europe was important, but only as part of a wider effort.'[40]

One of Heath's biggest problems as opposition leader was mercurial defence spokesman Enoch Powell. Powell's following in the parliamentary party was limited, but he did have the capacity to rabble-rouse and enjoyed some popularity amongst delegates at the party conference. He had strong views on immigration and in 1967 developed the habit of departing from party policy, always calling for a tougher line. In February 1968 the Labour Government rushed through a Commonwealth Immigrants Bill, 'bringing under immigration control citizens of the United Kingdom holding United Kingdom passports who have no substantial connection with this country, for example, by birth or paternal parentage . . . This legislation will not only apply a control to the present rush of immigrants from East Africa; it will also extend to persons in other parts of the world who have hitherto been similarly exempt from United Kingdom immigration control . . . There will be a special allocation of 1,500 vouchers a year.'[41] The Tories officially supported the Bill, guaranteeing its passage, though several notable names from their ranks joined Labour rebels and the Liberals in voting against its Second Reading on 27 February, including Michael Heseltine, Norman St John Stevas and Dame Joan Vickers. Iain Macleod abstained. In March 1968 Gallup found a 72 per cent approval rating for the legislation.[42] Despite this, overall approval for the Government had fallen to only 18 per cent, with 66 per cent of people registering disapproval. The Tories were doing well in by-elections and local elections, but Heath himself was still not winning over the electorate. His position remained vulnerable.

Labour followed up with a Race Relations Bill. The right wanted Heath to oppose it, but a small, liberal minority thought it deserved support.

Heath and the shadow cabinet were forced into an uneasy compromise, of putting down a so-called 'reasoned amendment' to the Bill, whose Second Reading was announced for Tuesday 23 April 1968, rejecting the Bill 'on balance'. On Saturday 20 April, **Powell** made a speech to the Conservative Political Centre in Birmingham that seemed to Heath and many of his shadow cabinet highly inflammatory. One section in particular caused controversy:

'As I look ahead, I am filled with foreboding. Like the Roman, I seem to see "the River Tiber foaming with much blood". That tragic and intractable phenomenon which we watch with horror on the other side of the Atlantic but which there is interwoven with the history and existence of the States itself, is coming upon us here by our own volition and our own neglect. Indeed, it has all but come. In numerical terms, it will be of American proportions long before the end of the century. Only resolute and urgent action will avert it even now. Whether there will be the public will to demand and obtain that action, I do not know. All I know is that to see, and not to speak, would be the great betrayal.'

Powell had planned to cause an immense furore and he certainly did. At first a spokesman for Central Office, caught unawares, told the press that Powell's speech was 'roughly in line with other statements that have been made on the subject',[43] but this line was never tenable. Liberal-minded Tory MP Nick Scott was the first of Powell's colleagues to respond. He said Powell was 'assuming the mantle of Governor Wallace of Alabama'. 'The Conservative Party is split down the middle,' declared Michael Heseltine, helpfully. 'The buck has been passed to Ted Heath, who has got to lead the party out of this most difficult and desperate matter.'[44] Within twenty-four hours of the speech, Enoch Powell's front-bench career was over. He wrote an extraordinary resignation later to Heath, offering his support from the back benches and asserting that 'I believe you will be Prime Minister of this country, and that you will be an outstandingly able Prime Minister, perhaps a great one.' I believe this must have seemed disingenuous to Heath and enraged him, for he never sent a reply, despite attempts to intercede by senior colleagues, notably Willie Whitelaw, in the interests of party unity.

This episode prompted one of the most passionate sections of **Heath**'s own memoirs:

'The content of the speech was deplorable enough, coming from someone who boasted of his scholarship, but the fictitious statistics, and references to alleged letters from constituents who could not be traced afterwards, were deceitful and disgraceful. The tone was still worse . . . All of this was in stark contrast to the line he took as Minister of Health in Macmillan's government, on one occasion telling the Cabinet that we could afford to stand up to the nurses in a pay dispute, "because I can bring in all the nurses we need from the West Indies". I was in the Cabinet Room at the time, and I heard him say it.

'The first I heard about Powell's speech was when the press started to telephone me at my father's home in Broadstairs, from tea-time onwards on the Saturday afternoon. I contacted Tony Barber, the Chairman of the party, but he too knew nothing. The accepted procedure with all public speeches was for the text to be sent to Central Office for reproduction and circulation, or to me personally for my information, but the convention had been ignored. Powell had waited until he got to Birmingham and then passed his speech to the agent there.

'I was appalled, and immediately recognised the immense damage it must have done to race relations in Britain and to the attitude towards our party among a large section of the population. Had I not sacked him, the party would not have had a Shadow Cabinet left. Quintin Hogg, Peter Carrington and Iain Macleod were particularly fierce about it. At around nine o'clock, I asked Willie Whitelaw, the Chief Whip, to get Powell on the telephone so that I could inform him of our conclusion. Willie returned to say that Powell had no telephone in his constituency home at Wolverhampton, but he was trying to get the number of his agent. He finally obtained this, and told the agent to contact Powell and ask him to telephone me at once. To Willie the agent seemed far from happy about doing this, but he was firmly told to get on with it.

'A short time later, Powell himself telephoned me. I informed him that I considered his speech to be racist in tone and liable to exacerbate racial tensions. I was, therefore, dismissing him from the Opposition front bench, after discussions with the Shadow Cabinet. Powell accepted this without protest and rang off. We never spoke again. The action I took, I am sure, was absolutely right and, although it caused friction between the party and extremists among the public, it saved our position with the majority of our people.'

Two days later, as Parliament resumed its activities after the Easter recess, shadow home secretary Quintin Hogg led for the Tories in the Second Reading debate on the Race Relations Bill. For once, an account of a debate in *Hansard* fairly crackles off the page. Hogg excoriated Powell and his speech, although Ivor Richard outdid him in both poetry and allusion by describing it as 'the sentiments of a Mississippi demagogue expressed in the measured accents of an ex-professor of classical Greek'. Powellites on the back benches supported their man, but largely went through the voting lobbies with their leaders, supporting the 'reasoned amendment' (as did Powell himself). The following day, the *Daily Telegraph* reported, without comment, its estimate that 97 per cent of the letters it had received about the furore had supported Powell; just 3 per cent favoured Heath.

In the week following Powell's sacking, Heath spoke with real feeling when he said: 'I am sorry that some of my secretaries have had to read the letters I have received . . . There has been a nasty, vicious reaction.' Despite early attempts to effect a reconciliation, it is certainly true the two men never spoke again. Occasionally I would see them in the same room and they studiously avoided one another. Heath had a unique level of distaste for Powell; and he and Michael Foot were the two public figures who refrained from making any comment whatsoever when Powell died in 1998 – even a bland 'we had our disagreements but he was a great parliamentarian' would evidently have stuck in their craws – and Heath once said to me how angered he was by Powell's apparent desire to be interred wearing his Brigadier's uniform – 'the bloody man never even fired a shot'.*

Heath regarded Powell as a mountebank and an extremist; a dangerous demagogue and (his word) a 'menace'. In later years he satisfied himself by deploying as simple an epithet as possible; as Heath's former researcher

---

* Powell was an intelligence officer in the Second World War.

Richard Bull recalls, the single, brutal and utterly uncompromising adjective 'evil' sufficed:

> 'It was in the context of prepping for the book. I asked him to assess his fellow candidates for the leadership in 1965. Maudling was described as amiably lazy. The subject of Powell was quickly dispensed with – that one word [evil] was all he would say, adding only that one should not shy away from such conclusions where justified.'

Heath did not 'suffer fools gladly' and behaved from the outset like a man who believed government was all but within his grasp. He also took an active and 'hands-on' interest in foreign affairs. Possibly it made him feel and – just as importantly – look more like a statesman, but he also genuinely enjoyed visiting new people and places. He would often boast that he 'never suffered from jet lag'. This was principally because he had both great stamina and also an enviable ability to fall asleep anywhere and at any time, however appropriate or inappropriate it might be. In his prime, he positively revelled in arduous foreign tours, sometimes, as **Douglas Hurd** recalls, despite the protestations of his staff:

> 'Mr Heath decided to visit the Gulf in March 1969, and took with him his Parliamentary Private Secretary Tony Kershaw and myself. It was the first of many foreign expeditions undertaken with him in the next five years, and also the most fascinating, except perhaps for the visit to China in 1974. It was clear from the beginning that we were about to strain the normal conventions which govern the attitude of the Foreign Office to overseas forays of the Leader of the Opposition. A briefing session at Mr Heath's flat in the Albany on 25 March before we left for the Gulf was a disaster. Mr Heath exploded in the face of Geoffrey Arthur, a senior Foreign Office official with much experience and a reputation for plain speech. The Foreign Office was accused of feebleness and bad faith. We were clearly set for a stormy ride.
> 'Mr Heath was at his best during the next crowded week of interviews with Arab rulers, punctuated by disagreeable meals and short bumpy rides in a small plane. He was immensely courteous and patient. He

remembered exactly the particular interests, history and idiosyncrasies of each ruler. He set out his own position with the right blend of deference and firmness. He enjoyed the company of these subtle men, and conveyed that enjoyment to them. It was a better display of diplomacy than any I remember during fourteen years in the Diplomatic Service. His moments of brusqueness and impatience were reserved for occasional British officials or businessmen. This was a contrast which marked almost all our foreign expeditions.'[45]

Heath was never a miser as such, but he always believed in economy and enjoyed combining business with pleasure or other good purposes, especially when long journeys were involved, as **Douglas Hurd** discovered later the same year:

'As early as August 1968 [Heath] had proposed in a speech in Canberra that stability against external threat could be helped by a new Commonwealth force which would include contributions from Britain, Australia, New Zealand, Singapore and Malaysia. At the end of 1969, he decided that he could carry the idea a stage further by going to South East Asia himself, much as he had gone to the Gulf that spring. Not that the East of Suez argument was the main reason for this expedition.

'His principal aim was to win the Sydney–Hobart race in *Morning Cloud*. This was a feat of organisation and daring in the face of great obstacles which only sailors can appreciate to the full. For the rest of us it was a symbol of something we already knew, that we were dealing with a remarkably determined and resourceful man. For the British public, if not for some members of the Labour Party, it dispelled the idea that Ted Heath's sailing had anything in common with the leisurely cruises of millionaires in pursuit of luxury and the sun. I doubt if Mr Heath has ever cruised in his life. During the six years that I worked for Mr Heath there were three *Morning Clouds*. I never set foot on any of them. He rightly preferred to keep that side of his life as separate as possible. Anyway once at sea I would certainly have fallen overboard or performed some other folly. It was therefore natural that I should fly out to Australia only after the race was over. It was not easy to disentangle Mr Heath from his crew, for hard celebration after an event is evidently as important a part of sailing as hard training before it. He managed to take a day off from the parties to see the Prime Minister, Mr Gorton, in Canberra, leaving Tony Kershaw and myself in Sydney to deal with a flood of congratulations.'[46]

Not everyone was impressed by the way in which Heath organised his life around his sailing. Cecil King, the sometime newspaper proprietor and Bank of England man, whose published diaries from the period are indispensable, more than once recorded both his own dismay at Heath's frequent absences and also that of some senior Tories. Although Heath was sailing competitively and not for reasons of leisure, the pursuit was and is an expensive one – a 'rich man's sport' – and the coverage back at home did not necessarily enhance his standing in the eyes of every elector. Harold Wilson and his cohorts made his absences for sailing a major theme of their sustained attempts to discredit him. Heath once revealed how this cut him to the quick, telling the parliamentary lobby: 'Here I am, pilloried by Labour MPs for going to sea in time of crisis. It's all right, apparently, for Harold Wilson to sit on an island and watch the boats go by. But it's absolutely wrong for me to be out there on board.'

Heath was all too aware of his own limitations in communicating and he was convinced the press had allowed itself to be seduced by Harold Wilson. Rather than responding with a charm offensive of his own in response to the poor press he was receiving, he sometimes became embarrassingly tetchy, for instance at a lunch with **Cecil King** in September 1967:

'Ted Heath for lunch, the first meeting for some months. He arrived tense, serious, and exceedingly difficult. After one and a half hours he left laughing, but what a lunch – the most difficult I have had in years. He was obviously deeply hurt by newspaper criticisms and the opinion polls, but battling on nevertheless. Was very critical of the newspapers always pulling down, never building up . . . He wouldn't agree that Parliament and the parties were held in low esteem; or that we were heading for a National Government. The present Government would disintegrate before 1971; there would be an election, the Tories would win, and on we should go . . . What emerged was (1) that Ted is deeply hurt by all the criticisms, and

(2) that he seems to have no understanding of the political atmosphere as I see it.'[47]

At around this time, Heath fell out badly with William Davis, the then financial editor of the *Guardian* and later editor of *Punch*, after Davis interviewed him and revealed in his article that they had lunched together in his 'exclusive Albany flat'. Months later, Heath saw Davis at a Stock Exchange lunch and objected to his presence: 'Either he goes, or I go'. Heath similarly could not contain himself when Wilson flew off for a parley with Ian Smith on Gibraltar during the Tory party conference in 1968 and a number of prominent journalists absconded to join him there. Heath barked at those who remained: 'I suppose you're frustrated to stay and listen to me at Blackpool instead of kneeling at the feet of Wilson at Gib.' Davis later commented that Heath might have enjoyed much more political success had he only 'lost his temper in public in the way he does in private', rather than projecting such a grey and passionless image to the nation.[48] Heath didn't help himself even when he was on generally good terms with someone. On one occasion the renowned *Sunday Times* photographer Kelvin Brodie took pictures of Heath for twenty minutes while he was being interviewed. Heath never acknowledged Brodie's presence, but, once he had gone, he praised him by name to the interviewer. This was utterly typical of Heath's awkwardness.

In this period, James Margach was very much the doyen of political and lobby correspondents. He found Heath impossible – a man who 'disliked journalists and distrusted newspapers'[49] – but did endeavour to understand him. He soon divined that playing the piano was Heath's way of releasing tension; and it fascinated him that this shy, introverted and difficult man would not only play, but play with great energy and passion, alone or with an audience. Before one interview with Margach, Heath arrived late, delayed by his struggles with the shadow cabinet. He apologised, then changed; and, upon his return, turned not to political matters but proudly showed off his Steinway grand piano, then played romantic music for half an hour before the interview. 'Do you play every night when you come home, even late from the House of Commons?' asked Margach. 'Yes,' replied Heath. 'Not every night, but very often. I've got very understanding neighbours and the walls are very thick.' 'But why?' asked the journalist. 'Does the great music give you release?' 'Yes,' confirmed the Leader of Her Majesty's Opposition. 'Music means everything to me when I'm here alone. And it's the best way of getting that bloody man Wilson out of my hair.'[50]

Patrick Jenkin was, by now, a well-established shadow spokesman on economic matters:

'In the House of Commons, Labour's legislation was being fought with skill and determination by the new team; some very good work was at last being done on policy research; and as the 1970 General Election approached, the Party was able to develop what was described as "the most sophisticated public relations exercise yet mounted in British politics". Within the Party, it was gradually recognised that Heath was bound to lead it into the election, and that people simply had to stop grumbling and get behind him. A new Director of Publicity (the excellent Geoffrey Tucker) began to find ways to improve Ted's presentations. His stunning victory in the Sydney to Hobart sailing race won him much praise; and the Selsdon Conference and its outcome brought welcome publicity for Conservative policies based on reducing the public sector, cutting taxation and promoting the private sector. We began to feel optimistic that Labour's interventionist policies, with their proliferation of unaccountable institutions, would be firmly put into reverse.

'Of course, Harold Wilson was still a formidable adversary. From the beginning of 1970, he ensured that wages were allowed to rise without check and that no unpopular measures were introduced. The consequence was that, between January and June 1970, the polls showed a swing back to Labour. By deciding on a June election, rather than in the autumn as many had expected, Wilson hoped that he would be re-elected before the inevitable price rises started to bite. He tried to pretend that he had thought of a spring or an early summer election as early as 1966, but the media had little doubt that it was the polls which determined the date.'

In the immediate run-up to the 1970 election, 'Selsdon Man' was born. Heath later claimed this term, coined by Harold Wilson, was misleading, because all that happened at Selsdon Park over the last weekend of January 1970 was a reaffirmation by him and his senior colleagues of policies that already existed, having been carefully deliberated over since the party lost power in 1964. This isn't exactly what he said at the time, when he was keen to express excitement at taking a united team into battle on a radical manifesto. What ultimately emerged from those discussions was the 1970 manifesto and also, as **Douglas Hurd** recalls, a very personal introduction to that manifesto from Heath himself:

'In the different, more confident atmosphere of 1970, the way was clear in Mr Heath's mind for a reforming Conservative Government. This Government should resolve to do in the 1970s what Peel had tried to do in the 1840s and Pitt in the 1780s. Those great Prime Ministers had shown that the aim of Conservative reform was not to enlarge the power of the state. It was to sweep away what was antiquated and inefficient in our public institutions, and create a new framework within which the individual could take his own responsibilities and create his own prosperity. New policies were not enough. The style and method of government also had to be changed. Mr Heath wrote a personal foreword to the 1970 election manifesto which revealed his own approach to politics more plainly than anything else in the campaign. It is a short angry piece which emerged hot from the years of frustration spent watching and despising Mr Wilson's style of government:

"During the last six years we have suffered not only from bad policies, but from a cheap and trivial style of government. Decisions have been dictated simply by the desire to catch tomorrow's headlines. The short-term gain has counted for everything: the long-term objective has gone out of the window. Every device has been used to gain immediate publicity, and government by gimmick has become the order of the day. Decisions lightly entered into have been as lightly abandoned . . .

"I am determined therefore that a Conservative Government shall introduce a new style of government: that we shall re-establish our sound and honest British traditions in this field. I want to see a fresh approach to the taking of decisions. The Government should seek the best advice and listen carefully to it. It should not rush into decisions, it should use up-to-date techniques for assessing the situation, it should be deliberate and thorough. And in coming to its decisions, it must always recognise that its responsibility is to the people, and all the people, of this country. What is more, its decision should be aimed at the long term. The easy answer and the quick trick may pay immediate dividends in terms of publicity, but in the end it is the national interest which suffers. We have seen that too often in the recent past. Finally, once a decision is made, once a policy is established, the Prime Minister and his colleagues should have the courage to stick to it. Nothing has done Britain more harm in the world than the endless backing and filling which we have seen in recent years . . .

"Courage and intellectual honesty are essential qualities in politics, and in the interest of our country it is high time that we saw them again. So it will not be enough for a Conservative Government to make a fresh start with new policies. We must create a new way of running our national affairs. This means sweeping away the trivialities and the gimmicks which now dominate the political scene. It means dealing honestly and openly with the House of Commons, with the press and with the public. The decisions which a Government has to take affect the livelihood and perhaps the lives of millions of our fellow citizens. No one has any business to take part in public life unless he is prepared to take such decisions with the seriousness which they deserve."

'This has always seemed to me a key document. Coming from a lesser man it might have been claptrap, but from him it was not. There runs through it a note of genuine puritan protest, which is familiar in British history, sometimes in one party, sometimes in the other. It is the note struck by Pym against the court of Charles I, by Pitt against the Fox–North coalition, by Gladstone against Disraeli, by the Conservatives in 1922 against Lloyd George. It is the outraged assertion of a strict view of what public life is about, after a period in which its rules have been perverted and its atmosphere corrupted. Commentators later reproached Mr Heath for not creating enough peerages, for failing to link arms in the corridors or gossip in the smoking room of the House of Commons, for refusing to flatter his critics. These crimes, if crimes they were, stemmed from his belief that the government of Britain was too serious a matter to be carried forward in the style of Mr Harold Wilson.'[51]

Another account of Heath's state of mind going into the 1970 campaign is provided by **Cecil King**:

'Lunch today with Ted Heath. We had lunch in his flat, the only other guest being Cowdrey, the Kent cricketer. People say Ted is cold, unfriendly, unapproachable, and all that kind of thing. But he was very easy to talk to, warm, friendly and forthcoming. I think it would be fair to say that he is no politician and certainly no Leader of the Opposition. He is essentially an able civil servant, but the Tories have no one better. He was naturally depressed as the polls, for no very clear reason, have taken a sudden turn to Labour and it is now generally assumed by the commentators and by Ted that the election will be in mid-June and will be announced on Sunday or Monday.'

From the outset of the 1970 campaign, whatever the polls indicated, Heath was wholly convinced he would win, but no one else shared his certainty. Indeed, hardly anyone else even believed he *could* win. That slippery old magician Harold Wilson dominated the field and seemed to have all the necessary sleight of hand; and there were scant signs in the public opinion polls that Labour might lose. During the campaign itself, Heath suffered the indignity of being warned by some of his closest supporters – the likes of Peter Carrington and Toby Aldington – that he would be well advised to plan in advance how he would conduct himself once he had been defeated by Wilson again. Heath was appalled and disappointed by such defeatism, but he never seemed to hold it against his friends and colleagues subsequently. They had simply read the polls and drawn the obvious conclusion.

Heath took the lead in what became a very unusual election campaign, fought by him as party leader not only through the increasingly decisive medium of television, but also out on the streets of marginal towns and cities. This happened almost by accident, as **Roger Boaden** recounts:

'On the first Saturday of the campaign EH addressed a meeting in Gravesend, a marginal seat. The High Street leading from the hall was pedestrianised and so we arrived at the back of the venue. Whilst the speech went ahead, I went outside to organise the cars and the Press Coach. The local Police told me we couldn't park outside, and would have to stay at the back. I enquired about the High Street and was told we would need to walk to the end and then we could join the cars and the coach there.

'To that point of the campaign the news coverage was becoming critical saying that EH was sitting in a studio all the time. Saatchi and Saatchi had designed a set which was used everywhere – in Central Office, at news conferences, on the platforms of meetings and rallies, and in the Party Political Broadcasts. The objective had been to establish a brand image which was appealing and efficient.

'This being a Saturday, none of my superiors were on duty at this relatively low key day of campaigning. So, I took the decision that we should walk down the pedestrianised High Street, meeting the thronging shoppers in the June sunshine. As EH finished I guided him through the hall to shake hands with the supporters in the audience, and as we reached the door I told him we were walking the three hundred yards or so to the cars. He told me he would appreciate getting some air and so we set off.

'For a while it took the press team, photographers and TV camera teams some time to catch on to what we were doing, and so initially we moved ahead quickly with EH striding out as he could. But as the press moved ahead of us taking pictures, we slowed, and the shoppers began crowding in. They quite literally mobbed EH, pushing forwards to shake his hand and pat him on the back, asking for autographs and here and there to stop and take photographs.

'One lady rushed up to him, threw her arms around his neck and kissed him, which brought a cheer from the sizeable crowd. Shopkeepers came out and invited him into their shops, which he did, shaking hands everywhere. He was smiling throughout, and laughing a lot as the good natured crowd followed every step of his progress. It was clear to me that this was good for everyone all round, and in particular for him, since he was now meeting real people, who were showing him a warm reception.

'Later that night, when finally back in Central Office, I had my ears chewed off by the publicists for daring to move away from the plan, and I was accused of messing up the campaign. However, the TV news coverage that night and the press attention on the Sunday gave a different view. The day of the "walkabout" had arrived.

'On Monday morning I was instructed to insert walkabouts wherever possible into every day's campaigning. At first I couldn't believe I had changed the direction of our campaign!'

Douglas Hurd recalls how doubts persisted about the party's chances right up to the wire:

'On the evening of 12 June 1970, after Mr Heath's speech at Manchester, I was standing at the back of the Free Trade Hall watching the crowds jostle their way out when a Party official told me that the *Daily Mail* next morning would carry an NOP poll showing us 12.4 points behind. It was the worst yet. There were only six days to go. I went to warn Mr Heath, but he had already left for the hotel. I hurried after him, but was too late. On his way up the stairs from the public lounge to his room a journalist gave him the news and asked for his reaction. I cannot remember his reply, but I can remember the blank look on his face.'

'I was so busy, that I didn't really ask myself if I believed we were going to win. Certainly I was surrounded by people who didn't think he was going to win, but I was loyal. Peter Carrington, who was chairman of the party, drove down to Bexley and saw Ted all by himself and apparently said, "If we lose, I think there will have to be a leadership election," but Ted brushed him aside and said, "No, no, we're not going to lose . . . relax, relax." Then, right at the end there was one opinion poll, ORC, which on the day itself gave us a slight lead and I did think, "Well, maybe we do have a chance." When we won, it was one of the most exciting moments of my life.'[52]

Even on election day itself, Heath was in a small minority in believing not only that he might win, but that he definitely was going to win. His principal aide on the day, **Roger Boaden**, recalls the pressure that had built on Heath as the number of doubters grew: 'I was rarely in any of the meetings, but each day on the campaign trail, I was conscious of his occasional comments, and the periodic visitations from senior Party figures for "private" chats.'

Eventually, however, the pressure found a release in 'an enormous outburst of emotion and frustration', as Boaden explains in this revealing scene:

'I spent Election Day, 18 June, with EH in his constituency of Bexley. He visited Committee Rooms, and travelled from Polling Station to Polling Station greeting electors and Party workers. Once the declaration of his result was made and he had celebrated briefly with his constituency officers, we set off in the Rover to Central Office.

'At first there was silence, until someone suggested we might listen to the radio. Bob West, the chauffeur, switched on just in time for an announcement being made: "That result confirms Edward Heath will be the next Prime Minister." We all applauded, congratulated him and waited. Suddenly, he slapped his hand on the side of his front seat, and said, "Bugger them, bugger the lot of them."'

CHAPTER THREE

Prime Minister (1970–1974)

Heath took office as Prime Minister in an unusual state of mind. In defiance of the relentless emotional and physical demands of a gruelling national election campaign, he had kept his head when all around him were losing theirs and blaming it on him. He had never lost his conviction he would win; and he was resolutely convinced the nation needed his leadership and his policies. A once-proud land was becoming the sick man of Europe; and it was to Europe he looked, for inspiration, for rigour, for renewed energy, for the stimulus that would force the land he loved to rediscover its greatness. He had no desire to set class against class, race against race or region against region. He was a 'One Nation' Conservative through and through, but he wanted to see all men (and women) of goodwill come together to refresh and renew – not to overthrow – the social contract that held the people together; to shake the body politic out of its complacency; and to goad British industry out of the torpor into which it had lately slumped. His overriding ambition was to take the United Kingdom into the EEC, but not shyly or apologetically, as a latecomer might slip through the back door into a party: he wanted the UK to walk tall as it embraced its continental destiny and that required him to lead an economic revival, even as he persuaded the latest generation of European politicians that the UK wanted to join the EEC in a positive spirit, not to spoil things for everyone else. Heath certainly had a vision, but it was essentially a rational one – technocratic and arrived at by a deliberative process, not a manic flash of inspiration. The key to everything was a healthy economy – 'expansion' as he termed it – and that was the first priority.

Journalist and writer **Terry Coleman** talked to Heath in Bexley on the eve of the 1970 general election. Heath was by now tired and careworn – and knew there was no more he could do to influence the outcome. Quite by chance – by his own admission, at the end of a singularly unsuccessful interview up to that point – Coleman suddenly hit a nerve by referring back to Heath's remark earlier that evening, when he had told an audience of Bexley constituents, which included a significant proportion of young people, that the key to everything was the creation of greater national wealth. 'Without exception?' asked Coleman. 'Without exception,' confirmed Heath:

> 'Then he came alive and spoke with a direct strength I hadn't seen in the two days I had been following him. "If you've ever been poor," he said, "you will know that . . . Look, the joy I've had today, seeing these young people, they've got an immeasurably freer life than I ever had . . . Without some prosperity you can't have a full life; travelling, theatre, books, books of your own and not borrowed from the library. This matters to me. I like to have things of my own. Pictures of my own, even if they are poor pictures."
>
> 'He did not, as I understood him, use the word "joy" as a politician would use it from the platform. He used it as a word one doesn't use often. He said it wasn't just materialism . . . But weren't friends, women, children, among these good things of life? He said of course they were, but let him tell me, you were a damn sight more capable of enjoying something if you didn't have to worry about not having enough. "There's an old saying of the Salvation Army: 'You can't cast out the devil on an empty belly.' And they're right."'[1]

The task of shaping the economic policies of the Heath government was entrusted to Iain Macleod, the new Chancellor of the Exchequer. His death, just weeks after taking office, had a shattering effect on Heath, as **David Howell** explains:

> 'The Heath Government was struck a terrible blow – perhaps even a mortal blow – within just a month of taking office, with the tragedy within a

tragedy, the sudden death of Iain Macleod, after an appendicitis operation. Had he lived, everything would have been different. Macleod sensed that we had to escape a whole imprisoning set of attitudes and assumptions if the country was to shake off its burdens and move forward: taxes had to be cut, regulations eased, the choking grip of militant trades unionism released and the machinery of central government reformed to make any of it possible. Macleod sensed all this, even if he did not fully understand where we had to start – which was right at the very heart of the central government administration. When appointed by Heath as shadow chancellor, he had re-joined the Tory mainstream, now the despised magic circle had melted away. "Come and see me soon," he scribbled on a card he wrote to me just after Ted had appointed him as shadow chancellor. "I have much to learn quickly. But then I learn quickly." Macleod's oratory and wit, in that penetrating, almost grating voice, would have been the ideal counterpoint to Heath's undeniably dull chant-speech style.'

Macleod was replaced as Chancellor by Tony Barber, whom Heath had initially appointed to lead the negotiations for accession to the EEC. He became part of Heath's inner cabinet – the small group of senior ministers whom Heath could call at any time, for reassurance, information or advice (the other senior 'trusties' being Peter Carrington, Willie Whitelaw* and Alec Home – but never Reggie Maudling or, still less, Keith Joseph or Margaret Thatcher). **Tony Barber** was certainly loyal:

'Whereas to Harold Macmillan the cultivation of one's political supporters was all part of the game, Ted seemed to find it distasteful to be pleasant to those he did not respect. Maybe he was right, for there is often something slightly hypocritical about political alliances. One other thing should be said about Ted Heath. For three years at the end of the sixties I was Chairman of the Party, Willie Whitelaw was Chief Whip and Jim Prior was the Parliamentary Private Secretary. We were all devoted to Ted

---

* When, just a week before polling day in 1970, Whitelaw acknowledged to him that the Tories might win, Heath responded, 'So you've decided to climb on the bandwagon at last!'

although he was not the easiest of leaders to "sell". But to his friends he was 100% reliable . . . One reason why there were no resignations from Ted's Cabinet was because he always allowed a full discussion on any major issue which was controversial. Whatever the result, ministers could not complain that they had not had a proper opportunity to put their case.

'There was an internal communicating door between Nos. 10 and 11 which was always unlocked. This meant that, unbeknown to the outside world and, more important, unbeknown to my Cabinet colleagues, I could see the Prime Minister at any time I wanted – provided only that he was free. A quiet word in the Prime Minister's ear before Cabinet could work wonders. It also meant that, if Ted had had a depressing day, he knew that he could always walk through to No. 11 and there would be awaiting him a bottle of his favourite malt.'[2]

Heath once said to me that the most important relationship in any government – bar none – was that between the PM and the Chancellor. Of course he was, at least in part, making a point about the cooling, then breakdown, in the Thatcher–Lawson relationship, but he meant what he said and the thesis is a powerful one. Only once did he struggle to demonstrate support to Tony Barber, which was in November 1970, when Harold Wilson rose in the chamber of the Commons to raise a point with Barber, who began his response with the fatal words 'I can tell the Prime Minister, who is getting up . . .'[3] He was then drowned out entirely for a time by triumphant cat-calls from the Labour benches. According to Barber, Heath was not amused: 'I looked around in vain for some solace from my own benches and then turned to the new Prime Minister. Ted did not think it at all funny. His face was expressionless. It took me quite some time to get the speech back on track.'[4]

Heath also retained within No. 10 an independent source of economic advice – Brian Reading, who had been on his staff since 1966. Reading's economic briefings to Heath are now readily available in the Public Record Office and, upon studying them, I did find myself wondering whether they were not, perhaps, a little too academic – abstruse even – for Heath. Frankly, I am not convinced he would have understood them. If he had fully comprehended and assimilated what he was being told, the history of the Heath

Government might have been very different, as **Brian Reading** himself explains:

'After the election it took several weeks before my appointment as one of the first special advisers was confirmed by the Cabinet Office – including full security clearance. Meanwhile Macleod, briefly Chancellor, died. The job was handed over to Tony Barber, an extremely nice man but hardly qualified for the job. This meant that the Treasury was able to dictate policy, which they could not have done under Macleod. Heath was more interested in Europe. He also had the greatest respect for Civil Service Mandarins from his former ministerial days. The Treasury was left largely to get on with implementing fiscal policy and any advice I gave Heath was dismissed.'

Reading goes on to list three specific pieces of advice that Heath chose to ignore: that technical changes should be made to the new 'Value Added Tax' system being introduced by the government; that this introduction should be softened by making changes to income tax; and that the government should be preparing for a possible recession rather than the recovery forecast by the Treasury. There was also a fourth example about the 1972 miners' strike that Reading considers was the 'most important' of all:

'I argued that the miners did a nasty, hard, dangerous and unhealthy job working underground. They were paid less than London secretaries. The value of the coal produced was insufficient to pay anything towards their wages. The miners' wage bill was met by the government, i.e. tax payers. I argued that it was wrong to fight miners' demands for more pay – everyone knew they deserved it. Instead the NUM should be told it could set miners' pay as high as it liked, but, at the same time, a list of pits would be produced showing which would then not be worth keeping open. They would have to choose between pay and jobs. Instead the government would be prepared initially to spend the money saved on retraining, redundancy payments, re-housing, pensions etc for miners who lost their jobs. The issue would become how generous the government would be to rescue miners from their nasty, hard, dangerous and unhealthy jobs working underground. Heath said "Brian, you don't understand politics."'

'I then decided I was wasting my time as an adviser whose advice was ignored. I accepted an offer from Alastair Burnet to become the first Economics Editor of the *Economist*. Alan Walters was rewarded with a knighthood for his work with Thatcher. I was rewarded for my six years with Heath with a glass of sweet sherry. This correctly sums up the value of my contribution compared with his . . . [but] make no mistake, I liked and respected Ted Heath while disagreeing with him.'

Reading may eventually have parted ways with Heath but he originally had high hopes for what the new government could achieve. He was not alone – as **David Howell** explains:

'We wanted less and better government and we wanted not just speeches, but also the management tools to help bring change about. We were sure that Ted Heath, the grammar-school boy, would cut through all the delay and obfuscation, re-direct the civil service machine and put us on a new and better path.

'The starting point of "New Style of Government thinking" was that the centralised corporatist state, as bequeathed by the Attlee Government, had failed and would continue to fail. The private sector could, on the whole, do better. Private enterprise could be harnessed to public purposes. In our naïveté we thought this was obvious to everyone. We thought it was understood that the liberalised market economy had to find new ways of working with the state, as in Germany – and to some extent in France . . . What we were really about were the actual mechanics of translating a heavily socialised economy into a free market and enterprise economy. It was in our eyes not just a question of making speeches about liberty and freedom and the market economy, however finely phrased, but of figuring out how these ideals might be turned into policy in hard, practical, step-by-step detail: how, in short, the transformation away from the state socialised era might actually be accomplished.'

A familiar face would soon be joining Heath in his private office at No. 10, in July 1970 – **Christopher Roberts**, who had worked with him during the attempt to take the UK into the EEC a decade earlier. Roberts recalls his experience of working for Heath:

'Ted showed remarkable qualities of patience and endurance, together with an ability to encourage allies and conciliate opponents. . . . This belies the reputation Ted acquired in later years for unreasonableness and poor handling of people.

'His staff enjoyed working for Ted, I believe without exception . . . I knew, of course, that on the occasions when Ted and I lunched à deux there would be long silences. Ted did not think it necessary to make polite conversation with his thirty-five-year-old Private Secretary, or to tell him at frequent intervals what a splendid job he was doing. I saw no need for this then, nor do I now. My colleagues and I knew that we would be left to get on with our jobs, and take as much responsibility as we could, as when I was asked to draft a speech for him on education policy, about which I knew little, without consulting the responsible Secretary of State, Margaret Thatcher. Fortunately I found a sympathetic senior official in the Education Department who was willing to help out on condition of strict anonymity . . . Ted was very hospitable to members of his Private Office. Any of us who enjoyed music were welcome at his weekend concerts at Chequers. We, and our families, were invited to his annual party at Number Ten after the Trooping the Colour ceremonies. And this hospitality continued after he left office, at his house in the Close at Salisbury and on special occasions like his eightieth birthday party on the Thames.'

Heath's great supporter **Peter Walker** was a natural choice for the new Cabinet:

'My wife Tessa and I turned on the television in London on the Saturday morning and saw Alec Douglas-Home and Iain Macleod going into No. 10. That afternoon we had to attend a wedding and we wondered what to do. Could we phone 10 Downing Street and say, if by any chance the Prime Minister wants a word, I will be at a wedding at such-and-such a church? Tessa went to the wedding and I stayed at home. The phone did ring and the Prime Minister asked me to be Minister for Housing and Local Government.

'I always remember the non-biased way in which he conducted Cabinet meetings. When I introduced a cabinet paper for the modernisation of the steel industry, Ted began by saying: "You all remember that the Secretary of State came a few weeks ago with a Bill for £x million for the coal industry and we all agreed to that – today he's coming with a paper for the steel industry and I know we won't make the same mistake again."'

Having served in opposition as an effective economics spokesman, **Patrick Jenkin** was a 'shoo in' as Financial Secretary to the Treasury in the new administration. Here he outlines the expectations and the challenges facing Heath as Prime Minister:

'The Selsdon Park weekend for the Shadow Cabinet had established the basis for what would become the policy of a new Government. As well as a commitment to renew the application to join the EEC, it was made clear that Heath's Conservative Party was determined to move firmly away from the 'Butskellite' compromises of the past and, instead, set a course towards smaller government; lower taxation; stronger competition; much less intervention in industry with an end to Labour's Industrial Reorganisation Commission; trade union reform rather than compulsory wage control; firmer control of immigration; and more selective social services, with an emphasis on concentrating help on those who needed it most. Considering that list, it is perhaps little wonder that it was later said Heath's manifesto commitments were quite close to the policies in the early years of the Thatcher Government.

'This was all given a much higher profile than originally intended by Harold Wilson's savage attacks on "Selsdon Man" – so much so that the public became well aware that a Conservative Government led by Ted Heath would be a change, not only from the 1964–1970 Labour Government, but also from previous Conservative Governments. Moreover, the public recognition that it was primarily to Heath that credit was due for the election victory gave him great authority, and he set about using it to promote his agenda.

'The experience of those who worked for him was of a very tough Premier determined to implement the policies on which he had been elected. The *New Statesman* quoted a senior civil servant as saying: "The new man at No 10 is the toughest operator since Neville Chamberlain. He knows what he has gone there to do and nothing will stop him. Nothing." Although his statement on taking office had spoken of a need to unite the nation, he did not hesitate to set about some measures that were bound to be divisive. In October 1970 he told the Party Conference: "We were returned to office to change the course of history of this nation – nothing less." He made it clear that economic growth was crucial to the achievement of his other objectives. He had a firm conviction, from personal and family experience, that economic well-being should have overriding priority. "Slow growth would aggravate all the social problems of poor housing and education, deprivation, racial tension, violence and crime" as one adviser put it.'

Jenkin, like so many other commentators on the Heath government, also points to the death of Iain Macleod as a crucial turning point:

'His first setback came very soon. After only a month as Chancellor of the Exchequer, Iain Macleod, having for years stoically coped with increasing pain, died in No. 11 Downing Street. It is hard to exaggerate the blow to the Government this caused. Macleod had been seen not only as the Party's most perceptive tactician, but also as its greatest trumpeter. As one colleague put it later, Macleod "had a skill unsurpassed in men of any party in my generation of raising issues in a big way, which commanded attention not only among his own party supporters, but amongst the country at large". I had been appointed as Financial Secretary to the Treasury and I was in tears after Robert Armstrong, then Ted's Principal Private Secretary at No. 10, phoned to tell me of Iain's death. As well as my very personal sense of loss, I was also very aware of the loss to the Government. I have never hesitated to assert that in what became my 50 years in Parliament, this was by far my worst day.

'For Ted Heath personally, it was an appalling tragedy. While his election victory had apparently enhanced his authority, the relative isolation occasioned by being at No 10, his belief that he was now entitled to press his views on colleagues, and his inability to understand why others did not always accept his opinions, all led to him once again being accused of failing to put the Government's case effectively. Indeed, one respected historian has written that: "It is arguable that it was in that first year that the Heath Government lost the communications battle and never afterwards got back on top of things."

'By April 1971, the Party Chairman was saying that recent polling "confirmed a good deal of other evidence we have that the Conservative Party is at present seen as unrepresentative, uncommunicative and remote, with little knowledge of or interest in the problems of ordinary people". Those final words embody perhaps the most chilling warning in political life – that a political party is "out of touch with ordinary people". This underlined the impact of Macleod's loss. There was no comparable figure in the Government with the will or weight to buttress Heath when he was right; and stand up to him when he was wrong.

'Although Anthony Barber was able eventually to put his own stamp on Treasury policies, I have clear recollections of him returning from Cabinet again and again having been overruled by Heath. He asked us, his junior Ministers, whether he should resign, but we advised him against this as it would serve only to draw attention to the problem and so undermine the Government's reputation for economic competence.

'Macleod's death had other malign consequences. Though the consequent reshuffle of Ministers was quite small, it brought into Government John Davies, a captain of industry, a former Managing Director of Shell and an influential Director of the Confederation of British Industry. Other Governments have chosen to appoint outside businessmen to be Ministers with very mixed results, but Davies's appointment to the Ministry of Technology and, later, to an expanded Department of Trade and Industry, was a disaster. He had no political experience, no gifts of oratory; and he tended to get bogged down in detail, finding the House of Commons a terrible trial. With rising unemployment, rising prices and growing Trade Union militancy, the Government's strategy came under pressure. Though it had started to implement the "Selsdon" economic policies, including abolishing the IRC and other interventionist bodies, the Government decided to undertake a full review of industrial policy; though this was done outside Davies's Department, his officials must have kept him informed. This led to one of the episodes in Parliament which left me having to respond to much Labour and Liberal derision, but which also undermined my confidence in Heath.'

Having been one of the first within the Heath Government to scent the troubles that would bedevil it, **David Howell** nonetheless ploughed on, even as his once close working relationship with Heath dwindled to almost no contact at all and he, along with other ministers, felt that senior civil servants had far more influence over Heath than they did:

'Something happened to Ted Heath once he became Prime Minister. The old sparkle vanished and my relationship with him faded away. Our reforms – and the whole New Style of Government package – were nominally adopted but the back-up was not there, interest trickled away and No. 10 sank into a quagmire of crises, with officials closing round the Prime Minister and suffocating all real radicalism. Despite these discouragements there were plenty of younger civil servants in some of the ministries who could see what we were driving at and welcomed the new emphasis on objectives and purposes in their work, but they were not the one in charge, so it soon became painfully clear our reforms were just "not on" – that familiar phrase resounding down the years and nowadays being used to frustrate any serious and fundamental reform of the European Union. As [Conservative MP] Ernest Marples had warned us would happen, the urgent ousted the important and we were lost.

'Almost the last time I was close to Heath and felt any real warmth between us was when he invited me to Chequers one wintry afternoon in January 1971. He was kind, interested and friendly, wanting to know how I was getting on, but I could feel things sliding away. He said that "they" were pushing him towards a prices and incomes policy, horror of horrors. Who were "they", though? The answer in part had come out of his study door just before I went in – in the distinctive form of three mandarins, namely Sir Burke Trend, Sir Denis Greenhill and Donald Maitland (later "Sir" and also Press Secretary at No. 10 in more civilised days, and after that – almost a decade on – my Permanent Secretary at the Department of Energy).

'The ostensible purpose of that Chequers afternoon was to give me a pay increase. Why? Because there was apparently no legal backing for a salary for a Parliamentary Secretary at the new Civil Service Department (CSD) and I was instead listed as a Lord Commissioner of the Treasury, at a salary of £3,000 per annum. The Prime Minister now told me I was also to become Parliamentary Secretary at the Department of Employment. It would involve a pay increase of £750 but would not involve me in any way with the work of the Department. He had obviously taken some trouble. We chatted on. He asked after my family, then came to the door to wave me goodbye and told me to take care of myself, watching as I drove away. It was the end of something. When I got back to London, the Permanent Secretary at the Employment Department, Sir Denis Barnes, rang to tell me that I would be answering Questions in the Commons on Employment matters and would I please attend meetings in his Department. So much for Heath's well intentioned assurance. As the ever-critical Ernest Marples was fond of saying, Heath was not really in charge.'

It was not long before some on the right began to have doubts about the Government's change of direction. In public **Norman Tebbit** remained loyal, but in 1971 he was already losing heart:

'The first six or nine months of Ted Heath's Government had been difficult. What none of us knew was that it was going to get worse. Worse both because of outside events such as the oil crisis and because Ted Heath himself was to desert the Selsdon programme on which he had been elected and retreat into corporatism, and from there into a mishmash of ill-considered centralist and socialist hand-to-mouth devices with no intellectual nor political cohesion, marked only by fits of obstinacy alternating with climb-down. He certainly understood the nuts and bolts of any issue with which he was concerned. Perhaps only Margaret Thatcher has shown a greater command of detail across such a wide range of issues but, for her, details are details, and they are built upon a general and usually consistent structure of belief and policy; for him details seemed always to obstruct commitment and obscure vision – except of course on Europe. However, at that time – before I had yet been in Parliament for a full year – I was unwilling to admit that my faith in the Prime Minister was faltering.'[5]

What of Heath himself during these first crucial months in office? **Douglas Hurd** describes those heady, early days of power:

'I had never seriously considered what my position would be if Mr Heath won the General Election of 1970. I vaguely supposed that I would con-tinue to work for him, but we had never discussed it. It would have tempted Providence to raise the subject with him during the election campaign, most of all in the last ten days when as a precaution we had to steel our-selves for defeat. So when he told me on the afternoon of 19 June to go to Ten Downing Street I had to ask how I should announce myself. "It's perfectly simple. Tell them you are my Political Secretary," he said, as if reminding me of some obvious fact which I had forgotten. The only remaining difficulty was that I had no idea what a Political Secretary was or what he did. Nor was there anyone I could ask.'[6]

Alan Simcock, who was already working in the No. 10 private office when Heath won the general election, can take us back to the very first moments of his premiership:

'Because Her Majesty The Queen had been all day at Ascot for the rac-ing, it was quite late before Mr Wilson could go to Buckingham Palace to tender his resignation, and even later before Mr Heath could kiss hands on appointment as Prime Minister and then come on to No. 10. One of my colleagues is reported as remembering that all the No. 10 staff were gathered in the entrance hall and applauded Mr Heath as he made his way to the Cabinet Room. My memory is different. Since it was so late, most of the staff had gone home for the week-end. A few from elsewhere in the building were still in the entrance hall, but I remember Sandy Isserlis greeting Mr Heath at the front door and bringing him more or less in silence down the corridor to the Cabinet Ante-Room.

'After Mr Heath and the group accompanying him had installed themselves in the Cabinet Room, we came to the first point at which the change-over made an impression. It was by then well into the evening, and it had been a long day for everyone. Mr Heath asked if "the No. 10 kitchen" could provide some food. I had to explain that there was no "No. 10 kitchen". There was the main kitchen under the State Dining Room, but that was staffed only on the occasions when there was a formal dinner or other function in the State rooms. There was also a kitchen in the basement where staff could prepare food for themselves. Apart from that, there was only the kitchen in the Prime Minister's flat. Nor was there anything in the adjoining Cabinet Office except for midday meals on week-days. I went on to say that, because we had thought that we would need to be working late, we had arranged some food for ourselves, and Mr Heath and his party were welcome to share it. (I had sent one of the No. 10 staff drivers to a nearby supermarket with some money to buy such ready-to-eat food as was available, together with some drinks.) Everyone ate heartily, but it later became clear that our impromptu supper was regarded as not up to scratch: various commentators reported the supper, suggesting that it represented a drop in the standards of public life. Later, in 1986, it seemed amusing that the first episode of *Yes, Prime Minister* included a scene in which the private secretary had to explain to the fictional Prime Minister the lack of catering arrangements in No. 10. Art does mirror life.

'Next day, it became clear that Mr Heath and the team working with him – William Whitelaw, Lord Carrington, Francis Pym, Douglas Hurd – were very ready to work with, and trust, the team of private secretaries that he had inherited. Even what could have been a difficult mishap was seen as proof that we were carefully working to make sure that nothing went wrong: the Cabinet appointments had all been agreed; the Cabinet members had accepted their posts; the necessary submission to The Queen had been sent to Buckingham Palace; and we were proof-reading the press notice to announce the new Cabinet. Then one of us noticed that no one had been appointed as President of the Board of Trade. The Board of Trade was a major government department – and one, moreover, that Mr Heath had headed in the last Conservative government. Mr Heath held a rapid consultation with his team, and the No. 10 switchboard was told to track down Mr Michael Noble in his Argyllshire constituency. Fortunately, he could be found and was delighted to be offered the Cabinet post. A further submission was quickly sent off to the Palace, and The Queen's approval obtained over the telephone. There was not time to re-type the whole of the press notice (in those days, press notices were produced on duplicators from wax stencils): Mr Noble's name had to be squeezed in at the bottom as a correction (the alignment of his entry was thus slightly different from the rest, but fortunately no one in the media noticed this and asked why). The whole exercise was completed in time for the 6 o'clock news. Mr Heath accepted what had happened with very good humour, and even suggested that he should have noticed the absence of a President of the Board of Trade. A good collaboration between his political office and the existing private office was under way.

'From the start, it was clear that Mr Heath was determined that everything should be done properly and in good order. I am sure that this was because he realised that there were people in the Conservative Party who would want to criticise him if they could claim that standards were slipping. At the same time, he had a conception of the office of Prime Minister which laid more emphasis on its representational role than Mr Wilson had. In great part, this was due to his overriding concern that the United Kingdom should join the European Communities. To achieve this, he needed to organise events and use No. 10 and Chequers in ways that went well beyond a simple office and house.

'An early example of this aim and the problems of achieving it came with the ministerial dinner on the eve of the State Opening of Parliament in 1970. There was a long tradition, dating back to the eighteenth century, that, on the eve of the State Opening, the Prime Minister entertained to dinner the members of the Government in the House of Parliament to which he belonged, while the Leader of the other House entertained the ministers in that House. Before dinner, the Queen's Speech was read to the assembled Ministers. Mr Heath naturally wanted to follow this procedure. When he was shown the draft invitation to be sent to the members of the Government in the House of Commons, he took exception to specifying "black tie". His recollection of these functions was that the proper dress was white tie and tails. Mr Whitelaw (Lord President of the Council and

Leader of the House of Commons) and Mr Pym (Parliamentary Secretary to the Treasury – that is, Chief Whip) were aghast: they considered that most ministers would regard it as an imposition to be asked to turn out in this dress, and thought there might be adverse comment in the media if ministers were photographed arriving at the front door of No. 10 in white tie and tails.

'Fortunately, the Chief Whip's office were able to find evidence that there had been a similar problem in 1951, when Sir Winston Churchill, returning to No. 10 as Prime Minister, had wanted to impose levée dress (tail-coat, breeches and silk stockings) as the dress for the eve-of-session dinner. The then Chief Whip had reacted to this in the same way as Mr Pym nineteen years later. The white tie and tails that Mr Heath remembered had been the eventual compromise. Given this Churchillian precedent, Mr Heath was prepared to concede and accept that the ministers could wear dinner jackets. Mr Heath was frequently prepared to concede if he could be shown to be following a Churchillian precedent.

'The Prime Ministerial flat in the roof storey of No. 10 was central to Mr Heath's life, both for work and relaxation. The flat was quickly re-organised for him after he took office. The main change was that the north-west room that had previously been the main sitting-room was turned into a bedroom for Mr Heath. As well as his bed and desk, it had a large settee and a number of armchairs, and could therefore (and frequently was) used for informal meetings, including the twice-weekly briefings for Prime Minister's Questions. It also had his clavichord and record-player. My memory is that when it was necessary to intrude on him in an evening, it was the clavichord in the flat that he was usually to be found playing, rather than the grand piano in the White Drawing Room on the floor below. In the morning, it was his practice to have his breakfast at a small table in this room, and then work on his red boxes until it was time to shave, bathe and dress for the first meeting of the day.

'Mr Heath was also concerned to ensure that the rest of No. 10 was up to the representational role that he considered essential. Substantial redecoration was carried out, some of which was also prompted by a renewed outbreak of dry rot in the western wall of the back part of the building. New pictures were also located for some of the State rooms, including the loan of a Renoir for the White Drawing Room, where his grand piano was placed. He also persuaded the Chequers Trustees to carry out there a similar programme of improvements.

'Like all my colleagues, I also had to support him by drafting speeches. Everyone who was involved in this task found it hard work: he was reluctant to turn his mind to a future speech and (except for set-piece speeches) rarely had a clear idea of what basic points he wanted to make. My first experience was with unpromising material – the opening of the World Cycling Championships in Leicester in August 1970, an engagement inherited from his predecessor. A couple of weeks beforehand, I put into his box a draft speech covering what it seemed necessary to say. It came back next day with a one-word comment: "Redraft". I discussed with the Sports Council what more might be said, and put a second draft into his box. It too returned next morning with the same one-word comment: "Redraft". My third attempt, which differed mainly in the opening paragraph, did not re-emerge: it was left in the box unmarked, and in the usual way went back to him with every set of boxes. Further reminders that the day for the speech was approaching also received no response beyond "I'll look at it". Eventually, on the journey to Leicester, he agreed to turn his attention from more interesting papers and read it through. He then delivered it with some verve, somehow making it sound quite a good speech. This sort of sequence was repeated on many occasions. Sometimes he added the variant of announcing when he stood up that he was not going to read the speech that had been prepared for him, but then delivered from memory more or less the draft that he had been given.

'A substantial part of my work for Mr Heath can best be described as the "stage management" of No. 10 and, for some occasions, Chequers. One of my tasks was keeping the diary and negotiating the timing of all the engagements that had to be fitted in. Mr Heath's wishes were a crucial part of this task: sailing week-ends were sacrosanct; he liked to go to Chequers for other week-ends and always wanted to sleep there when rehearsals for Trooping the Colour were held on Horseguards Parade (the military bands struck up at 6:00 am!); and he did not like early-morning meetings. Ensuring that the timetable, once settled, was adhered to, was another problem. On many days, my heart would sink when Mr Heath came into the private office at the start of the morning and announced "Alan, we must be flexible." This usually meant a new load of work re-jigging the timing of all the Cabinet committees, ministerial meetings and other events.

'A particularly difficult piece of time-keeping was ensuring that Mr Heath came down to the Cabinet Room for a meeting of Cabinet or one of the senior Cabinet Committees at 10:00 am. As said earlier, he would read his briefing over breakfast before shaving, bathing and dressing. I often had the dilemma of whether to wait a little longer for him to emerge, or go up to his bathroom to chivvy him. Such a dilemma was even worse when there was a State dinner for some important personage. Getting Mr Heath down to the front door of No. 10 to welcome the visitor was often a problem. The worst case was a State dinner for the Emperor of Ethiopia, Haile Selassie. In spite of chivvying, Mr Heath was still in his bathroom at the time when the Emperor was due to arrive. With a final warning, I went down to the front door just in time to see the official car drawing up. I found myself having to welcome the Emperor to No. 10, towering over his diminutive figure, while Mr Heath came galumphing (there is no other word) down the corridor from the lift.

'Another difficult element of the diary was the period after Prime Minister's Questions, every Tuesday and Thursday. Mr Heath's Parliamentary Private Secretary, Timothy Kitson, saw these times as the ideal opportunity for him to get Mr Heath to meet Conservative back-benchers in the Commons tea-room. It proved quite difficult to get Mr Heath to fall in with this. Time and again he would say that he needed to come back to No. 10 to work on his boxes, or would suggest it as the best time for some other meeting that needed to be fitted in. In the long run, the failure to take advantage of this kind of opportunity may have had serious results for him in 1974.'

Robert Armstrong worked with Heath almost through the entirety of his tenure as Prime Minister. His account of those days is invaluable:

'I was surprised to be told by my Permanent Secretary, Douglas Allen, on Wednesday 1 July 1970 that I was to be the new Prime Minister's

Principal Private Secretary, starting work next Monday. The outgoing Prime Minister had only just appointed Sandy Isserlis to the post, following the sudden death of Michael Halls, and the assumption had been that he would continue in post after the election. I was told that Mr Heath wanted someone from an economic department, and that, since he was thought to be a difficult man to get on with, a shared love of music might help me to establish a satisfactory working relationship with him. That proved to have been good thinking. And that appointment turned out to be the turning point in my career as a civil servant.

'So at nine o'clock in the morning of 6 July 1970 I went into 10 Downing Street to take up my new duties. I spent the day being taken round the house to be introduced to all the seventy or so people who worked there – except the Prime Minister. Then at 6.30 pm, as I was sitting with my predecessor to go through some secret papers, the door from the Cabinet room opened, and in came Edward Heath. He looked at me, and said: "Oh, you here? It's going to be very hard work, you know", and then he went back into the Cabinet room, closing the door, without giving me any opportunity of replying. No "glad to see you", or "come and have a drink". He was right, of course: it was very hard work. His greeting was characteristic: no pleasantries or small talk; business-like and to the point. That was how it was going to be.

'He was not good at the little things that oil the wheels of a busy life. When someone had done him some service he did not seem to be able to say "thank you" or "well done". And yet he seemed to be aware of his deficiency. He once said to a friend of mine whose brother was working for him: "I wish you would tell your brother how much I appreciate all he does for me; you see, I can't do it myself."

'I did not become sure that I was (as Jeeves would have said) giving satisfaction until I had been in No. 10 for over two years, when one afternoon William Armstrong, then the Head of the Civil Service, came in to tell the Prime Minister that he was proposing to post me back to the Treasury and promote me to be a Deputy Secretary there. When he came out I asked him how he had got on. He told me, with a wry smile, that the Prime Minister had said: "You must be out of your mind if you think that I am going to let Robert go. You can promote him on the spot and leave him where he is." This was very reassuring: not only was I providing him a service that he valued; we had become friends.

'Loyalty was one of his strongest and most consistent attributes. He was loyal to his friends, and to colleagues who were loyal to him. He was loyal to institutions of which he was a member . . . He was deeply loyal to his country. This became especially evident to me when we were in Singapore in January 1971 for a Commonwealth Heads of Government Meeting (CHOGM). The Prime Minister gave a dinner for the Prime Ministers of Australia, Malaysia, New Zealand and Singapore on board one of Her Majesty's frigates which was moored in the harbour. After we had drunk the Loyal Toast – seated, of course, in accordance with naval tradition – the party went on deck for a performance of Beating The Retreat by a contingent of Royal Marines. That great harbour was lined with ships of the Royal Navy, all brilliantly lit, and we all knew that in ten weeks' time the ships of the Royal Navy would be leaving their base in Singapore for the last time and forever, as a consequence of the decision by the previous British government to withdraw the British military presence East of Suez. When it came to the Last Post the Prime Minister and all his guests stood up. It was an intensely moving moment, and I doubt whether any British eye was dry. The Prime Minister's eyes certainly were not.

'Edward Heath was a very self-contained and private man. He had a group of personal friends, men and women, to whom he was consistently loyal, and whose friendship he kept separate from his political life. He had had a long-term girl-friend before and (so far as was possible) during the war, but he seems never to have asked her to marry him, and she eventually gave up waiting and married someone else. Perhaps he felt that his prospects were so uncertain that he could not be sure of being able to afford marriage and a family. Perhaps his ambitions were too strongly focused on a political career. But he never ceased to keep her photograph on his bedside table. I wondered whether he had resolved that he would never risk the possibility – the humiliation, as he might have felt it – of another such disappointment.

'Late in his life, in 1983, when he was not well, he told me that he was minded to spend the winter in Southern Spain. I suggested that that would be too far for his friends to come and visit him, and he might find himself very lonely. He said: "I have never been lonely until now." My mind went back to the day, early in the life of his government, when his friend and colleague Iain Macleod unexpectedly died suddenly after an operation. I was at home that evening and had not heard the news, when the telephone rang. It was No. 10: the Prime Minister wanted to speak to me. When he came on the line, he said, in a very flat voice: "Iain's dead. You'd better come in." I went in, and found the Prime Minister on his own, alone in his flat. It left me with a strong impression of the loneliness of his life, living on his own in the private apartment at the top of 10 Downing Street.

'Music was important in his life. He was a good musician: and music was a constant source of pleasure, and, like sailing, a refreshment which temporarily took his mind off his political preoccupations. He would sometimes come back to No. 10 in the early evening, and go upstairs to play his Steinway piano for a quarter of an hour. When he had a clear evening, it was his habit to retreat to the sitting room in the private apartment on the second floor of No. 10, have a light supper on his knee in the armchair and a glass of single malt whisky, read the papers in his overnight box, and play music on his record player. The music would often be by Richard Wagner or Richard Strauss, and would be played at the highest possible volume. If I had occasion to go up with a message or something, I would know as I left the Private Office that he was playing a record; by the time I reached the first floor I would know what he was playing; and when I went into the sitting room I would know that I had no chance of making myself heard unless he turned the volume down.'

The greatest economic evils at home – which jeopardised Heath's dream of taking a strong United Kingdom straight into a powerful, leading position within the EEC – were poor industrial relations, which were inextricably linked to a dangerous propensity to high inflation, which was contributing to poor economic performance, which was, in turn, further exacerbated by poor industrial relations. Heath was initially optimistic. He knew many senior trade unionists from his time as Minister of Labour, when he had earned a reputation as a fair, decent and practical person. In 1960, with Macmillan abroad and Rab Butler in charge, he had intervened in a potential strike on the railways and averted it, by bringing management and unions together.

In the middle of those critical negotiations, he had sent a message to Butler: 'Please make your decision in the next half hour. After that the pubs will be open and we will never be able to gather this crowd together again.'[7] Jack Jones* he had first met in Spain in 1938. As leader of the opposition, he had invited senior TUC men (including Jones) to his home at Albany, playing the 'Red Flag' for them on his Steinway.

Always, Heath held on to a profound belief in the power of reason and the ability of the British people to pull together in a time of crisis. Naively, as it turned out, he started out from that presumption that people could be persuaded to act reasonably and in the wider public interest – that trade unions would ultimately accept his policy of bringing them within the law of the land and also that they would refrain from demanding unreasonable pay settlements or threatening strike action, because the national interest demanded it. The approach in 1970 and 1971 was to reduce price inflation, mainly through cuts in taxation, then to argue that pressure for higher wages should be moderated because price rises had been slowed. Heath was, of course, to be bitterly disappointed. His attempt to reform industrial relations ended in rancour, with trade unionists in jail and the economy on the brink of collapse.

As the challenges to the state, the Government and the nation became increasingly nerve-wracking, Douglas Hurd would become ever more acutely aware of Heath's shortcomings as a communicator. On camera he could look stiff and he struggled to exude even a hint of the considerable warmth and sense of humour his close colleagues knew he possessed. I saw for myself a generation later that he was uncomfortably aware of his shortcomings in this regard. In his senescence, he overcame most difficulties by playing the 'age card' brilliantly. He had met so many people in his life that he rarely knew if he had met someone before. He therefore used the cunning opening gambit 'Hello, how are you?' – which was as close as possible to being neutral on this knotty question of 'used to employ'/'have met previously'/'don't know from Adam'. When he was Prime Minister, he had to do better than that and his flashing white teeth were not always, of themselves, sufficiently persuasive, as **Douglas Hurd** recalls:

---

* General Secretary of the Transport and General Workers' Union.

'When he became Prime Minister in June 1970 Mr Heath needed no persuading that communication was important. He had built up in Opposition a small team of advisers in this field whom he trusted and who had served him well. There was Michael Wolff, a close personal friend, who was content to be called a speechwriter but whose particular gift of weary wisdom had earned him a position of great trust and strength. There was Geoffrey Tucker, the Director of Publicity at Central Office. From outside the political world there were James Garrett, Barry Day and Ronald Millar, each bringing a special talent. There was nothing formal about this team. Different individuals were called in for different purposes. There was much painful wrestling with particular speeches or broadcasts; a good deal of wining and dining. The world was taken apart and put back together in many restaurants. All in all, it was a successful effort which proved itself in the election campaign of 1970.

'It was a private effort, and those who took part sought no headlines or advancement for themselves. What they did expect was the confidence of the man whom they were trying to help. They knew that they would not get this by flattery. On the contrary Mr Heath expected, indeed insisted on harsh criticism of his own public performances from those whom he trusted. He might then turn fiercely on his critics, and there would be a shindy; but next time round they would find that the criticism had been accepted. This method of proceeding caused anguish from time to time but I think that we would all, looking back, say that it was fun.

'This team were not out to create something called the new Heath, smooth, homogenised and empty. What they were trying to do was to help Mr Heath build on the strengths of communication that he naturally possessed. These were considerable. Find a group of forty or fifty serious people, perhaps student leaders or trade unionists or American journalists or Bexley constituents, and put Mr Heath among them with no microphone in sight and plenty of time ahead of him, and you might well listen to a striking feat of communication.

'Few political leaders can have such a range of detailed knowledge. This knowledge was combined with the belief that evidence rather than prejudice ought to be the foundation of political decisions, and that discussion among serious people was the best way of getting that evidence.

[109]

The tragedy was that gatherings of this kind, which were the best political meetings I have known, could only be occasional and limited in the
numbers of people they reached. For introduce a rostrum, a microphone,
an interviewer or a few thousand people and the result could be disas-
trously different. The voice might change its quality. The vocabulary might
become stilted, the tone defensive. The thread of the argument might be
lost in a mass of detail. Instead of speaking to people, Mr Heath would
too often speak at them. In trying to cure these habits Mr Heath was not
trying to create an artificial self. He was finding a way of transferring more
surely into public life the natural gift of private communication that his
friends knew well.

'Under the cares and pressures of office Mr Heath began to put aside
what he had learned about communication in the painful years of opposition. He was probably better at it in the General Election of 1970 and in
the European Referendum Campaign of 1975 than at any time when he
was Prime Minister.'[8]

The central role of communication in No. 10 is now a given but, although he
recognised its importance, Heath never gave it the highest priority. A case in
point came in spring 1971, when Heath's friend Bill Barnetson offered him the
opportunity 'to be the principal figure at the FA Cup Final' on 8 May (which
Heath's own team Arsenal would go on to win 2–1, adding the FA Cup to
their league title to complete a legendary 'Double'). He turned down this
golden opportunity because he preferred to go sailing. One cannot imagine,
say, Tony Blair, dropping such a 'dolly' catch. Heath also felt it was rather
frivolous to devote precious hours to honing a speech, when there were serious matters of state to which he might more usefully be attending. For his
team this was a nightmare, as **Douglas Hurd** recounts:

'The preparation of speeches can get out of hand unless the Prime
Minister takes a grip at each stage. I understand that Mr Wilson used to
do this. The chief complaint against Mr Heath's methods of work was
that often he did not. We often puzzled over this. It was not that Mr Heath
failed to understand the importance of speeches. He knew the magic of
words, and often talked about it. In fact I believe this was the trouble.

He was a perfectionist. We served up adequate drafts, which he saw were only adequate. It would take him hours to transform them – but the necessary hours were never there. They were swamped by meetings, and yet more meetings. So at the last minute the adequate draft was looked at, reluctantly approved, and unenthusiastically delivered. Next time of course would be different; but next time turned out much the same. It was a mystery and a tragedy that a man who possessed such a talent of exposition could not find a working method which turned it to good effect.'[9]

As Prime Minister, Heath was a natural target for everyone from satirists to blackmailers. He also continued his running battles with the press. When he 'entertained' Peregrine Worsthorne for a tea-time interview at No. 10, he initially offered the journalist whisky, then tea; and he then poured tea out for himself and did not give Worsthorne anything at all. His ultimate *bête noire* was probably *Private Eye*, whose editor, Richard Ingrams, despised him. On one occasion, **Richard Simmonds** thought a line had been crossed:

'When Ted was P.M., *Private Eye* reported that he had been in the same hotel bedroom in, I think, Cyprus as Christine Keeler, who was in part responsible for bringing down a Conservative Government in the so-called Profumo affair. It transpired that, in so many words, *Private Eye* was correct. However, there had been a ten-year gap between Miss Keeler's occupancy and that of Ted. I spent an hour drafting a note from Ted remonstrating with Lord Gnome. He took one look at my work and tore it up, saying: "Never, never, respond personally with denials to such matters. If you do, one day you will miss such an article and, because you have not denied it, the press will assume that it's true."'

At the time of writing, it is widely believed that nothing of the 1970–1974 administration outlived the 1970s, apart from the United Kingdom's membership of the European Union, which Heath championed and, at formidable personal cost, secured after a decade of superhuman determination and effort. That membership has never been less than controversial and many trace the roots of that unsettled relationship with the mainland and its political ambitions back to what they allege to have been a lack of honesty (and integrity) on the part of Heath and other pro-Europeans at the time of accession, about the ambitions within the EEC/EC/EU for political unity. Despatching that canard to perdition is not the principal aim of this book, but anyone who reads it with an open mind will surely accept that Heath was very open, candid and proud as he led the most pro-European government this nation has ever had.

Heath believed EEC membership was essential if the UK was to flourish again and he certainly did not pursue this objective with such single-minded determination in order to appease, or to endear himself to, public opinion. Between 1960 and 1967, the approval rating for an EEC application oscillated between 41 and 61 per cent. The 'Don't Knows' declined gradually, from 38 per cent in July 1960 to just 16 per cent in March 1967, but, after the Wilson Government shifted towards the EEC in 1967, the picture changed significantly, with the approval rating falling as low as 19 per cent in April 1970, just as the general election campaign began. Between August 1970 and November 1973, the approval rating fluctuated between 21 and 41 per cent; whereas the 'antis' varied within a much higher range, of between 59 per cent and 36 per cent. The younger a voter was and the higher his or her socio-economic class, the more likely it was he or she would be pro-EEC. In March 1972, men favoured entry by 46 per cent to 40 per cent; and women opposed it by 45 per cent to 34 per cent.

Heath had the greatest respect for Alec Home, the foreign secretary, but he knew from his experiences with de Gaulle in 1961–1963 that the crucial conversations would have to be with the French President – by now Georges Pompidou – which meant he would have to take a direct, active and personal interest in the matter, if the French veto of 1963 was to be reversed. Along with Robert Armstrong, **Douglas Hurd** was at his right hand for all but the most delicate and private of the high-level negotiations with the French:

'Mr Heath was remarkably free from bitterness against the French, who had confounded him in 1963. It would be a great mistake to suppose that he was ready to give the French whatever they wanted. On the contrary he saw them as tough negotiators with whom we would need again to bargain toughly. But he understood what the Foreign Office appeared to ignore, namely the real structure of the European Community.

The French had the veto, and on the question of British entry had already used it once. There was no question of them accepting British membership just because the Five wanted us in . . . If Britain wanted to enter it was to the French that we should pay attention. We must gain friends in France and outmanoeuvre our enemies. We must deal patiently with the French arguments, trying to meet those which had substance and to confound others which were merely propaganda. We must not try to organise the Five against France, for that was the best way to ensure that the French would again frustrate us.'[10]

Hurd accompanied Heath to the make-or-break summit in May 1971. As the moment of truth approached, suddenly all the advisers melted discreetly away (apart from two interpreters) and it all came down to the perspectives and relationship – of trust or distrust, mutual respect or disrespect, common interest or narrow, national interest – between two men, Heath and Georges Pompidou:

'The President and the Prime Minister were immersing themselves in the problem as a whole, testing the possibilities and each other's intentions and political quality. The answer would come, not piecemeal problem by problem, but all together at the end, Yes or No. The preparatory work had been enormous, the omens were favourable, but there was still a chance of failure. The agenda items provided the material of the discussion, but its essence was different. Mr Heath showed President Pompidou that the time had come to reverse the veto pronounced by President de Gaulle. Only Mr Heath can now say how this was done.'[11]

In his memoirs, **Heath** was very happy to do just that, and a sense of mischief, as well as a sense of justifiable pride, comes through very clearly:

'In our first session of talks, Pompidou stressed that what he felt was needed was an historic change in the British attitude. If Britain was really determined to make this change, France would welcome us into the Community. He regarded his own country and Britain as the only two European countries with what he termed a "world vocation" and

[113]

said quite explicitly that, if the political and intellectual prestige and authority of Britain were added to those of the Six, the Community would be greatly enriched. My task was to convince him that this was also what we wanted to see.

'I assured Pompidou that there could be no special partnership between Britain and the United States, even if Britain wanted it, because one was barely a quarter the size of the other. Through Europe, on the other hand, such a partnership was possible within a Community applying the same rules and working to shared principles. Our purpose was to see a strong Europe, which could speak with one voice after a full discussion of the world problems affecting it, and could then exert effective influence in different parts of the globe.

'Before we went to lunch on the Friday, President Pompidou took me to one side and said that we should resume, and aim to complete, our talks in the afternoon. I readily agreed, and we returned to the Elysée together for a further three hours' discussion . . . On Friday evening, we held our conference for the press, radio and television in the Salle des Fêtes of the Elysée Palace, a lofty and beautifully decorated room which has seen many splendid occasions in the life of France. It was also the scene of de Gaulle's press conference in 1963 when he had so astonished the world by announcing the French veto. The chattering ceased as the President and I took our places in the gilt armchairs on the platform. The air of expectancy was intense, for nothing whatsoever was known about our talks. It was obvious from the looks on their faces that the majority of the media believed that there could only be one explanation for the extended meeting throughout the afternoon and on into the evening, that we had found it impossible to reach agreement. I had not even confided in Douglas Hurd or in Michael Wolff, my senior political adviser, to their evident annoyance. They, too, obviously shared a fear of failure. Those present did not have long to wait for the answer.

'I had managed to convince President Pompidou, during twelve hours of talks, that Britain was genuine in its desire to enter the European family . . . It was marvellous to see the looks of astonishment on the faces of so many of those present. The President and I looked across at each other with delight, for we had secured success and also triumphed over the media. For me personally, it was a wildly exciting moment. Just forty years after my first visit to Paris, I had been able to play a part in bringing about the unity of Europe. It was an historic occasion. The negotiations were duly completed the following month in Luxembourg as the French negotiators, under orders from the Elysée, watered down their demands.'

One of those two interpreters was the diplomat and polyglot **Sir Michael Palliser**:

'Heath did it really on the basis of a very confident and trusting relationship with the French president. I saw the relationship developing between those two men and there is no doubt at all in my mind that Heath brought something off which probably no one else could have done.'[12]

In later years, **Douglas Hurd** would reflect on how that breakthrough was achieved and also upon the electrifying effect it would have on politics back home in the UK:

'It certainly was not done by giving way on every point raised from the French side or accepting every French analysis. President Pompidou was a serious man; he had to be convinced, not flattered. He had to believe that Britain was coming into Europe not out of despair, not to make trouble, but as a determined and capable partner. The winning round of President Pompidou was probably the greatest single feat of Mr Heath's premiership. In these talks he repaired the errors of twenty years of faulty French and British policy. A few years more and the errors might have been irreparable.'[13]

This left open the question of how to persuade Parliament to endorse the application. A vote on Second Reading (and therefore on the principle of the Bill) was scheduled for soon after the 1971 party conference season, on 28 October. Heath knew Tory MPs were overwhelmingly in favour of the application, but there were some hard-line rebels, including one or two within ministerial ranks, such as Edward (Teddy – now Sir Teddy) Taylor, a junior minister at the Scottish Office. Heath recognised the strength of Taylor's convictions, but valued him as a colleague, so devised a very pragmatic solution to the matter, as **Teddy Taylor** himself explains:

'Ted Heath was kind enough when Prime Minister to appoint me to a junior ministerial post in charge of Education and Health in Scotland, and we got on well together. However, when Ted decided to sign the Treaty of Rome I was so opposed to the project that I had to indicate that I would resign my post. Of course I have to admit that the great majority of politicians in Westminster and a great majority of my own constituents were in favour of the European venture and that supporters were regarded as forward looking, whilst we opponents were regarded as people living in the past.

'Ted Heath took me for a private discussion in the grounds of 10 Downing Street and emphasised that it would be sad if I was going to throw away a political career on an issue on which the vast majority of my colleagues disagreed with me. In fairness he was kind and considerate and at no time threatened me or abused me. I made it abundantly clear that leaving a government post was the last thing that I wanted, but I insisted that we could not ignore the fact that our democracy would be seriously undermined, that we would be creating problems with the growth areas of the world and tying ourselves into an area in structural decline. We had long and friendly discussions on the issue but neither of us changed our views.

'Of course I worried about my strong views on Europe and my disagreement with the PM. One of the things I did was to explain that I would resign from the government, that I would vote against the decision to join, but that if I lost I would wish him well and co-operate (I did this by not opposing the third reading) unless, of course, there were further treaties involving more surrender of sovereignty.

'A few months before the next election he invited me back to the Scottish Office and, quite surprisingly, later came to Southend to speak at an election meeting on my behalf. Of course I disagreed with Ted Heath on the EC but I have to say that he was one of the most honest and truthful politicians I encountered.'

The numbers were still tight and, with an overall majority of only around thirty and at least that number less than enthusiastic about – or downright opposed to – accession, Heath had a problem as the crunch vote approached. Clearly, it was not a realistic option to bully every last Tory MP through the lobbies, so a way had to be found to keep the all-but-one pro-EEC Liberals 'on side' and also to smoke out the many Labour MPs, headed by Roy Jenkins, who favoured entry but were under pressure from Harold Wilson (who imposed three-line whips) not to break ranks. As **Douglas Hurd** recalls, chief whip Francis Pym had a proposal, supported by Willie Whitelaw, but Heath was not easily persuaded:

'As a former Chief Whip Mr Heath believed in party discipline. In this instinct he was supported by another former Chief Whip, Mr Whitelaw. As Prime Minister, Mr Heath believed that the Government should use every means in its power to honour the agreement which it had reached with the EEC. He was supported in this by the Foreign Secretary, Sir Alec Douglas-Home. These views, so powerfully backed, were not easy to overcome. Nevertheless, they were overcome, and a free vote for backbenchers conceded. This was a turning point in the whole process of securing British entry.

'Francis Pym had no love of anarchy and no desire at all to endanger our agreement with the EEC. It was precisely because his convictions were so solid that his argument for a free vote carried weight. It was based on arithmetic. By the second week of October the Whips had reported on the mood of the Parliamentary Party. There were, as everyone knew, a sizeable number of antis. The conclusion drawn was that, so far as the Conservatives were concerned, the whipping would make little difference. From the other side of the hill, the information was less full.

'There was a considerable mass of Labour MPs whose position was unclear. Many disliked the line being taken by Mr Wilson and Mr Callaghan that the terms of entry were unacceptable. But these were not on the whole natural rebels. The chances of their following their own judgement might substantially increase if there was a free vote on the Conservative side. This would be true even if Mr Wilson attempted to whip them against entry.'[14]

Although Heath had publicly taken the position that 'every government is entitled to ask its supporters to support it on a major issue such as this', he did accept Pym's advice and Conservative MPs were given a 'free vote' on accession. The reality, of course, was that there was still considerable pressure on wavering MPs to toe the line and the principal import of the 'free vote' was not on the Tory side of the equation at all: it was contrived to send a signal to pro-EEC Labour MPs that this was not a matter of confidence in the Government. Sixty-nine of them duly voted in favour of accession, including senior figures such as Roy Jenkins, David Owen, Shirley Williams and Roy Hattersley. As the Bill progressed through the House of Commons, Labour MP John Roper and junior Tory whip Kenneth Clarke maintained a rota for pro-EEC Labour MPs, always ensuring just enough were absent – without going so far as to vote against the Labour line – to see that the Government got its business through. With echoes of RPM, sometimes the majority fell very low indeed. On the crucial Second Reading vote, the Accession Bill was passed by 309 votes to 301 – a majority of just eight. All but one Liberal supported the Bill, as did five of the eight Ulster Unionists. Thanks to an informal 'pairing' arrangement (sanctioned by Heath) that operated between the Government Whips' office (organised by Ken Clarke) and pro-EEC Labour MPs (organised by John Roper) the Government never lost a single division on the Bill throughout its passage and, on 1 January 1973, the UK would become a full member of the EEC.

Tony Barber was clear that EEC entry would never have been possible without Heath's remarkable determination:

> 'Although all the members of the Cabinet were committed to joining the EEC if we could get the right terms, I do not believe we would have joined without Ted's determination and resolve. Europe was, even in those days, a deeply divisive issue and, as the Government's popularity slumped, some were tempted to take the populist line that the terms were not good enough and that we should withdraw from the negotiations and "stand on our own feet". By joining the EEC the course of British history was fundamentally changed and it is no exaggeration to say that that change was brought about primarily through the perseverance of one man.'[15]

The principal domestic challenge for the Heath Government was the state of the economy – notably 'lame-duck' manufacturing concerns and the malaise of double-digit inflation. Heath found the situation embarrassing and wanted to do everything and anything possible to restore the UK to its former pre-eminence. Although the Selsdon Park proposals and the 1970 manifesto contained much talk of modernisation and shaking the nation out of its lethargy, Heath never wanted to break the so-called 'post-war consensus'. His preferred approach was to bring together those who could do most to alter (and improve) the destiny of the nation – businessmen, politicians, senior trade unionists – and appeal to their better nature and their patriotism. Bringing the trade unions formally within the law of the land for the first time was not, for him, a vindictive act sprung from a desire to emasculate, vilify or destroy. For Heath, it was just common sense. The Industrial Relations Act 1972 was a disaster. It was furiously challenged from the outset. It was too long and, in time, proved to be too complex and fundamentally unworkable. Robert Carr, who introduced the legislation, confessed in the 1990s that he had not fully understood the Bill himself as he took it through the Commons. When the new Industrial Relations Court started to send strikers to prison, it made martyrs of them and wrecked hopes that Heath and his ministers might maintain a cordial or constructive relationship with the TUC.

Another drain on energy and morale, time and goodwill, was Northern Ireland: the 'Troubles' were well underway by the time Heath became Prime Minister and escalated horribly in 1970 and 1971. Heath came into office enjoying the support of eight Ulster Unionist MPs, who took the Tory whip and made up more than half of his notional thirty-seat majority in the Commons, but this highly rational man, who carried what learning he had lightly and had no great interest in (or appreciation of) history, struggled to comprehend what made them and their voters tick – and why neighbour would turn so violently against neighbour. He had grown up in the embrace of the Church of England, but the austere Presbyterianism that seems to sweep straight in from the cold grey Atlantic and onto the craggy coastline of Antrim was entirely alien to him. One aspect of the schism in the Province he did eventually comprehend was the fact that Unionist Protestants are not 'British': they are Irish, with a very distinctive tradition of their own and an abiding, visceral unwillingness to see themselves assimilated into the

Catholic south, where they would be heavily outnumbered. Although he tried to appear balanced in his approach to Ireland, Heath had a great deal of sympathy with the perfectly peaceable majority of Catholics in Northern Ireland, who were being treated in many respects as second-class citizens, with little or no access to political power.

In early 1971, Cecil King was left with the firm impression that Heath 'had never considered a comprehensive solution of the Irish problem'.[16] That certainly changed, as an escalation of violence forced his hand. In conditions of considerable secrecy, Heath sent a delegation of Conservative Students to Dublin and Belfast, where they met paramilitaries from both sides and duly reported back on their findings. What Heath wanted to know was not whether the hard-liners were admirable or contemptible – he already had his own clear and settled views on that question – but whether there was any chance they might play a part in securing a lasting settlement. At that juncture there was not and, not long afterwards, Heath suspended the Stormont Assembly, imposed direct rule of the Province by ministers at Westminster and then worked tirelessly to bridge divisions and calm ancestral hatreds by building a power-sharing executive of just the moderate parties in the Province.

Heath was well aware from the outset that there could be deleterious consequences for the Conservative Party and its traditional Unionist allies if his initiatives were to prove successful. On 14 August 1972, he sent a Personal Minute (M80/72) to the party chairman warning that 'there are already signs that the Unionist Party, as we have known it, is a thing of the past'. **Heath's** impatience is apparent in this note, as is his yearning to see the familiar left–right politics of Great Britain supplant the sectarian cleavage in Northern Ireland:

'In these circumstances, I think it would be prudent for you and your colleagues at Central Office to examine how best we can maintain our position in Northern Ireland and our support for Northern Ireland MPs at Westminster. Personally, I do not believe that we can continue to maintain an alliance with a sectarian party based on and largely controlled by the Orange Lodges.

'In my view this leads to the adoption of one or other of the following alternatives. Either the Unionist Party, in whatever form it survives or is resuscitated, severs its connection with all Protestant bodies, including the Orange Lodges; and that means not having their automatic representation on the constituency committees or the Central Council. Or alternatively we extend our own organisation in Northern Ireland and fight seats there as the Conservative Party.'

Stratton Mills recalls Heath's travails as he struggled with the 'Irish Question':

'Ted was never sure-footed in dealing with Ireland. He was rather a typical Southern Englishman. He thought Ireland was tiresome and rather disliked Ulster Unionists as a breed, I always felt. He saw them as descendants from a long-distant past. He would never chat with the Unionist MPs at Westminster, or invite them for a drink to chat things through, as to where we were going.

'Brian Faulkner [Prime Minister of Northern Ireland] had been told by the Cabinet Office that talk of direct rule was "purely speculative" and never believed Ted was preparing the way for it. My impression was that Heath and Faulkner disliked each other. When [Faulkner] was told on 22 March 1972 that the Westminster Government wanted to assume direct control of law and order in Northern Ireland, he consulted his Cabinet and they unanimously agreed they would resign. So, on Friday 24 March, EH announced that the Stormont Parliament would be prorogued and direct rule imposed from Westminster . . .

'When Ted was pushing for a power-sharing agreement, my law partner from Northern Ireland, Robin Bailie, who had been in Brian Faulkner's Stormont Cabinet, happened to be in London and I asked Douglas Hurd if we could come and see Ted. He agreed to see us late in the evening, still wearing his dinner jacket after a night at the opera. One of the things I was pushing for was an increase in the number of MPs from Northern Ireland, should devolved government be restored. Ted's attitude was "There are quite enough Unionist MPs already" – heaving shoulders, end of conversation . . .

I was invited to attend [the power-sharing talks at] Sunningdale as an Alliance adviser, but I didn't really want to get involved. Those who did

attend, say that Heath would come into the room of the Unionist delegation and browbeat them and shout at them. There would be long silences
and, certainly, he was not attempting to charm. That was his style – very
strident and impatient. He couldn't understand why he couldn't solve
everything by logic. He bullied them and they cracked. In March 1974
he would have been able to retain a Conservative government if he had
maintained his relationship with the Ulster Unionists.'

The Good Friday Agreement of 1998, which paved the way to power-sharing
and relative peace in Northern Ireland, was not so very different from the
Sunningdale Agreement that Heath forged and which Harold Wilson threw
at once to the wolves in light of the close election result in 1974. It has
endured where Sunningdale failed for a host of interlinked reasons, including
an understandably greater weariness of violence, the increasing meaningless-
ness of borders within the EU and the consequent willingness of the heirs
of the hard-liners of 1974 to sign up. The card who proclaimed the current
arrangements to be 'Sunningdale for Slow Learners' was not so very wide
of the mark. In a very early draft, Heath's memoirs contained a reference
to the 'essential irrationality' of the people of Ireland. Robert Armstrong
wisely recommended its excision, lest it 'give grave offence'. In fact **Heath**
had explained himself with inoffensive clarity in 1985:

'I confess that I have always found the Irish, all of them, extremely difficult
to understand. Shortly after I became Prime Minister, I held a meeting
of the three Prime Ministers at Chequers. It was the first time that the
three Prime Ministers in these tiny islands had met for nearly 50 years. It
is astonishing that we could carry on in the modern world in such a way.

'I was struck forcibly by the fact that the Prime Minister of Northern
Ireland and the Taoiseach of the Republic spent a great deal of their time
reminiscing about their times together, the university to which they went
together, their education together, what they had done together and how
they were working out everything together. I was the odd man out, and
nobody cared about the odd man out because the Northern Ireland Prime
Minister and the Taoiseach were working so closely together. It has always
been said that we English cannot understand any of the Irish, and one just

has to accept that, although we are all part of the United Kingdom and the Republic of Ireland.'[17]

There were also continuing problems with South Africa and Rhodesia, and there was one moment of hubris followed by nemesis at the Singapore Commonwealth conference in 1971. As Heath was leaving, he found his route of exit blocked by Ugandan leader Milton Obote, giving a TV interview and proclaiming confidently: 'Yes, Heath is finished. He's out.' A coup took place in Uganda that night and Idi Amin took charge. Regime change in Uganda would have profound consequences for the Heath government and, in the longer term, for the nation, for Amin soon set about expelling tens of thousands of Asians from his country, depriving Uganda of their talents and industry and presenting Heath with a tough decision. In Heath's words, 'We did what any civilised nation would do, by taking the greater share of the migrants' – those who held UK passports. Peter Walker once said 'never under-estimate how difficult the right made Ted's life' and this episode was a case in point, as **David Hunt** recalled when he spoke at Heath's eightieth birthday dinner at the Savoy in July 1996:

'The one thing I will never forget was when you made a brave and courageous decision, to admit the Ugandan Asians, who were in trouble. Then, at the Conservative Conference in 1972, there was a rather innocuous motion on immigration, to be proposed by Mr Proctor, of Hackney South and Shoreditch. Suddenly we were told the motion would be moved by the President of Hackney South and Shoreditch, who, no one had quite realised, was a Mr Enoch Powell. There was much consternation and certainly Enoch was going to use the occasion to censure the Government. And you decided to tackle it head on – and I was the young David sent to slay the Goliath by moving an amendment to the motion. I shall never forget that debate, the courageous speech of Robert Carr, and the fact that by standing up to extremism, you struck a blow for freedom, for a multi-racial society and for making sure that, when we give people British passports, we don't take them away when they're in trouble. As Robert [Carr] said to me a few moments ago, when the chips are down, Ted is pure gold.'

Hunt paid a price for his stand, when he was deselected as candidate for Plymouth Drake. Things looked grim, but Heath did not abandon him:

'My political career was in ruins. I went back to my home the following day, sat down and turned on the television and there was our Prime Minister seeing off Dom Mintoff* at Number 10. Suddenly the phone went and it was the Prime Minister. And I shall never forget that conversation, Ted, because you told me, "If you stand up for your principles, you'll never lose, so you fight on and you'll win."'

Robert Armstrong was not the only future Secretary of the Cabinet to work in No. 10 while Heath was Prime Minister. **Robin Butler** (latterly Lord Butler of Brockwell), worked there too:

'It seemed to me that Ted Heath was a Prime Minister for whom government was both more important and more congenial than politics. His experiences as a young man whose early career had been punctuated by the traumas of a European and World War had framed his outlook and given him a deep sense of purpose, which he masked under a caustic exterior. I believe he was sincerely affronted by what he saw as the triviality of his predecessor's manipulation of, and skirmishes with, the media and political colleagues in the Labour Party. Hence the Conservatives slogan for the 1970 Election "Action, not words".

'However, he was not altogether at ease with his own colleagues in the Conservative Party. I don't believe that he was ever truly "Selsdon man". His experiences in the War had made him a One Nation Conservative who felt deeply the Government's responsibilities to all classes in society.

'My responsibilities included briefing him for Parliamentary Questions, which then took place on Tuesday and Thursday afternoons. This was a demanding task since Ted demanded comprehensive information on all aspects of each question's subject. I also had to check the *Hansard* record before it was printed.

---

* The Prime Minister of Malta.

'On one occasion I "improved" his answer by persuading the *Hansard* editor to omit a provocative parenthesis. Unfortunately the Labour Opposition detected this tampering with the official record and the Prime Minister had to go to the House the next day and make a personal statement of apology. This was something of a humiliation for a Prime Minister. Expecting that this might end my career in No. 10 or at least result in a severe dressing-down, I apologised abjectly as he was leaving the Chamber. He gave me a half-smile and said gruffly "Don't do it again" – and that was the end of the matter. This sort of kindness attached me deeply to him . . .

'It was the experience of myself and others that conversations with Ted were not easy because they were punctuated by long silences on his part. On the first occasion when I was on duty in the evening in No. 10, I had to go up to the flat at the top of the building to get his decision on an issue. I found him in his sitting-room listening to Wagner being played at high volume. He made no move to turn it down. I did my best to explain my question to him. When I had finished, he stared at me but gave no reaction. After a while, thinking that he had not listened or had not heard, I started again, somewhat louder. When I was only halfway through, he comprehensively answered my original question.

'Conversations on car journeys with him were similar. I would offer some comment, which would be met by silence on his part. I learned not to say anything further and, some moments later, he would offer a rejoinder. I came to find these slow-motion conversations both relaxing and enjoyable. They passed the time on long car journeys very pleasantly.

'Another of his characteristics which I found winning was the occasional indication that he liked me, even needed me. Several weeks could pass when I was only met by a glazed stare. But just occasionally the glaze would suddenly clear to reveal for a moment a look of real warmth and affection.'

On 20 January 1972, it was announced that the total number of people registered as unemployed had risen above one million. At Prime Minister's Questions, Labour MP Tom Swain slapped a copy of the early edition of an evening newspaper in front of Heath. Labour MPs then chanted 'Heath Out! Heath Out!' until the Speaker suspended the sitting for half an hour. The following week, Harold Wilson introduced a motion of censure, which mischievously stated the Government had been elected 'on the strength of a clear and specific pledge by the Prime Minister to reduce unemployment at a stroke' and censuring the Government for its 'doctrinaire and irresponsible policies [which] have forced the total of registered unemployed in the United Kingdom to 1,023,000 persons'. This cut Heath to the quick, for he too regarded so high an unemployment rate as unacceptable.

The phrase used by Wilson was carefully chosen to provoke Heath's ire. It was a favourite misquotation of something Heath had never said during the election campaign – and one that Wilson exploited to the full. In fact, Heath was never the felicitous wordsmith, as **Simon Hoggart** once explained:

'Ted Heath at no time said that he could cut prices "at a stroke". In the 1970 election, he spoke to a press conference. As the hacks assembled they were presented with the daily hand-out of news, comments and straight lies which the parties produce at poll times. That day's press release contained a long list of anti-inflation measures, and added, "This would, at a stroke, reduce the rise in prices". Heath never used the words, and probably did not know they were in the hand-out.'[18]

Heath was no monetarist, nor was he, in all honesty, much of an economist. He did, however, know that spending and borrowing more in the short term would stimulate demand and reduce unemployment – even if only in the short term. His rhetoric was now all about investing in infrastructure and creating a modern economy. I have no doubt he was sincere, but in his words there was, quite suddenly, what could easily (perhaps rightly) be regarded as a refutation of the 1970 manifesto. The seeds of rebellion were being sown – and more trouble was round the corner.

On 30 January 1972 came Bloody Sunday and on 9 February a State of Emergency had to be declared because of coal shortages caused by the miners' strike. Within days Lord Wilberforce recommended a generous settlement to the miners, which was accepted. When Wilberforce attended a private party in 1998, marking the publication of Heath's memoirs, I remember how nervous he still was to be in the same room as Heath, seemingly fearing a rebuke. A Government that had been elected on a manifesto promoting free enterprise and fiscal rigour now went into reverse. Ken Clarke believes the sudden reversal of policy was possible only because Heath dominated his ministerial colleagues to such a degree and no one dared stand up to him: 'Ted would not have got Iain [Macleod] to agree to go back to this poor man's social democracy which we went in for in the last two years.'[19]

One of the most fascinating files from the 1970–1974 papers at the National Archive dates from the early spring of 1972, revealing how Heath's patience was being tested to its (never very accommodating) limit. First of all, a magisterial note from **Douglas Hurd** to Heath, dated 21 February 1972, warned that the Government was consistently losing the publicity war on public sector strikes, principally, in his view, because the semi-constitutional role of the Department of Employment as a conciliator was inhibiting ministers from speaking out politically and making the wider, national-interest case for sensible pay restraint:

> 'Because of a possible, eventual need to conciliate, ministers are repeatedly advised not to enter into the substance of the dispute . . . The advantages of neutrality are not gained; the advantages of sustained advocacy are thrown away [EH noted in the margin at this point: "Well put"].'[20]

Burke Trend and William Armstrong immediately tried to persuade Heath that ministers could not completely divest themselves of their conciliation function, but Heath was not impressed. He sent a personal minute to the recently appointed Secretary of State for Employment, Maurice Macmillan, urging him to look at ways of enabling ministers to behave more politically and make the broader, public-interest case against excessive wage settlements in the public sector. He also sent a personal minute – and he heavily amended a draft of this by his officials – to John Davies at the DTI, urging far greater engagement with industry, to persuade the creators of wealth that the Government really wanted to work with them and had their best interests at heart. Heath's own scrawled addition runs thus: 'This requires an attitude in Government at all levels that it exists to help British Industry by all means possible to achieve its objectives in the national interest and confidence in industry that this is so.' Seemingly from a foreign trip in April 1972, **Heath** soon sent a dyspeptic telex message to No. 10, ablaze with frustration and impatience:

'I think it is essential that I send out a directive to all Whitehall departments emphasising the vital necessity of creating much closer working
relationships between the Government and British industry, between
departments and individual firms. I know the objections to doing this, but
I am not prepared to accept them any longer. I need a directive drafted
and I need to be advised as to how we can get this right down to the lowest
ranks in Whitehall and throughout all the regional offices. Kindly consult
and report urgently.'

What is so interesting is both the aggressive tone and also the desired objective – which, especially in referring specifically to individual firms – is miles
away from traditional, tri-partite corporatism. When an inconclusive and
rather defensive response came from John Davies in May, Heath was unwilling to accept defeat. What concerned him was 'not only the coverage . . . it
is the attitude adopted towards all those with whom [ministers and officials]
are dealing which is vital.'[21] On 28 June, Heath wrote to ministers, urging
them to spread the gospel of interaction between government and industry
as widely as possible – 'and the contacts should include contacts on the union
side as well as with management'. It is hard to discern what effect, if any, this
letter had, but these exchanges do suggest, in 1972 at least, that Heath was
willing to lock horns with his civil servants.

On 17 February 1972, Heath's favourite child, the European Communities
Bill, was passed at Second Reading by only 309 votes to 301; on 24 March the
Stormont Assembly in Northern Ireland was suspended; there were strikes
on the railways; and on 22 May Labour MPs cheered the Government's
Industry Bill, while Tories sat silent, dismayed. **Edmund Dell**, for Labour,
spoke for many Tories too:

'The greatest illusion the Bill shatters is that the Government prepared
themselves for office. In fact, they are searching wildly and desperately
for solutions to their problems. Our pragmatic Prime Minister, having marched his troops up the hill to laissez-faire and disengagement,
is marching them down to selective intervention on a massive scale.
With the enthusiasm of the convert, the Government have moved at a
stroke from the extreme of disengagement on the one hand to selective

squandermania at the other extreme, without precedent and without parliamentary control.'[22]

On 18 July Reggie Maudling resigned as Home Secretary after being implicated in the Poulson bribery scandal (he was grateful for Heath's support – 'Ted Heath acted like a true friend,'[23] he later wrote). In August there was another State of Emergency because of a dock strike. As the Government began to resile from its manifesto in the face of mass unemployment, no one was more discomfited by the reversal of policy than **Patrick Jenkin**, who was responding for the Government in the debate on the economy when everything abruptly changed:

'The first manifestation of what was later dubbed Heath's U-Turn came in the Budget debate in March 1972. The Budget itself, the second tax-reforming Budget in the 1970 Parliament, had been well received by the party and in the country; and, whilst sharply rising unemployment was certainly causing anxiety, it was recognised that this was the price that had to be paid for defeating inflation and for making industry more competitive. By then Chief Secretary, I had to wind up on the second day of the Budget debate.[24] Roy Jenkins, as Shadow Chancellor, had gone a bit over the top with his attack on the Chancellor, but John Davies spoke next with a dreary speech of nearly an hour's length in which, among other things, he spelt out the outcome of the Government's review of regional policy.

'Most of Davies' speech could perhaps be claimed to be consistent with the Government's strategy hitherto but it was in the final minutes that the bombshell came. He announced the formation of a new Industrial Development Executive, to be headed by a newly created Minister for Industrial Development. For a Government that had just abolished the Industrial Reorganisation Commission – and which was pledged to cut interference with industry – this was a major reversal of the policies of the previous two years. Moreover, the first sectors to be the focus of the Executive's attentions were to be the shipbuilding industry and machine tools – two dinosaurs of the old economy. So momentous was this "U-turn", and the secrecy in which it had been decided, that most Ministers had been kept in the dark. As I sat on the front bench listening to Davies speaking from the Despatch Box, I could scarcely believe what I was hearing, for this was the first I had heard of this radical U-turn. I have been back to look through the papers that crossed my desk in the weeks prior to the Budget, and there was nothing, absolutely nothing, that foreshadowed this shattering announcement.'

As soon as decently possible, Jenkin left the Chamber to seek out a senior DTI official able to tell him what was going on. Together they drafted a denial that the Industrial Development Executive represented any kind of change of direction for the government.

'This got me – and the Government – safely through in a House where the benches were mostly empty, with no vote at the end of the second day of the four-day Budget debate. However, it quickly dawned on the Government's own supporters that what had happened was that the Cabinet had lost its collective nerve; and when Ted Heath later announced his "Counter Inflation Policy" that damning verdict was confirmed.

'What I find it hard to forgive is that I had to wind up the debate with what should have been a routine exposition of tax and economic policy, only to be taken wholly by surprise by this policy bombshell. Certainly, the Treasury officials who worked with me on the Budget and who provided the first drafts of my speech for this debate can have had no inkling of what was afoot. The headline phrase "U-Turn" was not long in coming, and I was there when it happened.

'Why did Heath make this decision to abandon policies so clearly announced in the Queen's Speech in 1970, "to liberate industry from unnecessary intervention by Government"? He had been at the heart of the policy reviews that recommended this pledge; he had chaired the Shadow Cabinet seminar held at Selsdon Park which endorsed the policy; and he had masterminded the Manifesto on which the Party had fought and won the election.

'Ted Heath had deeply-held and lifelong convictions about the need to protect working people from the scourge of recession, stemming from his own experiences in the 1930s. It is my belief that, when confronted with the impact of the Government's economic policies on unemployment and on what he saw as the consequential social deprivation, those personal convictions took precedence over the Party's committed promises, as made at the election.'

In June 1972, **Cecil King** had lunch with Hugh Fraser:

'His main theme was the strong feeling growing up on the back benches against Ted Heath. They feel he is doing nothing about inflation and unemployment. Moreover, the Common Market issue is not going well. Last night the Government majority fell to five . . . In the last few days sterling has been weak on the exchanges and there is talk of devaluation . . . Fraser dined last night with Selwyn Lloyd, who said Ted's difficulties sprung from his working out his policy in detail before taking office. By the time he was in Downing St, things had changed and they were stuck with a fixed programme when what was needed was a different performance. Fraser thinks Ted has landed himself with an Industrial Relations Act that will not work and cannot be dropped; ditto with the Rent Bill; and with inflation the outlook is for rising prices but not for increased industrial investment.'[25]

In 1971 the CBI had adopted a voluntary anti-inflationary policy, curbing excessive price rises, which had helped to reduce inflation from around 10 per cent to just over half that figure a year later. In the autumn of 1972, **Heath** brought the CBI and the TUC together to try and persuade them jointly to contrive, refine and adopt a longer-term, but still non-statutory, policy of pay restraint in addition to continuing with the voluntary prices policy. He failed to persuade them:

'The Government and the CBI both made clear their strong preference for completely voluntary arrangements over the whole field, pay as well as prices, though they were prepared, for the sake of reaching agreement, to accept that voluntary arrangements should be supported by backing-up legislation over their whole range. The TUC representatives, on the other hand, had made it a prior condition that there should be statutory control of prices but they were not able to accept the introduction of similar statutory controls on incomes.'[26]

Two days later, on 8 November, Chancellor Tony Barber proposed a statutory – but temporary – incomes policy, which would come in three 'phases'. Heath and Harold Wilson had a running battle through much of the debate. On 22 November, the Government lost an important vote on new immigration rules, with the party openly split. As the nation prepared itself for accession to the EEC on 1 January 1973, neither the body politic nor the nation itself was in the best repair.

Just four days into 1973, Phase 2 of the incomes policy was announced. It came into effect at the beginning of April. The *de facto* abrogation of the Selsdon manifesto was nearly complete and 'Selsdon Man' was no more. The budget in March was broadly neutral, but unemployment was now falling. Progress towards a establishing a power-sharing executive in Northern Ireland was being made, but, again, events did not fall kindly for Heath or the Government. In May, answering a question from former Liberal leader Jo Grimond about Lonrho, which was doing everything possible to get around the anti-inflationary rules, Heath coined perhaps his most famous phrase: 'It is the unpleasant and unacceptable face of capitalism, but one should not suggest that the whole of British industry consists of practices of this kind.'[27] **Simon Hoggart** later revealed that this memorable phrase was the child of serendipity as well as artifice, because of Heath's vanity:

'He did say "the unacceptable face of capitalism", but he didn't intend to. Heath is short sighted, but usually too vain to wear glasses. Commenting on the Lonrho scandal in the House, he read from a script provided for him by Number Ten. But he couldn't quite make out the words typed on the page: "This is an unpleasant and unacceptable facet of capitalism" – a far less memorable phrasing.'[28]

Unemployment was now falling from its 1972 peak. By May it was down to 600,000 people. The voters of Northern Ireland reaffirmed their affiliation with the UK in a referendum and Heath travelled to Dublin, to meet his opposite number, Liam Cosgrave. There were more strikes and two ministers, Lords Lambton and Jellicoe, resigned in embarrassing circumstances. Fears over energy supplies were acute and Heath was somehow at once stubborn and also unsure about how to proceed. He was fast running out of patience with what he perceived as the sheer stupidity and unreasonable nature of so many of the people with whom he had to deal. He had a good relationship with TUC general secretary Vic Feather, dating back to his time as Minister of Labour, but Feather was shackled by extremists and could never deliver. He also liked and trusted Joe Gormley, notionally head of the NUM, but also in the thrall of the extremists. He found many of the so-called 'captains of industry' to be spineless and indolent. The only people he trusted were those who most closely surrounded him – senior civil servants and, usually to a lesser extent, ministerial colleagues. He became acutely aware of the difficulties he experienced in trying to persuade people he was on their side and understood their lives, their concerns and their fears. His natural inclination to isolation militated against his better judgement. He also mishandled colleagues during a stressful period for everyone.

As **Simon Hoggart** explained, Heath's sense of humour could count badly against him at times:

'Contrary to popular belief [Heath] can be a charming and amusing companion, with a fund of revealing anecdotes which he tells exceedingly well. Unfortunately, he has a peculiar, dry sense of humour which often sounds like, and is indistinguishable from, thoughtless rudeness. Take, for example, Mr John Nott who in 1973 was a junior Treasury minister under Mr Heath. He was fearful that all the money which was being printed was going to cause huge inflation, so he nervously approached his leader in the lobby asking if he could speak to him briefly after the Division. Before he could say what the subject was, he was curtly cut off: "If you want to resign, put it in writing." Was it a joke? Mr Heath's friends say it was. Mr Nott thinks it wasn't. There is one man who will never forgive, and there are plenty of others.'[29]

Douglas Hurd and his colleagues also despaired of Heath's reluctance to spend time reassuring his back-bench colleagues and making them feel their views and feelings were being respected:

'We wanted him to spend more time in the tea-room, more time going round; and he said "Well, I'm doing that already", but we knew he wasn't really. The truth is, he wasn't very good at that sort of tea-room chat, being nice to people. One of the main things about Ted was that his idea of a joke, his idea of being funny, was often taken the wrong way by other people who thought he was just being rude. This happened over and over and over again. He thought he had had a perfectly good conversation with someone – "very satisfactory really" – but that person had gone away fuming, thinking he hadn't been listened to.'[30]

Supporters such as **Sir Anthony Meyer** cannot have known whether to laugh or cry:

'He is one of the wittiest and most agreeable after-dinner speakers I have ever heard. But he finds it very hard to chat to MPs. He rarely came into the Smoke Room or the Dining Room, and never into the more informal Tea Room. There is a story of his then PPS saying to him, "Ted, you really must make an effort to be nice to some of the chaps. Why don't you go and have a drink in the Smoke Room one day?" Two days later the PPS was delighted to see Ted in the Smoke Room, chatting to a very senior back-bencher. The PPS crept up behind, just in time to hear Ted say: "That was a bloody awful speech you made in the debate yesterday." He was indeed his own worst enemy.'[31]

In a pre-conference message to party workers, dated 30 September 1973, **Heath** sought to explain his personal philosophy – and the reason they must continue to fight the good fight:

'The alternative to expansion is not, as some occasionally seem to suppose, an England of quiet market towns linked only by trains puffing slowly and peacefully through green meadows. The alternative is slums, dangerous roads, old factories, cramped schools, stunted lives.'

The Heath Government had attempted a reflationary policy, relying on the incomes policy as an effective means of restraining inflation, with little heed paid to the money supply. The time bomb went off sooner than expected, when October 1973 brought drama in the Middle East – the Yom Kippur

War, which directly led to a savage increase in the price of oil. A new, virulent strain of inflation was poised to manifest itself. Phase 3 of the incomes policy came into effect on 1 November, but it was soon overshadowed by another State of Emergency, declared on 13 November in light of dwindling energy supplies. Harold Wilson introduced another censure motion in the House of Commons. 'Whatever challenge may be made to the Government benches it has already become perfectly plain that the challenge will not be that of a viable alternative policy,'[32] declared **Heath** in his response to Wilson's litany of coruscating criticism. He then made an assertion – a boast even – that must have made the blood of many Tories run cold and stoked the funeral pyre of 'Selsdon Man':

'Those who represent the workers, the TUC, and the employers, the CBI, have had far greater opportunity to participate in every aspect of the management of the economy under this Government than under any previous Government. The whole House knows that to be true.'[33]

This was a defiant paean for a form of corporatism that many of Heath's colleagues had originally believed he wished to bring to a decisive end. Unemployment was still falling, but the oil price shock must have convinced anyone with a grasp of economics that the situation was not sustainable. Even Heath himself had to admit: 'We shall have to use a larger proportion of our national resources, a greater part of our wealth, to pay for the fuel we require until our own resources are sufficient to meet those needs.'[34] Inflation would soon be resurgent again and an economic downturn would follow.

It was astonishing that Heath never buckled, as **Douglas Hurd** relates:

'Under an immense work load the Prime Minister remained calm and unfussed. He was kept going by his own gifts of humour and courage. He held to a plan to tour north-east Lancashire on 22 and 23 November 1973. As usual this expedition out of London went reasonably well, and the contact with real life lifted his spirits. On the way back we had a long talk of a kind which was becoming increasingly difficult in London because of the pressures of time. I suggested that someone somewhere should be charting all the possible courses of the coal dispute. Although the Government had acted early and well to conserve stocks, it was hard to see the way through to a tolerable ending. Mr Heath was more concerned about oil. He felt that the Foreign Office might not be exerting its full diplomatic strength to safeguard supplies.

'On 27 November a meeting was called at Number Ten to brief the Prime Minister for his meeting with the Miners' Executive the next day. It should have provided a chance for that clear-headed analysis of the options before the Government, which was by then badly needed. Instead there was silence on the big issues and a confused, bitty discussion of trivial tactical points. I felt critical of the senior civil servants present, whose duty it should have been to force the discussion into some coherent channel. This was the third and final occasion when I felt that at a crucial moment they fell below what was required. The others had occurred after Bloody Sunday in Londonderry in 1972, and during the discussion of inflation in the summer of 1973. No one who was present at any of these three meetings could believe that the civil service runs this country.'[35]

Cecil King was not optimistic about Heath's prospects: 'A friend . . . went to see Ted about a propaganda department, and Ted's reply was that his job was to govern, not to explain. That remark explains a lot of Ted's mistakes.'[36] There was now much talk of a 'snap' election. The nation was in a state of crisis and the Conservative Party itself was in a state of panic. The following account from **Douglas Hurd** of life inside No. 10 at that time suggests that nothing short of a general election was now going to stand much chance of relieving the pressure that was building up within the body politic:

'By 11 December 1973 the Conservative Party was at its senior levels much alarmed. That morning at the Tactical Committee I was told that it was essential that the Prime Minister should broadcast without delay. There was no very clear notion as to what he should say; but that he should say something was evident to all. The next day Lord Carrington, as Chairman of the Party, forcefully supported this advice. At these discussions I was doubtful because I knew that Mr Heath disliked broadcasting when he had nothing positive to say. I also knew that although he might be persuaded to broadcast, a Prime Ministerial broadcast which the Prime Minister himself at heart disliked was not likely to be a great success. A broadcast should be used to reinforce action, not as a substitute for it.

'However, later in the week the three day week was announced and Ministers reached agreement on an economic package including drastic expenditure cuts. The broadcast was made on 13 December. It came over reasonably well, but there had been, as usual, too many hands at work on the text. This had been snatched from Michael Wolff and myself by Sir William Armstrong, and snatched back again by us a few hours before delivery. The hour that afternoon which the Prime Minister should have spent putting his personal imprint on what he was going to say was spent instead ironing out a last-minute difficulty which had cropped up over the creation of a new Department of Energy.'[37]

The fleeting success of the power-sharing talks at Sunningdale in December 1973 would quickly be forgotten, as Unionist voters turned against their traditional leaders. On 12 December a State of Emergency was again declared and on 13 December, in the grim broadcast to which Douglas Hurd refers, the three-day week was announced. Seen through contemporary eyes, that broadcast seems not only old-fashioned, but almost ingenuous, as Heath struggles to reassure a nervous nation, expressing his desire to speak 'simply and plainly', as he warns of 'severe restrictions on the use of electricity'. The production is crude; the voice monosyllabic and oddly unmusical; the tone bleak. On 17 December, there was an emergency mini-budget, featuring cuts to planned public expenditure. The so-called 'Barber Boom' was over and **Tony Barber** himself did not attempt to gild the situation:

'Over the past week or so, many have described the situation which we as a nation now face as by far the gravest since the end of the war. They do not exaggerate. The duty of the Government is to take whatever action the national interest requires, however severe, but equally to avoid measures which could make an already forbidding situation even worse.'[38]

Just a week before Christmas Day 1973, **Heath** himself opened a marathon debate about the state of the nation. This was no bravura performance, but

[137]

his command of facts and figures, as ever, impressed. He made no attempt to blame everything on external factors. It was time for the nation to pull itself together:

'As a nation, we have real prospects and opportunities ahead of us, thanks to the availability of energy supplies which will shortly be within our control, but we shall not be in a position to take those opportunities if we seek to tackle our immediate problems either by feebly giving way to inflation or, in anything but the short term, abandoning plans for expansion. The right economic strategy for this country is to continue the fight to reduce our domestically-caused inflation, to resume the expansion of the economy and the growth of output, to maintain the industrial investments on which our future prosperity and competitiveness depend and to increase our exports still further to pay for the oil and raw materials which we need to import.

'Only by following this strategy can we hope to avoid a disastrous and permanent lowering of the living standards of all our people. It must be clear by now to all, except a handful of people, that the right political and social strategy for the country is one of moderation and of good sense. We are in a situation where moderate men and women should no longer stay silent. Increasingly in the weeks to come their voices will be heard.

'The measures which I announced last week and the measures which the Chancellor of the Exchequer announced yesterday are severe because they are designed to meet an immediate crisis. But they were also designed to hold a fair balance between different sections of the community in our present difficulties. That is the spirit in which we shall continue to govern and it is in that spirit that we can claim and expect the support of the whole British people.'[39]

There is something at once heroic and honourable, awful and pitiable in this bleak account, again from **Douglas Hurd**, of Heath's decision to make an appearance in support of Conservative candidate Michael Spicer at the by-election in South Worcestershire, which had been prompted by the recent death of his sometime-admirer, sometime-critic Sir Gerald Nabarro:

'New Year's Eve 1973 was a splendid winter's day of mist, sun and frost. That afternoon I stood with a group of dignitaries waiting for the Prime Minister by the bridge at Upton-on-Severn. Michael Spicer, the Conservative candidate, and the officers of the South Worcestershire Association had the patient professional air of regimental officers awaiting briefing from their Commander-in-Chief on the eve of a particularly desperate battle. The sun declined, the mist on the Severn meadows thickened, the frost began to bite through our coats.

'The Prime Minister was late, not an unknown occurrence, though this time there was a reason. At last he arrived, almost too late to be photographed in daylight with Michael Spicer, and walked up the hill to the meeting hall past small enthusiastic groups of people. In the hall he gave the party workers a calm careful account of what had happened, and why we now had a three day week. It was in one way a remarkable occasion.

'Any other politician I have known would have seized and used the emotion hanging in the air. The country was tense, a struggle had begun on which our future seemed to rest. Here in this small market town the Prime Minister was talking to his supporters at the start of a crucial by-election. He had led them to unexpected victory in 1970, his courage and doggedness were immensely respected. He could have worked that audience to a pitch of fiery loyalty. He could have whipped them up against the miners. He could have sent them excited and enthusiastic into the streets. It did not occur to him to do so.

'What mattered to him was that they should understand the complexities of the issue, the objective facts and figures. He saw it as his duty to educate and inform, not to inflame one part of the country against another. So in one sense the meeting was a missed opportunity; but to those who wished to notice (a dwindling minority) it showed a Prime Minister who wanted to tackle not the miners, but inflation, the balance of payments and the desperate consequences for Britain of the oil crisis.'[40]

As the likelihood of an early election grew, it acquired the sense of being inevitable; even though the Government was less than four years into its term, there was a possibility of looking 'frit', as Margaret Thatcher might have put it. Heath's own constituency agent, **Jeffery Speed**, was not happy:

'At the end of 1973 it became increasingly apparent that an early General Election could not easily be avoided. Pressure went to the centre from the agents to avoid it at all costs, but if it had to be called then it must be held no later than 14 February, immediately before the new register of electors came into force. The advantage that the Conservative organisation had on the ground, at a time when nearly every Conservative and marginal seat employed a professional agent, meant that many more Conservative absent voters had been registered than by our opponents, an advantage that would be largely lost when the new register came into force. The decision to delay polling day until 28 February was justified on the grounds that a final (and predictably forlorn) effort should be made to reach agreement with the striking miners. The closeness of our (losing) national result proved frustrating, the Conservatives having polled 300,000 more votes than Labour, but gaining 5 fewer seats. We can only conjecture on how different it might have been if the agents' advice had been taken.'

In January 1974 the nation's grave economic difficulties were already being exacerbated by industrial action in the coal and electricity industries and also on the railways when, sensing the Government's weakness, militants in the NUM called a strike ballot. This would be Heath's Waterloo. He decided to set up a new Department of Energy, with Patrick Jenkin as its minister. **Jenkin** recalls how difficult negotiations with the miners became:

'One recollection of the 1974 strike was the miners' leaders' meeting in the Cabinet Room with Mr Heath and a group of Ministers. One of the miners asked why, as the Government had decided to pay the Arab oil sheikhs the oil price they were demanding, they could not also pay the British coal miners the wage increase they were demanding. This was met by an embarrassed silence. One delegate, Mick McGahey, an avowed Communist, made it clear that his objective was to bring the Government down. This threat, though disavowed by the Labour leadership, nevertheless contributed to what has been described by one Minister as a "siege mentality". For Ted Heath, who sought to embody a rational approach to politics and policy-making, McGahey must have seemed an inexplicable menace.

'The first miners' strike over the 1972 Pay Review had already demonstrated how effective their tactics of mass flying pickets could be, when they defeated the police efforts to keep open the Saltley coal depot in Birmingham. One Treasury adviser later talked of "Ministers looking over an abyss with the possibility of the country being plunged into a state of chaos not so far removed from that which might prevail after a minor nuclear attack". When the subsequent Wilberforce Inquiry awarded the miners most of what they were demanding, this not only shattered the Government's incomes policy but was a conspicuous personal defeat for Ted Heath. It led to a great deal of criticism by the Party, not least by its own Trade Union Advisory Committee, which attacked "the refusal, even abdication, of the Government to show itself willing to govern". What a stinging rebuke from one's own loyal supporters.

'Though Heath made efforts to find a better way of settling such disputes, first via tripartite negotiations, and then when those failed, by a Statutory Incomes Policy, it did not seem to be recognised that there was bound to be a repeat of 1972. His inability to convey to the country what he was now aiming at was a source of despair to his advisers – indeed, he even refused to admit that his policy had changed. Senior Cabinet Ministers were beginning to express their worries, but visceral loyalty to the Party, upon which Heath still seemed able to rely, prevented public dissent. There was some very vocal opposition from a few influential back-benchers, but effective whipping succeeded in concealing much of this from the Prime Minister. The U-Turns had seriously undermined the confidence of the "party faithful" in the leadership to the extent that, by 1974, there were increasing demands for change.

'Moreover, many felt that the constituencies had been largely ignored by the leadership. This disaffection sapped the readiness of party workers and volunteers to campaign in the election. Many local government seats had been lost between 1971 and 1974, with this being attributed by Central Office to "rising prices, unemployment and the Industrial Relations Bill" – in other words, to the failing counter-inflation policy.

'So, when the Miners turned their overtime ban into an all-out strike, with the devastating consequences already described, Heath was faced with having to choose: should the Government face down the strike or should he call an election? He was receiving conflicting advice. There were those who advised him that there must be no surrender. They believed that strong line was widely supported in the country: the Tories led Labour in the polls by 5 per cent, so a successful election could reinforce the Government's authority. Others feared that holding an election would only deepen the divisions in the country and could result in violence, with Tory candidates being pelted with lumps of coal.

'Ted Heath himself found it very difficult to decide; indeed, one adviser described the argument as "Ted against Ted"! Another said that Ted's real worry was the consequences of a Tory landslide: "It would sweep away the moderation which the post-war Tories went into politics to defend. It would be a triumph for the extremists!" If correct, this could be a really significant pointer to his whole attitude; it is as though he was more alarmed by his own party's right wing than he was by the left-wing trade unions.'

When Douglas Hurd left No. 10 to focus his energies on his own forthcoming election in Oxfordshire, Heath did not need to search very far and wide for a replacement. His new political secretary was a youthful member of the CPRS, **William Waldegrave**:

'I was thrown immediately into the thick of the crisis that ultimately brought down the government and with it Heath's career and his kind of Conservative Party. So, into that last winter we went: the country rationed on energy and petrol use; industry working a three-day week; All Souls lit by candlelight (as it should always be); Number Ten lit by French-made Camping Gaz butane lamps. I argued that we should challenge the extra-parliamentary power of the unions in an early election, running under the slogan "Who rules?" Heath was desperately tired after a long summer and autumn. He hung back from an early, confrontational election, seeing a far wider picture than I did. If he lost, he knew his historic Irish deal would collapse in the face of Enoch Powell's antique Unionism and Wilson's weakness in the face of the hard-line "loyalists" it encouraged (and so it proved). His achievement of securing British entry to the European

Economic Community would also be put at risk by Labour's opportunistic opposition and their promise of a referendum.

'Worst of all would be the kind of victory (we did not doubt it would be victory) he would win. He hated the idea of winning on what he saw as the divisive "Who rules?" question. He feared letting the right-wing genie out of the bottle, and a return to a pre-war, coercive Conservatism, with the unions suppressed by the victory of a party representing a hard, militant middle class. He did not want to see the end of the post-war attempt to make the Conservatives the party of one nation, outflanking class-based Labour. So, he delayed calling the election. And when he finally took the plunge, in February 1974, he agreed with his party chairman, Peter Carrington, that it was impossible to fight an election with the restrictions on broadcasting and the rest entailed by the electricity rationing of the three-day week. We would have to turn the lights on again. I thought this threw away our most powerful card: the sense of crisis, and that it would leave the country bemused.

'At Gravesend, traditionally the last big public rally of the election (there were open rallies, with real people – and hecklers – in those days), came a cry from the back of the hall. I believe the questioner was genuinely seeking enlightenment, rather than merely trying to cause trouble. "What can you do if you win which you can't do now with a majority of thirty?" he asked. We had no good answer. A series of upsets in the campaign – Powell's defection to the Unionists; an alleged muddle about what had been offered to the miners; a mishandled response to a clever apparent olive branch from the TUC – seemed crucial at the time. But they were far less important than the point raised by that Gravesend heckler. Still, it never occurred to me that we might lose.'[41]

Waldegrave discovered that 'Mr Heath was also a dominant Prime Minister in the structure of the government but he was a much less open arguer in cabinet. There was much less debate in cabinet and in cabinet committees as such. It was more a process-driven thing. The debate was a more analytical debate with senior civil servants, based on an attempt to find rational solutions. At such fraught times, it can become almost impossible to discern politics from public service.'

Robert Armstrong recalls the final days of the Heath Government:

'I have a vivid memory of the last meeting between the Prime Minister and his colleagues and the representatives of the Trades Union Congress (TUC). Ministers were looking for an effective guarantee that, if the coalminers were conceded a pay increase which did not conform to the counter-inflation policy, other unions would not seek to follow suit. It became clear that, with the best will in the world, the TUC could not offer such an unqualified guarantee. There was a long silence, as the Prime Minister considered the position, and then he finally made up his mind and said that the TUC's offer did not go far enough, and the meeting broke up.

'I have often wondered whether, if the meeting had been adjourned for half an hour, so that Ministers could have met separately and discussed the position, some compromise might have been found to avert the need for an immediate election, and so to create an opportunity to resolve the coalminers' dispute, bring to an end the three-day week, and open the possibility of holding an election later in the year, when circumstances might have been more propitious for the Government.

'That is one of the great "what ifs" of history. One consequence might have been the survival of the Sunningdale Agreement of December 1973 and a less troubled situation in Northern Ireland in the ensuing years. And, if the Conservatives under Edward Heath had won an election in October 1974, the political history of the next ten years might have been very different.'

Having faltered at the thought of calling a general election on 7 February, despite strong advice from Douglas Hurd and others to do so, Heath did soon decide to go to the country on 28 February. This would, perhaps, come to be the greatest regret of his life. 'Why,' **Douglas Hurd** later asked, rhetorically, 'having resisted so long, did the Prime Minister finally agree to a February election?':

'It was partly the deterioration of events, and in particular the lurch into a strike. It became almost impossible to see how a tolerable settlement could be reached without an election. But in my view, and I may be wrong, another argument was decisive. It had been there all along, but in Mr Heath's mind it grew steadily in strength. The more he studied the prospects, the more it emerged that oil rather than coal was the key. He had strongly practised and defended a policy of economic growth; it was now in ruins because of the oil price rise. The public expenditure cuts of December 1973 were only the first of the adjustments which would be needed.

'We were entering a period of lean years, perhaps many years of really harsh scarcity and impoverishment. The lean years would need new policies and a new vocabulary. There would have to be an end to promises. People would have to understand, because only with that understanding could their Government do what was needed. This was impossible for a Government elected in 1970, with policies and a vocabulary which were now out of date.

'The world had changed for Britain. Only a government which had explained the change and been re-elected after that explanation could succeed. I believe that Mr Heath would have liked this to be the main theme of the February 1974 election. In his own mind it was the main theme. It can be seen in his speeches and his broadcasts, and it constantly recurred in conversation.

'He disliked the election, he may for all I know regret it. I suspect that he would never have agreed to hold it at all on grounds of the coal dispute alone. It was the coincidence of the coal dispute with the disastrous change in our economic prospects which in the end clinched the argument.'[42]

Roger Boaden again helped to organise Heath's itinerary:

'I had tried to meet with EH for several weeks and, on Friday 8 February* I received a call to meet him at RAF. EH was late arriving, and therefore behind schedule. When he saw the amount of detail I wanted to discuss, he decided we did not have enough time. He asked if I had ever been to Chequers. I hadn't and so he said, "Good, be there at 2 pm. I have a business lunch and an evening meeting. I can fit you in between."

* The day after the election was called.

'I was surprised to find EH there to greet me as the door opened. First he showed me some of the changes he had made to the décor of major parts of the interior of Chequers, replacing dark colours with lighter hues, and natural wood. Eventually he said, "I suppose you want to work. What kind of music do you like?" I explained I was no match for him, but liked something of everything. "Ever listened to Mahler?" I admitted I hadn't, and he decided we would have some Mahler playing in the background as we sat down to go through the draft programmes. Tea was served, and we completed our work. I gathered up my papers, and we walked slowly to the door to return to my car. EH came out with me, and as we cleared the steps, a car drove up, and out stepped Hugh Scanlon.'*

Heath's constituency agent, **Jeffery Speed**, does not remember the election campaign fondly:

'Typically the political direction of the campaign seemed out of touch with the organisation. Every constituency had been put on alert by Central Office to receive a vital final message of national importance, to be delivered to every house during the last few days of campaigning. We all expected something dramatic which could transform the election. On the last Saturday evening before polling day, after a very active day and following a lively meeting, Ted and his closest advisers had supper in a private upstairs room at his favourite hostelry, The King's Head in Bexley village. A discussion ensued on the tactics for the final push in the last three days of the campaign; and it was clear that no one was aware of the whole Party having been put on stand-by for the eagerly awaited coup de grâce. I found myself sitting next to Sara Morrison, who was in the inner circle at that time. She seemed surprised to find me there and said we were expected to keep "as quiet as church mice", while the experts discussed their plans.'

Michael Heseltine has vivid memories of the run-up to the election, of the campaign itself and also of Heath's state of mind as he went to the country:

---

* Former Communist leader of the engineers' union.

'[Heath] saw, and I think his colleagues Willie and Peter Carrington also saw, that this was the closest to Civil War that a post-war government had come. And they were not prepared to do it.

'This is all about whether we should have fought the election on the 7th or the 29th, and people like me were absolutely certain that we should fight on the 7th. We knew that we'd lost the election, but then Gormley threw us a lifeline. "Who Governs" was a winning cry and, if we'd gone on the 7th, who knows? It is just possible we might have pulled the fat from the fire and won on the "Who Governs" issue. Harold Wilson, who caught us out in the last week on the issue of prices, took a different view, but he took it a fortnight later.

'I can remember the election campaign vividly – and, in the first couple of weeks, we were knocking them sideways. Wherever we went it was all "Good on you", "This is what we've been waiting for", then, on the Monday of polling week, it all went dead. It was the most extraordinary thing. I cannot explain it. The whole atmosphere had changed and Wilson's plan to catch us in the last week came to fruition.

'I think to say anything personal about Ted, you must think about this passing of the wartime generation. He was essentially a one-nation Conservative, he was not in the business of dividing the nation socially or fighting class battles, and he cared, he undoubtedly cared about the tough consequences of mounting unemployment.'

Douglas Hurd recalls the strain on his own relationship with Heath during this period:

'One of the advantages of being in his inner circle was that he noticed if you were feeling cross or disappointed. He had endless meetings during the last few days before the election was called – endless meetings with the TUC, wrestling, desperately trying to get an agreement – and I thought this was going too far. I didn't think simply buttering the trade unions up and hoping for the best was going to work – I thought we had to work out counter-tactics which could outwit them – and he came out of one of these meetings and saw me standing in a corridor. I wasn't very good at concealing my feelings. I had just been told that there was going to be another meeting and I thought, "My God, this is going on forever" – and he saw me and caught that expression on my face. "What are you feeling?" he asked, so I said "I think this is a mistake." "Oh well, he replied, "then you don't understand." We had that conversation quite often, but he believed right to the end, I think, that he was going to win, and that he deserved to win.'[43]

Brendon Sewill had played a leading role in the preparations for government; and he was also present during the brief, painful period of *Götterdämmerung*:

'Ted Heath inspired great loyalty both in his Shadow Cabinet, and in his Government. There were no resignations. Enoch was sacked but no one followed him. Keith Joseph had a plethora of original ideas but remained loyal to Ted. Even Margaret publicly supported all his policies. The same loyalty was evident in the Conservative Research Department during the years of opposition: although we had many bright young aspiring politicians (five of them went on to join Margaret's Cabinet) none expressed deep unhappiness with Ted. The reason was because we all felt he was a good man, desperately trying to do the right thing for Britain. And because he was so interested in policies and was prepared to discuss every policy in detail until he had got it right.

'Why did Heath fail? The obvious answer is the right one. He was defeated by the trade unions. In those pre-privatisation days, every basic industry was in the hands of one or two unions. A strike in electricity, or coal, or rail or the docks quickly brought the nation to standstill. It was always easier to pay up than to fight. So inflation accelerated, and eventually the miners, who had the benefit of public sympathy, delivered the final blow. Ted dithered over calling an election because he hated the idea of fighting the miners, most of whom he recognised as decent men – the sort of men whom he had served alongside in the war.

'During the February 1974 election he was too confoundingly upright to consider anything that might seem like playing politics. As part of the three-day week, television hours had been limited in order to save electricity. But when the election was called, Ted decreed that TV should go back to normal hours – with the result that many members of the public concluded that the fuel crisis had gone away, so why were we having an election?

'At that time I attended the daily Tory election strategy meetings over lunch at the St Stephens Club. I recall passionately arguing on a number of occasions that there should be a crisis meeting of the Cabinet to deal with various aspects of the fuel situation, and incidentally generate crucial Tory publicity. Heath did not attend the meetings at St Stephens – the meetings were chaired by Peter Carrington – but always the answer came back that the Prime Minister was not prepared to play politics in that way.'

For obvious reasons, Heath was able to devote only a few, precious hours to campaigning in Bexley. During the campaign, one of Heath's senior constituency officials told him that party workers had now canvassed the entire place. 'Then you'd better go back and canvass the doubtful wards twice,' he responded. Frank Johnson, in recounting that tale and praising Heath's gift for grumpiness, noted the seniority of the official concerned: 'There is no evidence that Sir Edward has ever been rude to the weak, the junior or those who cannot answer back.'[44] Heath again recruited talented young 'hopefuls' to cover for him. One such was **Richard Simmonds**:

'When campaigning for Ted in Bexley in the elections of 1974, it was my habit on the doorstep from time to time to reproduce Ted's statutory greeting for such occasions – in his slightly gruff tone, "How are you?", or, sometimes, "Where are you from?", which I suppose is on a par with Her Majesty the Queen's "Have you come far?" Jeffery Speed, Ted's wonderful Agent, used to tick me off for mimicking the great man. In Jeffery's office there were two telephones – one, the public number for the Conservative Association, and another reserved for Jeffery's contacts with Ted. One morning the hotline rang, and a slightly gruff voice inquired, "How are you getting on?" Jeffery, who was rather busy, replied, "Richard, I'm not in the mood to bugger about this morning," and slammed the phone down. A few moments later, it rang again: it was the Downing Street switchboard telling Jeffery that the earlier call from the Prime Minister appeared to have been cut off. On his next visit to the constituency, Jeffery told Ted the reason for his expletive and, when Ted came out of Jeffery's room, he looked me up and down, smirked, shoulders heaved, and he merely inquired, "How are you and your bloody cows?" Small talk was never his forte.'

Some reports of that campaign suggest Heath was on surprisingly good form throughout, despite the high stakes. After a rally at the Free Trade Hall in Manchester, he even broke off campaigning for a time, taking his entourage of staff and journalists to a bar and enjoying a relaxed couple of pints with them, until he was cajoled back on board his plane because he was in danger of wrecking the entire schedule. An anxious aide had warned him the plane was waiting. 'Who's paying for it?' asked Heath. 'We are,' he was told. 'Then it can wait, can't it?' It was certainly an eventful campaign, as **Roger Boaden** recalls:

'In the February 1974 Campaign Tour I travelled to Scotland with EH. We flew to Edinburgh, and made several constituency visits before ending up in Glasgow for a major rally. Our first visit was to a small town called Haddington, then part of the Berwickshire and East Lothian constituency, one of the key marginal seats – in fact Michael Ancram made one of the few Conservatives gains. It was an "unplanned" visit, a surprise to the local electors and supporters, a genuine "whistle-stop". It didn't quite work out like that!

'The Special Branch Superintendent who met us at the airport told me he had an intelligence report to expect disturbances at the open air meeting under way in Haddington. He asked me to travel with him in the lead police car to listen to messages. I did so and as we began our approach to Haddington for our stop, he received a call to tell him there was no sign of trouble, and we agreed to continue.

'Michael Ancram was addressing a crowd of two or three hundred supporters across the open space in front of the Corn Exchange. We got out of the cars, but within a few feet we were conscious of a growing crowd around us. No one in this crowd made any noise, but as the numbers quickly grew we were conscious that the increasing numbers were pushing us back towards the cars and away from the meeting of supporters.

'The Special Branch Superintendent decided he didn't like what was happening, and urged me to link arms with him, his four colleagues, and the two protection officers travelling with the Prime Minister. We had to work hard to resist the pushing from the crowd, and we experienced a real struggle to get Heath safely to the cars. As one of his protection team began to open the car door, I was aware a hand was pushing hard between me and the Scottish Special Branch officer. At once he yelled "grab that arm, he's after my f*****g shooter", but the arm was withdrawn as quickly as it had appeared, and we got EH into his car and away. I left moments afterwards in one of our convoy of vehicles.

'Later that night after the rally in Glasgow, I met with the Scottish Special Branch officer in the hotel bar. He invited me to sit down and suggested I took a large swig of the very large whisky he produced for me. What he told me in his broad Glaswegian accent was a real shaker! "If I was a supporter of conspiracy theories, I would record what we witnessed today as an assassination attempt. But I do not recognise any such theory, and therefore this has gone down as a major incident, with an attempt to get my weapon. I've a pretty good idea who was behind it. If I'm correct then he was after my weapon to embarrass me, and me alone. I hope we are both clear on this."

'I never heard any more about it, but I did have several disturbed moments when I contemplated what might have been, if that gun had been taken, and if it had been fired!'

The rest is history. The campaign was ill-starred from the off. Jock Bruce-Gardyne, by now no fan of Heath, was asked at an election meeting, 'If you win, what will you do about the miners?' He thought it prudent to be honest, answering: 'We'll pay them more money.' 'In that case,' asked his interlocutor, not unreasonably, 'what the hell's the election about?' At this moment, prompting general hilarity, the picture of Heath behind Bruce-Gardyne fell down off the wall.

Heath went to the country asking for a fresh mandate, but a haemorrhage of votes to the resurgent Liberals, who had been all but wiped out in 1970, was fatal to his chances. So the February 1974 election was lost not because of a swing to Labour, but because, despite Jo Grimond's valiant attempts to portray the Liberals as a party more radical than Labour, they were a natural recipient for the votes of those who had no stomach for the confrontational politics of the time. With some justification, Heath would interpret the considerable Liberal surge (from 7.5 per cent of the vote in 1970 to 19.3 per cent in February 1974) as a swing to the centre, not to the left.

In Northern Ireland, Heath's moderate Unionist allies, led by Brian Faulkner, were supplanted to a man by relative hard-liners who were all adamantly opposed to the Sunningdale Agreement in which he had invested so much time and energy. The Tories won more votes than Labour, but, crucially, won fewer seats. Over the following weekend, Heath tried to piece together a coalition, but his efforts were doomed. **William Waldegrave** gives a good summary:

'We got more votes, but fewer seats, than Labour. Parliament was hung. The Liberals, Scottish Nationalists and Ulster Unionists held the balance; but Labour was the biggest party. Wilson was as surprised (and perhaps as alarmed) as anyone by his near victory. Heath, concentrating now on the common ground on Europe, negotiated with Jeremy Thorpe's Liberals, seeking full coalition. He refused offers from the Ulster Unionists that would have entailed the abandonment of the Sunningdale Agreement and the betrayal of Brian Faulkner, the moderate Unionist leader, who had bravely backed it. Wilson, like most opposition leaders, had led Labour into an anti-European stance, and he was likely to give in to the hard men in Northern Ireland – two issues on which we had Liberal support. Right at the back of people's minds, however, there was another issue. The Prime Minister, and Conservative Central Office, knew all about the sordid scandal which ended in the assassination of poor Rinka the Great Dane that was about to come crashing down on Thorpe's head. An absolute veto on the use of any of this material during the election had been issued by Heath and Carrington – greatly, I believe, to their honour. But such knowledge did make Thorpe's demand for very high office, perhaps even the Home Office, as his reward for cooperation, implausible. Moreover, most of his party (though not some of his most senior colleagues, including Jo Grimond) was opposed to any serious negotiation with the Conservatives. In any case, even with the Liberals, the majority in the Commons would not have been secure, because of the hard-line Unionists and of nationalist gains in Scotland. As in 2010, the incumbent government, by not winning clearly, had lost. Heath stood down.'[45]

During a break in the final, fateful Cabinet meeting that was held that weekend, Heath found himself at a trough next to Peter Carrington in the gents. 'Why do people hate me so much?' he asked, plaintively. Within days, Harold Wilson would be back at No. 10, in charge of a minority government; and Heath's Steinway would depart Downing Street, for the last time. In a speech twenty-five years later, **Jim Prior** recalled the moment it all ended:

'As we sat round the Cabinet table, that fateful Monday morning in early March 1974, we knew we'd reached the end; and there was a silence and a stillness about the Cabinet room. We folded up our things and it was Margaret Thatcher who said she'd like to say a final word. She expressed our gratitude and our loyalty to a Prime Minister we liked and respected and whom we were honoured to serve. Ted, I think that is all that I can ever say: we were all honoured to serve you.'[46]

Heath would always believe the people of the UK got it wrong on 28 February 1974. He was never fully reconciled to that defeat. A private secretary of his from the early 1980s, Peter Batey, believes that was effectively 'the day [Heath] lost his faith in democracy'. There was something in that, but, deep down, he blamed himself – for his failure to communicate effectively the necessary facts and arguments to the people, for his procrastination about calling the election, and for his failure to spare the nation, as he saw it, the unnecessary travails of 1974–1979 and the even tougher medicine that followed.

Heath had lost his position and also his only home; upon becoming Prime Minister he had ceded his lease at the Albany to the Rothschilds. **Tim Kitson** recalls the period well:

'Ted couldn't stay in Downing Street when he had lost the job, but he hadn't got anywhere else and we'd nowhere to put him, so my wife and I let him move into our flat by Vauxhall Bridge, for six months. It was an awfully difficult period, but Ted wouldn't discuss things that went wrong. I don't think he felt that he'd done things wrong – just that things went wrong. He never used to show anger or frustration. He became silent. That was his way – to retreat into himself and become more introverted and reclusive. He always turned in on himself in those circumstances. It's probably true he went into a depression. He was very difficult to read in those circumstances. So far as the party leadership was concerned, I did say it wasn't going to be possible to hold it. He wasn't very keen about that. He reacted reluctantly, you could say. He had close political friends, such as Toby Aldington, but he didn't have amongst his colleagues in the Commons many "intimates" – Willie Whitelaw talked to him a lot and was very good about it all, but within the party generally he was very independent. He had always been independent as a child. He was close to his mother, but I didn't think he had a good relationship with his father and he and his brother didn't get on. After losing the leadership in 1975, he came down to Spain and stayed with my sister-in-law for a time. He went sightseeing and opened a golf course. That cheered him up a bit.'

Robin Butler believes that Heath's problems stemmed from a peculiar weakness in the negotiation room:

'It can be argued that what brought him down was his sympathy for those on the other side of his negotiations. In the talks at Sunningdale on Northern Ireland, he was much taken with John Hume, the nationalist leader of the Social and Democratic Labour Party – more so than he was with Brian Faulkner and the Ulster Unionists. As a result, he perhaps leaned over too far towards the nationalists in the Sunningdale Agreement.

'Similarly, in the dispute with the National Union of Miners which led to the downfall of the Government, he had good personal relations with the NUM leader Joe Gormley, and genuine sympathy with the mineworkers. He had to work within the straitjacket of the statutory prices and incomes policy but, within that constraint, he reached an informal agreement with Gormley about a settlement which the latter thought might be acceptable to his Executive. But the Executive, dominated by McGahey and Scargill, were unmoveable and the strike persisted.

'What brought about Ted Heath's downfall as Prime Minister was that he was a true one-nation Conservative who believed that Britain's economic problems could be solved by employers, unions and government working together. This was what drove the tripartite approach of his economic policy, disparagingly dubbed "corporatism". But the militants in the trade union were not willing to cooperate and the employers' organisations, particularly the CBI, turned out to be a broken reed in supporting him. It was not until the power of the militant union leaders was broken by a subsequent government giving voice to rank-and-file members through the secret ballot and new picketing laws that a more cooperative arrangement between workforce and employers was achieved.

'Eight years after Ted Heath left office, when I was being interviewed by Margaret Thatcher for the post as her Principal Private Secretary in No. 10, I felt it incumbent on me to tell her that I had believed in the objectives of what Ted Heath had tried to do. She gave me an old-fashioned look but, to her credit, she did not hold it against me and gave me the job. I have always been glad that I said it.'

William Waldegrave has his own view on why Heath's premiership did not last longer:

'Heath's loneliness throughout 1973–74 gives a clue to the weakness of his government. To be effective, leadership has to represent a movement, a group, a structure, and you have to have friends who represent those things, too. Heath had friends in relation to Europe (as well as enemies); and plenty of people had supported him, as I had, because he seemed to represent modernity, meritocracy and honesty, in contrast to Wilson's deviousness. But there was no "Heathism" and this was a source of weakness.

'I believe that Heath's embitterment started then, as he came to think that the British Establishment, and particularly the Conservative Party Establishment – which he had conquered from far outside its traditional borders – had failed him. There were no strong and confident structures to rely on: just himself, and he could not do it all. Something like this, I believe, was what he felt, and it was, of course, deeply unfair to the

Carringtons, Hurds, Whitelaws, Priors and the rest – including tens of thousands of loyal Conservative activists – who had supported him.

'It is perhaps a danger of the philosophy of the glittering prize – the conquest of the meritocratic *cursus honorum*, which had taken Heath from his humble origins to the top of Disraeli's greasy pole – that such conquest is an individual, solitary matter. No movement is represented by such an achievement; the long-distance runner is lonely. Disraeli himself, glittering prize-winner of all glittering prize-winners, was a lonely and somewhat ineffective figure once he had obtained power.

'Heath did adhere to one other profound ideology, in addition to meritocracy itself: his belief that the destruction he had witnessed in Europe after the war validated the drive to unify the continent as a bloc, a new near-national federation. This commitment did indeed represent a movement, in the civil service, in academia, in the serious press (led then by William Rees-Mogg's pro-European *Times*) and in elements of each political party – particularly those who had fought in the war. But it sat uneasily with the Tory Party, one strand of which had always been a quiet but insular nationalism. Heath once asked me, sitting in the back of the opposition leader's Rover, "Do you think the British people have still got it in them?" This was a question of someone who was romantic about Britain, and who had found himself in a depressed and depressing country he did not understand. He had thought he had understood it better than the pundits: after all, he had never wavered in his certainty that he would win the 1970 election, in spite of the polls. Douglas Hurd had a framed copy on the mantelpiece of the office in Number Ten where he met journalists of the edition of the *Observer* published on the last Sunday of that campaign. Its front-page headline read: "Labour 8% ahead: only a miracle can save the Tories now." Heath had been right then; conventional wisdom wrong. On another occasion, after a Königswinter Conference where he had made common cause in a European discussion with Shirley Williams and others, he said to me, "Those are the people we should be working with!"

'Heath's Europeanism was largely driven by his belief that a Europe with the UK genuinely at the top table gave Britain a better base for advancing its interests than did an Anglo-American alliance which, at least after the Casablanca Conference of 1943, had stopped having even the façade of equality. His fatal hesitation over when to call the first election in 1974 was due to his conviction that he was the only one who understood how much was at stake. His contempt for Wilson was not wholly unmerited, because the Labour leader would indeed give in on all the big issues. And the Conservative Party would indeed, in economics at least, revert to something much more like the party of the 1930s which Heath had fought over appeasement at the Oxford by-election of 1938, using high unemployment as an instrument of policy and drifting towards social reaction.

'"Making history is very tiring," Robert Armstrong told me during that February election, observing my doubtless bedraggled state late one evening in Number Ten. It is, even for the supporting cast. Heath had phenomenal strength of will and reserves of energy. But those last months of 1973 and early months of 1974 broke him, and with him the liberal Conservative settlement that had existed since the war. Forty years later, the realignment of British politics which began in 1974 remains incomplete.'[47]

No one has written in a more persuasive, or a better-informed, way about the trials and tribulations of the 1970–1974 Government than **Douglas Hurd**. He later argued that the seeds of that Government's downfall were possibly already sown, even before it took office in June 1970:

'As anyone who recalls the 1970 election campaign will know, Mr Heath and his colleagues won that election against and not with the tide of intellectual opinion. This made their feat more remarkable, but it also made their task more difficult. There is nothing tangible about intellectual opinion. There is no precise or visible obstacle against which Ministers bang their heads when that opinion is opposed to their inherited philosophy. But anyone who has held high office knows what such opposition means. The people talking round a common-room table, an editor's desk, a television studio, a company boardroom, are through the strange interweavings of British life more in touch with each other than they know. They have different ideas for society, but they edge towards a common view of what is actually possible, and they have the means to express it.

'A politician, moving rapidly from one of these rooms to another, meets different people of different political persuasions saying the same sort of thing about a particular situation. He is bound to be impressed. When this general comment runs in favour of what he is trying to do, he must be encouraged. The next government which tries to shift the balance of power away from the state and away from the trade unions will find, at least initially, that the general comment is on its side. It will be said that this advantage is nice but not decisive.

'If Mr Heath and colleagues lacked an intellectual groundswell on their side, that was not the reason for their eventual defeat. They lost because, despite the most strenuous efforts by the Prime Minister, the trade unions turned against the Government's economic policy, and in particular its attempt to limit wage increases. The trade union leadership, backed by the Labour Party, allowed the miners to break the Government. This had nothing to do with intellectual groundswells, with dons or journalists. It had to do with the brutal exercise of trade union power.

'We had a Prime Minister who believed passionately that realism should prevail if facts were reasonably presented. We had a Cabinet which, representing a modern Conservative Party, realised that in no way could that party prosper by setting class against class, however many warlike telegrams its supporters might send. Of all the charges now made against that Government, the charge that it sought or welcomed confrontation with the trade unions is the most absurd.'[48]

In the summer of 1994, Peter Hennessy (now Lord Hennessy) interviewed Heath for Rob Shepherd's ground-breaking Channel 4 television series *What Has Become of Us?* and tried to draw him out on what he had wanted to achieve, for and in the country, when he became Prime Minister. The response from **Heath** suggests that his intention, all along, was to underpin the post-war settlement, not to destroy it:

'What we wanted to do was to modernise. We'd done tremendous work as a shadow government planning all of this . . . so we had all of this on which to base our attitudes and our work when we took over. And you're quite right, we wanted to increase the efficiency of this country enormously . . . and if you can do it jointly with everybody else, so much the better. It avoids all the rows and you also avoid the dogma which has been the curse of recent years – that we know this and we're going to do this because it's our dogma and let's get on with it; all those who aren't with us are against us. That's not the way to run a country. You can't run a business like that either – and you certainly can't run a government like it. So yes, I wanted to modernise, I wanted to do it as far as possible on a consensus. But one always recognises there are some issues on which it might not be possible to get a consensus. Well then you have to take your own line in the best possible way.'[49]

Let the last word here on the Heath Government go to **Douglas Hurd**:

'There was a comradeship at Number Ten during that time. That is an overused word. By it I mean partly that there were very few quarrels or intrigues within the house. The atmosphere was wholly different from the strange enclosed bitterness described by Lady Falkender and by Mr Haines in their books about Mr Wilson's premiership. I am not saying here that our ideas were better or our ability greater, simply that we worked in greater harmony. That was partly because of the Prime Minister's personality, but not entirely. It was also, I think, because we believed that we were part of an enterprise which was attempting something unusual and worthwhile.

'It is nowadays a commonplace that Mr Heath and his colleagues lost their nerve because they were frightened of the political consequences of unemployment. I cannot write of arguments used at Ministerial meetings which I did not attend. Nevertheless I believe that the common explanation is exaggerated. It is true that Mr Heath felt strongly that the modern Conservative Party had to shake off the spectres of the past, of which mass unemployment was the most formidable. No one of Mr Heath's background and generation could easily dismiss rising unemployment as a statistical fiction or as unimportant. Despite this, the political advisers of the Government were at all times more concerned about inflation than about unemployment. We knew how the 1970 election had been won – we knew how the next election could be lost. At meeting after meeting we concentrated on the course of prices. No other consideration had in our minds anything like the same political importance.

'All governments make mistakes and pay a price. What distinguishes Mr Heath's Government is something different. He devoted himself to starting a new chapter of achievement in this country. The quiet revolution was not a phrase to be turned at a Party Conference and forgotten. It was the purpose of his political career. He and his colleagues had studied at length in opposition how it was to be achieved. They set to work on it in earnest. On the whole they were not successful. Some things they failed to achieve at all. Much was achieved in part, and then demolished by their successors. But the analysis was not wrong. The weaknesses they tried to cure were real enough. Indeed they have become much worse since they left office. Inflation, unemployment, lack of investment, overweening trade union power, industrial and agricultural stagnation, weakness in Europe and the world – the old problems, now aggravated, will have to be tackled all over again. The years of Mr Heath's Government should be regarded as a necessary first attempt, the rough work of pioneers.'[50]

CHAPTER FOUR

Out of office (1974–1997)

H aving tried to piece together a coalition and failed, Heath had to return, most ignominiously, to his old job, as leader of the opposition. It was not easy for him or for any of his colleagues. **Patrick Jenkin** recalls traumatic days for the Conservative Party:

'In the weeks following the election, there was a deep pessimism, not only in the party, but also right across the country. People began to ask "Is Britain governable?" The combination of poor economic performance, trade union militancy and the failure to reach agreement on a coalition, were all factors in this atmosphere of gloom.

'Heath emerged from the February election with all the confidence of his earlier years knocked out of him. Though some of his speeches in the House attacking the Labour Government provided some reminder of his undoubted skill as a Parliamentary debater, they won little praise from his back benches. He was still determined to advance his view that there must be a better way of conducting politics than the adversarial techniques of the past. He refused to consider standing down himself even if that might advance the cause of coalition; and he sought to portray himself as the champion of the case for a Government committed to the national interest. He was also determined to safeguard his great achievement of taking Britain into Europe, fearing that manoeuvring by Wilson might put that at risk.

'The party was in a pretty unhappy state and its MPs realised it was in no fit state to fight another immediate election. They were understandably eager to attack the new, minority Labour Government in the House, but they were reluctant to go so far as to defeat it in the division lobbies, just in case they brought it down and forced another poll. Ted's own position was grievously weakened now and I understand that over 100 Conservative MPs told the whips privately that he should stand down in short order, as his credibility was gone. With no overt challenge to his authority emerging, however, his own confidence did begin to revive and, by the summer, with an autumn election inevitable, he became, in effect, impossible to dislodge. Perhaps that explains why his aloofness, both from his supporters in the House and also from party members in the constituencies, appeared to intensify.'

To the crucial economic brief, the job in which he had once set out his own claim for the party leadership, Heath appointed Margaret Thatcher, initially as No. 2 to Robert Carr. I once asked him why. Those cool, blue eyes fixed me in a passionless gaze and he explained simply, 'because she was the best person for the job'. This is corroborated by **Tony Barber**:

'I told Ted about Margaret's experience at the Tax Bar and suggested that she might be a match for Healey. So she joined the opposition team and, sure enough, she was very soon scoring points off the Chancellor. Her success did not go unnoticed. It has been said that this was a mistake on Ted's part because it gave Margaret a chance to shine. But this is to misjudge Ted's motive, which was simply to strengthen the opposition Treasury team. Nevertheless, it is a fact that, by a stroke of good fortune – being given that opportunity by Ted – she considerably enhanced her chances of success when the chips were down and she stood against him for the Leadership.'[1]

Wilson was seventeen seats short of a majority, so there was never any doubt another election would come soon. Heath somehow persuaded himself that if he was indeed to return and be the saviour of the nation, with public opinion so divided and support for the larger parties at so low an ebb, it might

be better (and, presumably, more plausible in terms of electoral arithmetic) to take up the reins not of a majority Conservative Government, but of a Government of National Unity. Perhaps he was merely trying to be realistic, but the effect on the already shattered morale of the party faithful was baneful. With the trumpet sounding so uncertain a note, the Tory troops were understandably loathe to prepare themselves unto battle. During this period, **Stephen Sherbourne** had his first encounters with Heath:

'I was working in the Conservative Research Department and, every Tuesday and Thursday, I briefed him ahead of Prime Minister's Questions and I also attended Shadow Cabinet meetings. He appeared weary: with the job, which had no power; with his MPs who were restless; and with his shadow ministers, some of whom were on manoeuvres against him. Did he still want to be Prime Minister? I believe so. Partly as a matter of pride; partly because he was disdainful of what he perceived as Harold Wilson's superficial style; and partly because I suspect he believed that somehow he could meet the economic and international challenges.'

Just as 'election fever' signally failed to race through a weary and dispirited nation, Heath was hit by a brutal personal blow when he gave permission for Christopher Chadd, his young godson and the son of his wartime CO George Chadd, to sail on the third *Morning Cloud* boat in early September 1974, not in a race, but with a temporary crew who were moving the boat between harbours. **Owen Parker**, Heath's invaluable right-hand man during so much of his competitive sailing, tells the tale:

'They were unlucky enough to be caught by a freak wave, and the boat dropped off the top of it onto her side, losing two men overboard in the process. Unfortunately one of their harness lines broke and, in returning to look for Nigel Cumming who was in the water, they were struck by another rogue sea which washed overboard Mr Heath's godson, Christopher Chadd, as he was in the main hatch just making his way on deck. This time the boat . . . started to break up . . . Nigel and Christopher were not recovered and the survivors had to take to the life raft; they were eventually washed ashore in an exhausted condition.'[2]

EDWARD HEATH: A SINGULAR LIFE

Heath was a tough and resilient person – good qualities in both a wartime military officer and also a peacetime politician – but this was one of the handful of events in his life that would haunt him for the remainder of his days. George Chadd told him not to blame himself for the awful loss of his son, but I know Heath never totally forgave himself. He had little time to grieve, as Harold Wilson requested the dissolution of Parliament just a matter of days later. **Patrick Jenkin** takes up the tale again:

'When another election was called for 10 October 1974, the omens for the Conservatives were unpromising. Doubts about the leadership were perhaps the greatest concern, but other factors were in play too. The very mixed reception given to the various efforts to reform the party organisation had undermined morale in Central Office. The clear conflict between the Heathite policy of seeking a "National Coalition Government" and the case increasingly put forward by MPs for a distinctive Conservative approach was confusing the public. There was also a gap opening up on economic policy, with growing support both inside and outside the party for a really radical change in economic policies based on monetarism – the control of the money supply as the weapon to fight inflation – instead of the attempted control of prices and incomes. All this sent very mixed messages to the electorate.

'Unsurprisingly, the campaign was a dispiriting affair. Although great efforts were made to ensure that other senior Shadow Spokesmen were given prominent roles, the media concentrated their coverage of the Conservative campaign almost exclusively on the leader himself. Indeed, Heath seemed to be quoted on national TV and radio more than all other senior Conservatives combined. Unfortunately, if the message remained muddled and obscure to the public – "a rather woolly and nebulous programme" was the verdict of one commentator – it was hardly likely that Heath's main campaign speeches would provide the inspiration that could win an election.

'And so it proved: Labour was re-elected with a majority of three seats over all other parties combined – and a clear margin of 48 over the Conservatives. Harold Wilson had won three out of the four elections he fought as Labour Leader; Ted Heath had lost three out of the four he had

fought as Conservative Leader. Doorstep canvassing had reinforced the all-too clear message from the opinion polls: Ted Heath was significantly less popular than his Party.'

Heath had lost again – clearly this time – and his position as leader was under critical threat. Loyal whips set up dinners at which he could 'get to know' his back-bench colleagues. Ken Clarke described one such event, when he rounded up MPs from the Midlands. One of them was Ivan Lawrence, newly elected as MP for Burton. At the end of an excruciatingly stiff and uncomfortable occasion, with Heath at his most baleful and morose, Lawrence said to Ken: 'Until this evening I had not exchanged a single word with the party leader. After tonight I have *still* not exchanged a single word with the party leader.' Even the bombing of his house in Wilton Street by Irish terrorists just before Christmas 1974 – in many ways an appropriate cap to a ghastly year, though, fortunately, he was out of the house at the time – did not win Heath significant sympathy. Many of those who had previously been loyal now believed the name of Heath was unbreakably associated with defeat. He was also, despite the plots against him and the numerous other contenders for the unenviable title, determined to cling onto his long-held role of being his own worst enemy. Furthermore, although no one had resigned from his Cabinet, a total of 160 Tory MPs (around half the then total) had voted against the Heath Government – 100 of them more than once, and twelve of them more than fifty times. Heath did not want a leadership contest, but he was forced to recognise he had no choice: there must be one. **Julian Critchley** summed up his predicament very eloquently:

'Heath had made many enemies in the ten years of his leadership: he had led the party, despite being "Selsdon Man", from left of centre; and he had conspicuously failed to practise the political arts. His parsimony when it came to handing out the twice-yearly honours to clapped-out MPs was bitterly resented by those who sought consolation of a sort. He was also reluctant to flatter the simple. Most important of all, he had led the party to defeat in three of the four elections it had fought under his leadership. Shocked by February 1974, and humiliated by October, many Tory MPs

[165]

were only too ready to use the electoral machinery . . . to rid themselves of a man they saw as a political albatross.'[3]

Simon Hoggart suggests another, additional and subtler reason for Heath's fatal inability to rally his troops at his time of greatest need:

'Take the annual party for Tory MPs. Under Ted Heath this was thrown at some inconvenient time of year. Wives who wanted to come – that is, almost all of them – had to make a special trip down to London. Heath was often late in arriving, sometimes by three-quarters of an hour. Frequently he looked bored and could hardly be bothered to chat to anyone. This was a fatal mistake. Most men will put up with any amount of rudeness to themselves, but will never forget or forgive a snub to their wives.'[4]

Michael Heseltine recalls:

'By the time of the second election of 1974, which he lost, and the leadership challenge, I was shadow secretary of state for trade and industry. It was at this point that I began to know he had to go. I sat at the oblong table alongside Keith Joseph, opposite Ted. Keith would raise issues that seemed to me, as a new arrival at this top table, to be perfectly reasonable, about possible policy options and things that had gone wrong. Keith was the nicest man in British politics – courteous, softly spoken and intelligent – but Ted would turn on him, treating him abysmally, appallingly, I remember sitting there, thinking: "This man cannot heal the divisions in the party ever again. He cannot do it. He doesn't even try to listen." He had neither the instinct nor the willingness to reach out to those he knows have a different viewpoint to his. All he had to do was to say: "Yes, Keith, why don't you put together a team of solid policy makers and look at this, that or the other." That was all he had to do.

'That was why people like me thought he'd had his time. We had a career to make and he could never lead us back to power. I think Ted had reasonable regard for me, because he used to ring me up as time went on and Margaret was in power, to find out what was going on. I told him what I could. I don't suppose he ever knew I didn't vote for him.'

Speculation about Heath's future became ubiquitous. He was the story now; and his poll ratings were not good. Amongst Tory voters he had a 51 per cent approval rating; amongst Labour supporters, Wilson was running at 86 per cent. Labour led in the polls by 48 per cent to 34 per cent. Nonetheless, a clear majority of Conservatives in the country wanted Heath to carry on. Not so the 1922 Committee, whose members were not concealing their desire for an early contest as they busily agreed new rules for leadership elections. Eventually, on 14 November, Heath agreed that a leadership contest be held, with the date for the first ballot later set for 4 February 1975.

Willie Whitelaw was the bookies' favourite to succeed Heath as leader, but he would not stand out of loyalty to Heath. For a time, Keith Joseph seemed to be the likely challenger from within the shadow cabinet, but an ill-judged speech that had had a whiff of eugenics about it put him firmly out of the running. It was left to Margaret Thatcher to make that challenge. She had supported Heath for the leadership in 1965 and he promoted her so enthusiastically that she even appeared, as the third of a triumvirate with Peter Walker and Tony Barber, on the cover of Andrew Roth's 1972 study *Heath and the Heathmen*. Indeed, for a time she was laughingly referred to by political journalists as '"Mrs Heath"' – but now she had run out of patience with him. Hugh Fraser and Heath were the only other declared candidates. Fraser was a quixotic candidate at best, but he promoted himself as 'anti-establishment' and set out an astute critique of Heath and the effects of his leadership: 'What was a national party has lost the support of the great industrial centres, much of Scotland and all of Ulster. Our position is now worse than in 1945. Mr Heath is a man of character and ability, but he is no political leader. He is very efficient, but believes he can only lead if he is surrounded by like minds. The result is a total domination of the party by one man, a domination that reduced our party to its present state.'[5]

Heath sought to distinguish himself from his right-wing challengers: 'It is my belief and has been for all my political life that the death of the ideal of one nation would be a disaster for Britain.' Of the leadership election process itself, he asserted: 'I am determined to see the procedure through – I've been a fighter all my life and I shall go on fighting.'[6] He simply did not accept there was a case for replacing him, rejecting the suggestion that his electoral record meant he was a failure as leader: 'I don't think that's a very

sensible or rational approach.'[7] It was becoming painfully clear that many Tory MPs disagreed with him.

Patrick Jenkin recalls Heath's reaction to Mrs Thatcher's decision to run:

'Once Margaret had decided to run, she had the unenviable task of informing the incumbent of her decision. When she called on Heath to tell him this, the interview lasted for two minutes: he neither stood up nor invited her to sit, and all he said was: "If you must! You'll lose!"*

'The campaign was dominated by those who represented the "Anyone but Heath" view. Many of those who supported Margaret in the first round did so in order to ensure a second ballot, in which someone more acceptable (Willie Whitelaw, in many of their minds) might stand. Hugh Fraser . . . was not expected to get more than a handful of votes, and he didn't. All the polls showed Heath winning; all the press supported Heath; and most constituency chairmen supported him. Even though almost all of us felt depressed at the thought of Ted carrying on and thought he was now irrecoverably an electoral liability, not for nothing was it always said that "Loyalty is the secret weapon of the Conservative Party". The result of the first ballot was therefore a real shock.'

Kenneth Baker (now Lord Baker of Dorking) was Heath's second PPS, alongside Sir Timothy Kitson. He was with Heath in the Leader of the Opposition's room in the House of Commons when the results of the first ballot came in:

'Ted was sitting on the sofa at the window. He looked crestfallen as it became clear that he had been beaten in the first round. Although Margaret had not received the necessary overall majority on the first ballot, she had won 130 votes to Ted's 119. Ted decided to withdraw straight away, and with calm dignity he drew up in his own hand his resignation statement. As I left Ted's office I passed Reggie Maudling uncharacteristically

---

* This story has gone the rounds for forty years now, but Heath vehemently denied it to me – his comment being merely that 'I thanked her'.

rushing down the corridor and muttering, "The Party's taken leave of its senses. This is a black day." Ted was shattered. He had never believed the Party would turn on him in this way.'[8]

William Waldegrave has a slightly different, rather more apocalyptic, recollection:

'Tim Kitson brought the result of the leadership ballot into the big Commons office where some of us had gathered, and handed Heath the piece of paper showing that Thatcher had won the first round. There are two versions of what Heath said next: Kenneth Baker's, "So we got it all wrong then"; and mine, "It has all gone wrong, then." The version I remember is subtly but importantly different from Baker's. His means "we", and indeed "you – the staff", have messed up the election. Mine means that he was still thinking with the clarity that made him nearly great: that everything he had inherited, from Churchill, Macmillan, Butler and the other architects of post-war British Conservatism, was about to end. I know that he was so stubborn, and so ungracious and sour in defeat because he understood that the contest was not a matter of personalities, nor even of superficial policy differences. He realised that his defeat meant that a sea change was coming over the British right. It would be the end of the attempt to maintain the social contract and a reversion to far freer economics in which the government would not regard full employment as a possible – or even legitimate – object of policy. And it would begin the inexorable rise of anti-Europeanism in the party, which had the potential to undo what Heath regarded as his greatest achievement.'[9]

George Hutchinson blamed Heath's coterie for his humiliation: 'Mr Heath's advisers . . . displayed poor judgment and false instincts. With their loud, aggressive, pushing behaviour they were insensitive to the feelings of many Conservative MPs. Their methods were counter-productive, not least the astounding decision to advertise for support.'[10] A 'former close friend' (what a chilling description) told one newspaper that: 'Ted Heath lost yesterday because he ignored the little things in life which encourage and build up . . . After 1970, he spoke to me five times in 44 months as Prime Minister.

He could have chatted in the Smoking Room but didn't bother . . . Too many of us can tell the same story about him. Ted Heath believed it irrelevant to try to show human feelings.'[11]

Some years later, Tory MP **Nigel Fisher,** who had supported Mrs Thatcher's campaign and would write a more than serviceable biography of Harold Macmillan – reflected upon what Heath had endured:

'If the result was a triumph for Margaret Thatcher, it was a tragedy for Ted Heath. No one could have worked with greater dedication for his party and for the country; yet it had all ended in the personal humiliation of rejection by those he had sought so steadfastly to serve . . . Without a wife or children to turn to in times of trouble, Ted Heath must sometimes be a lonely man, and even those of us who, like myself, had contributed to his downfall could scarcely bear to think of his bitter disappointment. Like most of my colleagues, I wrote him a letter of genuine sympathy and soon received a magnanimous and generous reply in his own hand.'[12]

The morning after she was elected leader, Mrs Thatcher came to see Heath at his home, at her request. No one knows for sure exactly what transpired, but there are two basic versions. The Thatcher camp said this:

'[Mrs Thatcher] went to see Edward Heath at his house in Wilton Street to ascertain whether he would be willing to join her Shadow Cabinet and if so in what capacity. Until she knew his answer, she could not begin to fill the other positions. She came quickly to the point: "I have said publicly that I would ask you to join the shadow cabinet. Will you do so?" Heath at once declined and added that he intended to spend a period on the back benches. Mrs Thatcher then suggested that he might be willing to take charge of the Conservative Party's European referendum campaign from an official position. Again he refused.[13]

In his memoirs, **Heath** wrote that:

'Tim Kitson was approached by Mrs Thatcher's PPS, who asked whether

the leader could come to see me at my home at Wilton Street. It was suggested to Tim that she was going to offer me a job in the Shadow Cabinet. I received this message and, after careful consideration, I instructed Tim to take a message back saying that I had decided that I did not wish to join the Shadow Cabinet for the time being. I was therefore somewhat surprised when Mrs Thatcher arrived at Wilton Street at 10.30 the following morning.

'Mrs Thatcher was obviously and understandably flustered, but I congratulated her again on her victory in the second ballot. After these preliminaries, she said there was one point on which she would value my advice. How should she handle the press, particularly at the weekly press conference held in the lobby of the House of Commons, each Thursday? This press conference was used mainly to find out the attitude of the Opposition on the parliamentary business for the coming week. I told her that handling the press was an individual matter. We all had our own ways of dealing with them, and I suggested that she should develop her existing techniques. She thanked me, rose and said goodbye. It took only a few minutes.

'At the front door, where Tim Kitson was waiting to let her out, Mrs Thatcher asked to stay for a while longer, lest the press outside should conclude that the meeting had been a disaster. Tim took her upstairs as he was concerned that, if he took her to the downstairs dining room, they would be seen by the large number of press photographers who were waiting outside. Ten minutes later, he said goodbye to her as well. At no time during the meeting did she invite me to become a member of the Shadow Cabinet or to play any part on her front bench. This is confirmed by Tim Kitson who, standing in the hall, heard every word that passed between us, through the open door of my study.'

The two accounts may seem mutually inconsistent at first reading, but I am not sure they are: here was another example of the poor communications that had always characterised the relationship between Heath and Mrs Thatcher (and most other people too).

At Prime Minister's Questions, **Harold Wilson** paid a generous tribute to his vanquished adversary:

'While it has not escaped the notice of the House and the country over the years that the right hon. Gentleman and I have had our differences, and that neither of us has been diffident in expressing them, those differences have been political, representing a deep divergence of political philosophies. They have not been personal.

'He has made a most notable contribution to the work of the House and has done so much to make it a more workable institution. Increasingly, there will be time to appreciate what he has done for the processes and machinery of Government, and in many and indeed fundamental areas of policy. Those are matters which history as much as his contemporaries will be called upon to judge. But, Sir, in the House of Commons setting, in this Chamber and in the conduct of business behind your Chair, whether on Privy Counsellor terms or otherwise, he has been ever considerate and understanding, and always concerned to serve the best interest of this House and its Members.'[14]

Heath had lost so much in the course of just one year. Even his home was still boarded up after the IRA bomb attack ('The house sums up Ted,' said one friend – 'battered but not demolished') and he had lost his £8,000 per year salary as leader. He issued a brief statement – 'I offer my warmest congratulations to Mrs Thatcher on her election as leader of the Conservative Party in the House of Commons and wish her every success' – then went to Spain to nurse his wounds and grievances. Upon his return he immediately embarked upon plans to buy a new *Morning Cloud*, using the insurance money from its predecessor. He also celebrated his twenty-fifth anniversary as an MP.

The press could still sense blood in the political waters and constantly goaded Heath on the subject of Mrs Thatcher. One interviewer[15] grew desperate and asked him: 'You must like her hairstyle?' This was too much for Heath, who snapped: 'I don't believe in frivolity like that. I think politics is a serious business.' Didn't he feel betrayed, or even let down, persisted the journalist? 'They were all entitled to do what they did,' responded Heath, bleakly. 'They have their own ambitions, and it's a perfectly honourable thing to have ambition.' Was it honourable to have ambitions and at the same time betray loyalty? 'Well this is a very difficult question, which each individual has to decide for himself . . . or herself.'

In April 1975, Heath went to Germany with the LSO and André Previn. He conducted in Bonn and also attended a Königswinter event, at which he addressed some remarks to Federal President Scheel: 'Since the last conference you have ceased to be the leader of your party. You have become instead President of the Federal Republic. This is a very welcome way of dealing with such an event. Unfortunately it applies only to those leading parties under Republican constitutions!' At a Cricket Society lunch during the same period, Heath was the principal speaker. During the course of his speech, he made reference to overlooking a cricket ground on which women were playing. 'I have absolutely no objection to women playing cricket,' he told his audience. 'I just wish they'd left it at that!' An old friend of mine was the first person to laugh; and she was 'rewarded with a glint of a smile'. Wilf Weeks recalls another comment Heath made: 'Soon after he returned from his travels there was a meeting at Wilton Street to discuss the coming months and the party conference. It involved Stephen Sherbourne and Michael Young among others. The leadership election came up and to my surprise I heard [Heath] say that everything was going fine "until that woman threw her knickers in the ring".'

Heath was quickly energised as Harold Wilson sought desperately to resolve rifts in Labour over Europe by calling the first ever national referendum. Notionally the vote was on some very minor renegotiations that he had quickly completed with the EEC, but, in reality, it was about UK membership. The Conservative Party was overwhelmingly in favour of EEC membership, sharing Heath's vision of renewed British leadership in Europe. Its new leader Margaret Thatcher quickly resolved that she would allow Heath to be the leading Conservative figure in the campaign. She certainly had other matters that demanded her attention, as a new leader who was taking time to settle into the role. It also suited her purposes to allow Heath to restore his public dignity. There was no indication that she felt lukewarm about our membership – and photographs still circulate of her wearing an extraordinary jumper during the campaign, featuring the flags of the then nine EEC member states – but perhaps she already sensed that the EEC, with its founding document the Treaty of Rome calling for 'ever closer union', might one day head into uncharted waters that would be not to her taste. She passed on the referendum baton at the campaign launch on 16 April 1975 with an extraordinary show of warmth and deference:

> 'It is especially appropriate that we should open the Conservative campaign to keep Britain in Europe under your Chairmanship. Because you have done more than anyone else for the Conservative cause in Europe, and to see that Britain's place is in Europe.
>
> 'Naturally, it's with some temerity that the pupil speaks before the master, because you know more about it than any of the rest of us. I think there are four main reasons for Britain staying in the community. First, the community gives us peace and security in a free society. The peace and security denied to the past two generations. Second, the community gives us access to secure sources of food supply. And this is vital to us, a country which has to import half of what we need. Third, the community does more trade and gives more aid than any other group in the world, and fourth, the community gives us the opportunity to represent the Commonwealth in Europe. A Commonwealth which wants us to stay in, and has said so, and the community wants us to stay in and has shown it to be so.'[16]

Heath campaigned with renewed energy and vigour in the referendum campaign. He was a changed man and everyone noticed. He wanted to win the referendum – and he was determined to win big.

It was not only a question of the national interest: it was a matter of national honour. 'We gave our word,' he professed. 'We made a promise. We entered a commitment. And we signed a treaty. If one treaty is broken there is no reason why anyone should expect another one to be kept.' At a rally in Trafalgar Square on 4 May, he said this: 'It is those who talk loudest about international brotherhood – those on the far Left – who are most frightened about the big world. For people like Peter Shore, international brotherhood stops at Margate. Just look at those who want us to pull out of Europe, to become an isolated off-shore island . . . They all look so miserable! Who in their right minds would go on a desert island with them?' Debating with Michael Foot later in the campaign, he radiated scorn: 'I don't believe that sovereignty is something which you hoard up like a miser, and cover up in sacking and put in the cellar.' In May he addressed the Washington Press Club and earned a standing ovation with a speech about his hopes for Britain: 'It is my profound conviction that we will pull ourselves out of our current malaise. If you want to put that into simple journalistic prose, you can say "I'm Backing Britain".' He nearly missed the engagement when his flight was cancelled. He was told there was a cargo plane flying out, but the only passengers allowed were grooms. 'Then find me a horse,' he responded. They made him an honorary steward for the flight – and he travelled on the flight deck.

In his final appeal to the voters, **Heath** emphasised the political nature of European unity:

'Why was the Common Market formed in the first place? Quite simply, in order to stop a third European war this century. The wars of 1914 and 1939 were both triggered off in our own continent of Europe. On each occasion the old arch-enemies, France and Germany, were at each other's throats. Each time, Britain tried to steer clear of what was happening. But each time we found ourselves sucked in. The price we paid was immeasurable . . . The reality in the modern world is that no country, however powerful, can hope to be entirely independent – not even the US . . . We live in an interdependent world . . . Inside the European Community we can influence the development of Europe and so increase the effective sovereignty of Britain . . . If only we had had that increased sovereignty and influence in 1914 or 1931! Not one anti-European has so far been able to demolish this argument. Instead, they are shamelessly playing upon people's fears about food prices and jobs.'[17]

The day after the vote, as the results came in, Heath was in the ITN studio in London. There had been a landslide for Europe. At 4.30 pm he dashed off, changed his clothes and flew by helicopter from Battersea to Cowes. By 6.30 pm he was on board a racing boat. For six exhilarating weeks, Heath had toured up and down the land, speaking with an unfamiliar passion and eloquence; he had played a leading role in persuading Britain to embrace his European vision; and he had done much to restore his reputation amongst the British people. This may explain his state of mind afterwards, when he evidently persuaded himself that his political rehabilitation had been so comprehensive and profound that an offer of high office – perhaps, once again, the highest office of all – was now a possibility again.

His political secretary was now **Stephen Sherbourne**:

'I had started working for EH weeks before and it was a real joy to work with him in that campaign. It was a whirlwind six weeks. We criss-crossed the country, speeches delivered to every kind of audience, appearances on television and radio, articles appearing everywhere – and it would not have been possible without his trust in the people who worked with him (he knew how to delegate) and his unfailing good humour.

'He never lost his cool though although there were many occasions when he would have had good reason. Such as returning from Scotland in a tiny propeller plane, which could only take three passengers (EH, a secretary and me), when the secretary tapped the pilot on the shoulder to ask if he could possibly land somewhere, anywhere, so she could "pay a visit" and when, by the way, I was having to make use of the sick bag. Throughout the whole flight, EH sat stoically, just occasionally turning round to look at us quizzically, raising his eyebrows which was his way of saying both "I understand" and "for goodness' sake, get a grip".

'After the campaign had been fought and won, EH's reputation had risen considerably. People suddenly saw a more human and less wooden figure. The question was how would he exploit this?'

Heath now became a curious, idiosyncratic amalgam of bestselling author, international statesman, jobbing speech-maker – and back-bench Member of Parliament. For much of Heath's life, people speculated about how he could afford to live so lavishly. Part of the answer lay in the insight that he wasn't really 'lavish' at all. He could be very generous, but he also had a 'generous' sense of his own worth. His staff were always being exhorted to drive up speaking fees and, anyway, as a former Prime Minister, he received generous parliamentary and personal allowances; and, once he had a car and driver provided for him, plus around-the-clock protection, his travel cost him nothing. Each iteration of *Morning Cloud* was sold off (except in the case of No. 3, where insurance money had the same effect) to fund the building of its successor. He also made considerable money out of his books, both in the 1970s and also when his memoirs at last came out.

Perhaps the most significant development for him after he left office, however, was his association with the leading international accountancy firm Arthur Andersen. Until the mid-1970s, Arthur Andersen was overseen only by a board of people – partners and employees – from the firm itself. Then a decision was taken to set up a new body, consisting of eminent and inde-pendent persons from around the world, to perform a task akin to that of a non-executive board – looking carefully at the books, visiting offices, ensuring everything was ethical and efficient. Heath became one of the first recruits to the new 'Public Review Board'. According to Ian Hay Davison, who recruited him, 'an invitation to join the Public Review Board was accepted: £75,000 a year* plus free first class air travel anywhere in the world when-ever he wanted it for him and one or two staff'. Hay Davison also said that Heath was much the most conscientious of its members, reading his papers with immense care and insight; and always making thoughtful and telling contributions to meetings.

Heath became a familiar face at Arthur Andersen offices across the globe. This was by far the most significant outside interest he ever took on and, despite the growing scepticism of some of the British partners in the firm, especially as he became a much more isolated figure domestically when Thatcherism was at its apogee, globally the firm valued his services highly and it was only at the very end of his life, when he was no longer able to travel, that the association ended. I travelled with him on Arthur Andersen business in the 1990s and found it refreshing to discover how highly respected, almost revered, he could be elsewhere in the world.

As **Ian Hay Davison** explains, the early Arthur Andersen events proved to be a useful testing ground for a new technique Heath began to develop for his speech-making, of speaking without notes:

'His first task was to address the partners meeting in September 1975 at the Hilton in New York. He gave a brilliant, one-hour "tour d'horizon" of world foreign affairs without a pause and ending precisely on time. Asked

---

* The equivalent of over £500,000 in 2015 prices.

[177]

afterwards for the text for circulation to the firm we found that there were no notes: his entire speech was extempore. The same was true of many other long talks he gave to AA meetings: he memorised everything. I retired from the firm in 1983, but Ted stayed on until at least 2000, unwilling to give up the perks of what was in fact the only permanent employment he accepted in his retirement. The firm would ring and ask me how to get him to go, but I said that was then their problem.'

Heath began to establish the beginnings of his own, independent political position, whilst also dictating the first of his books – *Sailing: A Course in My Life*. In one article during the summer, he called for 'an accommodation' with the trade unions, in light of their 'capacity to wield immense power, indeed excessive power, across the community'. The political response required, he argued, was 'neither total resistance . . . nor total concession . . . treating trade unions like so many other bodies, as responsible participants within the democratic process rather than as rogue elements outside.'[18] He was beginning to isolate himself from Mrs Thatcher and her team.

Heath spent September 1975 touring the US and the Far East, delivering a series of lectures and playing the world statesman, musing on the dangers to liberal societies of international terrorism – and 'having to decide if, and how, restrictions on some freedom can be justified to preserve the greater freedom . . . There can be no relaxation, by the countries of the free world, in the defence of our liberties.'[19] When in Beijing in September, he received a 'surprise summons' to see Chairman Mao for an hour of talks – a remarkable honour, cutting across established protocol, which dictated that the failing dictator would see only heads of state, prime ministers or party leaders, for twenty minutes or less. Harold Wilson received no such invitation, apparently because the Chinese regime believed he and Labour were too 'Moscow-orientated'. In a Gallup poll, a majority of Tories (56 per cent) believed Heath was an asset to the party – the highest rating anyone achieved (Mrs Thatcher had 51 per cent).

Heath attended the party conference in October 1975 in Blackpool and shook hands with Mrs Thatcher on the platform, his appearance prompting a standing ovation from delegates. As soon as he left, however, he was caught up in a tangle of accusations and denials, when it was reported he had made disobliging remarks about Mrs Thatcher and Keith Joseph during his overnight stay at the seaside – calling them 'traitors' and 'maniacs'. He even considered returning to the conference from Weymouth, where he was attending the centenary dinner of the Royal Dorset Yacht Club, in order to clear the matter up. The situation was not helped when the contents of an hour-long telephone conversation about this, between him and his private secretary Stephen Sherbourne, were leaked to the press. A statement was issued: 'There is not a word of truth in this allegation. I am sick and tired, as no doubt Mrs Thatcher is, of those who are peddling such malicious accusations in an attempt to create dissension within the Conservative Party.' 'He's not sulking,' said Lord Hailsham. 'He just doesn't realise he's no longer leader.'[20]

Late on the night of Saturday 8 November, Heath returned home from a dinner in Lymington to discover that a bomb had been concealed by Irish Republicans under a parked car outside his home. Fortunately for him, it had been spotted and defused. Just hours later he attended the Remembrance Day service at the Cenotaph on Whitehall. It was rapidly decided that Heath should now receive around-the-clock police protection, which he retained for the rest of his life. Undaunted, he undertook a major, three-week book-signing tour to promote his book on sailing, right across the country. A month before publication, the initial print run of 40,000 copies had already sold out, half of them in the US. On 4 December at Harrods, he would sign over 1,000 copies at a single sitting, as he also did in Glasgow. On 10 December, a packed literary lunch was hosted by Foyle's in his honour, chaired by Lord Mountbatten and attended by numerous sailing luminaries. 'You don't know how much a gathering of this distinction can mean to a struggling young writer like myself – I shall go away fortified and encouraged.'[21] At a press gallery lunch shortly before Christmas, Heath used humour to fend off questions about Mrs Thatcher and the shadow cabinet: 'It seems to me strange, when so many people want to be in the shadow cabinet and can't be, that the one chap who doesn't want to be in it should be thought a criminal.'[22]

Heath had always taken great care, however busy he was with other responsibilities, conscientiously to nurse Bexley, never forgetting that he had snatched it from Labour by only 133 votes in 1950. Now he had been relieved by ungrateful parliamentary colleagues of his front-bench responsibilities, not unreasonably, his constituents hoped to see rather more of him; and his agent **Jeffery Speed** had some very carefully devised plans for ensuring Heath really 'worked his patch':

'Ted Heath, so far as I could tell, had never offered surgeries to his constituents, on the basis that most problems related to the local council, and if they needed to approach their MP they should write to him at the House of Commons, where he and his staff would deal with their concerns. As soon as his status reverted to backbencher, I mounted my campaign to persuade him to hold monthly advice bureaux by getting agreement from the council group leader that a rota of borough councillors would be established, to hold their own surgeries monthly and concurrently. Ted agreed to a trial period, provided the duty councillor would head off the nutters, and those with problems solely relating to the council.

'This worked well, and he quickly took to the whole experience, particularly as I arranged for surgeries to be followed by supper at a local restaurant or pub, with me and the Association Chairman. On the most memorable occasion I had arranged for dinner at the local up-market Chinese restaurant, for Ted plus the chairman and me and our wives, with his driver and protection officer dining at the next table. Ted greatly enjoyed acting as our host serving us with Sweet and Sour Lobster, a huge steamed sea bass, which he dissected with his chopsticks, and an array of luxurious classic communal dishes. The owner having said that he would accept no payment, Ted gave him a copy of his latest book *Sailing – A Course in my Life*, which I happened to have in my car, duly autographed and personalised.

'That book on sailing, and those on music and travels which followed, were the cause of many signing sessions, and I started to feel more like a literary agent, than a political one. He often went on signing tours by train (though I was not asked to accompany him outside our immediate area) and this gave rise to one cartoon in the *Daily Telegraph* showing a man at Bexley station asking for a RailRover ticket "because I need to see my MP!"'

Heath's attendance in Parliament was now somewhat intermittent, to put it kindly, but he did like to show his face on big occasions, for instance on 12 January 1976, when he attended a statement about the security situation in Northern Ireland and warned that 'it was possible for the previous Administration to deal with the situation in Londonderry only by the use of overwhelming forces'. Wilson, to everyone's surprise, reacted not with hostility but with warm praise for the 'experience, wisdom and knowledge' of his erstwhile opponent. In the same week, Heath won praise from the *New Statesman*, whose political correspondent wrote that 'now he is a statesman rather than a politician, he dips into the store of his experience, and hands out advice in such a way that one quite forgets what things were like when he was at the helm of state . . . I would certainly buy a used car from this man.' When Mrs Thatcher reshuffled her front bench in mid-January, there was no room on it either for Heath or for Peter Walker, though Douglas Hurd did become a junior spokesman on foreign affairs.

As 1976 progressed, Heath's diary was so busy that even his beloved conducting sometimes had to take second place – in a short space of time, he turned down an invitation to conduct the Chicago Symphony Orchestra and also an invitation from the former US Ambassador in London, Walter Annenberg, to conduct in Philadelphia. Much of Heath's travelling in this period was connected to his books and it was reported in May 1976 that *Sailing* had sold 88,000 copies, at £5.50 each. In the autumn his second book, *Music: A Joy for Life*, would be published. The initial print run was 94,500 copies, of which Heath would duly sign an estimated 12,500 copies. In 1976 he recorded a twelve-part LBC series on sailing, to promote the book. At Easter 1976, Heath went to Spain, opening a golf tournament at El Paraiso in a Good Friday downpour. He then enjoyed a cruise, spent an evening at a flamenco show and presented the Heath Trophy at a yachting regatta. The climax was a grand gala and banquet at which he was named 'Tourist of the Year'. His original itinerary included a bullfight – and a leading Spanish toreador was flown in – but Heath declined, instead visiting a sherry bodega at Jerez. He had formal audiences with the King and senior ministers – and reported back to both the Conservative and Labour party leaderships. On his return Heath said it was time to 'forget the memories and passions aroused by the Spanish Civil War and the memories of the Franco regime'. He also dubbed Gibraltar an 'anachronism' – and called upon Spain to open the border.

The journalist and commentator **Ian Waller** of the *Daily Telegraph* accompanied Heath on that Spanish trip and his analysis makes for interesting reading:

'I saw a totally different person from the distant, often arrogant and sometimes gratuitously offensive man I have known at Westminster for the past 20 years. He was relaxed, amusing and at times engagingly frank about the political world of Westminster. Also about some of those he met. After being harangued by a much bejewelled and rather vulgar English lady about her tax problems, that had forced her to emigrate to the Costa del Sol, he turned to me and said: "That's the sort of Tory I can do without." I happened to be with him as he was about to leave for the airport, on the way back to the Queen's birthday party at Windsor. I have always regarded Mr Heath as the model of efficiency, a highly organised man. But it was so like my own departures – a lost passport – where are the Traveller's Cheques? The way a man, particularly a bachelor, gets on with the young is no bad yardstick, and it was fascinating to see him with the Kitson children, affectionate without being patronising and clearly enjoying their company as much as they did his.'[23]

In May 1976, Heath's friend, adviser and confidant Michael Wolff died. In the weeks and months after, Heath showed particular consideration to Wolff's widow Rosemary, who told one journalist: 'Mr Heath is just one of the kindest and most generous hearted people I have ever known. He has been tremendously kind to me.' At one public function he brought her with him and publicly embraced her.

On 9 June 1976, mysterious reports appeared to the effect that Heath would be willing to serve under Mrs Thatcher in government (though not in a shadow role). He issued an immediate denial: 'There has been no change in the situation. I don't see how there could be any stories involving me because nothing has happened.' He did, however, cut short a trip to Singapore in order to support a censure motion against the Labour Government, which was lost by nineteen votes. He didn't speak and, according to one report, a 'Senior Conservative' commented after the debate: 'Ted just stared straight ahead like a man in his own world . . . Margaret could have done with all

Above: Edward Heath speaks to the people of Bexleyheath, Kent, while campaigning to win the seat, 15 September 1948.
Below: Heath, Jeremy Thorpe and Harold Wilson at the unveiling of a memorial to the late David Lloyd George, Westminster Abbey, 27 July 1970.

Left: Heath waves from Number 10 Downing Street after being elected as the new Prime Minister, 19 June 1970.

Below: Margaret Thatcher speaking at a meeting of the Conservative Party's campaign to keep Britain in the Common Market, watched by Heath, 17 May 1975.

"Er . . . Barber . . . about this . . . er . . . boom."

Above and below: Heath portrayed by the political cartoonist Nicholas Garland in the 1970s, commenting on the economic crisis (above, 13 July 1973) and Heath losing office (4 October 1974).

ADVENT: SELSDON MAN IS BORN TO DEMORALIZED TORY PARTY

SUCCESS: TO HIS AMAZEMENT HE WINS GENERAL ELECTION

TRIUMPH: JOINS E.E.C, WINS SAILING TROPHY, CONDUCTS ORCHESTRA

TEMPTATION: DECIDES TO HAVE SHOWDOWN WITH UNIONS, PICKS FIGHT WITH N.U.M.

DOWNFALL: STRIKES, BLACKOUT, 3 DAY WEEK, TO HIS AMAZEMENT LOSES GEN.ELECTION

RUIN: SEEN IN PUBLIC WITH JEREMY THORPE!

THE RAKE'S PROGRESS

Above: Bronze bust of Heath by Martin Jennings, 1991.

Above: Heath conducting the London Symphony Orchestra in *that* performance of Elgar's Overture *Cockaigne* at the Royal Festival Hall, 25 November 1971.
Below: Heath looks out from the stern of his yacht *Morning Cloud* at the start of the Fastnet race, part of the Admirals Cup, 1 August 1973.

Above: Heath and Annette Cole (Schmidt) at the bottom of the garden at Arundells, where the rivers Avon and Nadder meet.
Below: Celebrating his KG at Bignell Park with (l–r): Richard Simmonds, Roger Martin, Peter Luff, Erling Sorensen, Lindsey Martin, Michael Young, Sara Morrison, Rosemary Wolff and Ian Gilmour.

Above: Heath with Palestine Liberation Organisation leader Yasser Arafat, outside his Wilton Street home. The author is in the background, to the right.
Below: In Tokyo for the Praemium Imperiale in October 1999, with Mr and Mrs Oscar Peterson.

Left: At the Kunming International Horticultural Exposition, China, in 1999.
Below: With the Seligmans in the garden of Arundells: Olivia and Roderick (front), Madron, Nancy-Joan and Heath (middle), and Lincoln, Dominic and Olivia's husband Julian Turton (back).

the support she could get today and a "hear, hear" or some other gesture from Ted would have helped.'[24]

Efforts continued to bring Heath back into the fold. His former PPS Tim Kitson used a speech to send a thinly coded message to both Heath and the leadership: 'I, like all of you here, want to see the Conservative Party fighting the next election using all its talents.'[25] The *Sunday Telegraph* commented on 13 June: 'What . . . can be said with absolute confidence is that Mr Heath will never do to Mrs Thatcher what Mr Powell did to him: that is to say, give comfort to Labour in a general election. So presumably, when that moment comes, his innate loyalty to the Party, and concern for the country, will lead him to find ways of fighting hard on the Right side.' That same month, in a BBC interview with Robin Day, Heath said, 'It is . . . right when a new leader has been elected, then there should be an opportunity for the leader to do what she wanted and in her own way, and I thought I was able to play a much better part by sitting in the corner seat below the gangway.' Day was quoted in the *Daily Telegraph*, saying: 'The relationship between Mrs Thatcher and Mr Heath is as cold and distant as at any time since she ousted him as Conservative leader, and the general view in the party ranks is that Mr Heath is still sulking.' Heath responded tersely: 'That's absolute nonsense.'[26]

In July 1976, in the week of his sixtieth birthday, Heath tacked further away from the party leadership. He was increasingly uneasy with the party's drift towards liberal free-market economics, remaining wedded to concepts of social partnership and the effectiveness of an incomes policy:

'I fully and unequivocally support the agreement which the Government have reached with the trade unions. I do not believe that we should hedge about it. I do not view it as being in any way unconstitutional. It is a formalisation of what has been going on for many years in the Chancellor of the Exchequer's office in the Treasury before every Budget . . . We ought to recognise that to have an incomes policy which is, in the circumstances, quite a tough one, especially when we are on the upturn of the trade cycle, is a remarkable achievement.'

On 8 July, in an interview on BBC radio, Heath attacked Keith Joseph's penchant for contracting out policy-making to think tanks – 'I have no time for private armies of that kind'. On 9 July – Heath's birthday itself – journalist **Gordon Greig** asked:

> 'Won't the bitterness ever end? . . . For all the wishful thinking, a real rec-
> onciliation is just not on before the next Election – and may be superfluous
> after it. For Heath to accept a Shadow Cabinet place now would simply
> be to admit he was wrong. And to him the memory of his last General
> Election defeat is almost as fresh and deeply wounding as the outcome
> of the leadership contest . . . What is happening now is not a question of
> the Tory Party being too small for Mrs Thatcher and Mr Heath. A Tory
> Party without Ted Heath would be too small. There must be toleration, if
> not concern, for his uncomfortable situation.'[27]

The following day a senior party member was quoted thus: 'I have warned Ted that he is risking his own future by his behaviour. He must not do what Enoch Powell did and lose his political base. There is still a large fund of goodwill for him in the party, but he is increasingly alienating people.'[28] There was an undated letter to Heath from **Douglas Hurd** at around this time, which provides a flavour of the frustration and angst Heath was gen-erating amongst his well-wishers by his grumpy and surly behaviour:

> 'This is a bit of a *cri de coeur*! I very much hope you will be able when you
> speak this week to mention appreciatively what Geoffrey Howe is doing to
> sort out the differences in the Party on monetary and incomes policy, e.g.
> his immense speech to the Bow Group and his *Daily Telegraph* article . . .
> GH is groping (manfully, I think) for a set of general proposals which
> would repair bridges within the Party – and be roughly what a sensible
> Conservative Govt wd have to do . . . We simply can't afford to drift on,
> with you and the present leadership apparently at odds. No one who has
> ears can doubt the strength of your friends in the country and therefore of
> your influence in the election . . . But an election which we lose, apparently
> because of disunity, would be a disaster for you, Mrs T and all of us . . .
> I think you have quite enjoyed being a volcano on the edge of the plain,
> watching the tribesmen scurry about when you erupt – but I wonder if
> that period shouldn't come to a close!'[29]

In a major interview during that long, hot summer, **Heath** was in no mood for modesty, false or otherwise:

> 'I am not taking part in . . . the daily dog fight of party politics, but I am trying to deal with the really big issues . . . I can look back on the four years in which I was Prime Minister, in which I took Britain into the Community, and I believe that was a very great achievement. I think the historians looking back will say that it was the outstanding achievement of British politics, certainly in this century and probably for longer and I think also we had other achievements to our credit. We are going through a period now in which some people have lost their nerve and decry every-thing which was done during those four years, and others have allowed the myths to accumulate as to what is supposed to have happened . . . But we can resume our course, and our job is to persuade the rest of the country that it is the most meaningful course for them to take.'[30]

At the party conference in October 1976, Heath decided to speak. He had a seat on the platform, but he chose to speak from the rostrum below it. He was very nervous, so Rosemary Wolff attended with him. His presence dominated the conference for two days and he deliberately left before the last day. For once, he was on best behaviour. In a notable speech – the only one in which he endorsed his successor by name, albeit by using a wince-inducing multiple negative – he publicly accepted the policies set out by the leadership in its document 'The Right Approach'. The *Daily Telegraph* on 7 October claimed that his speech 'marked a welcome end to a divisive and unhappy period in Tory politics' – even though he spoke 'with a noticeable fall in his voice, which emphasised that the words were hard to say'. 'I have no doubt we would not flinch in future in taking difficult decisions which are in the national interest,' Heath told delegates. 'I have complete confi-dence they will be taken by Margaret Thatcher and her colleagues on the platform.' Heath won three ovations – two before his speech and one after. Mrs Thatcher reciprocated by referring to him in her speech: 'As Ted Heath said with such force on Wednesday, Britain is at the end of the road. As we all know, he is a man who never sold the truth to serve the hour. I am indeed grateful for what he said. Let us all have his courage.'

Veteran Tory columnist Ronald Butt made this comment: 'What matters now is to remember that the revolution that ousted Mr Heath was not just about personality: it was about policy, and that battle is over.' Then his old nemesis Harold Wilson stirred things up by saying that Heath 'had a lot more in him than he showed as leader of his party . . . But I don't think the Tories treated Ted right. We are seeing now the real Edward Heath . . . I think Mr Heath would still regard himself as combat worthy.'[31]

Despite all his misgivings and his sense of having been badly mistreated, Heath still enjoyed campaigning actively and the rune-readers sensed his commitment to the party was growing stronger. After the Tories spectacularly gained both the Walsall North and Workington constituencies at simultaneous by-elections on 4 November, he commented: 'I know after speaking to a great election meeting at Walsall that our people, racked with anxiety, will back the measures necessary to save our future. Let us Conservatives now rally the nation. We can beat this crisis.'

Mere weeks later, however, Heath was rebelling over devolution, telling the House of Commons on 16 December 1976:

'I do not think that in these circumstances anybody would expect me to vote against the Government's Bill. People know my history. I may be inflexible and very obstinate. On the other hand, it may be that I sustain my beliefs. My beliefs at the moment are that this devolution, to which I have been committed for a decade, is necessary and urgent. My purpose remains to keep the Union of Scotland, Wales, England and Northern Ireland. I believe that the best way of maintaining this Union is to have devolution.'[32]

It had been a busy year for Heath, and he chose to end it with a thirteen-day Caribbean cruise in the company of his old friend and frequent 'concert buddy' Moura Lympany – and the English Chamber Orchestra. The *Daily Express* on 22 December cheekily speculated: 'Miss Lympany, 60, whose two previous marriages were dissolved, would surely like nothing better than to become the first Mrs Ted Heath.'

Early in 1977, when tributes were paid to his old boss Anthony Eden in the House of Lords, Heath was the only MP to come and listen, but his parliamentary attendance was nonetheless the subject of adverse comment: in 1976/77 Heath voted in 46 out of 234 divisions – a proportion of 19.6 per cent, compared with 36.1 per cent in 1975/76. There was speculation that he might become a Knight of the Garter, joining Harold Wilson and, possibly, replacing Eden – but he was not yet ready to play the elder statesman. In fact, he remained busy throughout this period. By the end of 1977, for example, he had undertaken seventy-eight party speeches, thirty-six non-party speeches, ten major speeches abroad and ninety-four TV/radio/press interviews; and 1978 would be no less busy. He was scathing about Harold Wilson's virtual disappearance from politics since stepping down as Prime Minister: 'We were never similar characters. I don't recall one speech he's given about policy for the future since he left office. He always seems to be talking about the past.' Wilson was out of politics, he said, 'but I am still very much in it'.[33] And when he was asked about his future intentions during these years, Heath merely responded that, 'people will just have to keep on speculating'.

Much of the speculation was driven by his evident lack of commitment to the party leadership. In March 1978, during a debate in the House, a Tribunite Labour MP taunted Mrs Thatcher with a cry of, 'She's not doing very well is she?' According to witnesses, Heath lifted his head and gave a huge wink to the Labour benches. Then in mid-June it was reported that Heath had had dinner with the party chairman, Lord Thorneycroft, and discussed a heavy itinerary for the general election campaign that was widely expected to take place in the autumn. He would apparently be receiving full support from Central Office, including itinerary planning and visits to locations running into double figures, moving one 'associate' of his to comment, 'it would be bloody ridiculous for Ted to rush up and down the country calling for a Tory government and then refuse to serve in the Government once it was formed'.[34]

There was much talk about Heath becoming one of the first phalanx of directly elected British Members of the European Parliament, who were to be elected in 1979. Heath's view was that this was another method of 'trying to get rid of me', but many of his friends as well as his detractors thought this might be an appropriate outlet for his talents and energies, as **Richard Simmonds** explains:

'After he ceased to be Party Leader, Ted turned down a number of jobs, saying that he wanted to remain in the House of Commons. When it was announced that there were to be direct elections to the European Parliament, many friends thought that this would be ideal for Ted and Europe. A number of continental former Chancellors and Prime Ministers, Willy Brandt and Michel Debré (who twice said "Non" to British Membership of the then EEC) amongst them, had already announced their candidature. Douglas Hurd and others suggested this to Ted and got a negative grunt. In the end, I was asked to go and see him. We talked for half an hour, and he then asked me, "But why do you want me to go to the European Parliament?" In exasperation, having previously detailed my case at some length, I replied, "Because I want someone to carry my bags for me." This startled Ted, and he grinned and said, "I will ponder the matter and write to you." A week later I received a long hand-written letter, thanking me and others for their interest, and saying that he had thought long and hard, and it was the Commons for him. It was Europe's loss.'

On 5 July 1978, Heath made what was termed at the time a 'truce' speech, at the Penistone by-election, where he said the following:

'May I add a personal word? I can tell all of you here tonight that during this election campaign I shall fight just as hard as I have ever done for the return of a Conservative Government . . . I shall do so because I believe it to be in the best interests of Britain . . . I shall continue to play my part and . . . the change of leadership makes no difference to my determination to install a Conservative government once again in office. I wish Mrs Thatcher and her colleagues every success. Together we must fight hard to gain the victory we all want.'

The sighs of relief at Central Office were probably audible even in Yorkshire. Mrs Thatcher responded in gushing phrases: 'I welcome the warm terms in which Ted Heath has pledged his support. It will give added strength to the Conservative cause in the battles ahead. We shall all be working together for a decisive Conservative victory.'[35] By some counts, this was the sixth occasion on which the Heath–Mrs Thatcher rift had supposedly been repaired. It later transpired there had been several drafts of Heath's proposed comments and this section had, in fact, been toned down. Furthermore, Mrs Thatcher had the 'Penistone Proclamation' checked against delivery before her response was issued.

A few days later, Mrs Thatcher was asked about Heath when she was campaigning in Moss Side.[36] She had offered Heath jobs in Europe, she said, but he had refused: 'He is Mr Europe. He took us into Europe. Obviously, I always ask him if he is interested when appointments arise. That's the position. If you make too much of this, you'll do it wrongly. It is a matter of courtesy, no more than that – of clearing these things with him . . . I have no idea of the kind of job he might accept.' Of his words at Penistone, she said: 'It was a very, very warm statement from a reserved person. My colleagues in the House were, I think, as pleased as I was.' Did she have Heath's full support? 'Oh I do indeed. Ted is a very reserved person and therefore he delivered his speech in a very reserved way. But for him it was wonderful . . . I think the press have overplayed the differences between us. Now that there is this tremendous speech they are wondering why they have overplayed the differences.' Nine days after that, she said: 'I hope Mr Heath will fight a good, ebullient fight on behalf of the Conservative cause. He knows that as party leader I will form my Cabinet afterwards. I think he would like it that way. It leaves him freer.'[37]

The peace did not last long. On 11 October, in a television interview on ITN, Heath backed the Labour Government's proposed 5 per cent pay limit, just twenty-four hours after Mrs Thatcher had denounced it:

'I am sure the Prime Minister is right to say that this is the best judgement we can make about what the country can stand. I believe the British people think this as well. They have a deep-seated fear of another wage explosion . . . They have a deep-seated fear that our parliamentary democracy – the Government, the Cabinet and MPs – are going to be overruled again by one section . . . I am giving my own views, which are based on my own experience.'[38]

In his speech to the party conference the same week, he adhered to this view. If the Government's pay policy were to break down, he said, 'there is nothing here for gloating, nothing for joy – we should grieve for our country'. On 19 October, in a speech to Chelsea Conservatives, he explained his position in greater detail and explained why he did not see it as 'heresy': 'No government, no Prime Minister, no Chancellor, wishes to become involved in the complexities and intricacies of pay. They don't do it because they want to; they do it because they have to . . . The debate should not acquire the characteristics of a religious war – we are not having to choose between two different philosophies, each of which claims a monopoly of knowledge and certainty.'

Ten days later, Heath and **Wilf Weeks** travelled together to Yorkshire, to meet some old friends:

'One of the TV channels asked EH to take part in a discussion and documentary about the miners' strike which involved a visit to a colliery and miners' social club. The mood was amazingly friendly and the miners and EH got on like old friends. At some stage in the proceedings a swanky car arrived to ferry EH from the club to the top of one of the mine shafts. EH refused to be filmed riding in such a posh car and so a Cortina was produced and Heath, and EH else, was happy. One of the miners' officials told EH: "If we have to choose between you and Maggie, we'll have you."'

The NUM man was not alone in this view. On 10 November, an NOP poll suggested that, were Heath to replace Mrs Thatcher, the Tory lead would rise from 3 to 14 per cent. Asked who would make the best Tory Prime Minister, 55 per cent of those supported Heath, against 33 per cent for Mrs Thatcher. Her satisfaction rating was minus 13 per cent. Heath cannot have been upset by this. In autumn 1978, Jim Callaghan funked the chance to hold an election that he might, just, have won. Consequently, against all odds and expectation, the Labour Government had survived into 1979, which would have to be election year. On 1 March, Labour lost two more seats to the Tories in by-elections and, on 28 March, by 311 votes to 310, a motion of no confidence was passed in the Callaghan Government.

Simon Hoggart recorded Heath's reaction to this historic event:

'Jim Callaghan had announced the election, and the Conservatives seemed the almost certain winners. In the Conservative whips' office, the first bottles of champagne were being unpopped. Ted Heath walked slowly away from the Lobby, a look of resigned gloom on his face, like Sidney Carton with toothache. A Tory whip rushed up behind him, tapped him on the shoulder, and said, "Ted, come for a drink with us!" Heath slowly shook his head and walked on. "Just this once, this one time," pleaded the whip, but Heath did not break step, moving slowly through the sounds of revelry, alone towards his office. In the manner of a Buckingham Palace spokesman apologising for Princess Anne, one of Heath's assistants later told me that he had not realised at the time that Mrs Thatcher would be present at the piss-up. I wonder. He was certainly as glum as I have ever seen him.'[39]

Election Day would be Thursday 3 May. As Heath campaigned vigorously for the return of a Conservative Government, there was renewed (and predictable) speculation about what role he might play in it. 'Whenever I have been asked to serve my country, I have done so,' he told reporters. During the campaign Heath was the target of considerable vituperation from Labour, who evidently thought they could exploit the gap between him and Mrs Thatcher. Denis Healey described Heath as 'The Bourbon of Bexley'* and Jim Callaghan issued a mischievous warning to Mrs Thatcher about the lurking danger of Heath: 'He has an unforgiving nature. She will have to watch out. He regards himself as the natural leader of the Tory party in exile and who knows? One day soon he may be . . . one slip be her . . .' [mimics a throat slash] 'and what a happy band of brothers and sisters they will be . . . he cannot find anything good to say about his leader. It would stick in his throat. So what does he do? He abuses me.'[40] Heath warned in response that the UK faced a risk of becoming the 'ageing comic of the world'. He campaigned hard and certainly stayed loyal in public: 'We can settle for more of the same or we can opt for a new start. It is this start which Britain needs and it is a Conservative Government that will give Britain fresh hope.' On 1 May he broke off campaigning to pay generous tribute at a memorial service for Reggie Maudling. He must have sensed an

---

* Presumably meaning he never learned but also never forgot.

era was ending for him too. Heath was represented at the daily meetings of Mrs Thatcher's campaign team by Michael Young, who sensed at once that she had developed a certain contempt and even dislike for her predecessor, after four years of his sniping. It was via Young that she first sounded out Heath about the possibility of him becoming ambassador to Washington, in the event of a Conservative victory. Even before she won the election, she was planning to get him out of the way.

When Mrs Thatcher did lead the Tories back to power, Heath struggled to find anything positive to say about her. On election night he merely said he was 'delighted by the results, especially my own . . . I almost doubled my majority with a swing of 7 per cent . . . I am very happy about that . . . About my own future I have one aim, and that is to serve the party.' It didn't take long for that to change. Heath wrote a note of congratulation to Mrs Thatcher at once and went to stay with Charles and Sara Morrison in Wiltshire. On the Friday evening, the new Prime Minister sent him a short, hand-written and not unfriendly letter informing him that she had 'thought long and deeply about post of Foreign Secretary and have decided to offer it to Peter Carrington, who, as I am sure you will agree, will do the job superbly'. Heath let it be known that he would carry on as a backbencher. Peter Thorneycroft was unsympathetic: 'So Ted didn't get that job, but, you know, cabinet office is not a reward for long service in the parties . . . We all have different roles to play and I am sure Ted Heath will find a new role for himself.'[41] Heath later told the BBC's John Cole that he had reconciled himself to never serving as a minister under Mrs Thatcher when, on a flight from Geneva to Paris, he had read an interview in which she had asserted there would be no room in a government she led for anyone who disagreed with 'the central thrust of policy'.

Talking to Jean Rook days after the election, **Heath** sought to sound phlegmatic:

'I didn't think Mrs Thatcher would want me in her Cabinet . . . [I am] not bitter and not sad – in politics you have to learn to live with things. I wanted my party to win, to succeed. So I went on a nationwide tour to help, as was only right . . . But I don't know how anyone can accuse me of sulking . . . "Heath is sulking in his tent" – that's a typical, nasty press remark . . . In the last 4 years I've spoken at nearly 400 meetings and been all over radio and telly . . . I went up and down the country before the election and made 70 speeches and I think I did a lot to win the marginals . . . if that's supposed to be "sulking" I just don't know what they're talking about . . . If I'm wasted, that's for you to say, not I . . . I shall sit on the back bench, look after my constituency and make major speeches . . . You ask if I'm still ambitious. I am for my dream of a country that isn't torn apart, one that'll catch up with the world instead of lagging behind it as we have been doing.'[42]

So far as Mrs Thatcher was concerned, Heath had this to say: 'I want her to succeed for the party's sake and the country.' Did he like her, though, or dislike her, what did he make of her? 'No comment and dot, dot, dot . . .' Jean Rook noted that Heath had 'a removed, glacial quality that gains him admiration, but lost him his leadership' and asked about whether he planned to write some candid memoirs. He responded: 'I shall write the whole story and it will be the whole truth. I shall tell everything.' At the end of the interview, Jean Rook, who greatly admired Mrs Thatcher but always had a soft spot for Heath as well, could not contain her frustration any longer. 'I can't see why two great talents can't get together for the good of us all,' she told Heath. 'And if the rift's not your fault, if I were in your shoes, I'd be sitting here, tearing my hair and my nails with fury and frustration at being done out of a good job I know I could do.' Heath responded coolly: 'You're a very human person aren't you? I wouldn't think of carrying on like that. But I'm well known, aren't I, for being cold and inhuman?'[43]

Over the weekend of 12–13 May, Heath was sailing again, clearing his head and escaping from politics. There was another blow to come, which was, by any standards, poorly judged by Mrs Thatcher. **Michael Jopling** was the new Government chief whip and, on Monday 14 May, he suddenly found he had some fire-fighting to do:

'When Margaret Thatcher became Prime Minister in 1979, one of the first things she did was to send a letter to Ted Heath offering the appointment of Ambassador in Washington. He responded rather gruffly to say he was not interested and was seriously miffed that she had signed the letter "Margaret Thatcher" and not "Margaret". She was totally mortified that, in the hectic days of arriving at Number 10 Downing Street, she had unwittingly and abruptly contravened the conventions of Parliamentary courtesies. So she wrote another letter to apologise and instructed me, as the new Chief Whip, to deliver it in person. Indeed she made me watch her, as she signed it "Margaret". So, as a former Whip in his Government and a successor to Ted as Chief Whip, I went round to his home in Wilton Street to deliver it. I thought I might at least be offered a drink, but all I got was a grunt.'

Heath responded tersely: 'Dear Margaret, thank you for your note. As I have said, I do wish to stay in the Commons. I am sure you will be able to find somebody to do the job well. Yours, Ted.' He must have been incandescent with fury. He had already been sounded out more than once about this post, before the election; and each time he had made it clear he was just not interested. The *Daily Telegraph* applauded both his decision to carry on as an MP and also his general grumpiness: 'We do not always agree with Mr Heath's pronouncements. But long may he continue to annoy, inspire and goad his countrymen from below the gangway in the House of Commons.'[44] Heath now threw himself into the campaign for the first direct elections to the European Parliament. Speaking at Burnham, near Slough, on 17 May he said: 'No one in my generation can fail to draw the contrast of forty years ago. In 1939 we were sliding into a conflict that tore Europe apart. Now we are about to elect a Parliament that will represent our community of interests.' He was not included at the press launch of the Tories' Euro campaign, but Central Office did issue his speeches in full.

It seems almost incredible now, but sentiment within the Conservative Party – amongst paid staff and volunteers alike – was genuinely very, very positive about the EEC at that time and this was a positive campaign. In fact, Heath felt secure enough about that to make one of his few recorded criticisms of the EEC, when he said on 28 May: 'The budgetary contribution of Britain and some other countries is beginning to appear unfair, and a permanent form of adjustment must be found to rectify this.' Mrs Thatcher made one major appearance during the campaign – at a European Youth Rally on 2 June – at which she spoke warmly of the benefits of the free movement of labour and described herself and her colleagues as 'whole-hearted supporters of the Community and as resolute champions of the European ideal . . . Only if we pool our resources and share in each other's strength will free Europe survive. Only if we speak together can we expect the world to heed the voice of Europe. The new directly elected European Parliament will be one expression of that voice.'

That summer, not for the first or last time, Heath nearly died, in a disastrous Fastnet Race. Heath was, again, captain of the British Admiral's Cup team for the Fastnet; 316 boats started at Cowes, of which only 128 finished at Plymouth. No fewer than twenty-three had sunk or been abandoned and 165 were forced to retire – a total of 136 crewmen were rescued but fifteen died. *Morning Cloud* was 'picked up by a roaring wave and knocked down on her side' passing the Fastnet rock at 2.15 am, but righted herself. Just. After that lucky escape, Heath soon had another one when, as the first Western politician to visit Tibet in twenty-five years, the Russian-built plane on which he was travelling crash-landed, and two of its tyres burst.

For the triumphant party conference in October 1979, Heath had the perfect alibi: he was working in Brussels on the Brandt report. The preparation, publication and promotion of the report would keep him busy for much of the next few years. **Peter Luff** ran Heath's private office during this period. His memories of this period shed some light on the man – as opposed to the politician:

> 'Much has been written about his shortcomings (and there were quite a few including abruptness, intolerance of fools, a total disregard for punctuality and a reluctance to pursue tasks that did not interest him), but behind this formidable and often difficult man was, perhaps too cunningly concealed, a human being of real charm.
>
> 'One note, sent to him by the office secretaries, reminded him that it was my birthday. It came back with two words written on it: "Congratulate him". To those that did not know EH that may seem a little curt, but it was typical of his dry sense of humour. Once you understood his humour, you gained a deeper appreciation of this sincere, witty and really rather shy man.

'Imagining he would enjoy it, for a birthday celebration in July 1981, we took him to see the satirical farce *Anyone for Denis** and then on to supper at my home. His thank you letter read, "Thank you for your splendid birthday present in taking me to that ghastly play about M and D and for your most enjoyable hospitality thereafter . . . it marked a memorable occasion in the life of the office from which I hope you will all soon recover."

'It actually was a ghastly play, but watching him during the performance and talking to him afterwards it was clear he just didn't like the office of Prime Minister being mocked and that he disapproved of the nature of the personal attacks on Margaret Thatcher. I felt he respected her at all times – he often reminded people that was why he had put her in his cabinet in the first place. Initially his dislike appeared to be reserved for those around her who briefed against him. Latterly it became more personal, on both sides. It was significant, though, that Lady Thatcher attended his funeral. The joke was that she had gone to make sure he really was dead, but as I looked at her that day, I sensed she was there because she still felt something for the man who had first made her a minister.

'His shyness was the key to understanding him. He was relaxed talking to audiences of hundreds but so often awkward in private conversation. What he relished in those private moments was people who stood up to him, but he did not seem to realise how intimidating and rude he could appear. This meant that many simply deferred to him or were reduced to the kind of inanities that clearly bored him. It was a lesson I really only learned when my young fiancée, Julia, was talking to him at a social occasion and he was being difficult. To my amazement she said, "Oh for Heaven's sake, Ted, don't be so pompous!" Well, she may have said "Mr Heath", but it was still equally courageous. He stared at her, paused, said "Oh", paused again, said "Oh!" two, or three more times, and then the shoulders started to heave in that characteristic and very physical laugh of his, so beloved of the impressionists of the time. He was delighted, and so was I – delighted and relieved.

---

* A play by John Wells, about Denis Thatcher and his relationship with his second wife, Margaret.

'Another surprise was, in 1981, the diagnosis of hypothyroidism. His incessant tendency to fall asleep in public was dismissed by his friends as "That's Ted!", but I was not convinced. I bullied and cajoled his doctor, Brian Warren, into referring EH to a specialist. My conviction that he was ill was quickly confirmed and he cancelled all engagements and retreated for a period of convalescence to the Imperial Hotel in Torquay. His very private personality meant he would not disclose the nature of the illness, leading to much, perfectly understandable, speculation. Happily it was wrong and his condition was far from terminal. I greatly enjoyed my trips to Torquay to keep him up-to-date with events in the office and his constituency, since he was so relaxed and happy. One key to his happiness was his discovery of the joys of televised snooker and I soon learnt not to disturb him while a game was in progress . . . This was not the most likely passion for EH, but it was not the only surprise. I had to ensure he could attend a Rod Stewart concert and to get him tickets for the new West End production of "Oklahoma". He explained that this energetic, lively musical had burst into London just after the war with its young cast of singers and dancers and that it had reminded the wartime generation of the joy of living. So to the great opera composers that he loved and admired – Mozart and Wagner – add the names of Rodgers, as in Hammerstein.'

Almost unbelievably, Heath began 1980 by criticising the EEC again, this time for its lack of urgency. He was readily drawn into the controversy over whether British athletes should boycott the forthcoming Olympic Games in Moscow, in light of the Soviet invasion of Afghanistan. In the House of Commons, he developed a theme that was by now dear to his heart – that the Western powers needed to stop and reflect before engaging in 'gun-boat diplomacy' – because other nations and cultures do not think as we do, nor should they be expected to:

'The West has had no clear strategy of any sort whatever for the past six years, and from that springs the greatest danger to the world. That is what we are discussing today – the danger of a third world war because we stumble into it by mistake or by misjudgement. That is the real danger that we face today.

[197]

'We have long thought that people in the Muslim world wanted the Western way of life, that if they did not want it they ought to want it, and that in any case they were jolly well going to get it. What has now been shown in Iran, and is being shown elsewhere in the Muslim world, is that none of those things is true. There is a younger generation which does not want the Western way of life and which wants to go back to what it believes to be a simpler, older, authoritative – sometimes we would say authoritarian – way of life, according to the Muslim religion. I remember going into Tehran during last summer . . . There were 5 million cars, there were luxury hotels, the women were all liberated, and there were discotheques, alcohol and pornography – all the best that we could give them. How could they want to change that? But the fact is that they did, and we have to recognise it. We have to accept these facts in making a relationship with the Muslim world, otherwise we have no means of looking after our security and that of the developing world.

'The Olympic Games are a matter for natural differences of opinion. I happen to be one of those who take part in sport. I am proud that I have captained two national teams in international sport. I believe that we should keep politics out of sport. I fully accept that other people do not, but that does not alter my view. Nor do I think that having the Olympic Games in Moscow is only a question of prestige for Moscow. It is a question of prestige wherever the Games go . . . The question that I ask myself is this: "If the Soviet Union is as determined on aggression as is said, will abandoning the Olympic Games really stop it?" I find it difficult to believe that it will. But if individuals, teams or nations do not want to take part, it is fully up to them to take their decision.'[45]

Returning early from a conference in Europe to address a Young Conservatives' conference on 13 April 1980, Heath was critical of Mrs Thatcher's first threat to withhold contributions to the EEC budget, unless reforms were made: 'I don't see how in this country one can lecture trade unions about observing the law, or hooligans about behaving themselves, if the Government say they are going deliberately to adopt a policy of breaking international law.' He also said it was not a matter for him, whether or not he was asked to serve as a minister: 'In my experience one doesn't fill in an application form to ask to join a government. Things have to move the other way.' At around this time, there was more speculation that a big international job – this time as head of the World Bank – was beckoning. The more there was of this kind of speculation, the more resolutely Heath adhered to his avowed desire to stay in the House of Commons, firmly rooted below the gangway, serving as a thorn in his successor's side. According to one report, on his way home from the conference Heath asked Peter Luff: 'Peter, why do they find me so intimidating?'[46]

In full sail, Heath could still be magnificent in those days and, during a BBC Radio 4 all-nighter during the US presidential election in November, he found himself unexpectedly engaged in a live transatlantic exchange with Milton Friedman, the monetarist economist who had inspired much of the economic policy of the government at that time. Even the late, great Brian Redhead, in NYC for these purposes, could not break the two men apart as Heath laid into Friedman after he told Redhead that 'unemployment isn't important': 'You want to abolish the industrial base in the same way as is happening in Britain, in which smaller firms are going bankrupt more rapidly than ever before and big firms cannot make profits because of the high exchange rate of the pound sterling. We are realising this in this country and if you persuade Mr Reagan to accept that, then the future for the American people is really pretty bad.' Fortunately, added Heath, Reagan was 'too intelligent to follow the policies of ruinous monetarism as they appear to be followed in this country'. 'It's nice to have a chance to deal with that man for once,' commented Heath later. Labour MPs duly put down an Early Day Motion in Parliament congratulating him. Rather wanly, one of his 'aides' told the press that, although Mr Heath 'did not regret the remarks, he had not gone onto the programme with the intention of making them'. Heath had (unwittingly or not) crossed the line by insulting one of Mrs Thatcher's inspirations. At Prime Minister's Questions the next day, 6 November, she quoted Heath's own eve-of-poll message from June 1970 at him.* Indeed

---

* 'Once a decision is made, once a policy is established, the Prime Minister and . . . colleagues should have the courage to stick to it. Nothing has done Britain more harm in the world than the endless backing and filling which we have seen in recent years . . .'

Mrs Thatcher would often refer, in glowing terms, to the party's 1970 mani-festo, which, to her mind, proposed a radical change of direction for the nation, towards free enterprise and a smaller state – a forerunner of her own brand of fiery Toryism (or, one might argue, latter-day Gladstonian liberal-ism). On this occasion, Heath reportedly gave a 'half smile'.

Heath was always highly resistant to those who compared him with Mrs Thatcher, although they have a point. Until the battles with the miners became intractable and unemployment hit 1 million the government Heath led was in many respects proto-Thatcherite. There is an argument that, far from decrying Mrs Thatcher in the 1980s, Heath should have offered praise and taken a sly opportunity to bask in well-deserved, reflected glory; instead of which, of course, he simmered over with righteous (and all-too-often public) indignation. As **Michael Heseltine** said:

'He was the forerunner of what Margaret Thatcher became associated with. The Selsdon agenda was every bit as radical and far-sighted as what Margaret did; and, of course, in 1974, he announced the right to buy council houses. It is credited to her, but it wasn't her at all – it was Peter Walker and Ted Heath.'

Later on in that November, Heath dispensed with even half a smile as, in the House of Commons, he attacked the Government's policy of pushing up interest rates and the rate of sterling, as a means of constraining the money supply and squeezing inflation out of the system. This prompted a fierce counter-offensive from Mrs Thatcher's supporters in the Commons and, unexpectedly, one from the lady herself in an ITN interview broadcast three days later, in which she explicitly attacked the record of the Heath Government and likened herself to a firm nurse:

'Keep taking the medicine . . . shake out of it . . . Unemployment rose very sharply in Ted's time as well. He tried to overcome it by pumping money into the economy. We got an artificial boom and do you know where the money went? It did not go into investment or expansion. It went into the biggest property boom we've ever seen and I don't wish to see the like of that ever again. It did the Conservative Party immense harm . . . I am just as worried as he is about mounting unemployment. I hope he will admit that unemployment has gone on mounting for the last twenty years.'[47]

It was reported at the time that several ministers were most unhappy about her response, which made it all the more surprising that there were also reports that Heath was being sounded out about possible jobs.

Peter Luff has mentioned Heath's thyroid problem, which kept him out of action for the early part of 1981. Avid Heath-watcher **Simon Hoggart** perceived a change in Heath afterwards:

'The formerly aloof party leader, capable of deeply wounding a trusted colleague with a cutting remark, has gone. In its place there is a far more relaxed and amiable and energetic man. The secret of this startling change is his recovery from a serious and long undetected illness. For years he had been suffering from an underactive thyroid. The symptoms include lassitude, lack of concentration, irritability, and the disquieting habit of falling asleep without warning. Some of his colleagues now say that they could detect the first signs during his spell as Prime Minister; his mind would wander off during important meetings, or he would look unexpectedly drowsy. The illness is progressive but slow, so that friends, and even his own doctor, did not notice how severe it was becoming.

'Now his celebrated chilly remarks have been replaced by self-deprecatory humour. Earlier this year he gave a surprise party for two friends who had just married. One of the guests was Sir George Young, who had just been appointed (to a chorus of abuse from those who normally serve as the Downing Street hit-squad) race relations Minister. "Ah, the second most unpopular man in the Tory Party!" Heath beamed when Sir George walked in.'[48]

Although he claimed to have made a full recovery, Heath remained prone to narcoleptic moments, especially when drink had been taken. Watching him canvassing on behalf of the Conservative candidate during the Glasgow, Hillhead by-election in 1982, **Simon Hoggart** believed Heath was still playing a longer game:

'Heath is no fool, and he doesn't see the remotest chance of his leading the Tories again. Nor is he running through an elaborate game plan, designed to let him sidle back into power. What he does believe, however, is that a confused result in the next election might bring him back into the Cabinet. He has no intention of joining the Social Democrats, who have, he thinks, too strong a socialist leaning for comfort. But he has said in public that if the next election forced an accommodation between the Tories and the SDP, he would be willing to serve. And, though he doesn't mention this, everyone knows that the first condition made by the SDP would be the swift disposal of Heath's greatest political enemy. With her out of the way, who could resist the demands to find work once again for Britain's best-known unemployed man of destiny?'[49]

Also in Heath's private office during this period was Simon May, who went on to have an academic career of considerable distinction. His particular interest was in foreign affairs, with which Heath, then a sprightly sixty-something in robust physical condition, was very significantly engaged, usually seeing things for himself at first-hand, usually in connection with speaking engagements and/or his continuing role as the most active member of the Arthur Andersen PRB. **Simon May** sets the scene:

'It was extraordinary, as a recently minted graduate, to be invited to lunch with Edward Heath at his home in Belgravia. I was to be interviewed for a position as his assistant for foreign affairs, though it seemed prima facie bizarre that I could offer any advice at all to a man who had presided over so many major international events, from British entry into the European Community, to the independence of Kuwait, to the opening of full diplomatic relations with China, and had met almost every world leader from Winston Churchill and Helmut Schmidt to Mao Tse-Tung and Ronald Reagan.

'I was struck not only by his obviously powerful physical presence, with those piercing eyes and huge paws of hands, and his commanding forehead and demeanour of impenetrable privacy, but also by his instinctive meritocratic willingness to give a non-entity of a newcomer a full and careful hearing. There was nothing dismissive about him; you had to earn his contempt as much as you had to earn his respect. If you could hold his attention – by proposing something specific for which you could argue in the face of the sceptical reserve that could easily paralyze conversation with him – it didn't matter in the least who you were, or weren't.

'Perhaps presumptuously, I had arrived with ideas for how he might intervene in aspects of foreign affairs where a figure of authority, armed with no more than his own prestige and the capacity to be an honest broker, might seek, in the manner of Jean Monnet, to promote great ideals by winning acceptance among political, business and trades unions leaders for a small number of practical proposals for action that, if implemented, would form the nucleus of a new way of thinking and acting. They centered around European integration and – a then recent passion of his – international economic development and justice.

'I was treated to an extraordinary tour d'horizon of world affairs for nearly two hours, in which he reminisced freely about events and people he had known, never in great detail, indeed often in a surprisingly snatched, unstructured and even diffident way, but with an extraordinary capacity to recreate moments that had affected him deeply. In between we talked about music, a deep mutual interest, and the one topic on which he was never diffident or distant – though he could be outrageously, almost comically, self-confident about his judgement, such as when he accused the great violinist Yehudi Menuhin of being un-rhythmical.

'I found, from that lunch on, that as long as one stuck to world affairs and music one wouldn't be mired in the agonising silences for which he was so widely known. Any attempt to contrive conversation, or to discuss a topic that had no immediate emotional or practical urgency for him, would end in failure, and the harder you tried to arouse his interest the more decisively you would fail.'

Perhaps the most remarkable aspect of Heath's life during this period was his contribution to the Brandt Commission or, more accurately described, the 'Independent Commission on International Development Issues', established in the wake of a call to arms from Robert McNamara at the World Bank and which former West German chancellor Willy Brandt formed and chaired between 1977 and 1980, when it issued its first report. **Simon May** worked very closely with Heath on this:

'After European unification, "Third World" development, as it was then known, was Ted's second great international ideal. It was a late love – he took to it in earnest only after the oil shocks of the 1970s and the turmoil that would lead to the 1979 Iranian revolution. Like European unification, it was, for him, a moral ideal rooted in enlightened self-interest and to be pursued by pragmatic means – above all, the identification of mutual economic interest.

'Ted was convinced that the only way of taking action on the necessary scale was to forge a new global agreement between the key players in the West, the oil-rich world, and the resource-poor developing countries. Such an agreement must coalesce, he thought, around a very specific programme of action, in which North and South had powerful mutual interests, or else it would come to nothing.

'That programme was provided in the shape of two reports, published in 1980 and 1983, of the Independent Commission on International Development Issues, set up at the instigation of Robert McNamara, then President of the World Bank. It was chaired by Willy Brandt, former Chancellor of West Germany, and consisted of eighteen strikingly different personalities, from the former Swedish Prime Minister Olof Palme, to the Proprietor of the *Washington Post*, Kay Graham, from Abdlatif al-Hamad, then Kuwait's Minister of Finance, to Eduardo Frei Montalva, a former president of Chile.

'But for Ted's drive and vision there might have been no reports. The Commission had degenerated into a talking shop where a minority of its members would make content free interventions, rich in rhetorical bluster, occasionally lasting over an hour, to the despair of everyone except the speaker in question. Shortly before the first report was due, it had broken up in disarray with Brandt all but resigned to years of deliberation ending in failure. To break the deadlock Ted, in collaboration with Sonny Ramphal, then Secretary-General of the Commonwealth, went back to London and hammered out a draft, advised by such academic luminaries as Robert Cassen, which he then steered through the final meeting of the Commission with patient relentlessness. The result was the first Brandt report of 1979.

'It was followed in 1983 by a second report, also produced under the supervision of Ted and Sonny, assisted by a small group based in London, of which I was honoured to be one.

'Ted travelled the world giving speeches to huge audiences and meeting presidents and prime ministers in an effort to win support for the Commission's key proposals. No other member of the Brandt Commission, save Sonny Ramphal, engaged in this task with remotely his dedication, reach and success.

'In every session of the Brandt Commission that I attended, as well as in innumerable meetings with political leaders around the world, Ted was relaxed, gracious, witty and self-deprecating in a way that many failed to realise he could be. On our travels he was almost invariably superb company and seldom evinced the grumpy silence that was widely assumed to be his default mood. And, as with Europe, he had an extraordinary capacity to frame a great vision in a few simple sentences, aided by those trademark expansive gestures of his hands that seemed to trace the contours of new worlds.

'Whatever the rank order of his ideals, there is no doubt that for Ted politics was above all a moral calling. Power was secondary, a means to a higher end. For all his attachment to power, for all his mourning its loss, for all his resentment in ceding Downing Street to Harold Wilson or the Conservative Party to Margaret Thatcher, for all his famed sulking, his lodestars were always great moral ideals: the defeat of the Nazis, the integration of the UK into the European Union, the defeat of poverty at home and abroad. To paraphrase Jean Monnet, his unfailing ambition was to do something, not merely to be someone.'

One of Heath's finest speeches in the House of Commons came when MPs debated the Brandt Report in May 1980. Speaking entirely without notes, he showed a mastery of his brief that clearly bears out Simon May's belief that this was now a cause every bit as dear to him as European unity was:

'We ended up with total unanimity because we had come to the conclusion that we needed recommendations to recreate the world economy and not just to deal with individual items that affected individual developing countries.

'That is what is required today. It was done with the Marshall Plan, with America and Europe. It may be said that it is more difficult because there are more European countries and 105 developing countries. It is more difficult, but that is an institutional, organisational problem. However, if it is not solved we shall continue the slide into the economic abyss, and neither North nor South will escape.

'The two decades ahead for the coming generations will be bleak, but if leadership is prepared to take a grip on this and to ensure that instructions are given for the programme to be worked out, implemented and carried out in time, the comment that there is no hope for the developing world and no hope for us will be completely fallacious. Then we shall surmount our troubles. We shall overcome them. Once again, we shall be able to embark on a prosperous path and an expanding economy, and there will be hope for both North and South.'[50]

It is possible Heath never made any speech that more impressed colleagues across the House. Even Enoch Powell, who spoke immediately after him, was supportive, praising 'the breath-taking comprehensiveness and competence of the speech to which the House has just been listening'. A few weeks later, Heath received an extraordinary, hand-written letter, dated 8 July 1980, from the then Speaker of the House of Commons, **George Thomas** (later Lord Tonypandy):

'I have been intending for some time to write to tell you how deeply moved and impressed I was by your speech in the Debate on the Brandt Commission. You made the event into a major parliamentary occasion. I hope you will forgive me saying that I thought it to be one of the best speeches I have ever heard in my thirty-five years in the House. Suddenly the whole House is aware that you are undoubtedly our greatest World Statesman. Your vision of global problems and the practical measures you propose, have set a lot of our young MPs on fire. It is no mean achievement for one man to influence so many. I consider myself very fortunate to have been in the Chair for the greater part of your speech.

'Please forgive me for writing in so personal a way, but I do so because I believe you are directly in the tradition of the great Parliamentarians whose speeches have inspired the House of Commons during past centuries. Ever, George.'[51]

Heath increasingly used humour as a way of defusing potentially explosive disagreements with his fellow Conservatives and, at the 1981 party conference, coined one of his more felicitous phrases: 'Please don't applaud. It may irritate your neighbour.' Apparently Mrs Thatcher turned to her neighbour on the platform, and murmured: 'That's a good one.'

Heath's private secretary between 1982 and 1986 was **Peter Batey**, who noticed a big difference in Heath before and after the 1983 general election:

'My time as Head of the Private Office fell into two unequal parts, with the 1983 General Election as the watershed. The first part from the middle of 1982 until the 1983 General Election and the second from then until I left to go to China in 1986. In the first period there was still a sense that he might return to high office. That seems hard to believe from today's perspective, but it was only after Mrs Thatcher increased her majority in 1983 that it became clear she would not offer him a position in government. During the second period, he seemed more relaxed and easier to deal with from the private secretary's point of view.

'Dealing with Ted was often a challenge. He was never a man to be taken for granted. Getting a decision from him was not always easy, but once you had a decision there was no back-sliding or evasion and he was straightforward. He was not a man to blame those who worked for him and if he committed himself to something he pursued it with energy, not hesitation nor equivocation. He gave loyalty and expected it. He took responsibility – but the decisions themselves were sometimes hard to elicit. At other times, when the circumstances required it, he was quick and decisive.

'Hardest to judge was when to speak and when to remain silent. Long car journeys sitting next to him were initially intimidating when I first began work for him as a green (though I didn't think so at the time) twenty-four year old in 1982. Not one for small talk, he nevertheless enjoyed conversation and so sitting next to him for two or three hours at a time one had to gain a feel for when to say nothing, when to talk to the driver and the Special Branch officer in the front seats and when to address him directly. It took time to develop a feel for his mood. One useful tactic was to initiate conversation on a topical matter that one felt might interest him with the (frequently amusing and entertaining) protection officer and see whether he would rise to the bait. It was often hard to gauge when he was asleep: he lurked like an old crocodile waiting to pounce on a subject that roused him. Sometimes his interventions would be terse and sceptical, though usually amusing; at other times he would engage enthusiastically.

'He was generally at his best after a good dinner, surrounded by a preponderance of those whom he liked and trusted, with a large glass of malt whisky in hand when he would often open up with strings of anecdotes from all periods of his long political career and other aspects of his life.

'Malt whisky was one of Ted's basic requirements. He consumed prodigious quantities and it was the Private Secretary's sacred duty to ensure it was available wherever he dined or stayed overnight. Indeed one was expected to carry a bottle of the "medicine" as it was generally known in one's luggage in case of emergency. His favourites included Talisker and Glenmorangie. But he was also highly disciplined about alcohol. He appeared regularly on *Newsnight*, at 10.30 pm in the 1980s, and would not touch a drop before television appearances, no matter how tempting the wine at dinner. I once said to him while sipping a glass of Latour 1970 (one of his favourites which some generous host had kindly provided), "This is superb, surely you could have one glass?" "No," he replied. "I have tried that before, and the camera always picks up that flushed look, even after one glass."'

The 1983 general election had incalculable personal significance for Heath. Achieving what had seemed impossible twenty-four or even eighteen months earlier, when the Conservative Party lay for a time in third place in the national opinion polls, his supposed nemesis, Mrs Thatcher, had won a substantial three-figure majority in the House of Commons. A combination of the 'Falklands Factor' and a strong showing by the SDP/Liberal Alliance, which gravely damaged the Labour Party, had enabled the party to increase its majority in the Commons by around 100 seats, despite winning half a million fewer votes than in 1979. Heath must have realised that, for him, there was now no coming back. He hosted a party for new MPs. It was, by all accounts, a desultory affair. 'My wife and I stood there on his front room carpet for ten minutes, trying to exchange words,' said one attendee. 'I tell you, it was like getting stuck with the most tongue-tied constituent.'[52]

According to **Peter Batey**, Heath soon put the blow of the general election result behind him:

> 'Any disappointment was quickly dusted off and he set himself to continue his work in promoting the ideas and policies in which he believed without fear or favour. Reviewing a list of his major speeches for 1983–1985, it is clear that Europe and Third World development, building on his work as a member of the Brandt Commission, were the issues to which he attached greatest importance. He also continued to articulate his views on economic policy.'

In mid-January 1984, it was announced that Heath had acquired someone whom the *Sunday Times* described as 'one of the most promising young Tory MPs' – **Mark Robinson**, the recently elected Member for Newport West – as his PPS.

> 'Ted . . . gladly took me into his confidence and I had the privilege of discovering what a great raconteur he could be on all things political, both past and present, and how mischievous he could be in his comments on certain colleagues who had got too close to "that woman" simply to advance their careers, perish the thought!
>
> 'I was charged with setting up lunches, dinners and drinks at Ted's home in Wilton Street. At that time he wanted to meet as many members of the 1983 intake as he could "provided they were not beyond the pale". It was left to me to decide who might fall into that category and I must have got this more or less right as I was never ticked off for my choice of guests. Acceptances were high as most wanted to see where Ted lived and

his reputation as a good host was well known. After one of the lunches David Heathcoat-Amory took me aside and said in rather too loud a voice, "Mark, do you think you could persuade Ted to refer to Mrs Thatcher as the PM, not as her?" This was overheard by Nicholas Soames who bellowed, "I think we were lucky, it might well have been it."'

On 17 January 1984, Heath became the first former Prime Minister to vote against his own side, when he became one of thirteen rebels on the Second Reading of the Rates Bill, which would give ministers the power to 'cap' the expenditure of local authorities. It was one of the earliest responses to the 'Loony Left' Labour authorities, mainly in London and Liverpool, which were both morally and financially bankrupt – Section 28 of the Local Government Act 1988 being another. Heath's speech pulled no punches:

'The Bill . . . goes to the very root of Conservative philosophy, which has endured for centuries. It has always been Conservative philosophy that one of our main purposes in politics is to balance the power existing in our society. In particular, we have been opposed to the centralisation of power because we have throughout realised the intense dangers to freedom that that holds for everyone. The Bill deals with the balance of power between central and local government, and weighs it now heavily on the side of central Government.

'I ask what we would have been saying about centralisation and control from Whitehall if the Labour Party, as the Government, had introduced such a Bill. The complexity of the Bill will lead to an enormous growth of bureaucracy. Ministers themselves will not have the time to go into the details of each local authority and it will have to be left to civil servants. Those who are so strongly supporting the Bill but, at the same time in leaders in the press, are damning bureaucracy ought to think about that aspect of it. I do not believe that these powers should be given to the Minister.'[53]

That evening, in a lecture to the Foreign Exchange Dealers' Association, Heath attacked Mrs Thatcher's handling of the economy, calling for more investment in infrastructure and attacking 'naïve and simplistic' monetarism. He was also critical of the 'explicit decision to give and to continue to give inflation priority over unemployment regardless of all other considerations . . . the methods chosen to reduce inflation have been effective mainly by boosting unemployment . . . On both sides of the Atlantic there are governments who believe it natural and right to go their own way and devil take the hindmost: a national, selfish and often self-defeating view . . . Britain has suffered a recession deeper than any of her OECD partners. This has been due in part to policies deliberately pursued by the Government.'[54]

The coverage in the right-wing press the next day was damning. The *Daily Mail* headline was simply 'Traitor'. Heath responded by telling Robin Day: 'It is characteristic of the *Mail* to have a headline like that. If you differ from anyone you are a traitor. This is getting very close to the end of democracy as far as the *Mail* is concerned. It has no arguments, so it resorts to abuse of the grossest kind . . . A newspaper can say "all those members are calling him a traitor", but they don't have to give names or numbers to prove anything. It is a gross abuse of the freedom of the press and extremely dangerous.'

The *Daily Telegraph* was more subtle, with a pithy editorial that was spitefully sarcastic in tone:

'If Mr Heath did not exist, we would have to invent him. Although he says little that is witty or intentionally amusing, he has become one of our greatest comic characters. His corrosive dislike of Mrs Thatcher, his huge self-satisfaction, his infatuation with the Brandt Report, his conviction that the period between 1972 and 1974 was a brief idyll of enlightened and efficient government, his speeches, which set the world to rights, his sailing, his funny books, have marked Mr Heath out as a true eccentric who richly deserves the love and affection which have come his way since he gave up being Tory leader . . . If there is another politician who makes an equal contribution to the gaiety of nations, we do not know his name.'[55]

After Mrs Thatcher used the centenary luncheon of the parliamentary lobby to say she wanted to be remembered as the person who abolished consensus, Heath responded tartly: 'We always have to remember that in a democracy a time may come when the position of those in power will change. If a bitter legacy of non-consultation is left behind then those who take over will be animated by a similar spirit which cannot be good for the country as a whole.'[56] In March 1984 questions were raised about Mark Thatcher's interests in Oman. Heath was not being drawn: 'Mrs Thatcher has always maintained that the situation is absolutely proper and, of course, one accepts that.' Within ten days, 241 backbenchers had signed an early day motion from Edward du Cann supporting Mrs Thatcher. The press noted that Heath had not signed it. He never signed early day motions.

What did stir Heath into activity was the deadlock between the UK and its European partners over contributions to the Community's budget. When Mrs Thatcher made a statement to the Commons about the unsatisfactory European Council meeting in Brussels on 19–20 March, she was in feisty mood and made no apologies for vetoing a proposed budget increase that she regarded as inequitable to the UK. 'The Community is in a difficult situation,' she stated. 'We shall, however, persevere in our efforts to achieve a reform of its finances and to make its internal and external policies more relevant to the needs of today's world. I want to see a more effective Community, developing its full potential. That is the Community in which I believe.'[57] It seemed to be implicit in her words that, *in extremis*, she would withhold budget contributions. In a long 'question', Heath was generally statesmanlike and took care to be supportive. There was a sting in the tail, though: 'In these circumstances, is my right hon. Friend aware that many of us could not accept illegality in withholding funds from the Community?'[58] He received a chilly response. As soon as the statement was over, Heath hand-wrote a letter to Mrs Thatcher:

'Dear Prime Minister, I am writing to emphasise the last point in my question this afternoon – on which you did not comment – that I could not support, indeed I would strongly oppose, any act of illegality by HM Government affecting the European Community, just as I have always opposed illegality at home. However, as the Chief Whip will confirm, this is also the position of many senior members of the party in the House of Commons as well as many backbenchers who did not make their voice heard this afternoon. I hope that the Cabinet will appreciate this in any discussions it may have on these matters. Yours sincerely, Ted Heath.'[59]

There is no record of any reply being received, or sent. This marked the beginning of a new period of *froideur* between Heath and Mrs Thatcher. The next battleground was the Government's decision to abolish the Greater London Council (GLC). Heath had no truck with GLC leader Ken Livingstone or his left-wing posturing, but he thought abolition was vindictive and fundamentally undemocratic – and that there were better ways of addressing the problem. In the House of Commons, Heath sought to set out a philosophy in clear counterpoint to that of the Government:

'Worst of all is the imposition by parliamentary diktat of a change of responsible party in London government. It immediately lays the Conservative Party open to the charge of the greatest gerrymandering in the last 150 years of British history. That is what we, as a party, are being exposed to . . . The path on which the Government have embarked is very dangerous. Undoubtedly reforms need to be brought about both in the GLC and in the metropolitan counties. If one is to have those measures, one wants to bring them about with the greatest possible agreement. That means patience, examination and consensus about local government. The present path is extremely dangerous for local government, for the Conservative Party and for the Government because of the chaotic management that will result. It is extremely dangerous for our country to have local government treated in that way.'[60]

At Prime Minister's Questions the following day, Mrs Thatcher 'swung the handbag': 'In so far as there was a difference between (Mr Heath) and myself, I am sure that I was right.' Heath stuck to his guns a month later as the measure progressed, asking his one-time private secretary William Waldegrave, now the local government minister: 'Does he believe that it is morally or politically justifiable to change the political control of the authority in the capital city by edict of Parliament?'[61]

Despite these skirmishes, Heath was given a semi-official role in the party's 1984 campaign for the European Parliament. He was given an itinerary of eighteen visits – the first of which was in Orkney, about as far away from London as it's possible to get without entering the Arctic circle. One can only speculate that the Conservatives in Shetland (if there were any) refused to cooperate. He also went to the West Country. When a *Telegraph* journalist turned up for his press conference at Plymouth, Heath feigned delight: 'Ah, a national event.'

For the rest of that summer, Heath did not break too much of a sweat. In late June he visited Moura Lympany in Rasiguères and, together, they gave a concert with the Manchester Camerata of Beethoven's *Piano Concerto No. 2*. Heath was inducted into the Confrérie des Tastevins des Vignerons Catalans, donning ceremonial robes for the occasion. His speech of thanks was brief, to the point and, mercifully, light on the French language: 'I don't care what I do, so long as I have *beaucoup de vin*.'

In the early autumn, Heath made a private visit to Cuba, a 'rogue state' treated as a pariah by the US and its allies. He had meetings with Castro, made a couple of arranged visits and presided over a grand lunch with Castro's brother Ramon as a guest, but also took the opportunity to relax. He arrived home, via Bermuda, just before the Conservative Party conference in Brighton, which he had no plans to attend. Then the bomb went off in the Grand Hotel and, the next day, Heath came to sit on the platform during Mrs Thatcher's keynote address to the conference and the two of them made a big display of shaking hands at a party conference, for the first time in seven years, in an expression of solidarity and support after the bomb. He also went to visit Norman Tebbit in hospital.

In November 1984 journalist Kenneth Rose noted in the *Sunday Telegraph* that 'Edward Heath's hair, as white as snow a few months ago, now seems to have acquired a golden hue'[62]. The head of the office at the time, **Peter Batey**, recalls how this very public problem was resolved:

'The solution was expensive for me. I went (at my own – not inconsiderable – expense) to Grosvenor House, to have my hair cut by Edward, who cut EH's hair (I think "stylised" was the parlance, doubtless implying more than cutting and including colouring) at the time. I explained to him that I would prefer it if he would ditch the "Strawberry Blond" and go back to the "Dulux Brilliant White Emulsion". He said he would try but that he had used strawberry blond because EH said he wanted to look younger. I told Edward to be firm with EH and insist that strawberry blond didn't look quite right. My ploy worked and we remained permanently with the Dulux brilliant white thereafter.'

Heath began 1985 in Cassandra mode, warning about the dangers of mass unemployment and expressing a pious hope that ministers might do more to mitigate it:

'I stand here as an avowed advocate of what the Chancellor of the Exchequer described so elegantly as voodoo witchcraft. Perhaps I could explain to the House what I mean by that. It is simply that I regard the present level of unemployment in Britain as appalling. The situation north of Watford is shameful. To go to the north-east of England and find there more than 19 per cent overall unemployment, to find areas of male unemployment of 30 per cent or more, and to find in Consett 60 per cent juvenile unemployment is to me shameful.'[63]

In response the *Sun* newspaper ran an editorial describing Heath as the 'world's worst loser' and saying: 'Mr Heath waits for the call back to power. It will never come.'[64] The following week, Heath responded, point by point, repeatedly attacking any parallel between his situation and that of Alec Home, whom he had appointed as foreign secretary: 'No such invitation for any shadow cabinet or Government post has ever been made to me.' 'What is the *Sun* afraid of?' asked Heath. 'Only one thing. The truth. Why does it concentrate on character assassination? Because it has no intelligent answer to the political arguments now raging up and down the country. The *Sun* is the lackey of its financial bosses. Poor *Sun*.'[65]

Shortly after that rejoinder, he was interviewed for another Murdoch title by the Labour-leaning lawyer and playwright John Mortimer. It was 11 am. 'What would you like?' asked Heath, proffering his hand. 'Coffee? Cognac, bacon and eggs?' Was Heath happy, asked Mortimer. 'I've only been happy during three periods of my life,' he responded. 'When I was at Balliol, when I was at the Foreign Office, which many people say amounts to the same thing – and when I was Prime Minister.' 'Did it come as a terrible shock to you when you lost the leadership election to Mrs Thatcher in 1975?' 'You know what Clemmie said to Churchill when he lost the 1945 election? "It's the Will of God." And Winston said, "Well, then, God moves in a most mysterious way." Yes, it came as a terrible shock, particularly when all the predictions were OK.' 'What do you think Churchill would have made of the present government?' 'He'd have been appalled.' 'Do you think you'll ever be Prime Minister again?' 'No. Absolutely not.'[66] This interview coincided with Mrs Thatcher's tenth anniversary as party leader.

When the national miners' strike ended on 3 March, Mrs Thatcher had decisively achieved what he had failed to do: she had asserted the power of the state over the trades unions. Heath had never commented on the strike, he said, because he 'didn't want the Government to be distracted', but he did speak out about the rate of unemployment, which was over three million people. The so-called 'Budget for Jobs' in 1984 had not borne fruit. At the instigation of Peter Batey, Heath now produced an alternative budget, as part of a well-orchestrated outburst against the Government. Unemployment in some regions had tripled since 1979 and he wanted to demonstrate something could be done about it. His focus was on increased investment in industry, infrastructure and training. He put a figure on it too: borrowing £12 billion in 1985–86 instead of the proposed £10.5 billion. The 'Alternative Budget' went out on Channel 4 on 13 March 1985, in the week before Budget Day; and Heath's recipe for saving the nation was a dose of unreconstructed Keynesian economics. Sitting in his drawing room at Wilton Street, Heath quoted the CBI, which had recently warned that Britain was 'falling to bits'. What was needed, he said, was more public investment – and he prudently pre-empted his critics, one of whom appeared on the broadcast, claiming his proposals would cause interest rates to 'soar' and sterling to 'collapse'. It is also worth noting both the classic Heath use of 'we' instead of 'I' and also his closing dig at the prevailing Thatcherite slogan 'There Is No Alternative':

'What we really need is a Budget for industry – to help industry create jobs. We need to invest. The investment that I propose as a matter of priority would mean increasing public borrowing by £5 billion . . . We're always accused by our critics of wanting to "spend our way out of a depression" and of "throwing money at problems", but these are slogans not arguments. How can it be wrong to use the savings of our people to invest in their future? Successful businesses borrow, in order to expand and grow – and that is what we as a nation must do . . . We would all like tax cuts, but our priority must be the unemployed and the lower paid. The way to help them is not by cutting taxes at the moment . . . There is a much better way. There *is* an alternative.'

He followed up with a trenchant half-hour speech in the budget debate in the House of Commons. Roy Jenkins commented, 'I do not know what effect losing the leadership of the Conservative Party is said to have had on his temper, but it has had a remarkably good effect on the sense and sweep of his judgment and view of the world.'[67]

Having a home he could truly call his own was an ambition Heath had nurtured for many decades. While his father was alive, he had a room in Thanet to which he could return – which he did, often – and when he was first elected to Parliament, he rented a small bachelor flat at 88 Petty France. He did not entertain there and even his old friend Madron Seligman recalled being invited there only once, to change into evening dress before he and Heath went to an event together. His description seems extraordinary: 'A bed-sitting room with a kitchen and bathroom, a few water colours, but otherwise impersonal.'[68] When the lease there ran out in late 1962, he moved briefly into something similar, but by now he had set his heart on something more ambitious, where he could spread his wings, install a piano – and entertain, which seemed to him crucial for furthering his political career.

As soon as he had been elected as an MP, Heath put his name down for a 'set' at Albany, close to Piccadilly – 'an almost perfectly preserved Regency retreat'. When one did become available, early in 1963, following the death of Arnold Bax's brother, Heath wasted no time in seizing it. He relished having his own home at last and brought in a specialist interior designer, Jo Pattrick, to achieve the right effect of 'light and colour' and put his personal stamp on it, installing 'furniture that is comfortable and homely and modern'. The set was large enough for Heath to entertain and also to hold interviews or meetings with colleagues and he also acquired room for a housekeeper. He could also, for the first time, effectively display the beginnings of the art collection that still, at the time of writing, adorns his Salisbury home.

The expiry of Heath's initial lease at Albany coincided almost perfectly with his election as Prime Minister in June 1970, so he moved out, never to return. He had the state rooms at No. 10 renovated and gave Chequers a makeover too. When he lost office at the beginning of March 1974, it took him six months to find a house in Wilton Street, near Buckingham Palace, where he paid a modest, 'peppercorn' rent. For ten years, that was his one home. Twice he was targeted there by Republican terrorists, but he retained it until he stepped down from Parliament, in 2001. From 1985, however, it was merely a base for operations in London, to be used increasingly rarely – because his PPS, **Robert Key**, had gone far beyond the 'call of duty' and found him his dream home:

'Within a few weeks of me joining his team, Ted said how much he longed for a home of his own. He had told every estate agent in the south what he wanted – an attractive house not too far from London, not far from the sea (specifically the Solent), not in the centre of a town but not isolated in the country either. As it happens, that perfectly describes Salisbury – though I didn't tell him so at that time.

'Within months I was in the Cathedral, stewarding the Eucharist as usual, around the turn of the year between 1984 and 1985. After the service I caught up with an old school friend, whose mother had recently died and who had lived in a very beautiful Queen Anne house in the Close. I asked him if he would now come and live in the Close. He said he already had a nice house south of Salisbury, so Arundells, with sixty years of the lease yet to run, was being offered back to the Chapter of the cathedral.* They were now seeking to let the sixty-year lease through an agent in Salisbury. On Monday morning I went to the Agent and collected a brochure. That evening, after the ten o'clock vote, I went around to Wilton Street and said to Ted, "I've found your house!" We talked about it until after midnight.

---

* Heath soon discovered that two previous occupants, a canon and his sister, had lived to the ages of ninety-eight and ninety-four. 'I find that very encouraging,' he would joke.

'On Tuesday morning I was sitting at my desk in The House when the phone rang. It was Ted. "I hope they haven't sold my house! Can you come with me to Salisbury on Wednesday morning?" Within an hour he had decided. We returned to London and his lawyers, Freshfields, were on the case. In due course, they even managed to compel the Chapter to sell him the freehold at the market price prevailing at the time the lease was granted. This led to frosty relations with Chapter, which thawed when, in 1992, HRH Prince Charles devised the amazing "Symphony for the Spire" and Ted helped persuade some of the world's leading musicians and actors (including Placido Domingo, Jessye Norman, Ofra Harnoy, Charlton Heston and Phil Collins) to come and perform in a great fund-raising concert presided over by Prince Charles and Princess Diana.

'Ted loved entertaining in his newly-refurbished home. He brought with him his larger-than-life Italian cook. She sourced food local from Salisbury Market and local butchers. Ted loved his vegetable garden and served home-grown produce in season, but Italian broad beans in the pod, sliced and sautéed in butter, were not Broadstairs and were soon off the menu. Sue and I knew Ted well enough by this time to expect a phone call at lunch time on a Saturday, inviting us at short notice to fill his table the next day, because someone could not fly in from abroad that night. Several times Madame Pompidou, widow of the former French President, would be present. Another regular – and probably his favourite company – was Kay Graham, owner of the *Washington Post*.

'Soon I was PPS and Social Secretary, too. He would ask me to draw up a guest list for his Salisbury dinner parties. Sue and I had great fun! He came to supper at our very modest home in Woodfalls, a few miles south of Salisbury, where he was absolutely charming to our two little girls. He must have been happy, because he fell asleep in front of the fire! On one occasion Sue and I had been invited to dinner with friends who owned a lovely Elizabethan Manor on the edge of the New Forest. It was early days for Ted in Salisbury, so we asked June and George if we could please bring him. They were delighted and superb hosts. It was a snowy, icy drive there and back. Ted was on good form. He suddenly said, "Do your constituents often ask you out?" I said yes: I had known many of them since childhood. Ted replied, "I have never been invited to dine in the home of a constituent." How sad.

'In his last years in The House, Ted responded only occasionally to whips, even to three-line whips. He preferred life in Salisbury. There is no doubt he was lonely. A couple of times a week, he and his minder would go out to one of his favourite pubs in the villages round about. At least three still talk of "Ted's chair". People were very kind to him. He undoubtedly had the common touch. He never forgot his family roots and he had an easy relationship with the people he met in the pubs on weekday nights. To him they were the salt of the earth, representing all he loved best about his country.'

The internal redesign of Arundells was undertaken swiftly and decisively. Heath did not use Jo Pattrick this time, but Derek Frost, who lived more closely at hand. 'We did not set out to restore this house,' said Heath, 'but to recreate something new within it . . . I found it very exciting to use contemporary design ideas inside the house, but sometimes the difficulty for me was to visualise what Derek proposed.'[69] Early on in his time in Salisbury, Heath struck gold when he appointed a head gardener to bring order to the extensive grounds of his first and only true home. He recruited **Stuart Craven**, a musician who had once played with Mungo Jerry and stayed with Heath until the end of his life (and beyond, spending ten years in charge of the house after Heath's death, until he retired in 2015). From the late 1980s until Heath's demise in 2005, Stuart was as close to him as anyone was; and, in common with all of us who worked for him over the years, he knew all too well the chimerical nature of the man, from mischievous to magnanimous, from grim-faced to generous, from cantankerous to kind:

'His oft-quoted phrase of "there are two gardeners here, I have the ideas and someone else does the work" was typical, but his input was not much despite his protestations. The Seligman family bought him a good pair of secateurs for Christmas and he started to deadhead the magnolia blossom on the patio. When I returned he had fallen off the ledge and gashed his shin and promptly gave me the secateurs saying it was too dangerous.

Originally he had ideas of rounded, Italian-style borders, but I had to change a few things, such as the view to the rivers, as it was deemed too easy to shoot him from the opposite bank (a Home Office instruction). He liked to take the credit for everything to do with Arundells, even in my company, but always with a twinkle in his eye.

'After my divorce, about which he learned through a protection officer as I was reluctant to tell him my personal business, he called me up and gave me surprisingly fatherly advice about not trusting and moving on with my life, all of which I really appreciated. After asking me about how divorce affected me, he daily walked down the garden to find out how I was and whether I had been to the doctor etc. He was very caring and concerned, which certainly made me appreciate his loyalty, which I of course returned. A short while later he went on BBC *Question Time* and a question about divorce came up (I think they are aware of the questions beforehand). He spoke quite eloquently about his experience of how divorce affected his constituents, mirroring our discussion and, for a bachelor, got a round of applause!'

One of the most colourful accounts of Heath's life in Salisbury comes from Derek Frost's partner **Jeremy Norman**, who included the following section in his book *No Make-Up: Straight Tales from a Queer Life*:

'At ten o'clock one Saturday evening the telephone rang at our country cottage in Hampshire: it was Sir Edward Heath. "Those overpriced cushions you made for me are falling apart," he said, with a twinkle in his voice, not quite joking but not altogether serious either. He didn't know quite how to call someone just as a friend, without making a business excuse. The call was to Derek, Sir Edward's interior designer. Some half a dozen years previously, Derek had undertaken a major project to redesign and decorate Arundells, Sir Edward's magnificent Queen Anne house in The Close at Salisbury. The former Prime Minister had often demonstrated his wish to retain a friendship with us both, but always on unequal terms. He was invariably "Sir Edward" – while we were "Derek" and "Jeremy". It was clear to us that he was lonely and looking for an excuse to meet, either at his house in Salisbury or as our guest at our cottage on the Solent.

We sensed that, in his own highly inhibited way, he was reaching out to us as a gay couple. He undoubtedly felt comfortable in male company. With us he was relaxed and at ease.

'Old Ted, as we couldn't call him, was a great raconteur and loved his own stories about important people and world leaders he had known. "Chairman Mao gave me this hideous piece," he would declare with his characteristic unnatural laugh and heaving of his shoulders. The house was full of such memorabilia and photographs of world leaders and monarchs in silver frames on the piano. On one card President Nixon had added a hand-written note – "In our line of business you need a second string" – presumably a reference to his music and sailing interests.

'While Derek was decorating Arundells and for some time after, we would often visit. Heath's delight in his new home was evident. He had never before worked with an interior designer to create a stylish personal home. He relished both the experience and the result. He was happy getting down on the floor to examine samples of fabric and to pore over Derek's plans, his comments were always thoughtful and considered. Through the experience of working closely with him on so personal a project, Derek was able to touch an intimate part of his make-up. The long-buried gay designer gene expressed itself in his enthusiasm. His keen intelligence and appreciation of another's skill made him an ideal client; he learnt a great deal and gave a great deal of thought and attention to the matter. He discovered a newfound delight in decoration and design. He listened and learnt fast from someone who had much to teach about how to make the best use of available space and to achieve a harmonious and stylish result.

'His pride in the result was evident to see, but he was niggardly in his praise and often took credit for Derek's ideas. For some years after the job was finished, Derek would retreat to the study at Arundells with Sir Edward to discuss his long list of complaints and snags. It was as if he did not want to let go of either the experience or the relationship that it had engendered. 'Derek found it difficult to say no to such a prestigious client. Sir Edward pushed the limits of what could be considered fair and reasonable in free after-care service. We suspected that these frequent requests for help were his way of keeping in contact and not losing our friendship. He was an excellent client when it came to settling his account, but there were times when he stretched our patience with his niggling and petty requests.

'Although he could be quite entertaining, his conversation centred on himself; he never showed the slightest interest in our lives. His capacity for friendship rested solely on his entertainment and celebrity value; hence his loneliness. Our friend, Michael Wade, recalls a typical Heath reply to his question, "What do you consider your greatest achievement?" Always ready with a sharp rejoinder and conversation stopper, Sir Edward retorted: "Don't you think becoming prime minister is a sufficiently great achievement?"

'We discussed gay matters in relation to politics and I asked him for his views on issues such as the age of consent for gay sex. I asked him why he had voted against equality; he claimed that he had always favoured an equal age, but that politically it was impossible until now: "The rank and file of the party would never have stood for it," was his comment. Ever the politician, he put pragmatism before principle.

'As a gay man, I couldn't help but conclude that he was a deeply closeted gay man. He was clearly not rampantly heterosexual and, given that he was ambitious, it seems likely that he had decided early in life to sublimate his sexuality to his political ambitions. That he was right to do so was underlined by the tragic Jeremy Thorpe affair. At that period, at least, a political leader could not have risen to great heights and been a homosexual; he would have been discovered and exposed. His love of the organ (or so an organist told me), his exaggerated affection for his mother, his great artistic sensibilities and his bachelor, almost monastic, life lead me to the conclusion that if he had a sexuality – as nearly everyone must – he had to be inclined towards men. That impression was reinforced by his monosyllabic answers to questions about his love life and his one close woman friend: he clearly had something to hide. Sir Edward was a master at monosyllabic equivocation and evasion. "Yes, that's right," was all he would reply to the question, "Were you sad when she married someone else?"'

At the party conference of 1985 Heath was in dyspeptic mood. When his time as Prime Minister was criticised at a meeting, he responded by saying 'this conference is rigged', adding: 'That woman during my government was the biggest spender of them all, along with Keith Joseph.'[70] When he was presented at a restaurant with a marzipan bust of Mrs Thatcher, he ceremoniously cut it into four pieces and had it sent across to another table, where four cabinet ministers were dining.

In February 1986 the debate about selling British Leyland to General Motors had unhappy echoes of the Westland affair. Heath was cheered by many Labour MPs and not a few Tories too, when he expressed reservations to the new Secretary of State, Paul Channon, about what was proposed:

'I have been accused of many things in my life, but not of being isolation-ist. Moreover, I hope that he will not accuse me of being anti-American. I first went to the United States in 1939 as a student. I fought alongside the Americans. I have worked closely with four presidents of the United States. I am a great admirer of the Americans. Moreover, I admire what General Motors has done. I well recall one of the most famous phrases in history under President Eisenhower's Administration, that what was good for General Motors was good for America. That may well be true, but it does not follow that what is good for General Motors is good for Britain, and that is what concerns me.'[71]

Peter Batey's successor running the private office was **Richard Burn**:

'It is well known that Ted Heath disliked Margaret Thatcher and never forgave her from replacing him as Party leader, but it is not true that he always referred to her as "that woman" or that he did not recognise her capabilities. He was perfectly gracious to her when she went to his fiftieth anniversary party in Claridge's in February 2000 and went to her 75th birthday party later the same year, when the then party leader, William Hague, did not. I remember watching the television news with him when Edwina Currie, then a minister, was in trouble over tainted eggs, and asked him if she reminded him of Thatcher. "Oh no," he said, "there was much more to her." And then much later when Tony Blair was on the news, hectoring Parliament as he tried to justify the invasion of Iraq, which Ted Heath bitterly opposed, believing it illegal and likely to have disastrous consequences, I said (trying to get a rise out of him) "He's as bad as Thatcher", to which he immediately retorted, "No, he's much worse – Blair's evil." Hardly ringing endorsements, but he grudgingly recognised her strength of character.

'He had a great sense of humour and was often quite self-mocking among friends. When I worked in his office he would often ask my opinion after giving a speech. I tried to be honest although it was difficult to be too critical: luckily he was a very good speaker, particularly when talking off the cuff to an audience he liked. But occasionally, if I felt he hadn't been at his best, I might be lukewarm in praise. That normally elicited a grumpy response but if on the other hand I ever said he had spoken very well, he would say: "Oh praise indeed, the fool Heath has got something right!"

'I remember once sitting at my desk in his office when the phone rang and it was someone from an NGO asking if EH would be prepared to go to India to give a speech at a conference about aid to the developing world, also explaining that, unfortunately, they were unable to pay him a fee. I looked at his diary and discovered that, by chance, he was due to be in India anyway the same week. I rang him and told him about the speech and the coincidence of his being in India. "What's the fee?" he asked. I told him they were a non-profit making organisation and unable to pay a fee. "Well tell them," he replied, "that if they pay me a large fee, that will help them not to make a profit!" There was a long pause and then we both laughed. He did the speech without a fee.

'On one occasion (after I had stopped working for him) he was unable to use four tickets for Glyndebourne and asked if I would like to buy them, "to entertain my clients". I readily agreed and happily sent him a cheque. About two weeks before the opera, he rang up and said that, as it turned out, the event for which he had abandoned Glyndebourne had itself been cancelled, so he was free to go after all. My heart sank as I thought he would ask me to sell him back the tickets, but he had another solution: he would be pleased to come as my guest. That sort of practical joke was typical of him and those of us who knew him well understood that it was meant to be funny, as well as clever. Alas, people who did not know him rarely saw the amusing side of his pranks and deadpan remarks.'

The general election of 1987 was inevitably quieter for Heath than any other since 1950: although he did apparently visit twenty-eight constituencies, in support of friends and allies,* he felt no need to take any national profile. With the opposition parties still inflicting damage on one another with great vigour, Mrs Thatcher won more comfortably than expected, with a majority of around 100 seats. Once the election was over, **Heath** was quickly out of the traps, in the spirit of Nostradamus. In the debate on the Queen's Speech, he made it plain he did not see himself as a spent force, at least as a presence both baleful and baneful for ministers. Following a speech by David Owen, of whom he was never fond, he could not resist starting with a dig:

> 'In congratulating the Prime Minister, her colleagues and our party on their success in the election, I believe that it would be grossly unfair of me not to pay full tribute to the contribution by the Leader of the Opposition and the leaders of the alliance in that process. Their contribution was in all ways remarkable.'[72]

He went on to criticise the Government on devolution, crime, the debts of the developing world and, at some length, its proposals for reform of schools. He also identified the proposal that would cause the Government endless, ultimately mortal, pain, but seemed to believe ministers had already crafted an escape route for themselves. Perhaps he was joking:

> 'I am encouraged by the fact that the proposals in the Queen's Speech are all couched in terms that the Government could change, if persuaded to do so. They do not commit themselves to the poll tax: the speech states that fresh arrangements will be made. That gives the Government every opportunity . . . I hope that they will take advantage of every opportunity of accepting advice that we can give them . . . The characteristic of a poll

---

* Including Battersea, which John Bowis gained for the party, against the national trend.

tax is that it is not related to people's ability to pay, nor to the circumstances in different areas of the country. Those are two basic failings of the poll tax, quite apart from the administrative problems. The Secretary of State for the Environment last night said that he believed that it was right that tax should not be related to people's ability to pay. That is not a radical proposal; it is a reactionary, regressive proposal for the tax not to be related to people's ability to pay.'[73]

The 'Great Education Reform Bill' (known as the 'GERBIL') was taken through Parliament by Heath's former PPS, Kenneth Baker. It proposed a national curriculum, the power for schools to 'opt out' of local authority control and also extensive budgetary devolution to schools, which had already been pioneered in certain Conservative-controlled local authorities. At second reading **Heath** did not spare Baker's blushes:

'The extent of the Secretary of State's power will be overwhelming. Within the parliamentary system, no Secretary of State should ever be allowed to hold such a degree of power. He should surrender that power. There is no confidence in the claim that all the processes of consultation that the Secretary of State has mentioned will be effective or that the Secretary of State will take any notice of them.

'Opting out should be dropped completely. It will undermine the whole of the basic educational system of this country. The proposition of dictating to the universities what they should do, how they should do it and what will happen to their staff must also go. There is so much to be done and the Secretary of State could create a record for himself akin to that of Balfour and Butler. He will not do it this way. I beg my right hon. Friend to look at his predecessors and follow the line, both practical and philosophical, taken by them.'[74]

In January 1988, Heath spoke in support of the Protection of Official Information Bill that his back-bench colleague Richard Shepherd had introduced as a Private Member's Bill. He supported the liberal principles of the Bill (which did find their way into law in the era of the Blair Government) and deplored the Government's decision to impose a three-line whip against it, an act he believed was without precedent. The occasion produced one of his most impressive parliamentary performances and also one of the lowest majorities the Thatcher Government ever enjoyed – as it succeeded in killing the Bill (and creating considerable ill feeling amongst its own supporters) by 271 votes to 234. More than ever, Heath was effectively in opposition.

Despite these high-profile domestic interventions, Heath was still an inveterate traveller and there is a picaresque quality to the best tales from this period. There is the visit to China that descended into farce when Heath obediently sent his packing ahead to the airport and only then realised he had packed all his trousers. Peter Batey alone could remotely approximate the Heath girth, so Heath struggled into his trousers while Peter had to go to the airport swaddled in towels, until the luggage could be retrieved. There was also a trip to the then Soviet Union, during which a 'spook' from the British Council warned Richard Burn that the handsome young man assigned by their hosts to accompany the Heath party was a suspected 'agent provocateur', specially chosen for the fruitless task of attempting to catch the eye of the confirmed bachelor Heath and gain his amorous attentions. Much ribaldry ensued, with one of Heath's Special Branch protection offi-cers mirthfully exclaiming, within Heath's earshot, that 'They're going to roger Tubs* on the night train to Leningrad.' Needless to say, the sole object of Heath's affections throughout the trip was the private supply of whisky his entourage had provided for him.

When Nigel Nelson, Political Editor of the *Sunday People*, interviewed Heath in summer 1988, he was less than flattering about Heath's physical decline and sartorial sense: 'Ted Heath waddled into the room looking more like a Torremolinos tourist than a former Prime Minister,' he wrote. 'The one button holding his short-sleeved shirt together threatened to give at any moment, and the tight white shorts were so tight they were like a pair of incongruous hot-pants which seemed about to carve his midriff in two . . . but . . . 72-year old Mr Heath proved that his brain was as razor sharp as ever.' On one subject in particular, Heath was not far wide of the mark: 'I have attacked the Government's policy for the Poll Tax because I think it's absolutely unjustifiable. It's going to be very damaging to the party.' In the

---

* One of the many 'pet' names for Heath.

course of an hour, Heath did not mention Mrs Thatcher once by name and, when challenged on his parliamentary voting record (around 5 per cent) he simply responded: 'I spend a lot of time in my constituency and a certain amount of time abroad . . . A Government which has this size of a majority doesn't need to have everyone there.'[75]

On 20 September 1988, Mrs Thatcher travelled to Bruges and made one of her most famous speeches. Framed in terms that might arguably put her on the pro-European wing of the modern-day Conservative Party, this is the section of the speech that has achieved an immortality of its own:

> 'We have not successfully rolled back the frontiers of the state in Britain, only to see them re-imposed at a European level with a European super-state exercising a new dominance from Brussels. Certainly we want to see Europe more united and with a greater sense of common purpose. But it must be in a way which preserves the different traditions, parliamentary powers and sense of national pride in one's own country; for these have been the source of Europe's vitality through the centuries.'

Heath was indignant beyond words. He saw this speech as a complete abnegation of the pro-European attitude that had predominated in the party since the early 1960s. At the party conference in October, he set out to refute it. This felt like civil war. Jonathan Aitken was scheduled to speak before Heath, but spoke after him instead; and seemingly denounced not what Heath had said, but what he, Aitken, had expected him to say. Certainly there was nothing in Heath's fairly modulated words that justified Aitken's description of him as the 'unacceptable face of Conservatism'.

That same month, Heath was the surprising – and also surprised – recipient of the 'Parliamentarian of the Year' Award from the *Spectator*. It was an award he accepted with genuine pleasure and then cherished. At the end of May the following year, Heath himself went to Belgium, consciously flouting the well-established convention of not attacking one's own leaders when abroad, in his words, to 'wipe away the stain on its [the European Community's] principles and beliefs left behind last September by what is now known as the Bruges Speech by the British Prime Minister'. He was roundly attacked for his pains, even by former aides such as Douglas

Hurd and Kenneth Baker. He defended himself unapologetically: 'We have reached the stage where there is no point in going on talking in coded terms. Ex-Ministers have been doing that for ten years. One has to speak out because the situation is so serious.'

Many people were fascinated by how Heath's constituency party felt about his self-isolating position within the party and, every so often, journalists would go to Bexley, no doubt in the hope of uncovering splits or causing mischief. Heath's agent at this time, Tom Jolly, was an old hand and knew very well how to handle such expeditions. In any case, what the press found was a mixture of acquiescence in Heath's behaviour, resigned acceptance and dogged, personal loyalty to him. In my experience, the Bexley association was, in its views, much like any other – only those on the left of the party felt more able to speak out. Through a subtle admixture of charm, intimidation and sheer force of personality, for almost fifty years, half of which he spent as an outspoken and controversial self-appointed sage in the wilderness, Heath managed to inspire broad loyalty amongst the Tories of Bexley.

Robert Vaudry, who ran Heath's office between 1988 and 1992, was notably entrepreneurial in the role. The lunches in Salisbury went more 'showbiz', with the likes of Bob Geldof, Toyah Wilcox and Richard Branson in attendance. He once insisted that the great cellist Jacqueline du Pré should be invited and only reluctantly would he accept that her multiple sclerosis was far too advanced for that. Heath also befriended the rock star Sting and his wife Trudie Styler. For a fee that was paid to his charitable trust, he even advertised English cheeses ('Red Leicester?' 'No, I prefer Blue Stilton'). Vaudry realised how much Heath enjoyed publicity – 'He liked to be the centre of attention – it gave his life meaning' – and on a Friday he would sometimes call Chris Moncrieff of the Press Association, entirely off his own bat, to stir up a story in Heath's name. The following Monday, an amused Heath might comment, 'I was clearly very busy over the weekend!' Vaudry kept Heath off BBC *Question Time*, but did negotiate his appearance on *The Dame Edna Experience*, in which Barry Humphries, in his pink and flowery guise, asked Heath whom he had in his life to tell him when he had spinach on his teeth. Heath handled himself superbly, with a surprising lightness of touch.

In June 1989, the Conservative Party, which had been far more pro-Europe than Labour in the 1979 and 1984 European election campaigns, changed tack significantly, with posters about voters being fed a 'Diet of Brussels' should they neglect to vote Conservative. Many in the party were uneasy and, as she sought to calm the waters in the week before the European Parliament elections, **Mrs Thatcher** responded in a highly stage-managed way to a question from Tory MP Roger King asking her to confirm that no Conservative candidate was opposed to Britain's membership of the EEC:

> 'Yes, of course I confirm that, unlike the Labour Party, all our candidates in the Euro-elections believe that Britain's future lies in the European Community. A Conservative Government led by my right hon. Friend the Member for Old Bexley and Sidcup had the vision to take Britain into the Community . . . A successor Conservative Government have made such a success of Britain's membership.'[76]

Heath was seen to nod his head to this, twice, slowly. Nonetheless, he was appalled by the party's gradual conversion to an anti-European stance. In his memoirs, he described that Tory campaign as 'an object lesson in political inconsistency, as well as distortion'.

In a debate on Security and Intelligence later in the same year, Heath excoriated Mrs Thatcher's use of the No. 10 press operation, which was increasingly becoming involved in briefings against individual ministers who had fallen out of favour: 'They have used their press office at No. 10 in a way which can be described as corrupt – in a way which went far beyond not only the achievements but even the aspirations of any previous Government.'[77] Heath's principal media spokesman when he was Prime Minister, Sir Donald Maitland, later drew a strong contrast with that earlier era: 'There was never any occasion when I commented on the performance of any member of the Cabinet, for the very good reason that the Prime Minister never discussed his Cabinet colleagues with me . . . My relationship with Ted Heath was obviously a very close one, but on no occasion did that arise in any conversation he had with me, and I didn't expect it to.'[78]

Heath continued to travel, in particular to China, where he was feted as a statesman and old friend. As **Peter Luff** recalls, these visits were sometimes more than ceremonial:

'In April 1982, I went with Heath to Peking and met Deng Xiaoping. The conversation was formal but lively. I was struck by how often Deng laughed and by how often he spat. He sprung one big surprise about his vision for the future of Hong Kong. From nowhere came the unexpected idea of "One Country, Two Systems", clearly intended to be relayed immediately to the British government. The ambassador, Sir Percy Cradock, swore the Heath team to silence and quickly sent his telegram to London. But it seems Mrs Thatcher could not believe the Chinese would use Heath as the conduit for such important news and the British took no action to follow up on the proposal. Months of negotiating time were lost as a result of Thatcher's disbelief, born of the growing mutual antipathy.'

Through the late 1970s and the 1980s, it did seem Heath's policy of '*ouverture*' towards 'Red China' was the correct one and would continue to bear fruit. Critics called him an apologist, but, so long as China's internal affairs seemed to be moving in a positive direction – more freedom, a greater inclination to trade, frigid relations with the Soviet Union – his position was defensible. Then came the dreadful events in Tiananmen Square in July 1989, when hundreds of unarmed, peaceful demonstrators were murdered. So much for which **Heath** had worked, now seemed to have come to naught:

'Many of us . . . are still stunned by the trauma in Peking and other big cities in the People's Republic of China. I acknowledge immediately that I am one of them. No one believed that it could possibly happen. How could it happen when the people at the top had themselves suffered during the cultural revolution? Deng Xiaoping said to me: "I am here only because Mao Tse-Tung said that not a hair on my head was to be damaged." . . . We still need to know the whole story. Perhaps we shall never know it, but the ghastly tragedy was there for us all to see.

'The pernicious and dishonest journalist, Edward Pearce, has accused me of condoning the massacre. I have never condoned it for a moment. I am not ashamed that in 1972 as Prime Minister I brought about full diplomatic relations with the People's Republic of China . . . In my first discussions with Mao Tse-Tung I obtained from him, in the presence of Zhou Enlai, Deng Xiaoping and Hua Guofeng, an undertaking that nothing serious would happen in Hong Kong and that the changeover in 1997 would be peaceful . . . I could not possibly condone for one moment the massacre in Peking and the executions and shootings in the other cities that followed.'[79]

Unlike the gerontocracy in China, Mikhail Gorbachev and his supporters baulked at deploying brute military force to suppress the flowering of freedom. When the Berlin Wall came down in 1989, Heath and Vaudry were flown to Berlin for a live broadcast that Heath would undertake with Denis Healey. As the two old rivals and Balliol contemporaries were preparing to go live, Healey donned a joke-shop false eye, on a spring. The moment they were on air, he allowed it to drop into his lap. After the interview, Heath and Vaudry went to the Wall, which was being slowly demolished by the population, and walked through a gap. On the other side they were confronted by a group of nervous, young, armed border guards. Not for the first time, Heath's *sangfroid* stood him in good stead.

By 1990, Mrs Thatcher was in difficulties. Nigel Lawson had quit as Chancellor, widespread hostility to the poll tax was hardening and many of her fellow Conservatives were alarmed by her growing hostility towards Europe. The polls looked grim and there was a hint of mortality about the Government. She nonetheless attended a lunch at the Savoy Hotel in February, held to mark Heath's fortieth anniversary as a Member of Parliament. Heath's former PPS **Tim Kitson** paid this tribute to Heath:

'Those who have known and served with Ted Heath for many years will recognise in him the characteristics of a great parliamentarian: his honest belief in rational argument and debate as the means of reaching solutions and drawing out the truth; his straightforwardness and wit in speech; and his gift for friendship and unfailing courtesy towards other Members.'[80]

In early September the House of Commons was recalled during the summer recess, to discuss the invasion and occupation of Kuwait by Iraqi troops, which had taken place in early August. Mrs Thatcher was in her element, with much talk of resisting aggression. For once she did not have to resist any aggression from Heath, who welcomed the lead the United Nations was giving, made unsympathetic noises about Israel and sympathetic ones about Jordan; and then set out only one, very carefully calibrated, warning:

> 'I ask that we be careful in making absolute commitments, because on this occasion it is possible that Arab countries themselves will work out a solution to the security of their own region. That will not be easy, but it has been done on previous occasions.'[81]

A sizeable number of British citizens were taken hostage by the Iraqi government, for use as 'human shields'. Heath offered to go and negotiate their release. There had initially been indications from the Foreign Secretary, Douglas Hurd, that Heath's trip would carry the official sanction of Her Majesty's Government, but that had been withdrawn, apparently after Mrs Thatcher flew into a rage when she heard of it. During the party conference, Robert Vaudry organised, through Central Office, a room for a press conference. This gathering clashed with Michael Heseltine's speech at the conference, but journalists sensed the better story was with Heath. He was, he told the assembled throng, going to Iraq to lobby Saddam for the release of the hostages. Vaudry describes Heath's ten-minute opening presentation as 'the best I ever saw him' and the occasion on which he most clearly saw how and why his employer had become Prime Minister: 'I was so proud at that moment in time.' After questions they all had to make a quick exit, because Heath was hosting one of his traditional party conference dinners, at his home in Salisbury. The journalists, headed by the Press Association's legendary political editor Chris Moncrieff, later described how privileged they felt, to be part of the biggest story going. This was a far cry from all too many of these gatherings, where the gossip and food were plentiful, but everyone felt far removed from the mainstream of events.

When Heath left Arundells to travel to Iraq, accompanied by a number of British journalists, the police there mused to Stuart Craven that they might never see him again. Heath, Vaudry and Heath's personal physician, Jeffrey Easton, who had replaced the now-retired Brian Warren, flew first to Jordan, then on to Baghdad, where they met (and were charmed by) Saddam's foreign minister and confidant Tariq Aziz. At first they were told they were staying in the same hotel as the foreign press corps, but Heath objected (not least because the place was known to be bugged) and they were relocated to one of Saddam's palaces. Outside the British embassy, a crowd had gathered with 'Maggie Out' placards. 'I think they've got the wrong person,' said Heath.

When Heath and his sidekicks met the 'human shield' hostages, they were accompanied by a sizeable press pack and set about distributing, Santa-like, sackfuls of mail they had brought from loved ones. The Iraqis had in mind the approximate number of hostages they were willing to release but the negotiations were complicated by the fact that the names of the Westerners had been transliterated into Arabic and back into Roman script, making the lists all but useless. With the Ambassador, the group set about identifying those hostages whose medical conditions made their release most urgent. A total of thirty-three hostages were identified, about whom the British Embassy had been most concerned.

When Heath went to see Saddam, he had with him only an interpreter. Nonetheless a remarkable account exists of their meeting – an account that itself came to light in remarkable circumstances. If visitors from abroad come to Arundells these days, there is always a decent likelihood of them seeing something relevant to their home country and the excellent guides try to make a point of finding this out. On one occasion a visitor who had come to the UK from Iraq was shown a cartoon depicting Heath as a snake charmer, working his wiles on Saddam Hussein when he went to negotiate the release of the British hostages. The guide started to tell the story. 'I know all about that,' said the visitor, 'because I was there with him – I was the interpreter.' The guide encouraged the man to tell his extraordinary tale:

'We were invited to go into a room, where Saddam Hussein was sitting at a table, with two armed guards standing behind him. We sat down after the usual greetings and then Edward Heath turned to me and instructed me: "Explain exactly what I say. Don't change any of the wording. Tell him only a coward would hide behind the shirts and skirts of women and children." I thought at that point we were both dead. I steeled myself and said exactly that. The smile went off Saddam's face and the two guards behind him shifted on their feet, which made things even worse. Then Mr Heath smiled at Saddam Hussein and said: "Now tell him that, having met him, I will assure my government that he is not a coward and would never dream of doing such a thing." Then the smile returned to Saddam's face, the two guards relaxed and puzzlement spread on Saddam's face, as he weighed up what had happened and realised he had been cornered. Apparently it worked, because he then released a number of the hostages.'

When Heath and the released 'guestages' arrived home at Gatwick, a junior foreign office minister, Mark Lennox-Boyd, was there, but merely exchanged pleasantries and kept a low profile. Heath was not amused and some of his language was less than diplomatic. There was a danger the triumph might rapidly morph, in the words of Robert Vaudry, into 'another Heath vs. Thatcher scenario'. Fortunately it did not, largely because the mission was 'enough of a success for him to get away with it'. Heath flew straight off to Germany for a paid speaking engagement. In December, 100 more hostages were released, as part of the agreement Heath had negotiated. At an event at Buckingham Palace in November 1992, Heath and Her Majesty the Queen discussed Iraq with the first President Bush's Secretary of State, James Baker. Heath suggested to Baker that he should have gone to Baghdad, as he himself had done, for face-to-face talks with Saddam Hussein. Baker was not persuaded. In front of television cameras, Her Majesty intervened, saying: 'But he couldn't get to Baghdad, like you could.' 'Why not, Ma'am?' asked Heath. 'I went to Baghdad.' 'I know you could,' laughed the Queen, 'but you're expendable now.' Heath had little choice but to laugh.

After Mrs Thatcher lost the party leadership in November 1990, John Major defeated Michael Heseltine and Douglas Hurd in the contest to become her successor, thanks to the support of a substantial majority of right wingers in the parliamentary party, including his predecessor, Mrs Thatcher. Heath (who never disclosed his allegiance in this matter, but almost certainly voted for Heseltine in the first round and Hurd in the second) quickly warmed to Major in the 1990–1992 period and was particularly delighted when he stated, at the meeting of the party's Central Council in Southport on 23 March 1991 that, 'I want to place Britain at the heart of Europe'. An endorsement from Heath was more kiss of death than breath of life to a Tory leader, but when Labour introduced a 'no confidence' motion against the Government, specifically referring to the poll tax and only to the poll tax, just four days after Major's Southport speech, **Heath** made an unexpected, but sincere, well-intentioned and extremely powerful intervention:

'The main reason I want to speak is to give the fullest possible support to the Prime Minister, who has embarked on an enormous task and faces formidable problems. I am sad if what I say disappoints all those Opposition Members who have so strongly and loudly supported me during the past fifteen difficult years, but I am now in a position to say these few words. I believe that what the Prime Minister is doing is absolutely right – perhaps I say so the more strongly because I was one of those who previously said that the Government were absolutely wrong.

'In the debate during the passage of the *Local Government Finance Bill* on 17 December 1987, I summed up: "The poll tax is unfair and unworkable. It does not increase accountability and will be immensely damaging to the Conservative Party." The Prime Minister is now limiting the damage and leading the Conservative Party to recover from that damage.

'I am puzzled why the Opposition particularly asked that this vote of no confidence should be concerned only with the poll tax. I cannot recollect any other occasion in the House in the past forty years when a vote of no confidence has been limited to one particular subject . . .

'Why were they not prepared to give the Prime Minister all the credit for what he has done in restoring our situation in Europe? He has changed the whole position. Why were the Opposition not prepared to discuss the part that he played in the crisis in the Gulf? Why were the Opposition not prepared to discuss the dramatic step that he took in saying, within a month of taking office, that haemophiliacs will of course receive proper compensation for being infected with AIDS as a result of bad blood transfusions, something which had been argued about in a petty way for years? My right hon. Friend dealt immediately with all that, so why will not the Opposition give him credit for it?

'I just do not understand, except that they are not prepared to acknowledge the good things that have been done in the past 100 days.

I am, and I warmly congratulate the Prime Minister and his colleagues on that.'[82]

This vivid account from the sculptor **Martin Jennings** of dealing with Heath during this generally much more mellow period in his life is both revealing and hilarious:

'I had been commissioned to make a bronze portrait bust of Ted Heath for the Oxford Union and turned up at his house off the Close in Salisbury one hot August morning in 1991. I sat and waited in the garden with a coffee. Eventually Heath tacked lugubriously across the lawn and sat down, casting me a long baleful look. He did not appear to be looking forward to the business.

'The first thing I needed was a series of photographs of his top half to work from when he wasn't actually sitting for me. I asked him whether he could put on a suit and tie for the purpose. Releasing a huge sigh of despair he wandered back to the house, appearing what seemed like hours later wearing jacket and tie but having also put on what must have been the grubbiest pair of sailing trousers in his wardrobe. He was grinning broadly. Clearly it was all going to be a battle of wits.

'Modelling of the portrait took place in the large drawing room. Heath was a good hour late for most of the sittings which could be a problem not least because the morning was the best time to work. Invariably he fell asleep in the afternoon. As soon as his chin slumped onto his chest I had to down tools. A deep rumbling would emanate from him, the only sound apart from the buzzing of the odd trapped bee in an otherwise deserted house. During the pause I would take to watching out of the window as the two or three Wiltshire coppers consigned to guard the gates of his home idly toyed with their machine guns in the summer heat. What was I meant to do with this somnolent grandee? When eventually I managed to wake him after virtually yelling his name he would pull his head back and bark at me in turn: "I wasn't asleep! I was thinking!"

'The thinking bit of his face was interesting and I concentrated on it, furrowing the portrait's clay forehead like some of the Epstein busts I'd been studying. His nose, beloved of caricaturists, was of less interest to me than the primness of his mouth. Further down, the shelf of his stomach tugged against his jacket in waving sheets. At one point he turned to the sculpture and suggested I treat it to "a deal less neck". But how could I? The jowls were the man.

'Heath was provocative, rather like a bored teenager, but there was something very gratifying about his lugubrious wit. Before I drove off with the finished clay he told me in mock despair how feebly the work mirrored its subject. A few weeks later I had a call from his researcher to say that Heath rather liked it and wanted to buy a cast for himself.'[83]

Heath would bask in the *glasnost* of the Major era for some time to come and, remarkably, became something of an out-rider (albeit a freelance one) on Major's behalf whenever Mrs Thatcher sought to criticise or undermine him. Heath's most explicit – 'splenetic' is not too strong a word – attack on Mrs Thatcher came when, on Tuesday 18 June 1991, she had made a speech in New York attacking the European Community. Addressing 1,700 businessmen at the Economic Club of New York, she said it was time for the UK to look beyond the EC and 'begin to lay the foundations of an Atlantic Economic Community, embracing the EC, EFTA and the new democratic states of Eastern Europe on one hand, and North America on the other'. Europe was already dominating the headlines at home. On the Monday, there had been an attempt to bounce European foreign ministers into accepting a federal future for the European Community, which had prompted John Major to assure an uneasy House of Commons: 'A European super-state would not be acceptable to me or to the House – and in my judgment it would not be acceptable to the country.' Something inside Heath snapped and what followed overshadowed in its vitriol anything he had previously said – in public or even in private – about his successor. On *Channel 4 News*, Heath said of her New York speech:

'It is full of falsehoods – in ordinary English, lies – and every attempt to discredit the Community . . . She says that the European Commission is autocratic in its decision-making. It is nothing of the sort. It can only take decisions if ministers agree on those decisions. These are blatant falsehoods, and the history which she purports to put forward is again entirely false. She also is so ignorant that she does not realise we have a European culture as well as individual national aspects. Beethoven is European; Goethe is European; Michelangelo is European. These are all part of European culture and she has no realisation of that at all.

'What it is doing is showing that Mrs Thatcher is entirely out of touch with events in this country. She does not realise the situation John Major is having to deal with; she doesn't realise she was the cause of it; and she doesn't realise that in Europe she is regarded not just as irresponsible but entirely not to be considered at all in any way.

'She goes on talking about the results of freedom in this country; she shows no appreciation of the ghastly legacy she has left her successor. She doesn't realise she was pushed so unceremoniously out of No. 10 because of what she said about Europe – and the party wouldn't stand for it. She talks about the glories of the poll tax. Well, this country repudiated the Poll Tax because it was unfair, unmanageable and expensive. She talks about the great partnership with Reagan. She doesn't seem to realise Reagan is completely discredited in the US as a president.'[84]

In light of all that it's hardly astounding that Heath was invited onto every other news outlet. Later the same evening, he carried on where he had left off on BBC 2's *Newsnight*. He was asked whether the vehemence of his assault on Mrs Thatcher might not astonish people. He said: 'A lot of people won't be astonished because they are sick and tired of hearing this from Mrs Thatcher. We have held ourselves back now for ten years and the whole question is absolutely crucial as far as the European Community is concerned.' When he was asked what he thought of her warning that the Community was acting like a 'little club' and might exclude the new democracies of Eastern Europe, he retorted: 'The little mind is her own – minute, that's what it is.'

Surprisingly, during this period of heightened activity, Heath did at last turn some small part of his attention to the matter of his personal archive and a possible memoir. He recruited extra help and, in reality, extra company to add colour and interest to his time in Salisbury. The most notable recruit was American researcher **Jeff Stacey**, who first encountered Heath a year or two earlier:

'The first intimate view of Sir Edward's personal character for me came in the spring of 1990, when he came to the University of Michigan as the Deroy Visiting Professor. He was wined and dined by the President and invited to give a public address, but his specific role was to teach a two-week seminar to a hand-picked group of Honors Program students. I have to admit, that autumn prior I didn't even know who he was; but a mate of mine schooled me on the significance of this opportunity – "Thatcher worked for this guy" – and cajoled me to apply.

'On the seminar's first day the ten selected students were whisked off to a mansion owned by the university, used for wooing donors and never before seen by the likes of us. In a rather ornate library we situated ourselves on an assortment of grand leather sofas and then waited for this eminent individual, about whom we had been reading for weeks, to arrive. He finally did, and to our surprise, waddled straight past the finely carved lectern over in our direction and plunked himself down on a sofa, between myself and another student; he then slapped his hands on his thighs, looked around at us, and said, "So, what would you like to talk about?"

'We were more than a little taken aback and not at all prepared for so informal an experience. And so it was to be. So much so that by the end of our sessions and lunches I felt no inhibition at all in telling Sir Edward that I would be travelling to the UK that summer to study English and Irish literature; his instant response met my expectation: "Splendid; I shall look forward to your joining me for mint juleps on the Terrace." At the time I had not a clue he was referring to the most secluded bar in the land, jutting out over the Thames from the Palace of Westminster and requiring an MP in one's party to attend – nor that mint juleps are a southern American cocktail, and hardly British.

'To my surprise, halfway through the trip while traipsing around the grounds of the Salisbury Cathedral my professor surprised us by leading the way to Sir Edward's adjacent home, Arundells, to accept an invitation for tea. While my contemporaries gorged on mountains of scones and finger sandwiches, my professor and I fed on conversation with our host about Gorbachev and the prospects of the 2+4 talks – the end of the Cold War was in full swing.

[241]

'My second intimate view into Sir Edward's persona came at the tail end of that trip. I arrived in London suffused in Hardy and Yeats, eagerly anticipating meeting up with a mentor in the making. Some ten telephone calls later, my hopes seemed wrecked on the shores of a dubious private secretary; I decided to ring up his office yet one more time, and after languishing on hold for nearly ten minutes was about to put the phone down when the private secretary got back on the line and relayed an invitation from Sir Edward to me to attend Sunday lunch at Arundells.

'As fortune would have it, the other guests included two MPs, a Lord, a famous chef, and their respective partners. Literally awash in alcohol after some umpteen courses and sublime conversation right the way through, Sir Edward sensed my trepidation when I accepted a snifter of cognac that all the other guests subsequently refused. He poured himself the same, and beckoned me to join him in a window seat next to the drawing room's grand piano. Not long into the conversation he asked me what I planned to do after graduating from Michigan; when I smugly replied I would be attending law school in the US, he retorted snidely: "Why on earth would one ever do such a dreadful thing?" Roundly offended, I finally stammered a feeble question as to just what he meant (a year hence it would take me six months of working for him to discern when he was wielding that mordant wit of his and when he wasn't). His reply: "Why, you should come to work for me, of course."

'Suffice it to say, I never went to law school. That sole year working in London was simply the best year of my life, and that was due largely to Sir Edward. I found him to be intensely loyal to his staff, even to the point of being treated like the family he didn't have. I soon found myself invited to more speeches, interviews, openings, galas, and events of all kinds, than I could have imagined – the boss simply took myself and another researcher along for the ride whenever he could. My greatest thrills came in those Sunday lunches, before which he would ask me, "Whom should we invite along this time? The musicians, the economists, the journalists?"

'I came to believe that the infamous animosity between Heath and Thatcher had less to do with jealously and pique, and more to do with an honest assessment that she was doing a disservice to the country – from fighting a needless war with Argentina, to her "One of Us" embrace of Reagan, to the poll tax. After all, he had kept quiet in the House for quite some time, until he couldn't bear it any more, for not speaking up would have violated his principles. As to the inability of the press and public to distinguish between the two, it seemed he could not care less.'

Divisions over Europe were the bane of John Major's life, but whereas the 'noises off' from Heath and Mrs Thatcher were not exactly helpful, at least the arguments were being ventilated, the two extreme positions were being set out (not particularly persuasively) – and the battlefield was well outside the cabinet room. As he had in the Thatcher years, Heath served the function of an 'out-rider', providing cover for others who shared his misgivings about the state of the party. Furthermore, so far as Heath's reputation was concerned, he was in the, for him, unusual position of seeking to defend and consolidate the position of his party's leader. In November 1991, for example, with his 'pet' subject being discussed in Parliament, **Heath** could not refrain from making a speech:

> 'When the Prime Minister said, on his appointment, that he wanted Britain to be at the heart of Europe, my heart leaped with joy. That joy was echoed right across Europe. Other European countries said that the new British Government would be positive and co-operative and would put forward proposals for bringing about the completion of the European Community, for which they had been working for the past forty years. I believe that that is the Prime Minister's intention, which is why I shall strongly support him tonight.'[85]

After Heath had been on his feet for half an hour and began to draw his remarks to a close, his successor sought to make a point of her own. Their exchange was electrifying:

> **Mr Heath**: 'I have here a quote from [Mrs Thatcher], who said in the debate on the referendum [on 11 March 1975]: "It would bind and fetter parliamentary sovereignty in practice." I agree with her entirely. It would, and I see no reason to change my view, or her view, at this

moment or in the future. I do not believe in referendums as a means of government.

Mrs Margaret Thatcher: 'I know that I inherited that position from my right hon. Friend, and I loyally upheld it. Now, it looks to me as if three parties will be for a single currency and for sacrificing a great deal of the work that it has previously been the right of Parliament to do. How are the people to make their views known in this absence of choice? That was the particular point. My right hon. Friend will remember that our right hon. Friend the noble Lord Hailsham, made an interesting speech on elective dictatorship.'

Hon. Members: 'Oh!'

Madam Deputy Speaker: 'Order.'

Mrs Thatcher: 'Therefore, as he has been in the House longer than I have, will my right hon. Friend tell us how people can make their views known when all parties take the same view but each is divided?

Mr Heath: 'This is an occasion which constantly occurs in parliamentary history.'

Mr Budgen: 'Rubbish.'

Mr Heath: 'What a pity some people have such a limited vocabulary.'

As the 1992 general election approached, Heath offered full support to John Major and praised both his emollient approach on European matters and also the less stringent approach to economic policy that was emerging, as the country came out of its second slump in a decade. One does, however, detect another hand at work (presumably that of a politically ambitious member of his private office): 'He is an excellent Prime Minister and leader of the Conservative Party . . . the former banker who likes to say "yes".'[86]

After John Major led the Conservative Party to victory in the general election, it was announced that Heath was to become Sir Edward – a Knight of the Garter. Nothing in his life delighted him more than this elevation, which was in the personal gift of Her Majesty the Queen, whom he both admired and adored. He would never go to the Lords, he said: 'Sir Winston Churchill felt the most wonderful thing you could be was a Knight of the Garter and I agree with him.'[87] He was installed, a beaming smile on his face, on 15 June 1992. Before that, as Father of the House of Commons, he had to preside over the election of a new Speaker. He greatly admired Betty Boothroyd and subtly did everything he could to ensure she had the best possible chance of becoming the first woman to hold the office. When she defeated former Tory Cabinet minister Peter Brooke by 372 votes to 238, he gladly ceded the chair to her. A week after he was installed as a 'KG', Heath went into hospital for what was described as a 'routine operation' – which was, in fact, an elaborate procedure to rid him of bowel cancer.

An important factor – and significant source of inconvenience – for Heath in the years that followed would be the slender majority John Major won in April 1992 and the growing split within the party on Europe. In division after division during the 1992–1997 Parliament, every vote increasingly counted, as a combination of an unusually active Grim Reaper and three very different defections by disgruntled Tory MPs rapidly took the Government's majority precipitously down into single figures. Heath did not like this at all. John Major had the immense positive quality, in Heath's eyes, of not being Mrs Thatcher, but as the Euro-sceptics ran him ragged, for Heath the sheen rapidly came off him. Yet he was often required in the division lobbies. When I was in the Heath office for the final two years of the 1992–1997 Parliament, I found the whips extraordinarily helpful and accommodating. Just once did Derek Conway, then MP for Shrewsbury but later to return to the House as Heath's successor in Bexley, lose his cool with me, warning me (not unreasonably in the circumstances) that, 'if Ted wants to remain as a Conservative MP, he'd better come and help'.

Heath was certainly mellowing, but not everyone was persuaded and his enemies would still seek out opportunities to traduce him whenever possible. One example of Heath being misrepresented comes from **Michael Fabricant MP**:

'Not long after I was first elected, a rumour about Ted Heath and me started to do the rounds at Westminster – and then found its way into print. The suggestion was that he had asked me if I wore a wig – "Because, if you do, it isn't a very good one". Needless to say, it wasn't true. Ted Heath never made any such comment to me. However, this was a light and – to some people – amusing story, playing into Ted's grumpy image, so it was duly recounted and repeated in various other magazines and newspapers.

A couple of weeks later, Ted came up to me in a House of Commons corridor and said, "I am very embarrassed about what the press are claiming that I have said about your hair. I do hope you know that I would never dream of making such an impertinent and personal comment either to your face or behind your back." I later discovered that he had been genuinely upset by the story and I thought it rather decent that he should apologise so generously for something he had never done.'

Richard Bull was recruited to Heath's office in 1993 and worked there, on a temporary basis, in January 1994. He then worked full-time in the private office from July 1994 until September 1995. He recalls Heath's continued interest in foreign affairs during this period:

'Edward Heath . . . was – and remains – rare amongst recent Prime Ministers in having a strong foreign affairs agenda before assuming the premiership. Any opportunity to assert himself on the world stage was accordingly eagerly devoured. Familiarity with the subject matter was never going to stay a grasping hand.

'So, an invitation to alight on the complex terrain of Iranian politics was excitedly accepted even though Heath was not quite up to speed with developments following the Islamic revolution. Sir Edward was approached by Iranian born businessman Sir David Alliance (now Lord Alliance) to rebuild UK/Iranian relations.

'Armed with a patchy knowledge of recent Iranian history, Heath formed the strong view that the UK was losing out to EU competitors in trading opportunities with Iran because of the running sore of the fatwa on novelist Salman Rushdie imposed by the Supreme Leader Ayatollah Khomenei in February 1989, a few months before his death. Heath believed – with characteristic confidence – that his intervention would be decisive.

'I began to have misgivings during a conversation about our accommodation in Tehran. Used to wonderful embassies the world over, the prospect of a chargé d'affaire's villa (Britain having withdrawn its ambassador in 1989 on account of the fatwa) was not appealing. Heath wanted to make sure that the chargé would be sufficiently supplied with decent alcohol.

I reassured him, adding: "Of course that is particularly important in a dry country." "Dry country?" he retorted. "Dry country? What do you mean dry country?" I explained. I was met with absolute incredulity. And Heath had the last and, as he thought, decisive word on the subject: "When I visited the Shah in 1968, there was alcohol everywhere." His triumphant end to our discussion made manifest that he was locked into a view of Iran that had long been buried in the chaos of a bloody and ruthless cultural revolution.

'This intrigued me. It was as if he had stopped thinking following his departure from No. 10. The world that Heath left behind was fixed in his mind. Various explanations for this are possible. Of course, by 1995, Heath was not in the first flush of youth. And Iran had never been a focus of his policy. But these are for me insufficient explanations. I find more compelling the thought that the involuntary loss of power has profound psychological effects – for instance, Margaret Thatcher's thinking essentially froze in 1990. Heath was younger when he left office and he maintained vigour – participating in the Brandt Commission and the EEC referendum to give but two examples. But brooding on events takes its toll. It diverts attention. For Heath therefore, Iran merely had a new government which was less western orientated in its thinking.'

Richard Bull also remembers some revealing remarks made by Heath about John Major:

'Edward Heath was in my experience suspicious of intellectuals. They inclined to idealism and it was a perverse idealism which had disrupted the early years of his life. Even his European zeal was founded on very practical considerations. Heath was nonetheless proud of his university education, but Oxford was for him as much a finishing school as a place of learning. I sensed this most particularly over lunch one Friday following a particularly splenetic performance at PMQs by John Major. Heath found Major's ill temper and want of finesse troubling. He asked whether I would have so behaved at the despatch box. He warmed to his theme: "Of course you wouldn't. You know how things are done: you went to university." This was a rare direct personal criticism of Major in my hearing, but it was deep rooted. The personal criticism was not fuelled by Heath's increasing despair of Major's lack of direction on the European question: Sir Edward had his ideal of the politician. Major, one sensed Heath felt, was not of the calibre – or class – required. Oxford conferred on Heath the social status which he felt enabled him to join the ranks of the Elect. Nonetheless Heath was somewhat disappointed in the Major Government too. The period when I worked in the office was dominated by Europe. Heath was frustrated by the lack of purpose of the government. But in the leadership ballot of 1995, he gave short shrift to those MPs who urged him to vote for Redwood so as to make the way clear for a Heseltine challenge.'*

In this emerging 'Indian Summer', Heath took great pleasure both in meeting new people and also in being recognised. One summer's day in the mid-1990s, he was in a recording studio in West London. He had spent the greater part of a Saturday conducting an orchestra for a recording of Christmas music. Upon leaving the studio he enquired of his staff where would be a good place for an early dinner, as he was starving, having not eaten all day. They suggested the Berkeley Hotel, which Heath used regularly and was not too far away, but he declined as he didn't wish to go back into Central London. As a more convenient alternative, they suggested the Brilliant Restaurant in Southall, close to Heathrow, to which Heath readily assented. On arrival at the venue, Heath's staff spoke briefly to the owner, who made a great fuss of him and welcomed him with much aplomb to his premises. After several whiskies, dinner was duly served to Heath and his team. Heath ate with gusto and thoroughly enjoyed the food prepared for him. The restaurant was extremely busy and a large function was evidently taking place on the floor above, for dozens of people, beautifully dressed, were entering the restaurant and heading straight upstairs.

As Heath was coming to the end of his meal, a gentleman approached one of his staff and asked, very politely, if he might have a word with him. The man explained that he was one of the Ugandan Asians whom Heath,

---

* In contrast, Baroness Thatcher was very supportive of John Major's challenger. When he received eighty-nine votes, she commented, 'John Redwood's very respectable vote does justice to his decision to stand.'

as Prime Minister, had allowed to come to the UK, when he and his community were expelled by Idi Amin; and the celebration upstairs in the Brilliant that evening was to commemorate that event twenty-five years earlier. He explained that he and his fellow diners would be overwhelmed if Heath would agree to speak to them before he left the restaurant. Heath acceded to the request and proceeded to ascend the stairs to the first floor. Midway up, he turned and said, 'Well stitched up'. The Ugandan Asians were ecstatic that their saviour, by sheer coincidence, was available that evening to say some congratulatory words to them. On the following Sunday evening whilst ensconced in the corner of a pub in deepest Wiltshire, the team assured him they had had absolutely no idea that the Ugandan Asian party was taking place in Southall. Heath was not convinced.

The well-established lynchpin of Heath's private office by the time I arrived in 1995 was **Henrietta Rolston**, now Henrietta Mayhew. She told me that Heath saw the world as existing in three tiers: Her Majesty the Queen and her close family; Heath; and everyone else. She was only slightly joking:

'Getting to know someone when they are in their seventies is a strange thing. It's like being by a river as it nears the sea. So much has gone before that has determined its course. You only know what you see; you hear tell of the fast moving places, the middle course, but what you witness is the slow (and stately, we hope) progression of its later stages. By 1990, the slow moving feature of the political landscape that was EH was still in Westminster. I went to work for Mr Heath towards the end of 1990. At my interview he asked whether I liked opera and ballet, then fell asleep. I had been warned that this might happen, that you just had to wait and he would wake up again. OK. At his 80th birthday dinner at No. 10 Downing Street, it fell to no less a person than Her Majesty the Queen to nudge him back to wakefulness when he dozed off.

'I was a backroom girl, one of the two secretaries. Friends assumed that working for him would be grim, but it was a fascinating job, and Europe and his dislike of Mrs T didn't take up the 90 per cent of his existence that the press made out. Rosemary Bushe, who had become EH's constituency secretary in the 1950s, used to refer to EH as "The Great Man". I am sure he liked that, but by the time I got to know him we didn't think of him quite like that. Familiarity bred affection, jokes, wry amusement, a touch of cynicism and occasional wonder at his more grandiose tendencies.

'EH would generally come up to London, depending on the Whip, Tuesday to Thursdays and stay at Wilton Street, where Teo Lopez, his London housekeeper, would give him bacon and eggs for breakfast – a welcome contrast to the grapefruit and wholemeal toast regime in Salisbury. The Belgian chocolates were always hidden in the top left drawer of the desk, away from state intervention.

'After Mrs Thatcher went in 1990, there was a feeling of Glasnost, so it was a good time to be in the office. Justice had been done and unsurprisingly the press made much of his glee. Arundells had its own press line and it frequently rang with journalists wanting him to comment, stirring him up to rash pronouncements. If Mrs Thatcher had said something, then the press line would ring some time after 7 am, he would answer and then agree to go on the 8.10 slot. Caught in the trap again and again. By the time the Private Secretary arrived in the office, the damage had been done.

'If he had been married, there would perhaps have been some constraint on this, a wise head beside him to question the wisdom of even answering the phone to such a call. And perhaps a glance to steady the ship, tone down the comments. Not caring what the papers said about him, not expecting a good press, was very refreshing in a boss. Most people are terrified of bad publicity, but during my time in the office, EH never seemed bothered by it. But he did have a good relationship with many of the political correspondents. Each year, during Party Conference, he would take out his favoured political journalists for a long and jolly dinner – an amicable, open, on-the-record evening.

'His home life in Salisbury seemed very peaceful, at least until one of the "green-ink brigade", who used to write frequently, sometimes daily, appeared there one day. "Please tell Sir Edward that I would like to see him." She told the policeman. "I am telepathetically [sic] linked to him." The message went up. "Please tell her that if I am telepathetically linked to her," came EH's response, "she will know that I don't want to see her."'

I worked for Sir Edward Heath between 1995 and 2000. That was too long and I must confess I have some regrets about that period of my life. For an aspiring young Tory of my generation, having the name 'Edward Heath' on my CV was no bonus. After I lost my job as a special adviser in the summer reshuffle of 1995, I received an unexpected call from Charles de Lisle, known to me as a diary columnist on the *Daily Telegraph*. He informed me that he had been appointed to take charge of the production of the Heath memoirs, regarded in the world of publishing as the Bermuda Triangle of political writing.* He assured me 'The Book' would now be happening and Heath required a new private secretary to run his office while a team of eager young researchers scoured his archive and prompted his recollections, in order that a suitably comprehensive tome should emerge. I wrote a letter to Heath expressing puppyish interest; and I was summoned for interview.

The office was extraordinary – home to a mass of paper, a vast array of battered filing cabinets, a goldfish tank populated by two bloated inmates (one named, as Henrietta Mayhew reminds me, 'Sir James Goldfish' and one known as Saddam Hussein – 'named by the office, not EH') and eclectic, colourful trophies, presumably from Sir Edward's foreign trips (cowboy boots, a Torremolinos donkey; could there have been a pair of castanets?). I had entered the Twilight Zone. The conversation with Sir Edward himself was certainly not out of any conventional HR manual. He was terse, monosyllabic and seemed not especially interested in me. I bade him farewell and left.

For several days I heard nothing. I began to panic. Other possible job openings had been snapped up by eager young rivals. I called Charles de Lisle. Sir Edward was sad and resigned to not recruiting me, he said, because *he* had not heard from *me*. Apparently that was how it worked. I was first in a field of one and it was for me to accept. So I telephoned Heath late one evening, evidently catching him just after he had returned from the pub; and accepted the position. When he heard my voice, he obviously expected me to turn it down, and sounded really overjoyed when I said yes. It was the last time I ever felt myself to be in a position of strength vis-à-vis Heath.

---

* I subsequently discovered that Charles had lobbied Heath assiduously for this role for the previous five years.

Life was now very different. Many former colleagues treated me as they might a lost soul. When I introduced myself to my new colleagues in the office – the indispensable Henrietta and coolly detached Penny – I explained that my role would be different from that of Nick Edgar, my recently departed predecessor. Sir Edward now intended to make a series of keynote speeches on subjects other than Europe; and his memoirs were going to be written. I have never found it harder to disentangle contempt, pity and *ennui* from within a unison response. I suppose Henrie showed some pity and Penny erred on the side of languid contempt, but neither showed one iota of conviction that our employer would indeed rouse himself from the torpor to which he was now long and agreeably accustomed, to new, Herculean efforts. They had heard it all before and I quickly learned that here was a venerable oil tanker that had no intention of changing course by even one degree – and which was probably incapable of it.

It took time to get used to his ways. Once I proposed to send his apologies for an event he could not attend. 'Never apologise!' he told me firmly. 'Just send my regrets.' It unnerved me and, seemingly, I used a phrase to him in closing, repeatedly, which I have known myself to use before or since: "Okey doke". He never mentioned his disdain to me directly, but two colleagues in the office were rapidly instructed to warn me off using it ever again. Paddy Hunt – the wife of my previous boss, David Hunt – met Sir Edward at a party thrown by Lynda Chalker. 'I hope you're looking after Michael,' Paddy said. 'I thought he was supposed to be looking after me' he countered. Meanwhile a newspaper diary piece commented dryly: 'McManus now has the job of assisting the former PM in producing his memoirs. It is moving at a pace rather slower than the building of the Great Pyramid.'[88] Sometimes I sensed they felt sympathy towards me; sometimes it was more akin to pity. At the party conference at Blackpool, my job was to assemble a group of acceptable journalists for dinner at Sir Edward's regular hideaway, the Riverhouse at Poulton-le-Fylde. The food was excellent and the only other in-house guest was Cedric Brown, the controversial chief executive of British Gas. The dinner did not begin propitiously with Michael White of *Guardian* fame whispering to me as we filed in for dinner: 'You seem to have joined the care profession.'

In that first autumn, I had the opportunity to accompany Sir Edward to Tokyo, to attend the remarkable rituals and ceremonies associated with the

Praemium Imperiale. Before this trip, he must have sensed I was apprehensive. 'You don't like the Japanese, do you?' he asked me. I didn't think this was quite fair, so I just shrugged. 'Well, you must learn to like their money.' End of conversation. Around the same time I ill-advisedly bought a new dinner suit. It was rather baggy, with lapels that pointed sharply upwards. Sir Edward grunted at me when he first saw it: 'Isn't that terribly old-fashioned?' The next time I wore it was when I accompanied him to Tokyo for the annual presentation of the Praemium Imperiale awards. We both noticed at once that all our hosts were wearing dinner suits in the same style. He caught my eye and, afterwards, said to me: 'Well *they* don't know any better.'

Not long after came the principal rite of passage for any Heath staffer – the first trip to China. I soon learned how the Chinese revered him and how happy he was there; although, in truth, whilst he admired Chinese diligence, industrial development and history, by a cruel twist of fate, he didn't care for their cuisine, most of which he described privately as 'filthy' or 'muck'. Often he would play with the food in front of him and not a tittle of it would touch his lips, then he would proclaim it 'splendid' or 'delicious' as it was all cleared away. He didn't even like the ubiquitous green tea, which I loved. At a dinner with Peter Batey and other Europeans, at a private club, I heard him use the 'F' word for the one and only time, when someone asked him why Sarah Ferguson had taken to writing children's books. 'She's obviously got bored of fucking people,' he said. We all did a double take and he roared with laughter. At least I was spared the stress experienced by an earlier private secretary, when he had not appeared in the morning and the accompanying detective went to check on him, only to find him flat out on his bed, completely naked and showing no signs of life whatsoever. Help was summoned and everyone assumed he had perished until he reacted suddenly to all the fuss and asked gruffly, 'What's going on?'

There was one basic speech that Sir Edward would gladly make 'off the cuff', which all of us soon knew off by heart. It was his 'five superpowers' speech and, I can testify myself, it was an impressive speech to hear the first time. His argument was that most people in any given room had grown up in an age of two superpowers – the US and the USSR. Naturally, we, as a peace-loving, blissfully freedom-addicted nation, sided with the US. This situation had fundamentally changed. The USSR had been supplanted by

Russia – still a major force but not on the same scale – and other superpowers had grown up, notably China and India. Brazil was another possibility. So there was one 'super duper power' – the US – and these other superpowers. The thrust was, it was only through the EU that the UK had any opportunity to play a role in that big league. I subsequently discovered that the entire thesis – so brilliantly adopted and adapted – had come from none other than his old sparring partner Henry Kissinger, who had written a book on precisely these lines some years earlier.

The Major Years were, of course, years of 'Tory Civil War', at least so far as the media were concerned. Any hint of a rift and they would gleefully pounce. In the meantime, the Prime Minister and his ministers were patiently doing rather a good job, I feel, but that seems to have been of no account. After the abrupt ending of his 'wilderness years', Sir Edward was somewhat confused. Certainly he despised the Euro-sceptics – or 'Euro-septics' as he would term them, with a schoolboy's glee – as they clamoured for John Major to resile from the Maastricht Treaty or leave the EU altogether. Of course he was excessively concerned to protect what little remained of his personal legacy to the public life of the nation – but he also genuinely believed the future of the nation was at stake. In his eyes he had a duty to speak, but there was an ever-present danger that, in so doing, he would draw further attention to rifts within the Conservative Party and contribute yet another 'Tory rift' headline to the press cuttings file.

On Friday 12 January 1996 I travelled down to Salisbury to find him in an unusually dyspeptic mood. In his drawing room there was a single telephone, but three different lines came into it, one of which was a line exclusively for use by the media. When I arrived that line was blinking. 'It's been going all day,' he said, bleakly. It stopped. It started again. 'They all want me to comment on her speech.' The day before, in the Keith Joseph Memorial lecture, Mrs Thatcher had said this: 'I am not sure what is meant by those who say that the Party should return to something called "*One Nation* Conservatism". As far as I can tell by their views on European federalism, such people's creed would be better described as "*No Nation* Conservatism".' This had been interpreted as another salvo in the 'civil war' so, naturally, journalists wanted to fan the flames. 'I think you should ignore the calls and say and do nothing,' I told him, firmly. He cannot have been surprised; indeed he had been waiting for me to come and say precisely this. He regarded me with distaste. 'Typical of you,' he said after a brief pause. 'So weak. So we just let her get away with it?' I held my ground: 'As matters stand, Lady Thatcher stands accused of making mischief, of causing trouble for the Prime Minister, of dividing the party. If you keep your own counsel, she will stand accused and you won't. The story will just die and she will look disloyal.' He stared at me, for all the world like a petulant child who had been denied his favourite toy. 'Very well,' he said. 'Very well.' I was in disgrace – precisely because he knew I was right. Yet it would always be my decision, not his.

While 'The Book' was busily not happening, my private office team and I were fully occupied with preparations for Sir Edward's eightieth birthday. The birthday itself, on 9 July 1996, coincided with a state visit to the UK by Nelson Mandela, which kept him nicely busy for much of the day and evening, although I did arrange for him to be serenaded on the lawn of Arundells first thing, by a string ensemble from a local girls' grammar school, which was broadcast live on the *Big Breakfast* television show. On the following Saturday, 13 July, there was a gala concert in Salisbury Cathedral, which raised the necessary funds to renovate one of the 'spirelets' on the roof of the cathedral, then, the following week, there were two special dinners. The first was for around sixty people, hosted by John and Norma Major at No. 10 with Her Majesty the Queen the principal guest of honour (I think this was only the third occasion on which she had been to No. 10 as sovereign). The following night there was a dinner for several hundred friends at the Savoy Hotel. Excerpts from some of that night's extraordinary tributes are included elsewhere in this book.

Just five days after the birthday, **John Junor**, with whom he had a long-standing policy of mutual loathing, wrote a particularly vicious attack on him:

'There is one thing that has always puzzled me about Sir Edward Heath . . . How does he come to be so fabulously rich? He certainly did not inherit any family fortune . . . Nor has he ever earned very much . . . Yet he has always lived and acted like a grandee . . . He has a fabulous house within the cloisters of Salisbury Cathedral. Another in Belgravia. He has a superb art collection, including paintings by Sickert, Piper and Augustus John. And he has the lifestyle of a very rich man indeed.

For the benefit of posterity could he not tell us just how he has done it? Or is the answer quite simple? Could it perhaps be through having pursued a policy throughout his life of seldom if ever putting his hand into his own pocket?'[89]

Despite the overwhelming bonhomie of that celebratory month – or possibly because Junor's virulence jarred in so gratuitous and rebarbative a manner with it – **Sir Edward** was incensed by this onslaught. He brooded in Salisbury, then dictated a response:

'In his column on 14th July 1996 Sir John Junor chose the occasion of my eightieth birthday to make an unwarranted series of allegations against me under the heading "How did Sir Ted become loaded?" and then challenged me to answer them. "How does he come to be so fabulously rich?" he asked. I am not and I have never been fabulously rich and no-one else has ever suggested it. ". . . he has always lived and acted like a grandee" he states. For the first twenty years after the end of the War I lived in London in a bed-sitting room following which I lived in a flat costing £12.50 per week until I became Prime Minister and then lived at No. 10 where there were no charges.

"'He became an international yachtsman with a series of boats only a really rich man could afford" he declares, displaying his ignorance. The first *Morning Cloud* cost me £7,500. In it we won the Sydney to Hobart race overall, one of three great ocean races of the world. The Royal Ocean Racing Club covered some of our expenses and I then sold my boat for more than it had cost. I gave up sailing ten years ago.

"'It is true he has written books and gone on lecture tours," he declares, "but none of the books has ever been in the Jeffrey Archer money-making class." I agree that my books are not the rubbish which make Jeffrey Archer money, but John Junor ignores the fact that in the late 1970s I had three serious books, *Sailing*, *Music* and *Travels*, which were all bestsellers, not only in Britain and America, but in other European countries, in Singapore and in translations in Japan and China. "And I cannot believe he has ever received really serious money as a lecturer." It is obvious John Junor does not know what I receive for lectures. Why then should he make the allegations? He is in fact wrong.

'"He has a fabulous house within the cloisters of Salisbury Cathedral. Another in Belgravia." I suppose I must take it as a compliment that everything about me is described as fabulous. He confuses the cloisters inside the Cathedral with the Close, where my house is, outside it. The house I rent in London is a simple two-bedroomed house with rooms for the housekeeper. He praises my "superb art collection", but he has no idea whatever what it has cost me over a spread of forty years to collect drawings and paintings.

'Finally, he comments "he has the lifestyle of a very rich man indeed." This is ignorant nonsense as I am glad to say that we have seen nothing of each other for the last twenty years. "For the benefit of posterity," John Junor goes on to ask, "just how has he done it?" Yes, by continuous hard work, by savings and by avoiding every form of extravagance. "Or is the answer quite simple?" he continues. "Could it perhaps be through having pursued a policy throughout his life of seldom if ever putting his hand into his own pocket?" What a filthy insinuation to suggest that I have lived by begging, borrowing or stealing from other people. Yes, a filthy allegation but typical of John Junor.'

The letter was never sent. Sir Edward had heeded his own advice to others and resisted the temptation to become drawn into a public row with his detractors. For once I was not involved.

The next year (1996–1997) was gruelling. We were in the dying months of the Parliament elected in 1992 and there was an unmistakable whiff of the grave about the Major Government, whose majority in the Commons had dwindled, through single figures, to nothing. Sir Edward – for so long the absentee landlord, dropping in to Westminster infrequently, to deliver himself of major utterances on matters of great import – sometimes provided the vote that kept John Major in office. In September 1996, he was thoroughly dismayed by the Government's weakness on Europe, so there was nothing I could do to dissuade him from co-signing, along with Leon Brittan, Peter Carrington, Geoffrey Howe, Douglas Hurd and Willie Whitelaw, a letter to the *Independent*, marking the fiftieth anniversary of Winston Churchill's famous speech in Zurich about European cooperation. There was no intention to undermine John Major. *Au contraire*. The 'grandees' were seeking to shore up his position against the onslaught from the Euro-sceptics that was beginning to turn the party into an unelectable pandemonium:

'We believe that active British involvement in a strong European Union offers our country its surest guarantee of continued influence and prosperity in the world. From Washington to Tokyo, Britain's political voice counts because we are central to, not detached from, the interests of our continent . . . We have to find the confidence, as a nation and as a people, to make a success of our European destiny. The British instinct is to lead, not walk away. Our greatest patriots have never been little Englanders . . . For us now to rule out British membership of a single currency would be to betray our national interest. To countenance withdrawal from the European Union would be to court disaster. To commit ourselves, by contrast, to a positive role in the leadership of Europe is the most fitting tribute we can pay to Churchill's Zurich vision.'[90]

During the party conference Sir Edward warned that, whilst the sceptics would never relent in their demands, neither would they win the concessions on policy they wanted: 'They can't possibly change that, so the divisions with these people will remain.' During one debate on Europe, an anonymous note was brought in to him in the Commons chamber. Scrawled across it were the words 'Mr Heath for Prime Minister'. It came to the office with his addition: 'I agree.' He had been re-adopted to contest his Bexley seat again, but enthusiasm locally was growing subdued and, for one awful moment it seemed we might not have to nurse him through his fourteenth electoral battle after all. On 25 February 1997, the constituency chairman, Howard Ruse, wrote to him in the wake of a *Newsnight* interview in which he had said: 'There was a crisis in Tiananmen Square after a month in which civil authority had been defied. And they took action about it. . .' Then he began a new point, as was his custom, with the rather old-fashioned words – used as a form of breath mark by him – 'Very well. . .'

Many people had been 'deeply offended,' warned Ruse: 'I cannot recall you having been so isolated before, within our Party.' Ruse was under formidable pressure within the association and it was to his credit that he never buckled, as a difficult election approached. 'I must advise you . . . that many of your supporters simply cannot understand why you have chosen such a sensitive time as this, with just a few weeks before the General Election campaign, to be so outspoken and controversial and to outrage so many of those whom you will be asking to vote for you.' A few days later there was a 'High Noon' meeting in Sidcup between Sir Edward and the officers of the association. I did not attend, but I can well imagine how he used sheer force of personality to crush any putative rebellion. He must have sensed, however, that his days as their candidate were now numbered. Some weeks later that same interview caused us more pain and difficulty, when there was a wilful misrepresentation of his words in several newspapers, eliding his two discrete sentences together and claiming he had said the Chinese authorities 'took action about it very well'. That interview was not his finest hour, but the slur against him was as unfair as it was crude: although he could be selectively blind to the shortcomings of the Chinese regime, he had been devastated by the events at Tiananmen and it was clear this was a deliberate, conscious and vicious attack on him. The press refused to recant. It was my first – but far from my last – experience of the limitations of the self-regulatory system for the press.

Although no one (of course) dared to talk openly of this being the old warrior's last campaign, the general election campaign of 1997 felt like the end of an era. In the months before the campaign, he was uneasy. He knew perfectly well he could not be wholly immune from the unfavourable national tide. He had gained Bexley in 1950 by just 133 votes – helped by the intervention of a Communist candidate – and he had never, quite, turned it into an unassailably safe seat. So, just as his health was beginning to fail and he found himself, once again, increasingly out of sympathy with his fellow Conservatives, he knew he had a fight on his hands.

So, on the cusp of his eighty-first birthday, with a failing as well as a sinking heart, Sir Edward Heath KG MBE embarked upon his fourteenth consecutive general election campaign in Bexley. He agreed to spend several days a week in the constituency in the four weeks of the campaign and a rag-tag gang of former private secretaries, political colleagues and admirers was assembled, to augment the local support, which was vigorously orchestrated by his agent, Barry Fowler. It all felt like a throwback to happier times – the final foray of a once-great but now seriously denuded army. Despite the changed times, he insisted that certain traditions would be maintained. Despite his difficulties walking, he wanted to get out and meet people. So, on a Saturday morning, the car would deposit him on a shopping street and he would make off, in an extremely stately fashion, to 'press the flesh'. The car and detective would shadow him discreetly, ready to whisk him away when it got too much for him.

He had not had to campaign like this since the 1970s. We took him and Douglas Hurd to a large supermarket. He stood at the threshold and seemed momentarily lost for words. 'So much choice . . .' he began, then trudged desultorily into the aisles, in the hope of meeting some voters. In a smaller store, a dear lady, evidently unaware his hearing was failing him, pounced with zeal. She introduced herself. He didn't catch a word of it over the background din, but I gleaned she was the widow of a Bexley resident he had known well and who had died unexpectedly since she had last seen her MP. She persisted. 'You used to come to our house and play piano duets together,' she said, in a voice that would have carried to Erith. With great emphasis she repeated her husband's name. Sir Edward's eyes lit up with belated recognition. 'Ah yes,' he said with a broad grin. 'And how is he?'

The prospect for witnessing the old warhorse canter round the course one more time was too much to resist for the media. We had regular visits from television news and a very pleasant morning with that excellent journalist, **Jonathan Freedland**, who wrote an excellent account in the *Guardian* of his visit:

'The octogenarian parliamentarian is not pushing himself too hard. A gentle stroll up the High Street, a few handshakes, then a coffee break followed by a long pub lunch with his party workers. To save energy, Sir Edward does his door-to-door canvassing by car. The candidate only gets out when one of his younger volunteers finds a waverer worth meeting; otherwise he stays tucked up on the back seat.

'Still, he is prone to lapse into curmudgeon mode. "Come on, take hold of the situation" he tells one hapless aide* who has failed to nab a corner table in the pub. And don't get him on to the sleaze troubles bedevilling

---

* Anthony Staddon and I both lay claim to being this 'hapless aide'.

today's Tory party: "Neil Hamilton is an absolute shit," he says. But he is happy to send up his own reputation for pomposity . . .

'But the poignancy of the Heath situation is not purely personal. Watch him walk down the High Street, either ignored or greeted with zero formality – "Hello, Ted mate!" – and it's hard to believe one is looking at a former prime minister. No way Messrs Carter, Reagan or Ford would be treated so casually. "If I go to any other country in the world, I'm still called Prime Minister, the same way a president is always called Mr President," he muses.'[91]

Sir Edward's mood in the run-up to the campaign had not lightened when he learned that his former economic adviser, Brian Reading, had agreed to stand against him on behalf of Sir James Goldsmith's virulently anti-EU 'Referendum Party'. The Referendum campaign literature in Bexley did not deal in light and shade. Above **Brian Reading's** signature appeared the following:

'Joining the single currency is a step on to a bus, made in Maastricht, driven by Brussels, destination the Fourth Reich. Sir Edward Heath wants to push us on. The Lib-Dems wish us to board voluntarily. Labour wants on, but dare not say so. In Old Bexley and Sidcup I alone say, "let the bus leave without us".'

Heath regarded Brian's decision to run as an act of gross disloyalty. I liked Brian, having met him before, at an event in Jersey in September 1995. When my path first crossed his during the 1997 campaign, he told me that he had accepted the invitation to stand because, had he not, there would have been far more animus in the Bexley campaign and 'I didn't want to see Ted get hurt'. I tried to intercede with Heath and explain Brian's motives. He swatted me away. In **Brian Reading's** own account of that campaign, he says:

'I had no angst against Heath, just disagreed over Europe. I campaigned for just three weeks, going round in a van with a loud speaker on top – "Save the Pound, Vote Reading". To my horror the Referendum Campaign launched a vitriolic personal attack on Heath. I had no hand in this.

I therefore made a speech addressing the accusation that Heath had lied when taking us into the then European Economic Community.'

Anyone hoping the speech would denounce his old boss as a serial mendicant was, however, doomed to disappointment, as **Brian** confirmed again in 2016:

'It was my intention to disappoint those baying for Ted's blood . . . I don't have a copy of the speech because I never "write" a speech for myself, I do it in my mind beforehand. I remember exactly what I said, but not word perfect. I was appalled to discover how Goldsmith directed the campaign personally against Ted. I would never have stood had I known that in advance. There is a genuine case against EU membership because of the way it has developed. Ted's position was totally understandable given his experience and generation. He was not dishonest, but to my mind mistaken given the way things developed. To impugn an opponent because you disagree with him is reprehensible. Ted had many faults, but he was genuine.'

Brian's earlier account of the campaign then continues the story:

'Polling day came and I attended the count with my agent. Candidates and agents were allocated a room in which to wait and watch TV. Heath was ensconced with security personnel outside. When my agent attempted to enter he was told to "bugger off". He went to the Returning Officer who put the security man in his place. We joined Heath in the candidates' room. He was sitting in an armchair with a bottle of Malt Scotch and regularly replenishing his glass. He ignored me completely and went on drinking and watching the results on TV. So I ignored him. It would have been graceful if he had acknowledged that I had fought a clean campaign and offered me a drink. But then I had sinned by opposing him and he bore grudges.'

At the count, Sir Edward's mood grew more and more gloomy. 'My poor party,' he muttered. My colleague **Anthony Staddon** remembers the scene well:

'During election night itself, EH spent most of it immersed in the TV coverage via a small portable television in the polling station, watching impassively as Conservative MP after Conservative MP lost their seats. He took no enjoyment in this – in fact I think he was in shock. He was no fan of Michael Portillo, but I watched him closely as the result of his defeat was announced. There was very little emotion and he certainly took no enjoyment from Portillo's humiliation. He still cared very deeply about the Conservative Party and took no pleasure that his warnings had come to pass.'

At last the local count was complete – he was in, by 3,569 votes. Anthony Staddon broke the news, apologising for the close result. He shrugged: 'In the context of this evening, it's a minor triumph.' Up on the platform for the declaration, Heath talked animatedly to the Liberal Democrat and made a great (and rather rude) show of not acknowledging Brian Reading's existence in any way.

My gut feeling was that he had pretty much a neutral effect in the local campaign. For every constituent who voted for him out of habit, loyalty or gratitude, I sensed there was another who had simply had enough of him, of the rareness of his appearances, of his dogged reluctance to set up home locally and of his penchant for isolating himself politically. Others disagree. I know **Anthony Staddon**, who worked harder on that campaign than anyone, believes any other candidate would have lost Bexley for the Tories in 1997:

'Perhaps some people didn't vote for him because of his age and views on Europe (although these issues rarely came up on the doorstep), but my suspicion is his personal vote carried him through and it is worth noting that the neighbouring constituency fell to the Labour Party.'

He may well be right. Certainly, when people did feel personal loyalty, it was spontaneous, immoderate and a wonder to behold. Furthermore, his warnings about the direction of the Conservative Party, which had seemed both bitter and Cassandra-like, had now turned out to be just Cassandra-like: disbelieved at the time, but subsequently coming to pass. The legacy of the

Thatcher years was a party that had abandoned its supposed 'secret weapons': cohesion and loyalty.

We had got through, just; and what was left of the team gathered to wish Sir Edward good night. We sat and chatted for a while, then he stood up to go home, involuntarily farting very loudly in the face of one of his volunteers, Jay Dossetter, a young office intern from Kent, who was cured at a stroke of any lingering desire for further political entanglements. As Anthony Staddon comments: 'it cleared the room if I recall and was as good as any other post-election analysis of the Conservative Party's performance.'

CHAPTER FIVE

Final years (1997–2005)

F ive days after the 1997 general election, on Tuesday 6 May, Sir Edward and I attended a large literary dinner, to launch the second edition of his book *Music: A Joy for Life*. It was another occasion when the drinks flowed rather too freely and not much was achieved until two days later, when we transferred the private office back out of his house at Wilton Street and into the Palace of Westminster, where we soon learned everything was changed. Six members of the Major cabinet had lost their seats, including two of my own friends and mentors, Roger Freeman and Tony Newton. Gone too was David Hunt, my former boss. Sir Edward was no longer required to attend inconvenient division after inconvenient division. There were no close votes in the House of Commons until after 2001. The parliamentary Conservative Party – cut in twain and in a state of shock and grief – had now to conduct a leadership election.

Once it became clear Ken Clarke would run, I asked Sir Edward permission to help on his campaign. He agreed at once: 'Of course. We must save the party.' I took joint charge of Ken's media appearances.

Throughout that campaign, Ken was way ahead of his rivals in the polls – both amongst the general electorate and amongst remaining Tory supporters – and also in the internal party soundings that were taken, but his views on Europe were unacceptable to a majority of the 'rump' parliamentary party. He even tried to step down at the very end of the campaign, in the hope Michael Heseltine would prove to be a match-winning substitute, but he didn't; and he lost.

On that fateful afternoon, Sir Edward was sitting at the dining table in Wilton Street, contemplating what he always termed 'the work' – in other words, sifting through the increasingly thin gruel of mail that had arrived that day in the office. In truth, he was extemporising before, he hoped, he would travel the short distance to Central Office, to congratulate Ken Clarke as the newly elected party leader. The team were outside, listening to the BBC *PM* programme on the car radio, which would carry the announcement of the leadership contest live from just down the road at Westminster. After the result was declared, one went in and enquired whether Sir Edward was now ready to go and greet his new leader, Mr Hague. Silence, then a loud groan, followed by: 'My poor party! My poor party! I need a large Glenmorangie!' That Glenmorangie was the first of many. He then went straight home to Salisbury, in a state of despair.

Within ten days of that shared disappointment, I travelled to Hong Kong with Sir Edward for the handover to the Chinese on 1 July 1997, on a specially converted British Airways 747 that also had HRH the Prince of Wales on board, together with a variety of other high-profile guests. Once we arrived, we were left to our own devices, cared for not by the over-stretched government officials, but by my predecessors Peter Batey and Richard Burn. During a quiet morning the day before the handover ceremony, I slipped away to a Tower Records outlet on the other side of the island. In his book on music, Sir Edward had singled out, from a life-time of concert-going, one particular musical occasion that he had found to be the most singular and moving – a performance of Beethoven's *Violin Concerto in D* by Yehudi Menuhin and the Moscow Philharmonic Orchestra conducted by David Oistrakh. To my astonishment, while browsing in that shop I discovered a BBC Legends CD, which appeared to contain a recording of that very concert – at the Albert Hall in September 1963, when Menuhin and the Oistrakhs ("King David and Prince Igor") had alternated violin-playing and conducting duties. I bought it and, on my return to the hotel, went to his room. Richard Burn and Peter Batey were there, but he appeared to be fast asleep in his armchair. 'Oh no,' said Richard, amused. 'He's not really asleep – he hears every word you say,' whereupon he duly stirred, as though in assent. I roused him gently and handed him the CD with my compliments and a mixture of excitement and trepidation. He put on his spectacles and looked closely at it, seemingly as sceptical as I had been. Then he looked at me, suddenly moved. There was a hint of a tear in his eye. 'Oh,' he said, suddenly fully awake. 'Thank you. Thank you. I never, ever thought I would be able to hear this again.'

Not very helpfully, that same day, Sir Edward told a journalist from *Agence France Presse* that William Hague as party leader was going to prove an unmitigated disaster : 'A tragedy for the party. He's got no ideas, no experience and no hope.' These comments were widely reported. An anguished message arrived from the office in London. Were they to issue a denial? Playing the sulky child to perfection, Sir Edward confessed to having uttered those words, but cited supposed mitigation: 'The conversation was off the record.' I sighed. He glared. Although the damage was done, I went through the motions of trying to establish the fault of AFP in the matter. The journalist denied there had ever been any talk of 'off the record'. With well practised Gallic indignation, he claimed we were impugning his good name. William Hague was there in Hong Kong with us and I spent much of the flight home chatting with him and his wife Ffion, an old friend from my time in the Welsh Office. I didn't even feel the need to apologise. They understood.

The Tory meltdown had immediate and pernicious consequences for Sir Edward. True, he no longer had to come and vote in the Commons, but his status was now confined to that of 'Father of the House'. Most of the friends of 'Father Ted' had died or retired and he felt increasingly marginal to the Commons, to the party and to Westminster in general. He simply crossed the floor of the House and sat in the mirror image of the seat he had occupied since 1979, under the gangway. His neighbours now were not Tories at all, but Paddy Ashdown and his Liberal Democrats; and no one really cared much what he said, unless it was something wilfully destructive on a quiet news day (as in Hong Kong). My more immediate concern, however, was his memoirs. For two years a team had been employed to produce them and all we had to show for it was a handful of rudimentary drafts – and box upon box of photocopied documents. Meanwhile, deals worth around £600,000 had been signed – money he would have to repay unless a book was produced.

When the Ken Clarke leadership campaign was at its most stressful and frantic, I had received an urgent message to call Sir Edward. He was terse. 'Charles de Lisle has resigned,' he informed me. 'You had better think about what we do next.' It seems like a comical understatement, but the thought of producing a memoir really did present him with some profound difficulties. After he lost the leadership in 1975, he produced three books in three years, using the same method for all three. One of a small pool of secretarially trained assistants would attend upon him and, drawing upon his archive, he would dictate first-hand accounts of his adventures.* These would be typed up, manually corrected and submitted to the publishers. The true Heath dripped off every page. There was to have been a fourth book in this series, with the provisional title *The Future*; the kind of 'crystal ball' tome about the future that has most sane people running for cover. Fortunately it never emerged. At one point, however, in the very early 1980s, he signed a contract with George Weidenfeld, to produce a comprehensive memoir. Weidenfeld was said to have offered an advance of £350,000. He also sold on serialisation rights. Some time later, Michael Trend, son of one-time cabinet secretary Burke Trend and himself a future Tory MP, was employed to work on the book. His endeavours would be hampered by two main factors.

First of all, the Heath papers were not in effective or accessible storage. His then sole residence in Wilton Street was not remotely large enough to accommodate them all, so they were stored in the basement of a London hotel, where it was all but impossible to consult them. There was also no reliable index. Even more grievously, they were then damaged in a major flood. Many irreplaceable documents from the 1940s, 1950s and 1960s were lost in this way, including some that had provided the necessary material for the earlier books. The second, seemingly insuperable, problem was Heath's own state of mind. As this book should have demonstrated, well into the 1980s, he saw himself as a man with an important future contribution to make, as well as a past, and behaved accordingly. That deeply held belief proved to be wholly incompatible with writing a memoir. Perhaps he saw memoirs as things written by retired people, or perhaps he was simply unwilling to

---

* One of these assistants, Caroline Bowis (whom Heath greatly liked and respected), returned in 1997 to become his constituency secretary.

draw a final line, to sign off the proofs of his life, but the work ethos that had rapidly generated literary material in the 1970s – in the middle of a hectic schedule – had crumbled away in the much less busy man of later years. Michael Trend simply became the first of many who tried and failed to elicit a memoir out of Edward Heath. Nonetheless, if anyone proposed to write a biography about him – or interview him about a subject he found dull – he had a ready and convenient excuse for turning down their proposals: 'I shall say everything I have to say in my memoirs.'

By 1986 there was much speculation about the elusive tome. The putative author would merely confirm, 'there's no fixed publication date'[1] and tell people he was working hard on the project. In 1992, it was reported that, over a decade after signing the deal with Weidenfeld, he did now intend to begin serious work on his memoirs. In the 'Pendennis' column, Richard Brooks reported that the first four chapters had been drafted (though they needed 'beefing up', one of his staff had confessed). 'Part of Heath's problem is that he is somewhat averse to popping along to the Cabinet Office and other places where records are kept . . . He would have far preferred that the Cabinet Office came to him at his delightful house in Salisbury.'[2] This 'Mohammed' had no intention of rousing himself to visit that 'Mountain'. In 1997, supposedly two years into the serious process of writing, Heath struck a positive note: 'I am now at a stage of life when I can look back at the whole period with good judgement . . . many people, when they leave office, are so involved that their conclusions are often invalid.'[3] Unfortunately, the reality was that he was stubbornly refusing to engage, even though he was now paying four full-time staff on the book. He appeared to be deluding himself about his own intentions.

Much sifting of papers had taken place and research had been undertaken, but hardly any new material had been written. What had been written was about his early life and career and, although the quality was variable, it did generally bear the Heath imprimatur. Beyond that, he had simply refused to cooperate. At some level, I think, he believed he had done enough to fend off the importunate, incessant inquiries of those who wanted the book written through the very public gesture of employing a team; then he had carried on much as normal, rarely making himself available to them. One of the latest team, Richard Weight, now lived in Salisbury and took charge of wading through the mass of papers accumulated during the previous two years. The task was a dire one, leavened only by gallows humour – and Sir Edward himself was utterly demoralised and depressed by it all – the lowest I ever saw him. 'There's nothing,' he lamented. 'Nothing at all.'

I soon began to despair and it was during this time that I began to consult closely with (and rely greatly upon) Robert Armstrong. In consultation with him, I soon began to talk directly to Sir Edward's agent, the doyen (now as then) of London literary agents Michael Sissons; and also to Roland Philipps, his engaging publisher at Hodder & Stoughton, with whom he now had a contract to write the book. We all agreed the book must not be 'written by committee': it was being marketed as an autobiography, so there must be one voice and, so far as possible, that should discernibly be that of the supposed author. Neither Michael nor Roland left me in any doubt about the need for serious and rapid progress and I reported this back at the end of July 1996. For the next few weeks we sought in vain for a writer to take charge of this project and 'get a grip'. Numerous names were suggested but in the end all rejected, but some tangible order was being imposed upon the project. 'I hope you are at least enjoying some of this,' I said to him on one occasion. 'I am hating it,' he replied, without the flicker of a smile.

By the last week of August I was at the end of my tether. It was then that a friend suggested I take the job on myself. A penny dropped in my mind: my employer invariably preferred the tried and trusted and he would submit himself only to the imprecations of someone who had yet to establish his own, independent reputation. Just as importantly, not only did I already know him, his ways and his history, I had already produced a book with him, the revised version of *Music*. I set out my terms, which he accepted: I would need complete executive control over the project, I was to set aside all my other functions and I would need to draw fully upon the time of Anthony, who would be my No. 2. Once Heath had agreed to everything, he seemed as though an enormous burden had been lifted from him. We went out to a local hostelry, got pissed and then I worked late on a woeful draft about the woeful state of the UK economy in 1972.

My new role gave me my first opportunity to dig deeply into the life of my employer – and, indeed, to spend more time with him, both literally with the old man and figuratively with his younger self, as I pored over the stations of his life. I became a much more frequent attendee at his legendary Sunday lunches in Salisbury – it was very convenient to combine the conveying of papers between the office, my home and the Salisbury archive with a social occasion. And for Sir Edward it wasn't only about ensuring the work continued to progress over a weekend; I was all too well aware that he was lonely and relished having someone down there to keep him company.

It was that experience – acting as his amanuensis, stirring a range of what might be termed 'widely sourced' ingredients into a single literary soup – that opened up Edward Heath for me. I knew the contemporary curmudgeon all too well, but now I became acquainted with Teddy Heath, grammar-school boy and Oxford organ scholar. I learned of how, having seen Franco and Hitler at work with his own eyes, he defied Disraeli's dictum by following his conscience and opposing his party over appeasement in the 1930s; of how, like Shakespeare's Coriolanus,* he fought bravely for his people in war, but baulked at pandering and bragging to them, to make them love him for his exploits; of how musical and bookish 'Teddy' became 'Ted', the ruthlessly ambitious, relentless, tireless canvasser of Bexley. We spoke of Suez, of how, appalled, he was presented by a trembling and indignant Cabinet Secretary with the British copy of the Sèvres Protocol, whose existence his long-time hero Anthony Eden had mendaciously denied in Parliament, immediately prior to destroying it.

Anthony Staddon also recalls the momentous process of dragging Heath's memoirs out of him:

'We had to spend more time in Salisbury which normally meant taking the morning train from London for some time with EH (dictation, asking questions on various parts of the book) after he had read through his post. He would then break for lunch (to which we would be invited) before retiring for a brief nap and then starting again in the afternoon. His silences were legendary and rather disconcerting at first: I once timed one period of

---

* Brutus on Coriolanus (Act 2, Scene 1): 'I heard him swear, were he to stand for consul, never would he appear I' the market-place nor on him put the napless vesture of humility; nor showing, as the manner is, his wounds to the people, beg their stinking breaths.'

silence as long as six minutes and there was another time when I mumbled some excuse and left the room and returned ten minutes later only to find him as impassive as before. But you soon learned this was his way. By late afternoon he would normally have had enough and would start making noises about us having to take the train back to London.'

On Friday 27 February 1998, the first full draft was completed. It changed a great deal in the months that followed, but that was a true 'champagne moment'. Not long after, on 10 April 1998, the Good Friday Agreement was concluded. I was staying with Robert Armstrong in the West Country, working through our editor's comments. Together, we drafted a suitably statesmanlike response in Sir Edward's name and issued it: 'As Prime Minister at the time of the Sunningdale Agreement nearly twenty-five years ago, I recognise the magnitude of the achievement which this agreement represents, and I congratulate the two Prime Ministers and the leaders of the political parties in Northern Ireland on the statesmanship and deter-mination which have made that achievement possible.' Northern Ireland still faced an uncertain future, but the memoirs were now definitely on the home straight.

When Michael Jones of the *Sunday Times* went down to Salisbury in August 1998 to interview Sir Edward, to be published in conjunction with the newspaper's serialisation of the memoirs, he found his subject in expansive mode – in more than one sense. During their two-hour conversation, an entire bottle of champagne was downed. This was followed by a substan-tial dinner in a nearby village, with more wine, then multiple whiskies in a nearby pub, where one of the locals talked Mozart with Sir Edward. 'What a constitution,' wrote an admiring Jones afterwards.

The section of the book dealing with Margaret Thatcher's time as leader was evidently problematic for him – and turned out to be both the only chap-ter I wrote entirely single-handedly, and also the only one on which we did not receive a single comment from Sir Edward. I don't know if he ever even read this chapter, but I did everything I could to craft in it a positive, rational, one-nation critique of Mrs Thatcher and her administration, attempting to capture what I believed Sir Edward, from his unique vantage point during those acrimonious times, perhaps could and *should* have said – eschewing personal rancour and, instead, positing a rational, palatable and 'one-nation' alternative to Thatcherism.

As the date of publication loomed, local difficulties arose. One story of particular interest had been included in the book, as **Robert Armstrong** recalls:

'Late in the process [Heath] told us that when he was in command of a Royal Artillery detachment in Hanover in September 1945 he had been obliged to carry out the execution by firing squad of a Polish soldier in the British Army who had been found guilty by a court martial and condemned to death. Edward Heath said that it was this experience that had made him a supporter of the abolition of capital punishment. This story was duly included in the autobiography.

'When the book was published Nigel West said this story could not be true: there had been no executions by firing squad after the end of the war in Europe in May 1945. I did not think that Edward Heath would have made up this story: he was not that kind of man. So I made inquiries at the Ministry of Defence. Their records showed that a Polish soldier had been executed by a Royal Artillery firing squad in Hanover in September 1945. They did not show who commanded the firing squad; but that evidence convinced me that Edward Heath had been telling us the truth.'

The story about the firing squad appeared in the *Evening Standard* before the *Sunday Times* (which had paid a sum in the region of £200,000 for exclusive serialisation rights) had an opportunity to publish it. The latter newspaper was not amused. Sir Edward also found himself drawn into a civil case between the *Sunday Times* and Weidenfeld & Nicolson, over a pre-existing deal for serialisation. Both of these matters were essentially financial and possible to resolve. More seriously, journalists (one in particular, from the BBC) who had been putting together a story in connection with the publication of the memoirs had been down to the constituency – and all was not well there. There had been a most unhappy meeting of the Association's Executive Council on 1 July and, on 19 September, local party chairman Howard Ruse wrote to Sir Edward, after public discord between him and William Hague about the Euro. On the substance of the Euro issue, most Conservatives inclined to Hague, but loyalty to Sir Edward ran deeply. 'Although there were no formal resolutions made,' wrote Ruse, 'in my judgement the meeting generally agreed that it is not helpful to the recovery of the Party to continually be seen as so fundamentally divided.' Mischievously timed to coincide with the book launch, a BBC report claimed Sir Edward was under pressure to step down in Bexley. As a consequence, even on the day of the book launch itself, I was engaged in furious 'fire-fighting'. Somehow, that never carried over into the launch itself, which was overwhelmingly a joyous occasion, attended by the 'Great and Good' and also by many people who had contributed to the writing of the book over the years. Sir Edward astonished and delighted us all with his words, delivered from the staircase above us: 'Everybody here has been waiting twenty-five years for this day and I'm delighted that John Major, my successor – or rather my successor but one – is here!' Then to a cheer of relief and surprise he proclaimed: 'The Sulk is Over!'

On the evening of Wednesday 26 May 1999 the German Ambassador hosted a dinner in honour of Sir Edward, just as the three-month NATO bombing campaign against the residual Yugoslavia, which ended the Kosovo war, was coming to its conclusion. Alarm bells soon rang in my head as soon as Sir Edward began his speech after dinner – I had heard him opine on this topic before – but there was nothing I could do to stop this juggernaut. 'These people know no history. What they forget . . .' he began. My stomach tensed. I knew what was coming. '. . . is that in World War One the Serbs were our allies . . .' A little part of me died. '. . . in World War Two, the Serbs were our allies . . .' This was not the first time, nor the last, when the diplomatic skills of Edward Heath were found wanting.

The aged Heath still drew immense succour from the compliments of his attenuated army of supporters. Once, when he was on BBC *Question Time*, I faxed him a note halfway through telling him how well he was doing. The next day I took the 'work' to Wilton Street for him and we went through it. I was ready to go – or so I thought. 'You must be the most extraordinary person I have ever met,' he ventured. 'Thank you,' I responded, ingenuously. 'I was on *Question Time* last night and you haven't mentioned it once.' I blustered, told him he had done well, asked if the fax arrived OK – and left, chastened. He was over eighty years old; and still so insecure. That insecurity probably explains why he rarely discussed his health or admitted to any weakness. When Robert Vaudry once told William Waldegrave he might cancel an appearance because he had a cold, he was furious – the angriest Vaudry ever saw him. He did, however, until quite a late stage in his life, take a personal physician with him on overseas trips. He also took a close, even morbid, interest in the health of others – as most hypochondriacs do. It was a form of projected hypochondria. Whenever he saw Margaret Thatcher, he would comment, in a carefully calibrated voice that betrayed no emotion whatsoever – neither joy nor pain – that she looked 'dreadful', 'awful' or 'like death'.

On the one occasion when Sir Edward did confess to any feeling of frailty in my presence, I knew at once it must be serious. I was on my last trip to China with him and, after the mandatory visit to Beijing, he decided to attend a garden festival in Kunming, close to the border with Burma, which sits more than 6,000 feet above sea level. A car met us from the plane and we were transported to a splendid new hotel, to be received by the Governor of Yunnan Province. As we left that banqueting suite, Sir Edward asked Peter Batey and me for a private word: 'I feel dreadful,' he said. 'We must leave at the earliest opportunity.' Peter and I were both horrified. He had been at similar – or higher – altitudes before without any ill effects, but this time the altitude had left him gasping uncomfortably for air. He spent the night with a contraption that contained oxygen and relieved his distress – it looked like a balloon with a straw. I only began to believe everything would be alright after all, when he held up the balloon and giggled at it. The earliest possible escape was at lunchtime the following day. To my astonishment, in the morning he gamely asked to undertake a shortened tour of the festival we had come to see. Seemingly at death's door the evening before, he rallied to an extraordinary degree, as he chatted away with our hosts, who had evidently been warned they would be dealing with an invalid. Both Peter and I were more than impressed – we were dumbfounded. What a pro!

In 1999, Hodder & Stoughton decided to publish a paperback version of the memoirs. I sought to convince them that we should add a post-script, especially for this new edition. They were not persuaded, but going through my own archive in preparation for this volume, I found a draft of it that Sir Edward approved. Here is an excerpt from it published for the first time:

'When it came to choosing an appropriate title for this book in the Spring of 1998, my close friends and advisers came up with countless suggestions. None of them seemed to satisfy everyone, and everyone had their own favourite. From the literary reference of *The Heir to Adventure* to an unholy amalgam of Virginia Woolf and Roy Jenkins, *From the Lighthouse*, this debate ploughed on. My own best idea was *The Last Laugh*. Many of my friends liked this very much, my publisher liked it and, I have to confess, throughout everything it remained my own personal favourite. So much had been written about me "sulking in my tent" or being a "bitter" man. This title might have conveyed something of my true view of the world: a little sardonic at times, perhaps, but never I hope jaundiced. In the end, however, "wiser" counsels prevailed. The reviewers, I was told firmly, have the last laugh. It would be foolish to "lead with the chin" in such a way, to tempt fate. Well, the reviewers have now had their laughs and, I am delighted to report, most of them laughed with me, not at me. Perhaps, a year or so on, I am a little older and a little bolder and I hope that this postscript will live up to the mildly provocative title which was denied to the work as a whole.'

When Henrietta Rolston drew up a list of the '10 questions you are most likely to be asked about Sir Edward Heath', right at the top, inevitably, was the question: 'Does he really hate Margaret Thatcher?' By the late 1990s, I think the answer was 'no', but, by the accounts of some of my predecessors, there was definitely a time when the answer may have been 'yes'. Certainly he could never forgive her for what he regarded as an act of treachery, in challenging him for the party leadership in 1975 and wresting it away from him. She had been a loyal member of his cabinet, he would say, and she had gone willingly along with every policy. What was more, she had consistently fought tooth and claw for increased funding for her department, sometimes to the point of jeopardising Tony Barber's plans to get a grip on public expenditure. She had also signed the death warrants to more grammar schools than anyone else in history. This was all true, up to a point, but, in counterpoint, it must be remembered that, to accept Heath's claim that someone 'went along with every policy' is to ignore his brisk, even arrogant, management style, which was hardly one to encourage debate, still less to make anyone feel comfortable expressing a dissident opinion – just think of how he treated Mrs Thatcher in cabinet and Keith Joseph in 1974.

At an emotional rather than rational level, Heath certainly resented Margaret Thatcher. He resented the fact that she had the opportunity to analyse and learn from what went wrong for him in 1970–1974. He resented the advantage she enjoyed, through no judgement or initiative of her own, of facing a divided centre-left in 1983 and 1987, when the SDP/Liberal Alliance took votes predominantly from Labour, whereas, in 1974, the Liberal revival had taken place largely at his expense and that of the Conservative Party. He also found the Falklands conflict, which revived her prospects in 1982, genuinely distasteful and believed a peaceful solution was both possible and preferable. Out of loyalty he stayed his tongue. When she held her course as high interest rates and an over-priced pound painfully ground inflation out of the economy at the cost of three million people unemployed, he did not abase himself before her for her toughness, as others did: he despaired.

Margaret Thatcher's attitude towards Ted Heath is harder to divine. Her challenge to him in 1975 she seemed to regard as an unpleasant neces-sity, caused principally by his obstinacy and his stubborn belief that, having neglected them and taken them for granted for years, he could now bully disaffected back-bench MPs into keeping him as leader. Those friends who warned him to stand down gracefully after the October 1974 election had his best interests at heart. I can hear him even now, accusing them of being 'so weak', when he lacked the self-awareness and necessary, cultivated detach-ment to realise that the game was up for him. As party leader and Prime Minister, Mrs Thatcher did not always handle Heath well and she must have been aware of this. Only rarely – on fewer than half a dozen occasions – did she seek his private counsel or take advantage of his experience. She was also astonishingly insensitive and heavy-handed in her repeated attempts in 1979 to exile him to Washington.

She should also have been totally clear and explicit with him in any offer she wished to make in the Wilton Street meeting in 1975, instead of which she, ironically, in light of the 'Iron Lady' moniker she later assumed, allowed him to deflect her from her purpose and bully her into generalities. I experi-enced his penchant – and his undisputed gift – for doing that myself. It was very disarming and very frustrating. Consequently, he could come away from that meeting fully persuaded that she had offered him nothing at all. Her claim that she was met with monosyllabic hostility is highly credible and, in fairness to her, in the first instance he did comment that, 'in excluding me from the shadow cabinet, Margaret Thatcher has chosen what I believe to be the only wholly honest solution and one which I accept and welcome'. Her letter informing him she didn't want him as foreign secretary was unnecessarily terse and its ill-conceived successor about the job in Washington (Michael Jopling's story was new to me) laid the foundations for a feud. She never handled him well and her oft-attributed remark that, when dealing with him, she felt she was dealing with a woman rather than a man, helps to explain matters: she was far more adept at dealing with men than with women. In the final analysis, though, it was his reputation, not hers, that was sullied by his 'sulk'. After 1997, I sensed any residual animus towards Lady Thatcher drain out of Sir Edward. It was all receding into the middle distance. He would still make quips about 'that woman', but they lacked any sense of genuine savagery or scorn. Even before my time, the subject had become more one for humour than for genuine ill will. For instance, when he heard she had problems with her eyes and required a surgical procedure on them, he commented to Peter Batey: 'Even her eyes can't stand her.' There were a number of nuances and telling details in the memoirs and one I picked up was that, quite instinctively, when we were dealing with the period up to and including 1974, he referred to Margaret Thatcher as 'Margaret', yet, when we moved on to later (and, for him, less happy) times, he always spoke of 'Mrs Thatcher' or 'Lady Thatcher'. After the book had been published, I asked him about this. 'Well of course,' he explained. 'Before 1975 she was a colleague.' Perhaps it was because the party was in such dire straits now and all power and majesty had gone, perhaps the simple freemasonry of the 'Former Prime Ministers Club' had seeped into him – or perhaps he no longer had the energy for it – but I felt it was time to try and organise a rapprochement. Subtly but decisively a line needed to be drawn under one of the most protracted – and certainly the least edifying – political animosities of recent times. Yet there had been no serious, behind-the-scenes attempt to orchestrate a making up.

At the October 1998 Conservative party conference in Bournemouth, the organisers tried something new: instead of having serried ranks of party grandees and 'worker bees' across the platform, they opted for a handful of colourful, low round armchairs into which grandees could sink for the duration of each session. They also enquired whether Sir Edward would share the platform with Mrs Thatcher. I chatted the matter through with Mark Worthington – a former colleague now acting as my opposite number in Lady Thatcher's rather grander private office – and we agreed to try and make this happen. With some qualms, Sir Edward acceded to the request. When the historic morning came, he arrived on time for once, but in a most dyspeptic and disagreeable mood. All the way from the car to the conference centre, he was complaining: 'Have you seen the papers this morning? This used to be a serious party of government. Now all they can write about are those silly, bloody, damned-fool chairs.' I steered him into the Green Room, where Lady Thatcher was already waiting. Her eyes lit up and she bounded towards him. 'Hello, Ted,' she began, warmly. 'How are you? What ever do you think of those *ghastly* chairs?' He paused for a moment and, with an entirely straight face, shrugged his shoulders and answered: 'Oh, I rather like them.' Deflated, Lady Thatcher went to get a cup of coffee. I caught a twinkle in Sir Edward's eye. The rapprochement had some way to run, but it had begun. A mass of press photographers crowded around the two of them when they were on the platform together. One caught a hilarious moment when they both surreptitiously consulted their watches, at precisely the same moment. It made the cover of *Private Eye*.

A more overt sign of a thaw came when Sir Edward attended the grandly titled (and enormous) International Free Enterprise Dinner on 20 April 1999, held to mark the twentieth anniversary of Mrs Thatcher becoming Prime Minister. I attended too and we were both taken aback when, in her remarks, **Lady Thatcher** referred to 'Ted' by name. Her words were slightly double edged, in that she still focused not on the man or his (and, by implication, her) record in office between 1970–1974, but upon the 1970 manifesto. Despite ending on a somewhat jejune pun, however, this section from her speech was good-natured in tone and it was treated in the press as a tentative olive branch.

'Denis was always direct. When I first told him I intended to seek the Party leadership he said: "Good Lord! You must be mad, but I'll support you all the way." I suspect that Ted Heath, who's done us the great honour of being here tonight, would agree with at least half that statement.

'I would like to take this opportunity publicly to pay tribute to Ted as one of Britain's most forceful and effective Prime Ministers. Go back and read his 1970 manifesto: it's one of the boldest and best the Conservative Party ever produced – a document not for burning.'[4]

A few days later, Sir Edward was a last-minute substitute on the BBC *Any Questions* programme, along with another once-controversial politician, Tony Benn, who was also mellowing, at a dignified but perceptible pace, into a good-natured Vaudevillian. On the subject of Thatcherism and the Conservative Party, both Benn and Max Hastings were fairly excoriating and, when **Sir Edward's** turn came, he could not resist the bait and the joyous laughter of the studio audience speaks for itself. Heath–Thatcher was show business; it was box office; and it was good knockabout material by this stage, with any genuine malice faded and gone:

> 'Well, you won't expect me to share the sentiments we've just heard about a delightful and persuasive lady . . . [laughter and applause] . . . but one point I'd like to make is this – that in British politics, we never go for "name-isms" – we've never had "Baldwinism" or "Churchillism" or "Macmillanism" or "Attleeism" or "Wilsonism" – we just don't talk like that in politics, and it's been a mistake for her admirers to talk all the time about "Thatcherism". What concerns all of us in our party is Conservatism and that's what we've now got to concentrate on. And it's going to mean an enormous amount of hard work. Those . . . who want to press further and further to the right . . . are completely mistaken. What we've got to do is to regain the people we lost at the last general election; and that means producing policies which a large mass of voters will recognise and support again . . . we must get the young people back into our party.'[5]

Sir Edward dextrously combined vanity with self-deprecation when each panel member was asked to name his favourite personal accomplishment; and also to say what he 'would have liked to have had more of in his character':

'Well, I have a very modest approach to these things . . . I'm very proud of the fact I won the Sydney–Hobart race in Australia [applause and cheers] . . . only the second Britisher ever to do that . . . I was very proud of the fact that I conducted the London Symphony Orchestra in 1971 and went on conducting the world's great orchestras . . . and I'm very proud of the fact that I became Prime Minister and took Britain into the European Community [applause] . . . and if I'm asked then, what do I feel that I lacked then, quite frankly, it is the ability to persuade voters to vote the way I want them to vote.'

We were now approaching the fiftieth anniversary of Sir Edward's unbroken tenure as MP for Bexley (though parts of Bexleyheath and Sidcup had wandered in and out of his 'patch'). After the usual consultations, we chose Claridge's as a suitably prestigious venue and I persuaded Sir Edward that, although Peter Carrington was the obvious candidate to make the principal speech, he should also entertain Mrs Thatcher and Sir Denis on his top table, along with the Hagues and Norma Major. A great time was had by all and the following day, a handwritten letter from **Mrs Thatcher** arrived:

'My dear Ted, A very big thank you from Denis and me for the wonderful party to celebrate your fiftieth anniversary as an MP. Peter's speech and your own reply were perfect for such a great occasion. It was one of the happiest evenings I can remember – and a fitting tribute to your achievements and your splendid service to the Party. All good wishes, Yours ever, Margaret.'[6]

To my alarm, not long before I left the Heath office, he decided he wanted to make a speech in the Commons about the controversial question of the EU and fishing. This was not a good wicket for him and, for once, all the talk of speaking without notes was forgone. He asked for a brief, which Anthony Staddon provided. As soon as we saw him stand up to speak, we knew all was not well. His notes were on the green bench behind him. He had neglected to pick them up and, arthritically and with all the lithe flourish of a geriatric tortoise, he turned ponderously to retrieve them. Time slowed. He began to opine. He had not digested or understood the brief. He fumbled and mumbled. He got everything wrong. Anthony went ashen. As soon as this dire performance was over, I sought to reassure my young colleague, whose career had just flashed before his eyes. 'Come with me!' I cried. Off we went, from our eyrie in the Norman Shaw building and into the darkest, most rodent-infested recesses of the Palace of Westminster proper – to the secluded, rarefied *Hansard* room, where dazzlingly bright people turn the sludge of what is uttered in the chamber of the House of Commons into pellucid reported speech. I knocked and entered. 'Is someone doing Ted Heath's speech?' I asked. I did not need to ask. We could see the slumped shoulders across the room; we could sense the confusion and despair. We were ushered across. I have rarely felt more welcome. We talked the scribe through the briefing note; through what Sir Edward had 'meant' to say. Relief all round. Anthony was scandalised but pragmatic. We had saved the day. Sir Edward Heath only ever spoke on one more occasion in the House of Commons, when he bade it goodbye in a valediction that was wisely delivered without any supporting notes from anyone. I didn't hear it, but it reads well. Another triumph for the *Hansard* editors, perhaps?

By 1999, encouraged by my old friend and mentor Roger Freeman, I had found my way onto the Conservative Party's list of approved parliamentary candidates. To my delight, one of the first vacancies for which I applied – to be candidate for Watford – resulted in a call for interview. On the evening of Friday 10 March 2000, after a three-round process, I was selected. I was genuinely surprised but also had a sense of foreboding when, the next day, I called Sir Edward to inform him and he did not congratulate me.

My new second role, as a candidate for a target seat in my own right under the leadership of William ('Keep the Pound') Hague brought immediate strain to our relationship . He didn't like it one bit: 'Sometimes I shall be saying one thing and they will expect you to say something different,' he observed dryly. There was no good answer to that. I was experiencing for myself how his difficulties with communication could alienate those who were closest and most loyal to him. I hardly saw him again. On 13 March 2000 I faxed a message asking for permission to go to lunch with Robin Needham, my indispensable chairman in Watford, the following day. 'Agreed,' came the response, 'it's begun.' I could not fail to discern the ominous tone.

When I went on holiday to Edinburgh that summer, I returned to the office to discover Sir Edward had recruited my successor without forewarning me, or discussing the matter with me in any way. He felt his various gloomy and disapproving remarks during the past six months had given me fair notice. I concluded it wasn't worth the trouble to pursue it. Sir Edward suggested we have lunch to discuss matters. I could think of nothing I would less like to do, but my dad told me to accept. We had a tense lunch together at his favourite restaurant in London, Wilton's in St James's. I ordered gravadlax and Dover sole – the costliest items on the menu – and Sir Edward paid. We parted, if not reconciled, at least reasonably cordially.

The next time I saw him was a few weeks after I was defeated in the 2001 general election, when I was a guest at his eighty-fifth birthday party held on a boat on the Thames. After that I occasionally saw him at a musical event – a Prom or Glyndebourne – but, as his health deteriorated, I was never part of the inner circle who retained a place in his counsels. My successor, and his last Private Secretary, was **James Elder**, who takes up the story:

'As the 2001 General Election approached, there was mounting speculation over the eighty-four year old's future. However, before leaving the House, Sir Edward had one final duty to undertake in his role as Father of the House – the election of the new Speaker following the retirement of Betty Boothroyd. A certain amount of consternation was caused to the Clerk of the House by Sir Edward's new young private secretary, who raised the question of whether, as a Catholic, the leading contender, Michael Martin, was prohibited from holding the office. Further debate occurred as an unprecedented twelve candidates vied for the post, causing Tony Benn to argue for a change in the rules. In the event Sir Edward presided over the last speakership election under the old rules; a mammoth session lasting from 2.30 pm to 9.20 pm. The next day he announced his retirement, ending a fifty-year career in Parliament. Immediately following the announcement the traveller flew off to what was to be his final trip to China.

'Much of the next two years after leaving Parliament were dominated by the Saville Inquiry, ordered by Tony Blair in 1998 to re-inquire into the events of "Bloody Sunday". Sir Edward was determined to defend his reputation and that of the government he led, in the face of serious but wholly unfounded allegations, that there had been a "secret plan" to use lethal force against Republicans. He spent months in preparation for his evidence to the Inquiry, poring over thirty-year-old papers with his private secretary and lawyers; determined to defend his reputation and that of the 1970–74 Government. Indeed the desire for vindication provided a focus for his life now that he had left the Commons. Sadly, he did not live to see himself exonerated by Lord Saville, whose report was published five years after his death.

'Sir Edward's hospitalisation in Salzburg marked the beginning of a two-year slow but steady decline that would end with his death in July 2005. He was taken to the local general hospital in Salzburg, where he found the regime was not quite to his liking, as a stern Austrian matron forced the unwilling patient to take his daily exercise. He was therefore keen to return to the UK and arrangements were made to fly back to London. Unfortunately a TASS spotter noted the medevac plane and the identity of its illustrious passenger, ensuring that the patient faced a media storm on his arrival at the King Edward VII hospital. Although he was still unwell, this return to the public eye was not entirely unwelcome and he was buoyed up with messages of support from political friends and foes alike.

'A short stay in a nursing home in Buckinghamshire was followed by a longer sojourn in Jersey, where he was visited by close friends and sampled the Island's wide array of gourmet restaurants. When he returned to Arundells, the house had been fitted with a stair lift to accommodate his limited mobility. Although absolutely horrified when the idea was first raised, he grew to enjoy the process of descending in style to greet visitors.

'The post-Salzburg routine remained largely the same as before although somewhat scaled down, with regular evening drinks in local pubs punctuated by occasional visits to London for lunch with friends or to attend a concert. From a financial perspective this was less than ideal for the landlords as, in what must have been a real test of his strength of character, he had stopped drinking.

'As 2005 went on, Sir Edward grew weaker and weaker, his horizons narrowed and he took pleasure in the simple things in life. The flowers brought by his private secretary on his bi-weekly visits brought a smile of pleasure. With personal and political business at a standstill, it was his private secretary's sole duty to check on the ducklings in the river at the end of the garden and report back to Sir Edward. His closest friends and associates, knowing the end was in sight, made special efforts to see him "one last time".

'Sir Edward's eighty-ninth birthday was his last appearance. Summoning up his last reserves of strength, he made the immense effort to spend a little time with his guests. In the following days he gradually drifted off. Peter Batey and Richard Burn were recalled to say goodbye: Peter from his Best Man's duties at Mel Stride's wedding and Richard from the Far East. News of his abrupt decline somehow leaked out, so a statement was issued saying the end was near. Sir Edward died on 17 July 2005, surrounded by Lord Armstrong, Stuart Craven, Pamela Finch, Richard Burn, the nurse in attendance and myself.'

Following Sir Edward's death, I 'did some radio and television', but, surprising myself, I did not feel any grief. Was this, I asked myself, because he had lived a long and fulfilled life, or was there more to it? As we discussed this book, my one-time colleague **Henrietta Mayhew** shared with me her diary entry from that day. We did not compare notes then, but our reactions were remarkably similar:

'EH has died. Edward Heath. Today at 7.30 pm. James (Private Secretary) [Elder] rang. I'd heard he was "gravely ill at his home in Salisbury". How strange. It hasn't sunk in yet. I wish I'd been to see him recently and told him to make peace with his Maker. Did he? I wonder.'

I suspect he did make peace with his Maker. He was a regular church-goer, but a low-key one; and he had retained an interest in matters spiritual since his days at Oxford, when he and his friend Freddie Temple would discuss theological matters and then correspond about them with Freddie's uncle, William Temple, then the Archbishop of York and a future (during the Second World War) Archbishop of Canterbury. From an early age, Heath always liked to seek out the best possible advice.

Robert Key stepped down as MP for Salisbury in 2005, just a couple of months before Heath's death. Here he recalls the day of the funeral:

'Ted's Funeral Service in Salisbury Cathedral was grand yet simple. His coffin was taken from Arundells on a traditional two-wheeled hand cart. It was placed on a catafalque draped in purple, under the spire Crossing. The Cathedral was full. The choir and organ were at their glorious best. The Dean, June Osborne, declared "Edward, God has called you to his own," in the traditional words. It was all over for Ted in this world. Now his ashes lie under a simple slab, not ten metres from where his coffin lay and only thirty from the tomb of King John's half-brother, William Longespée, Earl of Salisbury – both of whom, when politics was the art of the possible, signed up to Magna Carta.'

I too attended that funeral service, but not the private 'family' cremation immediately afterwards. The tone in the Cathedral was sombre, but there were few tears; and the theme was rightly of a long life, well lived. In his admirable speech of appreciation, the Bishop of Salisbury, the Rt Revd David Stancliffe, spoke of a 'notable public life, lived with an integrity of purpose and an unswerving resolve', praised Heath's 'vitality of character' and described him (presumably without any fear of contradiction) as 'immensely hospitable, but not given to chit chat':

> 'Ted built bridges between countries and nations, between artists and ordinary people, between east and west, between young and old. No one can doubt his lifelong commitment to Europe, nor for that matter to the unity of the world. In this he exerted his fullest force . . . However well the individual voices of your orchestra or choir play, if they don't play in time, there can be no harmony . . . No sailor worth his salt thinks that you can just set a course, lash the tiller, and go below.'[7]

The final years of Heath's life were punctuated by events held in his honour – from his eightieth and eighty-fifth birthday parties in 1996 and 2001, respectively, to the thirtieth anniversary of his successful 1970 general election campaign. On each occasion – and again after his death – he was the recipient of warm tributes that tell us much about his life.

At the dinner held to mark the thirtieth anniversary of the Heath Government, **Lady Thatcher** made the following generous remarks:

'Tonight it's a privilege to congratulate Ted on his historic triumph in the year 1970, when once more we returned to power. And it was indeed, in 1970, his triumph – a victory against the odds and against the media. And it offers us all hope today, as we face the run-up to the next election. It was a good precedent and we shall strive to repeat it. Perhaps we can recapture the spirit of those days. I remember them well.

'The Government of 1970–74 was elected on a manifesto which in many ways set the tone for the manifesto of 1979. Ted's Government was wholeheartedly committed to the reforms needed to revive Britain, but we faced opponents who cared little for the law, or for the constitution. Had Ted's trade union law succeeded at that time, the country would have been spared many difficulties. That first attempt, upon which Ted so courageously embarked, was not successful, but he paved the way for our later reforms. Ted showed enormous courage and outstanding qualities of leadership in extraordinarily difficult circumstances.

'In the years since, he and I have not always agreed on every little detail, but I was – and I am – proud to have been a member of his Government, from which I learned so much. I cannot tell you everything – I am confined to two minutes, which is difficult for a woman – but I'd like to say, Ted has been one of the Conservative Party's most determined leaders and one of Britain's most innovative Prime Ministers and he is now, without doubt, our most distinguished parliamentarian. That is a record of matchless service to our country.

'Ted, tonight we honour you, and we thank you, for all you did for our party and for our country. I have only one more thing to say, Ted. Keep going: Britain still needs you.'

One senior Conservative who remained much closer to Heath after the traumatic experiences of 1970–1974 was **Ken Clarke**, who, when serving as a notably successful Chancellor of the Exchequer, paid warm tribute to him at his eightieth birthday dinner at the Savoy Hotel, London, on 20 July 1996:

'Ted is probably the last practising politician who has been a dominant figure throughout the entire length of my own political career. He's also one of the first people I can remember following. Our paths first crossed when

I was at Cambridge. He was enjoying himself leading our first attempt to negotiate our way into the European Community, so his life was dominated as ever by European affairs. On that occasion he was speaking extempore to students. It was typically conscientious of him to come back and keep us in touch with events, even while he was negotiating.

'A decade or so later I was one of the last bag-carriers in the government he led, serving as its most junior member – as a Whip, carrying through the European Communities Bill. I remember thinking at the time that this was the apogee of my life's desire, to be a Whip in a government in Westminster. It was a shortish government by the terms of this century, but actually it was historic, and historic because of that one towering achievement that mattered most to Ted; and also to the country.

'So many of the memories I have of Ted single him out from all the other Prime Ministers we've had for a very long time. For instance, every time we had the Opening of Parliament he would host a dinner at which he made his colleagues listen to Martin Neary's hand-picked group performing madrigals once the meal was over. It is sad to report that this is a tradition which has not endured. I enjoyed it enormously but I won't mention which colleagues, looking round, were subjected to agonies by this experience. There'll also never be another Prime Minister who wins the Sydney–Hobart yacht race.

'What Ted has now achieved magnificently is to make that tricky transition to an elder statesman. It wasn't comfortable. Ted is stubborn; Ted is difficult. He's been stubborn and difficult for a very long time, but at least he does now speak to me again, because I no longer work for the Boss that followed. He also now speaks brilliantly in the House. He may be the Father of the House, but he still makes witty, funny, telling speeches.

'It's a pleasure to see him there in the House, below the gangway surrounded by his enemies – not quite surrounded, they're behind him, all of them – and beating off these presumptuous youngsters, fighting the cause he's always lived. I have to say I enjoy seeing him, listening to him, witnessing him fighting off his enemies on that same cause that I've always followed him in, and to which I still attach myself. Ted is a man of principle, he's a man of courage, he's a man we all hold in very great affection, an eighty-year-old Member of Parliament and still the most distinguished statesman in the House.'

Denis Healey knew Heath for almost seventy years. Here is an edited excerpt from his tribute at that Savoy dinner in July 1996:

'Ted has so many friends, of whom I guess 200 are present in this room, from all walks of life. He and I have been friends for sixty years, since I went up to Balliol: both of us from grammar schools, both of us passionately keen on music, but also very devoted to politics; and there's never been anything between us except for Phil Kaiser, who separated us as Chairman of the JCR.

'Ted and I remained very good friends, although politically divided, ever since then. We even wrote to one another after joining the Army, as we both did, as soon as we had the chance when war was declared. We then went into the war together and we both came out as slightly different people. This is a secret which perhaps I am the first to reveal, Ted, that when you were at Balliol we all called you Teddy; when you came back from the war you were Ted and you've remained Ted ever since. And there was a toughness and determination there which, to many of us, was new. I came back from the war determined to fight communism, which I then rightly saw as totalitarian, both at home and abroad. And we've remained good friends ever since, because one of the things we learned, I think, from serving in the last war, is what people of all parties learn: that we are in fact all dependent on one another, that there very much is such a thing as society and our duty as politicians is to strengthen society and not to deny that it exists.'

Another Balliol contemporary, **Roy Jenkins**, was close to Heath both personally and politically, for over sixty years, though he, too, was always in a different political party. One evening the Playhouse Theatre in Salisbury hosted a conversation between Heath and Roy, with BBC journalist Edward Stourton in the chair. Roy began by saying: 'I remember well the first time I met Sir Edward – it was in the Common Room at Balliol.' 'Oh,' replied Heath, deadpan, smiling slightly and shrugging his shoulders, 'I have no recollection of that at all.' The packed house burst into laughter and applause. Roy's idiosyncratic and very telling turn of phrase is much in evidence in his tribute at the eightieth birthday event at the Savoy:

'I think the importance of anecdotes is that they should shine a shaft of light onto some hidden aspect of the subject's character. Well, I don't think there's a great deal that is hidden about Ted. For me, he is more and more a splendid caricature of himself. A bit curmudgeonly, increasingly extremely funny, and above all, massively unmovable by fear or tact or fatal desire to please. For me, he is a great lighthouse which, indifferent to the storms and to the spray, shines out a wholly dependable beam. I haven't had a serious quarrel with him since 1966, which must be a record I think. And that in spite of, should I say, one or two opportunities for ups and downs between us.

'From the time that I first saw him, sixty years ago, leaning against the club fender of the Balliol Junior Common Room after breakfast and reading *The Times* with great seriousness, his appearance has changed quite a lot. But not his beliefs or his essential style. He has always been faithful to a liberal internationalism and to his middle-way, compassionate and interventionist, vision of Conservative duty. He has never been deflected by his party moving further and further away from him. It has saddened him, perhaps irritated him even more, but curiously it has never made him question his party affiliation. He has just declined to notice his isolation. But, if that is not too inappropriate a phrase for the great European, it is a very splendid isolation.'

Another speaker on that star-studded occasion was **Sir Robin Day**, who had frequently been Heath's interlocutor for major television interviews when he was party leader and Prime Minister:

'I am here, really, because it was my privilege – and it was a privilege – to cross swords on television with Ted at critical moments in his career – moments of victory, moments of defeat, moments of triumph, moments of frustration – but he never bore me the slightest ill will. At least that was what I thought, until one warm afternoon at the Königswinter Conference in 1975. Suddenly, when we were discussing democracy and the media, Ted came in to make his first utterance since losing the Tory leadership and he said this: "I just want to explain why it is the political leaders get kicked out of office and lose elections. The reason is that people get bored by seeing the politicians interviewed all the time by the same boring interviewers." He went further, saying: "I have never understood why instead of getting rid of the boring politicians, we don't get rid of the boring . . ." The remainder of his words, I regret to say, were drowned in loud and prolonged applause.

'As Ted enters his ninth decade, this is no time for flippancy. The skies are darkening. A general election seems nearer and nearer and Ted has let it be known that, in Canada, the Conservative Party was reduced to two MPs. What worries Ted about that, if that happens here, is who would be the other one?'

Lord Heseltine also spoke at the Savoy dinner in July 1996:

'Ted is, actually, extraordinarily funny. I have heard him, in the House of Commons, keep his friends and enemies spellbound as he delivers apparently impromptu speeches laced with biting wit on the particular subject of controversy on which he chooses to speak. He never minces his words, he never qualifies his views, but he does it with a charm and a dignity and a humour which is captivating.

'I have had the privilege of attending his wonderful home in Salisbury, which means so much to him, where he is not the Ted we all have known in public life: he is another man, a human man, full of warmth, magnetism, wit and humour, charming and relaxed. It's quite difficult sometimes to square those shafts of humour and that relaxed man with the other sorts of jokes that Ted tells. You have to have been a Junior Minister in his Government to have experienced that piercing wit with which he passed you in the division lobbies of the Commons and said: "I think the speech you made last night was even worse than the one you made the night before."

'I've known Ted for over half his life, for forty-two years, since I had the effrontery as an undergraduate at the University of Oxford to ask him if he would propose me for the candidates' list of the Conservative Party. He agreed and I was immensely flattered. What is not known, is that on the basis of his recommendation I was turned down for the candidates' list of the Conservative Party, but then I've been blackballed for all the best clubs in London.

'Ted was the embodiment of that generation of politicians in my party who recognised that the age of Empire, the triumphant achievement of the Second World War, carried within itself a message which was difficult for the British people to understand and adopt, that a new world was dawning, a new sense of direction, a new opportunity for the British people, and that was called, in a word, Europe. I voted through the Commons in the long nights and the tensions of the 1970s to support Ted as he took us into Europe: the most controversial decision of the second half of the twentieth century, the biggest, the most dramatic, and history will prove, the most important and the most correct.

'I have seen the vilification which has been poured on Ted for that decision, and that is perhaps the nature of politics. You don't get immediate acclaim, you do not get universal acceptance, but what Ted will be singled out for, when petty men have passed away, is that rock-like tenacity with which he has stood for the things he believed, from the end of the Second World War to the eightieth birthday we celebrate today. He is a man of rock, invincible, determined, convinced – the highest principles of public life.

'The idea that Ted, who had fought with such distinction, for the causes in which he believed and to which Denis Healey has referred in the 1930s, who served our country with such courage and bravery in the Second World War, would sell out British interests is a travesty of the truth. He worked for Europe, like the leaders of other European countries, because he believed Britain would stand taller in the world of the next century as part of Europe than it would outside it. It was a total determination that Britain should excel that drove Ted into Europe.'

David Hunt (Lord Hunt of Wirral) also captured these sentiments perfectly, at the eightieth birthday dinner at the Savoy:

'Ted, you have done much to inspire many generations, but I don't know whether you've ever realised how much you did to inspire my generation to becoming involved in politics. Probably more than any other issue, on the question of Europe; because you gave such a clear signal, having learnt the lessons of history. In the second half of this century we had to entrench peace for generations to come by joining together in Europe. And when we all now recognise the important task that lies ahead, to be more positive about our European membership, it is really thanks to you that we're able to fight that battle from the heart of Europe. When I became National Young Conservative Chairman, you actively encouraged us when you were Prime Minister to come in and see you at Number 10. Indeed you gave me a small card with a direct telephone line: you said ring me any time and, to my amazement, I used to get through. We came in and told you our views on politics. I always remember in the corner was this marvellous man taking notes and every now and again you'd say, "Mr Hurd, will you see to that"; and of course Douglas has been seeing to that ever since. And when the history books are written, in the next century and the century after, and the century after that, you are the Prime Minister who will go down in history as perhaps having taken the bravest action of all, in taking us into Europe and entrenching peace for generations to come.'

Douglas Hurd, in a private interview in 2012, summed up Heath very succinctly:

'He was a strange man, but he was an absolutely fascinating man. Once one learned how to talk to him, which took a bit of learning, he was very worthwhile, he really was. I spent a lot of time with him, one way or another, and I never regretted those years. I owed him a lot and I learned a lot. He thoroughly enjoyed being Prime Minister. That's why he was so gloomy when he wasn't. He enjoyed it and didn't realise that it was going wrong. He wasn't conscious of his own failings.'

Lord Hurd's predecessor as head of Heath's office, **John MacGregor**, was close to Heath for over fifty years:

'Ted came from a modest, but hard-working, family background and always supported small businesses and wanted to help others to achieve: home ownership, self-employment and university being the way to a full life. What attracted him to politics was that it encompassed so many aspects of life. He truly walked with kings but never lost the common touch. Throughout his career, he strove to use all his faculties to achieve in whatever field – Oxford, music, politics, sailing. His pre-Thatcherite contribution was vast – and was never acknowledged. The public think those policies were all Margaret, but a hell of a lot of them were Ted.

'He had immense interests and enjoyed conversing and discussing with interesting people. I remember many conversations on overseas trips, to Washington and to Harvard for the Godkin Lectures, where I sat as a fly on the wall trying to remember everything while he was talking to the likes of Henry Kissinger, the American Secretary of State, and many others. He was driven by a strong belief that Britain could do better and so many of the things he believed in and did were Thatcherite – an incentive-driven tax policy, the drive against waste, privatising the Carlisle state brewery. He gave way to the civil service. He was a very good administrator – he was very logical and did his homework very carefully – but he was inspired by politics and a great believer in politics and in Parliament. He enjoyed campaigning. Yes, sometimes he just withdrew, but he always joshed himself out of it. Despite being seen as a lonely man, he really was very good at going around teas and so on. After losing the leadership, Ted could still have used his talents and had a huge influence, but he went into sulks and held grudges, which is a great pity.'

Charles Kennedy once found himself sharing a lift with Heath in Parliament. The former prime minister looked him up and down sternly and said, simply: 'I think I rather approve of you.' When MPs paid their tributes to Heath after he died, Charles made by some margin the most entertaining speech:

'If there is a book to be published in future when perhaps none of us is in this place, it is the book of Sir Edward's running commentary in my right ear of the contributions in advance of my own during Prime

Minister's questions, particularly his insightful running commentary of the contributions from the parliamentary Conservative Party. One particular occasion comes to mind. The Prime Minister had just returned from a much-vaunted third-way summit involving Chancellor Schröder, President Clinton and Prime Minister Jospin. At the beginning of that week the French behaved in a completely unacceptable way – a flouting of European law and a refusal to readmit British beef.

'The then leader of the Conservative Party [William Hague] was on to the issue like a shot at Prime Minister's questions. He had a cavalcade of questions and was making extremely good headway over this difficulty, understandably at the Government's expense. He finished with a great flourish, saying that it was so much for the Prime Minister's "much-vaunted third way", and that as far as his socialist friend Mr Jospin was concerned, it was more a "case of two fingers". He sat down to great cheers and the waving of Order Papers from the more Euro-sceptical sections of the parliamentary Conservative Party. At that point, the sphinx sitting next to me moved imperceptibly. He flicked a disapproving look, leaned over and said, "Such a vulgar little man."'[8]

Heath's latest successor as Prime Minister, **Tony Blair**, was in a jocund mood that day:

'Ted was very blunt in his manner, though once you got to know him he was very kind. I remember that I first met him at a parliamentary reception in the mid-1980s shortly after I became a Member of this House. He said: "Are you an MP?" "Yes," I said. "Which party?" "Labour," I said. "Well, you don't look like it or sound like it," he said. "What's more," he said, "as an Opposition, you're bloody useless." He then proceeded with remarkable insight to tell me exactly what we should have been doing.'[9]

Heath's successor as MP for Old Bexley and Sidcup, **Derek Conway**, had a characteristic tale to tell:

'Michael Brown, who is now a distinguished columnist in *The Independent*, is one former Member who will remember Ted with affection. He used to sit behind Ted when Ted sat in the seat that is currently occupied by [Mr Skinner]. He used to contribute vociferously and frequently to debates, and his comments made Ted more and more irritable. On the day that Michael Brown was appointed a Government Whip, he was wandering down the Library Corridor, when Ted came out of the Smoking Room – as a former Chief Whip, Ted had an enormous affection for the Whips Office. Michael expected Ted to amble by and ignore him, which he usually did, but on this occasion Ted turned around and said: "I see that they have managed to shut you up at last.""[10]

Labour MP **Sir Stuart Bell** also captured that special Heath humour:

'I may be the only Member of the House who shook Ted Heath's hand after the election of 1970. I had flown over from New York to celebrate a great Labour victory and I was sitting in my hotel a few yards from the Albany, where Ted Heath lived . . . I went down and stood among the crowds. As I stood there, finally they parted, a car came up, Ted Heath's hand jutted out of the window and I shook his hand . . . Years later, at the Inter-Parliamentary Union, when I saw Ted Heath and said, "I had my picture taken with you on the day of your election," he looked at me and said, "It didn't do much good, did it?""[11]

Even in his youth, **Gyles Brandreth** was a firm supporter of Heath's, and wryly recalls their first encounter:

'I knew Ted Heath. I liked him and admired him . . . [he] appeared regularly in my schoolboy diary. He was my leader and my kind of hero – even when things weren't going our way . . . Eventually, I got to meet my hero. He had become president of the Oxford Union in 1939. Thirty years later, I was keen to follow his example. But, unfortunately, on the day when I got my first chance to shake my hero's hand I was not feeling very well.

Friday, 28 February 1969
I was feeling sick. At 5.00 pm I was due in the Red Room at New College to be in the line-up for the sherry party to meet the

Rt Hon. Edward Heath, MP, Leader of Her Majesty's Loyal Opposition and my hero. At 4.30 pm I said, 'I'm not well enough, I can't face it.' At 4.45 pm I changed my mind and decided that it was important to go. I ran all the way. I burst through the door of the Red Room and joined the end of the line just as the great man was being brought down it. As he shook my hand and heaved his shoulders, I heaved mine and threw up all over his brown suede shoes. Yes, I met the Leader of the Conservative Party and literally vomited as I did so. I made my excuses and left.

Although he was out of office, as the years went, I continued to record our occasional meetings in my diary:

Tuesday, 28 February 1984

I have just had a cup of tea with Ted Heath. The way he cannot contain his vitriol against Mrs Thatcher is actually comical. He loathes her and assumes others must loathe her, too. I tried to steer him onto other territory – e.g. Broadstairs – but he kept coming back to "that woman". She is "ruining the country". I didn't like to tell him, but most people I meet think she's making it.

'In due course, I became an MP myself and started to see Ted on an almost weekly basis. I liked him, still. Perhaps, I liked him more because people said he was so difficult. He wasn't easy, certainly. You had to get use to his manner, but once you accepted that the conversation wouldn't always flow and that a grunt and a shrug might be all he was in the mood for that day, it was fine. He had a curious charm about him. If he liked you or was secretly amused by something he showed it in his eyes with a smile that was quite disarming.'

One of Heath's favourite journalists (he was not alone in this high opinion) was **Matthew Parris**:

'Ted used to invite a fairly random selection of journalists to dinner at his home in Salisbury when the Conservative Conference was in Bournemouth, or to the River House at Poulton-le-Fylde when in Blackpool. I was for a while one of the favoured ones. I think he had been struck (he often mentioned it) by my escorting his car on my motorbike wearing black leather biking gear, when he visited Derbyshire to speak during one euro-election campaign. As I arrived on one occasion he asked, "Who invited you?"

'I once heard someone ask Ted why Margaret Thatcher seemed to have taken so violently against him. "I cannot say," he replied. "I am not a doctor."'

Several contributors to this book took great pleasure in the company of Heath during what they sensed to be a surprisingly contented 'Indian Summer', in which his personality mellowed considerably. **William Waldegrave**, for example, is perfectly placed to contrast the senescent Heath with the very different man for whom he had worked in 1973–1975, who had laboured under the immense strain of public office at a time of national crisis, albeit when at the height of his powers:

'Edward Heath's premiership has almost been written out of history, at least by Conservatives. The winners write the first draft of history, and when Margaret Thatcher defeated Heath for the leadership of the Conservative Party in 1975 a new, resurgent version of the pre-war right defeated the liberal Conservatism built by Churchill and continued by Macmillan, Butler and the younger generation of Heath, Maudling and Macleod. I doubt that most of the Tory MPs who voted for Thatcher at the time understood quite what they had done; perhaps she did not understand it herself. Heath understood it very well: that understanding was the basis of his unrelenting subsequent bitterness. It was truly the end of an era.

'Heath was full of contradictions and oddities. He could instil passionate loyalty; but he could also be extremely offensive without apparent effort or, sometimes, purpose. He could be obviously vulnerable to hurt; but sometimes he seemed to have the insensitivity of a mule. He could be maddening to work for. "It's not quite right," he might say, handing back a speech you had written, as the speeding three-litre Rover arrived at RAF Northolt, where an aircraft was waiting to fly him to some great rally. The speech had to be issued to the press while he was in the air, so what was one to do?

'I had first seen Heath in action when he spoke to the Political Society at Eton in 1963. He had led the complex negotiations for Britain's entry into the EEC brilliantly, forcing the French to use their weapon of last resort – the veto – a huge defeat for their diplomacy. The meeting at Eton had been a bravura performance, treating the audience of eighteen-year-olds wholly as adults; in command of every detail; clear and witty. Here, I thought, was the modern Conservatism I was looking for. Although he did not replace Iain Macleod in my affections, he was a formidable representative of the progressive party of which I wanted to be a member. My first grown-up political act had been to write to Macleod in support of his opposition to the imposition of controls on Commonwealth immigration; I was a passionate opponent of hanging; I applauded Roy Jenkins's liberalisation of the laws affecting homosexuals; and I thought military action should have been taken against Ian Smith's unilateral declaration of independence in Southern Rhodesia. So, although for reasons of friendship and family ties I had mourned Sir Alec's passing as leader, I had welcomed Heath's election, particularly as Macleod would be at his side.

'Given the hopes I had placed in him, and the reasons for those hopes, it was hardly surprising that I could not allow myself to have any doubts about him, even by 1974. There was something about his unspoken assumption of your loyalty which made you respond. He took it that, if you were there, you were family: you understood, and did not need flattery or thanks; all that was a given. Of course, if he had misjudged, and you had not signed up in this unconditional way, you would see his behaviour as churlish ingratitude. But it was not so. I do not remember him ever thanking or flattering me in person; but he did both, movingly, in a little formal speech to my sister, Susan, doubtless knowing that I would hear of it.

'I think this explains the great mystery of Edward Heath: how did the popular young army officer, the supremely effective chief whip whose care and charm helped to reunite the Conservative Party after Suez, the subtle negotiator who outgunned the best French énarques, turn into the surly curmudgeon of later years? I think it was because his whole life had been based on a total commitment to and belief in a vision of a patriotic, liberal Conservative Party: he and it were family. So when that bond turned out to be conditional, premised on his delivery of continued success, almost everything he thought he understood turned out to be false.

'There is a touch of this in the infinitely more successful, and much luckier, Tony Blair: he genuinely thought – and thinks – that he created a family called New Labour which loved him and represented all the best in Britain. But in fact his tactical skill and his luck – like Clinton's, Blair's period in office happened to coincide with the easiest economic conditions since at least the First World War – delivered victories, and it was the victories that Labour liked. He seems genuinely perplexed that many of the members of that party, and many others, do not love him. How would Blair have done as a progressive Tory leader – which is what he most likely would have been if he had been born in 1920 – facing the catastrophes of 1973–4? His indomitable optimism and political savvy would certainly have carried him through much better than Heath. But would he have been any more courageous about the dangerous issues than Wilson?'[12]

Patrick Jenkin offers this summation of the enigma at the heart of Heath:

'His was by any standards a remarkable life. From humble origins, he had not only risen to the top in politics, but in the immensely competitive sport of Ocean Racing, and he had earned an enviable global reputation as an orchestral conductor. I remember saying at one point: 'Here you have a man with the ability to excel both in sport and in the performing arts. How can he fail to sweep all before him in politics?' Yet, that is precisely what he manifestly did fail to do. Although he succeeded in taking the UK into the EEC – a signal achievement which I have left others to describe – and though he rose to be Prime Minister of the United Kingdom, he eventually had to recognise his personal responsibility for his defeats in three of the four general elections he fought as Leader of his Party. I say this with great sadness. He had great ability; he demonstrated no lack of courage; and it was for me a huge privilege to have worked with him in the House of Commons. Yet, there was always something in his character which made it very difficult for him to build the close personal relationships with

other people that are so essential if a leader is to become a really successful statesman.'

Geoffrey Howe found himself moved to see Heath still fighting for the
cause closest to his heart as late as 2004, even as his ageing body was beginning to fail him:

'The last time I heard [Edward Heath] speak in public was to a group of
war veterans about a year ago. And amongst those ageing contemporaries, his message had begun to sound a little frail. But later the same day I
saw him as the guest of honour at a gathering of British students. They
had formed a bright, enthusiastic queue – all immensely eager to shake
his hand. It was a reassuring reminder that his spirit will indeed live on
– not just as a historic builder of the past but as an enduring architect
of the future. Would that every one of today's party leaders, who still
acknowledge that Britain's place is indeed in Europe, could show the same
enthusiasm – and above all conviction that they wish that mission to be
a success.'[13]

Brendon Sewill also knew Heath at the peak of his powers and suggests
an explanation for his behaviour during the 'wilderness years':

'Why did Ted come to hate Margaret? Why the long grump? Not just
because she had ousted him but because deep down he felt her policies
were dishonest, immoral and almost wicked. Yet out of loyalty to the Party
he was never able to enunciate those feelings clearly.

'Dishonest because she gained power by promising that monetarism
would stop inflation without admitting that it could only do so by creating millions of unemployed. I was never sure how far she and Geoffrey
Howe knew that would be the result, or whether they actually believed
the Milton Friedman mantra that sound money would solve everything
painlessly.

'Having grown up with the mass unemployment of the 1930s and
with his political formative years influenced by Keynes and the 1944
Employment White Paper with the hope that full employment was here

to stay (as indeed it was from 1945–1979) Ted felt deeply that curing inflation by throwing men and women out of work was immoral.

'Almost wicked to cause that amount of misery when there was a better, more rational way. Surely if only "all men of common sense" could agree on a method of limiting pay rises and preventing strikes, then the economy could continue to be run at full steam ahead, with full employment, increased business confidence and maximum production and welfare. Yet he could not say that without being laughed out of court. Enough to send anyone into the grumps!'

Stephen Sherbourne and Wilf Weeks worked for Heath between 1975–1980 and never lost touch with him. **Sherbourne** tells this very characteristic story of 'Heath humour': 'After four and a half years working for Mrs T in Downing Street, I wrote to EH to tell him that I was leaving. In typical Heath fashion, he returned my letter to me, on which he had simply written, at the bottom of the page: "So pleased you're becoming human again."'

Weeks tells this one: 'I asked EH to read some Old Testament verses at our wedding. He made quite a fuss about having to read about "creepy crawlies", but of course he did it perfectly on the day. He also asked me what we would like as a wedding present. I said anything but, please, not a *Morning Cloud* print. On the morning of the wedding a print of *Morning Cloud* was delivered.'

David Howell has been an invaluable and most generous contributor to this volume and his final analysis of Heath and the government he led is, in a pure and classical sense of the word, tragic:

'The Heath Government unfolded as a kind of tragedy in three acts. In Act One we have the great reformer, fresh from his triumph in destroying Resale Price Maintenance, coming from a modest background and free of the "grouse moor" and old Etonian mafia images which so worried the Party. His supporters and his young advisers strutted the stage, convinced that we were at last at a turning point of the Twentieth Century, both for Britain and the wider world, and Ted Heath would lead us there. Our champion is Iain Macleod. He, at least at this stage, is the Harry Hotspur, the Bolingbroke by Heath's side.

'In Act Two Macleod is dead – not, it must be said, in the Hotspur treachery mould, although his views about Ted were mixed – but struck down by heart failure in a weakened and wounded body. With his death the party nobles and barons start closing in. There is pressure to get rid of the young upstarts and courtiers. Errors are made, options are closed and radicalism fades.

'In Act Three, bad luck and bad timing converge and unite. There are rival counsels. Fools pronounce and urge. Ted is pushed this way and that and finally takes the fatal steps to destruction. I go back to those three high advisers and officials leaving Ted Heath's Chequers study that winter's afternoon – and to their colleagues ever hovering just behind the arras. All were wise, dedicated, experienced servants of the state. But their skill lay in managing situations, not changing them. Everything started from being "given" and had to be managed from there. Their views and judgments ran along a single valley, with no inclination to move laterally and see or connect with what might lie next door and over the mountain ridge. That kind of lateral thinking, and that kind of advice, had to wait another decade for its moment to come.

'For about twenty years after his fall, Ted Heath and I did not speak, until our paths crossed at a dinner at the Guinnesses' Hampshire house, when he suddenly, after a rather silent and sullen mealtime performance, began dilating on the good work I had initiated in changing the structure of government decades earlier. Then he closed down again – and had nothing to add about the many hours and days of preparatory work we had done together in the 1960s.

'Maybe the hostility afterwards was because Ted Heath felt I and others had let him down. Maybe it was because, along with others, I carried on serving his successor – because that is what you do in a political vocation, if asked. Maybe in his eyes we were all some kind of traitors. That is certainly a word he used about one of my colleagues who took the same path. Whatever happened, all sense of affinity was gone. I did not go to his funeral.'

From further outside Heath's natural political circles was American **Alyce Faye Eichelberger**, who relished a surprise invitation to lunch with him (offered after a chance encounter with me at the opening of an art exhibition) and proved that, even in his eighties, Heath had not lost his predilection for high-powered, successful and attractive women who relished standing up to him:

'Now, little girls from the sticks like me do not usually end up dining with prime ministers. As it turned out, thank heavens; this prime minister was not in the least inclined to discuss politics with the likes of me. Mr Heath was charming, humorous and very curious about me, which bespeaks the true calling of a great politician. Bill Clinton, by the way will also make you feel you are the most interesting person he's ever met. Thank goodness Mr Heath wanted to talk about me because that was the one subject I knew more about than he did. In his gracious company I became as relaxed as if I were at the church strawberry social in the garden of the Waco Methodist parsonage. He didn't expect me to talk politics; and I didn't expect him to talk Freud.

'I mentioned that I'd seen a baby grand piano in the front room and asked if he played. "Just a bit," he replied modestly, but very pleased by my interest, he offered rather timidly: "Perhaps you'd allow me to bore you with a few notes after lunch?" I was delighted. Ted Heath was about to become another of my English musician friends. After lunch we all moved into the drawing room where the Prime Minister gave us a private concert. I was pleased as punch to hear several pieces I loved from Bach to Beethoven, and even one Rachmaninoff. As I listened to the music I noticed beautiful models of sailing ships on the mantelpiece, which took on a special life with the waves of classical music in the background cascading over them. There were lots of photos of Mr Heath sailing and receiving trophies.

'When the other guests retired to the library for coffee, I stayed behind to admire the models. Mr Heath pointed out the model of the *Morning Cloud*, his first yacht that had won the Sydney to Hobart race in Australia. There was the silver framed photo of him receiving the Admiral's Cup here in England. "You just bulldozed over all of them, didn't you? You have won so much!" I quite genuinely gushed. The PM beamed.

'Our conversation turned to sailing, which, at that time, I was doing a great deal of with my newfound sailing friends. Mr Heath laughed at my own sailing exploits and asked if I would come on one of his river cruises from Westminster up the Thames to Greenwich where there would be a dinner, with music and a leisurely boat trip back admiring the lights of London. I attended several of those enchanted evenings. Mr Heath and I always had the best time chatting away about Rachmaninoff as if he were our neighbour down the street. The conversations were easy. We behaved as if we had known each other much longer than we actually did.

'I was his friend without portfolio. I didn't have an agenda . . . You see I had just entered my forties, I must have seemed like a young adolescent girl to him. One with whom he could laugh and chat and feel no sexual demands or romantic tension . . . I bantered, I flirted, and, as we say in Texas, around me, he could "let his hair down". We were an unlikely pairing but in Waco we would have called each other buddies.'

The journalist and newscaster **Alastair Stewart**, who became a good friend of his, also recalls Heath's attitudes to successful women:

'Ted was especially partial to powerful women: Sara Morrison, a board director of GEC, was a regular. Ted would give women more latitude then men in debate. I'm not sure it was out of courtesy; I think he just felt they often had more of interest to say. He became very fond of my wife Sally. She taxed Ted, once, on Chinese human rights . . Ted heard her out and engaged her in civil but forceful debate. On another occasion, much to my amusement, and I think Sally's, Ted regaled her with stories of the gifts his Chinese friends had given him. He beamed a Ted smile and asked her if she'd like to "come upstairs and see my silk hangings". Yes; the shoulders heaved.'

Another lunch guest at Arundells was the greatest Olympian of them all, **Sir Steve Redgrave**, who recalls:

'It was a great honour to be invited. My wife and I were one of the last guests to arrive. It did seem a strange atmosphere when I walked in. I found out later that Sue Barker's husband had been introduced to the other guests as me. I think there was a little bit of an embarrassment going around, but it didn't spoil my enjoyment of the occasion. I was very impressed with the level of detail. I had just been diagnosed as a diabetic and the chef had been briefed and was so kind. I loved the "Who's Who" of photographs on the piano of Sir Edward and some of the most famous people in the world. It was one of those rare occasions that you get invited to that is so special and the memories will always stay with me.'

David Harris was Political Correspondent of the *Daily Telegraph* and, subsequently, Conservative MP for St Ives (1983–1997), and recalls how attentive to details Heath could be:

'The press interest in him had escalated by the time of the General Election in 1970. On the eve of polling at his Bexley constituency office, I presented him with a book on ocean sailing on behalf of his "fellow travellers" from the press. Even we cynics could see that he was genuinely touched. Perhaps that was why he asked some of us to a reception at No. 10 shortly after he moved in. "Why don't you take out your wife to supper before going back to Orpington?" he asked when we said our goodbyes. How on earth did he remember where we lived at the time, a matter of complete insignificance to a Prime Minister?

'Years later, as an MP, I mentioned to him that my wife and I had been in Salisbury that weekend and had seen his superb house in The Close. "Why didn't you call?" he asked and, once again, I thought he might just have meant it.'

Heath's last PPS was Bedfordshire MP **David Madel**, who remained on good terms with his former boss in the final phase of his life, after they had both retired from the House of Commons at the 2001 general election:

'The last time I saw Ted was quite soon before he died, I was invited to Salisbury for lunch. On arrival an excellent glass of champagne, and the housekeeper said Sir Edward will be down in a few minutes. By then he needed a stair lift. Hello, he said, as the chair descended down the stairs, but then it refused to stop at the bottom, and took him upstairs again. Good bye, he said, you'll have an excellent lunch – which I did, and so did he, when the stair lift did eventually stop at the bottom to let him get off!'

The person whom Heath teased and goaded more than anyone – and who had entirely free licence to reciprocate in whatever manner she deemed fit – was **Sara Morrison**. Sara accompanied him to countless events and provided infinite support at times of difficulty. She was, to all intents and purposes, Heath's best friend in the world:

'When Ted was Prime Minister, I drew the short straw and went with him on a tour of three North Sea oil rigs in a tiny helicopter, which was, just, large enough to accommodate him, me and its pilot. On the way we dropped in to a Conservative event in the Highlands. I recall the pilot being frightfully subservient to Ted, so I was very much the opposite. When we landed I was first out. As a group of earnest Conservatives were walking towards us, I trod in a cowpat, slipped and fell over, absolutely flat on my face: Expletive-deleted. I looked up to see Ted with a grin that only I could see on his face. "Serves you bloody well right," he said out of the corner of his mouth, as he stepped over me and went to meet the greeting party, never looking over his shoulder ever again. I got up and did my bit too. "If I were you, I'd be very careful about which part of her anatomy you touch," Ted announced to our hosts. "She's just like her dogs – she rolls in every bit of dirt she can." Someone asked me if I'd like to be hosed down. "No thank you – I don't want to be wet as well." As we left, I exploded to Ted, "That was one of your more intolerable things – you might at least have been vaguely sympathetic." He shrugged: "It was fairly obvious you weren't hurt, so what do I have to be sympathetic about? You're going to smell all day and I'm going to be next to you." The pilot absolutely roared with laughter. When we arrived on each of the oil rigs, Ted apologised for me. "I should be very careful. Out in the wind she may be alright – she's smelling terrible today." Instantly, of course, that broke the ice, so I found myself giving him a picture on the way home – not telling him off for making fun of me, but advising him that in future he should be more natural in public, as he had been on this trip. "Why should I be? Most people wouldn't bother to appreciate it. There's no point in trying."

'I probably saw Ted once a week when he was in the country. I could never, absolutely to my satisfaction, understand why, with the experience of being chief whip, he managed to turn himself into a bad-mannered robot, so far as the rest of the world saw him. I never really got to the bottom of it. I think it was deep shyness, plus a deep loathing of the Tory Party which he loved. It is hugely underrated how the whole of the end of Ted's political life was done in by how the Tory Party treated him when he was first elected leader. I have always wondered if turning him into leader wasn't the day we absolutely wrecked the superb civil servant who, unfortunately, just happened to want to be a politician? The way the Tory Party treated him in those first few months was really inexcusable – the whole "Grocer" bit and all of that was really, really awful. That went much deeper than he'd ever admit.

'Even to me it became a joke about his bad manners. His point was that, "When there are people like you trailing around, who make an absolute virtue of convincing the masses that you're really lovely – if I wasn't like me, people wouldn't be saying how marvellous you were – think of that!" We heard him saying it, as a joke. He would often ask me to go and thank people and say how good a buffet had been – "You'll enjoy getting the credit for saying it much more nicely than I ever could, won't you?" It's true that, on one occasion, I was at a dinner with him and passed him a note saying, "Please talk to the woman on your right." In big writing, without folding the paper or any other attempt to prevent the woman seeing it, he wrote back: "Don't be so bossy – I have." It was one long giggle, really.

'It is sad Ted never decided to enjoy how enjoyable he could be. So much of his life was lived vicariously, through his "pets" – his friends. My children have never understood why the world never saw the Ted they saw as children – and still think of him as a dear, cosy old thing with a really good sense of humour. They loved him because he was constantly taking their mother apart. There's nothing more adorable for children than being told what a walking disaster their mother is. He would walk into the room and say, "I suppose she's late, surrounded by dogs and ready to make me do things I don't want to do – where is she?"'

To the very end of Heath's life, **Robert Armstrong** remained his closest confidant and, after the death of Madron Seligman, surely his closest and certainly his most appreciated friend. Here, he reflects briefly upon the final weeks of Heath's long and varied life:

'Once he was back at Arundells after being taken ill in Salzburg, restored to health but fragile, I used to visit him regularly two or three times a month, when I was on my way to or from my country home in Somerset. I was thrilled when, as I was leaving after one of those visits, only a few weeks before he died, he looked up as I was going out of the room, smiled, and said: "I am delighted that you come and see me." It seemed that he was conquering the inhibition of a lifetime, and was at last able to express his gratitude.

'How are we to account for the fact that this intelligent, ambitious, determined, self-contained and undemonstrative man was held in respect, admiration, trust and very often affection by his personal friends, by many (though not all) of his political colleagues and by the staff who worked with and for him? I shall not forget that evening on 4 March 1974 when the staff at 10 Downing Street assembled in the front hall to say farewell as he left for Buckingham Palace. Many were in tears. One member of staff said that it felt like saying goodbye to the father of the family.

'I think the answer is that what you saw is what you got: he could be difficult, he could be awkward; but he was not devious, he did not – perhaps could not – dissemble. He was, in a word, an honest man, a man whom people felt that they could trust. They were able to give him their loyalty because they knew that, if they did so, it would be reciprocated.'

So, in light of all these anecdotes and analyses and personal, first-hand accounts of him, who was Sir Edward Heath? What kind of man was he? Clearly he was a complex character. He was driven and, from an uncommonly early age, he was ambitious; but there's no sense in damning a politician for that. More interesting is the manner in which that ambition shaped the man. It drove him not only to Balliol, but to an unusual triumvirate of elected positions – President of the Oxford Union, President of the Oxford University Conservative Society and also, in some ways most impressively, President of the College Junior Common Room. Unless life was very, very different in the 1930s, holding high office outside the college was never an effective way of earning popularity within it.

When he left Oxford, Heath had seen for himself the ugly fervour that the Nazis could inspire in the people of Germany; and he had seen,

[309]

in Spain, what their death planes could achieve. He soon saw for himself how the German Wehrmacht could sweep the ragged Polish Army before it. He had no illusions of any kind, but he knew his duty. He signed up, he fought and he had a classic 'good war', showing conspicuous organisational skills, aptitude for leadership and hard work – and no want for courage. He went to war, as Denis Healey so memorably observed, as 'Teddy', but came back as 'Ted'. Thereafter, he single-mindedly sought selection as a Conservative candidate, then election as a Conservative MP. He didn't mind working a marginal. He merely saw it as a challenge. He built the best team around himself and relied on hordes of his friends from the various stations of his life to provide jovial and willing assistance, which they duly did.

In January 2016 I had a long talk about Heath with one of his oldest friends, the former Unionist Member for Londonderry, Robin Chichester-Clark, who, asked me, rather out of the blue, 'Did you like him?' It was the perfect question, a plum Yorker bowled deceptively at a weary batsman with half an eye on tea. 'No, not really,' I replied. 'I had a lot of respect and affection for him but no, I didn't really like him.' Even I didn't know precisely what I meant.

By the end of his life, Sir Edward Heath had no family – no family by blood ties. The only Mrs Heath in our lives was the very pleasant widow of his younger brother. My friend Alyce Faye told me years ago that we in his private office and his staff at his home – we were his family. He was the head of a family and, by accepting employment with him, I had become part of the family. The problem was, he was, by now at least, far removed from the model of a benign patriarch. Occasionally he would share a confidence or smile at a joke, but most of the time he was egocentric and distant, more like a spoiled child than a wise, oracular old seer. He never encouraged, praised but rarely and usually neglected to say 'thank you'.

Yet, I could recognise what this man had once been. It wasn't just that his known achievements gave him natural authority. He had remarkable presence and comic timing that a West End performer might envy and struggle to match. Those clear blue eyes could still penetrate a human soul. The problem was, he was marking time. He had survived a major cancer operation and his heart was failing. He had all the symptoms of what used to be known as 'dropsy'. Throughout his long dotage he must have been in constant discomfort or even pain. The network of contacts that he could once exploit to earn money for himself – or to rustle up a well-paid job to reward a loyal but departing protégé – had all but withered away. He was no longer in the business of nurturing; his horizons were limited to surviving – 'survival is all', as my old friend Nicholas Courtney used to say.

Heath could be kind, but he could also be thoughtless. He could be generous, but he could also be damnably selfish. Three critical episodes appear to have toughened his hide, making him unusually self-isolating and self-reliant: his experience of war; the departure from his life of his 'girl friend' Kay Raven; and the early death of his mother, just as his career was taking shape. As Peter Carrington told a BBC interviewer in 2015: 'Ted wasn't socially very easy. He took a long time to get to know people. One sign that you were his friend was that he started being rude to you.'[14] When preparing a celebration of Her Majesty the Queen's ninetieth birthday for the BBC, the excellent documentary film-maker John Bridcut was permitted to use home movie footage from the Royal Family itself. 'There is a lot of teasing,' he observed, 'which is how affection is expressed within this family, rather – as with many people of the Queen's generation – than by overt physical contact.'[15] Edward Heath was exactly of that ilk; indeed, he may even have learned this behaviour from first-hand observation of the family he most admired in all the world. Unfortunately for him, his teasing was not to everyone's taste, nor did it always seem appropriate.

Despite his undoubted capacity for generosity, he would more commonly count his pennies carefully and gladly refrain from spending them. He demonstrated a profound, lifelong sense of both social and financial insecurity. Fortunately for him, the basic activity of 'Being Sir Edward Heath' – with all his allowances, a car, a driver and police protection all provided by the taxpayer and endless invitations to eat, drink and travel at other people's expense – was remarkably inexpensive.

As soon as he could, when he moved to the Albany, in his forties, Heath hired a housekeeper and began to entertain, but he always felt inferior, compared with the gentry who traditionally dominated the Conservative Party; and they did not make life easier for him. He cultivated an extraordinary accent, an odd amalgam of Kent and 'crude posh' – another example, along with his excruciating attempts to speak foreign languages, of this keen musician's tin ear in most other respects. One of my colleagues from the 1990s told me a most revealing story, of a glorious summer evening in Dorset, as Heath's car glided through the estate of the Wiltshire Lord Lieutenant, Earl Digby, following a grand soirée. Taking in the glorious, verdant scene across the deer park, Heath commented simply and to no one in particular: 'Nothing affects these people.' That would never be true of him: he would never be rich enough, sufficiently well respected, or simply self-confident enough to feel that he was immune to the twists and turns of life, to changing economic circumstances or to the wider vagaries of fortune. That mattered to him. He always felt the need to prove himself, to justify himself, to demonstrate vigour and the power of argument.

So why did Ted Heath not prosper as party leader or, when he had the chance, as Prime Minister? When he expressed his disappointment to a military friend after Harold Macmillan kept him on as chief whip rather than giving him a department to run, apparently he was told: 'You cannot change the CO and the adjutant at the same time.' This consoled him, even as his obvious rival Reggie Maudling settled into his high-profile role as Paymaster-General. He would have been less amused to learn of what Dick Beeching, who became chairman of British Rail in 1961, subsequently related to Cecil King: 'Macmillan had said to him that he was surprised by the Tories' selection of Ted as their leader: that he was no political leader but an excellent staff officer.'[16] Heath's approach to politics appears to have been strongly influenced by his time in the military. As Andrew Roth put it, in June 1970, his 'style was more like a victorious commander moving into a command post he had stormed than the leader of an opposition party taking over the reins of government'.[17] He had melded men of every size, shape, class, origin and political persuasion into a single, highly effective fighting unit in the Royal Artillery, so now he just had to repeat the procedure, on a much grander scale. Then the UK could become the leading force, economically and politically, in Europe.

I am inclined to think that Heath as both leader and Prime Minster would have been better advised to appoint one or two larger, dissident personalities to senior roles – Hugh Fraser, Edward du Cann, John Biffen – rather than rewarding the 'Heathmen' as he did, often regardless of proven ability.

He arguably allowed personal dislikes and entrenched grudges to overcome his usual instinct, which served him so well as chief whip and also as skipper of *Morning Cloud*, namely to have around him the strongest possible team. Having been a firm but amiable chief whip, who eschewed the strong-arm tactics of political mythology in favour of more subtle and socially acceptable forms of persuasion, Heath as Prime Minister was also surprisingly short-tempered and impatient, remote and authoritarian. Despite his protestations, his determination to drive EEC accession through the Commons did leave a bitter legacy. **Ken Clarke**, who came into the House of Commons just as Heath became Prime Minister, did not expect Heath to fawn over him, but was evidently surprised by his lack of charm:

> 'He had no social graces whatever and this did get worse. He had no small talk and he came over publicly as stiff and awkward. His eventual fall from the leadership was because most of the party, including the more moderate people who agreed with his politics, didn't particularly like him and he wasn't very friendly or approachable. He certainly wasn't very clubbable . . . He couldn't think of anything to say, not only to members of the public, but also to colleagues who'd been in the House of Commons with him for years, and to whom he scarcely addressed a word.'[18]

Watching films of Heath as party leader or Prime Minister can still be a painful experience. In his broadcasts to the nation, he was painfully stiff. Meeting members of the public, as Ken rightly observes, he struggled to communicate. He had to dig deep for his big talk and his small talk. The matters that did interest him, however, really did interest him; and he believed it was entirely right that a senior politician should have a hinterland – and establish his (or her?) entitlement to carry on cultivating it when in office. He would tell the tale of visiting his mentor Harold Macmillan during the 'Night of the Long Knives' crisis in 1961, only to find him determinedly completing his reading of Dickens's *Dombey and Son*, on the eve of a demanding foreign trip. He enlarged upon his views in an interview with **Gyles Brandreth**, who asked if a similar approach would still be possible. Heath was in no doubt that it would and should be:

'It was that approach that allowed me my music, my concerts; it allowed me my sailing in the spring and the summer. It's a question of how you handle the job. I didn't interfere with departmental ministers just for the sake of it. I only became involved if something appeared to be going wrong.'

'When did that style of government begin to change?'

'With Harold Wilson. He was a workaholic. He had a small group around him and they met constantly, working into the early hours. They say Wilson was a great operator, but to what effect? There's nothing left of Wilson now.'

'And, of course, Mrs Thatcher only needed five hours sleep and never stopped.'

'Hmmm, yes, well. One saw the consequences.'[19]

Heath's principal modes of escape were, of course, music and sailing (see Chapter 6). Music gave him solace and a means of expressing his innermost feelings, which were surprisingly grand and romantic; sailing gave him physical exercise, leadership practice and an outlet for his competitive nature. Sailing also cut him off entirely from the world of politics and required complete concentration: playing music does the same, but listening does not, at least not necessarily. The problem with both these activities was that they had an elitist feel to them. Competitive sailing is a rich man's sport and therefore not accessible to most people. It was also too easily conflated in the public mind with the sybaritic pleasures of cruising on the Med or revelling in the company of millionaires in the South of France. The reality – cramped conditions, extreme physical exertion, testing oneself to the limit – was very different, but how widely was that understood? So far as music was concerned, friends and admirers knew that it was literally Heath's muse – the means by which he could give voice to warmer aspects of his complex personality, which for the most part remained subdued and hidden. His keyboard playing had a fluency that his verbal utterances, sometimes painfully, lacked. Yet his musical interests and tastes were far from demotic. As Bernard Donoughue once put it: 'He was high-brow Bach and Harold [Wilson] was middle-brow Gilbert and Sullivan – and there were political implications in that.'[20]

My father recently commented to me that Heath 'lacked inner confidence' and I think that gets to the heart of the matter. So too does the observation of Heath's one-time parliamentary colleague Nigel Fisher, that he combined 'intellectual arrogance with social diffidence'.[21] This helps explain why it was such an instance of historical misfortune for Heath that his period of dominance in his party coincided with that of Harold Wilson in his, for Wilson was everything Heath was not. He was an intellectual, not working class but lower middle class. He was 'comfortable in his skin' and had an easy manner, but he could also vex and infuriate Heath with minimal effort. During the 1966 election campaign, Wilson accused Heath of being too weak in his approach to the EEC: 'One encouraging gesture from the French Government and he rolls on his back like a spaniel.' As he read through that speech, Heath exploded: 'This is too sordid for words . . . lies . . . what a poisonous speech . . . absolutely filthy . . . nauseating, filthy insinuation . . . Wilson must be out of his mind . . .'[22] In his book about the period, Wilson does not conceal his pleasure at this palpable hit and the 'choice collection of epithets' he provoked from Heath.[23] Thereafter Heath began to call Wilson a 'squalid little man' and always referred to him as 'Wilson', both publicly and privately; Wilson invariably called him 'Ted'. How that must have infuriated him. With Wilson, nothing happened by chance.

Frequently there were explosions between them in the Commons, such as the occasion when Wilson and Labour MP Maurice Edelman pummelled Heath over a reception he had given for Jean-Louis Tixier-Vignancour, the French far-right politician who had defended the would-be assassins of Charles de Gaulle. Heath furiously attacked the 'slander by innuendo', which was, he said, 'typical of the Prime Minister'.[24] Five years later, when Wilson criticised his decision to expel 105 Soviet spies, Heath told Robin Day on live TV that his rival was 'contemptible'. Wilson intuitively recognised Heath's electoral weaknesses and exploited them ruthlessly. In response, according to Reggie Maudling, whenever Harold Wilson joined a meeting of the Privy Council, Heath would freeze with horror and distaste. Yet he took no pleasure in Wilson's loss of his faculties and the pitiful state to which this gradually reduced him. Furthermore, after his rival's death, he was invariably kind to Wilson's widow Mary, who was moved to tears on at least one occasion by Heath's consideration and kindness.

Heath also had the great misfortune of being a highly rational and essentially reasonable man who reached the political pinnacle, as Prime Minister, when the animal spirits in these islands were at their most irrational – and their most choleric. He tried to apply Kentish common sense to the tribal hatreds of Ireland, which had hardened over centuries. He almost succeeded. He tried to appeal to the better nature of the leaders of industry and, more particularly, the leaders of the trade union movement. He could not compute, or bear, the thought that they would prefer strife to cooperation; that they would allow their rivalries to dictate that mutually assured destruction was a more likely outcome than industrial peace and prosperity. He was not totally misguided. The likes of Vic Feather and Joe Gormley were, in large part, sympathetic to him – they liked him and trusted him, but they were not masters of their own destiny. In the unhappy, tenebrous 1970s, the decent and reasonable men simply could not deliver.

The result in February 1974 was the worst possible for Heath. Because the Tories won more votes than Labour, he could claim he had not really been defeated. Yet he palpably had. He was drained, frustrated and upset. He had to shoulder for himself responsibility both for the record of the 1970–1974 administration and also for the decision to go to the country when he did. He paid a price too for stubbornly adhering to the Sunningdale power-sharing agreement into which he had more or less coerced the Ulster Unionists under Faulkner, even though unionist voters had now rejected it at the ballot box.

He struggled for a decade or more to reconcile himself to the 'peasants' revolt' that saw frustrated, neglected, unappreciated back-bench MPs wrestle from him the leadership of the party that meant so much to him, but ultimately gave him so little fulfilment or peace of mind. It was perhaps understandable that, in the wake of his personal triumph in the 1975 referendum campaign and in light of Mrs Thatcher's struggle to endear herself to the electorate, Heath again came to see himself as a man with a future. He was a genuinely popular figure for the first time, often outpolling his successor. Many electors felt he was hard done by and they had made a mistake rejecting him in 1974. He seemed to embody a reasonable desire to bring calm and rational thinking to bear on the nation's problems, compared with the growing stridency of his party. Even after Mrs Thatcher won in 1979, he could be forgiven for believing a grateful nation might yet call upon his services: as unemployment rose inexorably and there were riots on the streets, the Tories in 1981 fell to third place in the opinion polls.

Like Shakespeare's Richard of Bordeaux, Heath never truly accepted the legitimacy of his successor (just one letter has been added to the original!):

> '. . . Show us the hand of God
> That hath dismissed us from our stewardship;
> For well we know, no hand of blood and bone
> Can grip the sacred handle of our sceptre,
> Unless she do profane, steal, or usurp.'[25]

John Junor once wrote that: 'Ted Heath has never been popular with the people closest to him. It has been said with a deal of truth that those who know him best love him least.'[26] That was simply not true. Junor's fellow journalist **Lynn Barber** came much closer to the truth, after interviewing Heath in 1998:

> 'What impressed me is that his personal staff, the people he sees every day, are deeply fond of him in a way that simply can't be magicked up by PR. His policemen trundle him out for excursions round the local pubs – he sits at one table with his Glenmorangie, they at another with their glasses of soda – while he chats to locals. This can hardly be part of their required policing duties – they must do it because they like him. While Heath was posing for our photographer, his housekeeper invited me into her cheerful kitchen for a cup of tea, and was raving away about "the boss" and what fun he was to work for. Housekeeper probably gives quite the wrong impression – Jeanne Cooper is not some servile, bun-haired retainer, but a lively, forty-something Australian. He interviewed her for the job in his office in the Commons and said: "Oh. I see you come from Perth" and then talked at length about Perth (which he remembered perfectly though he hadn't been there since the Sixties) before asking whether she could cook cordon bleu? Then she said: "Well. I'm getting there." He hired her. When I left, the policeman at the gate beamed and said: "Oh. I can tell it went well. Look! He's come to the door to see you off. He only does that if he likes someone!"'[27]

Edward Heath was a profoundly loyal person who expected ('demanded' sounds too strenuous) loyalty in return. I think of how readily, in 1998, he joined a number of other prominent citizens, defending the reputation of his old friend Martin Neary, who had been sacked as the organist at Westminster Abbey after alleged 'financial irregularities' had been discovered. He was loyal to institutions too – to the Conservative Party that he never left, to the monarchy and to Balliol. When my colleague Anthony Staddon was considering going to Oxford for an MPhil degree, I arranged for him to meet my old politics tutor at Lincoln College. 'Yes,' commented Sir Edward, 'but how is some don at Lincoln going to get him into Balliol?' His undemonstrative nature and his constant expectation of excellence from the people around him made him seem unappreciative. He expected the best and, ultimately took it for granted. Staff and colleagues who expected to feed on overt compliments went hungry. Simply working for **Heath** had to be a fulfilment in itself. That is why my colleagues and I so much appreciated his closing words at his eightieth birthday dinner at the Savoy, in July 1996. Characteristically, he could say 'thank you', but only when addressing a packed hall and not in more intimate surroundings, when sentimentality might, to his mind, have soured the atmosphere:

> 'I'd like to thank all my own staff over the last thirty years, many of whom are here tonight, who have helped us to achieve our successes, and who have had a major part in organising tonight's gathering. The tribute is due to them, very largely because they wouldn't tell me what was going on, but I have no crib to make about that because of tonight's success, which I hope you will agree should be shared amongst all of us. And so, thank you, every one of you. Thank you to all the politicians, all the artists, all the athletes, all the sportsmen, all those who have played some part in my life, thank you for all you've done, but not for me, thank you for what you've done for our country.'

Did Edward Heath stand for anything? Did he represent anything – at least anything that mattered? He certainly had his principles: he was patriotic and believed in freedom, democracy and public service. He also, despite his enthusiasm (and, in his mind, entirely consistently with it) adored

Parliament, respected its traditions and 'believed in it'. John Cole likened him to 'a businessman, a problem-solver: he tried something, and if that did not work, he tried something else'.[28] I think that is to underestimate him. He enjoyed politics. A man who had endured months of relentless, deafening ack-ack as he commanded a battery during the aerial defence of Liverpool was not easily disconcerted by a certain volume of 'incoming'. On the contrary: he relished it and, when deprived of it, he missed it sorely. He also relished leadership. He gave up sailing, he once told an interviewer, because 'we had fifteen years and won almost everything . . . There was no point in going on and starting to come down . . . I must be in charge on a boat, as in life.'[29] What a revealing remark, especially because he did not apply that principle to his political life: in mid-1996 he supplanted David Lloyd George as the longest-serving former Prime Minister in the history of the House of Commons. The occasion was marked, but only in low-key fashion, not least because so much of Heath's behaviour since 1975 had caused pain and embarrassment to his friends.

His one, overriding *cause célèbre* during those years was Europe. He watched, dismayed, as his party turned against the 'European ideal'. What he would never accept was that an ideal that had united Tories in the 1960s – closer European integration, founded principally upon vigorous, tariff-free trade – had been appropriated by Jacques Delors and others, who had a very different concept – that of a 'Social Europe'. Perfectly legitimately, Heath would demonstrate that the aspiration of ever-closer integration had been there in the Treaties from the start, but that was no longer the point. The direction and speed of travel were increasingly abhorrent to many of his colleagues. Mrs Thatcher was the first prominent Conservative to point this out – in her 'Bruges' speech, which so enraged Heath – at a time when the parliamentary party was not yet receptive to such talk. As that body of men and women was refashioned after the 1997 debacle, more and more in Lady Thatcher's image, the argument slipped completely away from Heath and he was not nimble enough to recognise that the ground rules had changed – and move with them.

On one crucial question, neither he nor the sceptics quite got it right. The sceptics – including Margaret Thatcher – encouraged the widening of the EU to the North, South and East, because they believed it would both entrench democratic values in newly liberated nations and also slow down the frenzied rush for closer integration. Heath opposed it, largely for that latter reason: he always envisaged the EU as an ever closer union of a smaller number of nations and peoples, whose living standards were broadly comparable. In a sense they fundamentally agreed and they were both wise: the disastrous combination of widening with deepening, which neither Heath nor Lady Thatcher ever envisaged or supported, has destabilised Europe and brought us to the precipice we now unhappily occupy. If only the debate could have been more rational and less visceral, the party might have united around a sensible, moderate proposition that might have won the day, both in the UK and more widely. In later life, Heath, the ever-rational and analytical 'énarque manqué', became a dogmatist. **Anthony Staddon** saw this at first hand:

'Having had a smooth route to the leadership of the Conservative Party and reached the top as Prime Minister, his fall from grace must have been hard to take, especially with the lack of a companion to help him cope with his defeat. He was a proud man who wanted to serve his country and enjoyed the responsibility of being Prime Minister. His opening line when contacting the office was always, "What's going on?" and this probably echoed his longing to be at the centre of political decision-making. The irony is that his record as a former Prime Minister was fairly impressive, but it was never going to fulfil him.

'I have no doubt that he would seek a leading role in the current referendum campaign if he were still alive today. While he would have been dismissive of David Cameron's renegotiation and general tactics, he would have approved of Cameron's recent speeches on the EU and his talk about sovereignty being illusory. There are echoes of Heath's own speeches on the subject in the 1975 Referendum Campaign and before – echoes that neither side would probably want to admit! I spent much time discussing European politics with him and it was a source of frustration that he never allowed himself to criticise the European Union in a constructive sense: he saw it as his role to defend the EU to the hilt. This was understandable given that joining the EEC was his main achievement and he often said that nobody else would defend the EU if he didn't. I suspect his contribution to the European debate would have been rather stronger and people would have listened more if he had taken a more constructive or nuanced approach to European developments. It would have been interesting for a recognised pro-European to identify elements of possible reform (in many respects he made the same mistake with China). For him, however, this would have been a sign of weakness.

'But the more I researched EH's views and speeches on Europe from the 1950s onwards and saw how the experiences of the 1930s and the war had moulded his views, the more impressed I was. His position remained remarkably consistent – while his opponents had changed their views many times. This was both a weakness and strength of his character. The essential point is that we did join essentially an intergovernmental community with some supranational elements; the European Economic Community of 1973 was very much an economic community in the shadow of de Gaulle's Luxembourg compromise, giving each member state an effective veto. The development of the EEC into the European Union, the use and extension of majority voting, the growth in powers of the European Parliament and the moving towards political and economic and monetary union came after Heath left Downing Street and long after he had any real influence on European developments.

'This is not to say that Heath wasn't a vocal supporter of further European integration or didn't foresee it to some extent – he was publicly calling for a common currency as far back as the 1960s. But a central tenet of the British system is ensuring accountability for the decisions taken by political leaders and to blame EH for the development of the EU absolves others – notably Margaret Thatcher – for the decisions taken during their own administrations. To blame EH for the current EU makes as much sense as blaming Clement Attlee or Nye Bevan for the state of the NHS today.'

In Chapter 20 of his memoirs, *in loco* Heath totally for once as his 'McManuensis', I tried to suggest what he might have said about politics during his long wilderness years – challenging, holding to account, doing his job, without alienating or allowing bitterness to take hold. Working on this book, I was struck powerfully by what John MacGregor said about this period – that he attributed Heath's periodic outbursts and sour mood to 'a form of depression'.

It is commonly stated that there are five stages of grief: denial, anger, bargaining, depression and acceptance. In an almost chilling way, it is possible to chart Heath's behaviour after 1974 using that scheme. Over the weekend of 2–3 March 1974, Heath was clearly in denial. He would not accept the cruel and ineluctable logic of the election result. Thereafter, as Peter Batey put it, he lost his faith in democracy. In the circumstances, the October 1974 result was much better than it might have been – but Heath had still lost three elections and won only one. He was marooned in denial. His backbenchers had had their fill of him. He would not accept it. Then came Margaret Thatcher and stage two, the anger. Bargaining with Fate was difficult enough for him; bargaining with the woman who had (to his mind) betrayed him was an existential impossibility. It was an anger that he would often turn against himself, resulting in a form of depression. Anger, depression and denial, then, in abundance, but acceptance remained elusive.

Let there be no misunderstanding: throughout this period, Heath was in most respects fully functioning. He retained a well-staffed private office and attracted high-flyers to work for him; they enjoyed his company, learned from him and, even today, remain devoted to him. He could be very funny and often endearingly childlike in his humour, as **Sarah Mansell** recently reminded me: 'During a taxi ride in Tokyo, our driver spent the entire journey on the phone, constantly saying 'hai' (which I think means "yes, ok I'm listening"). EH thought it was hilarious to say 'hic' straight afterwards so basically it was 'hai, hic' for about 15 minutes and I never saw him laugh so much.' He also retained his many friends and numerous organisations would pay good money to have him speak. He remained active in politics, joined the Brandt Commission, continued with his competitive sailing (at least until the Fastnet horror of 1979) and conducted great orchestras, but he had to confront one vast, unwelcome truth: there was no desperate, grateful nation begging him back into its service. That thought gradually ate away at him, denying him the final stage of the grieving process – acceptance – and trapping him within a closed circle of the earlier – and angrier and far more corrosive – stages of an unhappy emotional storm that sometimes seemed without end.

The key to acceptance – and to moving on from this state of depression and grieving – seems to have been the writing of his memoirs. At last he put his case and he rested his case. He hated the thought of signing off the proofs – they had literally to be wrested from his hands – but, once he had, a process of acceptance began. In the publication of those memoirs he found a form of vindication, a chance to tell his own side of the story, an opportunity to sign books again, even to bask in the Political Book of the Year Award, under the glowering gaze of Hugo Young, no fan of his and that year's ante-post favourite for the top prize. He found a form of closure. We are all dust, he seemed to understand at last – and he even appeared to accept the futility and the sheer waste of emotional energy inherent in his feud with Margaret Thatcher. The sulk was indeed over. It was not always enjoyable to play a part in that process. I think Sir Edward respected me, though he never seemed to like me very much; and I hope, in this book, by shining an honest and comprehensive light on the true nature of the man just when he has been posthumously traduced, I have done him, one last time, some service.

CHAPTER SIX

Sailor and musician

Edward Heath grew up by the sea and always had good 'sea legs', as he demonstrated when he sailed back from the US to the UK on the *Queen Elizabeth* in the Christmas recess of 1961–1962. The ship hit a terrible squall and the actress Olivia de Havilland later paid tribute to his steadfastness: 'He was extraordinarily steady in the storm.'[1] He would not, however, have considered himself a sailor. When he pottered about in a dinghy during his summer holiday in the south of France in 1965, there was a certain amount of media coverage (largely stimulated by Central Office, which was working hard to project a more 'human' image of the new leader), particularly because he ran aground. Gordon Knight, a schoolmaster and active member of Broadstairs Sailing Club, was intrigued. When he saw Heath on a jetty shortly afterwards, he had one of his pupils ask him when he might sail at Broadstairs. Heath then fell into talking with Knight, who pointed out he had been a paid-up, but non-sailing, member of the Club for years now, so wasn't it about time he did some sailing? He also offered to give him some lessons. Heath accepted the offer. During the Whitsun recess in 1966 he took his first lesson. Some years later he suggested he had health reasons for taking up this vigorous new activity: 'It was upon my doctor's advice that I first took up sailing – a decision which reduced my demand on pharmaceuticals.'[2] **Gordon Knight** recounted what followed to Marian Evans:

'The first lesson was not auspicious, for a Force 6 wind blew up and we were soaked. The boat was one third full of water, but Mr Heath had no fears. He was ultra-careful and his eyes sparkled; he obviously enjoyed every minute of it. After two or three lessons he would take the helm if it was calm and as he became more proficient he would sometimes race the boat and I crew. We didn't do very well that season, but we did win a second prize at the Broadstairs Water Gala. It should have been a first but it was a hazy day with visibility bad. It was my fault we didn't win, as I mistook the number of laps made by the boat in front. But Mr Heath was a good loser. He turned to me and said: "After that you have lost your job as First Sea Lord and Minister of Sport in the next Government!"'[3]

Heath's parliamentary colleague Dick Taverne once had to advise his wife on how to deal with Heath as a neighbour at a formal meal. He suggested she broach the subject of sailing. Heath warmed readily to this theme and explained to her what drove him to sail. It had nothing whatsoever to do with relaxation or leisure. He explained how he had set about identifying and then recruiting 'the best navigator, the best helmsman, the best boat'. In other words, sailing for him was about competing and, above all, about winning. It had other benefits too, for his physical and mental well-being. Heath's sailing career was indeed formidably successful and it also gave him frequent, short-lived but all-embracing escapes from politics: 'When I go ocean racing, there is great physical exertion. You're so preoccupied with racing to win you can't think of anything else. If you do, you lose. You race hard and it takes your mind off the problems. Then after a bath you climb into a berth, drink a malt whisky and, although the problems haven't changed, you come to them refreshed.'[4] In those days, racing yachts were not allowed to communicate ashore, but between 1970 and 1974, *Morning Cloud* did carry special radio equipment to link Heath with No. 10 and the police. It could have been very different:

'There was, however, a long to-do about security the first summer I was Prime Minister. Two advisers came in to see me and told me that, after some thought, they had decided that the best solution was to put two policemen on the boat. I said: "Do you know the trouble we go to, to save a pound here and a pound there? And you want to put two enormous thugs on board?"[5]

Having gone through various other scenarios, including replacing crew members and having a warship or helicopter follow the boat, all summarily dismissed by Heath, they had one last attempt:

'They would drop one of their chaps down on a ladder, strap me to it, haul me up and bring me home. I explained to my No. 2 on the boat that this would happen, and that we'd have to drop all sails to do it, and he said: "I'm not going to ruin a race just because they want to take you off." He told me they'd put a rubber dinghy overboard and that they could find me and take me off from that. Fortunately it never happened.'[6]

There would be danger and heartbreak too – the death of Heath's godson Christopher Chadd when the third *Morning Cloud* was hit by a freak wave and the brush with death that Heath himself experienced in the great storm that engulfed competitors in the Admiral's Cup in 1979. Sailing was an integral and vastly important element to Heath's life for over twenty years and, to his mind, it was never, ever about leisure: it was about competing and, above all else, it was about winning. Heath applied almost exactly the same principles to his sailing as he did to his political life. As in politics, he would be the leader, but he would assemble around himself what he believed to be the strongest and most coherent team available. There were five *Morning Cloud* boats and he and his crew would win both the Sydney–Hobart race in 1969, when he was leader of the opposition; and, when he was Prime Minister, the Admiral's Cup when he captained the British team. Only in the most extreme circumstances, even as Prime Minister, would he allow politics or the business of state to interfere with his sailing arrangements. This was understood by civil servants and party officials; and it was greatly appreciated by his hand-picked crew-mates, who evidently thought the world of their skipper.

Anthony Churchill was part of the crew of *Morning Cloud* during Heath's most successful period as a competitive sailor. He wrote this tribute in 2006, for the programme at the Heath Memorial concert in St John's, Smith Square:

'Ashore at the end of a successful 180-mile Cowes to Dinard/St Malo race in 1968, along the dockside above the St Malo lockgates, a chap came up to me and said he was thinking of getting his own boat and would I like to come and sail with him? This was Ted Heath. I was intrigued. Ted had been a recreational two-man dinghy sailor. In politics, though leader of the Tories, he was, according to the media pundits, soon to be tipped into the dustbin of history.

'Would I come and see him at his flat in Albany in Piccadilly? The building frowned, as if a prison. A ground floor corridor stretched for ever, with flats off to either side. I was shown into Ted's sitting room, a cavernous room sparse of furniture, dominated by a Steinway grand piano at the distant end. Ten minutes passed without an appearance. So, why shouldn't I while away time by an attempt at some choice Chopin on the piano? Still no Ted. Why not some Scott Joplin? That brought results. With the noise of a body falling down a narrow staircase, a small insignificant door burst open. "I heard your MAYDAY call of distress," he said, "and came instantly." It was a mark of our six-year relationship on various *Morning Clouds*, that dry humour which politicians perhaps seldom saw, straight to the point (I never dared play his piano again), yet kind.

'We talked over tea, on every subject, skirting round my teenage dabbles in politics, which he suddenly brushed aside. Would I sail on his projected ocean racing yacht? And would I introduce him to friends I'd raced with? I chose Jean Berger, Sammy Sampson and Duncan Kay, on-board comrades of years of racing. Ted chose Owen Parker who was, we quickly discovered, a tower of strength. So started the crew which won Australia's Sydney–Hobart race and was the backbone of the first years of *Morning Cloud*'s great victories. Ted's delight was in the choice of strong-willed people with all sorts of skills, gathering them together to make a formidable team. As with sailing, so with music and politics.

'Maybe he wasn't the best oboist, the best violinist, the best pianist, but he revelled in music and in putting together as conductor, heavenly, harmonious sound. In politics he may not have been the best Foreign Secretary, Home Secretary, Chancellor, but he enjoyed the role of primus inter pares, first among equals.

'In sailing, those who raced with him never had a rude word from him. No tantrums. Not for Ted the swinging of a knout, the raised voice. Calm pervaded. We made rational decisions in a rational atmosphere. And we aimed to win. We gained more than our fair share of victories, and were almost never out of the prizes. As individuals we were quarrelsome at times, childish, argumentative, but there was one who had our total and utmost respect, Ted. After a race we relished thorough group debriefings, which became ever more fun after he became Prime Minister and our venues became Chequers and No. 10.

'Ted's relationship with the sea was as varied as a kaleidoscope. A flat calm on the 600-mile Fastnet race and he noted he'd seen in the dawn water flashes of blue and purple and green enmeshed in bright contrast; he saw poetry in waves and he relished the challenge of mastery over that sometimes cruel mistress, the sea, that combination of wind and waves, racing against foe and friend in our peculiar brotherhood of ocean racing which draws us together in competition and comradeship.

'It was a human and heady time sailing with Ted. Whether he'd become Prime Minister or not. The sadness was that he had, in that role, so short a time to get the best from all around him, with his quiet intelligence and love. Love of sailing, love of music and, in politics, love of his country.'

No one was closer to Heath in his sailing life than Owen Parker, who died in 2008 and without whom Heath's remarkable transition into a successful international sailor could surely never have taken place. He sailed with Heath for twelve years. Parker would recount how Heath had woken him during the Sydney–Hobart yacht race saying that the boat was surrounded by killer whales. 'What should I do?' asked the Leader of Her Majesty's Opposition. 'Pray, sir, pray,' answered the wise old sea dog, then rolled over and went back to sleep. Another of Parker's favourite stories was of an occasion when he instructed Heath to 'bear away' – meaning to turn the boat away out of the wind. Heath responded by 'luffing', which is to say, turning into the wind. Without a hint of fluster, as a tutor might instruct a child, Parker added: 'Bear away the other way, sir.' Parker would also put his foot unobtrusively on the bottom of *Morning Cloud*'s wheel to steady the boat's course, when 'Sir' started waving to other sailors, usually on the way up the Hamble after a race.

In any case, if people waved, it wasn't necessarily at Heath: Parker was well known to everyone of note who was involved in sailing on the south coast.

Parker wrote at length about Heath and I am convinced that it makes essential reading in gaining an understanding of the man:

'As most people know, Mr Heath came to ocean racing from dinghies. The first *Morning Cloud* was the result of a visit to the London Boat Show, where Mr Heath looked at a lot of boats, liked the Sparkman & Stephens 34 and happened to meet the designer Olin Stephens on the stand, and finished up buying one. She was launched at Rochester in April 1969. She sailed with a certain amount of success that year and Mr Heath declared his intention of going in for the Sydney–Hobart race; this starts on 26th December, so fits in well with the Parliamentary recess.

'Now, all the others were paying their own way, but this was quite beyond my pocket and I told Mr Heath so, thus presenting him with a nice problem. The *Cloud* was a democratic boat, so how could he pay for one crew member and not all of them? He answered in the true democratic manner, as subsequent experience showed was his routine aboard. The crew were told the problem and asked to decide whether an exception could and should be made. They seemed to think that I could help them because they unanimously decided that I should come.

'Mr Heath used to get us together in his flat in Albany, off Piccadilly. We'd go there to breakfast, so as to thrash out our problems before the Skipper had to dash off to his parliamentary duties as Leader of Her Majesty's Opposition. We'd all sit round eating and talking while Mr Heath leaned back and soaked it all up. Then, suddenly, he'd make a decision and we would go on to the next point.

'Mr Heath was not able to spare the time for the first two races, and was to join us for one inshore race and then the big one; in the event, one of the earlier races had to be re-sailed after he arrived, so the Skipper was lucky. After a while this sort of life begins to get a bit tiresome, and just a little of the edge went out of us. That is, until Anthony [Sampson] announced that he reckoned we were fairly well placed.

'Mr Heath then showed some of his qualities as a leader, for nothing was too much effort for him as he encouraged us to greater efforts by his own example. We trimmed sails, baled, worked to windward, baled, tightened the backstay a bit more as the wind got even stronger, baled and fought our way up to windward. All this in a welter of wet gear, leaking diesel oil, cooking gas fumes and a fairly rough sea. "Things can only get better," said the Skipper, pausing to wipe salt spray from his face as he chucked yet another bucketful of water over the side. "Keep her going Sammy [Sampson], we'll get there one day." With 250 yards to go, we pulled away from the wind shadow and ghosted across the line.

'Then all hell broke loose. Every hooter, siren, gong and foghorn in the place started up such a racket as you have never heard. Grins all round on board, of course, and I've never before or since seen Mr Heath so excited. "Start the engine," he called when we had stopped chattering. But this was easier said than done, and it flatly refused to go, so we had to take a tow. But we didn't care, everything pointed to resounding victory, and that's what we had come for.

'Among the festivities was an invitation to Government House. In common with his invariable practice, whenever he was invited anywhere Mr Heath always replied "There's six of us you know" and we went everywhere as a crew. Anyway, this was obviously a fairly formal occasion, so we had to dig out our dark suits from the luggage which had been flown down ahead of us. "Guess whose is the only suitcase missing," grinned Mr Heath. Sadly anticlimax quickly set in, because Mr Heath had to get back to politics and we had to pack up the boat and return to England. . .

'The English manner of speech, of course, is a sure target for any Australians keen to take the mickey out of a Pom, and I have often been asked how they took to Mr Heath's almost exaggerated accent. I don't know what they said in private, but I do know that they found it impossible to understand how I, with my strong Hampshire burr, could come from the same country as the Skipper. But they quickly found that Mr Heath was a good mixer, as tough as they were when it came to competition (he was the first Brit to carry off their big one since John Illingworth won the inaugural race back in 1945), a man who asked no special favours, and was content to be judged on his merits. They particularly liked the way he was inseparable from his crew on all social occasions.

'When he was Prime Minister we all went to Chequers more than once, with everything laid on including a swim in the pool. After being treated like queens and having the chance to be shown around the official country residence of Her Majesty's First Minister, which we all read about but few of us ever see, no wife or girlfriend ever again complained about being a grass widow due to the "Cloud".

'I respect Mr Heath for being a great gentleman in the finest sense of that word. He thinks of others, not as a conscious effort, but automatically all the time. When we won the Sydney–Hobart race, the telegrams of congratulations poured in – there must have been nearly two hundred of them. He read every one of them out loud to the crew, and personally answered them all. When the request to appear on Australian television was received, he realised that it would mean a good deal more to the crew than to him so he asked us to do it for him; the boys pushed me forward and, indeed, I shall never forget trying to answer intelligently the questions of the interviewer, while having to ignore the ribald gestures of the rest of the lads secure behind the camera.

'It would be an unwise man who ignored expert advice on important points. I have already mentioned how we always put a lot of these things to the vote in *Morning Cloud*, but there are some where Mr Heath sounds the various views and then decides which one to adopt, others where he consults my opinion before making up his mind, yet others where he leaves it to me to get on with it, and some where he will decide on his own.

'Mr Heath is also a great leader, and it is right to say that the boat always goes better when he is on board. His presence lifts us, and he seems to know exactly how much to give us our heads and when to give us encouragement if we need it. On the final 24-hour beat to the finish at Hobart in 1969, conditions on board were very bad . . . We could easily have lost enthusiasm in the welter of chaos, and gone on like zombies praying for it all to end. Instead, we rose to new heights and fairly drove that boat to the finishing line in spite of the appalling conditions.

'He has evinced these same qualities again and again since then in lesser situations, and I like to think that he has come to have a respect for my own contribution. He has often shown this on occasions where a tactical decision has to be made quickly. He will start to discuss the various arguments for and against, realise that I want to get on with the job, and so will close the discussion abruptly. "All right Owen," he will say. "Do what you want. Only do it quickly and don't hang about." Then he may add with a grin, "But you'd better be right."'[7]

After Heath's death and not long before his own, **Owen Parker** was interviewed by a national newspaper and asked about Heath. He painted a straightforward picture of the man and his reasons for sailing. He also reminisced about the near-fatal experience they shared during the 1979 Fastnet race, when Heath had to have a bad gash on his leg stitched up in Plymouth after the race:

'His safety valve was sailing . . . He lived in a pressure cooker . . . I thought he was a bit of a lonely man, to be honest. I know he had his politician friends, but with us, we seemed to be a bit of a family to him. I could have sailed on any boat but sailed with the skipper for twelve years. That says it all. There was no politics on board; whatever was said afloat never came ashore and there was no alcohol. Mind you, we made up for it ashore. "Champagne if we win" was our motto . . . [In the 1979 Fastnet Race] we were rolled over to 210 degrees at two o'clock in the morning. Sir Edward was thrown out of the navigator's seat and Dave Arnold and Pat Lilley landed on top of him. He said nothing and we thought nothing of it until the next day when we saw dried blood on his leg.'[8]

Peter Dove became acquainted with Heath through his work, but ended up as a member of the *Morning Cloud* crew:

'I first met Ted at the London Boat Show in January 1969; he had just bought an S&S34, a new design by Sparkman & Stephens built on the Medway by Mike Winfield. The company for which I was working, Ratsey & Lapthorn, had been asked to make the sails for the boat and I needed to know what colour the new owner required his spinnakers to be; needless to say his colour of choice was blue.

'In September 1969 I was approached by Owen Parker to see if I would be able to go with the boat to Australia and race in the Sydney–Hobart race. Unfortunately my employers would not release me as they said I would not get back to England in time for the London Boat Show. I missed out on that one, but Ted was gracious enough to write thanking me for the sails we had made, which had withstood the test of the heavy conditions.

'I sailed on the boat a number of times in 1969 but never with Ted, as he had many commitments, but in 1970 I did the 'Round the Island' race with him. This is a classic race on the South Coast and most boat owners would wish to compete. Unfortunately Owen Parker was not able to race, so I became a point of contact.

'As Ted had recently been elected Prime Minister, his safety was of paramount importance. I had a telephone call from his office on the Friday before the race to see if I could meet a Squadron Leader at Hamble Point Marina, where the boat was based, as he had a lifejacket for the Prime Minister to wear. I said there were lifejackets on board – and also a life raft – so this would not be necessary, but was informed that this was something special. I duly arrived at the appointed time and found an RAF helicopter on land adjacent to the Marina, so I headed towards it. A gentleman in flying gear then jumped out holding a lifejacket, which he passed to me. I took it from him and nearly fell over with the weight of it; and told him Ted would not wear this and, if he did and fell over the side, he would sink to the bottom – only to be told that at least they would know exactly where he was.

'In the October of 1970 I was involved in early discussions about a new boat for the Admiral's Cup selection trials in 1971. We had had a number of meetings but in early December I was involved in a motor accident and finished up in hospital in Southampton. Ted rang the hospital to enquire how I was and to see if I needed anything. When the staff nurse arrived at my bed to say that the Prime Minister had rung and wanting to know how I knew him, I said it was through sailing. I was never quite certain if my treatment got better or worse after that, but at least he was caring enough to take the trouble to ask about me.

'In May 1971 the new boat was launched, and it quickly became apparent that the boat was quick and sailed well up to its rating. This gave the crew the opportunity to test sails and equipment and to play with the rating to get the very best out of the boat's design. The yacht also became a test bed to various new ideas and innovation. Ted would discuss these with the crew and some were literally taken on board, for he was not averse to trying new ideas.

'The selection trials for a three-boat British Team for the Admiral's Cup in August were held in the Solent and English Channel and, thanks to the boat's success, we were the automatic boat of choice with Sir Edward selected as Team Captain – a great honour for someone so new to the sport. One thing that Sir Edward achieved was to get together a very cohesive crew who all got along very well, with virtually no arguments and all very happy to pull well together.

'As a crew we have all kept in touch and have been able to enjoy many gatherings where we talked about the good times that we had with Sir Edward. Looking back over the years there was really only one incident which saddened Sir Edward's sailing and that was the loss of *Morning Cloud 3* and two of her crew. It was obviously discussed after the event at crew meetings to try and establish the turn of events, but no real conclusion was reached.'

In summer 2006, a year after Ted Heath died, I organised a memorial concert in his honour, at St John's, Smith Square, whose No. 32 used to be Conservative Central Office and has now become Europe House. The programme reflected his tastes. Of course. There was Elgar; there was Mozart; there was an orchestrated version of the piece Bob Farnon wrote in honour of Heath's sailing exploits; and there was the divine Catherine Wyn-Rogers, singing the gorgeous ballad 'Take Care of This House', by Leonard Bernstein, with whom Heath had a such a lively, playfully disrespectful and tease-strewn friendship. Lord Tom McNally subsequently wrote: 'I think the old curmudgeon would have been quietly pleased that such an eclectic gathering could still fill a hall to remember him with real affection.'[9]

This is an edited version of the essay I wrote for the programme book on that occasion:

'Sir Edward Heath was a man of paradoxes. He could be deadly serious, but he could also be unexpectedly and incredibly funny; he could be pompous yet he could also send himself up wonderfully, denouncing all "pomposi" everywhere; he could seem aloof and cold, but he was also capable of turning on the charm when the spirit moved him; and he was also an intensely shy and private man who loved nothing more than taking to the podium and conducting an orchestra in front of hundreds or even thousands of people. This last conundrum was the one that fascinated me most.

'So what did music mean to him? It was perhaps natural that someone with that introverted, private streak – and one so preoccupied with his own sense of destiny – should look to some private muse for inspiration. Ted Heath was also an intensely practical man, however, and the organ scholarship he won at Balliol was crucial for his development. It eased his financial worries and even enabled him to stay at Oxford for an extra year; a year he used to excellent and lasting effect.

'Yet there were undoubtedly times when I looked into those clear blue eyes of his and realised that, for this extraordinary and lonely man, music really was not just a means to an end; it was not about egotism or power or providing an answer to some deep need to create a personal space, using a wall of sound to supplement that famously terse manner. Music touched this man; it touched his soul. In so doing, it should have proved even to his gainsayers that he had one. Through music, the great campaigner for this country's European destiny also found a means of expressing his quintessential Englishness.

'When he notched up his unbroken half-century in the Commons, his parliamentary colleagues had a whip-round and I spent the money on beautiful scores by that other Sir Edward – Elgar, whose music he perhaps loved above all other – and Benjamin Britten, whom he had known personally and greatly admired. They were the obvious choices. The Britten volume was a facsimile of the manuscript score for Britten's opera *Peter Grimes*, which was premiered at Sadler's Wells just as the young Heath had been putting his life on the line for his beliefs, courageously fighting his way across Northern Europe as part of the army of liberation. As it happens, I did not select this in order to make some existential, political or biographical point; I did so at the suggestion of Donald Mitchell, doyen of Mahler and Britten scholars.

'Nonetheless, there was no disguising the symbolism of the choice. Grimes is the archetypal loner, one seemingly born to be misunderstood, generally misanthropic and especially uneasy with the distaff side. Yet he also retains a certain stark nobility, despite his tragic lapses into words and deeds that start with self-sabotage and ultimately lead him inexorably on to self-destruction.

'The Cathedral Close of Salisbury is certainly a less blustery and more clement port than the wintry coast of East Anglia, but sometimes it's hard not to conclude that Ted Heath too was one of our great tragic heroes: craggy and brave, too uncompromising for his own good and often recklessly indifferent to his reputation. Throughout the storms of his life, it was so often music that brought him solace – the 'joy for life' of which he often spoke – and tonight, together, we celebrate that in his honour.'

Edward (Ted) Greenfield (1928–2015) was chief music critic of the *Guardian*; and was the author of books on Puccini, Joan Sutherland and André Previn. He was for many years the doyen of writers and broadcasters and recorded music; and he was the most loyal of friends with Heath, never losing sight of his faults, but appreciating his virtues too. Ted contributed this very touching appreciation of Heath the musician for publication in that programme:

'It was a great occasion, certainly a first for a serving Prime Minister, when at the Royal Festival Hall in November 1971, Edward Heath raised his baton and conducted the London Symphony Orchestra in a revelatory performance of Elgar's *Cockaigne* overture. We all knew already that each Christmas from his undergraduate years at Oxford onwards Edward Heath had in his home town of Broadstairs conducted a carol concert. We knew too that as the organ scholar of Balliol College in the late 1930s he had been torn between music and politics as a career, but conducting the country's leading professional orchestra at a Royal Festival Hall gala concert in the full glare of world publicity was still a formidable challenge that he fully recognised and turned into a triumph both musical and personal.

'His performance of *Cockaigne* on that occasion told us not just of his musicianship and his understanding of Elgar – *Cockaigne* is a tricky piece to conduct with its kaleidoscopic changes of tempo and mood – but of his own character. If till then the general image of him was as a chilly, reserved figure, here was a man who in music revealed a warmth of response that took many by surprise.

'Within a year or so, soon after leaving Downing Street, he amplified that revelation in a book, one of the cherishable few which tell purely and directly of musical enjoyment, *Music: A Joy for Life*. There too a warmth and openness which few had suspected came out clearly. Plainly music fired emotions in him that he normally kept hidden.

'There were those who, maybe understandably, tried to decry his efforts as those of an amateur, but his presence on the podium regularly created a sense of occasion, and orchestras on whatever level responded accordingly. No one present in a packed Salisbury Cathedral for an eightieth birthday concert is likely to forget it, an electric occasion.

'Though he remained impervious to criticism, he was certainly gratified by praise for his musical efforts. I remember seeing him at a concert during his time as Prime Minister, when he referred with obvious delight to a review I had just written in *Gramophone* magazine, nominating his LSO version of *Cockaigne* as the one against which the new recording had to be judged. It plainly meant more to him than being praised for his political judgment.'

Music was Heath's great passion from his childhood until his death. He was a fine keyboard player; he established the Balliol Choir and organised concerts there; he composed incidental music for student theatre productions; and he conducted carol concerts each year (during peacetime) from the 1930s until the millennium. Those renowned Broadstairs Christmas carol concerts were latterly transferred to Bexleyheath, on the outskirts of his Bexley constituency, where he shared the stage, if not the podium itself, with an array of well-known sportsmen, television presenters and weathermen, who made the annual charitable appeal. Heath's mastery of the organ changed his life. Not only did it give him a creative outlet; it gave him an extra, highly fulfilling year at Oxford University. Yet that was as much a triumph of practice, effort and determination as it was of natural talent. He certainly loved music, as this entire section of the book demonstrates. His critics claimed his desire to conduct was just another manifestation of his desire to dominate and to meld others together into the instrument of his will. Perhaps they have a point – up to a point. There was also a simple, childlike joy in his music-making.

Heath's impressive musical mementos are scattered throughout Arundells, his former house in Salisbury. These include photographs from those concerts he conducted in his home town of Broadstairs from 1936 onwards; hairs (encased in resin) from the violin bow that Isaac Stern broke as he played Bach's *Chaconne in D Minor* at Chequers on 27 October 1973, at a concert in memory of Pablo Casals; a copy of the manuscript of a section of *Der Rosenkavalier*, signed by Richard Strauss; a case of Sir John Barbirolli's batons; and numerous other musical artefacts and manuscripts, including a first-proof copy of the score of Sir Edward Elgar's *Pomp and Circumstance* 'March No 3', annotated by the composer and signed on 6 August 1905. The drawing room at Arundells, which he often referred to as the music room, is dominated by the last of the Steinway grand pianos he owned.

Sometimes Heath was able to combine his political and musical enthusiasms, as witnessed, for example, by his indispensable role in the creation and nurturing of the European Community Youth Orchestra (latterly the European Union Youth Orchestra), which he also guest-conducted on tour in its early years: 'It was formed because someone wanted to show that there was more to the EC than merely fruit and vegetables and arguments about tariffs. We said that Europe and its history are much more than this; and although they might not have written it into the treaties, we can show that this is the case.'[10]

His most celebrated single appearance came when, as Prime Minister, he conducted Sir Edward Elgar's overture *Cockaigne* with the London Symphony Orchestra at London's Royal Festival Hall on 25 November 1971. This performance was captured by EMI for a best-selling LP record and then, in 1996, it was reissued on a CD that was produced to commemorate Heath's eightieth birthday. **Heath** had an hour's rehearsal with the musicians, the day before the concert. He began with a few words explaining his considered conception of the piece they would play together. It reminds us of how much more comfortable he could feel, expressing himself through music:

'Can I thank you first of all for your immense kindness in inviting me to conduct tomorrow night, I appreciate it enormously and I'd like to thank you. I asked that we should do *Cockaigne* for a number of reasons, but first of all because tomorrow is a gala night, and it seemed to me that *Cockaigne* as a gala overture was a showpiece, which the LSO plays better than any other orchestra, and it was therefore suitable to open a gala concert and I hope you agree with that. My general feel about *Cockaigne* is that it was composed at the beginning of the century when England was tremendously confident and when London itself was pretty cheerful and gay and I've always believed that *Cockaigne* should be played in that spirit and boldly, rather than a rather more reserved kind which we sometimes hear today. Once I remember a television interview went so far as to say it should be played with vulgarity – that was probably going a bit too far I think. Not quite vulgarity, but with plenty of confidence and verve and as a showpiece, so perhaps we could get on with that.'

Before Heath took to the podium to conduct the LSO that night, the orchestra's principal conductor **André Previn** gave him a generous introduction, which he must have relished:

'When he was at Oxford, Edward Heath at one point actually had to choose for his career between his two principal interests: politics and music. Politics aside, he even finds time for music today – he conducts a choir regularly and he finds solace and relaxation by playing the piano. In 1963, he was the chairman of the distinguished group that founded the LSO Trust. It was a position he relinquished only when he became Prime Minister. Now, a great many reasons have been suggested as to why we have invited him to be our guest conductor. The reasons up to, and including, the fact that perhaps this would allow me to ask that for fifteen minutes I could be guest Prime Minister. In actual fact we have invited him to be our Guest Conductor because he has been a staunch supporter and a loyal friend of our orchestra, the LSO, for a great many years. And also because he is a musician. Ladies and Gentlemen, Edward Heath.'

There was a good-humoured hubris to Heath's attitude towards his conducting 'career', though it is surprising to see the breadth of what he did conduct in public (including a full performance of Handel's *Messiah* and Dvořák's

Symphony No. 9). When he persuaded his friend Herbert von Karajan to allow him to conduct 'his' Berlin Philharmonic, the question of repertoire immediately arose. Playfully, Heath suggested Bruckner's mighty *Symphony No. 8*. When he did realise his dream of conducting the Berliners, he did so in a special televised concert in Paris in 1978 and in a much more suitable piece – Elgar's *Cockaigne* again. In the mid-1980s, his former parliamentary colleague Stratton Mills, now chairman of the Ulster Orchestra, proposed a full cycle of Mahler's ten completed symphonic works, to be performed by a combination of musicians from Ulster and the RTÉ Orchestra in Dublin, which contained a number of expatriate Hungarians to whom this music was second nature. He suggested to Heath that he might conduct the *Symphony No. 8* – known as the 'Symphony of a Thousand' because of its scale and ambition. It has defeated many a professional maestro. Indeed it is nigh-impossible to bring off successfully in the concert hall, as I have heard for myself on a number of occasions. Fortunately, Heath's 'security people' vetoed the idea almost immediately as being too dangerous and no one lost any face.

Heath guest-conducted a wide range of leading ensembles, including the Chicago, Cleveland, Utah and Bournemouth Symphony Orchestras. He chaired the LSO Trust prior to becoming Prime Minister and was accorded the very rare and privileged status of honorary membership of the LSO. In the 1990s, he conducted large-scale concerts in Salisbury Cathedral, in whose Close he made his home, to raise money for essential renovation work on the fabric of the building. Guest soloists included Ivo Pogorelich and Murray Perahia, with repertoire ranging from Schubert's *Symphony in B Minor* (The 'Unfinished') and Beethoven's *G Major Piano Concerto* to Heath's favourite choral work, the *Te Deum* by Anton Bruckner, sung by the Philharmonia Chorus and four distinguished soloists.

On one notable occasion, it was not merely politics but its more refined first cousin, diplomacy, that Heath intertwined with his musical passion, when, in 1987, he led a charitable appeal under the patronage of the late Queen Mother and the Vice-President of the People's Republic of China, to support the work of the China Welfare Fund for the Handicapped. The centre-piece of the appeal was a concert in the Great Hall of the People. **Heath** tells the tale:

'I had arranged to go to China in the spring of 1987, starting in Shanghai and then going on to Beijing. I received an invitation from the symphony orchestra in Shanghai to conduct them and, as soon as the China Central Philharmonic Orchestra in Beijing heard about this, they asked if I would conduct them in the Great Hall of the People too. Shanghai then came back and said that there was so much interest that they wanted me to do two concerts, which I accepted. Then came a further request to do a concert on the preceding night too, and I accepted that as well.

'The Great Hall of the People accommodates 8,000 people and . . . it was packed full. I was told that everyone of note was present, except Deng Xiaoping himself, who told me that because he suffered from deafness in one ear, he thought the seat would be wasted, which I quite understood. I went off to the western provinces after the concert and, whenever I walked into a hotel or along the street, people stopped and pointed at me and said: "The music man!" They had all been watching the concert on television that night, and it was calculated that some 400 million people had seen it.'

Heath had a meeting with Chairman Deng Xiaoping the day after the concert, 19 April 1987. Deng remarked that he had watched the concert live on television and had greatly enjoyed it. He also thought Heath might be pleased to know it was the first time he had ever known China Central Television to delay their nightly news broadcast to accommodate an over-run.

Heath made a handful of commercial recordings: a live recording of his concert debut in 1971 with the *Cockaigne* overture; another live recording for EMI of a Robert Mayer concert for young people; and an excellent LP he recorded of Christmas carols, to tie in with his book on the same topic. There was also a recording, made for the old Pickwick label, of the Triple Concerto by Beethoven. This was another instance of Heath falling for the unloved, semi-forgotten member of an otherwise celebrated canon (did anyone else ever name Beethoven's 'retro' and highly classical Symphony No. 8 as his or her favourite of the nine?). Readers can work out the significance of this (if any) for themselves. This is indeed an excellent recording and meant the world to Heath, for it was his first (and only) commercial studio recording of a multi-movement and serious piece, though the rave review it received in the *Penguin Guide* possibly had not a little to do with Heath's close friendship with Ted Greenfield, one of the editors.

The soloists were the Trio Zingara – violinist Elizabeth Layton and the piano–cello duo (professionally and personally) of Annette Cole and Felix Schmidt. Schmidt had played at Chequers with other students from the Menuhin School when Heath was Prime Minister. He was mortified when his cello spike slipped and he had to start playing his allotted piece again, from the start. When Heath met him years later, after hearing him perform at the Banqueting House, Whitehall for Yehudi Menuhin's 'Live Music Now' charity, he recognised Schmidt and recalled that Chequers incident clearly. He then asked him if he would like to do a concert with him. In due course a letter arrived and Schmidt was asked to play Schubert's *Sonata in A minor for Arpeggione and Piano* at a charity 'doo' in Bexley, accompanied by Heath. They rehearsed in Wilton Street and payment was a case of apples. Heath and Felix Schmidt performed a great deal together thereafter and Heath and the Trio also became a 'package' of sorts for concert promoters, performing the Beethoven *Triple Concerto* together. Felix Schmidt and Annette Cole were regular guests of Heath at Christmastime, along with the Seligmans. On more than one occasion, when it was time for the regular Boxing Day trip to Chewton Glen, a nearby hotel and spa, Felix and Annette, on the advice of one of Heath's policemen, temporarily disabled their car because neither of them wanted to be designated driver. They therefore got to travel with Heath, and Madron Seligman had to drive.

Music was the subject of the second of Heath's successful 'coffee-table' books in the mid-1970s and he used as a sub-title something his father had told him when exhorting him to practise his scales on the piano – that music would prove to be a trusty 'joy for life'. In what would become a dry run for the production of his much more substantial – but somewhat less heartfelt – memoirs twelve months later, in the winter of 1996–1997, once Heath's eightieth birthday celebrations were safely out of the way, I suggested to him that it might be a good idea to produce a second edition of *Music: A Joy for Life*. He was easily persuaded, as were the editorial team at the publisher, who had a handy link with Classic FM. A 'tie-in' radio series was agreed and we got to work. Sadly the book was no triumph. It was a worthwhile exercise, however, in that it demonstrated to me how to 'get a book out of Heath'. It's also a decent read and at the time of writing the remaining copies – which Heath bought up at a rock-bottom price – are still on sale at Arundells. One passage from **Heath**'s introduction to that second edition stands out:

'Beethoven wrote on the score of his *Missa Solemnis*: "It is from the heart, may it go to the heart." This inscription could speak for the whole of music. I have listened to, and loved, music for as long as I can remember. For performers, conductors and listeners, music transcends all boundaries of language, politics and culture. At its best, music is the purest and most moving form of art, and I hope that this book will, as its subtitle suggests, enable me to share with the reader some of the joy and unique inspiration that music can bring.'

Here is part of the transcript from an interview with **Heath** from the mid-1990s, when I was working with him on the second edition of *Music*:

'We always had musicians coming to No. 10. I remember Carlo Maria Giulini visiting and saying, "I'm told you have a remarkable sound system." I said, "I don't know if it is, but come upstairs and see." I put on Verdi's *Requiem* and he said, "This is tremendous. Is this my recording?" I said, "Yes – there's the label – you can see it is." These people don't recognise their own recordings. The same happened when I played the *Meistersinger* overture to Sir Georg Solti. He said, "It must be a German orchestra." But it was the London Philharmonic under Solti himself!

'I worry that some young musicians don't give two hoots about inter-pretation. Some come here to play and I say, "Do you know Paderewski's recording?" and they ask, "Who's Paderewski?" "Only a mere politician," I say, "but he is also one of the greatest pianists who ever lived." In a life in music one is often surprised. I was in Bayreuth once when a lady came up to me and said: "I am so pleased to meet you. I didn't realise you were interested in music at all. It is so nice to see you – when I get home I'll tell everyone I have seen you. I mustn't keep you any longer. Thank you so much Mr Wilson!"'

By the time I worked for Heath, his failing heart had caused his fingers to swell up, making piano playing difficult for him; and his hearing too was not what it had been, which condition was not helped by the old man's vanity that made him too proud to seek help in the shape of a hearing aid. By the mid-1990s, Arundells would more commonly shake to the sound of twenty-four-hour news (at an improbably high volume) than it would to the Terpsichorean muse. Nonetheless, for anyone whose heart sank upon discovering that a mischievous host or hostess had placed him or (especially) her in the immediate proximity of Heath on a *placement*, a good working knowledge of classical music was the best (perhaps only) guarantor of a conversation. Many of **Heath's** best stories, even those connected with politics, had a kernel of music to them, for instance this account of MPs engaging in something for which they have never been especially renowned, namely making a harmonious noise together:

'I recall one instance in the summer of 1951 when the Labour Government, with a majority of only seven, had been hard-pressed throughout the session and in particular on the Finance Bill, which had been dragged out day after day and night after night, until we were finally on a Sitting that had lasted continuously for thirty-two hours. At ten o'clock one night came the last vote on the Bill. Everyone was exhausted. As Junior Whip, I went to stand by the door where the Labour Members of Parliament were being counted by my opposite number. Suddenly, as I stood there, I heard a low sound beginning to well up from the Government lobby. The doors were opened and as the Labour Members filed through, the sound grew and grew. In that moment of supreme stress and strain, the Welsh Members were singing "Guide me, O thou great Redeemer, Pilgrim through this barren land", to the tune of "Cwm Rhondda", with all the passion of men and women who had reached a crucial time in their fortunes and had turned again to the childhood tunes of the Welsh valleys. As the words "Bread of Heaven, Bread of Heaven/Feed me till I want no more" swelled out and they burst into that wonderful harmonisation of "want no more", I felt sure it was giving them the strength to carry on the battle.'

The arrival of Heath as Prime Minister was followed, shortly afterwards, by his bold decision to cede his lease at the Albany and move all his possessions into his new home, lending his residency, in his own mind at least, an atmosphere of permanence. No image is more suggestive of his arrival than that of the Steinway team moving in his grand piano; and no single image more brutally captures his ejection from office less than four years later than the almost identical photographs of the same team removing the same piano, to be taken into storage for a time, for Heath had no home of his own to which he could immediately go. The adjective 'iconic' is over-used these days to a degree that denies it almost all meaning, but perhaps it might be apposite here. Heath loved music so much that his piano truly symbolised him.

Music was an integral part of his residency, both at No. 10 itself and also at the Prime Minister's weekend retreat Chequers, which he adored and turned into as much of a home as he had ever had. In fact he had both No. 10 and Chequers renovated and he loved to entertain at both his new homes. He felt he had earned it. At the heart of his busy social calendar were recitals, by musicians of all shapes and sizes, from world-renowned musicians such as the Stern–Istomin–Rose trio to pupils from the Menuhin School. Just as Heath would come to life in conversation when a musical thread presented itself, so, even in prose (a form of which he was scarcely an undisputed master) his sense of excitement could manifest itself clearly. Here is an abridged account from **Heath** himself, of the part music played in his premiership:

'When I moved into 10 Downing Street as Prime Minister, it was to become my home. I had no other. Moreover, when people came there I wanted them to feel not that they were coming to an office with an official residence and a flat over it, but that they were coming to a home with an atmosphere just like their own . . . and for me home meant music.

'One of the best-known photographs taken at the time I became Prime Minister showed my Steinway piano being moved into No. 10. After the breakdown of the first negotiations for Britain's entry into the European Community, through President de Gaulle's veto in January 1963, I had been awarded the Charlemagne Prize by the city of Aachen for my work in trying to create a wider European unity. With the prize money I bought a small rosewood grand piano from Steinway's which had recently completely renovated it. Built in 1922, it came from a vintage year – for pianos have good and bad years just like wines. Moura Lympany, the concert pianist, helped me to choose it.

'It was the first time I had had a piano of my own; until then I had relied on the one bought from Thornton Bobby's, nearly forty years before, which was at my father's house at Broadstairs, or on hired instruments. The Steinway was placed in a corner of the White Drawing Room on the first floor at the corner of No. 10 looking out over both Horse Guards Parade and St James's Park. It was the first time a piano had been permanently installed in the house since Arthur Balfour had ceased to be Prime Minister in 1906. Whenever an opportunity occurred I could easily get there for a few minutes' practice, particularly after a quick tray lunch or in the early evening after the day's meetings were over; often I would play late at night when I got back from official functions or from the House of Commons. Robert Armstrong once said to me that whenever they could hear the Steinway at No. 10 they all heaved a sigh of relief, knowing that for a brief time at least the demands made upon them would slacken. It was true that afterwards I would return refreshed and ready for the fray, but those interludes were beneficial for all of us.

'Another instrument that played an important part in musical life at No. 10 was the clavichord in the drawing room in my flat at the top of the building. This marvellous instrument was made for me by Tom Goff, the creator also of many modern harpsichords, who not only specialised in the construction of the instrument but also executed the beautifully inlaid decorative casing. Even among musicians comparatively little is known about the clavichord . . .

'The Steinway, the clavichord and the stereo were my own personal ways of making music, but I wanted music to enter more widely into the life of No. 10. Perhaps the most moving of all these occasions was when I entertained at 10 Downing Street the representatives of Northern Ireland and the Republic of Ireland, who were taking part in negotiations at Sunningdale over the establishment of the future relationship between the two countries. At the end of the first day's conference I had invited them all to dinner, but for reasons of security no one had been told where this would be, only that they would leave Sunningdale at seven o'clock; to their surprise they soon found themselves at No. 10.

'There had been no gathering like it in Downing Street before. For me it was an emotional moment. I was able to bring together round the same dinner table the representatives of those who had spent so many centuries quarrelling with Britain or with each other. Now at last a settlement seemed to be within our grasp. I was touched when John Hume and Paddy Devlin, two of the Social Democratic Labour Party representatives from Northern Ireland, came up to me and said: "We never expected to be inside No. 10 tonight. The last time we were at No. 10 we were lying on the pavement opposite in a protest demonstration and no one so much as gave us a cup of tea." I had asked Martin Neary to abandon the usual programme of madrigals and choose familiar songs that would appeal to our guests. Once the singers started there was no holding back the Irish. They immediately joined in and by the end of the evening they had taken over completely. The lilt of "When Irish Eyes Are Smiling" spread round the room. They went back to Sunningdale feeling better towards each other – and even perhaps towards the British.'

Another notable musical moment during Heath's premiership again involved the clavichord; he described it as a moment that would 'always remain of supreme importance to me'. **Robert Armstrong** describes the occasion, on the night of 28 October 1971, when the House of Commons had handsomely approved Britain's proposed membership of the EEC:

'The majority was a triumph, and there were many celebratory parties that evening, to all of which the Prime Minister had been invited and to many of which he wanted at least to look in. But immediately after the vote he came back to No. 10, where his father and brother and a few personal friends were waiting, and he sat down at his clavichord and played the first prelude, in C major, from the first book of J. S. Bach's *Das Wohltemperierte Klavier*. We listened in silence to the quiet, ordered sounds, and it felt as if he was expressing in his own way his profound feelings of fulfilment at bringing his country back into the mainstream of European civilisation.'

There is also a story from Heath's time as Prime Minister that Ted Greenfield received a call one evening, informing him that Heath wished to see him urgently, at Chequers. A government car was despatched to carry Greenfield on the forty-mile trip from London. Heath explained that a manufacturer had presented him with its most advanced record player, but it was so complex he couldn't get it to function. Greenfield examined it closely, reached underneath, turned on the power, and music filled the room. If that story is true – and sadly there is no way of verifying or disproving it – I suspect it tells us more about Heath's loneliness than anything else, though questions could be asked about whether this was an appropriate use of taxpayer-funded resources. We now live in very different times!

In December 1995, less than six months into my time in Heath's office, I received a call from a lady in Bonn. Apologising for the short notice, she said she was organising a forty-eight-hour, unbroken marathon of performances of music by Beethoven, for the people of Bonn. The festival was just days away, but they needed a big name to open it, with a keynote speech. There would be no fee but flights and hotel rooms would be provided. I asked Heath if he would consider it. The answer was blunt – 'Yes. If you write the speech.' I already knew this was special. No one *ever* wrote a speech for Heath. He prided himself on speaking without notes and he disliked wearing his reading glasses in public. He was a pro, though – he knew this one could not be left to chance. Furthermore, he knew I would enjoy this trip and I had to pay my way. So, for the one and only time in five years, I wrote a speech for him. Here is a long excerpt from it:

'There can surely be no other musician to compare, as a man, with Beethoven. Who could fail to be moved by his Titanic character, his disdain of the protocols of society, his growing deafness, his dedication of the "Eroica" and its subsequent, passionate destruction, the 'Heiligenstadt Testament' and all the other features of a life of such moral and creative strength. Like so many of his period, Beethoven drew inspiration from the brilliant characters of Homer, Plutarch and Shakespeare and from the democratic political revolutions of his time – yet he himself had a reputation for abrasiveness and rudeness.

'This was one of many contradictions in this extraordinary man, who, for all his scorn of society's mores, never dropped his "van", with its hint of aristocratic superiority. As a young man he was already regarded as

[349]

more than a little arrogant and sure of himself – and somewhat lofty. As the aged Haydn saw less and less of the young composer, he would ask of common acquaintances "How goes it with our Great Mogul?"

'Perhaps it is impossible to imagine the greatness without the loftiness, the sudden and wonderful bursts of creative activity without the impatience, the genius without the flaws. Nor must we forget that Beethoven was himself frustrated and troubled by his difficulties in dealing with other people – he desperately wanted his social graces to match his philosophical ideals, but his impatience and his growing deafness so often got the better of him. His deeply personal and confessional 'Testament of Heiligenstadt' gives us all a moving insight into the internal struggles that accompanied his immense creativity. Above all else, it reassures us of what we already know – that the composer of *Fidelio* was moved by love of his fellow men. Indeed, although he composed relatively little for it, the human voice often brought out the best in Beethoven.

'It is as well to be wary of drawing close parallels between political events and musical developments, but there can be no doubt that Beethoven was strongly influenced by liberal thought. For the bracing wind of freedom was already blowing strongly from the West – from the new Republic of America, from France and from the philosophers of England, and Beethoven rejoiced in it. There can be no more potent, more moving expression of freedom than *Fidelio*, to my mind by far the greatest opera mankind has wrought.

'Politicians and philosophers may squabble about the true nature of freedom, and many will always subvert its slogans and concepts to suit their own ends. But true freedom – freedom of thought and expression, freedom from the knock on the door in the dead of night, freedom from nuisance and harassment, freedom to develop and to live a fulfilling life – these are the freedoms which continue to inspire me in politics, and they are the ideals which inspired Beethoven and his generation.'

When we arrived at the packed (and very large) hall for the opening ceremony, Heath was as good as gold, delivering my carefully prepared script word for word. He liked the speech and the audience liked it too, demonstrating their excellent linguistic skills by laughing at any instance of gentle humour, even before the translators had a chance to repeat them in German.

The Heath sense of humour was dry as dust and this trip produced the sole occasion on which I witnessed him truly helpless with laughter. Inevitably, no great thought or subtlety had gone into the 'trigger line'. After watching Sir Roger Norrington conduct the opening concert of the Beethoven marathon, we were invited to a private dinner with the singers, though not, for some reason, with the conductor himself. As we began to dine, Heath turned to me and said, in a stage whisper, 'These people really should realise, they can't compensate in this way.' The remark seemed odd. I looked quizzical. Who was compensating, for what, and in what manner? Somewhat dyspeptically, with a jabbing gesture, he explained: 'The beard, the beard.' It dawned on me: Sir Roger is follicly challenged, or, more bluntly and demotically, he is a bald man with a beard. 'Oh,' I replied jauntily, 'you mean Mr Upside-Down Face!' To my astonishment, like a tubby schoolboy hearing a dirty joke for the first time, the aged former Prime Minister completely lost his dignity and self-control and started giggling uncontrollably. He ended up gasping for breath, he had laughed so much.

So was Heath much of a musician? I write for *Gramophone* magazine, so I suppose I ought to know. Daniel Barenboim (whom, allegedly, Heath once described as a 'monkey with a stick', though I never found any reliable attribution for this unlikely remark) once mentioned Heath in an interview and said he was a great admirer of his 'because of his passion for music'. 'But he's not the greatest of conductors, is he?' asked the interviewer, Douglas Kennedy. Barenboim paused. 'He sails better than I do,' he replied, somehow both diplomatically and mischievously, with a twinkle in his eye.[11] I witnessed one or two near disasters. There was a performance in Salisbury Cathedral – the acoustic no help – when the first movement of Beethoven's *G Major Concerto* almost completely disintegrated. I also remember several string players in fits of giggles during a rehearsal of Schubert's great 'Unfinished' Symphony at the same venue. I dread to think what prompted that. It is important for a conductor to lead, to keep the beat slightly ahead of the band, but, like most amateur conductors, Heath tended to slow down as he conducted, sub-consciously waiting for the musicians to catch up. He loved Bruckner's *Te Deum*, but, when he conducted it to mark his eightieth birthday, I thought it would never end. Nonetheless, the accumulated power of the piece was a wonder to behold.

I have talked to several musicians who played under him. They all agree – he was a gifted amateur, neither more, nor less. One pianist, called in at short notice to rehearse and play a Mozart concerto with Heath as conductor, recalls the concertmaster of the orchestra whispering to her as she arrived, 'whatever you do, don't look at him'. Any competent concertmaster knows how to nurse an orchestra through all but the most complex piece, although it does help if the person on the podium gives the occasional cue, to brass, woodwind and percussion – and Heath could be unreliable in his cuing. At a rehearsal of Tchaikovsky's intricate *Rococo Variations* in Prague, he once neglected to cue the end of a horn solo – such that the poor soloist seemingly did himself a mischief holding a note and had to be replaced for the concert itself. In his party piece, the *Triple Concerto*, the three soloists could, if necessary, take charge between them and keep things on track. He took it all deadly seriously, of course, and he was deeply wounded when a European journalist accused him of 'massacring Mozart' (the overture to the *Magic Flute* with the ECYO) and had a dig at his sailing credentials. 'The chap who wrote that was not even a music critic,' said Heath resolutely. 'I don't think we need worry about him and his headline, with its cheap sneer at sailing.' I went to several rehearsals by Heath, by which time, of course, he was an elderly man. They were brief and to the point; and his comments were never technical. What he did, however, was constantly to exhort the musicians to play with greater flexibility and feeling.

In Heath's defence, as a young man he certainly was technically very good as a keyboard player and, even if his (untrained) baton technique was deficient, I saw at first hand that he had a good musical mind. The Balliol organ scholarship – and the installation of a new chapel organ, which he supervised – amply testifies to that. He also genuinely adored music. In late 1969 and early 1970, Heath and Bryan Magee (later to become a Labour MP) made an *Omnibus* film for the BBC – 'The Other Edward Heath'. Speaking about music, Heath is, in turns, sincere, endearing and child-like in his enthusiasm, most notably when he is showing off his stereo system (which he characteristically pronounced 'steer-ee-oh'). Filmed talking to conductors of the calibre of Edward Downes and Carlo Maria Giulini, he seems unusually relaxed and happy – as though with colleagues. Invited to present the Edinburgh fringe award in 1969, he reveals his playful and anarchic side, praising 'the real purpose of the Fringe

– to provide new, original, creative work'. In an excerpt from a Broadstairs carol concert, he is as relaxed, cheerful and game as can be. Perhaps most telling is his intense love of Beethoven's only opera, *Fidelio*: 'The whole theme is the freedom of man – and the influence of good and the influence of evil . . . and, in the end, good triumphs over evil. Well this, as a philosophy, sums up the whole of what life is about . . .'

Heath also thought long and hard – possibly deeply – about music, as this passage demonstrates:

'I find the opening bar of Beethoven's *Fifth* the most controversial of any orchestral piece, though I seldom hear it discussed amongst conductors. The normal practice is to emphasise its three quavers equally, with a tendency for the main emphasis to come automatically on the first. Two bars later, however, as soon as individual instruments begin to play the same phrase in the way in which it is valued in a complete bar, the emphasis naturally comes on the second of the quavers. The contrast between the second version and the first, coming so quickly after the opening bar, is so marked that I find it jars. Moreover, it is difficult to justify intellectually. I have yet to hear the performance, however, in which a conductor tries to reconcile the two.'[12]

I don't think music-making for Heath was about the exercise of power, as some have claimed. Far more often for him, as several contributors to this collection have testified, it was to the gentle clavichord that he often turned for musical fulfilment. The last clavichord he owned had the slogan *'plus douceur que violence'** on it – 'a fair motto for life', he once said. It was a means of expression; an opportunity for him to reveal the warmer, more romantic side of his nature. This was implicit in the repertoire he loved most. I write this having just heard a performance of Mahler's *Symphony No. 2* – 'The Resurrection' – which was one of Heath's lifelong favourites. With its non-liturgical but profoundly spiritual and uplifting finale on the theme of the resurrection of the soul, this piece is the epitome of the grandiose, overtly emotional music that Heath adored and more fastidious music lovers eschew

* 'More gentleness than violence'.

at all costs. How odd to think Mahler died just five years before Heath was born.

For concert promoters and working musicians, Heath was above all 'box office': he would get 'bums on seats'. Wisely, as in his sailing, he would surround himself with good people, in particular top soloists, who were more than capable of covering up any of his deficiencies. There is merit in Ted Greenfield's summary: Heath's conducting exploits gave infinite pleasure to him and also much pleasure to others. Perhaps the best parallel is to think of Dr Samuel Johnson's expression, from long before political correctness took hold: 'Sir, a woman's preaching is like a dog's walking on his hind legs. It is not done well; but you are surprised to find it done at all.'

As the revised and updated version of *Music: A Joy for Life* neared completion in early 1997, the question arose of whom to ask for an appropriate introduction. Heath and I agreed that the perfect person would be another old friend of his, **Yehudi Menuhin**, the distinguished violinist, conductor and all-round humanitarian and citizen of the world. He opened his tribute with an apposite quote from Shakespeare's *The Merchant of Venice*. It provides the perfect coda for this section of the book:

'"A man who has no music in himself, nor is moved with concord of sweet sounds, is fit for treasons, stratagems and spoils." How imperative it is, therefore, that, of all professions, it is politicians who should ideally "carry music in themselves", from their earliest days, so that, attuned to song and through singing, they should have learnt to listen – to listen to others and eventually to that still small voice in their own hearts which is so often drowned in the business of living; to remember; and through memory of sounds, to make into one the realms of thought and emotion. Edward Heath had this "joy for life", which is music, from his earliest years. I firmly believe that it is in infancy that the seeds of a benign and happy old age are planted.'

Coda: Heath, sex and the allegations of 2015

From his adolescence onwards, Heath had to tolerate endless speculation about his sexual orientation – or lack of it. 'You can't imagine Teddy kissing a girl, can you?' said Heath's mother to his first sister-in-law. 'But he says he loves them all a little bit.' In the dying days of the Second World War, Heath attended a 'liberation dance'. According to his fellow officer Major Harrington, Heath could not wait to leave: 'Captain Heath did not stay at the dance overlong . . . After the CO left, he retired to his makeshift office in a local garage, to do more planning.'[1] Not long after, at his selection meeting in Bexley, Heath would say: 'I have no prejudice against matrimony. I just think that it is not a matter that should be rushed.'[2] He was true to his word.

His bachelor status certainly did not help him in politics. It marked him out and caused much speculation, which evidently (and understandably) irritated him. In his first BBC interview as leader, Heath was asked by Robin Day whether being a bachelor would lessen his electoral appeal. He responded, rather tartly: 'I don't really see how you can expect me to decide that. I don't really think so.' Day persisted. Had Heath, he enquired, ever thought of taking 'any personal initiative in that matter?' Heath responded laconically: 'No. You have recently taken one on, but I have not got one in mind, at least not yet.'[3] This was not the only occasion on which he wisely used humour to deflect this line of questioning. Around the same time, a woman reporter asked what he intended to do about a hostess at No. 10, should he become Prime Minister. 'Is that a proposition?' he asked.[4]

Asked a few months later whether he would make a better Prime Minister were he married, Heath appeared to have given the matter more thought and replied: 'I don't know. It would depend to some extent on the woman, wouldn't it? What I do know is that a man who got married in order to be a better Prime Minister wouldn't be either a good Prime Minister or a good husband.'[5] Heath's friend and contemporary Ian Harvey did exactly that, though, marrying Christopher Mayhew's sister principally to ensure he could have a political career. I think it is very much to Heath's credit that he did no such thing. He had too much integrity. He certainly had plenty of opportunities, but the kind of women who would throw themselves at him were precisely the kind of women with whom he felt uncomfortable – as he saw them, subservient and simpering. An early example was a secretary at the *Church Times* who was so smitten with Heath that she followed him everywhere and (even) predicted he would become Prime Minister one day. He could not bear that; an attitude that never changed. Cecil King, a seasoned Heath-watcher, understood this: 'Ruth* thinks Ted is fond of me; I think he is fond of her and finds the friendship of an intelligent and musical woman, with no possible axe to grind, very welcome.'[6]

Heath's father once said: 'Of course, we would be very pleased if he got married, but that is up to him . . . It would be good for him. I've tried to talk to him about it sometimes, but it's no use. He's married to politics and that's all there is to it.'[7] Unsurprisingly, Marian Evans, first wife of Heath's brother John, devoted a substantial (but not unkind) section of her 1970 book to this burning question. Here is an excerpt that gives a flavour of what must really have upset Heath about her book:

'[Mummy] and I would often speculate about Teddy and girls. We knew they liked him a lot and thought he liked some of them too. It wasn't as though he didn't notice girls or feminine things. He was always very quick to spot a new dress, hair style or perfume, and as his mother was not a woman to wear curlers or look other than immaculate he had a high

---

* Cecil King's wife.

standard of female beauty. Once when we were speaking of someone we thought he liked very much he dismissed her because she had thick ankles, though we thought he would have admired her fantastic brain! . . .

'I've often thought that had Teddy married it would have been to a woman who was prepared to devote herself to him and not have a career of her own.'[8]

Asked by one interviewer whether his 'shell' had protected him, Heath answered: 'It has prevented other people trying to cause damage and, to a certain degree, the feeling of pain. Music has helped there too. I never like to think of it as being an outlet, but it has enabled me to live a much fuller life . . . I was brought up not to go around shouting one's own wares, so I have never done so. Perhaps that was my mistake.'[9] Perhaps the most durable rumours of entanglements with the distaff side involved the oft-married concert pianist Dame Moura Lympany, who, by all accounts, would have been very happy to be the first Mrs Heath – and Katharine 'Kay' Graham, publisher of the *Washington Post*, who had been widowed in 1963. There is a hilarious passage in Marian Evans's book about the latter:

'Perhaps the most ridiculous story was the one soon after the [1970] general election. American inspired, it was picked-up all too eagerly by our newspapers and I believe was little more than sensation. This was the rumour that Teddy and wealthy American widow Mrs Katharine (Kay) Graham were "smitten with each other". A US columnist claimed that Teddy and Mrs Graham . . . were seeing each other every night in London and the woman had extended her visit to this country after the election. Mrs Graham promptly denied the story. Next day an interesting theory as to how the story started appeared in the *Daily Mail*'s Charles Greville diary. It seems there was some confusion between their names and those of a couple with similar names – a Ted Leith and a Kate Grahame, the girl an American.'[10]

When her memoir was published in 1997, Heath said to me, *en passant*, that she had been 'very nice in it about our affair'. This was certainly an unusual remark, coming from Heath, but I merely stored it away until recently, when I obtained a copy of Mrs Graham's memoir. In it, Heath is mentioned just twice, and the story of their 'alleged romance' – as Mrs Graham puts it – runs along similar lines to that told by Marian Evans.

It wasn't quite as simple as that, because Kay Graham later served on the Brandt Commission with Heath and certainly became a confidant of his. Robert Vaudry recalls that she used to stay at Arundells and rather take the place over – 'she was very comfortable with him, very relaxed and at home'.

Heath met Moura Lympany in 1961; and she introduced him to a range of her many musical and theatrical friends – including Joan Fontaine. She became a regular concert companion of his and gossip columns frequently suggested they might end up as a couple, though she again dismissed such suggestions as 'nonsense' in her memoir.

The journalist Lynn Barber interviewed Heath in 1998, in connection with the forthcoming publication of his memoirs. She was intrigued by what – if anything – made him tick sexually:

'According to Kay Raven's cousin, Pamela Hill: "I honestly don't think there was, on her side, any romantic attachment." Anyway, she married a pilot in 1951 and died of cancer in 1978 . . . Dame Moura Lympany . . . told Cockerell that during Heath's premiership, someone came from the 1922 Committee to beg her to marry Heath, but she was in love with someone else at the time. Anyway, Heath knew nothing of this proposal! On the homosexual side, we have Margaret Thatcher's remark to Sir John Junor: "When I look at him, and he looks at me, I don't feel that it is a man looking at a woman. More like a woman looking at another woman" – and Barbara Castle's comment about his redecoration of Chequers, that he made everything look "so much more feminine – another clue to Heath's character?" John Campbell mentions an MI5 claim that he had an affair with a Third Secretary at the Swedish embassy, and Alexander Waugh, the music critic, tells a story about Heath's enthusiasm for a young German cellist called Felix Schmidt, whom he pestered with invitations and promoted so vigorously that one concert agent thought he was Schmidt's manager. But such stories hardly amount to "evidence"; all we can say with certainty is that Heath is a bachelor who has totally repressed whatever sexuality he might have had.'[11]

Perhaps the mystery of Heath and his sexual nature was solved, intuitively, not by someone close to him, but by someone who, to the best of my knowledge, never met him but held him in high esteem, Kenneth Williams. In his published diaries, I was astonished to discover that Heath featured prominently. Williams evidently admired him very much indeed and, reading not too much between the lines, recognised some of his own qualities in Heath. In his diary on 23 May 1971, Williams recorded: 'Wrote to Edward Heath saying I admire him very much: do hope he gets us into Europe.' Against the odds, I located a copy of the letter in Heath's shambolic archive. Writing from the Cambridge Theatre, where he was performing in *Captain Brassbound's Conversion* by George Bernard Shaw, Williams in fact wrote: 'As one who so much admired you during the Election Campaign – knowing the tremendous odds which you faced – I just wanted to let you know that I, and many others like me, still feel that admiration and affection as well.' I noted with approval that Douglas Hurd had Heath respond personally. Is it too much of an imaginative leap to conclude that Kenneth Williams – the reclusive, frustrated, self-repressing, occasionally self-loathing, high-profile, high-achieving but congenitally dissatisfied gay man who found the thought of physical intimacy with others repugnant – sensed Heath was a similar soul?

No one will ever for sure know about Heath's sexuality, but it was certainly something about which people would ask when I worked for him. I therefore pondered it long and hard, without any chance of coming to a definite conclusion. Often I would watch him closely in the hope of seeing someone – a waiter or waitress, a flight attendant, easy on the eye, male or female – catch his eye, but ne'er was there a flicker that I could discern. This seems to have consistently been the case with him, at least as far back as the 1960s. I was not the first Heath staffer to wonder, as **Jeff Stacey** can confirm:

'The fourth researcher [on the Heath memoirs], also American, decided one day at Arundells while the boss was away to establish once and for all what his sexual preferences (if any) entailed. I would have nothing to do with this plot and tried to dissuade him from carrying it out, but, when I returned after a weekend in London, my colleague reported that he had searched Sir Edward's bedroom and private library high and low, coming up with nary a single piece of paraphernalia. The boss was thereafter cleared of any such suspicion.'

In the absence of outright evidence, I reasoned the matter through. If Heath had been sexually attracted to women, then why on earth would he have denied himself the pleasure of dalliances or long-term relationships with them? In his pomp, he was pretty dashing, not hard up, with a substantial public profile. At one point he was both a leading politician and a UK team captain in international sport. There seemed to me only one credible answer to the conundrum. The downside was that it was totally unoriginal. I expressed my opinion forthrightly in a book I wrote in 2011 about the tangled history of the Tories (who stand, if for anything, for personal choice and freedom) and LGBT rights in the UK, to which they have only belatedly (and only partially) converted:

> 'The author of this book worked for Sir Edward Heath between 1995 and 2000 and was left in no doubt whatsoever that Heath was a gay man who had sacrificed his personal life to his political career, exercising iron self-control and living a celibate existence as he climbed the "greasy pole" of preferment. This is the obvious, default explanation for Heath's bachelor status, bouts of narcissism and notoriously prickly relationships with women – and there are plenty of reasons for subscribing to it, contrasted with few (if any) for rejecting it.'[12]

To my disgust, when allegations were made, in the summer of 2015, about Heath abusing under-age young men, this quotation was wheeled out, as if it were in any way supportive or indicative of allegations of illegal activity with boys, when, if anything, the opposite is true. So too were the words of Jeremy Norman, included in the section of this volume dealing with Heath's later life in Salisbury, referring to the way in which Heath in old age relaxed into the company of gay men and became a supporter of LGBT equality. I don't believe any of the nonsense about Heath bothering boys or going to prostitutes or cruising on Hampstead Heath. He was a very fastidious man, who disliked physical contact of any kind. That wasn't an act, put on for show.

I suspect Heath never had much of a libido at all, nor do I believe he ever had an intimate relationship with anyone – but I do also agree with a colleague who once said to me, during a conversation on this topic, that dismissively to dub anyone 'totally asexual' was to deny them their very human identity. I think that is right. So, to my mind, Heath still must have made a conscious decision at some point – an ordinance of self-denial – and diverted his energies elsewhere. There are numerous tales – not least in this volume – of Heath being disappointed when women to whom he was well disposed went off and married other men. Certainly he was fond of several of them and could be charmed by women, but it seems to me his disappointment was simply (and understandably) that he could no longer count on being the focus of their attention; and it would probably be inappropriate for each of them, once married, to be his 'plus one' at social events. How typical of Heath to demonstrate a mixture of selfishness as well as propriety.

Even if, as I and many others believe, Heath had no sexual desire for women, he could, of course, still have found a wife. There are plenty of precedents for that, especially in politics. Finding a wife could have made Heath's life easier in so many ways: certainly he would have avoided all those awkward questions, dark hints or 'hello sailor' *doubles entendres*. No, Heath decided early in life that this part of his life would be closed off. In some respects this helped him, enabling him to devote his energies and time to other matters, but it would also, crucially, have given a wife to Caesar. Political wives (or husbands) can be invaluable sources of sincerely well-intentioned and entirely confidential (though not always excellent) advice and provide a way of letting off steam. For all his legendary rudeness to women, he didn't do perhaps the cruellest thing of all, by marrying one. All of which brings us back to the allegations of 2015, which, at the time of writing, still hang over the name and reputation of Heath as the investigation continues, spawning various lubricious and ludicrous website posts and rants.

On 20 April 2015 a BBC researcher contacted me with what seemed to me a mystifying line of questioning. Had I attended Coombe Hill Junior School, he asked? Slightly warily, I confirmed I had. Was I there in the spring and summer of 1979? I confirmed this too. That was my final year before going to grammar school. He asked me if I recalled a road traffic accident, in which a child from the school had been killed or seriously injured? I had no such recollection – and it's not something one would likely forget. He then ran a number of names past me, none of which I recognised. The researcher was reluctant to give too much away, but I pressed him. It subsequently became clear I had been contacted as a consequence of the investigations by the Metropolitan Police into allegations made against a number of public figures, by someone operating under the pseudonym 'Nick'. One senior detective had described his claims as 'credible and true'. A team at the BBC had realised that 'Nick' had made one crucial slip, because, amidst all the vague allegations, he had made one – just one – that was time- and place-specific and therefore verifiable, claiming a boy (a victim of abuse) had been deliberately run down and killed outside Coombe Hill in the spring of 1979. The BBC was now seeking to track down former pupils of the school who had been there at that time – ideally in their final year – as both 'Nick' and the alleged 'victim' supposedly had been.

I called an old schoolmate and he, too, had no recollection of any such incident. What we both did vividly recall was that there had been at the school a poor little girl who had been born with a hole in the heart. When she – not unexpectedly – died, the excellent head teacher, Mrs Keane, had suspended the normal activities of the school for a time and held a special, unified assembly. It was a traumatic, unforgettable event. If one of our peers had perished in an accident, that would surely have been indelibly seared on our minds. I consulted my father, who was working at the time in the Education Department of the Royal Borough of Kingston upon Thames. Any such event would have crossed his desk at once and he too is certain this was fantasy. He checked with his former colleague Mike Dale. The answer was clear: no, this had not occurred. The local press too looked into it and found no record of such an occurrence.[13] The BBC duly produced a broadcast that discredited 'Nick' utterly and the Metropolitan Police Operation Midland ended soon afterwards, amidst a flurry of grudging semi-apologies. Harvey Proctor, a living victim of the witch hunt, has spoken and written eloquently of the human consequences of what occurred. He, at least, is protected by the law of defamation. Heath does not have that privilege. The BBC investigation, which was criticised by the police, had tugged at the one verifiably loose thread in the cloth of deceit woven by 'Nick', which was now falling to bits.

On Friday 31 July 2015 I received an email, forwarded from my personal website, from a journalist on the *Mirror* newspaper. 'I wonder if you could give me a call when you have a moment,' it read. 'Working on something to do with Ted Heath that I would like to discuss with you.' I called the journalist and he explained he had got wind of a story about Heath, to the effect that he had been accused of using the services of a 'madam' in Salisbury to procure young men. I laughed it off. I thought no more of it until the following Sunday evening, 2 August 2015, when I received a lengthy email from a colleague. Here is an excerpt:

'Tomorrow at 12.30 the Independent Police Complaints Commission [IPCC] will issue a statement announcing that they are investigating Wiltshire Police in relation to a case from the early 1990s.

'A young Detective Constable was prosecuting a woman for brothel keeping. He was approached by her solicitor who said that if the case wasn't dropped then she would allege that she had procured boys for Edward Heath. He then referred this information up the chain of command. Then the case may have been dropped. Nothing further then happened until the police officer, who had by then risen through the ranks, reported the facts to his senior officers. They then referred the matter to the IPCC who have now decided to oversee an investigation.

'The difference between this situation and the trickle of vile allegations that have appeared on the internet over the years, is that this will be the first time that an official body has announced an investigation in to an allegation involving (albeit tangentially at this point) Sir Edward. The police intend to deploy officers outside the house tomorrow to ensure order (albeit it could also have the advantage for police PR of implying an investigation in to Sir Edward). They expect that the announcement may lead to camera crews turning up and there may be protesters.'

I was stunned, and hoped that what seemed to me a non-story would come to nothing. Unfortunately that was not to be. On the next day, Monday 3 August, the IPCC did indeed announce it was going to investigate the conduct of Wiltshire Police, in connection with a claim that 'a criminal prosecution was not pursued when a person threatened to expose that Sir Edward Heath may have been involved in offences concerning children'. In May 2016 the IPCC found there was no evidence to support this allegation, although a separate investigation continues to look into a number of complaints that have arisen since the call for victims at Arundells was made.

In life Heath was not totally immune to far-fetched allegations – for instance, in January 1984 an alleged rapist claimed Heath had appeared in pornographic photos, along with a detective sergeant – that had been stolen by the police. That claim was rapidly dismissed. The announcements in 2015 by the IPCC and Wiltshire Police, however, led directly to a wild outburst of media speculation that has caused such damage – possibly irreparably – to the posthumous reputation of a statesman who is no longer protected by defamation laws.

What has been so striking since then is that, so far as I can ascertain, no one at all believes what has been alleged. They have good reason. While certain newspapers took advantage of the story as something colourful with which to fill their front pages in August, traditionally the quietest news month of the year, more thoughtful columnists in the classier elements of the press – notably the *Telegraph* and the *Sunday Times* – soon righted the balance by stating obvious and salutary facts: there was no evidence; an ugly climate of fear was being created; and Heath was unable to defend himself.

Gradually, the storm abated, calm discussion ensued – and widespread scepticism about the allegations gradually took hold. On 30 August, it was reported that the former police officer who had exposed Jimmy Savile as a wholesale child sex offender, Mark Williams-Thomas, had warned that the witch hunt against Heath was being led by individuals who were 'not evidence-focused, preferring to pass off rumour as fact and, very worryingly, in a few cases, putting pressure on victims of child abuse, which has led them to name high-profile people as offenders . . . The police job is to investigate an allegation and collect evidence or challenge the allegation made . . . Yet none of this has properly occurred before going public, with unsubstantiated allegations, and totally trashing Heath's reputation.'[14]

In considering the allegations, some of us who knew Heath well have gone through a three-part process. The first question we asked ourselves was whether we believed Heath would have desired sexual contact with underage men or boys. Not one of us, based on hundreds of years of combined experience of the man, believed he would. Nothing appeared to suggest it. If that was Heath's penchant, he made a superhuman and 100 per cent successful effort to conceal it.

The second question was, even if Heath had harboured such desires, would he have succumbed to them? In this context we can speak meaningfully

of the iron discipline he possessed and also of the extraordinarily busy life
he lived, first as an ambitious young politician who either worked or travelled, or enjoyed music or sailed, in every waking moment. He had so very
much to risk from any illegitimate liaison; and he was so driven to succeed.
It seems most unlikely he would risk it, even if he did want it. This was, let
us remember, a man who harboured leadership ambitions until the 1980s –
when he was almost seventy years old.

The decisive 'clincher' for me – not unrelated – is the third point, which
is how Heath lived his life, from the time he became a whip (and, incidentally,
someone responsible for monitoring any moral turpitude or peccadilloes
amongst his colleagues). Between 1951 and 1965, politics was already his life.
He put in hours, in Parliament, in Bexley and out on tour that barely gave
him a moment's privacy or peace. From 1965 until 1970 his life was controlled
utterly by his private office; between 1970 and 1974 he was Prime Minister;
and, after 1975, he had constant police protection and surveillance.

Peter Batey trawled through his private papers and archive on a number of occasions and remained a friend until Heath's death:

> 'There was nothing in his private papers, my extensive discussions with
> him and frequent travel with him to suggest Heath was homosexual. Most
> of his friends and staff were male, with the exception of his secretaries and
> housekeepers, but this was hardly uncommon, both for his time and for
> Westminster. In many ways he was naïve. We had to advise him against
> using the term "cruising" in his memoirs when referring to a holiday as we
> thought there was a risk it could be misconstrued and used against him. He
> meant the term innocently and was genuinely taken aback when the risk
> was explained to him. The historical allegations of paedophilia are shock-
> ing and I cannot believe them, based on my time working for him and my
> extensive dealings with him for the remainder of his life. Ted Heath fought
> for his country in the Second World War, served his country in Parliament
> and in the governments of Winston Churchill, Anthony Eden and Harold
> Macmillan, eventually rising to become Prime Minister himself. He even
> represented his country as a sportsman. He does not deserve this.'

A politician whom I greatly admire, **Norman Tebbit**, who admits he did not like Heath, calling him a 'cold fish', wrote a fine piece in defence of his posthumous right to fair treatment and a fair 'trial':

'Now, 10 years after his death, when he is no longer here to defend himself, there has been a sudden storm of allegations that Heath was a particularly foul pervert who found pleasure in the sexual abuse of young boys. There are, his accusers declare, questions to be answered. Indeed there are, but Ted Heath is unable to answer them, while his accusers have free rein to canvas throughout the media for victims to come forward to denigrate him.

'If we are looking for justice, then this is a dangerous step to have taken. Who do we think will answer this call? Perhaps some of those disturbed people who may sincerely believe, among their many fantasies, that they have suffered wrongs or abuse at the hands of those in power. Or maybe those who are excited at the thought of a moment of fame. Or, the worst of the bunch: those tempted by the prospect of financial gain . . .

'As to Mr Heath, none of us can judge because he cannot speak. I did not like him, but that does not make him a pervert. His claim to justice is no less valid than those who claim to be his victims.'[15]

In these pages there is a comprehensive portrait of the man – of a decent, shy, sometimes frustrated, often difficult, rarely charming, wantonly brusque, proud, public servant who always believed in fairness and who loved his country – and who never hurt a fly. Heath was very different, yes. He never married. He had to deal with innuendo all his life. He may have been gay ('So what?' most younger readers would say – and good for them), but in death he has been treated abominably. What does it say about us as a society that we can hand out such treatment to people who have so faithfully served their country?

As I have explained in this book, I struggled to get on with Edward Heath, but I do retain a certain affection for him and I also admire him for his manifest achievements. I also believe passionately in his entitlement to fair treatment in death – his right not to have people wantonly trash the 'immortal part' of himself – his reputation. Only time will tell, but I hope and believe the investigations by Wiltshire Police will ultimately exonerate Heath of these gruesome allegations and his reputation will be restored.

Acknowledgements

My thanks are due, first and foremost, to the excellent team at Elliott & Thompson: to Jennie Condell, who took direct charge of the project; to Pippa Crane, senior editor at E&T, who remained stoically calm, patient and good-natured in her dealings with a highly eccentric author and his (almost) catastrophically over-long manuscript; and to Alison Menzies and Ollie Dewis, the PR team who have done such sterling work, making people aware of this book's existence. Jonathan Asbury has been a sensitive and good-natured editor, dextrously leading the way in boiling down 250,000 words to something closer to 150,000 words without diluting substance, flavour or pertinence.

Nicholas Garland was Ted Heath's favourite cartoonist – his former home in Salisbury still contains a substantial display of Garland originals – and it was appropriate, essential even, that his brilliant work should be represented in this book. His immediate willingness to grant me the necessary permission was characteristically generous.

So many other people also made this book possible and receive my heartfelt thanks:

My father, Noel McManus, not just for his help with the text of this book, but also for almost half a century of support, encouragement and sustenance.

Georgina Jayne – for support and help, way and beyond. Some of those speeches made the cut, at least in part . . .

Nicholas Robinson, for numerous V&Ts and also for setting up the

website for the book (along with several others for me, including www.michael
mcmanus.org.uk).

Guy Black, Gavin Fuller and Ed Taylor, all at the *Telegraph*, without
whose assistance the historical research for this book would have been all
but impossible.

Peter Batey, who has contributed – and continues to contribute –
so generously to help consolidate the personal and political legacy of
Sir Edward Heath.

Neil Carmichael, the excellent MP for Stroud, who does more than
anyone else to keep the flame alive in the House of Commons.

Other friends who helped in various ways, sometimes directly, some-
times indirectly and sometimes just by being a friend: Liam Abrahams,
David Alliance, Catherine Bailey, Tom Baker, Tristan Beint, David Benson,
Edward Bickham, Slaven Bilić, Richard Blackford, Lisa Bowerman, John
and Caroline Bowis, Steve and Stella Broster, Peter Bull, Jo Carr, Chris
Collins, Martin Cullingford, Iain Dale, Nick Denys, Jo Frey, Mark Gallagher,
Matthew George, David Gold, Sarah Graham, Ben Gummer MP, Theo
Hadlow, Richard Harrington MP, Nick Hurd MP, Paul Kendrick, Sarah
Kennedy, Jane Kersley, Andrea Knowles, William Kwok, Shaun Ley, Ken
and Carol Lucas, Jeremy McIlwaine, Patrick Maddams, Fraser Massey, Pete
May, Ian MacGregor, Will Meyerhofer, Nigel Morris, James Naughtie, Sian
Norris-Copson, Lee Ormsby, Giles Peel, Lisa Pritchard, Carolyn Quinn,
Sakuntala Ramanee, Mikey Robertson, Lewis Robinson, Tracy Rodger,
Charlie Ross Mackenzie, Howard Ruse, Mathew Rutter, Barry Ryan,
Dominic Seligman, Lincoln Seligman, Olivia Seligman, Roderick Seligman,
John Sessions, Jae Shannon, Rob Shepherd, Tim Shipman, Helen Smeed,
Karen Summers, Donald Sumpter, Anthony Teasdale, William Timmins,
Eleanor Updale, Gerry Wade, Margareta Waymouth, David 'Wooders'
Wooding, Peter Wright and Michael Young.

I owe a profound debt of thanks to all my contributors for their generosity and patience, starting with David Howell and Patrick Jenkin, who
both made such considered and substantial, first-hand contributions, adding
enormously to the authority of this book.

To have one former Secretary of the Cabinet in such a book may be
regarded as a coup; to have two looks like star billing. I am so very grateful

to Robert Armstrong and Robin Butler, along with their former colleagues Christopher Roberts and Alan Simcock, for contributing their memories of Edward Heath, Prime Minister, from their time in the No. 10 Private Office.

That distinguished quartet are part of an almost unbroken run of forty years of private and political secretaries, from the time Edward Heath became leader of the Conservative Party until his death in July 2005; and all the surviving members of that human chain have contributed memories, reflections and assessments to this book, which lend it both colour and authority: John MacGregor, Douglas Hurd, William Waldegrave, Stephen Sherbourne, Wilf Weeks, Peter Luff, Peter Batey, Richard Burn, Robert Vaudry and James Elder.

Profound thanks for contributions go also to Geoffrey Adams, Lord Baker of Dorking, Roger Boaden, Gyles Brandreth, Richard Bull, Robin Chichester-Clark, Anthony Churchill, Michael Cockerell, Lord Cope of Berkeley, Pete Cracknell, Stuart Craven, Peter Dove, Lord Dykes, Alyce Faye Eichelberger Cleese, Michael Fabricant MP, Patrick Guthrie, David Harris, Ian Hay Davison, Lord Heseltine, Lord Hunt of Wirral, Lord Jopling, Robert Key, Barbara Lewis, Sir David Madel, Sarah Mansell, Lady Susan of Mar, Dr Simon May, Henrietta Mayhew, Heather Millican, Stratton Mills, Sara Morrison, Jeremy Norman, Matthew Parris, Lord Prior, Professor Brian Reading, Sir Steve Redgrave, Mark Robinson, Nick Rundle, Felix and Annette Schmidt, Brendon Sewill, Richard Simmonds, Jeffery Speed OBE, Dr Jeffrey Stacey, Anthony Staddon, Alastair Stewart, Elaine Tarsh and Sir Teddy Taylor.

Thanks are also due to everyone who gave permission for me to reproduce material, in particular Lin Menuhin and Menuhin IP Management GmbH and the Parker family (for the late Owen Parker).

Notes

CHAPTER ONE **Early life (1916–1950)**

1   *Sunday Express*, 15 August 1965
2   Hutchinson, George, *Edward Heath: A Personal and Political Biography* (Longman, 1970), pp. 8, 10, 14, 15
3   *Sunday Express*, 15 August 1965
4   *Mail on Sunday*, 13 November 1988
5   Hutchinson, *Edward Heath*, pp. 12–13
6   *Sunday Times*, 3 February 1985
7   *Sunday Express*, 15 August 1965
8   *The Times*, 11 January 1975
9   Hutchinson, *Edward Heath*, p. 18
10 Hutchinson, *Edward Heath*, p. 34
11 *Sunday Express*, 22 August 1965

12 Laing, Margaret, *Edward Heath: Prime Minister* (Sidgwick & Jackson, 1972), pp. 72–73
13 Hutchinson, *Edward Heath*, pp. 41–42
14 Hutchinson, *Edward Heath*, p. 43
15 Hutchinson, *Edward Heath*, pp. 47, 50–51
16 *Sunday Express*, 22 August 1965
17 Evans, Marian, *Ted Heath – A Family Portrait* (William Kimber, 1970), pp. 108–109
18 Hutchinson, *Edward Heath*, pp. 60–62
19 *Daily Telegraph*, 9 September 1977

CHAPTER TWO **Rise through the ranks (1950–1959)**

1   House of Commons, 26 June 1950, Cols. 1959–1964
2   Laing, *Edward Heath*, p. 101
3   Eden, Anthony, *Full Circle* (Cassell, 1960), p. 549
4   Laing, *Edward Heath*, pp. 101–102, 105–107
5   Evans, *Ted Heath*, pp. 90–91
6   Evans, *Ted Heath*, pp. 89–91
7   Speech, 14 June 2000
8   *Hansard*, 30 October 1956, Col. 1275
9   *Hansard*, 1 November 1956, Col. 1716
10 House of Commons, 20 December 1956, Col. 1457

11 Hutchinson, *Edward Heath*, pp. 83, 85
12 Eden, *Full Circle*, p. 549
13 House of Commons, 17 May 1961, Cols. 1390–1400
14 From records held at The National Archives
15 Ibid.
16 Letter from Harold Macmillan to Heath, 26 December 1962, from records at The National Archives
17 Roll, Eric, *Crowded Hours* (Faber & Faber, 1985), pp. 113–115
18 Hutchinson, *Edward Heath*, p. 129

19 Laing, *Edward Heath*, pp. 159–160, 161
20 Laing, *Edward Heath*, pp. 183–184
21 House of Commons, 10 March 1964, Cols. 255–269
22 Laing, *Edward Heath*, p. 161
23 Laing, *Edward Heath*, p. 162
24 Whitelaw, William, *The Whitelaw Memoirs* (Aurum Press, 1989), p. 53
25 *Observer*, 16 June 1965
26 Laing, *Edward Heath*, p. 157
27 *Daily Mail*, 19 July 1965
28 Interview with Lord Walker of Worcester, 15 January 1998
29 *Daily Telegraph*, 29 July 1965
30 House of Commons, 29 July 1965, Cols. 727, 736, 738
31 *Daily Telegraph*, 30 July 1965
32 House of Commons, 2 August 1865, Col. 1085
33 Laing, *Edward Heath*, p. 182
34 Ibid.
35 Ibid.
36 *Daily Express*, 20 September 1965

37 *Illustrated London News*, 18 September 1965
38 *Spectator*, 14 January 1966
39 Adapted from Hurd, Douglas, *An End to Promises* (Collins, 1979)
40 Ibid.
41 *Hansard*, 22 February 1968, Col. 659
42 *Daily Telegraph*, 14 March 1968
43 *Sunday Telegraph*, 21 April 1968
44 *Daily Telegraph*, 22 April 1968
45 Adapted from Hurd, *An End to Promises*
46 Ibid.
47 King, Cecil, *The Cecil King Diary 1965–1970* (Jonathan Cape, 1972), Tuesday, 26 September 1967
48 Margach, James, *The Abuse of Power* (WH Allen & Co Ltd, 1978), p. 158
49 Margach, *The Abuse of Power*, p. 157
50 Ibid.
51 Adapted from Hurd, *An End to Promises*
52 Ibid.

CHAPTER THREE **Prime Minister (1970–1974)**

1 Coleman, Terry, *Thatcher's Britain* (updated edition, Corgi, 1988), pp. 76–77
2 Barber, Anthony, *Taking the Tide* (Michael Russell, 1996), pp. 75–76, 97
3 *Hansard*, 4 November 1970, Col. 1107
4 Barber, *Taking the Tide*, p. 102
5 Tebbit, Norman, *Upwardly Mobile* (Weidenfeld & Nicolson, 1988), pp. 105–106
6 Adapted from Hurd, *An End to Promises*

7 Roth, Andrew, *Heath and the Heathmen* (Routledge & Kegan Paul, 1972), p. 138
8 Adapted from Hurd, *An End to Promises*
9 Ibid.
10 Ibid.
11 Ibid.
12 'Battling for Britain', *The Top Job*, BBC Radio 4, 16 October 2000
13 Adapted from Hurd, *An End to Promises*
14 Ibid.
15 Barber, *Taking the Tide*, pp. 75–77

16 King, Cecil, *The Cecil King Diary 1970–1974* (Jonathan Cape, 1975), 6 March 1971

17 *Hansard*, 27 November 1985, Cols. 898–899

18 Hoggart, Simon, *On the House* (Robson Books, 1981), p. 150

19 'Edward Heath Day', BBC Radio 4, 26 July 2015

20 Adapted from Hurd, *An End to Promises*

21 Manuscript note dated 28 May 1972

22 *Hansard*, 22 May 1972, Cols. 1095–1096

23 Maudling, Reginald, *Memoirs* (Sidgwick & Jackson, 1978), p. 193

24 *Hansard*, 22 March 1972, Cols. 1522–1648

25 King, *The Cecil King Diary 1970–1974*, 21 June 1972

26 *Hansard*, 6 November 1972, Col. 623

27 *Hansard*, 15 May 1973, Col. 1243

28 Hoggart, *On the House*, p. 150

29 Ibid., p. 10

30 Adapted from Hurd, *An End to Promises*

31 Meyer, Anthony, *Stand Up and Be Counted* (Heinemann, 1990), pp. 63–64

32 *Hansard*, 19 November 1973, Col. 973

33 Ibid., Cols. 973–974

34 Ibid., Cols. 985–986

35 Adapted from Hurd, *An End to Promises*

36 King, *The Cecil King Diary 1970–1974*, 5 December 1973

37 Adapted from Hurd, *An End to Promises*

38 *Hansard*, 17 December 1973, Col. 952

39 *Hansard*, 18 December 1973, Cols. 1176–1177

40 Adapted from Hurd, *An End to Promises*

41 Adapted from Waldegrave, William, *A Different Kind of Weather, A Memoir* (Constable, 2015)

42 Adapted from Hurd, *An End to Promises*

43 Ibid.

44 *Spectator*, 6 May 2000

45 Adapted from Waldegrave, *A Different Kind of Weather*

46 Speech, 14 June 2000

47 Adapted from Waldegrave, *A Different Kind of Weather*

48 Adapted from Hurd, *An End to Promises*

49 *What Has Become of Us?*, Channel 4 series, 6 June 1994

50 Adapted from Hurd, *An End to Promises*

CHAPTER FOUR **Out of office (1974–1997)**

1 Barber, *Taking the Tide*, p. 80

2 Parker, Owen, *Tack Now, Skipper!* (Granada Publishing, 1979), p. 73

3 Critchley, Julian, *Heseltine, the Unauthorised Biography* (Andre Deutsch, 1987), pp. 44–45

4 Hoggart, *On the House*, p. 100

5 *Sunday Telegraph*, 2 February 1975

6 To Michael Cockerell on BBC *Midweek*, January 1975

7 Ibid.

8 Baker, Kenneth, *The Turbulent Years* (Faber & Faber, 1993)

9   Adapted from Waldegrave, *A Different Kind of Weather*
10 *The Times*, 8 February 1975
11 *Daily Telegraph*, 5 February 1975
12 *Sunday Telegraph*, 13 March 1977
13 Ibid.
14 *Hansard*, 6 February 1975, Cols. 1554–1555
15 *Daily Telegraph*, 29 March 1975
16 Speech to Conservative Group for Europe, 16 April 1975 (www.margaretthatcher.org/document/102675)
17 *Daily Express*, 3 June 1975
18 *Daily Telegraph*, 29 August 1975
19 *Daily Telegraph*, 18 September 1975
20 *Observer*, 12 October 1975
21 *Daily Telegraph*, 11 December 1975
22 *Daily Telegraph*, 18 December 1975
23 *Sunday Telegraph*, 30 May 1976
24 *Daily Telegraph*, 10 June 1976
25 *Daily Telegraph*, 12 June 1976
26 *Daily Telegraph*, 26 June 1976
27 *Daily Mail*, 9 July 1976
28 *Daily Telegraph*, 10 July 1976
29 Heath Archive
30 *The Times*, 23 August 1976
31 *The Times*, 13 October 1976
32 *Hansard*, 16 December 1976, Col. 1787
33 Pendennis, *Observer*, 19 February 1978
34 *Guardian*, 14 June 1978
35 *Daily Telegraph*, 8 July 1978
36 *Daily Telegraph*, 8 July 1978
37 *Daily Telegraph*, 18 July 1978
38 *The Times*, 12 October 1978
39 Hoggart, Simon, *Back on the House* (Robson Books, 1982), pp. 26–27
40 *Guardian*, 1 May 1979
41 *Daily Telegraph*, 7 May 1979
42 *Daily Express*, 11 May 1979
43 Ibid.
44 *Daily Telegraph*, 19 May 1979
45 House of Commons, 28 January 1980
46 *Sunday Telegraph*, 6 July 1986
47 Reported across the newspapers on 30 November 1980
48 Hoggart, *Back on the House*, pp. 157–158
49 Ibid.
50 *Hansard*, 16 June 1980, Col. 1190
51 Heath Archive
52 *Sunday Telegraph*, 6 July 1986
53 House of Commons, 17 January 1984, Cols. 184–188
54 Carried in all the newspapers, 18 January 1984
55 *Daily Telegraph*, 18 January 1984
56 *The Times*, 20 February 84
57 *Hansard*, 21 March 1984, Col. 1050
58 Ibid., Col. 1061
59 Heath Archive
60 House of Commons, 11 April 1984, Cols. 425/428
61 House of Commons, 10 May 1984, Col. 1121
62 *Sunday Telegraph*, 18 November 1984
63 *Hansard*, 15 January 1985, Col. 227
64 *Sun*, 21 January 1985
65 *Sun*, 21 January 1985
66 *Sunday Times*, 3 February 1985
67 *Hansard*, 25 March 1985, Col. 63
68 Laing, *Edward Heath*, p. 120
69 *The Times*, 4 January 1992
70 *Daily Telegraph*, 11 October 1985
71 House of Commons, 5 February 1986, Col. 325
72 *Hansard*, 2 July 1987, Col. 665

73 Ibid., Cols. 667/668

74 *Hansard*, 1 December 1987, Col. 795

75 *Sunday People*, 14 August 1988

76 *Hansard*, 8 June 1989, Col. 366

77 *Hansard*, 2 February 1989, Col. 488

78 Harris, Robert, *Good and Faithful Servant* (Faber & Faber, 1990), p. 92

79 *Hansard*, 13 July 1989, Col. 1176

80 From the brochure marking Heath's fortieth anniversary as an MP

81 *Hansard*, 6 September 1990, Col. 752

82 *Hansard*, 27 March 1991, Cols. 985–988

83 Jennings, Martin, 'I once met . . . Ted Heath', *The Oldie*, February 2008

84 Reported across the newspapers, 19 June 1991

85 *Hansard*, 21 November 1991, Col. 457

86 *Daily Telegraph*, 20 March 1992

87 *Evening Standard*, 9 June 1992

88 *Independent*, 22 September 1995

89 *Mail on Sunday*, 14 July 1996

90 *Independent*, 19 September 1996

91 *Guardian*, 16 April 1997

CHAPTER FIVE **Final years (1997–2005)**

1 *Daily Mail*, 9 September 1986 – and something of an understatement!

2 *Sunday Times*, 12 January 1992

3 *Daily Telegraph*, 28 March 1997

4 Speech at the International Free Enterprise Dinner, 20 April 1999 (www.margaretthatcher.org/ document/108381)

5 BBC Radio 4, 30 April 1999

6 Heath Archive

7 *Guardian*, 26 July 2005

8 *Hansard*, 18 July 2005, Col. 1079

9 Ibid., Cols. 1075–1076

10 Ibid., Col. 1081

11 Ibid., Cols. 1079–1080

12 Adapted from Waldegrave, *A Different Kind of Weather*

13 First published in *House Magazine*, 25 July 2005

14 *Impressions of Heath*, BBC Four, 2015

15 *Radio Times*, 16–22 April 2016, p. 11

16 King, *The Cecil King Diary 1970–1974*, 5 March 1971

17 Roth, *Heath and the Heathmen*, p. 210

18 Speaking on BBC Four, August 2015

19 *Sunday Telegraph Review*, 14 November 1999

20 'Edward Heath Day', BBC Radio 4, 26 July 2015

21 *Sunday Telegraph*, 27 February 1977

22 Widely reported across the newspapers, 24 March 1966

23 Wilson, Harold, *The Labour Government 1964–70* (Pelican Books, 1974), p. 283

24 *Hansard*, 28 June 1966, Col. 1596

25 *Richard II*, Act 3, Scene 3

26 *Mail on Sunday*, 19 January 1997

27 *Observer*, 4 October 1998

28 Cole, John, *As It Seemed to Me* (Weidenfeld & Nicolson, 1995), p. 81

29 Interview by Pamela Coleman, *Sunday Times*, 1999

CHAPTER SIX **Sailor and musician**

1 *Guardian*, 23 August 1971
2 *Northern Echo*, 15 September 1971
3 Evans, *Ted Heath*, pp. 95–96
4 *Sunday Express*, 18 March 1984
5 *Sunday Times*, 5 September 1999
6 Ibid.
7 Parker, *Tack Now, Skipper!*

8 *Daily Telegraph*, 2 August 2005
9 *House Magazine*, 17 July 2006
10 From Heath, Edward, *Music: A Joy for Life* (revised and updated edition, Pavilion, 1997)
11 *Daily Telegraph*, 4 April 1992
12 Heath, *Music: A Joy for Life*

Coda: Heath, sex and the allegations of 2015

1 Roth, *Heath and the Heathmen*, p. 49
2 *Bexley Observer*, 14 November 1947
3 Reported in the *Daily Telegraph*, 29 July 1965
4 *Time*, 6 August 1965
5 *Observer*, 16 January 1966
6 King, *The Cecil King Diary 1970–1974*, 6 March 1971
7 *Daily Telegraph*, 16 October 1976

8 Evans, *Ted Heath*, pp. 106–111
9 *Mail on Sunday*, 13 November 1988
10 Evans, *Ted Heath*, pp. 111–112
11 *Observer*, 4 October 1998
12 McManus, Michael, *Tory Pride and Prejudice* (Biteback Publishing, 2001), p. 61
13 *Surrey Comet*, 16 October 2015
14 *Sunday Times*, 30 August 2015
15 *Telegraph Online*, 6 August 2015

Bibliography

Alexander, Andrew & Watkins, Alan, *The Making of the Prime Minister* (Macdonald Unit, 1970)

Baker, Kenneth, *The Turbulent Years* (Faber & Faber, 1993)

Barber, Anthony, *Taking the Tide* (Michael Russell, 1996)

Blake, Robert, *The Conservative Party – From Peel to Major* (Arrow Books, 1998)

Campbell, John, *Edward Heath: A Biography* (Pimlico, 1994)

Cole, John, *The Thatcher Years* (BBC Books, 1987)

Cole, John, *As It Seemed to Me* (Weidenfeld & Nicolson, 1995)

Coleman, Terry, *Thatcher's Britain* (updated edition, Corgi, 1988)

Critchley, Julian, *Heseltine, the Unauthorised Biography* (Andre Deutsch, 1987)

Day, Robin, *Grand Inquisitor* (Weidenfeld & Nicolson, 1989)

Deedes, William, *Dear Bill* (Macmillan, 1997)

Eden, Anthony, *Full Circle* (Cassell, 1960)

Evans, Marian, *Ted Heath – A Family Portrait* (William Kimber, 1970)

Fisher, Nigel, *Harold Macmillan* (Weidenfeld & Nicolson, 1982)

Goodhart, Philip, *Full-hearted Consent* (Davis-Poynter, 1976)

Graham, Katharine, *Personal History* (Phoenix Press, 2001)

Harris, Robert, *Good and Faithful Servant* (Faber & Faber, 1990)

Heath, Edward, *Travels* (Sidgwick & Jackson, 1977)

Heath, Edward, *Music: A Joy for Life* (revised and updated edition, Pavilion, 1997)

Heath, Edward, *The Course of My Life* (Hodder & Stoughton, 1998)

Hoggart, Simon, *On the House* (Robson Books, 1981)

Hoggart, Simon, *Back on the House* (Robson Books, 1982)

Hoggart, Simon, *House of Cards* (Elm Tree Books, 1988)

Home, Alec, *The Way the Wind Blows* (Fontana/Collins, 1978)

Howe, Geoffrey, *Conflict of Loyalty* (Macmillan, 1994)

Hurd, Douglas, *An End to Promises* (Collins, 1979)

Hutchinson, George, *Edward Heath: A Personal and Political Biography* (Longman, 1970)

King, Cecil, *The Cecil King Diary 1965–1970* (Jonathan Cape, 1972)

King, Cecil, *The Cecil King Diary 1970–1974* (Jonathan Cape, 1975)

Laing, Margaret, *Edward Heath: Prime Minister* (Sidgwick & Jackson, 1972)

Lympany, Moura, *Her Autobiography* (Peter Owen, 1991)

Macmillan, Harold, *At the End of the Day* (Macmillan, 1973)

Margach, James, *The Abuse of Power* (WH Allen & Co Ltd, 1978)

Maudling, Reginald, *Memoirs* (Sidgwick & Jackson, 1978)

Meyer, Anthony, *Stand Up and Be Counted* (Heinemann, 1990)

Norman, Jeremy, *No Make-up: Straight Tales from a Queer Life* (Elliott & Thompson, 2006)

Parker, Owen, *Tack Now, Skipper!* (Granada Publishing, 1979)

Patten, Chris, *East and West* (Macmillan, 1998)

Roll, Eric, *Crowded Hours* (Faber & Faber, 1985)

Roth, Andrew, *Heath and the Heathmen* (Routledge & Kegan Paul, 1972)

Smith, David, *The Rise and Fall of Monetarism* (Penguin Books, 1987)

Taylor, Teddy, *Teddy Boy Blue* (Kennedy & Boyd, 2008)

Tebbit, Norman, *Upwardly Mobile* (Weidenfeld & Nicolson, 1988)

Thatcher, Margaret, *The Downing Street Years* (Harper Collins, 1993)

Thatcher, Margaret, *The Path to Power* (Harper Collins, 1995)

Trewin, Ion (ed.) *The Hugo Young Papers* (Allen Lane, 2008)

Whitelaw, William, *The Whitelaw Memoirs* (Aurum Press, 1989)

Williams, Kenneth (ed. Davies), *Diaries* (Harper Collins, 1994)

Wilson, Harold, *The Labour Government 1964–70* (Pelican Books, 1974)

Worsthorne, Peregrine, *Tricks of Memory* (Weidenfeld & Nicolson, 1993)

Young, Hugo, *This Blessed Plot* (Macmillan, 1998)

Ziegler, Philip, *Edward Heath* (Harper Press, 2010)

Index

Königswinter 156, 173, 290
Kosovo 274
Kunming 175
Kuwait 202, 204, 233

L

Labour party 16, 18, 19, 32, 45–48, 49,
50, 55, 59, 65–67, 71, 76–78, 82, 90,
94, 97, 117, 118, 124, 125, 128, 143,
151–152, 156–158, 161, 162, 165, 167,
173, 178, 179, 181–183, 187, 189, 190,
199, 210, 215, 224, 230, 231, 237,
261, 263, 295, 296, 300, 315, 316,
345, 352
Lambton, Lord 53, 132
Lancashire 135
Lawrence, Ivan 165
Lawson, Nigel 90, 233
Leith, Ted 357
Lennox-Boyd, Mark 236
Liberal Party 3–4, 7, 8, 45, 50, 54, 56, 64,
97, 118, 132, 151–152, 209, 277
Liberal Democratic Party 261, 263, 267
Lilley, Pat 333
Lindsay, Sandy 6
Liverpool 9, 210, 319
Livingstone, Ken 213
Llandudno 37
Lloyd George, David 81, 319
Lloyd, Selwyn 23, 131
London 3, 4, 10, 37, 40, 45, 57, 91, 93, 98,
121, 135, 166, 175, 197, 204, 205, 210,
213, 218, 219, 232, 242, 248, 250,
256, 257, 267, 268, 270–272, 283,
284, 287, 292, 305, 340, 349, 359
Londonderry 136, 181, 310
Lonrho scandal 132
Lopez, Teo 250
Low Countries 10
Luff, Peter 195–196, 199, 201
Luxembourg 114, 321
Lympany, Moura 186, 214, 347, 357, 358

M

Maastricht 254, 261
MacGregor, John 56–57, 293–294, 321
Maclean, Fitzroy 22
Macleod, Iain 16, 41, 42, 55, 57, 61, 62, 71,
73, 88, 91, 127, 298–299, 302
death 89, 91, 95–97. 107, 303
Macmillan, Harold 21, 23, 25, 28–30, 33,
38–42, 73, 89, 107, 169, 170, 280,
298, 312, 313
'Night of the Long Knives' 313
Magee, Bryan 352
Maitland, Sir Donald 97, 231
Major, John 236–237, 239–240, 243, 244,
245, 247–248, 254, 255, 257, 274
Manchester 84, 150
Daveyhulme 45
Mandela, Nelson 255
Mann, Anthony 8
Mansell, Sarah 322
Mao Tse-Tung 178, 202, 222, 232
Margach, James 78–79
Marlesford, Lord 67
Marples, Ernest 97–98
Marshall Plan 206
Martin, Alec 4
Martin, Michael 283
Masefield, Peter 10
Maude, Angus 65
Maudling, Reggie 41, 47, 51, 52–54,
57–58, 75, 89, 129, 168, 191, 298,
312, 315
May, Simon 202–205
Mayer, Robert 342
Mayhew, Christopher 356
Mayhew, Henrietta see Rolston, Henrietta
McGahey, Mick 140, 154
McNally, Tom 335
McNamara, Robert 203–205
Menuhin, Yehudi 203, 254, 266, 343
School 346
Meyer, Sir Anthony 134
Millar, Ronald 109

INDEX